The
MX Book
of
New
Sherlock
Holmes
Stories

Part XXII – Some More
Untold Cases
(1877-1887)

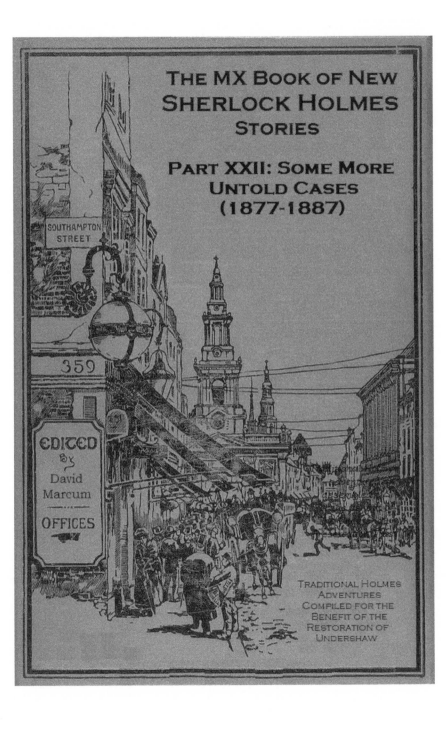

THE MX BOOK OF NEW SHERLOCK HOLMES STORIES

PART XXII: SOME MORE UNTOLD CASES (1877-1887)

SOUTHAMPTON STREET

359

EDITED By David Marcum

OFFICES

TRADITIONAL HOLMES
ADVENTURES
COMPILED FOR THE
BENEFIT OF THE
RESTORATION OF
UNDERSHAW

ISBN Hardback 978-1-78705-656-5
ISBN Paperback 978-1-78705-657-2
AUK ePub ISBN 978-1-78705-658-9
AUK PDF ISBN 978-1-78705-659-6

Published in the UK by
MX Publishing
335 Princess Park Manor, Royal Drive,
London, N11 3GX
www.mxpublishing.co.uk

David Marcum can be reached at:
thepapersofsherlockholmes@gmail.com

Cover design by Brian Belanger
www.belangerbooks.com and *www.redbubble.com/people/zhahadun*

CONTENTS

Forewords

Adventures

(Continued on the next page . . . .)

(Continued on the next page . . . .)

These additional adventures are contained in
Part XXIII: Some More Untold Cases
(1888-1894)

These additional adventures are contained in
Part XXIV: Some More Untold Cases
(1895-1903)

(Continued on the next page . . . .)

(Continued on the next page . . . .)

PART III: 1896-1929

PART IV – 2016 Annual

(Continued on the next page . . . .)

PART V – Christmas Adventures

(Continued on the next page . . . .)

PART VI – 2017 Annual

(Continued on the next page . . . .)

PART VII – Eliminate the Impossible: 1880-1891

PART VIII – Eliminate the Impossible: 1892-1905

(Continued on the next page . . . .)

Part IX – 2018 Annual (1879-1895)

(Continued on the next page . . . .)

Part X – 2018 Annual (1896-1916)

Part XI: Some Untold Cases (1880-1891)

(Continued on the next page . . . .)

The Adventure of the Silver Skull – Hugh Ashton
The Pimlico Poisoner – Matthew Simmonds
The Grosvenor Square Furniture Van – David Ruffle
The Adventure of the Paradol Chamber – Paul W. Nash
The Bishopgate Jewel Case – Mike Hogan
The Singular Tragedy of the Atkinson Brothers of Trincomalee – Craig Stephen Copland
Colonel Warburton's Madness – Gayle Lange Puhl
The Adventure at Bellingbeck Park – Deanna Baran
The Giant Rat of Sumatra – Leslie Charteris and Denis Green
        Introduction by Ian Dickerson
The Vatican Cameos – Kevin P. Thornton
The Case of the Gila Monster – Stephen Herczeg
The Bogus Laundry Affair – Robert Perret
Inspector Lestrade and the Molesey Mystery – M.A. Wilson and Richard Dean Starr

Part XII: Some Untold Cases (1894-1902)

Foreword – Lyndsay Faye
Foreword – Roger Johnson
Foreword – Melissa Grigsby
Foreword – Steve Emecz
Foreword – David Marcum
It's Always Time (*A Poem*) – "Anon."
The Shanghaied Surgeon – C.H. Dye
The Trusted Advisor – David Marcum
A Shame Harder Than Death – Thomas Fortenberry
The Adventure of the Smith-Mortimer Succession – Daniel D. Victor
A Repulsive Story and a Terrible Death – Nik Morton
The Adventure of the Dishonourable Discharge – Craig Janacek
The Adventure of the Admirable Patriot – S. Subramanian
The Abernetty Transactions – Jim French
Dr. Agar and the Dinosaur – Robert Stapleton
The Giant Rat of Sumatra – Nick Cardillo
The Adventure of the Black Plague – Paul D. Gilbert
Vigor, the Hammersmith Wonder – Mike Hogan
A Correspondence Concerning Mr. James Phillimore – Derrick Belanger
The Curious Case of the Two Coptic Patriarchs – John Linwood Grant
The Conk-Singleton Forgery Case – Mark Mower
Another Case of Identity – Jane Rubino
The Adventure of the Exalted Victim – Arthur Hall

PART XIII: 2019 Annual (1881-1890)

Foreword – Will Thomas
Foreword – Roger Johnson
Foreword – Melissa Grigsby
Foreword – Steve Emecz
Foreword – David Marcum
Inscrutable (*A Poem*) – Jacquelynn Morris

(Continued on the next page . . . .)

PART XIV: 2019 Annual (1891 -1897)

(Continued on the next page . . . .)

(Continued on the next page . . . .)

Part XVII – (1891-1898)

Part XVIII – (1899-1925)

(Continued on the next page . . . .)

Part XIX: 2020 Annual (1892-1890)

(Continued on the next page . . . .)

The Adventure of the Matched Set – Peter Coe Verbica
When the Prince First Dined at the Diogenes Club – Sean M. Wright
The Sweetenbury Safe Affair – Tim Gambrell

Part XX: 2020 Annual (1891-1897)
Foreword – John Lescroart
Foreword – Roger Johnson
Foreword – Lizzy Butler
Foreword – Steve Emecz
Foreword – David Marcum
The Sibling (A Poem) – Jacquelynn Morris
Blood and Gunpowder – Thomas A. Burns, Jr.
The Atelier of Death – Harry DeMaio
The Adventure of the Beauty Trap – Tracy Revels
A Case of Unfinished Business – Steven Philip Jones
The Case of the S.S. Bokhara – Mark Mower
The Adventure of the American Opera Singer – Deanna Baran
The Keadby Cross – David Marcum
The Adventure at Dead Man's Hole – Stephen Herczeg
The Elusive Mr. Chester – Arthur Hall
The Adventure of Old Black Duffel – Will Murray
The Blood-Spattered Bridge – Gayle Lange Puhl
The Tomorrow Man – S.F. Bennett
The Sweet Science of Bruising – Kevin P. Thornton
The Mystery of Sherlock Holmes – Christopher Todd
The Elusive Mr. Phillimore – Matthew J. Elliott
The Murders in the Maharajah's Railway Carriage – Charles Veley and Anna Elliott
The Ransomed Miracle – I.A. Watson
The Adventure of the Unkind Turn – Robert Perret
The Perplexing X'ing – Sonia Fetherston
The Case of the Short-Sighted Clown – Susan Knight

Part XXI: 2020 Annual (1898-1923)
Foreword – John Lescroart
Foreword – Roger Johnson
Foreword – Lizzy Butler
Foreword – Steve Emecz
Foreword – David Marcum
The Case of the Missing Rhyme (A Poem) – Joseph W. Svec III
The Problem of the St. Francis Parish Robbery – R.K. Radek
The Adventure of the Grand Vizier – Arthur Hall
The Mummy's Curse – DJ Tyrer
The Fractured Freemason of Fitzrovia – David L. Leal
The Bleeding Heart – Paula Hammond
The Secret Admirer – Jayantika Ganguly

(Continued on the next page . . . .)

The following contributions appear in this volume:
The MX Book of New Sherlock Holmes Stories
Part XXII – Some More Untold Cases (1877-1887)

The following contributions appear in the companion volumes:
The MX Book of New Sherlock Holmes Stories
Part XXIII – Some More Untold Cases (1888-1894)
Part XXIV – Some More Untold Cases (1895-1903)

Editor's Note:
Duplicate Untold Cases

In some instances, there are multiple versions of certain Untold Cases contained within this volume. Each of these are very different stories and do not contradict one another, in spite of their common jumping-off place. As explained in the Editor's Foreword, no traditional and Canonical versions of the Untold Cases are the definitive versions to the exclusion of the others. They simply require a bit of additional pondering and rationalization to consider what was going on in Watson's thinking, and why he chose to present them in this way.

In this volume, the reader will encounter several versions of "The Darlington Substitution Scandal" – *Enjoy!*

Editor's Foreword:
Watson's Obfuscations
by David Marcum

Obfuscate:
> Merriam-Webster –
>> 1 – a: to throw into shadow, darken;
>>> b: to make obscure
>> 2 – Confuse
>
> *Dictionary.com* –
>> The act or an instance of making something obscure, dark, or difficult to understand

Watson obfuscated. Without a doubt. To pretend that he did otherwise would be rather naïve.

We have obvious evidence or this, and also that which is much more indirect and must be inferred.

That isn't to say that Watson is an actual *liar*, with the habitual and intentional regular misrepresentations that this word implies. A true liar cannot help him or herself. Such a person chooses falsehoods over truth with the same lack of thought as when taking a breath. Some liars do so occasionally, while others do it dozens of times per day in the very visible public eye, regardless of the damage that they cause.

When Watson obfuscated, it was for a reason.

Consider: Watson wanted to record his Sherlock Holmes's various investigations so that the public would be aware of his friend's abilities, and so that credit for the solution of his investigations would be properly pointed in Holmes's direction. At the end of their first shared adventure, after Holmes explains how he followed the scarlet thread of murder through the tangled skein to a correct solution, Watson cries: *"It is wonderful! Your merits should be publicly recognized. You should publish an account of the case. If you won't, I will for you."*

Holmes replies, *"You may do what you like, Doctor."* – likely little realizing just what he had let himself in for.

A moment later, Watson added, *"I have all the facts in my journal, and the public shall know them."* And so they would – but it would be nearly seven years before that occurred. Watson made that promise in early March 1881, but *A Study in Scarlet* wouldn't be published until late November 1887, in *Beeton's Christmas Annual.*

In the meantime, Holmes continued to investigate, and Watson continued to assist him – more and more as his health improved following his grievous mid-1880 war injury, and also as Holmes's practice continued to grow and thrive. We view those cases now as something from a long-ago time, stirring within us longings for those mysterious gaslit streets and foggy nights. Sometimes we tend to forget that when Watson first began publishing in 1887, those stories were essentially contemporary. Adventures might occur in streets or locations that no longer exist, but they certainly existed then. Our Heroes made their way across London in hansom cabs and growlers, and while those are long gone, that was the norm then. And when Watson was writing about Holmes's cases, they weren't recountings of events that had occurred decades before – some had happened only a few months before they were published.

Consider "The Red-Headed League", which took place in October 1890. (There is a bit of confusing contradiction within the story regarding this date, but that will be addressed in a moment.) Watson, then married for a couple of years and living in nearby Paddington, relates how he'd stopped by to visit Holmes and found him in consultation with Mr. Jabez Wilson concerning the rather comical pawnbroker's recent connections to the mysterious aforementioned League, and his subsequent grievances against them – for they had been paying him steadily for months to spend his mornings copying the *Encyclopaedia Britannica*, and just that morning he'd found that this unusual post had been terminated without any previous warning.

As expected, the matter resolved satisfactorily, and Watson recognized that this was a tale that should be shared. He probably wrote up his notes to a certain degree within a matter of days, and added them to an ever growing stack of narratives. Then, just a few months later – specifically on May 4th, 1891 – Holmes was presumed to have died at the Reichenbach Falls, which gave Watson even more motivation to recall the promise that he'd made on March 6th, 1881, at the end of *A Study in Scarlet*: "*Your merits should be publicly recognized. You should publish an account of the case. If you won't, I will for you.*"

As of the spring of 1891, Watson had only published two accounts of Holmes's cases, *A Study in Scarlet* (in late 1887, in the aforementioned *Beeton's*), and *The Sign of the Four* (in February 1890, appearing first in *Lippincott's Monthly Magazine*). With the idea of paying tribute to his fallen friend, Watson, assisted by his friend and literary agent, Dr. – and later Sir – Arthur Conan Doyle, approached the publisher of the recently formed *Strand* magazine – itself only in business since January 1891 – and arranged for some short sketches of Holmes's cases to be published, beginning with "A Scandal in Bohemia" on June 25th, 1891. The world was electrified – and soon after the obfuscations began to creep in – sometimes from carelessness or accidentally, and sometimes because Watson had no choice.

For example, from the distance of so many years, it's difficult to know exactly which names within The Canon are accurate, and which have been *adjusted* due to Watson's effort to protect the players. It's entirely possible that Jabez Wilson's identity was true as presented – for there is some argument that his modest pawn shop could only have benefitted by being associated with such an interesting story – Wilson could have dined out for the rest of his life on his version of it, were he able to overcome the personal embarrassment at his own gullibility. But as those initial two-dozen stories were published in *The Strand* between June 1891 and December 1893 (when "The Final Problem" appeared to a stunned and dismayed public), it's obvious that some facts must have been changed to protect those involved.

For instance, "The Boscombe Valley Mystery", which occurred in June 1889, was published in October 1891, just a little over two years later. It ends with a dying murderer's confession that is to be kept secret – and yet, here is Watson publishing it to great interest in a widely read magazine when the events were still somewhat fresh in the public mind. But some delicate obfuscation was occurring here. Try finding Boscombe Valley on a map. And if the location was disguised, then it's likely that the names were as well. What other information was smudged and altered to hide the specifics while providing the gist of the cases, while also making sure to highlight Holmes's brilliance?

Of course, if locations and the names of involved parties could be changed, then dates could be altered as well. There are a number of chronological inconsistencies within The Canon that can be blamed on all sorts of reasons – a misreading of Watson's handwriting by a careless typesetter is always likely. Certainly similar carelessness by Watson's Literary Agent was another reason, as he failed to pay enough attention to the preparation of Watson's works for publication while he was instead distracted by his own lesser-known efforts. And of course, Watson certainly made some intentional changes for reasons of discretion.

As early as the publication of *The Sign of the Four* in 1890, there are unexplained discrepancies. We know that the case occurs in 1888, because it says that 1882 was six years earlier. But then a letter, supposedly sent that first day of the investigation, is postmarked "*July*", while just a couple of chapters later, Watson comments that it's a "*September evening*". The internal evidence seems to set this case in September 1888, and the reference to July is likely a printer's error – Watson's short-hand notes probably said *"9"* when referring to the month that the letter was postmarked, but the printer read it as a *"7"*.

Other dating errors can be found elsewhere in The Canon – simply examine "The Red-Headed League", where Watson says that he had called upon Holmes *"one day in the autumn of last year"*. Since this adventure was published in *The Strand* in August 1891, most chronologicists place it in 1890. (This year is later confirmed in the story.) But then it gets tricky. Watson said it was *"in the autumn"*. And yet, in regard to publication of the first advertisement for the League, Watson writes: *"It is* The Morning Chronicle *of April 27, 1890. Just two months ago."* April is *not* two months ago from the autumn – and in just a few lines *"autumn"* is narrowed down to *"October"*. The hapless client, Jabez Wilson, then reports that eight weeks have passed from his initial interview and hire by the curious League to that very same morning, when he decides to visit Holmes, after discovering this notice pinned at the office where he has been laboring:

The Red-Headed League
is
Dissolved
Oct. 9, 1890

For a Sherlockian chronologicist, this ought to be pure gold: An actual firm date as a jumping-off place. The day that Jabez Wilson visited Holmes was October 9th, 1890. But . . .

. . . the events of the story clearly take place on a *Saturday* – in fact, they *have* to occur on a *Saturday* to make any sense – and October 9, 1890 was a *Thursday*! So our solid date, the one fixed point we can grab when trying to date this case, is ephemeral.

And that throws the whole thing open to interpretation or adjustment. All of the major chronologicists still agree that "The Red-Headed League" occurs in October, and most – but not all – still put it in 1890. But in October 1890, some favor October 4th, or 11th, or the 18th – all Saturdays, but *not* October 9th. Gavin Brend will only say October 1890 without picking a specific day. Others choose entirely different years – Baring-Gould 1887 and Ernest Bloomfield Zeisler 1889 – and even then, they don't set it on October 9th, instead picking October 29th or October 19th respectively, because both are Saturdays.

And what to do about that pesky April reference when Jabez Wilson was initially hired, eight weeks before his visit to Holmes? It can't have been *April* as listed, but it could have been *August*. That fits, and the

4

realization that someone – again, the typesetter at The Strand? The Literary Agent? – mis-read Watson's notes, perhaps taking the abbreviation *Au* for *Ap*, becomes the most likely explanation for this inconsistency.

So is this tempest in a chronological teapot due to careless errors, or did Watson have some reason for deliberately confusing the facts? Sidney Paget's original *Strand* illustration had the October date, which serves as a confirmation, seemingly showing *Oct. 9, 1890*:

with a little square of cardboard hammered on to the middle of the panel with a tack. Here it is, and you can read for yourself."

He held up a piece of white cardboard, about the size of a sheet of notepaper. It read in this fashion :—

"The Red-Headed League is Dissolved. Oct. 9, 1890."

Sherlock Holmes and I surveyed this curt announcement and the rueful face behind it, until the comical side of the affair so completely overtopped every other consideration that we both burst out into a roar of laughter.

"'Well,' said I, 'the gentleman at No. 4.'

"'What, the red-headed man?'

"'Yes.'

"'Oh,' said he, 'his name was William Morris. He was a solicitor, and was using my room as a temporary convenience until his new premises were ready. He moved out yesterday.'

"'Where could I find him?'

"'Oh, at his new offices. He did tell me the address. Yes, 17, King Edward-street, near St. Paul's.'"

"I started off, Mr. Holmes, but when I got to that address it was a manufactory of artificial knee-caps, and no one in it had ever heard of either Mr. William Morris or Mr.

THE DOOR WAS SHUT AND LOCKED.

But a closer look (see next page) even brings that into question, as it isn't clear if the month is *Oct.* or something that maybe starts with an "*A*", or if the date is a *9* or a *4*. (As the image isn't reproduced brilliantly here, an independent investigation by the reader is strongly encouraged.)

And the date isn't the only possible obfuscation in this story. Jabez Wilson is initially interviewed by "the League" and subsequently employed for eight weeks at *7 Pope's Court, Fleet Street*. No such location can be found. (A much more likely candidate is Mitre Court, leading from Fleet Street to King's Bench Walk.) Strangely, while this address is changed, as is the location of Wilson's pawnshop in "Saxe-Coburg Square" (probably Charterhouse Square), another address listed in the

5

narrative, 17 King Edward Street, is accurate and can be visited today – although the buildings look nothing like what was there in 1890.

In some cases, such as "The Second Stain", Watson avoided giving a year at all, being careful to avoid any hints as to when this sensitive matter occurred. (Sharp Sherlockian chronologicists, however, have mostly settled the question anyway.) In other cases, Watson provides specific dates that must be disregarded.

For instance, there's "Wisteria Lodge", which begins with Watson's statement that, *"I find it recorded in my notebook that it was a bleak and windy day towards the end of March in the year 1892 . . . ."* – which is clearly impossible, as at that point in 1892, Holmes had been presumed dead for ten months and was somewhere in the area of Tibet. This, too, is likely a misreading of Watson's notes, seeing the *"5"* in *1895* as a *"2"*.

In *The Hound of the Baskervilles*, the inscription on Dr. Mortimer's walking stick indicates that it was presented in *1884*, and a little bit later, Holmes refers to this date as *"five years ago"*. Easy enough to do a little math and come up with a time-frame for *The Hound*: Autumn *1889*. And yet . . . .

If Watson met Mary Morstan in *The Sign of the Four* in September 1888, and certainly married her not long after (as well as purchasing a medical practice which would consume some of his time – although not all of it!), then how is it that he's still living in Baker Street in Autumn 1889, eating breakfast and with plenty of time to leave both Mary and his practice to go away for weeks, journeying indefinitely to Dartmoor in Sir Henry Baskerville's company?

And then there's "A Scandal in Bohemia", in which Watson states that he hadn't seen much of Holmes since his marriage, and he says that he's stopped by to visit "*on the twentieth of March, 1888*". So if he didn't meet Mary Morstan until *September 1888*, who exactly had he recently married several months before that?

And then there's "The Noble Bachelor", in which Lord St. Simon – Was that his real name, or was it obfuscated? – is listed as having a birth-date of 1846, and Holmes says that he's forty-one years old. A little basic math then tells us that this adventure occurs in 1887 – but at the start of the narrative, Watson explains that "*It was a few weeks before my own marriage, during the days when I was still sharing rooms with Holmes in Baker Street . . . .*" So we know that Watson met Mary Morstan in September 1888, but Autumn 1887 was just a short time before his marriage (NOBL), and he was already married in March 1888 (SCAN), and he was able to go away for weeks in Autumn 1889 (HOUN). Clearly there is conflicting information.

As a Sherlockian Chronologicist, I've long been satisfied with the obvious solution that Watson had a *first* wife before Mary Morstan. This first wife's existence somewhat clears up some of these chronological problems. It was William S. Baring-Gould who initially posited this first-wife's existence in *Sherlock Holmes of Baker Street* (1962), his brilliant biography of Holmes, naming her Constance Watson *née* Adams. Baring-Gould speculated that Watson, at the time of publication, adjusted the dates of those stories that occurred while Constance was alive, or didn't mention her by name, in order to protect the feelings of his second wife, Mary. Without knowing what was in Watson's heart, this explanation is as good as any – and goes to show that the Good Doctor was willing to obfuscate when necessary.

And now, turning this lumbering ship of an essay toward the theme of this current set of books, another obfuscation was used when discussing what has come to be known as *The Untold Cases*.

In "The Problem of Thor Bridge", Watson tells us that:

Somewhere in the vaults of the bank of Cox and Co., at Charing Cross, there is a travel-worn and battered tin dispatch box with my name, John H. Watson, M.D., Late Indian Army, painted upon the lid. It is crammed with papers, nearly all of which are records of cases to illustrate the curious problems which Mr. Sherlock Holmes had at various times to examine. Some, and not the least interesting, were complete failures, and as such will hardly bear narrating, since no final explanation is forthcoming. A problem without a solution may interest the student, but can hardly fail to annoy the casual reader . . . Apart from these unfathomed cases, there are some which involve the secrets of private families to an extent which would mean consternation in many exalted quarters if it were thought possible that they might find their way into print. I need not say that such a breach of confidence is unthinkable, and that these records will be separated and destroyed now that my friend has time to turn his energies to the matter. There remain a considerable residue of cases of greater or less interest which I might have edited before had I not feared to give the public a surfeit which might react upon the reputation of the man whom above all others I revere. In some I was myself concerned and can speak as an eye-witness, while in others I was either not present or played so small a part that they could only be told as by a third person.

Thank heavens Watson maintained this amazing tin dispatch box, wherein can be found so many more incredible Sherlockian adventures beyond the pitifully few sixty of them that came to us by way of a detour across the First Literary Agent's desk. By some counts, there are over one-hundred-and-forty additional *Untold Cases* referenced in The Canon – the number goes up or down based on the interpretation of what was truly one of Holmes's cases, or if he was just referring to some affair in which he wasn't associated, or even if a missing comma means one case or two, (as in "*the repulsive story of the red leech and the terrible death of Crosby the banker*", which may be one case or two, and the same for "*the Addleton tragedy and the singular contents of the ancient British barrow*").

Over the decades, as lost Watsonian manuscripts have been discovered all around the world, some confusion has occurred when multiple versions of an Untold Case appear, leading some Sherlockians to wonder which is the actual *true* version, and which is a clever *fake*? As I explained in the foreword to *The MX Book of New Sherlock Holmes Stories: Some Untold Cases* (Parts XI and XII, 2018), there are over two-dozen legitimate versions of that most famous Untold Case *The Giant Rat of Sumatra* (as mentioned in "The Sussex Vampire"), and more have been added since then (listed here, in no certain order, except for the first):

- *The Giant Rat of Sumatra* – Rick Boyer (1976) *(Possibly the greatest pastiche of all time)*
- "*Matilda Briggs* and the Giant Rat of Sumatra", *The Elementary Cases of Sherlock Holmes* – Ian Charnock (1999)
- *Mrs. Hudson and the Spirit's Curse* – Martin Davies (2004)
- "The Giant Rat of Sumatra" – Leslie Charteris and Denis Green. [Originally broadcast on radio on July 31, 1944 as part of the *Sherlock Holmes* radio show, script reprinted in *The MX Book of New Sherlock Holmes Stories: XI – Some Untold Cases (1880-1891)* (2018)]
- *Sherlock Holmes' Lost Adventure: The True Story of the Giant Rats of Sumatra* – Laurel Steinhauer (2004)
- *The Giant Rat of Sumatra* – Paul D. Gilbert (2010)
- "The Giant Rat of Sumatra", *The Lost Stories of Sherlock Holmes* – Tony Reynolds (2010)
- *The Giant Rat of Sumatra* – Jake and Luke Thoene (1995)
- "The Adventure of the Giant Rat of Sumatra", *Mary Higgins Clark Mystery Magazine* – John Lescroart, (December 1988)
- "The Case of the Sumatran Rat", *The Secret Chronicles of Sherlock Holmes* – June Thomson (1992)
- "Sherlock Holmes and the Giant Rat of Sumatra", *More From the Deed Box of John H. Watson MD* – Hugh Ashton (2012)
- "The Case of the Giant Rat of Sumatra", *The Secret Notebooks of Sherlock Holmes* – Liz Hedgecock (2016)
- "The World is Now Prepared" – "slogging ruffian" (Fan Fiction) (Date unverified)
- "The Giant Rat of Sumatra", *Sherlock Holmes: The Lost Cases* – Alvin F. Rymsha (2006)
- "The Giant Rat of Sumatra" *The MX Book of New Sherlock Holmes Stories: XII – Some Untold Cases (1894-1902)* – Nick Cardillo (2018)
- "The Giant Rat of Sumatra", *The Oriental Casebook of Sherlock Holmes* – Ted Riccardi (2003)
- *Sherlock Holmes and the Limehouse Horror* – Phillip Pullman (1992, 2001)

9

- *Lestrade and the Giant Rat of Sumatra* – M. J. Trow (2014)
- "No Rats Need Apply", *The Unexpected Adventures of Sherlock Holmes* – Amanda Knight (2004)
- *The Shadow of the Rat* – David Stuart Davies (1999)
- *The Giant Rat of Sumatra* – Bob Bishop (2019)
- *The Giant Rat of Sumatra* – Daniel Gracely (2001)
- "The Giant Rat of Sumatra", *Resurrected Holmes* – Paula Volsky (1996)
- "The Mysterious Case of the Giant Rat of Sumatra", *The Mark of the Gunn* – Brian Gibson (2000)
- *Sherlock Holmes and the Giant Rat of Sumatra* – Alan Vanneman (2002)
- "The Giant Rat of Sumatra" – Paul Boler (2000)
- "The Giant Rat of Sumatra" [Radio Broadcast, April 20th (or June 9th), 1932, July 18th, 1936, and March 1st, 1942] – Edith Meiser (Now Sadly Lost)
- "The Case of the Missing Energy", *The Einstein Paradox* – Colin Bruce (1994)
- "All This and the Giant Rat of Sumatra", *Sherlock Holmes and The Baker Street Dozen* – Val Andrews (1997)

The list shown above is by no means a complete representation of all the Giant Rat narratives. These are simply the ones that I found when making a pass along the shelves of my own Holmes Collection. The thing to remember is that *in spite of every one of these stories being about a Giant Rat, none of them contradict one another or cancel each other out to become the only true Giant Rat adventure.*

The fact is that there are lots of different versions of the Untold Tales. Some readers, of course, don't like this and will never accept *any* of them, since the First Literary Agent didn't handle them between Watson and the light of day. Others, however, only wish to seek out the sole and single account that satisfies them the most, therefore dismissing the others as *"fiction"* – a word that I find quite distasteful when directed toward Mr. Sherlock Holmes. Quite a few are more interested in favoring one version or the other because some certain author wrote it, and they hope that naming this work as their favorite will earn them a fleeting glance for their flattery.

My approach is that if the different versions of the Untold Cases are Canonical, and don't violate any of the same rules that define what types of tales appear in these anthologies – no parodies, no anachronisms, no actual supernatural encounters, and no portrayals of Holmes as a murderous sociopathic creep with absolutely no redeeming value whatsoever – then they are legitimate.

Some people can't get their minds around the fact that there were a lot of Giant Rats (in one form or another) causing mayhem in London during Holmes's active years. In fact, each of the Giant Rat adventures listed above is very different – comedy or tragedy, police procedural or gothic horror, London-based or set in the country – and in any case – and here's the point – *Watson obfuscated!*

Not counting printer's errors or Literary Agent carelessness, Watson changed all kinds of things to make the story interesting to general readers – as compared to how Holmes wished his cases could be presented: Dry factual studies for the interested study. (*"You have attempted to tinge it with romanticism,"* he complained some months after the publication of *A Study in Scarlet, "which produces much the same effect as if you worked a love-story or an elopement into the fifth proposition of Euclid."*

Watson brilliantly knew his audience, and he wrote the narratives in a way that would immediately capture the reader's attention, and yet not cloud the issue with too much of the lesser-known tedium of detective work, and also leaving out other unrelated matters which would cause confusion.

For example, when preparing a story for publication, he would often give the impression that it was the only thing currently on Holmes's plate, and possibly the only matter to occupy his attention for weeks, when in fact Our Heroes were constantly busy, and the many cases in which they were involved were truly a *tangled skein.* Watson sometimes gave the impression that Holmes went for weeks in fits of settee-bound depression between cases, when in fact he was constantly working in this or that direction upon a number of cases, each intertwined like incredibly complex threads in *The Great Holmes Tapestry.*

In spite of constructing the stories so that they were self-contained, some mentions of other cases – the Untold Cases – were unavoidable, and as students of The Master's life and methods, we can only be grateful for the small bits that we've been given and what we can glean from them. And one thing that we know by way of stories from Watson's Tin Dispatch Box is that sometimes he obfuscated by naming different cases with the same general catch-all title – an obfuscation that, for whatever reason, was important to him.

For example, there have been many different and varied stories about Holmes and Watson's 1894 encounter with Huret, the Boulevard Assassin, as mentioned in "The Golden Pince-Nez". Confusing? Contradictory? Not at all. Holmes simply rooted out an entire nest of *Al Qaeda*-like French assassins during that deadly summer. There are a lot of tales out there relating the peculiar persecution of John Vincent Harden in 1895. No problem – there were simply a lot of tobacco millionaires in London during that time, all peculiarly persecuted – but in very different ways – and Watson lumped them in his notes under the catch-all name of *John Vincent Harden.* Later Literary Agents, not quite knowing how to conquer Watson's personal codes and reverse-engineer who the real client was in these cases, simply left the name as written.

There is no need, as some do, to pick a favorite version of the Giant Rat or the Abergavenny Murder. There's no reason to think that only one of the variations is true, thus negating or neglecting the others. A previous favorite iteration doesn't have to be scrapped because some other later Literary Agent's attention and approval must be sought and curried. Watson took the time to record *all* of these versions, and all can be respected and enjoyed as part of the overall life of Sherlock Holmes. There are many already out there to read, and over sixty more of them in this collection, and still others to come in days ahead. Enjoy, and take Watson's Obfuscations as an important part of playing The Game.

* * * * *

"Of course, I could only stammer out my thanks."
– *The unhappy John Hector McFarlane,* "The Norwood Builder"

As always when one of these sets is finished, I want to first thank with all my heart my incredible wonderful wife of over thirty-two years, Rebecca, and our amazing son and my friend, Dan. I love you both, and you are everything to me!

Also, I can never express enough gratitude for all of the contributors who have donated their time and royalties to this ongoing project. I'm constantly amazed at the incredible stories that you send, and I'm so glad to have gotten to know all of you through this process. It's an undeniable fact that Sherlock Holmes authors are the *best* people!

The contributors of these stories have donated their royalties for this project to support the Stepping Stones School for special needs children, located at Undershaw, one of Sir Arthur Conan Doyle's former homes. As of this writing, these MX anthologies have raised nearly $70,000 for the school, with no end in sight, and of even more importance, they have helped raise awareness about the school all over the world. These books are making a real difference to the school, and the participation of both contributors and purchasers is most appreciated.

Next is that group that exchanges emails with me when we have the time – and time is a valuable commodity for all of us these days! I don't get to write as often as I'd like, but I really enjoy catching up whenever we get the chance: Derrick Belanger, Brian Belanger, Mark Mower, Denis Smith, Tom Turley, Dan Victor, and Marcia Wilson.

There is a group of special people who have stepped up and supported this and a number of other projects over and over again with a lot of contributions. They are the best and I can't express how valued they are: Larry Albert, Hugh Ashton, Derrick Belanger, Deanna Baran, S.F. Bennett, Craig Stephen Copland, Matthew Elliott, Tim Gambrell, Jayantika Ganguly, Paul Gilbert, Dick Gillman, Arthur Hall, Stephen Herczeg, Craig Janacek, Mark Mower, Will Murray, Robert Perret, Tracy Revels, Roger Riccard, Geri Schear, Brenda Seabrooke, Shane Simmons, Robert Stapleton, Kevin Thornton, Charles Veley and Anna Elliott, I.A. Watson, and Marcy Wilson.

I also want to particularly thank the following:

- *Otto Penzler* – I've been aware of Otto for ages, and I owe him so much in so many ways. When I was a lad, I obtained, by way of my parents as gifts, two of his reference books, *The Private Lives of Private Eyes, Spies, Crime Fighters, and Other Good Guys* (1977) and *Detectionary* (1977). These books provided incredibly useful information to me, an urgent mystery fan living in a part of the country where such information was rare. Later, when I had my first job, I used my very first pay check to purchase *The Solar Pons Omnibus* from Otto's justly famous Mysterious Bookshop.

  In the mid-1980's while in college, my deerstalker and I were able to visit New York and the store (in its original location) for the first time, and it was something of a religious experience. At some point I was brave enough to correspond with Otto (back in the days of letters instead of emails), and later, when I wrote my own first book of Holmes pastiches, *The Papers of Sherlock Holmes* (2011), he sold copies of that mostly unseen original edition in his store.

  Over the years I've been back to New York on a few occasions, always stopping in at The Mysterious Bookshop – which, along with West 35th Street to see Nero Wolfe-related locations, and the same for Ellery Queen's house on West 87th Street, were really the only places I cared about visiting in NYC. In January 2020, I was able to visit Manhattan again, for the first time in over a decade, for my first journey to the Sherlock Holmes Birthday Weekend celebration.

Each year at that time, there's an Open House at The Mysterious Boosksshop for Sherlockians, and that, along with the famed BSI Dealer's Room, were the main reasons that I'd always wanted to go during the January event. The Open House was planned for Friday, but I went to the store on Thursday afternoon, so I could look around at my leisure – particularly along the entire back wall of the store, covered entirely in Sherlockian shelves – in order to accumulate a stack of Holmesian items for my collection.

When I was finished, I rather timidly asked an employee if Otto was there, and if I could say hello. In a moment the man himself came out and greeted me most wonderfully, making me feel at home and as if I'd been a weekly in-person visitor to the store for decades. Before that afternoon was over, he had me sign a massive stack of books that I'd written or edited – fulfilling a personal bucket list item of being able to autograph books at The Mysterious Bookshop – and he'd also taken me down to the incredible basement collection of still more Sherlockian items. I was also able to visit with him some the next day during the more hectic official Open House.

I'd tried for years to recruit him to write a foreword for these books, and I'm very happy that I've finally succeeded. Otto Penzler is a living legend, and has done so much for so many. It's wonderful to have him be part of these books, and a personal thrill for me. Thank you, Otto.

- *Roger Johnson* – I'm more grateful than I can say that I know Roger. His Sherlockian knowledge is exceptional, as is the work that he does to further the cause of The Master. But even more than that, both Roger and his wonderful wife, Jean Upton, are simply the finest and best kind of people, and I'm very lucky to know both of them – even though I don't get to see them nearly as often as I'd like, and especially in these crazy days! In so many ways, Roger, I can't thank you enough, and I can't imagine these books without you.

14

- *Steve Emecz* – When I first emailed Steve from out of the blue back in 2013, I was interested in MX re-publishing my previously first book. Even then, as a guy who works to accumulate *all* traditional Sherlockian pastiches, I could see that MX (under Steve's leadership) was *the* fast-rising superstar of the Sherlockian publishing world.

  The publication of that first book with MX was an amazing life-changing event for me, leading to writing and then editing more books, unexpected Holmes Pilgrimages to England, and these incredible anthologies. When I had the idea for these books in early 2015, I thought that it might, with any luck, be one small volume of perhaps a dozen stories. Since then they've grown and grown, and by way of them I've been able to make some incredible Sherlockian friends and play in the Holmesian Sandbox in ways that I'd never before dreamed possible.

  All through it, Steve has been one of the most positive and supportive people I've ever known, letting me explore various Sherlockian projects and opening up my own personal possibilities in ways that otherwise would have never been possible. Thank you Steve for every opportunity!
- *Brian Belanger* – Brian is one of the nicest and most talented of people, and I'm very glad that I was able to meet him in person during the 2020 Sherlock Holmes Birthday Celebration in New York. His gifts are amazing, and his skills improve and grow from project to project. He's amazingly great to work with, and once again I thank him for another incredible contribution.

And last but certainly *not* least, **Sir Arthur Conan Doyle**: Author, doctor, adventurer, and the Founder of the Sherlockian Feast. Present in spirit, and honored by all of us here.

It was particularly unusual editing this collection through the spring and summer of 2020, as the world faced a deadly globe-spanning pandemic. Many people ended up being stuck at home, and my first thought was that a number of them will take advantage of that newly carved-out time – although for terrible reasons – to write. However, it soon became apparent that everyone's lives were turned upside down to greater or lesser degrees, and even if they had the *time* to write something, they didn't necessarily have the *heart* to do so. I was concerned that this set of anthology volumes might not have enough stories – at least not to the level which many have come to expect and look forward to.

But as people found their footing and their spirits, the stories began to arrive, more and more of them – both for these books, and also for other Sherlockian anthologies that I'm editing at the same time. It's been amazing, and it showed that in these dark times, people have found great comfort in writing about Holmes and Watson and those bygone days, and also that they want to share those tales with others who will find comfort as well.

For everyone who dug deep and found a way forward and is a part of this collection, and for all of you who will be reading it, thank you so much.

As always, this collection has been a labor of love by both the participants and myself. As I've explained before, once again everyone did their sincerest best to produce an anthology that truly represents why Holmes and Watson have been so popular for so long. These are just more tiny threads woven into the ongoing Great Holmes Tapestry, continuing to grow and grow, for there can *never* be enough stories about the man whom Watson described as *"the best and wisest . . . whom I have ever known."*

David Marcum
September 25th, 2020
The 132nd Anniversary of Holmes
asking Watson what he makes of
Dr. Mortimer's walking stick . . . .

Questions, comments, or story submissions
may be addressed to David Marcum at

thepapersofsherlockholmes@gmail.com

Foreword
by Otto Penzler

Everyone reading this extraordinary series of books discovered Sherlock Holmes in his or her own way. No one wrote of that magic moment more compellingly than Ellery Queen (in this case, Frederic Dannay, one of the two cousins who collaborated under that memorable pseudonym) in his essay collection, *In the Queen's Parlor*.

When I was ten years old, P.S. 9, my elementary school in the Bronx, offered what I imagine was common in those long-ago days but which I fear may be less common now: A library class. Once a week, our teacher would walk us down to the school library, where Miss Gibson would talk about how to use about books. We were shown the proper way to open a book, learned the rudiments of the Dewey Decimal System, and absorbed her cheerful talks about the wonders of reading.

For the second half-hour of the class, we were allowed to take any book we wanted off the shelf and read. I pulled down an anthology (title unknown, now), scanned the table of contents, and was intrigued by the title "The Red-Headed League."

I was instantly captivated by this Sherlock Holmes fellow and by the utterly bizarre notion of someone with a particular hair color being hired to copy the *Encyclopaedia Britannica*. Totally immersed, I was crushed when the bell rang, signaling the end of the class.

No, no, no. Wait. I have to know what this all means.

Mercilessly, the class was herded back to home room. Never was a class so eagerly anticipated as the following week's library hour.

Eventually, I learned that there were more stories like this one. I bought *The Complete Sherlock Holmes*, the Doubleday edition with that magical introduction by Christopher Morley, read it more than once, and lamented that there weren't more stories about that odd but curiously likable detective.

Happily, I was wrong. There *are* more stories, and this volume – all the volumes in this worthy series – prove that life always offers hope.

Otto Penzler
New York
April 2020

"Fond of Queer Mysteries"[1]
by Roger Johnson

We're all fond of queer mysteries, of course, or we shouldn't bother with this book. And among the queerest (strangest, oddest, most curious) are those that are merely referred to by John H. Watson in the chronicles of his friend Sherlock Holmes. We're familiar with sixty of the great detective's cases – the number of which we know nothing is potentially infinite, of course, but these particular volumes are concerned with the investigations that are tantalisingly hinted at, sometimes with a little detail.

That detail can provide the spark that our imagination needs to re-create one of those unpublished stories. Who among us hasn't wondered what could possibly link a politician, a lighthouse, and a trained cormorant? Or just why Holmes claimed that world was not yet prepared for the story of the giant rat of Sumatra?

Some of the hints relate to the solving of a crime. There's the Camberwell poisoning case, "*in which, as may be remembered, Holmes was able, by winding up the dead man's watch, to prove that it had been wound up two hours before, and that therefore the deceased had gone to bed within that time – a deduction which was of the greatest importance in clearing up the case.*" That's reasonably straightforward. More problematic is the "*dreadful business of the Abernetty family, which was first brought to Holmes's attention by the depth which the parsley had sunk into the butter upon a hot day*". Naturally we wonder what was so dreadful, and what the parsley in the butter had to do with it – but more puzzling yet is how the "*dreadful business*" was *first* brought to Holmes's attention by that seemingly trivial matter. (The essential clue, I fancy, is that the parsley *did* sink into the butter. Real parsley would tend to float, even on melted butter, which suggests that there was something very wrong with one or the other on the Abernetty dining table.)

A few of the unpublished accounts fall into the category of the seemingly impossible, such as that of the cutter *Alicia*, "*which sailed one spring morning into a patch of mist from where she never again emerged, nor was anything further ever heard of herself and her crew.*" Or the enigma of Mr. James Phillimore "*who, stepping back into his own house to get his umbrella, was never more seen in this world*".

Even more nightmarish is the mental image of "*Isadora Persano, the well-known journalist and duellist who was found stark staring mad with a match box in front of him which contained a remarkable worm said to*

18

be unknown to science". (The female name "*Isadora*" has encouraged more than a few to assume that Mr. Persano was a cross-dresser, ignoring the obviously correct explanation that it's a persistent mis-spelling of the male "*Isadore*".)

The hints that Watson offers range from the sensational to the apparently mundane. On the one hand, for instance, are the "shocking affair of the Dutch steamship, *Friesland*, which," he says, "so nearly cost us both our lives", and "*the repulsive story of the red leech*", which may or may not be connected with "*the terrible death of Crosby the banker*". On the other are the case of Mrs. Etherege, who recommended Holmes to Mary Sutherland because he had found her husband so easily "*when the police and everyone had given him up for dead*", and that of Mary Morstan's employer Mrs. Cecil Forrester, whom he helped "*to unravel a little domestic complication*". They all offer the opportunity to take up residence at 221b Baker Street, where we can let our imaginations work in tandem with the logical methods of Sherlock Holmes

Roger Johnson, BSI, ASH
Editor: *The Sherlock Holmes Journal*
July 4th, 2020

NOTES

1. "Well, Mr. Holmes, what do you make of these?" he cried. "They told me that you were fond of queer mysteries, and I don't think you can find a queerer one than that." (Hilton Cubitt, in "The Dancing Men")

Conan Doyle's Legacy in 2020
by Steve Emecz

Undershaw
Circa 1900

The MX Book of New Sherlock Holmes Stories has now raised over $65,000 for Stepping Stones School for children with learning disabilities and is by far the largest Sherlock Holmes collection in the world.

Stepping Stones is located in Undershaw, the former home of Sir Arthur Conan Doyle and the fundraising has support many projects continuing the legacy of Conan Doyle and Sherlock Holmes in the amazing building.

One of the amazing projects we have funded is to enable Stepping Stones to be a broadcast location for video using Zoom, including live events. This has proved to be incredibly timely with the global pandemic restricting movement and access. We have even broadcast a live Sherlock Holmes play *A Scandal In Nova Alba* by Orlando Pearson from Undershaw, including fans from over a dozen countries around the joining live!

The Doyle Room at Stepping Stones, Undershaw
Partially funded through royalties from
The MX Book of New Sherlock Holmes Stories

MX Publishing is a social enterprise – all the staff, including me, are volunteers with day jobs. The collection would not be possible without the creator and editor, David Marcum, who is rightly cited multiple times by *Publishers Weekly* and others as probably the most accomplished Sherlockian editor ever.

In addition to Stepping Stones School, our main program that we support is the Happy Life Children's Home in Kenya. My wife Sharon and I have spent seven Christmas's with the children in Nairobi. Due to the global pandemic we won't be visiting Africa this year.

It's a wonderful project that has saved the lives of over 600 babies. You can read all about the project in the second edition of the book *The Happy Life Story.*

There are very interesting parallels between our work in Africa and the UK – we have Zoom video enabled Happy Life, saving them tens of thousands of dollars in saved travel between their locations. In 2020 we're very proud of our *#bookstotrees* program where every book bought on our *www.mxpublishing.com* website results in a tree being funded at Happy Life. We reached our target of 1,000 trees (and still going) in August.

Our support of both of these projects is possible through the publishing of Sherlock Holmes books, which we have now been doing for twelve years.

You can find out more information
about the Stepping Stones School at:

www.steppingstones.org.uk

and Happy Life at:

www.happylifechildrenshomes.com

You can find out more about MX Publishing
and reach out to us through our website at:

www.mxpublishing.com

Steve Emecz
August 2020
Twitter: *@steveemecz*
LinkedIn: *https://www.linkedin.com/in/emecz/*

A Word From
Stepping Stones
by Jacqueline Silver

Undershaw
September 9, 2016
Grand Opening of the Stepping Stones School
(Photograph courtesy of Roger Johnson)

"Life is infinitely stranger than anything which the mind of man could invent."

– Arthur Conan Doyle

Apt words to describe current times.

Amidst the uncertainty and ongoing challenges, I have been fortunate enough to have recently joined the wonderful community here at Stepping Stones School, where we spend our days in this wonderful building, steeped in literature and history. Now that the school has re-opened after lockdown and we are reunited at Undershaw, we appreciate our school, our surroundings, and each other even more than ever. It is a privilege to lead the school and its students into the future in this most treasured setting, and we remain ever-grateful to you for your ongoing support.

Jacqueline Silver
Headteacher, *Stepping Stones,* Undershaw
September 2020

"Undershaw," Hindhead, Conan Doyle's House.

24

Sherlock Holmes (1854-1957) was born in Yorkshire, England, on 6 January, 1854. In the mid-1870's, he moved to 24 Montague Street, London, where he established himself as the world's first Consulting Detective. After meeting Dr. John H. Watson in early 1881, he and Watson moved to rooms at 221b Baker Street, where his reputation as the world's greatest detective grew for several decades. He was presumed to have died battling noted criminal Professor James Moriarty on 4 May, 1891, but he returned to London on 5 April, 1894, resuming his consulting practice in Baker Street. Retiring to the Sussex coast near Beachy Head in October 1903, he continued to be associated in various private and government investigations while giving the impression of being a reclusive apiarist. He was very involved in the events encompassing World War I, and to a lesser degree those of World War II. He passed away peacefully upon the cliffs above his Sussex home on his 103rd birthday, 6 January, 1957.

Dr. John Hamish Watson (1852-1929) was born in Stranraer, Scotland on 7 August, 1852. In 1878, he took his Doctor of Medicine Degree from the University of London, and later joined the army as a surgeon. Wounded at the Battle of Maiwand in Afghanistan (27 July, 1880), he returned to London late that same year. On New Year's Day, 1881, he was introduced to Sherlock Holmes in the chemical laboratory at Barts. Agreeing to share rooms with Holmes in Baker Street, Watson became invaluable to Holmes's consulting detective practice. Watson was married and widowed three times, and from the late 1880's onward, in addition to his participation in Holmes's investigations and his medical practice, he chronicled Holmes's adventures, with the assistance of his literary agent, Sir Arthur Conan Doyle, in a series of popular narratives, most of which were first published in *The Strand* magazine. Watson's later years were spent preparing a vast number of his notes of Holmes's cases for future publication. Following a final important investigation with Holmes, Watson contracted pneumonia and passed away on 24 July, 1929.

Photos of Sherlock Holmes and Dr. John H. Watson courtesy of Roger Johnson

The
MX Book
of
New
Sherlock
Holmes
Stories

Part XXII: Some More Untold Cases (1877-1887)

32

The Philosophy of Holmes
by Christopher James

Do not let your vices exceed your virtues.
Always choose the strongest tobacco
and hide it where it cannot be found.
Only brush the teeth you want to keep.
A disordered house is not always the sign
of a disordered mind. Sleep is overrated.
Venture out in the rain only if you must.
A good ulster is worth two umbrellas
Wear a hat to suit the season. Do not
be afraid to wear a dressing gown past noon.
Listen to your friends, but measure yourself
against your enemies. A doctor in the house
is worth two in the bush. Never explain,
never apologise, never say never.
Memorise the train timetable and know
the names of your cabbies. Only drink claret
on Thursdays. Only bet on a certainty.
Listen more than you speak. If you plan
to break the law, watch where you drop
the ash from your cigar. Make time for music.
Never overlook a trifle. Eliminate the impossible.

The Terror of the Tankerville
by S.F. Bennett

"**G**ood heavens!" I exclaimed as we dawdled over breakfast one morning in the late autumn of 1889. "Why, Holmes, here is mention of your brother in *The Times*. Something about a charitable bequest?"

"Yes, Mycroft did mention something of the sort." He ran a lazy eye over the article I had passed him. As he read further, he gave a wry chuckle. "Listen to this: '*Mr. Mycroft Holmes, presenting the donation to the Fund for Decayed Authors on behalf of the Diogenes Club of Pall Mall, spoke of the necessity for generosity at a time of great hardship for many. "It is a regrettable truth of our age that the poor are always with us," said Mr. Holmes. "Therefore, it is incumbent upon us to follow the Biblical example of being open-handed towards one's brothers and the poor and needy of our land."'* Dear me, what a pompous fellow Mycroft is!"

"It sounds most generous to me."

"My dear Watson," Holmes said evenly, "when have you ever known the members of the Diogenes to rouse themselves for anything other than their own interests? Have you not seen in the press lately speculation about the nature of a man who would begrudge a matchstick girl her ha'penny, yet spend five guineas on a bottle of claret? Several of the neighbouring clubs have already come under fire for what has been decried as 'untrammelled decadence'. No doubt Mycroft had wind that the Diogenes would be next. This is nothing more than an attempt to pour oil on troubled waters."

"All the same, the amount in question is considerable."

"They can afford it," Holmes said dismissively. "And worth the expense to keep the wolves from their door, I dare say."

"You disapprove," I noted.

Holmes replaced his cup in its saucer with a sigh. "I have reason to count my membership of such institutions as nil. How may one seek to solve the world's mysteries if one retreats from it?"

"That is a very narrow view," I countered. "There is more to it than that. Why, the companionship of one's fellows – "

"Which appeals to me even less, present company excepted. Forgive me, Watson, but you speak as a clubbable man. You have become habituated to the routine. Had you half my experience with such places, you would never set foot across any of their thresholds again."

I smiled. "Surely you exaggerate, Holmes."

35

"Not at all. Some of my most interesting cases have originated from those who count themselves as clubmen."

"For instance?"

"Major Prendergast."

The name struck a chord and it took a moment for me to remember where I had heard it before. "Of the Tankerville Club? He recommended you to that poor devil, Openshaw. I recall you mentioning something about an accusation of cheating at cards."

"There was rather more to it than that."

Holmes rose and filled his pipe. I gathered he was in a restless mood and, with no case at hand, had deigned to enlighten me on the error of my ways and the shortcomings of clubs in general. As it happened, with rain pelting on the windows and no calls upon my time, either professional or domestic, I could think of no better way to pass a desultory morning than to hear of one of Holmes's early investigations. Over our years of association, he had tantalised me with many a passing reference to some obscure case of which I had no knowledge and on which he would later refuse to be drawn. So rare were the times when the humour took him to share that he invariably commanded my undivided attention.

"The accusation of cheating was dire enough to warrant the Major's misery, but it was not that which brought him to my door. The man was in fear of his life!" A waft of blue smoke rose from his pipe to the ceiling as he eyed me mischievously. "Would you care to hear about the case? I realise that Mrs. Watson is away, but one wouldn't wish to be the reason that causes you to neglect your home."

"My home will keep well enough," I said, settling myself on the sofa and waiting for him to begin. "And I am burning with curiosity."

"Well then," he began, "you expressed surprise at seeing my brother's name in the paper. However, had you been a subscriber to *The Times* in the March of 1877, you would have seen Mycroft's name attached to mine as my next of kin in a notice of my sudden death, along with some florid words about the promise of youth cut short or some such nonsense. The line was from Marlowe's *Doctor Faustus* as I recall: '*Cut is the branch that might have grown full straight, And burned is Apollo's laurel bough*'. I remember Mycroft being particularly pleased with his choice at the time. He still quotes it at me regularly whenever he is in one of his less forgiving moods."

"But, my dear Holmes, do you mean to tell me he believed you were dead?"

"Ostensibly. And half of London with him."

"What of the other half?"

"They do not read *The Times*. Nor, I dare say, do they care one jot for the passing of feckless young men who dabble in crime and find themselves the victims of it. However, my quarry did and that was worth the doing of it." He made a small expression of triumph. "To say nothing of the fact that it was nearer to the truth than either Mycroft or I would have wished it to have been."

"Your life was threatened?"

"Quite so," he mused. "But for a stroke of good fortune, my 'branch' would indeed have been 'cut', as Marlowe has it. Such is the folly of youth."

He took a seat in his usual fireside chair.

"Admit that you are intrigued, Watson."

"Shocked, certainly."

"'*Needs must when the Devil drives*'," he said grimly. "And never was there such a devil as Colonel Francis Afton." He drew thoughtfully on his pipe. "You see, Watson, your influence is pernicious. I have developed your habit of beginning at the end of the tale and neglecting the facts of the case."

"Would you mind if I took notes?" I asked, reaching for my journal.

"By all means. Someone may find it of use at some later date. *Spectemur agendo*, as Ovid has it. Although," he added, "if I am to be judged by my deeds in this instance, any sane man would have recommended a less perilous occupation than that of consulting detective. Are you ready?"

I nodded, pen poised over the page.

"Capital!" A dreamy, faraway look came into his eye as he delved into his memory. "It began, as did many of my early cases, with a chance encounter with the man who was to present me with an opportunity to exercise my skills. You will remember I wasn't so well known in those days. Consequently I was obliged to take whatever came my way. It was a disheartening experience, I will not deny. Having presented myself to the world, I expected the world to come calling. Instead I found myself frequently disappointed and burdened with debt.

"The consequence of this was the necessity to fall upon my brother's goodwill. This he tolerated to some extent. To his credit, he didn't exactly discourage me, but neither did he encourage me. The exception to this rule was in the case of Major Prendergast.

"As it happened, I found myself going cap in hand to my brother when I had neither coke for the fire nor coat for my back. I expected another lecture on the wisdom of my choice of career. What I found instead was Mycroft attempting to offer solace to a gentleman who appeared to be on the verge of breaking down. Only those who have ever witnessed my brother's sorry efforts in this field will understand when I say he was failing miserably. Scarce had I been admitted into Mycroft's rooms than the fellow clasped his hands to his face and began to rend his hair.

"'Courage, sir!' Mycroft reprimanded his unhappy guest. 'Standards cannot be allowed to slip because you face ruin. The other tenants will be complaining if you keep this up.'" Holmes gave a soft grunt of laughter. "As I say, Mycroft's idea of sympathy is somewhat lacking."

Having met his brother, I could well believe what he was telling me.

"You will understand that this isn't the usual reception one expects when one calls on Mycroft," Holmes continued. "My curiosity was naturally aroused – especially when his landlady made her presence known to insist that the noise be kept down.

"'What the deuce is going on?' I wanted to know when he had ushered her out and closed the door on prying eyes.

"Mycroft glanced imperiously down his nose at me. 'What business is that of yours, sir? Although from the sight of you, Sherlock, the reason for your being here is evident. Tell me the amount and I shall send you a cheque. Now be gone with you.'

"I wasn't about to let petty financial concerns deter me. I stood my ground.

"'Who is this?'

"'Major Prendergast,' said he finally and grudgingly. 'Prendergast, this is my younger brother, Sherlock. Prendergast *idles* for Queen and country, and consequently never has any money. That is something the pair of you have in common.'

A thin-faced, sandy-haired man of five-and-forty years with his cares worn freely for all to see, the Major pulled himself together enough to acknowledge my presence.

"'In my case, the fault is my own,' said Prendergast, rising to his feet. 'Forgive me, I should never have come. I didn't know where else to turn.'

"'Indeed. Goodnight, Major,' said Mycroft, opening the door for him. 'You too, Sherlock. We have had quite enough excitement for one night.'

"I ignored him. Patience has never been my brother's strong suit.

"'What is the nature of the problem?' I asked.

"'A gambling debt,' said Prendergast. 'Or rather, the results of one. Should I leave this house, I believe I will never make it to the end of the street alive. *He* will kill me, Mr. Holmes.'

"One should never revel in the misery of others, but I will admit that this presented possibilities. 'Who wishes to kill you?' I urged.

"'Colonel Afton!' He choked back a strangled sob. 'You aren't familiar with his name, I can see that. To him I owe this debt, and I fear he will demand it in blood!'

38

"I looked to my brother for an explanation, for Prendergast was near insensible with terror.

"'Prendergast is the second cousin of a certain government minister,' said Mycroft wearily. 'We have some slight acquaintance on account of being members of this same club where the unfortunate debt was incurred.'

"That told me nothing. In those days, Mycroft changed clubs as regularly as his collar. Unable to find one that met his requirements, he eventually decided to set up his own. Thus did necessity give birth to the Diogenes.

"'My club is the Tankerville,' said the Major when I urged him to tell his tale. "I lost a great deal of money at cards. No small sum, Mr. Holmes. Indeed, just shy of £5,000.'

"He took a deep, steadying breath and began to toy with a small gold band set with a diamond chip worn on his fourth finger. Rather a tawdry item, much battered and marked, I observed, which sat incongruously with the cut and style of his clothes. A piece of some sentimental value clearly, for it was a size too small for him and fashioned for a lady, yet not a memory of some past love to be kept safely on the watch chain, but instead something he needed to hand immediately. From this and from the little he had told me, I gathered that Prendergast made his money at the gaming tables and this ring he counted as his 'good luck' charm. You may have noticed that even the casual gambler is a fellow of many superstitions. Where to sit, which way he turns upon entering the establishment, the objects he believes enhances his 'luck' – all these may be of importance to the devotee of the game of chance. I have written a monograph on the subject, if you are interested."

"I'm told white heather or a rabbit's foot has been credited with the same properties," I commented, "which much the same efficacy, I should imagine."

"Do you deny then that you have a tried-and-tested ritual when it comes to your own wagers?" Holmes said, his gaze darting in my direction. "I know, when you choose *that* chair and the same stump of a pencil with which you refuse to be parted, that you are making your selection for the day's race meetings."

I shifted slightly in my seat. He was, as usual, correct. I hadn't realised it was that obvious.

"In the case of Major Prendergast," Holmes continued, "he readily confirmed what I had already deduced. 'I rely on cards and horses for my income,' he said. 'God knows there's little else I'm good at, save soldiering, and those days are long over. A bullet through the liver in the colonies put paid to that. Well, I've been somewhat down on my luck of late, and when several fellows at the club asked me to join them for whist, I leapt at the opportunity. However, I soon found myself out of pocket. I have never had such a run of bad luck. On the final hand, I thought my fortunes were turning. I was mistaken.'

He shook his head, whether out of regret or disbelief, I was loath to say, although both were applicable to Prendergast's situation.

"'I didn't know what to do, gentlemen,' he continued. 'I hadn't such a sum to pay them. I was facing ruin and my reputation with it. And then, in the depths of my despair, Afton offered me a lifeline. He was willing to cover the debt.'

"'That was most generous of him,' I said. 'What did he want in return?'

"'Certain assurances. I have a maiden aunt of advancing years of whom I have expectations. Afton offered me an advancement on any future inheritance, from which he would receive his initial sum and plus half again as interest.'

"'Most unwise,' said Mycroft. 'What if the lady had changed her will?'

"'Afton had thought of that,' said Prendergast. 'He was prepared to accept that risk in return for me agreeing for him to take out an insurance policy on my life.'

"I glanced over at Mycroft. It sounded a dubious arrangement if ever there was one.

"'Well, I accepted,' said the Major. 'What else was I to do? We signed a contract and made the necessary arrangements that very night. The next morning, I attended the offices of the insurance company and the policy was issued.'

"'Did you not think it odd that a stranger would be willing to help in this manner?' I asked.

"'I fear I did not,' he admitted. 'I was grateful beyond words. He was very good about it too. Anything to help a fellow member of the Tankerville and a fellow officer, he said. He was willing to take my word as to the situation with my aunt and made our deal before he had ever confirmed it with her. Well, that is where my problems began. My aunt was furious when she received the letter from Afton informing her of our arrangement. She cut me out of her will that same day. That left the life insurance policy.'

"His hands had begun to shake.

"'It was only when I read the finer detail that I realised the danger I had unwittingly fallen into. In the event of my death, by whatever means, Afton stands to receive £20,000. Dear heavens!' he wailed. 'I am worth more dead than alive!'

"'You have been very foolish,' said Mycroft. 'That much is evident.'

"'I went to Afton, offering to pay back everything I owed,' said Prendergast. 'I was confident I could win enough at the tables to clear my debt. I explained my predicament and he was willing to accept my terms for payment of the original sum plus interest. He was really rather reasonable about it, considering the circumstances. The policy was to remain active, however. Well, I thought no more of it until today.'

"He paused in his tale and wrung his hands earnestly.

"'There has been an accusation made that I have been cheating at the tables,' he said in anguish. "It is unfounded, I swear it, but until my name is cleared, I'm barred from my only source of income. If I cannot pay what I owe, then I am a dead man.' A sheen of sweat appeared on his face. 'I have faced such horrors in my life, gentlemen, that I cannot begin to describe. But will confess that the prospect of what might happen in the next few hours fills me with an unspeakable terror. For tonight, as I was headed home, I was certain I was being followed.'

"'Did you see who it was?' I asked.

"'No, I was terrified to look behind me,' he said. 'I ran the length of Pall Mall, not knowing where to go for the best, until I remembered having seen Mr. Holmes entering this building. Your brother has been good enough to offer me refuge in my hour of need. But God knows what is to become of me now!'

"'And here he has been ever since,' said Mycroft gruffly.

"I took my brother aside, out of Prendergast's earshot. 'What do you intend to do with him?' I enquired.

"'He is not my responsibility,' my brother countered.

"'His relative – the aunt – must be informed.'

"'He has. She wants nothing to do with him. She wants to distance herself from any scandal.'

"'Then the money must be found.'

"'What do you want me to do, Sherlock, adopt him?' Mycroft looked affronted. 'It is onerous enough supporting you without taking on other people's waifs and strays. Do you imagine I can simply lay my hand on such a sum?'

"'If you send him away, you will sign his death warrant.'

"'That is not my concern. I happen to believe that a man's debts are his own affair,' stated Mycroft. 'That is a lesson I trust you one day will learn.'

"'You leave me no choice,' I said. 'If you will do nothing, then I shall accompany him to his home.'

"My brother has two inches on me in height when he can be bothered to make use of them. He attempted to do so that night, to little effect, for I

41

wouldn't be forced to back down. Mycroft has his faults, but he can usually be relied upon to do the right thing in a crisis, once his conscience is pricked.

"'Very well,' said he, sighing with annoyance. 'I shall have someone collect him and deliver him to Dover. A trip to the Continent should put him beyond this Afton's reach.'

Holmes stretched out his legs and bent his eyes upon the fire. Outside our window, the rain was growing ever heavier, blurring the line between grey sky and grey buildings.

"Well, Watson," said he, once he had refilled his pipe, "the thing was done and we managed to get Prendergast away without incident. He left England dishonoured without a penny to his name, save the clothes upon his back and that small gold ring. That he was alive was the greater victory. I didn't discount, however, that Prendergast's fears had been nothing more than the product of his own fevered imagination. After all, there was nothing to say that Afton was planning his murder to recoup his losses.

"It was the insistence on the insurance policy that told me my instincts weren't at fault. I fell to wondering how many others hadn't been so fortunate. That there had been others – of that I was certain. Once a criminal establishes a successful pattern, he invariably holds his course.

"It was no easy thing to set myself upon Afton's trail. Scandals of this nature tend to be kept within families, so that it seemed to me that my first port of call should be to the insurance companies themselves. I discounted the larger associations – losses in the order of £20,000 would raise more than a few eyebrows and warrant a strenuous investigation. They were also more likely to turn down such an application. Therefore, it was to the smaller companies I turned.

"It was at the fifteenth such office I tried that I finally found my mark. The agent, Mr. Martin Warner, had blanched at the name of Colonel Afton, and it had taken some convincing on my part that we shared a mutual interest before he would tell me what he knew of the gentleman.

"Three years before, so Warner told me, a policy for life insurance had been taken out on Simeon Henry Phinn, in the amount of £30,000. The premium had been paid by Afton and he was named as the sole beneficiary. Phinn was twenty-eight years of age at the time and comfortably expected to outlive the policy, which had clauses at to the exact circumstances in which the contract would be terminated. Warner had no problem in doing so. Since the 1744 Gambling Act, it hasn't been legally possible to take out life insurance on another person unless a legitimate insurable interest can be demonstrated. The debt gave Afton that interest, and he paid a higher premium than usual to include a clause stipulating that payment would be guaranteed even in the event of the suicide of the insured. He also required that the policy be indisputable, whereby the power of the company to contest a claim was removed.

"All was well and good, until the unfortunate Phinn was found dead in his rooms at the Albany, an empty bottle of laudanum beneath his bed. To spare the family, misadventure was the official verdict of the inquest, and the policy paid out. According to Warner, the sum brought the company to the verge of bankruptcy. Others, he said, hadn't been so fortunate. He had had his suspicions at the time, but since Phinn had been found in a locked room and the key had been on his person, the investigation proved fruitless.

"I was willing to trust to Warner's impressions, however. As he said, why was the key on his person? Why would a man about to take his own life take care to stow it in his pocket? And why was the laudanum *under* the bed? If, as he argued, it had fallen from his dead hand, why were his arms well inside the limits of the bed when he was found?

"A most sagacious fellow, Watson! From his own enquiries, he had found at least eight other companies with whom Afton had held one of these policies over the course of ten years. Following his successful claims, they had been forced to close their doors.

"All of this would seem to indicate some wrongdoing on Afton's part. However, in the cases identified, suicide had claimed the lives of five and accidents the other three. Furthermore, by dint of my own efforts, I was able to identify six other companies where the policy had been terminated by immediate payment of the debt and interest, no doubt by relatives fearful of the consequences.

"You will understand my dilemma. The fact that Afton had been willing to accept payment in some cases, coupled with the nature of the debt and the inherent fear of disgrace that drives a man to take his own life, could have indicated that we had cast aspersions over a man who had, in fact, done nothing wrong except extend the hand of largesse. I was compelled, therefore, to visit any surviving relatives of Simeon Henry Phinn to learn of their impression of the fellow.

"Of the family, only his mother would talk to me. The father had died a year after the son, of a 'broken heart', according to Mrs. Phinn. When it came to Colonel Afton, the lady was firm in her convictions.

"'My son would never have taken his own life!' she declared.

"'The debt was considerable,' I said. 'How can you be sure?'

"'Because he had no concept of honour, Mr. Holmes. The debt was nothing to him. Indeed, I received a letter from him, the morning he was found dead, saying he intended to leave the country to escape his obligations.'

"At my request, she produced the letter. Despite Mrs. Phinn's assurances to the contrary, I could see how Phinn's talk of 'going away' might be construed to have another meaning.

"'He was a wastrel,' said Mrs. Phinn. 'He knew all the sins of the world and revelled in them. We could do nothing with him. But for all that, he was my youngest boy. The money would have been found. Had he told us of his predicament, I would have sold everything I owned to deliver him from this fate.'

"And then, when I thought I'd heard the last of it, Mrs. Phinn had one final revelation for me. 'His death killed his poor father, of that I am sure,' said she. 'He was scandalised that Simeon had dared to presume upon an inheritance. He cut him off without a penny. Then came the accusation of cheating. It sent him into a rage. But he had a good heart, Mr. Holmes. He would have forgiven Simeon, given time.'

"Here at last was a pattern. 'Cheating?' I asked.

"'At cards,' the lady explained. 'He was expelled from his club on account of it. He died that same night.'

"'And the name of this club?'

"'The Tankerville.'

"Now some will tell you that coincidences occur with greater frequency than the universe might allow. However, I contend that they shouldn't happen in the same club with the same accusation levelled at a member who owed a debt to the same gentlemen. You will agree it was a step too far. And with the trail cold after so many years, it was evident that a vigorous investigation was necessary on my part. Predictably, Mycroft was less convinced.

"'Out of the question!' said he when I put it to him.

"'All I need is your recommendation for my membership of the Tankerville Club,' I told him. 'A letter disinheriting me at the appropriate time will also be required.'

"As good as his arguments were to the contrary, he was at the mercy of greater forces. The Prime Minister had learned of Mycroft's part in helping a man accused of cheating leave the country and was less than impressed. This, coupled with the swelling scandal that threatened a senior member of government, eventually swayed his decision.

"So it was that several days later, I entered the Tankerville, adopting the demeanour of a gadabout with fine feathers and a careless attitude when it came to money. If I was right, then I was certain I would attract Afton's attention. Sure enough, after a week at the gaming tables, I was approached by two fellows who invited me to join them for baccarat. I can hold my own at the card tables, but against these two, I soon found myself out of my depth. A finer pair of cardsharps I have never encountered. Oh, it was very artfully done. False shuffles, bottom dealing, holdouts – I learned a thing or two that night.

"I allowed the game to continue, recklessly doubling my stakes out of sheer bravado, suspecting that this was the first act in Afton's drama, and by the end of the evening, I had losses of £6,000. I wrote them notes promising to pay by tomorrow and retreated to the Smoking Room to drown my sorrows with a brandy. It was then I was approached by another man, who introduced himself as Colonel Francis Afton.'

"Afton was tall and wiry, nearing his sixth decade, with a thin but well-favoured face, searching brown eyes, and greying hair starting to recede at the temples. Injury had put paid to his military career, for he had a stiff gait, and took his seat opposite mine with some difficulty. On his gold watch chain, he wore a large opal, rough-cut and polished, a fair amateur effort.

"There is a popular belief that opals are unlucky, but here was a man who either laughed in the face of superstition or had some personal reason for keeping it on his person. I came to the conclusion that both were applicable, and in the case of the latter, I later learned he had found the opal in question in Australia and had attempted the cutting himself. Again, no minor feat, for opals are liable to be damaged in the process. Here then was a man of considerable pluck. His military record bore out this observation. He had been in the Crimea at Inkerman with the 20th Foot, where he had served with distinction. How he came to be lending money to impecunious young men was a story that was worth the hearing.

"'Mr. Sherlock Holmes, isn't it?' said he. I gestured for him to join me. 'I hear you had some bad luck tonight at the tables.'

"'A trifle, sir,' I replied.

"'Perhaps to you. A small fortune to others.' He took a sip of his brandy and considered. 'Do you have the means to pay it?'

"'Eventually.'

"'Ah.' He placed his glass with care on the table. 'In my experience, Mr. Holmes, such men do not count patience as a virtue.'

"'That may be true. However, I have no other option.'

"'Well,' he said, sitting forward in his chair in the manner of one about to share a confidence, 'what if I were to tell you that I am in a position to cover your debt?'

"'Why would you do that?' I replied.

"He shrugged. 'I was young once. I know how it is to be hampered by lack of money. Besides, if a gentleman cannot help a fellow of the same club, then what the devil use is membership?'

"All very plausible and not in the least believable. As I expected, the lure was about to dangled in front of me and the spider was ready to pounce.

"'And what do you get in return?' I asked.

"He took out his cigarette case and offered one to me. 'A consideration. Tell me, do you have any expectations of your relatives?'

"'I have only a brother,' I said, lighting my cigarette from the match he offered. 'You may know him: Mycroft Holmes. He is a member of the Tankerville too.'

"His eyes narrowed in an effort of remembrance. 'A largish fellow, given to sitting in corners and complaining about the noise?'

"I nodded. 'He allows me a small annuity. Such are his miserly ways that I should be kept poor if I had not the advantage of living by my wits.'

"'You are his only relative,' Afton said thoughtfully. 'What if we were to consider this a loan against your future inheritance? I trust you are named in his will?'

"I confirmed that I was and so the thing was done," said Holmes, rising from his seat to ease his cramped limbs. A turn about the room allowed me to catch up with my note taking, and by the time he had taken a look out of the rain-washed window and drawn the blind in disgust, I was ready to document the next chapter in the tale. He took up position before the fire and continued in leisurely fashion.

"We drew up a temporary contract that evening and the money was paid. The next morning I presented myself at the offices of the insurance company. My concern that they would recognise me was unfounded, despite the company being one of the many I had visited during my preliminary investigation. The requirements were met and the policy duly drawn up and stamped.

"The next stage in this grim farrago was the letter that Afton sent to Mycroft. I was with him when he received it. I was present to read his reply, disinheriting me forthwith. When he signed his name, he sighed, laid down his pen and pinched the bridge of his nose.

"'I have just given Afton a mandate for your murder,' said he heavily. 'Tell me you know what you are doing, Sherlock.'

"I outlined my plan. I would go to Afton to offer an alternative, whereby I would pay him back the sum in instalments, plus interest. Afton would accept naturally, to avoid raising suspicions. Then soon after, a spurious accusation of cheating would be made to cut off my only source of income. When, or indeed if, he tried to kill me, then our own trap would be sprung.

"It went exactly as I expected. The agreement was made and I continued with my rash behaviour. Several nights went by and I was again

46

approached by the same gentlemen as before at the club. We played a few hands, during which I was allowed to win, and then came the uproar. A marked card was discovered in the pack and the finger of guilt was pointed at me. I was ejected from the club that same night and told not to return. Thus, I found myself in the same position as the unfortunate Major Prendergast.

"In order to give credence to my new lifestyle, I had secured rooms in one of the better parts of Westminster. It was to these that I now returned. I walked, to give whomever was following me a chance to show their hand. I was, however, disappointed. Unlike Prendergast, I couldn't detect the presence of a silent assassin and made it to my door unchallenged and unharmed. I was beginning to think the Major had been of a fanciful disposition until I checked under my bed and found an empty bottle of laudanum already in place. They had no need to follow me. They knew where I lived. The scene for my murder was set.

"What I didn't know was how they would accomplish it. I had taken the precaution of checking that the window was secure and removing the key from the front door. It hadn't saved young Phinn, but there was no point giving my would-be murderers easy access by turning the key in the lock from the other side. Satisfied the room concealed no lurking creatures ready to sink a poisoned fang into my flesh or gas leaking from a damaged mantel, I lay on my bed in the dark and waited.

"I was convinced an attempt would be made that night, following hard on the heels of my disgrace and removal from the club. If I wouldn't jump of my own accord, then I would be pushed. The clock counted away the hours and time passed. Then, as the distant chimes of Big Ben heralded three in the morning, I became aware of a faint hiss. I sat up, straining to determine the source of the sound. Certain it was coming from the window, I attempted to head in that direction. It was at that moment I experienced an entirely involuntary giggle."

Holmes drew on his pipe, releasing a great cloud of smoke that hung before the lamp and took on an amber hue. "I think you know me well enough, Watson, to know that I am not a man given to 'giggling'."

"I have heard you laugh many times," I admitted.

"Quite so. But a giggle, at a moment of extreme concentration, is quite unlike me. The one I could dismiss, but then it was followed by another and another, until I was quite helpless with laughter. I realised the seriousness of my situation. I was being systematically poisoned with nitrous oxide. How I got to my feet, I shall never know. I remember being as weak as a new-born and the mere effort of getting up was exhausting. By some method, I made it to the window, only to find it fastened exactly as I had left it. I fumbled with the catch, except my fingers were all thumbs

47

and appeared to be made of lead. The room itself felt like it was tilting, a strange experience, which only served to increase my feeling of confusion.

"I was dying, Watson, and if I hadn't a fragment of sense remaining to me in those final minutes, I should surely have perished. Instead, I took up the chair and hurled it through the pane.

As if reliving the moment, his breathing had quickened and a touch of colour stained his pale cheeks.

"Never have I been more grateful for the lungful of London air that came through that broken glass," he went on. "I breathed deeply and the fog in my mind began to clear. I had my answer as to how young Phinn had met his death. One would hope the average doctor could tell the difference between a death caused by laudanum and another due to nitrous oxide. However, in this case, the mountain of evidence pointed to the former and anything which deviated from this had been dismissed as an anomaly.

"As to the method of delivery, on inspection I found a small plug of wood on the floor. In my absence, a hole had been drilled through the corner of the window frame and concealed with this plug and a thin coating of paint and grime. When a tube or small pipe was inserted from the outside, the plug would be dislodged and the gas allowed to permeate the room. But for the rug beneath the window, I should have been alerted by the sound as it hit the floor. It isn't often I'm forced to admit to a mistake, Watson. However, but for the greatest of good fortune that night, I should have paid the ultimate penalty for having been found wanting in that respect. It was a salutary lesson in the necessity for observation.

"Nor did I have my culprit. Whomever had done this had scaled a drainpipe with a cylinder of nitrous oxide to my window on the third floor. No mean feat for the average man, let alone the Colonel with his old injury. I already knew he employed lackeys – the cardsharps at the club were proof enough, and this agile fellow was evidently another. Armed with this, I persuaded my brother to go along with the pretence that the attempt on my life had been successful. He played the part of a grieving relative to perfection. The notice of my death duly appeared in the press and bought me another day to complete my investigation.

"Nitrous oxide is not something to be found on the shelves of the local chemist shop. It must have been stolen to order, for it isn't the first thing a thief might think to take. By mid-morning, at the expense of good shoe leather, I had located an aggrieved dentist in Chelsea whose premises had been burgled several days before. A cylinder of nitrous oxide had been stolen, and with it a small piece of gold that had been removed from a patient's tooth earlier in the day.

48

"An easy thing to overlook, yet a valuable clue! I set my Irregulars to work and, by the end of the day, I had the name of a pawnbroker in Aldgate who had accepted the gold in settlement of a debt. A personal call and a sovereign eased his conscience and bought me the identity of the thief, John Finch, a former acrobat in a travelling circus who performed under the name of 'The Flying Finch' until a weakening of his constitution brought his career to an end. The prospect of the hangman's noose soon loosened his tongue once the police arrived. If further confirmation was needed of his part in the crime, an empty cylinder of nitrous oxide was discovered in his rooms. He had kept it in order to sell it for its value as scrap metal. See, Watson, how pernicious is the misery of poverty. Even with the sum he was to receive from Colonel Afton, he had kept the incriminating evidence in order to get a few pennies more.

"After that, it was a question of waiting for Afton to make his move. Accordingly the next morning, I attended the office of the insurance company with two constables and Inspector Moncrief from Scotland Yard. The colonel was not slow in making his claim."

At this point in his narrative, Holmes smiled with a degree of satisfaction.

"You may imagine his surprise when he saw me. Bluster turned to insults when Moncrief told him his accomplice had implicated him the deaths of Simeon Henry Phinn and several other men, killed variously by nitrous oxide poisoning, accidents, and slayings arranged to look like suicide.

"'Curse you, Holmes!' the fellow raged as they wrestled the handcuffs on him.

"'Why did you do it, Colonel?' Moncrief asked him.

"Seeing all was lost, the man calmed and sneered. 'The money, why else?'

"'That's pretty cold-blooded, sir, if you don't mind me saying.'

"'What other value were they?' Afton declared, reserving his bile for me. 'I have seen a thousand men die on the battlefield who were each worth ten of these idle wretches. Better that their deaths have some profit to me than that they fritter away their meaningless existence to the detriment of everyone else!'

"Such was the end of the case. Afton's accomplices at the club were apprehended and Prendergast vindicated. I dare say he does have good cause to remember me. For myself, I was richer for the experience. Neglect of the smallest detail is a mistake I have never made again."

At this, Holmes sighed and his gaze moved far beyond the confines of our smoky room to a place somewhere in the distant past.

"As they took Afton away, I saw a glint of fire in that fine opal of his as it caught the light. Did you know, Watson, the Romans believed the opal gave the wearer the power of invisibility, making it an attractive talisman for thieves and robbers? Equally, some in the medieval world equated it with the 'Evil Eye' of legend, and credited it with the ability to bring misfortune. How apt it should have been the gemstone of choice for Colonel Afton."

He tapped out his pipe and threw it onto the mantel.

"But come, enough of this gloom. The rain is stopping. Lunch is called for, my dear fellow, followed by a walk through the park and then a concert."

"There is a comic opera at the Savoy tonight," I suggested.

"Not my first choice," said Holmes, "but fitting, given the tale you have just heard. After all, *voluntary* laughter is the best medicine!"

"I have heard of you, Mr. Holmes. I heard from Major Prendergast how you saved him in the Tankerville Club scandal."
"Ah, of course. He was wrongfully accused of cheating at cards."

– John Openshaw and Sherlock Holmes
"The Five Orange Pips"

50

The Singular Affair of the Aluminium Crutch
by William Todd

Sherlock Holmes had always been a creature of Bohemian and slovenly habits. He seemed more at home discarding superfluous paraphernalia onto the floor or in an ashtray or under a chair (or in a slipper!) rather than putting them what I would regard as their rightful place. And when it came to the systematic filing of his past cases and the little trinkets he would sometimes keep, he was just as slapdash. He had them cloistered away in a tin box using a system of categorization as seemingly unbreakable as Vigenère's Cipher. This box would travel arbitrarily from room to room. I might find it under our dining table one day and next to the hearth on another. I have even seen it used as an extra area to place chemistry beakers during an experiment. Its particular spot at any given moment depended wholly on his predilection that day.

So, it was with intrigue that I gazed upon my flat-mate one dreary April day in '88 as he rummaged through a chest – the box's current home. He had just pulled an aluminium crutch from the back corner and was examining it with an expression of fond reminiscence.

"Good morning, Watson," said he without taking his gaze from the crutch.

"Doing some spring cleaning?" I mused as I poured a cup of tea from a setting on a side table.

"Don't be ridiculous," was Holmes's glib reply. "The place is clean enough for my benefit. No, I was just reacquainting myself with one of my old cases. It was when I was first establishing my bona fides in my days on Montague Street. A young woman, Joan Costello, was brutally attacked and forced-upon in her flat in the dead of a sultry summer night. The intruder, I was able to establish, was her stepfather. The authorities barely gave him a second look, for they thought he had an ironclad alibi, and no investigation beyond that was pursued. I, fortunately, was able to demonstrate the contrary. At any rate, it seems the wretch, Mr. Charles Newcomb, has just been released from almost a decade at Wormwood."

"That doesn't seem to be an adequate amount of time to be jailed," I replied with more than a bit of exasperation. "The consequences for crimes such as what this poor girl most likely endured should be of the most severe kind."

51

"Agreed, my dear fellow. The only saving grace that kept him from a much dire fate was the fact that an insomniatic, old widower living in the flat above her heard the muffled cries and went down to check on Miss Costello. When he knocked on the door, her stepfather, whom she couldn't identify in the almost absolute darkness of the room, escaped out through an open window and down a fire escape to the street below before he completed the act. The young lady is now married with children and wants to make sure there are no further altercations – since there are still family ties – and has employed me to that effect. It is a little beneath me, I think, but I acquiesced out of a certain . . . *client loyalty*, shall we say. I will have a word with Mr. Newcomb to let him know that he is being watched and to have no contact whatever with his stepdaughter. Anything even appearing untoward on his part shall be dealt with swiftly and harshly. I believe the warning and the fear of reincarceration shall be all that is needed to prevent a second attempt."

Pointing to the crutch I asked, "Was that part of the investigation?"

"This? Oh, no. I have been bitten by that anomalous insect which is often a scourge on the human psyche – *nostalgia*. After going over and reacquainting myself with some of the finer points of the Costello case, I refiled it but found this old aluminium crutch in the back corner, which drew my mind back to another case that involved a friend – well more of an acquaintance than a friend – from my university days. Oh, it wasn't a remarkable case in any fashion with regard to my investigative capabilities, so I doubt it would have sufficient substance to interest you, but I daresay it is a memory I look back upon fondly."

"If it was such a pedestrian circumstance, why have the keepsake at all?"

"Precisely because I very nearly lost my life in bringing it to a successful conclusion."

He tossed the crutch over to me, almost making me spill my tea. "What can you make of it? It is very telling in and of itself, and I was able to discern much just from its examination."

I replaced my cup on the setting and turned the thing over in my hands. "Well, the first obvious thing one can gauge from it is the height of the individual." I then stuck the leather-padded top of the crutch under my arm, standing slightly tiptoed as I did so. "He is taller than me, but I daresay it looks as though it would fit easily under your arms, so he would be a bit shorter than you. I would venture the owner to be about six feet tall."

Holmes clapped his hands. "Bravo, Watson! Why a *he*? Could it not be a woman's crutch?"

"Although it isn't out of the question for a woman to reach that height, it is, however, unlikely, generally speaking. And you have already mentioned a friend from university as its owner, so I ventured the owner as male."

He sat in his chair next to the hearth, animatedly threw one leg over the other, and, with the thinnest of grins, replied, "I find fault in your assumption."

"On what point did I err?"

"I said he was an acquaintance from my university days, but I didn't mention the owner of the crutch having gone to university *with* me."

"Quite right, quite right," I replied a bit subjugated at my mistake.

"You are nevertheless correct," Holmes then interjected. "Correct speculation is as accurate as a correct proof. Pray tell, continue."

I looked it over more intently. Assessing a person's height wasn't all that difficult a fact to establish. This is where most normal men's acumen ended, yet this wouldn't have even scratched the surface of Holmes's intellect. Doing my best, I then added, "It is made from aluminium. Even a decade ago, an aluminium crutch would have been a relatively expensive purchase compared to wooden crutches, so I would guess the owner was of some wealth."

"Correct. You are doing splendidly thus far."

"I see no inscriptions, nothing that would give away its owner, though by what it is made of alone, I would venture to guess this is a personally purchased crutch and not one received at hospital."

"That is merely a variable on the wealth of its owner, so no points for that. Go on."

"I don't see what else I can glean from it . . . Oh, wait," I said pointing to some scrawl down one post. "It looks as though someone began to write something." The scrabble was hard to make out. "I believe it says, *Don't F*. But that could mean just about anything – *Don't Fall*, perhaps, since it is a crutch. Maybe a friend etched it, being cheeky about their friend's clumsiness at the act which precipitated and necessitated the crutch."

"Then why is the *cheeky* inscription not finished?"

"Obviously, it was interrupted. The owner left it unattended for a time, perhaps while bathing or toileting or sleeping. There are any number of possibilities as to how the scribble got there. And I only offered that as a possibility. And without a second letter to the missing word, it could mean almost anything."

"Yes," Holmes replied with some little disappointment. "Well, we shall get to that little cipher in due course. Moving on – do you not also see the scratch on one side, just below the grip?"

"I do, but what would that tell me?"

"Look at the other side."

I turned the crutch over. It was unblemished. "What am I looking at?"

"What side of the crutch would tend to become marked with use?"

I thought for a moment, then offered, "The outside, but if you are referring to *which* crutch this is – right or left – I can make the blemished side the outside regardless of the side I place the crutch on. It is just a matter of turning the crutch in my hand."

Holmes sighed, "That is when you next examine the grips and the tip. The side of the grip resting inside the palm would be cleaner and smoother from wear. The leather-wrapped brass-guard at the tip would wear more to the inside, as most people splay their crutches outward slightly. It is a right-hand crutch. I must say, I had thought that having watched me work for several years now, you would have garnered a little more knowledge of my methods. You had shown much promise at the beginning of this little exercise."

I smiled. "Yes, but you have the advantage of hindsight. Did you pick up on all this straightway when *you* first examined the crutch?"

He shot a look at me which gave me the answer in no uncertain terms.

"Of course you did," I answered apologetically. "And how did you come by it, anyway? It is a grey day outside and rain is imminent. I found you lost in this recollection, so now you have a willing audience. Tell me this *singular affair of the aluminium crutch*."

"I shall. Come, sit – but don't be disappointed at the plainness of the events."

I settled in the chair opposite Holmes after having refreshed my tea. "So firstly, how did this gentleman come to having to use the crutch – or is that part of the story?"

"No, the crutch predates the story. Its owner's name is Simon Van Pelt. His family was of some wealth – horse breeding, I believe – with an estate in Surrey. He was left lame after being thrown from his horse at a young age. As was symptomatic of his rather verbose personality, it was a story that he freely and bombastically expounded upon to every available ear at university, whether you were interested in it or not. In my case, as we had many classes together, that rumination was heard *ad nauseam*, whether it was to me he was retelling the story, or I was within earshot of him telling another. It may well be that it was the only memory of note in an otherwise boring and pampered life."

"A-ha!" I exclaimed. "After hearing that, I believe I was right with my first postulation, *Don't Fall*. Or at least that was what the scribbler intended to write before being interrupted."

With a perceptible sigh being my friend's only retort to my theory, Holmes then took a more comfortable position, lit a cigarette, and started as he gazed off, living the memory once more . . . .

"It was early September of '77. A Monday – the third, if memory serves. The day had been sunny, warm, and a bit breezy, as I recall. It was late afternoon, and I had just returned from an errand – I believe to send a telegram. It must have been a trivial matter, for the particulars of it escape me now. When I returned to my small flat in Montague Street, upon the stoop at my front door lay that crutch. Well, at that time I didn't have the services of you, or Mrs. Hudson, or my Baker Street boys, so I started with just this singular clue and nothing more."

"So what information did you glean from the examination of the crutch, and where did it lead you next?" I asked.

"I examined it much the way you just did. I was, however, able to extract a few more points that you missed." He pointed at it, and I examined the area he pointed to. "The most telling being that horizontal scratch on both posts just below the grip. Do you see it?"

"I do," I replied. "What information could that supply?"

"Vital information. As you may know, Montague Street, and my old flat, in particular, isn't far from St. Bartholomew's Hospital."

"Of course. Only about a mile or so, I believe."

He nodded affirmation. "Might you also be aware of a certain dreadful metallic protrusion arising from the door frame at the main entrance?"

I smiled knowingly. "I have ruined more than one sleeve on the old twisted bit of metal or nail or whatever it is . . . dreadful thing. I have complained more than once to have whatever it is embedded in the door frame removed, but it has fallen on deaf ears. It is still there to this day."

"And as you well know, I had used the services of Barts' morgue and chemistry laboratory on more than a few occasions for experiments."

"Of course. It is where we were first introduced."

"Precisely. So it seems we both know from experience about getting caught up on that dreadful doorway. As I examined the crutch, I noticed the scratch on the posts while puzzling over that scrawl etched into the metal. With my proximity to a hospital and the horizontal scratch that would match in height the protrusion on Barts' door, I decided there would be the best place to start my queries. I tossed the crutch into my flat for safekeeping and headed to the hospital.

"When I arrived at Barts, I searched out my friend Stamford, whom you may remember brought us together. 'Ah, Holmes,' he said with a wide smile. 'It has been some time since I last saw you here. You look well.'

"'Indeed,' I replied. 'I have been immersed in some interesting cases of late that have kept me from my customary chemistry experiments. One curiosity, in particular, happens to be a singular aluminium crutch that has been recently placed on my doorstep.'

'Ah, yes. I took it by your appearance that Van Pelt found you.'"

"'Van Pelt?'" I replied.

"'Yes, Simon Van Pelt. I thought your presence here meant he had found you. He came here specifically to search you out. He had been in several times over the past few months with some chronic ailments due to a riding accident from his younger days. I attended him a few times and quite by chance your name was mentioned, and he said he knew you from university.'"

"'I am familiar with the man,' I said, recalling the name, 'although I haven't seen him in almost two years. It is unfortunate, but I wasn't in when he called on me. I found his crutch on my steps. How long ago was he here?'

"'It can't have been more than an hour-and-a-quarter ago. In quite the hurry, too.'

"'Did he mention the nature of his inquiry?' I asked.

"Stamford shook his head, 'No. Only that it was urgent he see you. I think he may have wanted to put that large cranium of yours to use. He seemed eager. No – *vexed* would be the better sentiment.'

"'Was that all?' I asked.

"'That was it. The entire exchange lasted less than a minute. I gave him your address with some cursory directions in case he was unfamiliar with the area, and he hobbled out as fast as he could.'

"I thought for a moment, turning about some ideas in my mind, then asked, 'Did he happen to leave the same way he entered?'

"Stamford thought momentarily then replied, 'By Jove, he did not. How did you know that? He hobbled down the west wing and out the doors at the end of that corridor. I thought nothing of it at the time, for it would be a more direct path to Montague Street rather than going around the hospital.'

"'Thank you,' I replied.

"I turned to leave, but Stamford stopped me in my tracks. 'This may just be a coincidence, but based on how Van Pelt was acting, I doubt so – within minutes of him leaving, a big, burly chap came rushing in. He looked around with the face of a madman. Upon not seeing the object of his quest, he turned and left just as quickly as he entered. I didn't think of it at the time. However, this conversation makes me believe I now know for whom he was looking.'

"'What did this gentleman look like?'

"'Oh, he was no gentleman by *any* stretch of the imagination, Holmes. Big as an ox, jagged scar down his right cheek from his eye to his upper lip, and if the look he wore was meant for Van Pelt, the poor chap was in trouble.'

"I knew who that behemoth was, for I had dealt with him once before. His name is Elias Mudger. He was a notorious shylock, and his methods of extracting overdue payments were positively medieval. My intervention on a case cost him a handsome sum, and if my name had been brought up by Van Pelt at all, that would have given Mudger license to be even more brutal in his retribution."

"Yes," I said knowingly, "I seem to remember that moniker across several headlines some years ago, though I must say he seems to all but have disappeared. My hope is the disappearance means he's currently in the docks."

"Patience, Watson," Holmes reprimanded, flashing a droll grin. "The story must be told correctly and chronologically, or I may end up with one of your tales!"

"My apologies," I replied stolidly. "Pray, continue."

Holmes gave me a passing detached smile and resumed. "I left Barts putting what little I had together in my mind. Van Pelt had something of import to relay to me, obviously having something to do with money owed to Elias Mudger. Van Pelt had stopped at Barts, searching me out, and from there made his way to my flat when he learned of my whereabouts. But Mudger was on his heels. Van Pelt got as far as the steps to my flat before he was overtaken by Mudger. He was probably strong-armed into a waiting carriage and taken away before anyone knew what had happened."

"Did he not come from money?" I asked. "It seems out of place that someone of such high standing would even be associated with such a brute as Mudger."

"Deep pockets do not preclude an individual to amass an even deeper debt. Indeed, wealth may even exacerbate one's proclivity to take on debt. But a few bad wagers can make your liabilities outweigh your assets in the blink of an eye. And if those liabilities are owed to Elias Mudger, your prospects of repayment without some kind of physical retribution are slim. Without knowing the particulars, I believe this is what happened to Van Pelt. He was wagering with sums of money he didn't have and amassing losses he couldn't repay – no different than an addict, only his vice was gambling and not opium.

"Now, it was only a hunch, but I knew of a waterman service not far from Barts where Mudger operated one of his dens. I decided that if getting his quarry off the street and out of the public eye as quickly as possible

57

was his first concern, Mudger would most likely take Van Pelt there. And I knew I had very little time to waste.

"I had a hansom drop me off several buildings north of the waterman's service entrance, and I paid him an entire night's wages to wait in case I needed his services later on – it was a prescient notion and well worth the sum, though at the time money was a bit tighter than it is today. I then went by foot to the waterman's office, but found it locked with a placard on the door that read *Closed for Boat Repairs.* It was then that I knew my deduction had been correct, for every reputable waterman had more than one boat to avoid having to close when one was being repaired.

"I next had to ascertain where in the building Van Pelt was being kept. It was a small, derelict structure, three storeys high, and roughly forty feet from front to back, with a fifteen-foot storefront. I deduced the entire edifice to have twelve to fifteen rooms, front-to-back and top-to-bottom, not counting any rooms below ground.

"First, I looked up the front of the building. A second-floor window was open, and a curtain flickered in the breeze. I doubted Van Pelt would be there or the window wouldn't be open, allowing potential ears to hear Mudger's handiwork. I then stole down a small walkway between the buildings, looking through windows, trying to discover in which room they might be keeping him. Each room drew a blank until I finally arrived at the back of the building. There, through a slit in a pair of dark curtains pulled shut, I saw him – Simon Van Pelt – sitting in a chair with his hands tied behind him. He was sitting at an angle to my line of sight, but there was no mistaking the man. His lip was bloody, and his face was swollen and bruised. Mudger and two of his thugs were standing about talking amongst themselves, on occasion taking a break only to slap Van Pelt across his face for good measure."

"Those thugs!" I exclaimed.

"This was tame compared to what they had planned, of that I was sure. Even so, Van Pelt looked worse for wear.

"The situation became more dire when my ears finally registered a queer monotonous sound coming from my right. It was the thrum of a steamboat idling, docked at the waterman's pier about fifty feet down a gravel embankment. It was small for a steamer, the kind one would use with larger parties than what a wherry could hold or when one was in a hurry to get up or downriver."

I replied with some distress, "That would be the perfect place to torture someone – out in the middle of the Thames with no one around. Then, you could just weigh the body down and toss him overboard, never to be seen again!"

Holmes took a long drag from his cigarette and replied in a puff of smoke, "Precisely, my good man, and that presented me with some dilemmas that needed swift answers. This was most definitely a three-pipe problem, but I was without my pipe, or the time in which to smoke it."

Here he lingered for a long moment, a dramatic pause in the little act being played out for this captive audience of one. Holmes got up and poured himself a cup of tea. Finally, as he reseated himself and took another drag from his cigarette, I exclaimed, "What happened next? There is no need for histrionics."

He gave a mischievous smile. "What is the point of a good story without theatrics? Shakespeare would have never become the literary icon he is without them."

I crossed my arms defiantly and replied, "Then I don't want to hear any lamentations from you when I take a bit of literary license in retelling any future cases."

"*Touché*," said he as he slouched languidly in the chair.

"At that point," I interjected to fill the void, "why not go the constabulary? Certainly catching Mudger with Van Pelt tied up and worked over would have put an end to it."

At this he replied, "Ah, Watson, ever the bastion of prudence, especially with hindsight as your guide. The thought had occurred to me, but I didn't know how much time I had before the cat got away with the mouse. I didn't want to take the chance of leaving, only to return to an empty room, and I would then have all but signed his death warrant, for I wouldn't have known where to find him after that. No, given the choices I had, I believe that I made the right one."

I stopped him. "So at this point, had you actually formed a plan of action?"

"I would like to say I had, but I would be lying. I was very much cobbling it as I went. My technique wasn't as refined as it is all these years later. Though my natural abilities may be something at which to marvel, there is something to be said for the instruction one gains with experience."

"Well, what was your next move?" I asked with more than slight excitement.

"I couldn't just walk down to the pier and the waiting boat, for the way was clear and gave me nothing behind which to conceal myself. At any point, a casual glance out the window and I would have been found out. That surely would have meant the end of Van Pelt. There was also a waterman present keeping himself occupied in the pilothouse. Between the two, it was inconceivable getting myself onto the boat unseen from my current location. So I quickly made my way back to the street and hurried to the other side of the next building over, upstream from the water taxi.

Behind this building was another, smaller pier, as many businesses along the river have their own piers. I went out to the edge and, after relieving myself of my coat and shoes, I quietly submerged myself into the Thames. I let the current take me down to Mudger's waiting boat so as not to be found out by the waterman who, as far as I could tell, was the only person on board. Once I floated down to the boat, I grabbed hold of a piece of rope that dangled over the side near the stern. There, hidden from all, I weighed my options as I waited for Mudger and his cargo."

"Well, did you have to wait long?" I asked. "The Thames isn't a body of water either in temperature or cleanliness in which to spend much time before becoming detrimental to one's health."

"The waterman went below deck momentarily – I think perhaps to the engine room. While he was engaged below, I extracted myself from the water and found concealment under a tarpaulin at the back of the boat. Luckily, I didn't have to wait long. Within minutes, just as the waterman came up from below, I heard the voices of Mudger and his two thugs approach, along with a hooded Van Pelt. I witnessed through a small gap in the tarpaulin as he was forced along, being held up by the two brutes as he limped, dragging his left leg along as best he could. His mumbled protestations told me that he was gagged underneath the hood as a further precaution. Mudger tailed behind them, glancing furtively about, and I feared the worst when I saw Mudger carrying a sledgehammer."

"I will not lie," I gasped. "I am forever astonished at the brutality employed by the lower elements of society. It seems that humanity has left them altogether, and I almost wonder if they had ever even been born with it."

"Indeed. There does seem to be a missing piece to certain individuals' souls, leaving them dark and empty and more animalistic. No, I take that back, for even animals kill only for sustenance and self-defense. They don't inflict nor take pleasure in – as far as can be observed – the barbarous and determined mutilation of another animal. Some people, I have come to realize, are either created outright or fashioned by their environment to be even baser than animals. Mudger was certainly one of these."

"You will get no argument from me on that account. Please continue."

"The waterman untied the line from the dock, and he took his position in the pilothouse. Soon we were off, twisting our way out into the middle of the Thames with the sun just above the horizon. In a few short hours, nightfall would overtake us.

"With the waterman thus occupied, I quietly extracted myself from the tarpaulin and made my way to the steps that led below deck. Here, I couldn't see the men, but I could hear them. Or more precisely, I could

60

hear Mudger, for he did most of the talking. He said, 'Ye do realize that I'll get me money one way or 'nother. Surely, yer father would be more 'an willing t'pay yer debt for ye.'

"Van Pelt's reply was stilted and mumbled. Mudger had obviously decided to keep his captive at least gagged, though I wasn't certain whether the hood was still in place. All I could make out of Van Pelt's muffled response was, ' . . . if you just give me more time.' His voice was soft and fearful.

"'But ye now owe twice a what ye borrowed. Surely I were quite clear how this worked an' the penalties invoked when payment weren't met. Gamblin' wasn't meant for those whose pockets ain't as deep as their desires.'

"Again,, the reply was longer than what I could make out, but I heard, ' . . . but that sum is too much . . . a lifetime to repay . . . my father won't — '

"To which Mudger replied, 'I think ye do yer father a disservice in how far he would go t'save his only son.'

"There was a disagreeing tone in Van Pelt's reply. I made out, ' . . . me a disservice . . . how much you think my father cares.'

"Mudger replied in a tone that chilled even me, 'Well, that is the conundrum we currently find ourselves in, now ain't it?' I then heard the hard and rhythmic thud of the sledgehammer as it tapped against the floor. 'As I see it, a strongly worded letter demandin' payment in exchange for yer life might not do the trick. So that's why I intend t'give yer pawr some . . . visual assistance, shall I say. That's a nice signet ring ye got there.'

"'It's yours,' Van Pelt pleaded through the gag. ' . . . should . . . should fetch . . . money.'

"'Oh, not enough, not nearly enough t'even wet me lips. But I'd be willin' t'bet that the ring, along with the finger it sits on, sent t'yer father would be more 'an enough incentive t'pay yer debt for ye. And jist t'make sure I am fully compensated, I may take this hammer, here, an' give ya a matchin' set of legs.'"

"Well, what on earth did you do? What *could* you do, being outmanned three to one?"

"The odds were definitely stacked against me, for not only did I have Mudger and his henchmen, I also had the boatman to contend with. My hope was that he was preoccupied enough with the maneuvering of the boat that I had little to worry about from him, although being in Mudger's employ gave me no confidence in that sentiment."

"So what was your plan of action at this point?"

"It seemed to me that Mudger's intention was only to wound Van Pelt and not kill him. That, at least, gave me more options than I'd had, for he

61

was known to be just as content with taking a life as repayment than in trying to extract debt by the usual means. This is what made Mudger the last resort for those requiring this particular service."

"That makes no sense," said I. "Murdering the one owing you money all but ensures that you will *not* get your money."

"Agreed. Killing to most money lenders is a self-defeating proposition, for they would never get their money back. Mudger, however, had more money than he could ever spend in a lifetime from a very lucrative career thus far. Only the worst gambling habitualists would dare take on debt from him, but take it they would, and it made him wealthy. Even as a man with no taste in the finer things of life, he considered himself a member of the *nouveau riche*. In accumulation of wealth, he was certainly that, but that was where his culture ended. It wasn't until after the accumulation of all this wealth that he became more inclined to wrest compensation by other means. The man, it seemed, got a sick gratification from extinguishing the life from his debtors. And the more you owed him, the worse your end would be if deadlines were not met. In Van Pelt's instance, however, he must have caught Mudger in good humour with his inclination only to separate the man from his finger as a distinct possibility."

"What was your next move then?" I asked with bated breath. I must confess here that although this wasn't by any account a showcase of Holmes's unique abilities in detection, it was, nonetheless, a thrilling and daring narrative – one I could easily see being penned by the likes of Charles Dickens or Henry James.

"Mudger needed stopped," Holmes went on, "and from my vantage point I had but one way to do it, and only by implementing it would I know whether or not it was a good idea. I surreptitiously made my way past the ladder to the pilothouse, where the waterman seemed oblivious to my presence, and to the engine room down the stairs on the port-side of the boat. From there I extracted a little trinket from the boiler and made my way back topside.

"It was time to try and get Mudger and his thugs up from below deck. While under the tarpaulin, I had noticed a Very pistol secured to the inside panel on the starboard side of the boat. This I secured and promptly shot the flare into the tarpaulin. Quite a raging fire ensued. I had hoped the fire would draw everyone topside and it did. The waterman heard the pistol shot and turned around as I hid at the bow of the boat, waiting for my mice to take their bait.

"'Oi!' the waterman yelled. 'We got a fire up here!' He immediately idled the boat and came down from the pilothouse as Mudger came up from below.

"'What're you yappin' about?' Mudger asked as he made the top step. When he saw the fire he exclaimed, 'What the bleedin'. . . Ye only had one job, Paxon! How on earth did ye let this happen?'

"The waterman, Paxon, replied, 'I was doing my job piloting the boat, just like you wanted me to. I ain't got eyes in the back of me head, now do I?'

"He looked around the boat expectantly, but not yet seeing me, yelled back down to his cohorts, 'Get up 'ere an' help me! The bloody boat's on fire!'

"I laid in wait as Mudger's two associates, along with Van Pelt, scurried up the steps, grabbed buckets, and, scooping up water from the Thames, did their best to douse the flames."

"Wait, what? Van Pelt helped?"

Holmes beamed a full-feathered smile at me. "Of course, he did. Did you not know that it wasn't Van Pelt who got onto the boat?"

"Of course I didn't know that. Why would I?"

"You will be up to speed shortly. I produced myself from the front of the boat and watched silently behind them. Mudger, who was filling buckets from the side of the boat and handing them off, must have felt my presence and stopped in his tracks. He turned his head in my direction and said over his shoulder, 'How nice of ye t'finally show yerself, Mr. Holmes. I knew it'd only be a matter of time.'

"All five men stopped what they were doing and turned to me. The man wearing Van Pelt's clothes looked nothing like Van Pelt besides having his general body type, which was no doubt why he was removed from the building hooded. Certainly, a gag would have sufficed to keep him quiet while they boarded the boat, and the excessive use of the hood was telling."

"So this was a trap?" I asked, flummoxed.

"It was. I knew from the moment they came out through that back door that I was being set up. But please, let me continue. It shall all come out in the wash."

"By all means," I replied.

Holmes went on. "'So, where did I fail in my little ruse?' Mudger asked. 'How did you know?'

"'I commend you on your help's acting abilities. They truly played their part well in treating Van Pelt's stand-in as cruelly as they would have treated the man himself. But they might have overplayed their hand. They manhandled him so severely, he forgot which was the lame leg. He limped on his left leg when I know that Van Pelt's right leg is impaired. Your substitute also speaks much softer than Van Pelt. The gag was a commendable attempt at rectifying that problem, but not quite good enough.'

"He shrugged. 'All that mattered, in the end, was ye gettin' aboard this here boat. See, I been plannin' this revenge for some time. Ye cost me a fair bit a coin a while back, ye did. Now, I'll get me recompense in spades, even if I don't see a single pound of what ye cost me.' He cracked his knuckles. 'This'll be more fun than anything I coulda done with that money anyway.'

"As a low whistle began to emanate from below deck, I asked him, 'Before attempting to extract your *recompense,* you would be doing me a great favor by answering how Van Pelt got involved in this little subterfuge?'

"'Ye're in no position to ask for anythin' besides mercy – which ye will not get. But I feel generous, so I'll allow it. Van Pelt's got a yap as free-flowin' as his pockets. He mentioned ye durin' one of our little impromptu conversations. He knew ye'd been gettin' more popular with yer detectin' exploits and thought that by throwin' out yer name, I might go easy on him and extend a bit more credit. He thought I might fear the genius that is Sherlock Holmes if he ever decided to sic ye on me. He had no idea that ye'd stuck yer nose in my affairs once already. Well, I couldn't pass up this opportunity, so I went easy on the boy and gave him the extra coin he was lookin' for. But from that point on, I planned t'use him for me own retaliation.' Mudger then let out a devilish laugh. 'The little cripple never even knew he'd been used! At least not 'til it were too late.'

"'And *this*,' I said with a sweep of my hand, 'is the revenge you came up with? I am truly disappointed.'

"'Yer here, ain't ye. I think it worked out pretty good, even if ye did figure it out in the end. Too little too late, though, cuz ye got nowhere t'go. Yer my main course, Mr. Holmes. Afterwards, me dessert shall be finishin' what I started with the gimp Van Pelt. This night will be remembered for a long time as a glorious night!'

"'So, it shall,' I replied, 'but not for the reasons and by the people you think should glory in it.'

"As the fire continued to burn behind them, Mudger and his blackguards made their way to me, taking slow deliberate steps. As they closed in, I reached into my pocket and retrieved the little memento I had taken from the engine room earlier and tossed it onto the deck in front of them. None of the four men seemed to understand its significance so I elaborated. 'That happens to be the valve that opens and closes the steam pipe to the boiler. It is now permanently closed.'

"By doing that," I said astonished, "you were putting everyone at risk, for the boiler could only handle so much pressure before it exploded, and surely everyone on board would perish!"

"Precisely. However, my gamble, I had hoped, would pay – for me at least – before the realization of that outcome. Unlike you, however, not an eye gazing upon me understood the import of that statement."

"No doubt your next move involved an eye-roll," I quipped as I sipped the last of my tea.

"You know me all too well, my good man," Holmes replied with a grin. "I then expounded to my obtuse audience, 'Once the pressure in the boiler reaches a climax it will explode, and this boat will be but a pile of toothpicks on the Thames.'

"'Put it back on!' one of Mudger's henchmen exclaimed.

"'I cannot. I broke it off the pipe. The process is now irreversible.'

"'I can't swim,' he whispered to Mudger.

"'Me neither,' said the other thug and Van Pelt's doppelganger in unison.

"'Well, as it turns out," I said, "I am rather a good swimmer.' With that, I turned and jumped over the side of the boat."

At this, Holmes got up and stretched his long legs, leaning against the mantel as he continued. "Once in the water, I heard Mudger bellow, 'I never ran over a man with a boat before. This ought t' be a jolly good time!' He then waved to the waterman to resume his place at the helm of the boat. 'I wanna have a front-row seat when this here boat splits yer head in two.'

"I turned and swam as fast as I could towards the shore where our little excursion started."

I got up from my chair at this point in the story as well, refilled both our cups, and then decided to stretch my legs and remain standing for the duration, setting myself up across from Holmes.

"With that," Holmes continued, "the boat came around as the other men began to squabble amongst themselves and run around the deck of the boat, looking for, I can only assume, something to keep them afloat in the water when they abandoned ship."

I then asked, "Did Mudger not give any credibility to your warning about the boiler? It seems that he was more preoccupied with the possibility of doling out bodily harm than the prospect that his own life was in peril."

Holmes waved off the statement as he lit another cigarette. "There are those who seem to think that natural laws – in this case, the laws of thermodynamics – somehow do not apply to them . . . until they do. And unfortunately, the chain reaction experiment that I had initiated wasn't as precise in its timing as I would have liked. I had no idea when the boiler would reach that penultimate point. The fact that it hadn't right away, I believe, gave Mudger and his cohorts a false security that it wouldn't happen at all. He arced the boat around and headed right at me."

"My word!" I exclaimed. "What could you do at that point?"

"Well, I couldn't out-swim a boat. My only option was to dive, in which case I would need seven or eight feet to make sure I was below the level of the propellers as they passed above me. This I would have to do as many times as needed until I got my intended result with the boiler.

"The boat was closing in on me now – fifty feet – and even at that distance, the whistle from the building pressure was now audible. Mudger's compatriots seemed to have resigned themselves to the boat, no longer looking about for a floatation device but standing idly on the deck preparing to watch the outcome of what they thought was about to happen. Apparently, if Mudger wasn't worried about the boat exploding, neither were they.

"Now, even at a distance of thirty feet, I could see the wildness blazing in Mudger's eyes from the bow of the boat as it barreled down upon me, its engine screaming in protestation. At the last moment, I took a deep breath and retreated into the depths of the Thames. I pushed and pushed, sinking deeper into the murky waters. I couldn't see them in the muck, but I could feel the disturbance of the propellers as they passed above me. I looked up to try and catch a glimpse, a specter of the boat passing above me, backlit against the setting sun, when suddenly, there was a brief splash and a moment later a dull roar and a flash directly above. There was a precipitous, watery convulsion that emanated from the explosion that sent me deeper into the depths. At my lowest point, before I was able to finally make my ascent, I believe that I was some twenty feet below the surface of the river. With my chest now burning for air, I shot back up as fast as I could. Finally breaking the surface, I sputtered for breath and expelled the dirty Thames from my lungs. All around me were bits of burning debris from the boat, but I couldn't make out clearly what it was I gazed upon from detritus in my eyes. However, it was obvious that the wreckage was in such small pieces one can only imagine what the explosion had done to Mudger and his henchmen.

"Exhausted but now free to take a more leisurely pace, I swam back to the pier and pulled my spent body from the Thames. I watched as nearby boats converged on the scene of the explosion. It would be some time before the constabulary was able to piece together – no pun intended – whose boat had exploded and who was on board.

"Now depleted of any vigor whatsoever and soaking wet, I made my way back up to the door from which Mudger and his minions exited earlier, for I still needed to find Van Pelt, and I didn't know if he would be guarded, or by how many. The danger, unfortunately, wasn't yet over."

I said, "I imagine it lessened considerably compared to the circumstance from which you had just extracted yourself."

"My end, my dear fellow, could be met just as easily on dry land as it could on a boat or in a river. I would have been a fool to not be as prepared at that point as I had been in the middle of the Thames."

"Of course."

"I found the door unlocked, so I surreptitiously entered into a darkened hallway that made its way down the entire length of the building. All the doors coming off this corridor were on the left side. The hall was littered with old boards and building material – a refurbishment that was much-needed but never carried out. At the end of this hall was a staircase that led to the upper storeys of the building. The first door opened into the room where I had previously seen Van Pelt. It was empty. There was an open door against the far wall that presumably led to the next room. I went through it, and my hunch had proven correct.

"It seemed that every room had a doorway that opened to the next room so one wouldn't have to go into the hallway to go from room to room. At any rate, it was in this second room that I found Van Pelt, still tied to the chair. He was wearing only his undergarments, was gagged, and was barely conscious. And luckily enough, he was unguarded. Apparently, Mudger felt that in his current state Van Pelt couldn't and wouldn't be able to work himself free. His arrogance was a blessing to me, for even though I know the Asian martial art of baritsu, which has come in handy on several occasions over the years, I hadn't yet recovered sufficiently from my swim for it to be of any practical use if confronted by one or more of Mudger's men. That is especially true if they were anywhere near the size of the behemoths on the boat.

"I nudged Van Pelt back to reality as I set about untying him from the chair. When he looked upon me with his one good eye and gingerly felt his swollen cheek he said, "'Oh thank God!'

"'Quite the predicament you got yourself into,' I said as I finally, completely, released him from his straps.

Looking around with a bit of astonishment, Van Pelt asked, "'Where is Mudger?'

"'At the bottom of the Thames, I should think,' I replied as I lay sprawled upon the floor next to his chair, finally able to catch my breath.

"'My God, man, how did you manage to pull that off?'

"'It wasn't easy.'

"'When I realized I'd been taken for a fool, I tried to fix it.'

"'I know,' I replied. 'I noticed the little warning you began to scrawl on your crutch as Mudger's men closed in. You didn't finish it, but I surmised that you were warning me *Don't Follow.*'

Van Pelt laughed and slapped his knee, "'Good old Holmes! I knew if anyone could get me out of this mess it was you. But I hardly thought you would have been able to guess what that partial message was going to say. How did you know?'

"I shrugged. 'Sometimes it's easier for me to just say I knew instead of trying to explain *how* I knew. That shall have to suffice. If that scrawl on the crutch was your caution to me, from that point on I at least had to entertain the thought that this was a deception and somehow, I was the object of it. Mudger anticipated killing two birds with one stone, using our mutual association against us.'

"Ah," I replied at this revelation. "So, the little mystery of the scribble on the crutch is now solved."

"Indeed. Now you know your little conjecture was mistaken. One must take in the totality of the situation, and in doing so, you will find that the possible word combinations to that little phrase are lessened considerably."

"Is that the end of the story?"

"Unfortunately not. After a few minutes respite, I wrested my tired and wet body from the floor as Van Pelt remained seated, taking inventory of his wounds. 'Well, I believe those debts you owe are no longer,' I said.

"'I appreciate that,' Van Pelt acknowledged.

"'You need to reign in that desire for wagering. I may not be able to remove you from the next spot you get yourself into.'

"'That's just it, Holmes,' he replied, now more animated and verbose as he regained some of his vigor. 'The amount I owed to Mudger isn't even mine. I met a woman – '

"'I see the problem already.'

"' – at the tracks who loved betting ponies. She said she had inside information on a guaranteed win from a trainer with a horse in one of that day's races. With a bit of flirting, she was able to pry the information from him. The odds-on favorite was having a hoof problem of some sort, but its owner refused to pull the horse from the race. The trainer who had given her this little report had the next best odds with his horse, and felt that he was a shoo-in to win.'

"'The next conundrum she faced wasn't having any money to wager. She came from a bit of old money, but her brother who lived in India managed her portion of the inheritance. She was awaiting her monthly allowance, but feared the wire wouldn't come through before the late race. I myself had already lost a tidy little sum on one of my family's own horses from an earlier race, so I'd had my fill of wagering for the day and had nothing handy to lend – certainly not the sum she was looking for. I knew of Mudger, for I had borrowed from him before – *and* paid back, mind you,' he emphasized. 'I introduced her to the man, who is always rambling about the tracks on race day, but he was reluctant to give her the loan. It was a handsome amount she was asking for, and he didn't know her.'

"'Another bit of information that should have raised suspicion,' I interrupted. 'What I knew of Mudger told me that unfamiliarity rarely played a role in whether or not he would lend money to an individual. That alone should have made you question the whole affair.'

"'I know that I should have, but it isn't often that I get a second look from a lady with my game leg. It never occurred to me that I was being played. Well, Mudger said he'd let me borrow the money and after that didn't care what I did with it so long as it was paid back. Reluctantly, I agreed. I didn't want to do it, but she was quite a handsome little creature, and I confess to being a bit smitten. She didn't even seem to mind my crippled leg, which made her all the more alluring. She assured me that it was a guaranteed win.

"'I think I can surmise the ending,' I replied. 'The horse didn't win, the woman disappeared, and you were stuck holding the bag.'

"Gingerly feeling his jaw, Van Pelt said, 'I surely wish you were around when this transpired. Mudger had set me up good to borrow money that I was now on the hook to repay. I think this is a common practice of his, which is one of the reasons why the man has amassed such a fortune. Well, he got pretty hot at me for not even attempting to repay, and I told him I wouldn't. As far as I was concerned, *he* bet on that horse through that woman in his employ and lost his own money. He obviously didn't see things as I did. I did mention you in a fit of frustration and anger, hoping he would drop it, but once I mentioned you, he seemed even keener at getting the money from me.'

"I helped Van Pelt out of the chair. 'Yes, he lost quite a little sum of money on my account as well. He no doubt saw this as a way of getting back at both of us.'

"'And so I shall.'

"We both turned to see a soaking Elias Mudger in the doorway, chest heaving, eyes full to overflowing with animosity."

"Reading my astonished expression, he said, 'I never said that *I* couldn't swim. I jumped ship only a few seconds before she went up in a fireball. As ye can see, I'm a big man, so me stroke may not be as refined as yers, but I made it t'shore, nonetheless.'

"His eyes were fixed squarely on me. I nudged Van Pelt away from me. 'You need to get out,' I said.

"Mudger shooed him off. 'Yes, get away little fly. I'll deal with ye shortly. This here will be between me an' Mr. Holmes.'

"Van Pelt, already beaten and weak, tried to stand on his own, but with his maimed leg only fell to the floor and slowly crawled to the door that led to the next room."

"'Don't go too far,' he said to Van Pelt laughing. 'This won't take long.'

"So you ended up having to defend yourself against a man the size of a mountain," I said.

"Yes, but that mountain expended much more energy than did I when swimming in from the middle of the Thames. All things considered, I would say it was about as fair a fight as I could have asked for. He lunged at me, but I was able to escape his grasp. My hope was to tire him even more than he currently was before I attempted any actual hand-to-hand fighting.

"But I was still out of sorts from my swim, and when he lunged at me a second time, in my attempted escape I fell over the chair Van Pelt had been tied to. When I found my legs again, I was up against the wall with nowhere to go.

Mudger closed in, and I took up a defensive posture for my last stand. Then, something I hadn't expected materialized right before my eyes. Hopping on one foot with a large wooden board clutched in his hands, Van Pelt threw himself at Mudger, screaming wildly. Mudger turned to Van Pelt, taken aback at Van Pelt's abandon, and was rendered momentarily immobile. It only took the blink of an eye, and Van Pelt smashed that thick, wooden plank against the side of Mudger's head. There was an audible crack, a sudden spray of blood, and Mudger fell to the floor."

"I slid down the wall and watched as the lifeless eyes of Mudger stared blankly back at me. Van Pelt, almost hyperventilating, crawled his way beside me, and we both sat silently looking at Mudger's dead body.

"After some moments of silence, what started as a nervous chuckle from Van Pelt turned into riotous laughter from both of us.

"'I must say, Van Pelt, that I didn't think that you had that in you,' I finally said.

"'Nor I, old chap. I guess I figured turn-about is fair play. You help me, I help you.' He swallowed hard. 'I've never killed a man before.'

"'It was self-defense, completely justified,' I replied. 'He wasn't going to let either of us leave here alive.'

"'Now, what do we do?'

"'You shall go home, pretend this never happened, and never place another bet as long as you live.'

"'Hear hear! You will never see me in a betting line ever again. What are you going to do?'

"I shall take the responsibility for all of this. I am of a growing standing within the constabulary these days, and I'm sure they will take me at my word – whatever I decide I tell them. Rest assured, the Van Pelt name will not be mentioned in my account.'

"'Much appreciated.' He looked himself over and laughed. 'I'm not sure how exactly I'm going to get home without drawing attention to myself. I seem to be without my wardrobe at the moment.'

"'I have a waiting cab up the street. I'll fetch it and have him take you home.'

"I stood and helped Van Pelt to his feet.

"'How can I ever repay you?' he asked as I helped him hobble to the front door.

"'By never needing my services again,' I said.

"'Say, did I ever tell you about how I got this lame leg?'

"'And also by never telling me that awful story again.'

"Erupting in laughter once more, Van Pelt said, 'You've heard it then?'

Sensing the story was now finished, I grabbed the aluminium crutch and handed back to Holmes. "Why on earth do you still have the crutch?"

"It was totally forgotten at the time. Exploding boats, near drownings, and homicide will sometimes do that, Watson. I sent him a telegram the next day to let him know I had it for safe-keeping. His reply was that had several extras to keep himself ambulatory, but he would swing by my flat and pick it up the next time he was in the area. I never saw him after that, so it ended up with all my other little trinkets."

"And was he true to his word?" I asked. "About the gambling, I mean?"

"Besides a letter of thanks along with remuneration for my services which I received about a week later, Van Pelt has been utterly absent from my thoughts. I don't know if that means he no longer wagers on horse races, but at least he has never gotten in over his head to the point of needing my services."

"Well," said I with an air of satisfaction, "that was quite the story, Holmes."

"Possibly, but I'm sure that you would agree that it doesn't reach the level of sophistication of the many previous affairs I've been fortunate enough to have utilized my unique abilities."

"Maybe not, but what the story lacks in intellect it makes up for in excitement."

"If righting the wrongs of the world, if bringing about justice from injustice, were only done for the mere excitement of it all, I fear, my dear fellow, that the lion's share of evil in this world would ever go unpunished."

"Never a truer statement said," I replied.

> *"Here's the record of the Tarleton murders and the case of Vamberry, the wine merchant, and the adventure of the old Russian woman, and the singular affair of the aluminium crutch, as well as a full account of Ricoletti of the club foot and his abominable wife."*

– Sherlock Holmes
"The Adventure of the Musgrave Ritual"

The Trifling Matter of Mortimer Maberley
by Geri Schear

During the first few months that we shared our Baker Street accommodations, I thought Sherlock Holmes was the oddest man I had ever met. However, seeing him in action as he brought the case that I have tentatively titled *A Tangled Skein* to a successful conclusion, I was full of admiration. I hoped he and I would settle into a mutually satisfying friendship. This hope was tested, however, during the last week of March. I had come down with a bad cold and spent several days feeling quite sorry for myself. Workmen were hammering outside my bedroom window, making my head ache, and so I huddled up by the fire, croaking, coughing, and sneezing. Holmes spent those days in his own room, even taking his meals there.

"If you will not confine yourself to your bedroom, Watson, I must confine myself to mine," he said, showing not the slightest sympathy for my aches, my fever, and my unpleasantly swollen nose.

By the Feast of Fools, I was over the worst. My temperature was back to normal, the sneezing and coughing had ceased, and I no longer sounded like a frog with catarrh. I had not seen Holmes or, indeed, anyone but Mrs. Hudson's maid in several days, and I was, I confess, feeling rather forgotten.

Someone knocked at the door below and my spirits lifted. Perhaps one of my cohorts had called to inquire after my health. Sadly, I was doomed to disappointment, for it was not the welcome visage of a close companion that entered our apartment, but the sour countenance of a choleric gentleman, flushed of face, black of hair, well-dressed, and with the air of one used to obedience.

"Excuse me," he began, as he hovered by the door. "I see you are rather under the weather."

"I'm on the mend," I replied, "I am Dr. Watson. Please come in and sit by the fire. How can I help you?"

"Well," he replied, "I was looking for a Mr. Sherlock Holmes. A policeman at Scotland Yard suggested he might be able to help me."

"Sit down, do," I said. "Holmes!" My voice cracked and croaked. I tried again, "*Holmes!*"

A door banged open and seconds later my friend exploded into the room. "What the devil is the meaning of that bellowing?" he demanded.

"A client," I said, nodding towards our startled guest.

Immediately my friend's demeanour softened. "Indeed," he said.

"This is Mr. Sherlock Holmes," I said. "And you are?"

"My name is Mortimer Maberley," the other replied, with a slight bow.

Moving his armchair some distance from me, Holmes sat in a regal manner and indicated our guest should take a seat on the settee. "My sympathies on the loss of your brother," he began.

"Thank you, but how did you – "

I was, I confess, as bewildered as our guest. Holmes looked very pleased with himself.

"There is a certain creativity in how one interprets the data, I confess," he replied. "But the facts themselves are plain enough. The callouses on your hands are unique to the furniture maker's trade, and the smell of – " He sniffed the fellow's hands. " – linseed oil, rosin, and beeswax confirms it. Forgive me – it is my business. When I see a man who is quite obviously a carpenter, whose name is Maberley (who has not heard of Maberley and Sons?) it seem probable that you are a member of that illustrious family. The newspapers not two days ago told of the sad demise of Mr. Douglas Maberley. From his age, I deduced, therefore, that the deceased was your brother."

"You are quite correct. Yes, sir, in every particular. Why, I thought it was witchcraft!"

"Perhaps, then, it was your mother who passed on some six years ago?" Holmes continued.

"Yes, by Jove! But how could you possibly know?"

"Ah, that's where creative interpretation comes in. Although your mourning armband is brand new, to honour your brother, your mourning clothing is about six years old. Observe the style of the lapel, Watson, much in fashion around '75. Additionally, observe the repositioning of the buttons, allowing for an increase in girth since the outfit was last worn. I deduced, therefore, that you suffered a loss approximately six years ago. I surmised it was your mother."

"Bravo, Holmes!" I cried. He bowed slightly, pleased with my approbation.

"I can see why the detective at Scotland Yard sent me to you, Mr. Holmes. You are undoubtedly the cleverest man in the kingdom!"

My companion smiled slightly at the praise. "Please have a seat, Mr. Maberley, and tell me how I can be of service. You may speak freely before Dr. Watson. There is no more discreet man in the empire."

I flushed with pleasure at this kind words.

Maberley said, "As you said, my brother died on Wednesday. I am convinced he was murdered by his wife."

Holmes sat back in his armchair, his eyes lidded, and his hands forming a steeple. "Tell me the facts," said he. "Start at the beginning. Omit nothing."

Maberley took a moment to settle his thoughts, and then he told us his tale. "As you said, my father owns a furniture-manufacturing company in Harrow Weald. In his youth, he was full of plans and ideas, and the business profited accordingly. He married my mother in 1848, and she, in due course, gave him two sons, my brother Douglas in 1849, and me six years later.

"In his youth, Douglas was a giant of a man, taller and heavier than our father. He stood six-foot-six and was as broad as he was tall. As he was graced with a fine appearance, he had no lack of admirers, but he showed no interest in anything other than travel, and in demonstrating his great strength to one and all. My parents doted on him, as did I.

"Douglas's role in the company was to procure wood, and to this end he travelled around the country seeking the best timber available. During one trip to Scotland, he became acquainted with the Grady family of Taynuilt in Argyll and Bute. He stayed with them whenever he ventured up north and did much business with Mr. Oliver Grady. Douglas seemed particularly taken with Charlotte, Grady's only daughter. For a time, we all expected him to come home and announce his engagement. However, that did not happen. Not then.

"When I was seventeen years old and Douglas twenty-three, my brother decided that he wanted to travel further afield. He said it would enable him to examine other types of timber and open up new sources of wood for the business. My parents were reluctant to let him go, but Douglas always had a strong will, and early in 1872, he left. Over the next three years he travelled abroad, and he successfully established contracts for us with a number of timber cutters in America, Canada, and India. He sent us samples of the wood and I, as a master carpenter, was delighted to have such a variety to choose from. Other than the contracts, however, we found Douglas was a poor correspondent, and we heard little from him, save for the occasional letter.

"After an absence of three years, he returned at last, but he was a much changed man. Where once he had been solid bulk, he was now slender, almost emaciated. His thick black hair had thinned, though his moustache was as luxurious as ever, and he seemed to catch cold easily. He dismissed the concerns of my father and said it was merely the result of being so active while he was away. He was, he said, determined to continue his work as usual, and within a week, he was back on the road.

75

As we now had a plentiful supply of lumber, his focus now was on locating places where we might sell our wares. He returned home at the end of every week or two, and he would spend whole days in bed, resting.

"Within a month or two of Douglas's return, our mother died. The three of us, my father, brother, and I, scrubbed along well enough with the assistance of our housekeeper, Janet, and the maid, Meg.

"The business continued to thrive. Douglas had a keen eye for a bargain, which kept our costs low, and he'd found a number of businesses that paid well for high-quality items, which I designed and made. My father managed the day-to-day running of the shop, though he seemed to lose interest after our mother died. We were very successful. Indeed, a large number of the furnishings in these islands were came from Maberley and Sons.

"About three months after our mother died, Douglas surprised us by saying he had decided to marry. My father and I had not known he was courting anyone. It transpired that he had maintained contact with Charlotte Grady, and they had reached an understanding even before he left on his wanderings. He brought her to London to meet us. My father and I were both very taken with her. She was a soft-spoken young woman, tall, yet somewhat delicate in appearance, and seemed happy to take over the running of the house.

"Now I must come to the most recent events.

"Ever since his return home from his travels, my brother suffered with a stomach complaint. Charlotte prepared hot milk for him every evening, to ease his pain. In time, she and my father began to join him in this ritual. However, I dislike milk, and nothing could induce me to partake of it. I did, however, sometimes drink hot cocoa. This brings me to the events of this week."

Holmes leaned forward in his seat, his thin face burning with interest. "Pray be very particular as to the details."

Maberley closed his eyes and seemed to be thinking. Then he continued, "On Sunday evening – yes, it is Friday today, it was certainly Sunday – Douglas was feeling out of sorts. He ate breakfast but had nothing else the rest of the day. That evening, he refused his dinner and said he wanted nothing but his hot milk. Charlotte made the drinks as usual for all of us. A short time later, we retired, but a few hours later, Douglas began to howl with pain, and vomited violently."

"A moment," Holmes interrupted. "Was your sister-in-law the only one to make the drinks? It was not left to the servants?"

"No, indeed. Douglas insisted that no one made it to his liking the way Charlotte did."

"Do you know if the same milk was used for all of the drinks?"

"Yes, Mr. Holmes. The doctor asked the same question. The servants confirmed that they had set aside a jug of milk from a gallon urn for the evening's nightcap, as was their custom. Everyone's sugar came from the same bowl."

"And he ate or drank nothing else?"

"Nothing, Mr. Holmes, not even water."

"Thank you, that is very clear. Pray continue."

"The next day, Monday, Douglas spent much of the day in bed while Charlotte attended him. I was kept busy at work, but when I returned home that evening, I found he was no better.

"He consumed nothing all day and vomited several times. That evening, as usual, Charlotte made the drinks. Despite his pain, Douglas drank most of his, but within minutes, he vomited it up. I pitied my poor brother, but I assumed this illness would pass like his previous attacks. However, by Tuesday morning he was in agony, and so the doctor was called."

"Who is the physician?" I asked.

"Dr. Frederick Tennant in Harrow Weald. He has been the family's physician for several years."

"I have heard of him, though I have never met him. He's a Barts man, I believe. Very sound."

Maberley continued. "The doctor came and examined my brother and seemed very concerned. He took samples of the milk and sugar to run some tests, just to make sure there were no contaminants present."

Holmes said, "But surely if either had been contaminated, you all would have suffered the ill effects."

"That was Charlotte's objection, but the doctor said in light of my brother's history of gastric problems he might be unusually susceptible to some germ or other.

"For three days Douglas lingered, getting progressively worse. He could tolerate little but water, and he was insensible most of the time. My father and I were kept busy with work, but we stayed at Douglas's bedside as often as we could, and my sister-in-law tended to him. Alas, he was raving and confused most of the time, and howling in agony."

"Did the doctor see him again?" Holmes asked.

"Yes, he came every day. He suggested that Douglas was suffering from a particularly bad flare-up of his old complaint. I admit my brother had suffered frequently with his stomach, but never as bad as this. The doctor agreed and admitted he was troubled.

"Tennant told us to give Douglas water and a little broth, as much as he could tolerate, but nothing else."

"Nothing else?" I asked. "Milk is generally considered soothing for gastric upsets."

"We had observed, my father and I, that it seemed particularly difficult for Douglas to tolerate. He vomited violently every time he drank even a little. Despite that advice, however, my sister-in-law persisted in giving it to him, claiming he had begged for it and she could not refuse him."

"Do you believe that was true?" Holmes asked.

"I never saw him asking for anything, and as I said, he was not coherent."

"It's possible, surely, that he mentioned milk in his delirium, and she misunderstood," I said. "I have seen such patients rave about any number of strange things."

Holmes did not seem convinced by my explanation, however. He shook his head slowly, then said, "Pray continue."

Maberley resumed his narrative. "For three days my brother lingered in the most dreadful agony, his symptoms never abated. At my direction, my sister-in-law was never left alone with him – either my father or I, or one of the servants always remained with her.

"On Wednesday morning, he suddenly sat upright in the bed and cried, 'The milk!' Then he fell back dead." Maberley paused, overcome. "I notified the police but . . . ." He spread his arms, palms up, in a gesture of hopelessness. "She killed him, Mr. Holmes. I know it."

"Who is the policeman in charge?"

"A fellow by the name of Gregson."

"Ah. Did he conduct an investigation?"

"I would not deign to call it so. Cursory, indeed, was his inquiry. He spoke to me, to my father, my sister-in-law, and the servants. He said there would be an autopsy, and he would follow up with the doctor regarding the samples he had taken. I've heard nothing since, and so this morning I called into Scotland Yard. Gregson said he had received the report and nothing untoward was found. When I remonstrated, he directed me here."

Holmes sat back in his chair and shook his head. "Why are you so certain that your brother's life was ended so unceremoniously by your sister-in-law? On the face of it, there is no evidence to suggest foul play. By your own admission, your brother suffered recurring medical problems. You all drank the milk and added the sugar without any ill effect. The medical report shows no toxins were present. What makes you think that your brother was murdered, Mr. Maberley?"

"It is a million little things and nothing at all, Mr. Holmes," he cried. "It is Charlotte's insistence on giving him milk contrary to the express direction of the doctor. It is the way she smiled throughout his suffering.

78

Her sigh of relief when he breathed his last. Then, not half-an-hour after his death, she announced she did not mean to wait for the funeral but wished to leave for her family home in Scotland the next morning. My father and I insisted she was required as a wife to remain until he was laid to rest. After that, she may do as she wishes. None of her behaviour was that of a devoted wife." Tears were in his pale eyes, and his baby-faced skin flushed with emotion. "My brother was a fine man, Mr. Holmes, but the woman he married was always a disappointment. Whatever light he thought she possessed when they were courting shrivelled to nothing within a month of their marriage."

"I gather he was unfaithful to her," Holmes said.

Maberley did not, for a moment, reply. When he did at last speak, his tone was defensive. "He was a man and he behaved as men do."

"Not gentlemen," I retorted.

"Did your sister-in-law stand to gain by your brother's death?" said Holmes.

"No, his share in the business comes to me, and the house belongs to my father. I just want to know the truth, Mr. Holmes. I can see you are a clever man. I will accept your findings, whatever they may be. I know your time is precious. I would not trouble you unnecessarily. You may name your own price."

"My professional charges are upon a fixed scale," said Holmes. "I do not vary them, save when I remit them altogether. You will, I am sure, be willing to defray any expenses that I may incur in my investigation."

"Most certainly."

Holmes rose to his considerable height, stretched his back, and yawned. "Thank you for bringing this little puzzle to my attention, Mr. Maberley. I will look into the matter, but you should not raise your hopes that I will uncover evidence against your sister-in-law. Still, we shall see. Give your contact information to Dr. Watson, and I shall be in touch."

"Thank you, Mr. Holmes, thank you," Maberley said, shaking my friend's hand vigorously.

After Maberley left, Holmes sank back into his chair and seemed lost in thought. At last he roused himself.

"I must go out, Watson."

"Can I be of service?"

He hesitated. "You are unwell. I would not wish to be the cause of your relapse."

"I feel much better. I believe the fresh air will do me good."

He stared hard at me, and for a moment I wondered if he could assess my temperature from where he stood. What he saw satisfied him, however, and at length, he nodded.

"Very well. I trust you know your health best. We leave in five minutes."

With the thought of escaping our stuffy rooms, breathing air as fresh as London could provide, and the possibility of some excitement, I already felt enormously better. In Baker Street, we caught a cab and headed for Scotland Yard.

"If we are fortunate," Holmes said, "we may catch Gregson and see what he can tell us. He is as lacking in imagination as his rival, Lestrade, but he is not without wit."

"Do you really think Douglas Maberley was murdered?"

He contemplated for several moments before replying. It was a mark of his character that he avoided the flippant and the ill-considered remark.

"There is something decidedly odd about the affair. Certainly, Mrs. Maberley's behaviour raises more questions than answers. We need more information before we can form a reasonable hypothesis."

"On the face of it, there does not seem much to investigate."

"True. The lack of scientific evidence is frustrating. Then again, there are many ways of poisoning a man other than ingestion, are there not? Does not Shakespeare tell us that Hamlet's father was murdered by Claudius pouring poison into his ear?"

I stared at him astonished. "I had no idea you were familiar with the plays of William Shakespeare."

His mouth curled into an amused smirk. "My knowledge of the plays is limited, I grant you, but I am not quite the ignoramus you think me."

"I think you're far from an ignoramus, Holmes. There are simply some odd omissions in your knowledge."

"As I have told you, I retain only that information which is pertinent to my work."

When we arrived at Scotland Yard, we were pleased to find that Inspector Gregson was at his desk, poring through a large stack of files.

"Mr. Holmes, Dr. Watson," he greeted us, and indicating we should sit. "What can I do for you, gentlemen?"

"I am looking into a case in Harrow Weald. The death of a man named Maberley. His brother said you were the investigating officer."

"Oh, him," the inspector said, with a grimace. "He insists his brother Douglas was murdered, most likely by the man's wife, but I found no evidence of wrongful death. I think the notion was put into his head by the family doctor, fellow called Tennant. He was suspicious of the man's symptoms and preserved samples of the last things Maberley had ingested before his illness. Tennant admits the dead man had a long history of illnesses of various sorts, particularly stomach maladies. However, he says he acted on instinct."

I had expected my friend to dismiss this as a valid reason, but to my surprise, he said, "Upon such trifles, cases are made. One must always listen to the small voice of intuition, particularly when it comes from experts. Most often, it is reason bypassing the conscious mind. Of all the tools in the detective's arsenal, intuition is one of the most important. Indeed, I would place it second only to logic."

Gregson and I stared dumbfounded at Holmes. Indifferent to our reaction, he continued, "For form's sake, may I see the chemical analysis, Inspector?"

"Yes, I have it here somewhere . . . ." Gregson rummaged through his papers. Eventually, he retrieved the report and handed it to my companion.

"Yes. The milk and sugar contained nothing of interest. Did you interview the dead man's wife?"

"Charlotte Maberley, yes. I'll grant you she's an odd character, and I had the distinct impression she was trying to hide something, but what that might be, I have no idea."

"What did you make of her relationship with her brother-in-law?"

"There's no love lost there. She is either terrified of him or holds him in contempt, perhaps both. It's plain she was once a beautiful woman, but the years of her marriage have not been kind. She's a fragile-looking thing who barely speaks above a whisper. I noticed a bruise on her left jaw. When I asked, she said her husband was raving and accidentally struck her."

"Did you believe her?"

Gregson lit a cigarette and took a long pull before replying. "The bruise was starting to yellow. Certainly, it's possible it had happened during the early days of her husband's illness, but she had other injuries, too. Her right wrist was swollen, and there was some discolouration around her left eye. Again, I cannot say with any certainty that she had not incurred those injuries before her husband's fatal illness."

"There is too much ambiguity surrounding this case," said Holmes. "Too much supposition and too few facts. What about the background of the family members? Did you learn anything of interest there?"

Gregson pulled his notebook out of his coat pocket and flicked through the pages. "The deceased was a strong, determined man with an unshakable will," he read. "The father is nearly sixty, and I had the impression he is more of a figurehead than an active member of either the family or the business. He is soft-spoken and meek, more like his daughter-in-law than his son, the brash and bold Mortimer Maberley. There was one curious thing though . . . ."

Holmes's eyes glinted in expectation. In an idle tone he said, "And what was that, pray tell?"

"The father seemed afraid. I cannot point to specifics. It was merely an impression I got. I asked him how he got on with Mrs. Maberley and he said she was a very sweet lady. As to his son Mortimer, he would say only that he was a hard worker and a fine carpenter."

"How did he get on with the deceased?" I asked.

"Ah, there's the thing. He said they got on well enough, but it didn't ring true." Gregson looked slightly embarrassed. "I'm afraid I have no facts to offer, here, Mr. Holmes. It was an impression, nothing more."

Holmes must have been in one of his more genial moods, for he patted the inspector on the arm and said, "Again, the intuition of an intelligent professional is of enormous value." Gregson blinked in surprise and smiled.

"You ordered an autopsy, I assume. Have you received the report yet?"

"No, Mr. Holmes. It hasn't yet been conducted. There are quite a few others at present. I doubt I'll receive anything before Monday or Tuesday of next week."

"And the corpse is in the Kew Morgue?"

"That is correct."

"We shall go take a look. Oh, and do you have the address of the family doctor?"

"He's in Harrow Weald, on King's Way."

We decided to go to Kew first.

The body of the late Douglas Maberley lay upon a slab, covered with a dingy grey sheet. He was a tall man – taller even than Holmes – shockingly thin, and his head was balding. To contrast this, the fellow had a luxurious moustache, carefully waxed and curved into handlebars. It was a splendid specimen, and I suspected the man had been justly proud of it.

Sherlock Holmes studied the corpse in minute detail. As *rigor* had passed, the dead man's body was malleable, which facilitated examination. Holmes spent several minutes studying the palms and soles with his magnifying glass.

"Ha!" he exclaimed. "Yes, I begin to see."

Next, he pried open the dead man's mouth and examined it closely. At last, he stood back.

"What do you make of him, Watson?"

"Without conducting a proper autopsy, my conclusions must, necessarily, be limited. However, I observe he is extremely thin, almost to the point of cachexic, the skin seems intact other than a number of lesions on the palms of his hands and the soles of his feet. There is no evidence of foreign substance in the ears."

"So much for the Hamlet theory." He chuckled.

"Yes, indeed. It is evident the poor fellow suffered from chronic illness for some time."

I pried open the mouth. "There are old lesions on the palate."

"More evidence of a chronic condition," said Holmes. "I was foolish not to have seen the potential in this case. If I am correct, this is utterly unique. Yes, by Jove!" Then, he turned abruptly, and led the way out of the morgue.

"I don't suppose you'd care to tell me what has so excited you?" I asked.

He chuckled again. "Come, Watson, you are a physician. You have seen what I have seen, heard what I heard. Surely you have formed some conclusions?"

"I am reminded of some cases I witnessed in Afghanistan, but I cannot quite see . . . ."

"Afghanistan, indeed. And India, Watson, India!"

I confess I was no wiser from this pronouncement, but I had learned, even during our brief acquaintance, that my companion would not reveal his secrets until he was quite certain of his facts.

"Where now?" I asked.

"Harrow Weald. First to see what Dr. Tennant can tell us, and then we shall call upon the Maberleys."

The journey to Harrow Weald didn't take long and soon we were walking up the hill to King's Way, where Dr. Tennant kept his surgery. Fortunately, the young doctor did not have a busy morning, and he greeted us cordially.

"Good morning," said my companion. "I am Sherlock Holmes, and this is my friend and colleague, Dr. Watson."

"Ah, yes, I've been expecting you," the doctor said, waving us into a pair of seats. "Mr. Maberley said you might call upon me."

"You attended the late Mr. Douglas Maberley during his last illness?"

"I did, Mr. Holmes. I had treated him and all the Maberleys for the past five years, ever since I came to Harrow Weald. Douglas suffered from a number of illnesses, most notably a stomach complaint."

"What was your diagnosis?" I asked.

"Chronic gastritis, probably contracted during his travels. That was before my time, of course, but I was advised that he had been a hale and robust fellow in his youth."

"But he was not so upon his return?"

"No, Doctor. He was subject to frequent colds and various gastric disturbances. He was a frequent visitor of my predecessor, Dr. Davis. He never regained that raw good health of his younger years."

"We have been to the morgue and viewed the body. He was emaciated."

"Yes, he was always extremely slender, and during his final illness became more so."

"What did you make of the lesions on his hands and feet?"

"A chronic condition. He said he began to notice the black spots during his time in India. He had tried a number of ointments and lotions, but nothing helped."

"What can you tell us about his most recent illness?" Holmes asked, "What were his chief complaints?"

"As with his previous conditions, he complained of severe abdominal pain, constipation, diarrhoea. During this final illness, however, he seemed in agony, to the point where he was almost delirious. He could retain nothing, not even water. He vomited copious amounts and had no control of his bowel."

"You did not think to hospitalise him?" I asked.

"I suggested it, but his wife objected. She believed that she could tend him better on her own and, frankly, there was little we could do for him in the hospital that could not be done in his own home."

"What was your diagnosis?"

"A severe case of gastro-enteritis, exacerbated by a stomach ulcer. That was my official diagnosis."

"And the unofficial?" asked Sherlock Holmes.

"I cannot discount the possibility that Mr. Maberley ingested some toxin. I should add that Mr. Mortimer Maberley was convinced that his brother had been deliberately poisoned. I had the milk and sugar tested, as they were the last things he consumed before his fatal illness. The results were negative."

After we left the doctor's office, we walked the short distance to the home of the Maberleys on Torver Road. The house was a simple red-bricked building, with a front garden that was coming to life with daffodils. A lilac bush filled the air with its heady scent. After a week of feeling under the weather, I felt positively invigorated by this evidence of springtime.

Holmes knocked on the door and we were admitted by a petite barrel of a middle-aged woman who identified herself as Meg.

"Come in, sirs," she said, with a respectful curtsey. "We was told to expect you. If you'll wait here a moment, I will let Mr. Maberley know you are here."

84

The hallway smelled of beeswax. The mahogany table and the crystal vase that sat upon it shone. The bright yellow daffodils were fresh. A man in this house was dead, but life continued without interruption.

A moment later, we were ushered into the parlour. It, too, spoke of luxury, elegance, and charm. In contrast were the inhabitants. Mr. Mortimer Maberley rose and introduced us to his father, the stooped, grey Lionel, and his sister-in-law, Charlotte. The young woman must have been breath-taking just a few years earlier. Tall and pale, with once-golden hair, and a fearful expression, she reminded me of Keats' *"Belle Dame Sans Merci"*. Once she had ordered the maid to bring coffee in a voice barely above a whisper, she sat on the sofa beside me.

Holmes seemed irked at having to partake of social niceties when there was a case to be solved, but there was no avoiding it without appearing rude.

The coffee arrived and I offered sympathies on Holmes's behalf and my own. My companion sent me a brief, approving glance. I then engaged Mrs. Maberley in conversation about Scotland. As she spoke, she seemed to come back to life, and her lilting accent became more pronounced. At last, the coffee was drunk, and we could return to the grim matter at hand.

"Have you had time to form an opinion yet, Mr. Holmes?" Mortimer Maberley asked.

"I have reduced my number of hypotheses to three, but I need to clarify some points before I determine which is correct. May I speak with Mr. Lionel Maberley alone?"

Mr. Mortimer Maberley and Charlotte swiftly left the room.

"Well, now, Mr. Maberley," Holmes began. "I believe you can tell us a great deal about this situation."

"I don't know so much, Mr. Holmes." The old man did not meet my companion's eye.

"No? Then let me begin by asking you: Do you believe your son was murdered?"

"No!" A deep flush covered the man's cheeks. "Absolutely not."

"Mr. Douglas Maberley was greatly changed upon his return from his travels, I gather?"

"Yes. He was thin as a rail and was balding. His energy was much less than it had been. He also developed a very delicate stomach. He had been so robust before. I should not have let him go."

"And his temperament, too, was altered, was it not?"

"Indeed, very much so." Mr. Lionel Maberley shook his head. "He was so changed upon his return that his own mother hardly recognised him. He had been a kind and cheerful young man, always ready for an adventure, afraid of nothing. As a boy, his laughter filled this house night

85

and day. But the man who returned was volatile, moody. He had developed a temper and a cruelty that had not been there before."

"He struck his wife."

"He did," the man replied without hesitation. "I was ashamed of how he treated that poor woman. He was a disgrace. He struck anyone whom he believed had crossed him, even in minor matters. The only one who escaped his savagery was Mortimer. The two were as close as they ever had been as children."

Holmes looked kindly upon the grieving father. "And all of this because of the bad habit he had picked up in India, was it not?"

The old man stared in astonishment at my companion. "How in the world did you know that, Mr. Holmes?"

"The change in appearance and temperament, the nightly ritual of hot milk. It was a simple deduction, confirmed by the appearance of the corpse."

"It was the work of the Devil who set him upon such a path. It stole the golden boy who was my son and replaced him with a thing of evil. No one had a hand in his death, Mr. Holmes, but I tell you truthfully, I am not sorry he is dead. That is a terrible thing for a man to say about his own son, but it is the truth. My son died the day he left this house."

"I appreciate your candour, Mr. Maberley. I think there is only one small matter upon which I need clarification. Would you ask Mrs. Maberley to come in?"

After the old man left the room, I said, "Your three theories, Holmes – murder, accident, or natural causes?"

He nodded in approval. "You see, do you not, Watson, how this terrible situation occurred? There is also the remote possibility of suicide, but I think it highly unlikely. Who would wish such a death upon oneself? Still, I cannot rule anything out until I have spoken to Mrs. Maberley."

The woman joined us just moments later. She sat nervously before us, a handkerchief in her hands twisted round and round. Holmes spoke to her very gently.

"You were very young when you met your husband, I believe."

"That is true. When I first met him in Taynuilt he was kind and gentle. That was twelve years ago. I was hardly more than a child, just fourteen years. When Douglas came to buy wood from my father, he always brought me a treat. He was a gentleman through and through. He often wrote to me, even when he was away travelling the world – such sweet letters. I thought myself very fortunate when he asked for my hand."

"When did you learn of the draught that he was taking?"

"However did you know about that, Mr. Holmes? I did not learn of it until after we had been married for two or three months. One night, after everyone had gone to bed, I found him fixing a milk drink for himself. He said he had developed a condition while he was in India and the draught helped. He would not tell me what the medicine was, but he said he took it once a day to prevent recurrence of his condition. He pleaded with me not to tell his father or brother about it. He did not wish to worry them."

"And they never found out?"

"I think Mr. Lionel Maberley suspected. We never spoke of it, you understand, and I may be in error, but that was my impression."

"Where was it kept?"

"I do not know. He was very secretive about it."

"Did he purchase it at the chemist's?"

"No. It came in the post from India. Douglas said he had a doctor there who had treated him, and there was no one else he would trust to prepare so delicate a medicine. Those were his very words."

"He took it in his nightly drink, I gather?"

"Yes, Mr. Holmes. He put the dose in the cup in the morning before he left for work, and I simply added the sugar and hot milk to it in the evening."

"Well, that sounds unnecessarily dangerous," I cried. "Anyone might have taken the cup and drunk from it, becoming violently ill, or even dying."

Holmes looked at me, amused. "Oh, come, you must realise that would not happen."

"Why ever not?"

"Can you think of no reason?"

I thought through every possible scenario, but still could not determine what Holmes meant.

"Let me give you a hint: Lionel and Mortimer Maberley are both clean-shaven."

This seemed even more bewildering.

"No?" Holmes said. "You saw the body of Mr. Douglas Maberley in the morgue. What would you say was the most remarkable thing about his appearance?"

"He was emaciated . . . The moustache! He drank from a moustache cup!"

"Precisely! Well done. Yes, the cup with the shield to prevent the wax in a gentleman's moustache from melting into the hot liquid. They are quite *de rigueur* at present. In addition, I surmise the cup was kept on a top shelf so neither of the servants could reach it and see the poison within. As you will have observed, my dear Watson, Mrs. Maberley is taller than average. It would have been no difficulty for her to reach the cup."

"That is exactly what happened, Mr. Holmes," said the widow.

"But something happened during this past week. Before he took ill, he was particularly violent." To me, he added, "You observe the bruises on the lady's cheek and wrist are approximately a week old."

I nodded in agreement. Mrs. Maberley stared at him in astonishment. "Yes, Mr. Holmes. Douglas had failed to secure a contract that he had been working on for months, and on Saturday came home in high dudgeon. His father was the first recipient of his fist, and I was next. He raved all day, and I thought that he was going to retire without taking his medicine, but he drank it as usual."

"Thank you, Mrs. Maberley," said Holmes. "You paint a very clear picture. Now, if you please, tell me about your late husband's last illness."

"Douglas had been out of sorts all day Saturday and Sunday. Little things seemed to vex him, and we all felt the lash of his tongue. Mr. Lionel Maberley told Douglas that he should not fret about the contract. Though losing it was a disappointment, it did not have any significant impact on the business. The shop was doing well, and the other gentlemen seemed in good spirits, although Mr. Lionel also suffered from my late husband's ill temper."

Here she hesitated.

"Come, come, Mrs. Maberley," Holmes said softly. "Do not shy from the truth now. You decided to stop adding the concoction to his drink."

She stared at him in astonishment and then burst into tears.

"I meant no harm. I thought how kind and gentle a man he had been before he left on his travels. When we were first married, he had been reluctant to tell me anything about the medicine and why he took it, but after a few months he spoke to me about it. Often, he ranted to me that if he had known at the first how it would ruin his life, he would never have begun."

"And so you decided to stop giving it to him."

"Yes."

She began to weep, and Holmes looked at me helplessly. I sat beside her and held her hand, speaking soft words of comfort. After a few minutes, she calmed. She dried her eyes and said, "When I saw how ill he became after missing just one dose, I realised what a mistake I had made. I tried to give him more milk, this time with the draught, but he was too ill to take it and vomited it up immediately.

"All night long, I sat with him. He was in agony, had soiled himself, and was vomiting repeatedly, though he had little in his stomach except water. He seemed confused and rambled. Oft, he called for people I had never heard him mention. We were all with him on Wednesday morning when he breathed his last. I was relieved that he was finally out of his pain. Then Mortimer began to accuse me of wilfully causing my poor husband's death and I was in terror of him, of what revenge he might try to wreak upon me. In his own way, he is as cruel as Douglas, though with nothing like the reason. I thought to go home to Scotland, to my family, but that incensed him even more. If it had not been for Mr. Lionel's kindness, I do not know how I would have managed."

Holmes listened to this impassively. When Mrs. Maberley fell silent, and her tears ceased to fall, he said, "Thank you for your candour, Mrs. Maberley. Watson, will you ask the two gentlemen to return?"

A few minutes later, we were all gathered together again. Holmes said, "Mr. Douglas Maberley's death was accidental. There was no malice intended."

Briefly, he reviewed the dead man's history with his "medicine" and its unfortunate effects.

"Mrs. Maberley intended only to try to wean him from the, ah, medication. She could not have known what the consequences would be."

"I don't understand," Mortimer Maberley said. "What was this medicine? Why was it so harmful to him to stop taking it?"

"It is not known in general British society, but it is popular among certain groups around the world, particularly in India. It is not uncommon for some among the British troops in that land to take what is known as the 'Tanjore Pill'. It is arsenic. Your brother was what is known as an arsenic eater.

"Who knows why Mr. Maberley began to take it. Possibly it was the result of a dare – he took great pride in his strength. Or perhaps he became convinced of its medicinal qualities. Whatever the reason, we likely will never know.

" I suspect he was taking several grains a day. The dosage would be fatal to most people, but he had built up an immunity. However, the impact on his body was devastating. You saw his frequent bouts of gastric upset. His weight loss, the lesions on his hands and feet, and his frequent ill-temper were other symptoms. Unfortunately, once dependent upon the poison, his body was unable to tolerate its absence – hence his final illness and subsequent death. Mrs. Maberley intended only to wean him from the poison. She could not know how devastating the result would be."

True to his word, Mr. Mortimer Maberley accepted Holmes's finding, and handed him what was, I gathered, a sizeable cheque.

That evening, as we sat by the fire in Baker Street, I said, "So it was merely happenstance that took Maberley's life."

"Oh, no, my dear Watson," Holmes said. He sat back in his armchair and lit a pipe. "Mrs. Maberley knew exactly what she was doing. Those final blows on Saturday decided her, but I have no doubt she'd been contemplating it for some time."

"What? You mean she murdered him? Deliberately?"

"She had reached the end of her endurance. She emptied out the poison that he had left in the cup and washed it thoroughly. Of course, my own experiments have revealed that arsenic cannot be completely removed by washing, but what remained would not have affected a man used to such a substantial dose."

"But she regretted her actions. She tried to give him another dose the next day when she saw how ill he became."

"Did she? She told us that she did not know where the arsenic was kept. I believe she searched the house in hopes of finding it so she could give him a fatal dose. However, when she could not find it – I suspect Maberley kept it on his person – she decided that omitting the arsenic was a better option. Much easier to claim it was a mere accident. Moreover, I suspect Mr. Lionel Maberley was well aware of her actions. He said himself: He was not sorry his son was dead. He, too, had suffered from the fellow's brutality."

"How could she have known of the dangers of omitting a dose?"

"Almost certainly her husband told her. I'm sure she had asked him to stop taking the arsenic, possibly during one of his previous bouts of illness. He would have explained how dangerous it would be for him to do so."

I thought about the conversations we had had at the Maberleys' home, and the report of Charlotte Maberley's behaviour during the man's final illness. Her smiles, her sigh of relief when he died, her desire to flee to Scotland immediately.

"But, Holmes, shouldn't you tell Gregson? If you are right, she is a murderess."

He shook his head. "I am not employed by Scotland Yard. Even if the case came to court, there is nothing to prove the man was murdered. He took the arsenic himself, and his own father will testify for Charlotte. In this instance, I think a higher justice is served."

We sat back in our seats, smoking our pipes, lost in our own thoughts. I was thinking about the case when suddenly Sherlock Holmes sneezed three times in quick succession.

"Damn it, Watson!" he croaked from behind a handkerchief. "I've caught your blasted cold!"

"I believe that my late husband, Mortimer Maberley, was one of your early clients . . . ."

"I remember your husband well, madam," said Holmes, "though it is some years since he used my services in some trifling matter."

– Mary Maberley and Sherlock Holmes
"The Three Gables"

Abracadaver
by Susan Knight

"There you are at last, Watson," said Sherlock Holmes, buttering a piece of toast. "I was thinking you must have slept in this morning, until I observed that your top coat was missing. And now I see from the mud on your boots that you have been walking in the Regent's Park."

In fact, I had just then returned from a morning stroll in that very place, having been awakened early by the unseasonal sunshine on that sharp November day. However, on this occasion, Holmes's perspicacity failed to astonish me, since as he knew well I am often in the habit of enjoying the delights of the nearby park. Now quite invigorated, I was ready to partake of the devilled kidneys that Mrs. Hudson had provided for our breakfast.

I was so engrossed in filling my plate that it was only when I had taken my first mouthful that I noticed Holmes looking at me with a small smile on his face.

"You have a healthy appetite, my friend," he said. "I envy you."

Indeed, in my professional capacity as a doctor, I had frequently been concerned at my friend's haphazard eating habits. He often went without altogether and, when he did finally sit at table, he took little relish in his food, seeming always preoccupied with something else. At this moment, he was waving a letter in my face.

"I received this in the morning post," he said. "It is from Mrs. Cecil Forrester and I find it, I have to say, as eccentric as one might expect from that person."

Holmes had recently assisted the said lady, a widow of enormous girth in her middle years, in a little domestic unpleasantness, the exposure of her steward. This man had, as it turned out, been embezzling her funds little by little over time, hoping presumably by that means to avoid notice. This Arthur Alexander fellow, however, proved no match for Holmes, who soon got to the bottom of the business. It was a sad enough case all the same because the said steward, a well-built and charming young man to all outward appearances, had become a firm favourite with Mrs. Forrester, and might indeed have been a beneficiary of the lady's will, had insatiable greed not overcome him. Alexander had escaped prison only through the good offices of Mrs. Forrester, an outcome I personally regretted, feeling that a bout of hard labour might do the young man the world of good and bring him to his senses. Instead, the kind-hearted lady had provided him with the wherewithal to leave England for South Africa, to start a new life.

"What does she say?" I asked.

"See for yourself." He offered me the letter, inscribed on the elaborately crested notepaper of the family, Mrs. Forrester having been an Honourable before her marriage, a title she still used on occasion. The shaky handwriting was presumably that of the lady herself.

I read what she had written and started to laugh.

"She offers two tickets for the Egyptian Hall this very night!" I cried. "In grateful thanks. Is she quite serious?"

"Yes. I should have taken it for a joke, too, had I not been acquainted with Mrs. Forrester's whimsical character." And he picked up the said tickets from beside his plate.

"Will you go?"

Holmes languidly took another piece of toast and stared at it, as if it might provide the answer. He sighed.

"Do you really consider that I should relish the prospect of a night at England's 'Home of Mystery', as I believe the place likes to call itself?"

Indeed, the Hall, a striking edifice in the style of an ancient Egyptian palace, and once a private museum, had become the location for shows of magic and spiritualism.

"It might be fun," I said.

The look he gave me was, had I been some lowly insect, utterly crushing.

"I find," he said, yawning, "that I am far too preoccupied with my monograph on the refinement of porcelain during the Yuan Dynasty to think of 'fun'. However, it would seem a shame for the tickets to go to waste, and I suspect that you yourself would not be averse to a night out . . . ." He paused and looked quizzically at me. I have to confess that my friend knows my little weaknesses. I do enjoy a good show.

"Well," I replied, "as you say, Holmes, in the light of the lady's generosity, we should not want the tickets to go to waste. Who knows? The Great Maskelyne might be on the bill."

"Good," he went on, "and I was thinking that it might be a kindly gesture to take Mrs. Hudson with you. She gets out so little and has been so very good to us." So patient with Holmes's many quirks and unreasonable demands, I thought. "Unless of course you have anyone else in mind."

"Not at all," I replied. "Assuming Mrs. Hudson is free, it would be my pleasure to escort her."

Thus it was that, later that evening, myself and our good landlady, all a-flutter, took a cab to Piccadilly, where the Hall was situated.

Mrs. Hudson regarded with admiration the exotic frontage, with its carved sphinxes and scarabs inset into square cut stone pillars. "I have passed by here on many occasions, Doctor," she said, "but I never thought of entering it. It is quite a thrill, I can tell you."

I was delighted for her and admitted that it was a thrill for me as well, even though I was disappointed to learn from the lavish programme that those famed masters of illusion, Maskelyne and Cooke, would not be performing that night. It seemed that they were away on tour in the United States.

The interior of the place was even more splendid than the outside: The great hall, lavishly adorned with more Egyptian motifs illuminated by sparkling chandeliers, leading through to the theatre itself. Our seats were well placed near the stage, for which I thanked the thoughtfulness of Mrs. Forrester.

Unfortunately, Mrs. Hudson, being of short stature, found that her view of the stage was effectively blocked by the head of the tall person in front of her. She would have to bob and bend continually to see around him. To change places with me would have proved of no avail either, since the person before me was as lofty as his neighbour.

It was at this point that the gentleman to Mrs. Hudson's left, on overhearing our dilemma, most courteously proposed that, since there was no giant in front of him, she take his seat, he being a man of at least equal height with Sherlock Holmes himself. I could see that our landlady was torn – it provided a much better prospect, and yet to change places would have put this unknown gentleman between herself and myself. A solution was finally found with him taking my place – a remove which, in the event, proved fateful.

I managed to exchange a few polite words with the kind gentleman before the start of the show. He informed me that he was a Mr. Hartley Jameson and that he was visiting London on business from Birmingham, where he owned an engineering company. He took Mrs. Hudson for my mother, which I think rather displeased that lady. In mitigation, I whispered to her that Mr. Jameson was evidently a very short-sighted gentleman, in dire need of a new pair of spectacles.

Soon enough the lights went down in the auditorium and a Mr. Charles Mellon, as described in the programme, started to play a suitably eerie overture on the pianoforte, a piece I recognised as the *Danse Macabre* by Saint-Saens.

"Ooh, Doctor Watson," Mrs. Hudson whispered, "it quite sends shivers down my spine."

I had to agree and must add that, in retrospect, the piece proved only too horribly appropriate.

Mr. Mellon finished with a flourish, we applauded heartily, and the heavy red velvet curtains swept back from the stage to reveal a scene more Far Eastern than Egyptian, with a painted backdrop depicting a waterfall plunging down a mountainside to a pagoda quite similar to the one in the Gardens at Kew. A small round man stepped forward. This was our *compere* for the evening, a Mr. Harold Quincy, who in addition proved to be a fine tenor when he regaled us, accompanied by Mr. Mellon, with renditions of *Come into the Garden, Maud* and *The Lost Chord*.

He then introduced the first act as Chinese Plate dancers come all the way from Peking, which explained the design on the backdrop. Mr. Mellon obliged with suitably exotic-sounding music. (I believe it was from a comic opera I once had the pleasure of attending – namely *The Mikado* by Messrs Gilbert and Sullivan, and thus Japanese in inspiration. But let us not quibble.) Six young ladies with Oriental features, in Chinese straw hats, tight-fitting embroidered blouses, and what I believe these days are called "bloomers", emerged from the wings, each clutching several long bamboo rods on which they had set plates a-spinning. They danced gracefully and performed other breath-taking acts of acrobatics while continuing to spin the plates. Such consummate skill. Clearly the plates could not be stuck to the poles, and yet we had to marvel that the performers managed not to drop a single one.

Mrs. Hudson whispered to me as we applauded that she was glad Phoebe wasn't present to see the show since she might be inclined to try the trick for herself – Phoebe being our clumsy young scullery maid, renowned for the amount of ware she somehow managed to break.

The next act was a gentleman named Felix Grau, a facial artist with an amazing mobility of expression, able to mimic with the aid of wigs and lights the features of several great personages of our time. I laughed particularly at his William Gladstone, our Prime Minister, stern-faced and side whiskered. Mr. Grau captured him to the life.

The act that had replaced Maskelyne and Cooke's celebrated illusions then followed. This was a magician of whom I had never heard, perhaps because he came, as the *compere* informed us, all the way from Paris. Monsieur Fantôme was his name, and he was accompanied by a pretty assistant, all dizzy curls and rosebud lips, somewhat scantily clad in the way of the French. Fantôme introduced this young person to us in his strong accent as Veronique.

He performed several tricks which I felt were appreciated more by Mrs. Hudson than by myself, since they were from the familiar run-of-the mill repertoire of linking rings, colour-changing scarves, and the

95

production of a rabbit from a previously empty hat. Holmes, I felt, could have explained the deceptions in an instant. However, they were well received by the crowd – including Mrs. Hudson.

Next, an upright cabinet was wheeled on to the stage. When M. Fantôme opened the door, we could see that there was room for a person to stand inside and he invited Veronique to do so. She feigned reluctance, perhaps because M. Fantôme was at the same time holding a fearsome looking sword that he had taken from a side table where several more of the same were lying. She tested the blade and apparently found it sharp, because she shook her curls vigorously and said, "*Non, non, non.*"

For a moment, M. Fantôme looked nonplussed at her refusal, but then called upon the audience to persuade her. With one voice we exhorted her to "Go in!" and finally, she was prevailed upon to do so. M. Fantôme then shut the door upon her, locking it with a big key. Brandishing his sword, he thrust it with some force through a slit in the side of the cabinet. We gasped as it came through the opposite side and Mrs. Hudson clutched my arm in fear. The magician continued with the other swords until the cabinet quite bristled: surely anyone within must have been impaled. Mrs. Hudson squeezed my arm tighter.

M. Fantôme then called to Veronique, but there was no reply. Looking worried and shaking his head, he removed the swords, one by one, calling out each time to no avail. At least no blood was visible on the blades and Mrs. Hudson relaxed her grip somewhat.

With a flourish and the word "Abracadabra!" the magician swung the cabinet door open. Out stepped Veronique, none the worse for her ordeal. We cheered and applauded wildly.

M. Fantôme then addressed the audience again, challenging some brave Englishman – quipping "if any such there be" – to enter *La Boîte de la Mort*, The Cabinet of Death. At the same time, Veronique descended from the stage and cast her eyes over us. Several gallant gentlemen raised their hands, offering their services. It seemed, however, she had fixed upon my neighbour, Mr. Hartley Jameson, who, I believed, had not been one of those to volunteer. Nevertheless, he took her hand and followed her willingly enough, smiling back at me as he climbed up on to the stage, to the cheers of the audience.

Still smiling – And how can I ever forget that smile? – he entered the cabinet and the door was closed upon him. As before M. Fantôme plunged the swords, each one now offered to him by Veronique, through the cabinet wall. One, two, three, four . . . They all emerged from the other side.

"Are you well, Monsieur?" the magician asked each time, to which our erstwhile neighbour replied that he was.

And then the fifth sword. As Fantôme drove it in, there came a frightful cry such as I have never heard before and hope never to again, a scream of more utter agony and terror than I ever heard in all my time serving in Afghanistan.

At first the audience thought that it was part of the trick, that Mr. Hartley Jameson was a stooge acting out a previously agreed role, but then came the blood, the blood flowing out from under the cabinet door . . . Some people still laughed, but then fell silent. This was no trick. This was real.

M. Fantôme stood frozen. After a pause, amid a shocked silence, the curtains swung across the stage, blocking our view. Almost immediately, Quincy, the *compere*, came forward and announced, "Ladies and gentlemen, there has been a most unfortunate accident. I wonder if there is a doctor present here."

I had already leapt to my feet and made my hurried way on to the stage. The sight that greeted me there was truly dreadful. The cabinet door stood open revealing its grisly contents: The body of Mr. Hartley Jameson hanging impaled upon a sword while blood still flowed from a wound in his abdomen.

Examining him, I shook my head. There was no sign of life. M. Fantôme, standing at my side, moved to pull away the sword, but I halted him, merely pushing the door closed again, to hide the horrid sight.

"The police will wish to see this as it is," I said.

"The show cannot go on then?" asked the *compere*.

"Of course not!" I was shocked that he would even think it might. "But no one should leave the Hall until the police arrive."

Shaking his head, Quincy stepped out in front of the curtains to make the announcement to the horrified audience, requesting them to stay calm and to remain in their seats for the time being.

"How could this have happened?" I asked the magician.

"I know it not," Fantôme replied. He explained how the other swords had been trick ones, with retractable blades and a mechanism that sent their apparent tips out through the opposite side of the box. "But someone must have placed a real sword among the others. *O, Dieu, quelle horreur!*" He clutched his head. "But where is Veronique! Perhaps she knows more."

We looked around to find that young person huddled on the floor, sobbing and being comforted by one of the Chinese dancers

"*Mais c'est ma faute!*" she muttered. "It is my fault." And she collapsed into a further wail of weeping.

I was on the point of crossing over to tend to her when someone new rushed through the curtains on to the stage. To my enormous astonishment, it was none other than Sherlock Holmes, his face haggard with concern.

"My dear Watson!" he exclaimed, observing the blood on my hands. "You are injured but alive. Thank God for that."

I have to say I was rather surprised at his passion and soon reassured him that I wasn't injured in the least, the blood being that of Mr. Hartley Jameson. I opened the cabinet door to show him the poor man.

"Most astonishing," he said, viewing the scene with his customary marked attention

"But why," I asked, "did you think that I was the victim? And whatever brought you here in the first place?"

"To answer your second question first," he replied, "I decided this morning that it would be a courtesy to write to Mrs. Forrester, thanking her for the tickets. Imagine my surprise and shock when she replied by the evening post that she knew nothing of the matter." He looked at me with a frown.

"She didn't send them?" I said. "But who then?"

"That, my friend, is the question. I realised immediately that something was seriously amiss, and with all haste came here to try and prevent a catastrophe. When I asked Mrs. Hudson where you were, she told me that something frightful had happened and pointed to the curtains. My dear fellow," and I cannot help but think I detected some strong emotion in his usually measured tones, "I feared the worst."

"Well, you can see that I am unhurt, but that the poor fellow there has suffered a fatal accident."

"An accident!" replied Holmes. "I think not. This is no accident."

"What then? Surely not murder?"

"Oh, indubitably. But why *this* man? What has he done to deserve such a fate?"

"It has surely to be random," I said, explaining what little I knew about Mr. Hartley Jameson.

"You mean, he was sitting beside you?" Holmes asked, with a fresh gleam in his eye. "That is most significant."

"In fact, he was sitting in my seat." I then recounted how we had exchanged places so that Mrs. Hudson might see the stage.

"A-ha!" Holmes exclaimed. "Well, it seems you have had the most lucky escape, but at a terrible cost to this fellow."

"You think that I was the intended victim? But how can that be?"

"You, or perhaps me, since the tickets were intended for the two of us."

"Good Lord!" I cried, looking at him in horror.

"Who picked out Mr. Jameson to come on stage?"

I indicated the magician's assistant, Veronique. Holmes went over to her and spoke in low tones. She looked up at him with a tear-stained face, and replied at length and with emotion. Then he came back to me.

"What did she say?"

"It is most interesting. She claims that some fellow gave her a golden sovereign to pick out the man in Row B, Seat 15."

"Did she not think it strange?"

"I think she considered it well-paid for a moment's work. The man told her he wished to have a laugh at the expense of his friend."

"Some laugh!" I commented. "Was she able to give a description of the fellow?"

"In some detail. He was of tall stature, having a face adorned with thick black whiskers, and wearing a hat pulled down over his eyes."

"A disguise, then?"

"Possibly."

I considered the matter. "So whoever sent us the tickets, this stranger presumably, thought that either you or I would be in that very seat. Poor Mr. Jameson. If only he hadn't been so quick to be polite."

"You and Mrs. Hudson may be grateful that he was."

I could not deny the fact as it related to myself, but added, "Oh, Mrs. Hudson was at no risk. Fantôme specified a man. An Englishman, actually."

"An Englishman?"

"A brave Englishman. I think it was supposed to be a French joke."

"Ah."

We were interrupted then by the arrival of the police, in the familiar wiry form of Inspector Lestrade, along with a couple of uniformed constables, as well as Armitage, a doctor often employed by Scotland Yard.

"No need to say anything just now about our suspicions," warned Holmes. "I first wish to look further into the matter myself."

Lestrade was evidently most surprised to see us but, on hearing of the circumstances – we didn't mention how we had obtained the tickets – was inclined to put it down to a lucky coincidence. I told him what I knew, and what I had observed, no more and no less.

"It would seem," Lestrade remarked, "to be a tragic and most unfortunate accident, although," and here he looked around, lowering his voice, "I shall be investigating that Frenchie, just in case."

Holmes and I left him to his work and at last rejoined poor Mrs. Hudson, who had stayed abandoned in her seat. She is a woman of considerable character, however, and wasn't inclined to hysteria on this occasion, unlike some of the other ladies in the theatre who were displaying, in various degrees, fits of the vapours.

Permission was soon given for all of us to leave the Hall, which we did, having first provided names and addresses to the constables and theatre staff. Holmes, Mrs. Hudson, and I elected to walk back to Baker Street, since any cabs we spotted were already taken. Although it was a cool and foggy night, we walked briskly and it wasn't unpleasant to be outside. In fact, I was glad of it, to clear my head. Of course, the conversation soon turned back to the terrible events of the evening.

"Did Veronique have anything to say about the substitution of the swords?" I asked.

"Only that they all look alike to her. In fact, she trembled at the thought that if the magician had picked up the real sword when she was in the box, it might have been she who was the victim." Holmes looked at me. "Think, Watson. Did anyone touch the swords between the two tricks?"

"Not that I saw."

"But of course, you weren't looking. I suppose that you only had eyes for the young person." Holmes recognised too well another of my weaknesses, that for a pretty face. "It is the traditional magician's ploy of diverting attention," he said.

"A man did appear from the side of the stage," Mrs. Hudson interpolated, "just as the young lady came down into the audience. "I noticed him fiddling around as if adjusting things. I cannot testify that I observed him place a new sword on the table but, as you say, Mr. Holmes, we were all distracted at the time. He may have done."

"Mrs. Hudson, as I have often remarked, you are a perfect treasure!" If Holmes had ever said such a thing, it was certainly not in my hearing, but never mind that. "I wonder," he went on, "if you can describe the man further."

"I am sorry, Mr. Holmes. Just that he was young and in a regular suit. Not a stage costume."

"A suit!"

"Rather a shabby suit. I remember thinking it a little strange at the time. In such a fancy place, you know. The men who wheeled the cabinet on to the stage previously were both in costume."

"You see," said Holmes, clapping his hands, "how it pays to be observant at all times."

"I have learnt it from you, Mr. Holmes." Mrs. Hudson smiled modestly. "You are an excellent teacher."

"Sad then," Holmes said, clapping my arm to offset the harshness of his words, "that Watson is such a poor pupil."

The next morning, Holmes and I set off to interview Mrs. Cecil Forrester, having first sent a telegram to warn of our imminent arrival. We took a train to Camberwell and from the station walked through that most delightful suburb to Addington Square and the elegant house wherein the lady dwelt. She expressed great delight to see us again, her plump features wreathed in smiles of welcome that soon turned to horror when she learned what was the matter.

"I haven't yet seen the newspapers," she said. "What a terrible business!"

She was dressed, I thought, somewhat too youthfully, given her age and shape, in a gown of mint green, festooned with ribbons and frills and perhaps rather too tightly laced, making bulges where there should be none. That said, we had always found Mrs. Forrester a lady of extreme good-nature, one who found it hard to see the bad in people – which had made her an easy prey for the villainies of her steward.

"I need to ask you some questions, Mrs. Forrester," Holmes said.

"Not hard ones, I hope." Her grey curls, under a lacy mop cap, bobbed coquettishly as she spoke.

"No, nothing to be concerned about. It is just on the matter of the tickets for the show."

"Well, Mr. Holmes, as I previously communicated to you, I had nothing to do with that." She rang a bell. "But let us discuss this further over tea. At this time of day I always feel the need for some sustenance, you know, and I'm sure you would like to taste some of Cook's gingerbread. She made it fresh this morning, especially for you."

Since it wasn't long past breakfast time, Mrs. Forrester's hunger might be wondered at and yet, as I have mentioned already, she was a stout woman, whose girth flowed across the sofa upon which she was seated. The way she attacked the plate of cake subsequently brought in by the maid showed that her appetite was in no way diminished by bad news.

"The question," Holmes said, when he had finally managed to get the lady's attention back to the matter in hand, "is who might have appropriated your stationery." He produced the original letter and showed it to her. "If this notepaper does indeed come from your house."

She took it and studied it.

"Oh yes. It is identical. How very strange. Though it is not my hand, you know. Very like, perhaps, but I pride myself on the excellence of my copperplate."

She rang the bell again and asked the maid to send for Miss Sarah.

"I am sure I cannot think . . . Perhaps she will have some better idea, Mr. Holmes," she said. "You must have met my children's governess, Sarah Willis, at the time of the . . . er . . . unpleasantness."

"No," Holmes replied. "We have not yet had that pleasure."

"Ah, well," she replied. "As for pleasure . . . The poor girl isn't endowed with a lively personality, I am afraid, and as for her person . . . I have tried to urge her to make more of herself, you know." Mrs. Forrester paused thoughtfully to munch on her cake, and then continued. "Like myself, Sarah was greatly upset by the . . . the unpleasantness, you know. She seemed to have been under the foolish impression that she and Arthur had some sort of understanding." Mrs. Forrester smiled at some memory. "Oh, he could charm the birds off the trees, that one."

Holmes bowed his head as if in understanding, although I'm sure he took both women for arrant fools to let their heads be turned by such a trickster.

"Is it not strange, Mr. Holmes," Mrs. Forrester went on, "how misfortune seems to follow some people around? Sarah is only now returned from visiting the death-bed of her mother and is understandably quite out of sorts. I was the same when Herbert died – you know, my dear dear husband." And she pressed a delicate handkerchief to her eyes. "But here she is . . . ." She smiled at the newcomer. "Sit down, my dear. This is Mr. Holmes and his friend Dr. Watson. You will recall how they helped out when . . . well, you know . . . ."

Mrs. Forrester clearly did not like to call a spade a spade.

The young woman nodded and sat herself down, no answering smile gracing her lips. As Mrs. Forrester had implied, Miss Willis was a person entirely without charm or attraction of any sort. Flat of figure, her colourless hair was pulled back in a tight bun, and she wore thick spectacles, surely too heavy for her thin face. Her black dress was so plain it might have suited a missionary. Indeed, a silver crucifix hung around her neck.

Her employer then explained the business and showed her the letter.

"How very strange," the girl said, in low tones, peering at it. "I cannot think . . . ." She looked up at us, "unless . . . unless Mr. Alexander took some sheets before he left."

Arthur Alexander, the disgraced steward.

"Of course," said Mrs. Forrester. "It has to be Arthur. He was very bitter against yourself, you know, Mr. Holmes, and it would be quite in his character to play a trick upon you."

It was rather more than that, I thought, but let it pass.

"Perhaps," Holmes replied. "But surely Alexander left for South Africa. Did you yourself not provide him with a ticket to do so?"

"That is true," said Mrs. Forrester. "Well, in that case, I am sure I do not know . . . ."

"We did not see him onto the ship," the companion cut in with some asperity. "He may not have gone at all. I am sure he didn't wish to, and only agreed because the alternative was Newgate Prison."

She regarded us with some defiance. Could she still have feelings for the fellow despite his villainy? Surely not, since, as Mrs. Forrester had informed us at the time, she had been as much a victim, in her own way, as the lady herself, having lent the man from her own meagre savings. All the same, if he had spoken soft words to her, the sort that a plain girl such as herself might never have heard before nor since, then maybe she forgave him on her own account.

"You are right, my dear," Mrs. Forrester was saying, "he may not have gone at all. Oh dear." And in her distress she took another piece of gingerbread, while Miss Sarah Willis sat rigid on her chair, hands neatly folded in her lap on top of her mourning dress.

It seemed to me that the case against the steward was convincing. He would have borne a bitter grudge against Holmes and myself, a bitterness that might easily have turned to an obsessive desire for revenge. Of course, there were questions remaining: How had the young man managed the change of swords, for instance? Had he obtained casual work at the Egyptian Hall? Was he the person spotted on stage by Mrs. Hudson? Had he disguised himself with a black beard, to bribe Veronique into picking out Holmes or myself from the audience? The answer to all these seemed to be in the affirmative. Oh, Holmes might deride my powers of deduction, and yet I felt this time I found my way to the bottom of the matter without any help from him.

An even more pressing consideration suddenly struck me. Alexander's murderous attempt against Holmes and myself had failed. It was of paramount importance, then, to lay hands on the scoundrel before he realised that he had killed the wrong man and came looking for us.

Holmes meanwhile was lost in thought. Suddenly he jumped up.

"Well Mrs. Forrester, Miss Willis, thank you for your time. Watson, we must be off."

Mrs. Forrester looked surprised. "But Mr. Holmes, you have hardly tasted the gingerbread."

"Indeed, we have," he replied. In fact, I had consumed my portion, but Holmes had not, the confection merely crumbled by his nervous fingers over his plate. "Our compliments to your most excellent cook."

Indeed, I thought – and yet Mrs. Hudson's gingerbread is most definitely superior.

"Well," Holmes said as we made our way back from Camberwell, "what did you make of that? Most enlightening was it not?"

"Indeed, "I replied. "It all points to the steward."

"You think so, do you?"

I looked askance at him, but he was merely smiling to himself, seemingly absorbed by the view from the window of the train.

We weren't long back in Baker Street, considering what we had discovered – at least, Holmes was sunk into an armchair smoking his infernal pipe, while I tried to see what might be wrong with my theory and finding nothing – when the doorbell rang. Soon afterwards Mrs. Hudson showed Lestrade up to our rooms. He came in rubbing his hands and smiling broadly.

"It seems the case is solved," he said. "I thought you would like to know that we shall have no need of your skills on this occasion, Mr. Holmes."

"I am glad to hear it," my friend said. "But pray explain."

"The Frenchie and his girl have run off. A clear indication of their guilt, wouldn't you say?"

"Hmm," Holmes replied. "And you have them in custody, I suppose."

"Well no. Not yet. But we have it on good authority that they are making for Dover. No doubt to take the ferry back to France. The Kentish police have been alerted and are looking out for them at this very moment."

"I am afraid, then," said Holmes, "that your jubilation is somewhat premature, Lestrade. Of course, I don't know the source of your information, but I should be more inclined to congratulate you if the fugitives were captured, and had confessed. No, I fear there is a long way to go yet, my friend."

Lestrade looked momentarily abashed, but soon recovered. "You are merely envious, Mr. Holmes, that you haven't been able to solve the crime yourself."

"On the contrary," Holmes stated, to my surprise as much as to that of the policeman, "I rather think that I have. And yet there are certain points that I need to clarify before I am absolutely certain."

"Well, well," Lestrade replied. "We shall see. I expect to hear back from my officers in a short while and will certainly keep you up to date on our investigation."

"I suppose," I said, after Lestrade had left us, "that you meant that you were hot on the track of this Alexander fellow."

Perhaps Holmes hadn't heard me, for he picked up his violin and started scraping a few chords and arpeggios, my hint to leave him well alone.

Over the next few days, I had to spend some time at Barts Hospital. It was in truth quite a relief, after the excitement of the last while, to be in that humdrum world, attending to the sick, dressing wounds, and performing the occasional amputation, although I admit I was somewhat wary going about my business, and eyed askance any new patient if they happened to be a young man of attractive appearance. I had seen Arthur Alexander only once and couldn't recall his features with any precision. I didn't wish to find myself alone with him in case he persisted with his evil plan.

This peaceful time could not last, of course, and on the fourth morning I was hurried from my boiled eggs by Holmes insisting that I accompany him to Scotland Yard.

"I have received word from Lestrade," he said. "They have him."

"Alexander?" I asked.

"No, no, no," said with some impatience. "Fantôme. Lestrade has kindly invited us to sit in on his interrogation."

"You think he will confess after all?" I asked.

"To what?"

"Well, murder of course."

Holmes merely emitted a cynical harrumph and, in his excitement to be off, nearly pulled my arm from its socket.

The magician looked much reduced when we saw him again, in his shabby civilian suit, far from the splendours of the Egyptian Hall. The interview room provided a dismal enough setting, its bare plastered walls stained with rust – or possibly blood – its rough table and hard chairs set on a cold stone floor, the dim and flickering gaslight casting a mournful pall over all.

Holmes sat back in the shadows, the tips of his fingers joined, his head thrown back. Was he bored? Lost in thought? Was he listening intently? I am afraid even now I'm often unable to read his mood. Lestrade meanwhile was leaning forward on the table, facing the Frenchman in a threatening manner and bombarding him with questions.

The little man, at first downcast and even sullen, soon reared up and protested his innocence with Gallic fervour. How could he, Fantôme, have committed such a frightful deed? Why? He didn't even know this Monsieur Jameson. His hands flew about as he spoke, and I could tell that Lestrade was not one iota impressed with such a foreign carry-on. Yet as I thought back to my arrival on the tragic scene, I remembered how shocked Fantôme clearly had been at what he'd done. I didn't believe then that he had knowingly run the victim through with his sword, and I didn't think so now. Lestrade, however, wasn't convinced.

"If that is the case," he asked, "why did you run away? Didn't you think that it would indicate your guilt?"

"But Monsieur," Fantôme pleaded, "I cannot deny that it was I who struck the blow that killed the man – in front of an audience of a thousand. I am guilty of the deed. So then Veronique . . . ."

At the mention of this name, Holmes leant forward.

"Veronique said I must fly or you will send me to the guillotine."

"Not in this country, we don't," said Lestrade. "Not in England. Nothing so barbaric."

No, we hang you by the neck until you are dead, I thought.

"And where," Holmes cut in, "is the fair Veronique now, might I ask?"

Fantôme shrugged. "I do not know."

"She didn't flee with you."

"No."

"Ha!" And he leaned back again, Lestrade throwing him an inquiring look to which he didn't respond.

"But please to remember," Fantôme continued, "that it was Veronique who handed me the sword."

"You'll have to do better than to blame an innocent young lady." Lestrade was clearly intent on pursuing his quarry to the end.

"But she is not – ?" Fantôme started.

"What?"

Holmes rose to his feet. "She is no mademoiselle. She is not French. Isn't that the case?"

"*Oui*. Not French. No. Just for the act she pretends."

"Not French!" I exclaimed. "Well, I must say, she sounded French."

"Oh, zat is easy, *non*, to make ze pretence." Holmes had resorted to a terrible fake accent and Lestrade and I regarded him aghast. "But you see, my friends – " (Back to the Queen's English, thank goodness.) " – when I spoke to her in what I took to be her native tongue, it was immediately clear to me that she understood not a single word."

"It is true," Fantôme replied. "She is *une Anglaise*."

"And one I think that hasn't been in your employ long?"

"That is also true, monsieur. In fact, she offered her services to me just before the opening night. You see, my assistant, Claudette, had gone missing. At such a time! *Parbleu!*" He shook his head. "Claudette who has been with me for three years . . . . Who is like a daughter to me! Gone! I am at the end of my wits. Suddenly, this Veronique arrives and tells me that she has experience as an actress. To be quite honest, messieurs, I took her on like that." He clicked his fingers. "I could not complain. She was not Claudette, but she worked well enough until that night so terrible."

"And then she impressed on you the need to run away. Good, good," said Holmes, rubbing his hands together.

"We must find this Veronique, or whatever her name is, as soon as possible," I said.

"I am afraid we have no leads on her," Lestrade remarked. "She seems to have disappeared into thin air, like in one of this fellow's trickeries." And he chuckled at his own joke.

"Not at all," Holmes said. "I know exactly where she is. If you're willing to accompany me, gentlemen, I think we can clear the matter up tonight."

Lestrade's jaw dropped. "And Fantôme?" he asked.

"Oh, you can let him go," Holmes said. "He has nothing at all to do with it."

"Well now, Mr. Holmes," came the gruff reply, "I don't think I can do that just yet. No, indeed. This fellow seems like a slippery customer to me, with his fancy French ways. I will keep him under lock and key for the time being, until you can prove his innocence to me beyond the shadow of a doubt."

Holmes gave a resigned nod. One cannot argue with Scotland Yard.

I had no notion at first where we were bound and Holmes was giving nothing away. He is something of a showman after all, producing solutions to crimes in the way a magician will pull a rabbit from a seemingly empty top hat. So it was only when we reached Blackfriars Station that I realised we must be returning to Camberwell. Indeed, the three of us – Holmes, Lestrade, and myself – soon boarded a train heading thither.

"I don't suppose," Lestrade said, "that you would care to enlighten us, Mr. Holmes."

My friend simply put on that rather annoying enigmatical smile of his and leaned back, extending his long legs across the carriage floor and placing the tips of his fingers together.

"All in good time, Lestrade," he replied. "All in good time."

It seemed that he was in a philosophical frame of mind and the subject of his musings on this occasion was the female of the species.

"Women, you know," he started, speaking out of what he no doubt considered his great experience of the sex, "are creatures utterly under the sway of their passions. They aren't rational the way men are. They let themselves be carried away by their emotions, and if those emotions are strong enough, then let mankind beware."

"Hmm," commented Lestrade, no doubt thinking of Mrs. Lestrade, a formidable woman, as I had heard say, who ruled her husband with a rod of iron, capable of reducing, in the domestic sphere, the lion of Scotland Yard to a meek lamb.

For my part, I couldn't keep silent. "I know of several women," I said, "who are quite as rational as men, and on the other hand men who are quite irrational and likely to be carried away by their passions."

"Of course you do. And yet I would argue that those are men who have given in to the feminine element in their psyche. Have you not read Briquet's treatise on the subject of hysteria?"

I had not, though I was aware of the fellow's arguments. Nevertheless, I stuck to my own opinions which were not gleaned from volumes of psychology, but from my own observations of the world.

The train soon pulled into Camberwell Station and again we walked the short distance to Addington Square. A pall of fog hung over all and the air, even in this usually pleasant suburb, was rank with the smell of coal dust. By the time we reached the Forrester house, our coats and hats were beaded over with droplets of moisture, as was my moustache, no doubt. I almost felt inclined, on reaching the refuge of Mrs. Forrester's hallway, to shake myself like a dog.

The lady of the house was again expecting us, so I presumed that Holmes had sent her another telegram. The presence of Lestrade, however, seemed to discommode her not a little – a frequent reaction, as I have noticed in the past, of even the most innocent when face to face with a Scotland Yard detective. Yet was she indeed innocent? Perhaps it was she after all who had sent us the letter to lure us to the theatre. For what reason I could not imagine, however, and despite Holmes's earlier disquisitions on the shortcomings of the female sex, I could hardly believe that the eminently respectable Mrs. Forrester had any great passions to hide, except perhaps in regard to gingerbread and other such tasty comestibles.

We had been shown again into her parlour, but this time Holmes insisted that we didn't want any tea, answering for both Lestrade and myself, who might not have refused so readily. Clearly this was to be no social visit.

"I do not know what more I can tell you, Mr. Holmes," Mrs. Forrester said.

"It isn't you that I wish to question," he replied. "I wonder, could you send for Miss Willis."

This young person entered soon after, displaying a scowl of reluctance on her thin face that certainly added nothing to her attractions.

"Ah, Miss Willis," said Holmes genially. "So good of you to join us."

She nodded coldly.

"I might have expected," he went on, "that you would have returned to the theatre by now, to your acting career."

108

Mrs. Forrester gave a start of astonishment (as did Lestrade and I), but the governess regarded Holmes coldly.

"I have no idea what you're talking about," she said, fingering her crucifix.

"Come, come, Veronique – or whatever your real name is. That will not do, you know. Did you really think, no matter how skilled the disguise, that you could fool Sherlock Holmes? Did you not think that, despite those absurd spectacles, I would not recognise the same eyes that had wept so convincingly on the stage of the Egyptian Hall?"

Veronique! It could not be. I rather agreed with the young woman that my friend had, for once, to be mistaken. This skinny scarecrow, with her faded hair and pinched mouth, the fair and seductive magician's assistant? No, never!

"You are indeed a skilful actress," he continued, "able to switch characters in an instant."

"Mr. Holmes, I have to protest," Mrs. Forrester interrupted. "I really think you must be barking up the wrong tree, this time. Miss Willis came to me with the very best of references. Indeed, perhaps they glowed a little too brightly with respect to the poor girl, but Mrs. Standish is a woman of the highest integrity and wouldn't have sold me a pup."

"Can I remind you, Mrs. Forrester," Holmes said, kindly enough, "that references can be forged as much as letters containing tickets for the Egyptian Hall. I suspect that you did not contact Mrs. Standish personally to check if she had indeed had Sarah Willis in her employ. Although – " And here he looked across at the still expressionless girl. " – she is so devious in her ways that there might indeed be a Sarah Willis who once worked for Mrs. Standish as a governess – only, I can assure you, madam, this person is not she."

"Oh dear," said Mrs. Forrester, "oh dear, dear, dear."

At last, Lestrade, who had been sitting silently all along, broke into the conversation.

"What's all this about a letter with tickets?" Having received the explanation, he went on. "But why should Veronique hatch such an elaborate plan in the first place?" He shook his head. "I agree with Mrs. Forrester. This time you're being a bit too clever by half, Mr. Holmes. I still think the Frenchie is behind it."

"Remember, Lestrade," Holmes replied, "what we were discussing on the train?" (Hardly a discussion, I thought.) "The overpowering and all-consuming passions of womankind. I have uncovered evidence that Willis was in league with Alexander." He turned to Mrs. Forrester. "They entered your employ at about the same time, is that not so?" She thought for a moment, then nodded. "Their intent was to rob you, a trusting widow, of all that you possessed. Lucky for you, then, that I was able to thwart their devilish plan, although I admit that, at the time, I considered Alexander to be solely responsible."

Here the young woman shifted slightly in her seat and a smirk played over her features.

"But while Willis was devoted to Alexander," Holmes continued, "he for his part felt no obligation to her. He despised her and only used her of necessity. Once her usefulness was exhausted, he wanted no more of her and happily sailed off to South Africa, abandoning her here without a second thought."

"That's a lie!" The girl was as last stung into replying. She stood up, tearing off her spectacles and casting them from her. Her eyes blazed and at last I began to see that she might indeed be Veronique. "He loved me! Yes, he did. He loved me with all his heart. It was you, Mr. Sherlock Holmes, who took him from me. You!"

The quiet and plain companion was now quite transformed into a hellcat. She looked ready to jump on Holmes and scratch his eyes out.

"So he has written to ask you to join him in the colonies, has he?" There was a cruel and sarcastic edge to Holmes's tone.

"Damn you!" The oath broke from her lips. Mrs. Forrester exclaimed in shock, while Holmes smiled.

"I thought not."

I should have abhorred his harsh treatment of the girl more, had I not then recalled the fate of poor Mr. Hartley Jameson.

"The wrong man died, then," I said to her, "from your point of view, that is."

"Yes. It should have been him." And she pointed a quivering finger at Holmes. "Why was it not him? It is true," she went on, frowning, "I did not know exactly what he looked like except that he was tall and lean and often in the company of another man." Turning back to me. "You, Dr. Watson . . . So when I peered through the curtains before the performance started and saw you talking together like old friends, how could I not think that this is was the celebrated Sherlock Holmes? I rejoiced at the sight. You had fallen into my trap, and now I was to be revenged on the men who had ruined my life and taken from me the only person I have ever loved. I handed Fantôme a real sword – yes, I did, knowing its deadly power. But it is you two responsible for the death of Mr. Jameson, not me. Not me!"

She sank on the chair, exhausted and overcome. It was impossible for me to feel pity for her. Yet I detected an expression of sorrowful sympathy on the wide face of her employer.

Lestrade needed no more evidence – Had she not confessed? – and sent forthwith to the local police station for a vehicle to convey the girl to the prison at Holloway.

There is little more to relate. Fantôme was cleared of all involvement in the crime. We had feared for a while for the fate of Claudette, his previous assistant, but as it turned out that she had simply been bribed by Willis to disappear. If the magician considered her like a daughter, Claudette apparently did not reciprocate with any sense of filial duty. Her loyalty was easily bought for a few sovereigns. Nevertheless, the magician forgave her and she returned to his employ where, for all I know, she has remained ever since.

Veronique – or Willis – was found guilty of the murder by proxy of Mr. Hartley Jameson, and still languishes in Holloway Prison.

The young man who had wandered onto the stage during the fatal performance, as observed so closely by Mrs. Hudson, turned out to have nothing at all to do with the business, which just goes to show that one can be too observant sometimes. Just as well that Holmes didn't allow himself to be distracted by that particular detail.

As for Mrs. Forrester? Her betrayal by trusted persons in her employ did not weigh on her for very long. She wrote Holmes a letter on her by now familiar crested notepaper in a fine copperplate informing us that she had found a most suitable replacement for the wretched Willis. This person had come with the most impeccable recommendations – although, the lady added, this time she had been sure to confirm them.

"*I do not think,*" the letter concluded, "*that I shall have any trouble with my new governess, a Miss Mary Morstan, a most attractive and intelligent young woman. Perhaps you and Dr. Watson will have the pleasure of meeting her someday.*"

As indeed we did, but that is quite another story.

> "*I have come to you, Mr. Holmes,*" *she said,* "*because you once enabled my employer, Mrs. Cecil Forrester, to unravel a little domestic complication. She was much impressed by your kindness and skill.*"
>
> "*Mrs. Cecil Forrester,*" *he repeated thoughtfully.* "*I believe that I was of some slight service to her. The case, however, as I remember it, was a very simple one.*"
>
> "*She did not think so . . . .*"
>
> – Mary Morstan and Sherlock Holmes
> *The Sign of the Four*

The Secret in Lowndes Court
by David Marcum

It was the coldest March that I could recall, and I was glad that morning to have no requests for my attention. In those earlier days in Baker Street, my health was still somewhat precarious, although it was then approaching three years since I had been wounded in the Battle of Maiwand. Joining Sherlock Holmes on his investigations had done wonders for my recuperation, forcing me to set forth when I might otherwise have chosen to sit by the fire and sip whisky. My own brother had started down that path for far smaller reasons than a shattered shoulder and a grazed subclavian artery, and I was always aware that such snares could entrap any man before he knew it, and if he wasn't ever vigilant.

Having no regular practice of my own, I would divide my time between Barts as needed, and occasionally as a *locum* for various doctors whom I had come to know around the city. More and more I found myself participating in Holmes's cases, as time and health permitted, and early on he had made it clear that any fees that he earned which involved my assistance were to be shared. "If you were called in by another doctor to consult on a medical case," he had explained soon after I had assisted in the arrest of Jefferson Hope, "you would not expect to take your valuable time and offer your opinion – the result of years of training and experience – for free. Neither would you think it acceptable to pay from your own pocket any expenses incurred along the way – transportation, lodging, and so on. As a professional, you expect to be treated as one. You have earned that right. I, too, am a professional in my own way, and I demand the same. When I request your services, it is more than simply asking you to join me as a friend – although that aspect is not to be negated. Your presence and participation are part of that which is offered by my little agency, and as such, the client will be responsible for that payment."

Then he had dropped into his chair with a rueful smile. "Although I must admit that at times my professional charges, which I never vary except when I remit them altogether, do get remitted more often than they should. It has been my experience that sometimes the most challenging and interesting cases come from those who can least afford to pay for them." Then he sat up a bit straighter. "Nevertheless, we shall each of us, you and I, stand upon our professional dignity and demand proper remuneration whenever possible. We can but try."

Now, looking at Holmes's latest client, I suspected that this might be one of those instances when his fee might be remitted yet again.

Often in those days, Holmes's mornings were not very different from those of a general practitioner who opens the door to a steady stream of patients with a variety of complaints. The difference, or course, is that a doctor quickly learns that nearly all of the complaints fall into three or four typical categories, each requiring the same type of treatment, whereas Holmes's cases tended to be much more unusual. Of course, he would sometimes become weary of the tediousness of some of their stories, for as he'd explained once early on, "There is a strong family resemblance about misdeeds, and if you have all the details of a thousand at your finger-ends, it is odd if you can't unravel the thousand-and-first."

The amateur writer in me never tired of listening to the curious tales presented by Holmes's clients, one after another, and finding interest in their stories, as well as their diverse backgrounds. Holmes, however, with a thousand (or more likely ten-thousand) details at hand, would strip away all the frippery and froth in an instant and see the bones of the matter exposed underneath, in the same way that Sir Jasper Meek or Penrose Fisher, or any of the best doctors in London, could instantly recognize a disease – even a rare one like Black Formosa Corruption – because they had seen it presented so often before.

As I recall, that morning had been rather typical, with three or four clients already having come and gone. One was a young woman who had a bundle of her dead grandfather's letters, in which her recently acquired young gentleman seemed to have too great an interest. Five minutes of glancing through them, followed by a few questions about the grandfather's seafaring background and a look through the *Gazetteer*, was enough for Holmes to advise her to look behind a framed map (which she confirmed that she owned, in spite of not knowing how Holmes could have been aware of it) for a set of stock documents, hidden long ago, and now no doubt worth a fortune. (As she left, I added my own professional advice: Avoid the young gentleman in the future.)

After a couple of other similar consultations and a second cup of coffee, the morning continued with the announcement by Mrs. Hudson of one Ernest Wilson. He was a compact fellow of perhaps forty-five. His suit was well-kept, but not new. He had gray hair that was perhaps overdue for a trim, and it was pressed down in a ring-shape encircling his head, no doubt from wearing the cloth cap that he had clutched in his hands. He looked from one to the other of us rather nervously, but seemed to relax quickly – although not completely – when Holmes invited him to the basket chair before the fire.

113

"Thank you for your time, Mr. Holmes," he said, glancing my way with a bit of uncertainty. I had seen this before, but for the most part I no longer felt the need to apologize and offer to retreat upstairs to my bedroom, as I had done when Holmes and I first began sharing rooms, or even to the present when a client of recognizable importance professed a matter to be of the utmost secrecy. Usually Holmes indicated that I should stay – sometimes, it seemed, as a way to assert his authority over the client more than a wish for my presence – but there were still occasions when I *was* excused. In Mr. Wilson's case, there was no indication that I should leave, and thus I picked up my notebook to jot down a few points as the man told his story.

"You may not remember me, Mr. Holmes – "

"Of course, I do, Mr. Wilson. You're the manager of the messenger service in Regent Street, around the corner from the Union Bank in Argyll Place."

Wilson's eyes widened. "I am indeed. Thank you. Thank you." He paused for a second, as if some great honor had been accorded and had left him speechless. Then, in an effort to regain his train of thought that was visible to both Holmes and me, Wilson continued.

"As you say, I'm the manager, and have been with the company, at that location, since I was a boy. I started running messages when I was just a lad, a number of years before you two young men were born, I expect. It was a local concern then – we've since been absorbed by a larger organization – and as I came up, I took on more and more responsibility, so that when old Mr. Jeeter retired, I was given the reins. It's steady work, and necessary, and if one keeps an eye on all the moving pieces, there isn't too much that can go wrong.

"When I first started, I lived with me mum, not far out of the Seven Dials, and thank heavens I escaped from there, as many of my young mates did not. With what I earned, we were able to move to a better neighborhood, and there we stayed. Mum died a few years ago, but I remained there in our old rooms, by myself, until the middle of last February, just over a month ago, when we – that is, the other tenants and me – learned that the building had been sold to a nearby brewery so that they could demolish it and expand their building. Well, there wasn't anything to do but look for somewhere else.

"The same day that I learned I'd have to move, I was returning from delivering a package – as I've never risen so high that I don't still do some of that for myself – and I was quite fortunate to notice that a room had just become available near my place of employment – in Lowndes Court, just off Carnaby Street, not three or four blocks away from the service. It's an

114

easy walk, and there are probably six or eight pubs a couple of minutes in any direction, should I wish for a little something at the end of the day.

"It's a small house, smaller than this one, and the lease is held by Mrs. Denbigh, a widow of about my age. It seems that her previous tenant, an old man who had been a bank clerk, had dropped dead at his desk one morning a week or so before, and after his sister came and cleared out his things, she needed a new lodger. The rate is reasonable, including meals and laundry, and after I saw the sign in her window and knocked on her door, we had concluded the arrangements within fifteen minutes.

"I'm not one for change, you understand, but I had no choice. I'm satisfied with where I work, and I was happy with where I lived, until I had to find somewhere else. But this is definitely a satisfactory solution to my problem."

I could see that Holmes was becoming impatient, and to Wilson's credit, he perceived it as well. He hurried onward toward the meat of his story.

"I've lived there for just a month now – at Number 8 Lowndes Court. In all that time, there's been nothing unusual whatsoever, and I've simply picked up and carried on with my life the same as before – I just turn a different direction at the end of the day to walk home. But yesterday morning, as I was finishing my breakfast, Mrs. Denbigh knocked and asked to come in.

"That was a bit strange, as she usually waits until I've gone for the day to collect the dishes, along with any laundry which I've set aside. She seemed upset, and wanted to speak about something, but had a difficult time finding a way to start. I've seen this over the years with my lads at the service – when they've made a mistake, or something that should have been easy has had a complication, and they fear that they've handled it the wrong way. The best way forward is simply get them to tell it, and I urged Mrs. Denbigh to share what troubled her.

"'Have you heard any . . . noises in the night?' she asked.

"'What noises?' I asked. Truth be told, the house could burn around me and I might not wake up – it used to worry my mum something terrible.

"'Footsteps – that's how it started,' she said, as if she were embarrassed about it. I couldn't think why, until I suddenly understood what she might be thinking. She didn't mean a burglar. 'And then the knocking began.'

"'Do you think that the house might have a *ghost*?' I tried not to smile and make her feel foolish.

"She couldn't look at me then, as if hearing it said out loud, in the bright light of morning, made her too ridiculous. And yet, she'd decided to ask me about it, and she pressed on, instead of letting the matter drop.

115

"'Yes. No. Oh, I don't know, Mr. Wilson! I've never heard anything like these noises before, in the entire twenty years that I've lived here. For the last week they've happened every night – softly at first. Just a single knock on the wall outside my bedroom, as if a piece of plaster has crumbled loose and fallen in the wall, or been knocked loose by the passage of a mouse. I'm a light sleeper, or I might not have noticed it – at least, when it began. But once I hear it, then in a few minutes – five or ten I suppose – there will be another, and it sounds intentional, as if someone had thumped a knuckle on the wall, and not as if the house is simply creaking as it settles for the night. Every night that I've heard the noises, they've begun the same way.'

"'Every night, you say. And you've heard them for a full week?'

"'Yes, although who can say when they started before I noticed them? They might even . . . might have started . . . .'

"Her voice trailed off then, and I knew what she was implying – that old Creech, the man who had lived there before me – was back somehow. I laughed aloud then, and her eyes narrowed. She didn't like being mocked.

"'You're thinking that it's your former tenant,' I said, trying to sound serious. 'But that's silly, Mrs. Denbigh. Surely you don't believe in ghosts.'

"That made her a little angry, I think. Her eyes narrowed and her nostrils turned white. 'I am sure that I don't know what to believe, Mr. Wilson,' she said tightly. 'I apologize for wasting your valuable time.' And she would have left in anger if I hadn't risen and asked her to stay, and to tell me more of what had happened.

"'Has it just been the knocking, then?' I asked.

"She shook her head. 'The first night I heard steps, somewhere in the house, but I couldn't tell from where, It was a sliding sound, with an occasional thump – the way that old Mr. Creech would walk around up here at night in his slippers.' She took a step forward, and put a hand on my arm. 'Have you heard him? Has he been up here as well?'

"I shook my head. 'But the walking was only the first night? After that it was the knocking?'

"She nodded. 'That started the night after I heard the walking – even last night. When I'm fully awake, it stops. Afterwards, I can't go back to sleep. It's a wonder the last few nights that I've managed to fall asleep at all, afraid of what I'll hear in the darkness, but when I do hear the knocking, I wake up, my heart racing. Are you sure that you haven't heard anything?'

"I shook my head and forcefully kept myself from smiling this time. 'I sleep so deeply that your Mr. Creech could be leaning right over my bed and I'd never know it.'

"I'd mistakenly made light of it once more, in spite of trying not to, and that only seemed to upset her yet again, but instead of turning to leave this time, a strange look came over her face, and she rushed on with her story. 'But it isn't just the knocking and the walking around. Now . . . now, last night – he's written me a warning!'

"This, then, sounded more substantial. One might have thought that she was dreaming the other, no matter that she insisted she was awake. After all, I've only known the woman for a month, and while she's presented herself most sensibly during that time, I cannot really say if she might be the type to hear things that aren't there. But if there was actually a warning – something written down – well, now there was something to be going on with. As we say at the service, if it isn't written it doesn't exist, and this sounded like proof.

"Aware that the morning was getting away from me, I asked her to explain, but she said that she'd better show me instead. I nodded, and she led me downstairs – my two rooms are on the first floor, same as yours here, gentlemen – and then along the hallway beside the stairway to her own chambers at the rear. (The ground floor front is let to a key shop.) Of course I hadn't been to this part of the house before, but there were no surprises about it – She has a parlor with windows looking out over a small court, and a bedroom just beside it, and a small kitchen."

"And the basement?" interrupted Holmes.

"The door to the downstairs is underneath the steps going up to my rooms. It's located just outside of Mrs. Denbigh's sitting room."

"And who lodges above you?"

"No one – I'm the only lodger. Above me is just the attic, nothing more. It's a small house."

Holmes nodded for him to continue.

"In the parlor, she led me over to the fireplace. The wall there is papered – some sort of pink flowers, very small – and there, alongside the mantel, was the word '*Revenge*', written in soot."

Holmes glanced at me. Just two years earlier we had seen something of the sort scrawled on the wall of an abandoned house in Brixton. In that case, the same word – but then in German – had been inscribed in blood, located above the body of a dead American. It had been a most thrilling affair, especially to me in those early days of my recovery, and I wondered if Wilson's narrative might end up as another tale of vengeance spread across many decades and continents before coming to a grim conclusion in an old house in the heart of the British capital.

"Is the word still there?" asked Holmes, his features alert with interest. I knew that he would wish to examine it, and that he'd likely be able to glean a number of useful details.

Wilson shook his head. "Mrs. Denbigh washed it away later that day."

Holmes's eyes narrowed. "Describe it then."

Wilson glanced away for a moment as he reviewed the image in his mind. "The letters were even – none larger than the other – and each about a foot tall."

"All capitals?"

"That's right."

"And about how wide? Did they crowd together, or appear to get closer together at the end of the word, as if the writer had planned poorly and was running out of room?"

"No, they were evenly spaced – about six inches wide each, and an inch or two apart."

"Ah, a ghost who plans accordingly beforehand. What you describe would have been over four feet wide."

"That's right. It was at eye-level, and you couldn't help but notice it. There's plenty of room on that side of the mantel."

"And one would assume that the ghost – or whomever was responsible – dipped a finger into the fireplace to access this make-do ink."

"I thought of that. I looked in the fireplace, but Mrs. Denbigh had already built up the fire that morning. I did see some small droppings of soot across the slates in front of the fireplace leading off to the right, toward the message."

Holmes nodded. "A man after our own hearts, Watson! Possibly an important detail – for why would a phantasm need soot to write a message at all? Wouldn't such a creature be able to inscribe it with green flames, or with some sort of ectoplasm from 'The Other Side'."

Wilson nodded. "My thinking exactly, Mr. Holmes. Someone real – not a dead man – had been in those rooms. But even if it wasn't a ghost, it's still something that is a worry to Mrs. Denbigh."

"Agreed. And you say that this occurred yesterday morning?"

Wilson nodded.

"What did you do next?"

"There wasn't much that could be done. It was a bright morning as you'll recall, and the idea of ghosts seemed silly in the daylight. I mentioned that I needed to get on to work – Mrs. Denbigh didn't seem too pleased about that! – but I promised to think on it during the day."

"Does she not have anyone else that she can call upon for assistance?" I asked.

"It seems not. Her husband died fifteen years back – he was a brakeman for the railway, and there was some sort accident. She's mentioned that fact a number of times in passing. There were no children. If she has anyone else – a parent or brother or sister perhaps – I'm not aware of them. She doesn't have any photographs of family in her parlor, although there might be something of that sort in her bedroom."

"You've waited a day to approach me. What happened next? May I assume that there were developments last night?"

"Last night, and this morning as well. Throughout yesterday, I considered the problem, and decided that there was nothing to be done except hide myself last night and try to catch the person who was getting into the house. When I returned yesterday evening, I explained my plan, intending to settle myself in a little alcove near the front door, where I'd be out of the way when someone passed by – either entering somehow by way of the front door, or coming up from the basement."

"Is there a back entrance?" Holmes asked.

"Yes, but it's in the basement, so if someone were to enter that way, he or she would still have to climb the stairs and pass me in the alcove."

"Is there a separate entrance into the house by way of the key shop?" I interrupted.

Wilson nodded. "I thought of that, but I examined the connecting door in the front hall quite closely after I returned home, and it was locked and seems to be secure. The light wasn't the best there, but I could see that cobwebs across the doorway were too old to have been made since the night before, and they unbroken."

Holmes nodded appreciatively, and Wilson continued. "I also looked around a bit down in the basement, but saw nothing that seemed unusual. The rear door was locked up tight, and the door to the front areaway beneath Lowndes Court has a couple of solid locks, and while someone might be able to pick them, or even have copies of the keys, there's nothing there that revealed itself to me.

"After my little supper, I read for a bit and then went downstairs, knocking on Mrs. Denbigh's parlor door and letting her know that I was getting on station for the night watch. She seemed concerned that I'd be too far away, being near the front door, to know if anything happened, but I'd already arranged a comfortable chair in the alcove, and settled in to wait for whatever happened. However, gentlemen – and I hate to admit it – but . . . well, I fell asleep. I never heard a thing. This morning I awakened early, rather shamed that I'd been unable to stay awake for one night, and crept down the hall toward Mrs. Denbigh's parlor. She wasn't up yet, and the house wasn't making a sound. There, written in the same place as the

119

morning before, and duplicating it as if traced in the same spot, was the word '*Revenge*', again spelled out in soot.

"It was quite early, and the fire wasn't built up yet, so I looked closely and saw where there were places in the soot where a finger had likely dipped in to be re-inked. I took the time to examine the letters more closely, and it was apparent to me then – and I should have noticed it the first time – that each letter would have taken a number of strokes to complete, for a little bit of soot inked on each finger doesn't go far when writing seven letters that are each half-a-square-foot in size."

"What was Mrs. Denbigh's reaction when she saw this morning's message?" asked Holmes.

"Or more specifically," I amended with a smile, "when she learned that you had fallen asleep at your post?"

Wilson looked rather sheepish. "She said she'd heard the knocking again, and when I first spoke to her, she was a bit scared. When she saw the writing, she clung to me in fear. But then, when she heard that I'd slept through it all, she wasn't as upset with me as I would have thought. It seemed to please her in some strange way – proof that an intruder could enter once again, even with someone nearby. I believe that it further solidifies her belief that she has acquired a ghost."

"A ghost," Holmes added, "who dips a phantom finger into fireplace soot in order to physically convey his thoughts." He uncrossed his legs and straightened in his chair. "So you have now decided to consult with me."

Wilson rubbed his face. "I don't know what else to do. The woman asked for my help, and I could certainly hide again tonight, and this time make much more of an effort to stay awake, but then what? I want to stay in Mrs. Denbigh's good graces, and help her if I can, but I'm not sure just what I've gotten myself into. Suppose I do catch some fellow slipping through the house tonight. Do I try to trap him? Do I hit him over the head? Do I try and hold him until the police arrive, taking a chance that he'll do me an injury in the meantime?" He shook his head and sighed. "This is not my line at all. That's when I thought of you."

"And Mrs. Denbigh? Her thoughts about this consultation?"

Wilson shook his head. "I didn't tell her. I hadn't really decided when I left for the day. Instead, I simply said that I'd take care of things tonight for sure. That seemed to please her. Then, not long after I walked into work, I recalled you, Mr. Holmes – you were there last week, I believe – and my mind was suddenly clear on the matter."

Holmes tapped his lips two or three times, and then said, "This almost certainly falls into two or three likely categories. I'm aware of something like it ten or fifteen years ago in Saxe-Altenburg."

120

Wilson's eyes lit up. "That fills me with great confidence, Mr. Holmes! Although this matter has only intruded into my life for a couple of days, I'll be happy to have things return to normal. I don't like change, you see."

"Yes, I believe you mentioned that." He stood. "Doctor Watson and I will do a bit of research and let you know something before the end of the day."

Wilson and I rose as well, and he offered his hand, first to Holmes and then me. "Very good. I'll look forward to seeing you."

When the manager had departed, I looked at Holmes with an expectant raised eyebrow. "Pah!" he cried. "I shouldn't interfere at all."

"Indeed? Then why do so?"

"Because that messenger service is well-run and convenient, and I don't want to get on Wilson's wrong side. I fear that this will end badly for one of us." He glanced at the clock. "Nearly noon. Surely Mrs. Denbigh can be found at home. Would you care to accompany me?"

I did, and in ten minutes or so we were well-bundled against the cold and making our way by hansom toward the client's lodgings. We had held to our own thoughts down Baker Street and then into Marylebone Road, and it was only as we turned along Park Crescent, and so into Portland Place, that I sensed that Holmes was ready to speak.

"You indicated some familiarity with the matter."

"I did. It's as clear as if she'd pretended to fall into a stream so that he would rescue her, and then fall hopelessly in love."

I laughed at the image. "So that reference to some matter in Saxe-Altenburg . . . ?"

"That's real enough. The second daughter of Ernst I – the Duke – contrived something along the same lines to catch the attention of an aloof young man that she'd picked as a husband. The fellow was too dim to realize that he was being played like a fiddle, and set about trying to 'protect' her from the ghost that was following her about – that only she could see, mind you. I believe that they now have four children, and someone wrote a rather dull epic poem about it."

"I doubt," was my response, "that Mrs. Denbigh has read that poem. We must give her credit, I suppose, for coming up with the scheme on her own – if you're right."

"Oh, I'll admit it could be something else. Old Creech could have, in his misbegotten youth, stolen the Lost Fire Emeralds of the Yupik and hidden them within in the house, and now a vengeful tribesman, the last survivor of his people, has made his way on foot across the frozen wastes of the polar icecaps to chase Mrs. Denbigh out of her bedroom so that they can be retrieved. But the simplest solution is best: After a month, the

121

widow has set her cap on the new lodger, who is too unaware to see the fate that she has planned for him. He did say, I believe, that she chided him for staying too far away from the parlor – and her bedroom – last night. I suspect that, in her own ineffectual way, she probably hinted that he should wait in her chambers for the ghost to arrive – a fact that probably eluded him, and thus he didn't feel the need to mention it. When he instead went the other direction, toward the front of the house, and in fact then fell asleep, it was easy for her to reload her guns with another message. Tonight, but for our intervention, the poor man might have been lost!"

"Holmes!" I said with mock surprise. "You hinted that this might end badly. I can agree that he might need to move if he finds this distasteful, which would be a bad ending for him – for you'll recall that he doesn't like change – but matrimony with the woman might end up being the best thing for the man! Don't disparage it, and don't charge in like wild bull and spoil something just because of your cynicism."

He glanced at me with a glint in his eye. "No promises, Watson. We'll see what sort of impression this woman makes. In the end, you might agree what saving Wilson is of the utmost importance."

And in fact the woman in question made a rather winning and pleasant impression after all. The hansom let us out in front of a small house, rather mashed between two larger buildings, as if in the past age when the city was being constructed, builders had started from either end of the court and worked toward each other, and when they met in the middle, their poor planning hadn't left quite enough room for a full-sized structure, and so the modest little house was built instead. The door to the residence was crowded to its left side, while the right held a modest little key shop – now dark, and with a sign on the door indicating that the owner would return by two o'clock. The entrance to the shop was reached by a little concrete "bridge" over the open space of the areaway below, and it had been added some years after the house's original construction, whenever the front ground floor was converted into a business requiring a second entrance. Those in the countryside might not have seen such an arrangement before, but in London it is rather common. A steep little metal stairway went down between the two doors to the areaway.

Holmes rang the bell of the residence door, and within a few moments it was opened by a slender and somewhat careworn woman in her middle-forties. The lines on her face, however, seemed more likely to have been caused by smiles rather than frowns – although when Holmes introduced us and explained our purpose, a frown was what presented itself.

"I had thought," she said, with rather tight lips, "that Mr. Wilson would be taking care of this matter for himself. I didn't expect that he would confer with outsiders."

"I understand," said Holmes smoothly. "But he had some legitimate concerns that whatever is going on might be more than he could handle – and he wanted to make sure that you didn't come to any harm along the way."

I glanced at Holmes to see if there was any sarcasm to his comment, but his face was open and without guile. When he then asked if he might look around the house to see if he could determine what was going on, the woman allowed it, although clearly she still wasn't pleased.

After closing the door, she led us back along the hall to her parlor. I noticed the closed and locked door to the key shop on the right side of the entry way, and then the stairs on the same side, leading up to Wilson's rooms. The left side of the hall ran smoothly to the back of the narrow building, where it ended at a widened area consisting of four doors. One, directly in front of us and closed, presumably led to the lady's bedroom. A second, on our right, was well-lit by sunlight from the south-facing window, and was clearly the parlor. The third door beside it led into a small kitchen, and the fourth was underneath the stairs – leadng down to the basement, according to our client.

The parlor was small but pleasant. The papered walls, tasteful decorations, and comfortable-looking chairs made it seem like a good place to spend time, and the warm little coal fire was a treat after our cold journey from Baker Street.

I didn't venture too far into the room, instead leaving things as untouched as possible for Holmes. Although I'd only been accompanying him on his investigations for a couple of years, I'd long-since learned the correct way to behave when entering an area where interpretations of evidence might be possible – and crucial.

It was quite obvious that, unlike the previous day, Mrs. Denbigh hadn't yet wiped away the word which defaced the wall to the right of the mantel. Holmes slowly made his way across the distance between the doorway and the fireplace, while I simply watched. Our hostess noticed my gaze, and stated, "I have no idea why anyone would seek revenge against me, Doctor."

I was tempted to ask – simply making conversation – whether she had seen any vengeful Yupik lurking in the neighborhood, but I feared that my attempt to privately amuse myself would only make for an awkward exchange. Instead, I asked her how long she'd lived there, and she began to chat more freely, stating that she and her husband had obtained the lease nearly twenty years before, not long after their marriage, by way of a small inheritance combined with what he earned from the railway. When he was killed, a small settlement had given her a bit of financial security, and enough besides to remodel the larger front area of the house into a shop.

With the income generated from that source, and also taking in a lodger to fill the space upstairs that she didn't need for herself, she'd maintained a comfortable-enough living.

Holmes finished examining the carpet, and then moved wider afield, still looking down as he criss-crossed the room, even investigating the window opposite the fireplace where it was unlikely the "ghost" would have needed to venture. After only three or four minutes of this, he finally turned his attention to the sooty message upon the wall. This received less attention than I would have suspected, and he never looked into the fireplace at all – knowing that the day's new fire would have likely destroyed the signs that Wilson had seen where someone had dipped a finger into the ashes.

Murmuring something about with Mrs. Denbigh's permission he would now examine the rest of the house, Holmes briefly visited the kitchen and then opened the door to the basement – without actually receiving said permission – and vanished downstairs. He was gone for quite a bit longer than I would have expected, and my conversation with the landlady went from polite to strained to conclusion, and we stood in silence for an awkward long time awaiting Holmes's return. We finally heard him climbing back upstairs, whereupon he shut the door to the basement and, without a word, turned and went down the hall before then ascending to Wilson's rooms.

Mrs. Denbigh seemed about to object, but then she held her tongue – perhaps uncertain of her ground when she considered that Holmes was acting as Wilson's agent. Her dilemma was short-lived, as my friend returned almost immediately, joining us in front of the fire, which had remained quite pleasant to me, even in my coated condition.

"It's a very curious situation," he said, rather noncommittally, I thought, considering his earlier theory as to the source of the threatening message. Perhaps there was more to it than he'd let on, or possibly he simply wished to present his findings to Wilson, and thereby let the manager decide how to proceed. Additionally, he spoke rather quietly – or so it seemed to me – as if he didn't want to be overheard. It gave the conversation a seriousness that had previously been missing.

"We can see the writing on the wall. Can you tell us more of the noises on the first night?"

She nodded. "I described it to Mr. Wilson as if someone were walking, but that's not quite right, I suppose. It was a sliding noise, and it seemed to be all around – I couldn't say that it came from within this room, or the hall, or anyplace with certainty."

"And he also mentioned knockings."

It seemed as if she had momentarily forgotten that. "Oh, yes. There's that too. But the noises seem less important somehow than if someone – some *thing* – is inside the house and writing threats upon my wall." Her eyes pointedly glanced toward the fireplace. "Yet I'm certain that Mr. Wilson can manage this. I . . . I don't have money to hire a detective to spend hour after hour here trying to catch my ghost. In fact, you might scare him away."

"Wouldn't that be the purpose of the exercise?" asked Holmes with an innocent tone. Only someone who knew him would spot the humor in his narrowed eyes.

"Why, yes. Of course. But if the ghost does decide to leave, you will still keep investigating, day after day, to make certain he's gone, and I can't afford that kind of expense."

"I believe that Mr. Wilson took on that capital outlay for this matter when he hired me, madam, but I do see your point. In any case, I suspect that this matter will resolve itself rather sooner than later. Tell me," he added, "do you have a relative, or a friend, whom you might visit this afternoon? The doctor and I want to keep an eye on the house when it's empty, to see if anything unusual occurs."

Mrs. Denbigh frowned and seemed to want to ask a question, but then she nodded. "Anything to get this finished, I suppose. I can go see my old aunt in Norbury. I've been meaning to do so – it's been several months."

"Promise me that you will go? Excellent. Then for now the doctor and I will leave you, but we hope to have news for you by this evening."

She seemed puzzled, but also relieved that we were departing. After she shut the door behind us and we reached the pavement, I intended to stop and question Holmes, but he took my arm and led me down the street. Glancing back, I saw that the door had reopened, and the lady of the house was looking our way. Nearby, a stout man was unlocking the key shop, apparently having returned early from his errand, as it was still somewhat before noon.

When we were several blocks away, Holmes hailed a hansom and directed the driver to drive north along Regent Street. It was crowded, and we made poor progress.

"Your mood changed," I said. "After you had been downstairs."

He nodded, his face grim. "As you recall, Mrs. Denbigh told Mr. Wilson that the 'walking' sounds occurred about a week ago. I believe that those were real, even if she wrote the message on the wall herself."

"So that's established then?"

"Without a doubt. The pattern of her footsteps beneath the message tell the whole story."

"She might have stood there to examine it."

"No. The footprints shifted slightly from left to right, back and forth, as would someone who was carefully writing each letter, and then turning back repeatedly to the fireplace, bending down and obtaining more soot."

"And the knocking that she reported?"

"That was false, to gin up her story. She nearly forgot to mention it until I asked, and her facial expressions were clearly less sincere than when she described the initial walking sounds. I suspect that she truly heard the mysterious noises a week ago, and probably was made sincerely nervous. From that, she developed the idea of a full-blown haunting, intended to serve as an excuse to lure Wilson into her clutches."

"But back to my original question: What changed your level of interest after visiting the basement?"

"You recall that Wilson said he examined the basement to see if intruders had entered that way? What he failed to mention, no doubt thinking it of no importance, is that a portion of the basement under the key shop is walled off from the part used by Mrs. Denbigh – no doubt done when the shop itself was built following the death of the lady's husband. There is also a connecting stairway between the shop and their segment of the basement.

"There is a connecting door between the two sides of the basement, and it was well locked, with no signs of recent passage as Wilson said – which is likely why Wilson didn't mention it as a factor. Knowing that the key shop upstairs was closed, I had no hesitation at picking the lock to see what was going on in that half of the basement.

"Do you recall what happened just a week ago?" he asked, seemingly switching course midstream. I wracked my brain. Did he mean one of his own cases? Or something more generalized? Then it hit me.

"The Fenian bombing in Mayfair!" I exclaimed. "On the fifteenth, I believe. And they placed a second bomb at the offices of *The Times*, but it failed to explode."

"Precisely. And what do you think that I found in the basement of the key shop?"

"Good Lord," I muttered. "Dynamite?"

"Nine full cases of it. Enough to destroy several blocks in every direction around that woman's house should it go off – not to mention countless public structures if they have a chance to use it elsewhere."

"And she isn't aware of it," I said, half as a question, and half hoping it to be true.

Holmes agreed. "If she was a part of such a thing, she'd have no need to take in a strange lodger, just weeks before the plot was due to be executed. If she needed a lodger to complete the picture that she is just an innocent landlady, one of the Fenians could have filled the bill. I'm

126

surprised that they didn't think of it – putting one of their own there when she advertised the rooms – but perhaps the timing was wrong. Possibly Wilson arrived right after she placed the sign, just in time to rent the rooms before someone else could present himself as another lodger. In any case, if she was in on the plot, she certainly wouldn't have started all this foolishness about having a ghost, and taking the chance on attracting attention to the place, in the very week that the bombers were laying low and sitting on a deadly amount of explosives."

At that point, he spotted something and had the driver pull to the side and wait. Then he hopped down and danced through the crowd until he reached an idling lad of twelve or so – whom I recognized as Silas Thurber, one of his more steady Irregulars. They spoke for a moment and coins were exchanged before the boy dashed away and Holmes regained his seat in the cab, informing the cabbie to now take us to Scotland Yard with all possible speed.

"Gregson, I think," he said. "I believe that he's been involved in the formation of some sort of special branch to address the bombing problems."

The inspector was in a conference related to the very issue of which we'd been speaking, and when he heard that Holmes was there to see him, he immediately excused himself and led us along a hallway to an unused office. There, Holmes told him succinctly about our initial skeptical visit to examine Mrs. Denbigh's house for evidence of ghosts, and then what he'd found in the basement.

The inspector instantly perceived the gravity of the situation. "Are you sure that this landlady isn't involved? And what about this Wilson fellow?"

Holmes explained his reasoning as to why they weren't connected with the dynamiters. "No doubt this key shop was set up to appear as an innocent cover for the Fenians, right in the heart of London." Gregson nodded, and was all for immediately raiding the place, but Holmes had a different plan.

"I asked Mrs. Denbigh to get out of the house later today. One can only hope that she will do so as promised. If she doesn't, we can still proceed, but I'd feel better if she was gone. In any case, I propose that we get an anonymous message to the owner of the key shop – Randall, according to the name upon the door – that all is known. It should convey just enough to get him moving without really telling him anything. He may flee on his own, in which case we follow *him*, or he may assemble his men in order to move the dynamite, and we'll follow *them* – rather like spotting a single bee and marking his path until he leads you to the hive. We can try to take the whole nest of them. Granted, arresting Randall now and confiscating his cache of explosives will solve the immediate problem, and we might very well get some more names out of him – but then again we might not. I believe that in this way we can bag most, if not all, of the gang."

Gregson rubbed his face with one of his big hands and nodded. "I'll get some men around the place."

Holmes shook his head. "No – or at least not too close. I've already taken care of surrounding the building, as well as the neighborhood in every direction, with a veritable army of my Irregulars. Let them work in close to these men as they escape, so that no suspicions are raised. Have your men ready to arrest them when they've gone back to ground elsewhere in their other hidey-hole."

The inspector reluctantly agreed and returned to his meeting to quickly brief those who were waiting to learn why he'd been called away. Within a half-hour, we – along with the inspector – were on our way back to the area around Mrs. Denbigh's building.

We left our vehicle several blocks away, and Holmes stood patiently for a moment until Silas Thurber came out of a nearby alleyway to report. "The lady left not long after we got there," he said. "It's just the man in the key shop now."

"Good. And Dungiven?"

"We've fetched him. He should be here in just a few minutes."

And he was. Michael Dungiven was one of Holmes's agents that I'd met on a few previous occasions. He was from Ireland, and could lay on the accent so thick that he became nearly unintelligible when needed. Fiercely loyal to the Crown, he often provided information about Irish criminals when requested by Holmes. (Interestingly, he hadn't yet met Gregson, and after these events he was recruited into the newly formed Special Branch, serving with great heroism and distinction until his tragic death some nine years later, during the period following Professor Moriarty's death when the London underworld violently fought to fill the vacuum left by the destruction of that criminal's evil web of crime.)

Holmes quickly explained the situation, and Dungiven nodded. He really only needed to convey one thing to Randall, but his quick intelligence perceived the deeper aspects of the matter. He turned and set off for Lowndes Court, while we waited impatiently. He was gone for no longer than ten minutes, before approaching us from a different direction than that in which he'd departed.

"Any difficulties?" asked Holmes, while Gregson balanced impatiently from one foot to another.

"None," said Dungiven. "He was curious about who I was, but I dropped a couple of names he'd likely know, and that seemed to convince him. I was in and out in two heartbeats nearly. He's on the telephone, and he was starting to call someone as he watched me leave. I believe that things are in motion."

That proved to be correct. We strolled until we reached an alley, whereupon Holmes led us through to the Lowndes Court end, where we had a view of Mrs. Denbigh's building. Within half-an-hour, a dray wagon with a couple of draft horses drew to a stop in front of the key shop, and half-a-dozen men leapt down and pressed inside. Within a minute they were lugging crates to the back of the wagon like ants carrying cake droppings back to their hill.

"The question," said Holmes, "is whether Randall shall stay or go — Ah! He's locking the door and joining his fellow plotters."

"I'm glad that we listened to you, Mr. Holmes," said Gregson in a low tone. "That dray wagon could be followed by a man in a bath chair. We'll have them, and no mistake."

"You might want to hold off, Gregson — at least for a few hours — once you know their destination. You can pick off the ones that leave, and perhaps others might arrive in the meantime, even someone higher up in their organization."

Gregson frowned, considering whether it was worth taking the chance of possibly losing track of those that he'd just seen over the reward of a bigger catch. Then he nodded.

It was a gamble that paid off. The Irregulars followed the wagon as it crossed London to an old warehouse in Hackney, not far from Sutton House. There, Randall supervised the unloading of the dynamite, which was carried inside without incident. The Irregulars kept up a running contact with the police during the journey across the city, racing ahead on side streets and anticipating where turnings would occur. Later that evening, several other big fish did arrive as Holmes had suggested, and Gregson decided then to make his move. The raid swept up nearly a dozen men, including two who were definitely implicated in several previous bombings. More important, an additional quantity of dynamite was discovered in the warehouse that dwarfed that which had been moved from the key shop. We had found the Fenians explosives depot.

That night, Holmes and I knocked on Mrs. Denbigh's door. She answered with a surprised look, explaining that she had just returned a few minutes before from visiting with her aunt and was in the process of preparing Mr. Wilson's dinner. When asked if she could pause that and fetch him, she agreed, and soon we were in her little parlor, where Holmes was explaining the full details of the arrest of the lady's storefront tenant.

Both were shocked, and they glanced at one another as if they had just survived some great tragedy. "You've saved our lives is what you've

129

done, Mr. Holmes!" said Wilson. "What if that dynamite had blown up during the night?"

"Or what if the police had caught wind of it on their own," added Mrs. Denbigh, "and arrested us without the benefit of your deductions that cleared us beforehand?"

"That's right," added Wilson. "You not only saved us, but you cleared our good names as well."

The two of them then chattered together, sharing remembrances of Randall that each recalled, indications that should have let them know what the man was really about. I waited for some mention of the knocking ghost and the warning of "*Revenge*" to be uttered, but they never seemed to get around to it, and neither Holmes nor I were inclined to remind them. In a very short while, we excused ourselves, and they seemed happy to let us go, as their conversation now was of the type that excluded all but themselves.

"Perhaps," I said, outside and pulling my coat tighter against the chill, "they'll recall in a few minutes that the question of the writing upon the wall wasn't adequately explained."

Holmes shrugged. "She'll likely concoct a reason that satisfies him – that Randall was somehow getting into the main house and trying to scare them away. It won't make any sense, of course, but people in love don't have any respect for logic."

"You saw it too, then," I said. "The dam between them has been breached."

"Indeed. Mrs. Denbigh's plan might have worked anyway without any of this, but the addition of a dash of danger in the form of dynamiters was just the extra ingredient to make Wilson gobble down the whole cake."

I laughed. "A curious metaphor. Perhaps it will be a wedding cake."

And so it turned out to be. Later that year I saw the announcement of their marriage in the newspaper. I mentioned it to Holmes, who was expectedly indifferent, but I found myself the tiniest bit peeved, as if we should have been invited somehow for helping them, in our own modest way, to complete the arrangements. However, after another moment's thought, I found that I was relieved that we hadn't been asked to attend. Perhaps, I realized with a start, just a bit of Holmes's antipathy was rubbing off on me – something that I vowed to resist with more effort than before.

He turned into one of the district messenger offices, where he was warmly greeted by the manager.

"Ah, Wilson, I see you have not forgotten the little case in which I had the good fortune to help you?"

"No, sir, indeed I have not. You saved my good name, and perhaps my life."

– Dr. John H. Watson, Sherlock Holmes, and Wilson
The Hound of the Baskervilles

Vittoria, the Circus Belle
by Bob Bishop

I have been criticized in the past for over-sensationalizing my narratives. Sherlock Holmes has repeatedly made the point that the general public should not be pandered to in their taste for the *outré* and the bizarre. He feels, rather, that it would benefit my readership intellectually to learn more of the mental processes by which he has been able to unravel convoluted but otherwise mundane conundrums. For that reason, perhaps, I have shied away recently from reporting some of the more unusual cases with which we have become involved. My editor – however, responding, I dare say, to a drop in readership – has begged me to indulge him by putting on public record one of our more out-of-the-ordinary adventures. I feel inclined to accede to his wishes on this occasion, and so, with apologies to Holmes's sensitivities on the subject, I offer the tragic case of Vittoria, the Circus Belle.

It was brought to our attention by our old friend, Inspector Lestrade. He arrived one breezy March morning, unannounced, at our Baker Street lodgings, entering at the door so precipitously it seemed as though the wind must have propelled him through it.

"Thank goodness you are at home, gentlemen!" he exclaimed. "I have never needed your help more!"

"Good morning to you too, Lestrade."

"Sorry, Mr. Holmes, but I am at my wit's end," said our visitor, beginning to pace back and forth.

"If you would take a moment to sit down," Holmes said, sitting himself, "you can tell us what has made you so excitable, and simultaneously relieve the wear upon our Turkish rug. Watson, why do you not ring for Mrs. Hudson and ask her to bring up some tea?"

"I really don't want tea," Lestrade said, rather brusquely I felt, though he did eventually sit down. When he was a little calmer, Holmes invited him to explain what it was that had made him so agitated.

"It's a murder, Mr. Holmes," he said. "At least I think it is. It might just be a terrible accident. But if it *is* a murder, I shall have to arrest the whole blessed lot of them, because I can't for the life of me say which of 'em did it, for they are all accusing each other. And what's more, if I don't do something quickly, they'll all have upped-sticks and gone by tomorrow. What am I going to do?"

"Start at the beginning?" suggested Holmes.

"The beginning? Yes, right. Well, I don't suppose you have heard of Hildebrand's Circus and Menagerie?"

"No," said Holmes. "Not my sort of entertainment."

"I think I have seen posters," I said. "Though actually, I don't go to circuses either."

"Well, there's this bunch of performers and freaks who have winter quarters in a farm down Hounslow way. You should see them, Doctor – all weird shapes and sizes, and most of them mad as hatters. Well, on Monday the local force got called in, and on Tuesday they called in the Yard – "

"And now, on Wednesday, the Yard is calling in us," said Holmes, rubbing his hands in what looked like satisfaction. "But you haven't explained why. A murder? Surely that is every-day fare at Scotland Yard? Why do you need help from me?"

"Tomorrow at first light they will be packing everything up and heading for Brighton. Given time, I have no doubt I could see my way through the tangle, but in just a few hours . . . ? That's why I need you to come down with me now, Mr. Holmes, this very minute, to see if you can tell me whether there has been a crime committed or not, and if so, which of them it was done it." Before he had even finished this imperfect sentence, Lestrade was on his feet again. I looked across at my friend. He was still relaxed in his chair, so I remained in mine.

"Before I say whether I will help you or not, Lestrade," he said, "I insist that you sit down again and give me a coherent account of the incident. You might like to begin by telling us who is the victim, and the circumstances in which his – or her – body was discovered."

Lestrade sat down again. "The victim is a her," he said. "'Vittoria the Circus Belle' is the name she goes by . . . *went* by, that is, the poor girl. They found the remains of her in a lion's cage on Monday, first light. Mauled to death, she was. My colleagues had never seen a sight like it – enough to make the most experienced copper throw up his breakfast – "

"Yes, yes. I am sure – a horrible sight. You haven't seen the body yourself, then?"

"No, and I don't want to. In any case, there isn't much left to see, I'm told. They had to gather bits of her up from every corner of the cage."

"What makes you think it wasn't an accident?"

"Because we found something else in the cage."

"And that was . . . ?"

"Some rope. And a chair! The beast's tamer, Maximillian, swears there was no chair kept in the cage, so I ask myself – Why should that girl go into the cage of a wild beast in the first place, of her own free will? And, given that she did, what reason would she have to take a chair in with her? She wouldn't be going in there to sit and read it a bed-time story, would she?"

"So you take the presence of the rope and chair as an indication that murder is more likely than accident?"

"I do."

"Although I have rarely visited a circus," Holmes said, "I have seen colourful posters displayed, depicting a lion tamer using a chair as his only defence to keep the beast at bay. Perhaps this unfortunate young woman took a chair into the cage with her for the very same purpose?" By way of demonstration, Holmes leapt to his feet and took up a wooden dining chair, holding it by the back, with its legs extended towards Lestrade, in a fair imitation of a lion-tamer defending himself from a ravening beast. Lestrade looked momentarily alarmed.

"I suppose that is a possibility," he conceded. Holmes replaced the dining chair and returned to his fireside seat.

"That, of course, would do nothing to explain why she entered the cage in the first place," he conceded. "Explain to me your own interpretation, Lestrade. What do you think happened?"

"It seems someone tied her up to a chair and left her there, defenceless, to be devoured by the lion. That is what I think."

"I see. And why did the lion not attack this person, while he – or, of course, she – was tying Miss Vittoria into her chair."

"I don't know. Except that it didn't."

"Hmm. You have already interviewed the staff and performers, I presume?"

"Certainly. All day yesterday. I have my notes here." Lestrade took from an inner pocket a much-used hard-backed note-book and opened it mid-way through its sheaf of pages."

"Good, then. Introduce us to some of your suspects. I suggest you commence with the lion-tamer. Maxwell, I think you said his name was?"

"Maximillian," I corrected.

Holmes frowned at my interruption. "He must surely be on top of your list, as the only person in the camp who had easy access to the animal, as well as a degree of control over its behaviour."

"He was the first person I spoke to. He has a twirly, black moustache – "

"Is the moustache relevant?"

"Not really."

"So, let us stick to the facts which are, or we shall be here all morning."

"Well, as you said, Maximillian was the first person I questioned. He was very distressed, and fiercely protective of Rajah . . . ."

134

"The lion?"

"Yes." Lestrade consulted his note-book. "Said it was ordinarily a gentle beast, and must have been provoked to . . . do what it did. He was working in the ring with it until nine o'clock on Sunday evening. They are preparing a new routine for the season opening in Brighton, you see. Anyway, he took the animal back to its cage just after nine. He is quite certain that the cage was completely empty when he locked it up."

"Apart from the lion."

"Apart from the lion, yes. He then went to dine with the wife of the owner, Captain Hildebrand."

"Just the wife? Not the owner as well?"

"I didn't ask. No – wait! Hildebrand didn't return until lunchtime on Monday. He had been abroad, interviewing some Russian trapeze artistes." Lestrade returned to his notes. "No – sorry – they were Lithuanian. Anyway, Maximillian went to feed Rajah at six o'clock on Monday morning. It was then he found – "

" – That the animal had already eaten."

"Well . . . yes."

"Who was it who summoned the police? Maximillian?"

"Let me see . . . ." Back to his notes: "No, it was Iago."

"They have very colourful names, these circus folk. Pray tell me about Iago."

"Iago is a knife-thrower. Vittoria has been his assistant. She would stand against a board while he threw knives at her." Holmes raised an eyebrow. "Well, not *at* her, exactly," Lestrade corrected. "All around her. The poor man was very distressed. He has no one to throw knives at now, you see, and they are due to open at the weekend."

"I should hope," I couldn't resist saying, "that the lack of an assistant wasn't the only reason for the man's distress?"

"One would hope not, Doctor, but as I said before, they're a rum lot, all of them."

"Tell us about some of the others whom you interviewed," Holmes demanded.

"Well, I spoke to the boss man, of course. Hildebrand. He only got back from his trip abroad after it all blew up, so he couldn't be a suspect. Still, I thought it best to talk to him – to see if he had any inside information, as it were."

"And did he?"

"He wasn't at all helpful. Swore a lot. Said it was just a terrible accident, and blamed the girl herself for going into the cage. Good as asked me to brush it all under the carpet so that they could pack up and get on the road tomorrow. No help at all."

135

"Introduce us to more of your colourful characters. Help us to get a whiff of the circus."

Lestrade laughed out loud, in spite of the seriousness of the situation. "You wouldn't want a whiff of the circus in your lodgings, Mr. Holmes, I can tell you!" he chuckled. "Some of those animals smell dreadful! I wouldn't want to go within a hundred yards of the camels. Beats me why folk will pay one-and-sixpence to go and gawp at those smelly old flea-bags!"

"So let us confine ourselves to the humans," Holmes said. "Up to now we have only met the lion-tamer, the knife-thrower, and the circus owner. Who else came under your scrutiny?"

Lestrade went back to his notes. "We spoke to Petronella. She's covered from head to foot in tattoos. Was a good friend of Vittoria. Very upset, she was. When we got her to stop wailing and crying, she said we should arrest Maximillian on the spot."

"Why?"

"Because he is more of a brute than his animals, apparently. I asked her if he had a particular grudge against Vittoria, but she just burst out wailing and weeping again. Couldn't get any more out of her."

"Does this Petronella have any circus skills?" I asked. "Or does she just sit about on a stool for people to admire her tattoos?"

"She can tie herself up in knots," Lestrade said. "She folds herself into a suitcase, apparently."

"Handy for travelling," Holmes quipped. It seemed to me my friend was displaying more levity than the gravity of the situation demanded, but he can never resist teasing Lestrade, who often fails to notice it. The policeman consulted his note-book and told us next about the two clowns, Biffo and Algernon. Biffo, we discovered, was a dwarf, who was also a mute.

"We interviewed them together," Lestrade said. "As the dwarf couldn't talk, and never stopped pulling faces at us, it was a complete waste of time talking to him. The other clown, Algernon, seemed like a decent enough fellow. He told us we should talk to Bendigo, the strongman. He said Vittoria and Bendigo had been lovers, but had a falling out a week or so back. He had seen the strongman following her about recently, and watching her when she didn't know he was there. It seemed like our best lead so far, but it came to nothing."

"Why was that, I asked."

"Because Bendigo had put his back out the day before, trying to lift the rear axle of a trailer out of some mud. He's been laid up in his caravan for two days, unable to move. We did manage to speak to him, though. He told us there was only one person in the circus who hated Vittoria enough

136

to kill her, and that was Zelda, the snake dancer. Zelda. She claims to be Iago's wife. Might even be so, for all I know. Anyway, Bendigo said Zelda had told Petronella that she was sure that Vittoria had something going on with Iago. But Iago said – "

"Enough!" said Holmes. "I can't take in anymore! I need to meet these people in the flesh."

"So you agree with me there has been a murder done, do you, Mr. Holmes?"

"Beyond question."

"But which of them is the murderer?"

"The lion," said Holmes. "What we need to work out is, who was his accomplice, and I cannot do so from this armchair. How about it, Watson? Are you in?"

"I'll get my hat," I said.

I suppose that I had expected our journey to end beside a huge, colourful tent, erected on a village green. Instead, on the rural fringe of Heston village, we found ourselves in a muddy lane which led eventually to an even muddier farmyard with a cluster of barns scattered around it. The smell Lestrade had warned us about hit us when we were only part-way down the lane. By the time we reached the farmyard, it was over-powering. In a small fenced-off enclosure, close to the road-edge, stood two moth-eaten camels and a llama. They ambled over to gawp at us, the camels moving their jaws around in a grotesque circular motion the whole time, like sailors working on plugs of tobacco.

"Watch out for those brutes!" Lestrade said. "They spit." We gave them a wide berth. In a field on the other side, half-a-dozen well-groomed ponies skittered about, tossing their silky manes and tails as they leaped and pranced to the command of a very small woman wielding a very long whip. The horses were altogether a much more attractive sight than their smelly, sulky neighbours in the opposite field. Lestrade led us past the pony field and made straight for the largest of the barns. Its winnowing doors stood wide open, and we could see a circus ring had been constructed in the interior of the building. Multi-coloured curved wooden blocks made up the edge of the circle, and a thick layer of sawdust carpeted its interior. On top of the sawdust was stretched a stout tarpaulin, decorated by white stars, and in the middle of this groundsheet, a sizeable trampoline had been erected. Up, over, and all about this trampoline, five men in leotards bounced and dived without ever becoming entangled. Presumably this was the troupe of tumblers, so recently recruited from Lithuania.

I was fascinated, and would have paused to watch, but my companions were already heading out of the matching open doors on the opposite side of the barn. I hastened after them. They had entered a barnyard, strewn with straw on top of a deep bed of mud. In places, the mud was oozing though the straw. At the rear of the yard, backed up against a block of single-storey buildings which could have been stables and pig-sties, stood a number of brightly-painted caravans. Some had people sitting on their steps, others displayed no signs of life at all. Lestrade walked up to the largest van in the collection. It was decorated in a colour-scheme in which muted browns and creams dominated, but its curved roof was metallic, and shone in the spring sunlight as though it were made from beaten silver. As we approached, a tall man in glossy black boots and silky white britches appeared in the van's open doorway. A flight of steps led up to it, and the four of us – Holmes, myself, Lestrade, and a uniformed constable name Jarvis, all gathered at the foot of them.

"You again?" growled the man, fixing his angry gaze upon Lestrade. "What do you want this time?"

To his credit, Lestrade didn't attempt to answer the man's question. "Mr. Holmes, Dr. Watson," he said, "this is Gervais Hildebrand, the ringmaster and circus owner."

"*Captain* Hildebrand," the man snapped. "Who the Devil * are your two cronies? More Scotland Yard detectives, I suppose? For goodness sake, man, I have told you it was an accident. This is a dangerous place. We take precautions, but accidents happen. Now go away, and leave us alone. We have a full run-through this afternoon, and we leave tomorrow for Brighton."

"You will not be leaving at all if I decide to arrest the lot of you!" Lestrade snapped back. "These gentlemen are helping me with my enquiries, and I'll thank you to treat them with respect."

"I'll treat them with the lash end of my whip if they get in my way!" shouted Hildebrand, and with this last threat, he turned on his shiny heels and disappeared into the van, slamming the door after himself.

"Quite the charmer," commented Sherlock Holmes. "Are you certain he was absent at the time of the incident?"

"Regrettably, yes. It would have been a pleasure to collar him for it, but the Middlesex force insist that he arrived from the station with his foreign friends and a cart-full of luggage several hours after they had been called in."

"Then let us waste no more time talking with or about him," said Holmes. "Now, which is the van belonging to the animal trainer?"

Lestrade indicated a red-and-green wagon further down the line. As we set off towards it, the small woman with the large whip appeared from the direction of the circus barn and headed towards us.

"Who is this?" I asked.

138

"She is Hildebrand's wife, Clementine," Lestrade said.

"Poor woman!" I exclaimed. "To have to live with that bully – why, he could crush her underfoot like a beetle, if he felt like it!"

Our Scotland Yard colleague swept off his hat as the ringmaster's wife approached our small circle. "Good day to you, Mrs. Hildebrand," he said.

"Inspector," she responded, giving him a deferential nod. "So, you have returned to us. Does this mean you have more questions to ask?"

"We do. This is a most serious matter. Your husband doesn't appear to understand the full gravity of the situation."

"Oh, he understands it," said the woman. "He just believes he can bluster his way out of it. Now, who is it you wish to see? We have a run-through of the new programme starting in an hour, so nobody will be off the site."

"I should like to visit the scene of the accident," said Holmes, choosing his words with care. "I think, perhaps, your trainer, Maximillian, would be the best person to accompany us, under the circumstances."

"Of course," said the owner's wife. "Max will be with his animals at this time. I shall take you to him." With a few short bounds, she hopped up the wooden steps to her caravan and opened the door wide enough to call inside, "Gervais, I am escorting these policemen. Start without me, if you need to." And without waiting for a reply, she pulled the door shut again and ran back down the steps. "Come along," she said. "It is round the back."

Holmes and I looked at each other. This remarkably small woman seemed to have no fear of her blustering bully of a husband. Things aren't always as they first appear. We followed her across the straw-littered yard. At the back of the large barn was a smaller one, with no visible doors or windows on the yard side. A narrow alley led between the two buildings, and Clementine Hildebrand was already disappearing down it. We followed. The entrance to the smaller barn faced a sunny field, in which several gaily-painted flat-bed wagons were drawn up. Each was surmounted by a cage with iron bars all around it. All the cages were empty. A zebra was wandering free, munching at the grass. An ostrich strutted about like a giant, shaggy goose. On the far side of the field, several heavy horses grazed, the familiar amongst the bizarre. We found Clementine waiting for us at the door to the barn.

"Be careful in here," she said, standing aside to let us enter. It was dark in the barn, and the air was redolent with unfamiliar smells. As our eyes adjusted to the dim light, we saw cages similar to the ones outside, but standing flat on the floor of the barn. Some of them were occupied by shadowy shapes. Immediately inside the doorway, looking to my right, I

139

was shocked to find myself face to face with an enormous tiger. Its amber eyes were fixed on mine with an unblinking, malevolent stare which quite unnerved me. Suddenly, the powerful beast emitted a roar and, springing forward, flashed a viciously-clawed forepaw between two of the bars of its cage and took a swing at me. In the nick of time, the ringmaster's wife hauled on my arm and, with surprising strength for one so small of stature, dragged me roughly out of the big cat's reach.

"I told you to be careful!" she said. "Don't stand near the cages!" I didn't plan on doing so again. A short but muscular man in jodhpurs and an open-necked shirt had appeared from the barn's gloomy depths and was talking to the tiger in soft tones. The animal presently stalked to the back of its cage and lay down, its tail still thrashing, but otherwise calm. The man, whom I took to be Maximillian the lion-tamer, turned his attention to the small party who had invaded his territory. He did, indeed, possess a fine black moustache, I noted – waxed and twisted into tight curls. As he came towards us, Clementine detached herself from our group and went up to him. She spoke quietly, using much the same tones he had just employed to address the tiger. I fancied I saw his moustache loose some of its bristle, as he came over to us and bowed his head in a silent, Oriental greeting.

Lestrade spoke first. "Maximillian, I have returned as promised, with two colleagues who are experts in the analysis of crime." I felt strangely honoured, never having quite considered myself in that light. Lestrade continued: "I trust that, as promised, you have left the cage where the body was found unoccupied, and untouched?"

"It is just as you saw it. Follow me."

From his appearance, I had anticipated that his voice, like his appearance, would carry hints of a Mediterranean, possibly Italian, antecedence, but his English was as good as my own. The lion-tamer was striding off towards the far side of the barn. We followed him obediently. He paused at a cage which contained a single occupant. A sleepy-looking lion with a magnificent mane was stretched out behind the bars, languidly licking one forepaw in the manner of a domestic cat relaxing by someone's fireside. It wasn't as large as the tiger. Was this the savage beast who had so recently ripped apart and devoured a human being? It was hard to believe. The lion turned its head slowly and fixed me with a stare which seemed to single me out from our group as its weakest link. I believed it.

"I told you, that animal should be destroyed!" Lestrade was saying, angrily.

"And I told you, I will not do it!" responded the tamer with passion. "Rajah is no more to be blamed for killing the girl than your cat is for catching a sparrow. He is a wild, noble creature – it is in his nature!"

If he was a wild, noble creature, I thought, then it was in his nature to stalk the plains of Africa. Why did the lion tamer find it acceptable to keep him locked in a cage, and make him dance for his supper? I said nothing, however. Maximillian was working himself up into a fine anger. "If you provide him with meat, he will eat it. I will not have him blamed for this, and he will not be wantonly slaughtered. You will have to kill me first!"

Clementine placed a calming hand upon his arm. "They haven't come to shoot him, Max" she said. "They are not armed." (This was not strictly true. I had my service revolver with me, though it would remain in my pocket unless I found myself *in extremis*.) The lion's defender allowed himself to be pacified, and we passed on down the line of cages, past two pacing lionesses, to a cage which stood empty, with its door chained shut. Maximillian withdrew a large key from his waistcoat pocket and unlocked it for us. The scene which met our eyes in the cage interior brought home the true horror of what had taken place.

Although those body parts which had remained after the lion ate its fill had been gathered up and removed, the evidence of the attack was visible in all its gory realism. Dark blood-stains covered the iron cage floor. Shreds of flimsy, blood-stained clothing were scattered everywhere, and a wooden chair with one leg broken lay on its side in a corner of the cage. There were also fragments of frayed and bloodied rope scattered around. The inference had to be that the victim had been attacked whilst bound, and presumably gagged. What a truly appalling way to meet one's death!

Upon stepping into the cage, Holmes became instantly transformed into the man of action. "Light!" he exclaimed. "We need more light! Don't touch that, Lestrade! I need you all to get out of the cage – you, too, Watson! Out! Out!" I found myself shooed out of the open door. So much for my brief elevation to the rank of crime expert. Maximillian dispatched two lads who had been cleaning out empty cages to throw open the big doors at the end of the barn. Suddenly light flooded in. I watched as Holmes picked his way around the debris, examining everything in minute detail. Occasionally he muttered to himself in frustration or satisfaction. Lestrade and his constable, Jarvis, stood on either side of the opened door to the cage, as though on sentry duty. Neither spoke to the other.

Maximillian and Clementine had withdrawn themselves to a position close to the cage of one of the lionesses, an animal which paced endlessly in the confined space as though in emotional distress – which, quite conceivably, it was. I noted that the lion-tamer and the circus owner's wife appeared to be very comfortable in each other's presence. Their heads were pressed very close together as they whispered to each other. Had they, possibly, enjoyed more than just a meal together on the night of the killing, I wondered? If so, they would do well to confess it, for it would give them both a solid alibi. I decided it was time to earn my keep as a detective. Standing watching Holmes at work was contributing nothing at all. I walked over to the whispering couple and introduced myself as Sherlock Holmes's associate. His name wasn't familiar to either of them, and carried no weight. I decided to press on. "I wonder if I might ask you both about the night of the killing?" I began.

"We have already told your Chief everything," Maximillian replied, rudely. "Why don't you ask him?" I kept my composure, as Holmes would have done. "He isn't my Chief," I said. "Inspector Lestrade has engaged us as independent experts. I am afraid that we may need you to answer some questions more than once. It is possible that the gravest of crimes has been committed here, and until we are satisfied that it hasn't, then I'm afraid you may be put to some inconvenience in the interests of justice. Now, sir, would you please tell me your actions on the night of the attack, being precise as to times?" The animal trainer confirmed the timings of his actions on the fateful evening exactly as reported to us by Lestrade, up to the point when he went to take supper with Clementine Hildebrand. In her turn, Clementine told us that she had worked her ponies from five until shortly after seven, before stabling them, rubbing them down, and supplying them with fresh hay and water. She had then gone to her caravan and prepared a meal.

"Was it just the two of you dining together?" I asked. I noted that they exchanged looks before confirming that yes, it had been just the two of them. I continued, addressing the woman alone. "What time, approximately, did Mr. Maximillian leave your caravan, Mrs. Hildebrand?" There was no mistaking the look of panic which she flashed in her companion's direction, and I felt that look alone had given me the answer that I needed. When I told them that my only purpose in asking such personal questions was to establish who was where and when, in order to eliminate suspects, they admitted that they had been together all night, until Maximillian left the van just before dawn to commence feeding his animals. Feeling that I had achieved something useful, I disclosed my findings to Holmes when he finally came out from his examination of the cage, and we had a brief moment alone.

"So I think we can eliminate those two from our list of suspects," I told him. "They have confessed to me that they spent the whole night together."

"Unless, of course, they were lying to you, for the exact purpose of establishing an alibi," he said. "You did question them separately, I hope, to make sure that they told the same story?" I felt a little less with pleased with my achievement, then, but Holmes wasn't interested in dwelling upon my failures.

"Come and look at this, Watson," he said, and drew me over to the side of the cage he had just left. Without entering again, he pointed to some scuff marks on the cage floor, clearly visible from the outside. They formed an approximately straight line from the back of the cage to the front, at a point about two feet from one of the solid side walls of the enclosure. "What do you make of those marks?" he asked.

"It looks as though something has been drawn along the floor from back to front," I said. "Perhaps they were made by a stick or an iron rod?"

"Hmm," said Holmes, and set off to search through the assorted circus paraphernalia which was stacked against a nearby wall of the barn. There were iron cage parts, brightly coloured props of every shape and size, and sections of timber shuttering, all painted in the circus's predominant colours of red, green, and white stripes. He was particularly interested in one of the items of shuttering, which was the outermost piece of several similar sections, all stacked together. It was a wall of timber, about eight feet in height, twelve in breadth, and a good three inches in thickness, rather like an exceptionally stout piece of garden fencing. I judged that it was probably an end-section from a dismantled cage. Holmes seized it by its outer edge and gave it a tug, managing to drag it away from its companions only an inch or so before he gave up, panting. Lestrade and the uniformed man came over to join us.

"What are you doing, Mr. Holmes?" Lestrade asked. "Need any help?"

"Yes," said Holmes. "Could you step away please, and not move around too much? You are disturbing the floor with your boots." He was bending down now to examine the barn floor between the stack of boarding and the cage. What he saw pleased him. We tried to see what he was seeing. There was a thick layer of dust over the rough concrete, much disturbed by the marks of many feet. I couldn't see how one set of prints could be any more significant than any of the others. Then suddenly I saw what Holmes meant. Although largely obliterated by the numerous footmarks which criss-crossed it, I was able to make out drag marks leading from the board Holmes had moved so very slightly and the empty cage which represented the murder scene. Before I could say anything, Clementine Hildebrand came over to us and addressed Lestrade.

"We have a dress rehearsal to stage, Inspector, and everyone has to prepare. Do you have any objections to our starting on time?" Lestrade looked at Holmes for guidance.

"Not at all," said Holmes, much to my surprise, for he had hardly interviewed any of Lestrade's suspects. "But before you begin, I wonder if I might have a brief word with Biffo, the clown?"

"You won't get anything out of him!" said the lion-tamer. "He's a mute."

"Nevertheless," Holmes replied, pleasantly, "I should like to meet him. Perhaps you could ask him to come here now? And Lestrade – would you announce to the company that they are to leave their vans open for police inspection during the performance?"

"They won't like that," said Clementine at once. "Policemen poking around in the vans when the owners aren't there? Our vans are our homes!"

"Oh, I'm certain they will not object," Holmes said, still with a friendly smile. "Unless, of course, you think some of them might have something to hide?"

"Of course not!"

"Excellent, then. Please tell Biffo that I shall be waiting for him here." And he sat down on one of those circular tubs upon which the circus animals performed, carefully dusting it first to keep the seat of his trousers from being soiled.

"What do you want me to do, Holmes?" I asked, as the others set off out of the barn.

"Go with them and watch everyone's reaction when Lestrade asks them to leave their vans open. If anyone objects more strongly than the others, report back to me at once."

I left him sitting there and went after the others, wondering why he had singled out the mute clown, when other performers seemed to have more to hide – Zelda, the snake dancer, for instance. If she really suspected that Vittoria was out to steal her husband, that would surely give her the strongest motive of anyone to commit a murder. As I left the barn, I saw that some heavy closed wagons had been brought into the paddock, and men were manhandling stout bundles into them. We hadn't even considered the army of people who laboured behind the scenes to convey the circus from site to site across the country. How would it ever be possible to find the guilty party amongst this small township, all of which was due to move on the next day? I began to understand how Lestrade felt.

There was much frantic activity going on in the main barn when I arrived. The trampoline and its starry mat were gone, and the sawdust inside the ring had been raked level. Beside the ring, in what looked like an enclosure built of sheep folds, five bandsmen were tuning up their instruments, which added to the general hubbub. Gervais Hildebrand had now donned his full ring-master attire, complete with scarlet coat and top hat. He was strutting round giving orders. He had in his hand a coiled whip, and it was easy to believe that he was quite capable of using it on anyone who got in his way. A man in a conical hat and a suit of glittering gold and silver sequins was juggling Indian clubs. I guessed this must be Algernon, the clown who had been so helpful to Lestrade the day before. I had expected him to be in big boots and baggy trousers with a ridiculously oversize painted smile on his face, but he was a white-face, one of that superior sort of clown who never receives the custard pies.

It was easy to identify Petronella. Although she wore tights and a leotard, those of her extremities which were visible were covered in complex inked designs. She had been limbering up on the ringside, and now dropped her torso to reach both head and hands between her legs, and scuttle round the ring in a grotesque imitation of a spider. Most of the women appeared young, although so heavily made-up it was hard to judge. Nearly all wore what could best be described as burlesque costumes, with highly ornate laced bodices over frilly blouses, teamed with very short, flounced skirts and tights in a colourful variety of harlequin stripes, whorls, and diamonds. Although at a distance they looked quite glamorous, close up there was something tawdry and rather sad about them.

After searching the crowd of performers for some time, I was able to identify Zelda, the snake dancer, because she was carrying around a wicker basket with her name painted on it. It wasn't difficult to guess what was slithering around inside it. She went to speak earnestly with a man sitting on a straw bale, aloof from the bustling activity all around him. He wore no costume at all. Could this be her husband, Iago, unable to perform today because his partner had been eaten by the lion? Of all the performers mentioned by Lestrade, the only one that I couldn't identify was Bendigo, the strongman. Presumably he was still laid up in his caravan with a bad back.

There were others in costume, not mentioned by Lestrade at all, as well as a regiment of rope-pullers, prop-handlers, and general roustabouts. I estimated there must be close on fifty people milling around, without even counting the children who scuttled everywhere, getting in everyone's way, and receiving cuffs and curses from all and sundry. I doubted that even Holmes would be able to solve this murder in the time-frame imposed upon him – there were just too many possible suspects. It looked to me very much like a lost cause.

Clementine, who had been in earnest conversation with her husband, crossed over to the band corral and spoke to the leader, a trumpeter whose scarlet coat boasted more loops of gold braid than those of his fellow musicians. He signalled his men for silence, then nodded to the drummer, who gave three loud bangs on his huge bass drum. The entire barn fell silent. Hildebrand jumped up onto one of the ring curbs and gestured for the assembled company to draw closer. He then stood down and allowed Inspector Lestrade to take his place.

There were sympathetic nods as the policeman paid tribute to the dead girl, and spoke of the terrible shock her brutal death must have been to the entire company. He spoke of the urgent need to establish beyond doubt the true circumstances of her death, and to apprehend the murderer if it could be shown not to have been an accident. Murmurs began to arise from the assembled body. Lestrade waited until they subsided. I was impressed by his control of the crowd, especially the manner in which he had the company on his side with his first remarks. Although Holmes is inclined to belittle the man, he has clearly not risen to the rank of Inspector without some merit.

He moved on to explain how he appreciated the company's need to proceed with their dress rehearsal with a minimum of interference, and how, to that end, he would need each van, wagon, and kiosk to be left unlocked, so that his officers could complete their round of routine checks. No private possessions would be interfered with, he promised. This time there were several angry voices raised in opposition.

The crowd became restive. During his speech, I had worked my way round until I was standing in a position slightly behind, and to the left of Lestrade, so that I could see as many of the assembled faces as possible. I couldn't make out anyone who seemed more alarmed or angry than anyone else, for this last announcement had generally gone down very badly. The volume of vocal opposition was swelling when the air was split by what sounded like a pistol shot. It was the ringmaster who, back up on the ring curb next to Lestrade, had cracked his whip over the heads of the crowd.

The murmurs died away. In the ensuing silence, Hildebrand asked the company whether any individual was refusing to permit his or her van to be inspected? Not one voice answered in the affirmative. The company were released, to make their property available for police inspection as required, prior to the scheduled run-through, which would commence promptly at three o'clock. I joined the general outflow from the barn and went to report back to Holmes.

When I went down the passageway between the two barns, I found my exit blocked by a tunnel of iron hoops. This must be the passage by which the big cats would be moved to the circus barn for their moments of glory in the ring. There was no getting past it, so I retraced my steps, intending to walk right around the big barn and approach the smaller one from the paddock side. I hadn't taken more than a pace or two beyond the alley, however, when I spotted my friend, standing amongst the straw of the yard with his back to me. At his side was a very small man in full clown

146

costume, who gave an elaborate bow as I watched, and scurried away in the direction of the performance arena, as fast as his very short legs would carry him.

"There you are," I said, as I reached his side. "It looks as though I have just missed meeting your friend, Biffo."

"So you have," he said. "One of the nicest men you could hope to encounter."

"What a shame that he must have been unable to answer any of your questions."

"On the contrary. He answered them most eloquently."

"Indeed? So the little fellow isn't a mute, after all?"

"He has no speech, but there are other ways to be eloquent, my dear chap. Let us find somewhere to sit and exchange our information."

We found some dry straw bales in an open-sided hangar at the rear of the yard and sat there. I gave my brief report on how Lestrade's speech had gone down, offering praise where it was due. "Whatever you say about him," I concluded, "the man certainly knows how to handle a crowd."

"So does the average schoolmaster, but that doesn't make them all brilliant detectives," he said, dismissively. "Now tell me, was everyone on Lestrade's list of suspects present?"

"I think I identified all of them. Oh – except for the strongman, who must still be laid up."

"Interesting. And did anyone who was present object to a search of their van?"

"Most of them did, but there were no outright refusals."

"Excellent!"

"Is it? I think they were too wary of that Hildebrand character to object too loudly. He really is a terrible bully, but at least, on this occasion, he supported Lestrade."

"I imagine that his wife told him that he had to. Bully or not, I think he is afraid of her. I wonder if he knows about her infidelity? If he does, that could account for his permanent bad temper – unless, of course, he was born like that."

"Holmes, you haven't told me how you managed to converse with that clown. Did you find out anything from him?"

"Just about everything I needed to know. The net is closing in, Watson."

"Is it? You have a suspect then?" I asked, surprised.

"I do."

"For heaven's sake, fill me in properly. What did you find out from Biffo? And how on earth did he talk to you if he can't speak?"

147

"He is very good at dumb-show. We also drew pictures in the dust. I suspected when Lestrade told us how Biffo kept making faces at him that he probably had some information to impart. Lestrade was the dumb one not to realise it."

"So what was his information?"

"His van is next to that occupied by Bendigo, the strong man. He saw Vittoria enter Bendigo's caravan at about six o'clock on the Sunday evening. He indicated that he heard them shouting at each other before he left his own van, and went out to practice his routine with Algernon. When he got back, all was quiet, and he thought no more about it until he heard what happened to the poor girl."

"He told you all this in dumb-show?"

"That, and by drawing pictures in the dirt."

"Biffo can't tell you, though, whether Vittoria might have left Bendigo's van later, fit and well, now can he? He wasn't there."

"True, but his evidence only served to confirm what I thought I already knew."

"You already suspected Bendigo before you met Biffo?"

"Oh, yes. Didn't you?"

"No, I didn't! I haven't suspected anybody. There are just so many of these people. It seemed to me that any one of them could have done it. Just a minute, though. Aren't you forgetting that Bendigo put his back out before all this happened? He's been laid up ever since."

"Ah, yes. His bad back. Many people would have seen him lift the trailer axle out of the mud the day before the murder. It was simple enough later to claim he had damaged it. Back injuries are easy to claim, and very hard to prove, are they not, Doctor?"

"Well, yes, that is true. Let me see, now . . . he claimed to have hurt his back on the afternoon before, so he must have been planning the murder, and his alibi, well in advance."

"Actually, I think her death could quite possibly have been accidental."

"Oh, come now! You can hardly throw someone to the lions accidentally!"

"We can discuss the finer details later. It is time to brief Lestrade and at least get him to haul the man in for questioning." So saying, Holmes rose to his feet, and at that very same moment we heard the band strike up a rousing march tune. The rehearsal was under way.

"Do you know which is Bendigo's van?" I asked as we crossed the yard on our way to report our suspicions to Lestrade and his constable.

"Yes," said Holmes. "It's that one there. Our suspect has just walked out of it!" About twenty yards ahead of us, an enormous fellow, built like

148

a Clydesdale, was walking away from his caravan steps, and taking giant strides across the yard, heading towards the farmhouse. His back was straight as a plumb-line, I noted.

"Quickly, Watson!" Holmes said. "Now is our chance!" Before I could even reply, he was running towards the caravan which the muscle man had just vacated. In two bounds he was up the steps and, peering first through a window to check no one else was there. Then he pushed open the ornate wooden door and vanished inside. I followed him with one hand in my pocket, grasping the stock of my revolver – just in case it might be needed.

Inside the caravan, everything was very tidy. The rear wall had a bunk bed set over the top of a bench seat, both of which stretched the full width of the van. There were cupboards and shelves everywhere, to make best use of the space, a small sink with a draining board, and a wooden dining table, but no chair. The boards which made up the floor gleamed with fresh polish. As I entered the van, Holmes was on his knees beside the little table.

"Watson!" he cried, "Look at this!" I crossed to where he knelt and saw his finger tracing a set of scratch marks on the polished boards. "See!" he said, "A chair normally rests here. You can see the scratches of all four legs where it has moved around. Where is that chair now, I wonder?"

"In Rajah's cage," I answered. "Nothing could be clearer."

Holmes withdrew from an inside pocket the magnifying lens he always carried with him. He used it now to examine minutely the edges and corners of all the built-in furniture along the walls. "What are you looking for now?" I asked. "Surely we have enough to take to Lestrade?"

"Go and stand guard outside," he replied, "I just need a few more minutes to satisfy myself on one point, and we don't want to be taken by surprise. I fancy this fellow could handle himself well enough in a fight." I turned to do as bidden, taking my revolver from my pocket as I went. It wasn't more than three or four paces to the door, but before I reached it, I heard a heavy footfall on the wooden steps outside, and the door was thrown wide open. Silhouetted in the open frame was the same giant of a man we had seen heading in the direction of the farmhouse. He had a pail of water in his hand.

We stared at each other for the briefest of moments, while he took in the fact that two strangers were ransacking his home, and I debated whether to charge at him and hope that he would fall back down the ladder, or fire my weapon at a fellow human being, something I had rarely done since leaving the army. I waited too long. With a swipe of his mighty arm, he swung the full bucket across his body and caught me in the chest with it. The bucket made solid contact, and I was knocked violently back against the caravan wall, striking my head against a shelf-edge. Soaked, winded, and seeing stars, I felt myself sliding down the wall. At the same time, I heard a loud explosion from outside the van as the pistol, which I had already cocked, flew out of my hand and discharged itself on hitting the ground. That was the point where I blacked out.

From out of the suffocating blackness which enclosed me, I heard a distant voice that I thought I recognised. Surely that was Holmes? So he was still alive? *I* was still alive? Every part of me hurt. I think I blacked out again. Gradually, gradually, consciousness crept back, until I was able to open my eyes and make out a blurry group of figures gathered round me. The light was very bright. I closed them again. Minutes passed, before a babble of voices penetrated my bruised brain.

"I think he's coming round."

"Thank goodness for that!"

"Keep back – give him air!"

"Watson? Watson? Can you hear me?"

"I can hear you, Holmes," I mumbled, my lips feeling as though they were carved out of lead. "Stop yelling in my ear, will you?" Finally, I managed to open my eyes again and keep them open this time. I was in a caravan. Not the same one. The concerned face of my best friend was the first that I recognised, hovering over mine. Behind him were two women. One was Clementine Hildebrand, the other was unfamiliar to me. However, the glistening python wrapped round her shoulders told me it must be Zelda, the snake dancer. I saw pictures on the walls, all depicting the same woman in striking poses, and always adorned with snakes. I deduced that they had brought me into her caravan, and felt grateful, although I could have done without the python, which had unwound itself a little from her shoulders, and was regarding me with slit-eyed curiosity. Suddenly I remembered Bendigo. Where was he? Had he escaped? Why hadn't he killed us both? I tried to sit up, and it hurt very much indeed.

"Try not to move, old chap," Holmes said. "You're still a bit groggy." I felt this was an understatement, but I let it pass.

"Where is Bendigo?" I asked, allowing him to lower me back down onto the soft, white pillow. I liked the lace trim round the edge of it, and the sweet fragrance which arose from it. Much nicer than my own . . . I felt myself drifting away again. Somehow, I forced my mind to concentrate, and my heavy eyelids to remain open. "Bendigo," I said again, "Have we lost him? Has he got away?"

"Lestrade and Jarvis have taken him away in chains," Holmes said. "He put up quite a fight. It took four men to pin him down and handcuff him."

"Why didn't he kill you?" I asked. "He almost killed me!"

"He might well have done, if your pistol hadn't gone off. He had me by the throat when they all rushed in and dragged him away."

"He was dangling from Ben's fist like a rag doll," said a man's voice. I saw the man I had cast as Iago lurking at the foot of my bunk. That made sense: Zelda and Iago. Iago and Zelda. Married. Shared the same caravan – with how many snakes? I wondered.

"Like a rag doll," Iago said again. "You should have seen it."

"No thank you," I said. I could imagine it, and that was quite enough: Sherlock Holmes dangling from the fist of an angry, crazed giant. Being shaken like a rag doll. I wouldn't have liked to have seen that. I drifted off again, this time deep into the arms of Morpheus, for a very much-needed sleep.

My memory of the rest of that day is very patchy. I know that it was past midnight when we returned to our Baker Street lodgings, and I know I slept again until almost eleven o'clock the next day. It was a great relief to find my head was clear. I got up, dressed and shaved, and went down to our sitting room, where Holmes was doing something with some test tubes. He never rests.

"My dear fellow!" he exclaimed. "How are you feeling?"

"Much better," I said. "But curious. I need you to fill me in on the bits of yesterday I missed." A thought occurred to me. "It *was* yesterday, wasn't it? I haven't been out for days, have I?"

Holmes laughed. "No," he said. "It was only yesterday." He rang the bell for Mrs. Hudson. "Would you prefer a late breakfast or an early lunch?" he asked.

"Neither," I replied. "Just a pot of tea." So that was what Mrs. Hudson provided, along with home-baked biscuits and her solicitations concerning my health. After she had departed, I finally persuaded Holmes to sit down and answer the nagging questions which remained.

"How did you decide that it was Bendigo who was the murderer?" I asked him. "You seemed to think I would have suspected him, too."

"You saw me try to move that piece of shuttering in the barn," he said. "I am quite strong, but it was too heavy for me."

"Why were you so interested in it anyway?"

"I asked myself why Maximillian saw nothing when he put Rajah back in his cage. It was obvious that the girl must have already been there. She could never have been put there later, strapped to a chair, without the lion either escaping, or attacking both her and her murderer. When I saw those cage sections stacked together, I reasoned that one of the spare walls could have been slid between the end bars to make a false wall and hide

151

anything set up behind it. Only a very strong man could have dragged that wall section across the floor and slid it through the bars in that way."

"Two men together might have done it."

"Possibly, but that would have involved a conspiracy, and the simplest answer is usually the best. Lestrade told us that Bendigo had taken it badly when Vittoria broke off their relationship. He was probably both hurt and angry."

"But to plot to kill her in that terrible way – only a lunatic could think up such a terrible revenge!"

"I told you yesterday, I don't think he planned it. She went to his van, and they argued. We don't know why, but I would guess he wanted her to come back to him. She refused. He hit out, and with his extraordinary strength, he hit her much harder than he intended. I found a faint trace of blood against the kitchen sink edge, where I think she hit her head. I believe she died there in his van. That was when he decided to put her in the lion's cage so that the animal would be blamed for killing her. After Maximillian put Rajah back in his cage, Bendigo only had to return to the barn and drag away the false wall, so that the lion discovered the body. As we were reminded yesterday, a lion will eat any meat that is fed to it."

I shuddered at the thought. One thing still made no sense to me. "Why strap the body to his kitchen chair? It would have been so much simpler to carry just her body into the barn, and toss it into the space behind the false wall. Why sit her in a chair at all?"

"I have been asking myself that, and I cannot give you a definite answer. The fact is that he did it, and perhaps he may one day be persuaded to tell us why. If you want my opinion, though, for what it is worth, I think he did it because he loved her."

"I don't follow."

"Perhaps, at first, he did take the body down and leave it on the floor of the cage. But he was horrified that he had killed the woman he loved. He couldn't bear to see her lying there, crumpled and broken. I think he went back to fetch his chair, and placed her in it, so that she had some shred of dignity when he looked upon her for the last time."

It wasn't the most satisfactory of explanations, but to this day, we haven't thought of a better. The jury didn't share Holmes's view that Vittoria the Circus Belle's death wasn't planned and executed by a crazed murderer, and Bendigo never spoke out in his own defence. He accepted the inevitable fate which awaited him and, I'm told, went to the gallows with dignity and resignation.

I think that he had nothing left to live for.

I leaned back and took down the great index volume to which he referred. Holmes balanced it on his knee, and his eyes moved slowly and lovingly over the record of old cases, mixed with the accumulated information of a lifetime.

"Voyage of the Gloria Scott," *he read. "That was a bad business. I have some recollection that you made a record of it, Watson, though I was unable to congratulate you upon the result. Victor Lynch, the forger. Venomous lizard or gila. Remarkable case, that! Vittoria, the circus belle. Vanderbilt and the Yeggman. Vipers. Vigor, the Hammersmith wonder. Hullo! Hullo! Good old index. You can't beat it*

– Dr. John H. Watson and Sherlock Holmes
"The Adventure of the Sussex Vampire"

NOTE

As Lestrade had warned us, the ringmaster's speech was peppered with the foulest expletives, which I propose to omit, or replace, for the sake of propriety. – JHW

The Adventure of the
Vanished Husband
by Tracy J. Revels

"They say he is dead, sir. The police have told me to abandon all hope, to accept that he is surely gone, never to be seen again until Judgement Day. My employees, my neighbors – all tell me to turn my thoughts to the future. Even my pastor tells me that I am sinning to pine so for Teddy, and that I must accept this misfortune with Christian fortitude, but I tell you I cannot bear it, for it is not true! A wife would know – she would feel it when her husband perishes!"

This outburst came with a full-bodied howl of pain, a sound that seemed impossible for such a thin, bloodless woman to produce. Mrs. Edwina Etherege rocked back and forth on the sofa with a black handkerchief clutched to her face. She was a lady of some forty years, tall and as thin as a scarecrow in a field. Her sharp, pale face was marred by a birthmark almost the size of a strawberry on her left cheek. Her dark hair was shot with gray, and her gown bagged in awkward places, indicating a sudden loss of weight. As a physician, I had immediately suspected a cancer, or some other cruel disease, might be attacking her.

"Madame, please, calm yourself," Holmes pleaded. "I am willing to hear your case. But you must gather your nerves. Doctor?"

"No, I not wish a sedative," she hissed. "I have been given too many pills and draughts. I only want to be heard, by someone who will believe me."

"Some cool water then," I suggested. With trepidation, she accepted a glass as Holmes continued to reassure her that he would listen to her problem. My friend could be gallant when he chose to be, and as soothing as a nurse if the occasion required it. The lady composed herself.

"Forgive me, sir. It is only – so many people have tried to convince me that I am insane for believing as I do, that he yet lives. My husband – Theodore Etherege, my Teddy – went missing a month ago today. He left home for an evening's entertainment and never returned. They found blood, and his clothes, his bag, and his gold watch, in his room at the Langham Hotel, but they did not find his body."

Holmes nodded. "I recall reading something of it in the newspapers. But let us have it from you, from the very beginning."

"Then I must tell you things that are humiliating to me," Mrs. Etherege said. "I fear that if I withhold them, you might lack some essential clue. I told these things to the police and was openly mocked. I pray you will be more charitable."

"I promise I will only seek to help you," Holmes replied.

Reassured, the lady began her tale.

"I am London-born. My father operated a clothing store on Tottenham Court Road. We sell both new and used attire for working men and women – sturdy boots, painters' smocks, maids' uniforms with aprons and white caps, as well as a large selection of mourning attire for ladies. I was an only child and raised in the business – it became my schoolroom, my world. As you can tell, I have no beauty, and I know that I lack any feminine charms. My entire life was given to assisting my father in the shop. I suppose I entertained some girlish fantasies of a wedding day, but when I turned twenty and all my female friends had married and were becoming mothers, I accepted the spinster life as my cross to be borne, doubling my efforts to be a good daughter and businesswoman, if I was never destined to be a wife."

"On the very morning of my thirty-fifth birthday, my poor mother died. Father mourned only until the funeral was past. Then, to my horror, he began going out to music halls and pubs, as if he were a young man again. Mother had been in her grave less than a season when Father revealed to me that he had fallen in love and wished to remarry. His intended was barmaid from a tavern who would not agree to share a house with a stepdaughter who was almost twice her age. Father ordered me to find a husband – As if such a matter were as easy as going out to buy a bouquet of flowers! – or consider becoming a nun.

"It was in this time, in such a dreadful state of mind as you might only imagine, that I met Teddy. He had been hired as a clerk at the jewelers' next door, and often we would find ourselves sitting on a bench behind our respective businesses. He was such a young man – he had just turned twenty-one – and so thin, so I began bringing food to him out of pity. We fell into companionable conversation, and in this way, I learned something of his life. His father was a Scottish baron, but Teddy was the product of an indiscretion, born on the wrong side of the blanket. His father had never claimed him, though he had provided for Teddy and even sent him to the University of Glasgow. But Teddy's high spirits had led to his expulsion from school and his estrangement from his natural father.

"'He says he will give me a portion to set myself up, if I marry a respectable girl. But it must be soon, for he has allowed me only until the end of the year to find a bride.'

"I could not help to laugh at the way his situation seemed a strange reflection of my own. I told him of my father, and of the horrible slattern who had turned his heart against me.

155

"'Will you take the veil?' he asked.

"'No – I have no wish to embrace the Roman faith.'

"'Then . . . do you suppose you could see your way to marry me?'

"Mr. Holmes, it was the strangest proposal in British history. I objected that he was a young and healthy man, and I an older lady. Besides, we were not in love with each other.

"'Do you not think we could see our way to love, Miss Edwina?' he asked. 'Let us play at it for a fortnight. I shall be your gallant suitor and you shall be my sweetheart. Let us see if the roles become us.'

"And, so, we did, Mr. Holmes. For two weeks we courted as earnestly as any young lovers might. We went to dances, we attended religious services, we were tourists at the Tower. Through it all, we came to enjoy each other's company. At the end of the allotted days, Teddy asked me again if I would marry him, and this time I said yes.

"However, I was too much of a shopkeeper not to haggle to some degree, and Teddy likewise felt that we should have some special agreements between ourselves since ours was a most unusual union. I was to retain control over the shop should I inherit it from my father, and he would retain a portion of his father's settlement, which he would keep in a separate bank account, for his own use. The strangest part of our pact, however, was the understanding we had about his 'sabbaticals'."

"Your husband was to become a teacher?" I asked.

"No – we merely chose the term because others seemed . . . offensive. Teddy freely confessed to me that he would need time apart, that he had a great many intellectual interests which I clearly did not share. Teddy loved music, theater, and art. It made sense – he had been to college. He had been exposed to the life of the mind. I am as dull as a brick. Teddy enjoyed attending the opera. My idea of a pleasant evening is one spent at home, knitting by the fireplace. All Teddy asked was that, twice a year, he would have a week to himself, where he might spend his time away from home in a nearby hotel, here in the city, and I would not follow."

"And you agreed to this?" Holmes said.

"Yes. Do you think I am a terrible wife?"

"On the contrary, Madame, I think that if more spouses were amenable to a sensible measure of freedom, we would have fewer separation cases, and definitely less murders. But do continue."

"We were married at Christmas and moved into the rooms right across the street from the store. A modest but comfortable allowance arrived from my husband's natural father, and my own father began to plan his nuptials. However, I never acquired a stepmother."

"Your father changed his mind?"

"No – death claimed his bride! She was killed when an omnibus overturned on Regent Street. My poor father was heartbroken. He followed her to the grave not long after, and so I inherited the store and our old home in the apartments above it.

"For five years, Teddy and I were happy. I ran the store while he enjoyed himself, reading books, painting pictures, playing the cello. We were contented and peaceful. Even when Teddy took his 'sabbaticals', there was never any hint that he had broken his marriage vows. He would return from his little adventures with programs from the theater and museums, sketches that he had made, and always some kind and thoughtful little trinket for me."

"Your husband was – *is* artistic?"

"Oh yes," the lady said, her face suddenly alight with pride. "He calls himself a mere amateur, but he has wonderful talent, even if pursued only as a hobby. But now I must brace myself, for this part of my tale is . . . difficult, even now.

"Last year, in the spring, we had the sudden, unexpected, and joyful hope of a child. Teddy was giddy with excitement and painted a nursery with a ceiling full of stars. Then one morning I awakened with a dreadful pain, and the child was no more. I nearly died in the weeks that followed. When at last I recovered, the doctor was firm in his ruling – I was foolish to long for a baby at my age and, with my fragile health, another would kill me.

"After this, a coldness developed between us. I think that Teddy, who had so gamely embraced a rather unconventional wife, now began to see clearly the differences in our ages. He asked for more and more time apart, and I meekly gave it to him, as I threw myself into my work at the store. I prayed that he only needed time to adjust his mind to our new restrictions, and that we could still be a faithful pair, even with the changed circumstances.

"Exactly one month ago, I woke before daybreak to find him pulling his carpetbag from our wardrobe. I asked him where he was going.

"'Madame Miranda plays tonight at the Royal Albert Hall – her last stop before America. I must see her!' He noted my frown, and as a placating gesture he held open the bag. "See, it is packed for only one night – I am just taking my evening clothes. I will stay at the Langham, my usual abode.'

"I forced myself to smile and bid him to enjoy himself. He kissed me and was gone.

"I thought nothing of it the rest of the day. Jack, my chief shop clerk, was hot – he claimed that some wares had been stolen. I served our customers while he fretted, and at night I took a lonely meal before retiring

157

early. I was surprised, upon waking, that Teddy was not home – he usually returns in time for breakfast. Then, to my horror, a police inspector and a pair of constables came knocking on the door, asking me to identify a bag, a watch, a wallet, and two suits of clothes. I protested that while these were indeed Teddy's things, he surely would not have abandoned them. At that instant, one constable muttered that there was a great deal of blood in his room at the hotel. I fear that I fainted."

"Since that time, there have been no developments. I have my store, which is successful, and there is an insurance policy, which I cannot bear to look at yet, much less to place a claim upon. I am not embarrassed by any financial need, but . . . Mr. Holmes, I love my husband! I have searched my feelings and I cannot believe, for one instant, that he is dead!"

My friend has listened to this recitation most intently. He began to waggle his fingers in the air, like a conductor about to summon his orchestra to tune.

"Mrs. Etheredge, will you be guided by me?"

"You are my last resort, sir."

"As I have been to many. This is what I would have you do: Tomorrow, you will retire to the seaside for a short holiday. This is not beyond your means, I take it?"

"No sir. I have a childhood friend who lives in Brighton and who has been imploring me to call on her."

"Excellent! Do you have servants?"

"Only one maid."

"Take her with you. Lock your rooms when you go, but leave the key with your man at the store, along with instructions to permit us entry. Doctor Watson and I will visit your abode while you are gone. We will disturb nothing, I promise. I will also pay a call on the inspector who handled your case. I believe that you mentioned upon your arrival that it was Gregson?

The lady scowled. "Yes."

"An old acquaintance, which is fortunate. He will be more candid with me than he might be with another. Do leave you friend's address, so that I may reach you quickly if necessary. And finally – do you have a photograph of your husband?"

"Yes. I thought you might require it."

She gave Holmes a *carte de viste*, which he in turn passed to me. It was an image of the couple made, I presumed, on their wedding day. Theodore Etherege was a short and reed-thin man, clean-shaven and with such a youthful face he could easily have been mistaken for a son rather than a husband. Mrs. Etherege had been somewhat stouter on her bridal morning, making it all too clear how grief had taken its toll on her health and looks.

"You have hope?" the lady asked my friend.

"Your case presents some intriguing qualities, Madame. I do not wish to make promises, but I think I can throw some light into your darkness."

"Then bless you, sir. All anyone else does is call me a fool."

"Tell me, Gregson" Holmes said, "how does a gentleman as naked as Adam in the Garden of Eden depart from a London hotel and not be noticed by its guests, desk clerk, or porters?"

The inspector nearly spat out his coffee. We three had been enjoying a most delicious repast at Simpsons and had just moved to the dessert.

"Ah, I should have known you had something up your sleeve, Mr. Holmes. It's that blasted Etherege business, isn't it? Poor old crow, taking on so over a young husband who's been dead for – what, a month now?"

"I have heard the story from the lady. Now let me hear it from you."

"There's not much to tell. Mr. Etherege checked in about four in the afternoon – he was something of a regular. The desk clerk knew him by sight. Etherege mentioned that he would be going out to hear Madame Miranda play, and at seven the clerk noted his departure in his evening clothes. He came back just before eleven and asked to be awakened at six. The boots was sent up to roust him when the time came. There was no response to his taps, but then the door, which was unlocked, swung open. The poor lad got quite a fright – there was blood in great arcs across the walls. The gentleman's attire was thrown about the room, but his gold watch and his wallet were on the nightstand. The room's key was later found beneath a chair."

"Was there any money remaining?" I asked.

"Less than a shilling. Robbery was clearly a motive, as we later learned Etherege had closed out his personal bank account and had a great deal of cash on his person, perhaps as much as five-hundred pounds."

"Yet the thief and presumed murderer left a fine gold watch behind." Holmes lifted his cup, favoring the inspector with a sardonic eye. "The abandoned attire was complete – not tattered or torn?"

"Yes. A grey tweed business suit, which the clerk recalled Etherege wearing, along with a white shirt, brown tie, and a bowler hat. The pieces were thrown about the room. The evening suit was also Etherege's – his initials were on the linen – and while it had not been damaged, it was found flung to four corners. And before you ask, there was no broken furniture, but the chairs were all upended, and the washbasin spilled out."

"Was the footwear also found?"

The inspector rolled his eyes. "You have quite the obsession with fashion! Yes, we found two pair – grey boots and black shoes."

"What about a nightshirt or pajamas?"

Gregson scowled. "We found none. Perhaps he was carried away in them."

Holmes arched an eyebrow. The Scotland Yard man sputtered.

"It is the only thing that makes sense! As you said, he couldn't have exited the building in a state of nudity! We have his wife's evidence that he had only the two sets of clothing with him, and that he was at the hotel for just one night. And then there was the blood." Gregson stabbed into his slice of cake. "It was like that business from Lauriston Gardens, blood all about. I remembered how you figured the blood had come from Jefferson Hope's nose. This was much the same, though more of it. My theory is that someone came back to the room with him and cut his throat after he had changed into his sleeping clothes. The murderer then carried his victim to another room and hid the body in a trunk. I spoke with the night porter – as you know, he unlocks the doors for any guest who departs after eleven p.m. There was a lady or two – one in deep mourning – a family of six with an Irish nurse, and several fellows who left for the late trains, taking luggage with them. I've tracked down five of those men, but as one departed for India on a packet – well, there's more work to be done."

Holmes's expression was that of a man with poor digestion, despite the remarkable cuisine we had just consumed.

"Gregson, do you mean to tell me that you are looking for a man who carried a dead body in a trunk all the way to India?"

The inspector bristled. "I'll have you know that the man I have in my sights has been a suspect in three other strange disappearances. Plus . . . ." Here he lowered his voice and cut his eyes around at the neighboring tables. "I have my suspicions about Mr. Etherege. I do not believe his 'sabbaticals' were as innocent as his wife claims. And all that love of art and music – such a man is bound to meet an untimely demise."

The next morning, we found ourselves at the Ethereges' shop in Tottenham Court Road. It was a sizable establishment, with a look of comfortable prosperity. The clerk, who introduced himself as Jack Keller, was a spry older gentleman with greased hair who immediately brought out his mistress's key and led us upstairs.

"I feel very bad for her, sir. I don't think she's had a solid meal since it happened, and I hear her crying in her office every afternoon."

"Mrs. Etherege mentioned that on the day her husband departed there had been a theft in the store, one that distracted you throughout the day."

160

The old man sighed. "I am ashamed that I worried her over it, sir. It's just that I despise a thief. Lower than a rat, a thief is! I have to keep a good eye on the shop, especially our used items. I always check my inventory, every day, I do. And to think a lady would do such a thing!"

"If you did not see the thief, how do you know the villain's sex?" Holmes asked.

"By what was stolen, of course! It was a widow's ensemble, for a slender lass, with a big hat and veil, a shawl, and black boots to match. Plus, a little purse, all of it used, and not terribly fine, though respectable enough. Worth maybe a pound or two, no more, as it was last year's style."

"How did the thief get in?" I asked, trying to imagine some poor woman in desperate need of a black dress. "Had any window been broken?"

"No, sir, and the doors were locked. That's what puzzled me so much. How could a whole dress walk away like that?"

"How indeed?" Holmes mused.

The Etherege apartments were perhaps some of the strangest we had ever explored. They seemed to be completely divided by taste rather than utility. There was a small parlor, stuffed with bric-a-brac, potted palms, a gilded birdcage, and a mantel covered in silly trinkets. But a second room was airy and vast, well-lit and designed to showcase a Turkish rug and a collection of Oriental divans. Several large paintings hung on the wall. Holmes observed them with the care he usually devoted to bloodstains.

"They call this new style 'Impressionistic'," he said. "I do not recognize the artist, and the choice of scenery is rather unique – no field of flowers in France, but the smokestacks and dreary lanes of Glasgow." He turned away and together we explored the rest of the chambers. There was only one bedroom, with a single wardrobe, which held a meager amount of both masculine and feminine garb. Holmes moved on to a room fixed up as a study, with a sizable library and a cello propped beside a chair. Holmes opened a desk drawer and riffled through some papers.

"I had hoped for something revelatory – perhaps I have found it. Listen to these notes, Watson. '*Sunset at Cliffs*', fifty pounds. '*Birds and dogs*', five pounds. '*Field below Old Gate*', fifteen pounds. '*All must be paid to St. Clyde*'."

"'*Paid to St. Clyde*'? That has an ominous ring to it, like some type of code. Perhaps Mr. Etherege was being blackmailed over this secret life he led."

"You scintillate today, Watson. But we have learned enough here, I think. Let us take our leave."

We returned the key. Holmes took a moment to walk around the store, pausing only to ask the clerk a final question.

161

"Did Mr. Etherege help with the business?"

The man sneered. "Does the Queen do her own cooking? Much too fine for the trade, that one was! If you ask me, Mrs. Edwina is better off rid of him. Only thing he ever did right by her was that insurance policy."

"Indeed?" Holmes leaned on the counter with the air of a practiced gossip.

"Oh yes – took it out about eight months ago, just after the . . . well, it's not mine to say but . . . ."

"After their hopes of a child were disappointed."

"Exactly, sir. I think he felt guilty in some way. Told me he wanted to be sure she was always provided for in case he should die. Only decent and manly thing he ever did!"

Holmes thanked the clerk for the intelligence and then led me from the store, swinging his cane jauntily.

"Do you have plans for this weekend, Watson?"

"None to speak of."

"Excellent! Let us take a brief journey and savor some Scottish Lowlands air."

"And Mrs. Etherege's case?"

He smiled. "I am engaged in solving it."

Holmes could be the most maddening of companions when he chose. At times, he would grasp a mystery to his person, concealing his clues as deftly as any magician ever palmed a coin. Holmes insisted on spending the remainder of the afternoon on an idle ramble through a number of picture galleries. Later, Mrs. Hudson provided such a savory supper that I nodded off on the sofa, only to be awakened by Holmes shaking my shoulder and bidding me to take up my bag, as our cab was at the door. A short time later, we were aboard the Scotch Express to Glasgow, along with a number of weary business travelers. I tried to engage Holmes in conversation, but he waved away my questions and recommended a book to me, the *Lives of the Artists* by Giorgio Vasari.

Needless to say, I was soon asleep as our train chugged through the countryside.

"It is simplicity itself," Holmes finally said. We had secured rooms at a small hotel and set out on foot to the city's outskirts. The weather was fair and the sky a sweet shade of blue that a Londoner seldom sees. "The entire case began with a basic question – where does a man goes without his clothes on?"

"To his bath, one would hope."

162

"You are the soul of wit this morning! Clearly, Mr. Etherege did not exit the hotel in such a state of undress. So the gentleman changed his attire and, with it, his entire person. No one noticed his exit because he did not exit as himself. He returned to his room after the concert and removed his evening suit, but did not don his business attire. Instead, he put on clothing that made him invisible. Tell me, how does a male guest in a hotel become invisible?"

"He adopts a disguise that makes him fit in. He appears to be a clerk or a porter."

"It won't do, Watson. The Langham, while large, is still too insular. A strange porter or clerk would be hailed by a regular employee as an imposter. What other types of individual might depart?" He elbowed me, none too gently. "Think of the most obvious, Watson. A man will not be recognized by his fellows, even by men who knew him well, from his previous stays at the hotel, if he exits as – "

"A woman?"

"Exactly!"

"But – where would he have acquired women's clothing?"

"That perplexed me for a moment, especially as the gentleman was not of such proportions that he might have taken one of his wife's cast-off dresses. But the theft from the shop solved that difficulty, especially when the clerk revealed what had been stolen. A black dress, a heavy shawl, a thick veil – the costume of mourning would shield a male nicely, especially a male as delicately made as Theodore Etherege. Since he possessed keys to his own establishment – even if he rarely assisted there – he could merely grab the desired items on his way out early that morning, after making a point to his still-abed spouse that he had only a suit of evening clothes in his bag."

"But why such an involved deception?"

"Let us work through it. We know that Etherege left the hotel sometime between when he was last recognized, just before eleven at night, and before the boots found the disarrayed room at six in the morning. Recall that at the Langham, the doors are locked after eleven p.m., so that the porter sees all who exit after that hour. The porter mentioned opening the door for several individuals, including a lady in deep mourning. Mr. Etherege clearly did not intend to go home in such garb! It could have been possible he was bound for some unsavory assignation, but the blood in the room hints otherwise. He was leaving forever, and he wanted everyone to think he had been murdered, so that his wife would receive his insurance settlement. But why leave just after eleven – what was essential about that time? Here, imagination is necessary. Clearly, our friend Teddy would wish to put distance between

163

himself and London. What train would he be most likely to take if fleeing the metropolis, keeping in mind that if secrecy was of the essence – and clearly it was – he would hardly want to exit the train at a lonely station, where some bored agent would notice a lone 'woman'. No, he would need to make his exit with a crowd. What train would satisfy that requirement? A quick consultation of railroad schedules tells us that the great Scottish expresses bound for Edinburgh and Glasgow leave just at midnight. Now, could I discover which one he was on?

"Mrs. Etherege remarked on her husband's skill as an artist, and the paintings in his apartments confirmed that this was not mere spousal flattery. Artists frequently return to sites of inspiration, and Mr. Etherege had painted the same scene of Glasgow at least three times. When one considers that clue, along with the fact that he had emptied his bank account a day before his departure, one sees the strong probability that he intended to trade his London life for one in the Scottish Lowlands. A-ha! – here is an inspiring vista."

We had stopped in a field only a mile from the old city. There were several artists at work, all of them in loose smocks and rugged trousers. Holmes slipped the photograph of the Ethereges from his vest.

"Do keep in mind that he may have, in the interim, begun to change his appearance further by growing a beard. Do you spot our man?"

"Good heavens! I do – that one!"

Together, we crossed the field and came up behind the thin little fellow. He was so obsessed with his brushes and palette that he did not even react until we stood just behind him, blocking his light.

"Would you step aside?" he asked.

"If you will tell me why you abandoned your kind and loving wife, perhaps I shall," Holmes answered, his tone as dark as a judge pronouncing sentence. The man spun around and went white beneath the first hint of a copper-tinted beard.

"I – I am sure – I do not understand – "

Holmes gestured toward the other painters. "Shall we tell them of your flight northward in widow's weeds? Or do they know it already?"

"No! Heavens, no – lower you tone – for God's sake, do not . . . ."

He dropped his head. His brushes fell into the grass. After a moment, he began to sob.

"Am I under arrest?"

"I am no representative of the official forces," Holmes said. "Only an agent employed by a most noble lady, whom you have grievously wronged."

"Yes . . . God forgive me, but . . . I thought it would be better. Please, sirs, give me just a moment to gather my things. Sit with me, and I will tell you my story."

A half-hour later, we were seated at a small café. Mr. Theodore Etherege ordered coffee. Holmes sat across from him with folded arms.

"I suppose Edwina has told you how we met. It is true, I am the natural son of the Baron of Strathclyde, who gave me one year to find a bride and turn from my 'dissolute way of living'. My father knew that I preferred a much more Bohemian lifestyle, with the freedom to express myself in my art. I wanted to live and to love the way that I pleased, but I simply could not afford it. I confess I only married Edwina because my time was running out and I had no practical talent for making a living.

"I did not expect to love her – but I did, at least at first, when being married was a novel status. Edwina is pleasant and kind, and completely devoted to me. But I also found her dull and boring. I have a mind meant for higher things, sharper thoughts, a greater enjoyment of life's pleasures, no matter whose god they offend! Can you imagine the torture it was, year after year, to keep company with a woman whose idea of art was a picture on a teapot, and whose idea of a beautiful song was a music hall ditty? When I married her, I thought my unconventional nature would be content to be compressed into a few weeks a year, but I was soon growing restive. And then . . . when I thought I would be a father . . . a new and more fulfilling life appeared to be opening before me. I imagined a child with my gifts, my insights, my joys. But as you surely know, our hopes were crushed."

"And you abandoned your good wife," I snapped. "You made her feel responsible for your selfishness!" Holmes raised a hand, preventing me from further speech, even though I found myself boiling with outrage. The man nodded, his face bloody with shame.

"Yes, I did wrong, and I know it. But the loss of our child showed me a bleak future. I could imagine Edwina growing old, and my time for painting, for art, for living life, for my other loves, running out as I waited patiently for her to die. I began to plot a way to be free of her. I had my father's settlement – he was faithful to his promise, and I had barely touched those funds – and I was also having some small success as an artist."

Holmes inclined his head. "You are becoming well known as 'The Glasgow Impressionist', though under the pseudonym of St. Clyde. I saw a number of your pictures in a gallery on Oxford Street. Yet your wife never knew of these commissions – she who was so proud of your talent."

Etherege passed a pale hand over his brow. "She was . . . patronizing me. She did not understand anything."

165

"You do her a disservice," Holmes said.

"Truly I did not wish to hurt her!" the man wailed. "That is why I took out an insurance policy. It will pay handsomely, if only the police will pronounce me dead."

"Thus, the blood in the room, to stage a murder scene," Holmes said. "Animal blood, of course?"

"Yes, bought that day from a butcher in Whitechapel. I had an urchin lad make the purchase for me, in a bottle, and paid him well for his silence. I wanted to make it look as if some terrible fight had occurred in my room. It struck me as rather hideous, which was the effect I wanted. I threw the bottle out of the window when it was done."

"And the dress was stolen from your own store."

"Edwina's store," he corrected. "I was familiar at the Langham. I could have gone to another hotel, but I always went to the Langham, and didn't want Edwina to question any change in my habits. I needed to leave on the night train, to come back here, the place where I was educated. Where I have friends, and where my best work has always been done. In school we would act out Shakespeare as they did in the olden days with lads playing the female parts – as I was so slight, I was always cast as Juliet or Ophelia. I knew I could manage a dress and a heavy veil. It was merely a matter of slipping out of the door of my hotel room when no one else was around. I had no luggage, of course – nothing more than the purse – but I had closed my bank account and so I had plenty of money. I also have a friend here, who was much astonished to see me in such attire, but still admitted me when I arrived."

"You have behaved most disgracefully."

"I . . . I know. Perhaps you will not believe me, sir, but every day that I have been away I have . . . I have regretted how I treated Edwina. I thought I would feel free, like a prisoner released from his shackles, but I do not. I thought I would find love, but I have not. Even my pictures seem wretched to me now. It is as if my hand no longer knows how to hold a brush, or my eyes the way to see the light as it falls upon the scenery. But what can I do?"

"Go home," my friend said.

"I cannot. She has given me up for dead."

Holmes scoffed. "The police have given you up. Your neighbors, your employee, your wife's pastor have written you out of the land of the living. But would I be here if your wife truly believed you dead?"

The man stared at my friend. "No, of course not. But . . . she . . . is not . . . angry?"

"Women are incomprehensible creatures," Holmes said. "I have learned that they are impossible to predict. Some hate with the fires of hell, others love with greater purity than the angels. You have deserved the former and have been granted the later."

My friend rose from his chair as the pathetic man gaped up at him in surprise.

"Come, Watson. It has been some time since I have been in Glasgow, and I should very much like to visit the University, to examine their collection of medieval charters. Mr. Etherege, I give you good day. My companion and I will return to London on Monday."

"And my wife?"

"I leave her fate in your unworthy hands." Holmes removed a folded paper from his vest. "She is currently visiting a friend in Brighton. Here is her address."

When we returned to Baker Street, Holmes found a letter from his client, as well as a substantial cheque for his services. Holmes glanced at the letter, then handed it to me with a command to read it aloud.

My Dear Mr. Holmes,

My husband has returned. I confess I screamed very loudly when he suddenly appeared at my friend's doorway, all bearded and rough like some Scottish highwayman. He explained everything. He spared me nothing. He told me how he felt he had no longer loved me, and that he had hoped I might be comforted by a financial settlement, instead of his presence. He said he should go and live his life apart from me, that he was unfit to be my husband. He was a most pitiful specimen.

I have asked him for only one thing – a fortnight to see if I may convince him that there is more to our love than he imagines, that his presence is more valuable to me than all the riches of India or China, and that I would never ask him to suppress his talents or his nature. We have discussed this at some length and have agreed to the experiment.

Thank you, Mr. Holmes, for believing in me, even as I have believed in him.

Yours very gratefully
Edwina Etherege

"A remarkable and formidable woman," Holmes said. "Let us hope the gentleman realizes the prize he possesses. I wonder if I shall ever hear of them again?"

> *"I came to you, sir, because I heard of you from Mrs. Etherege, whose husband you found so easy when the police and everyone had given him up for dead."*

– Miss Mary Sutherland
"A Case of Identity"

Merridew of
Abominable Memory
by Chris Chan

"Thank heavens you're back, Doctor. I'm at my wit's end trying to figure out what to do next."

Our landlady, Mrs. Hudson, was rarely flustered, but this evening, she seemed terribly shaken.

"What on earth is the matter?"

"Well, you've been gone for three days visiting your army friend, and Mr. Holmes has been away for even longer, working on another of his cases. This morning, a gentleman knocked on the door and insisted on coming inside. Well, I tried to tell him I didn't know when Mr. Holmes would be back. It might be a few minutes, or it might be a few days. He didn't care. He said he had no idea who this Mr. Holmes was, but I could show him in when he arrived. He was adamant on waiting in your rooms, even though I said that I didn't like leaving a stranger there with both of you away. But I couldn't stop him. He just staggered up the stairs, sat down in a chair, and said that he needed rest. He wouldn't listen to a word I said, and to the best of my knowledge, he hasn't stirred from that chair."

"Not since this morning?"

"Well, if he's gotten up to stretch his legs, I haven't heard him. I've been checking in on him every hour, and he's starting to gather dust, he is. Mind you, I'm not in the habit of doling out free meals to strangers who show up at the doorstep, but I don't think he's eaten a crumb since he arrived. Do you know what he said when I asked him if he'd had his dinner?"

"What?"

"He said, 'Dinner? What's that?' And then he turned his head to one side and started staring at the window. Only the curtains were drawn. That's a very odd duck, if I do say so myself. I think you'd better see what he wants, hadn't you?"

"Absolutely! Did you give you his name or tell you why he came here?"

"I asked him, and I tell you, his answer made the hairs on the back of my neck stand on end. Shall I tell you what he said?"

"Yes! Please don't keep me in suspense!"

"Very well. He told me, "I don't know. Don't ask me again." And then he closed his eyes and wouldn't say another word, not even when I spoke directly into his ear."

I was dumbstruck. "Are you saying he claims not to be able to recall his own *name*?"

"Exactly. I thought he was having a joke at my expense at first, but when I looked at him closely, I didn't see the faintest hint of a smile. It makes no sense to say this, but I think he meant it."

"But that's absurd."

"With all due respect, Doctor, you should be telling him that, not me."

I saw the justice in this comment, and I hurried up to our rooms and opened the door. I saw no one at first, until I approached the fireplace and discovered a small, elderly man sitting in one of the high-backed chairs.

He didn't appear to notice me until I cleared my throat. His body quivered and he finally looked up to meet my chilly gaze. "Who are you and what do you want?" he demanded.

It took a bit of effort, but I managed to keep the asperity I was feeling out of my voice. "My name is Dr. John Watson and this is my home. May I ask who you are and what you're doing here?"

My guest didn't seem upset or surprised by my reply. "Are you sure?"

"Of course I am. I know for certain who I am and where I live. Can you say the same?"

He clenched his jaw. "This is my home." He paused. "I think it is." His voice quavered and cracked. "I thought it was."

My annoyance vanished as I suddenly realized that this man might be suffering from some sort of stroke or dementia. "Sir, I am a medical doctor, and I think I should examine you to see if you are – "

"No!" His voice grew so loud and shrill that I felt my eardrums vibrate. "I won't be touched! You can't! You have no right! This is my house! Leave me alone!"

Involuntarily, I took a couple of steps back, but regained my composure when the suddenly enraged man shook and deflated like a punctured balloon, until he was just a frightened and lost-looking old fellow.

I approached him again. "Sir, what is your name?"

He looked agonized. "My name? Don't you know?"

"I do not, sir. I'm afraid we're strangers."

"How bizarre. I wonder what you're doing here, then."

"Sir, what is your name?"

"I . . . I think I know. I ought to know it. I just need time to think of it. Give me time. Give me time!" He clasped his head in his hands and rocked back in forth in the chair. I placed my hand on his shoulder in an attempt to steady him, but he slapped my arm away immediately. He was quite frail, so he caused me no pain by striking me, and my overarching emotions were of concern for him rather than annoyance.

The next two hours followed the same pattern. I would attempt to examine him, he would fight me off. I would ask his name, he would be unable to answer. Then he would ask me my name and demand to know what I was doing in his home. When I would patiently re-introduce and re-re-introduce myself, he would become disoriented and confused. All attempts to come close to him were rebuffed, and I was starting to grow frustrated when the door swung open and Holmes made his welcome return.

After greeting him and quickly apprising him of the situation, the familiar interest glint entered Holmes's eye, and he strode over to the fireplace without even taking off his coat. "Good evening, sir. My name is Sherlock Holmes."

"Who?"

Holmes was compelled to repeat his name thrice, each time receiving the same response, until he finally asked for our guest's name, and received a response similar to the ones our guest gave me.

Looking thoughtful, Holmes rang for Mrs. Hudson. When she arrived, he asked for tea and scones. He filled a cup and handed it to our anonymous visitor. "Your tea, sir."

"My . . . tea?"

"That is correct. I suggest that you drink it while it is hot."

Obediently, our guest took the cup and sipped. When its contents were nearly emptied, he started sagging, and the cup tilted and began to slip from his fingers. Holmes snatched the cup from him before the dregs spilled, and chuckled as he sank his teeth into a scone.

"Holmes, what did you put into that tea?"

"A bit of sugar. It disguises the taste of the mild narcotic I slipped into the cup."

"But you can't just go about knocking out people with drugs!"

"This is a special circumstance, Watson. Our guest is clearly ill and will not allow us to examine him. This is the most efficient and humane way to subdue him." Scrutinizing our visitor as he slipped into unconsciousness, Holmes took a sip from a teacup that I presumed was devoid of narcotics. "I think he'll be more amenable to an examination now. I suggest that you start immediately. The dose I gave him was so tiny that I doubt that he'll need more than fifteen minutes or so before awakening."

Setting my last lingering concerns about medical ethics aside, I started to look over our guest. He was not in the best health. The fact that he quite likely hadn't consumed any nutrients or water in the last few days – aside from his recent cup of tea – had left him weak and dehydrated. Yet it was clear that he had been in decline for some months previously, and from the pallor on his skin and a handful of other indicators, I suspected that he was in the advanced stages of some sort of cancer.

I voiced my initial diagnosis to Holmes, who was in the middle of his second scone. "Could his disorientation be due to a brain tumor?"

"Anything is possible. I need to examine him more closely. It's possible that a stroke or an aneurism, or simply senility, has caused this."

"Or a blow to the head?"

"That's possible, yes." Our guest's head was largely bald, but as I examined the eggshell-colored fringe along the edges of his skull, I noticed a little brown patch the size of the nail on my littlest finger. "Holmes! Look at this!" I pointed to a small piece of metal that was sticking out of the back of his head. "What is that? Could it be a *nail*?"

"There's no head to it, and the edge is rough, like it was snapped off . . . An ice pick, perhaps?" Holmes picked up his magnifying glass, nodded in response to my warning not to touch the metal projection, studied the wound, and handed the glass to me. After examining it, I returned it to Holmes and informed him, "I would say that this man was stabbed in the head, most likely with an ice pick. The wound almost certainly caused lasting brain damage and probably permanently impaired his memory."

"Abominable. Is it possible to remove the weapon to study it?"

"At this point, I would strongly advise against it. To pull out the weapon might cause even more damage, and would possibly even kill the patient. Perhaps a skilled surgeon specializing in brain disorders might be able to operate, but to attempt to do anything with the wound here would be so foolhardy that any doctor who attempted to perform such a procedure might justifiably be expelled from the profession."

Holmes shook his head. "That is unfortunate on multiple levels. Yet now that you know the cause of this man's memory impairment, you can say with certainty that he requires proper medical attention?"

"Of course! Not only for his wound, but for his malnutrition, dehydration, and general illness as well."

With a nod, Holmes crossed the room and summoned our page-boy. When he arrived moments later, Holmes told him, "Go and fetch an ambulance at once. Inform them that we have a gravely ill and wounded man here, and he requires urgent medical attention. Quickly now."

As the lad sprinted away, I shook my head. "It's amazing that the man was able to walk and retain so many of his cognitive functions after suffering such a terrible wound, but such things do happen – though in his condition, I'm not sure whether to dub him lucky or not."

"Where there's life, there's hope, Watson, and in any case, we have to make use of the precious time we have before the ambulance arrives and takes away our guest." Holmes immediately started searching the pockets of the unconscious man. I started to make some sort of objection, but Holmes waved a dismissive hand at me. "If we are to find out who attacked this man, we will need all the information we can obtain, and first on the list is his name."

After completing his preliminary search, Holmes sighed. "No wallet. The man was the victim of a pickpocket."

"Surely he could have simply misplaced his wallet or left it behind. We don't know how or where he received his injury."

"First of all, I will draw your attention to these greasy smears and coal-dust on the inside of this poor man's pocket where most men keep their wallets. This man's hands haven't been washed recently, but they are not nearly at that level of uncleanliness and are well-manicured. Obviously another hand, not his own, dipped into his pocket and extracted his wallet. No doubt some filthy denizen of the streets saw our visitor in his discombobulated state and thought he was a wealthy and easy mark, so he picked his pocket."

"He? There are female pickpockets, you know."

"If you were to look at the size of the dirty smears in that pocket, you would know it was unlikely that a woman's hand could have created that level of damage. We also know that he was attacked at night, inside a building where he felt comfortable and safe and where he was prepared to spend a substantial period of time – though not, most likely, his own home."

I was still smarting from Holmes's rebuttal to my female pickpocket remark, so I said nothing, and Holmes, looking disappointed at my missing my cue, continued. "You'll note that our guest is clad in evening wear. Quite expensive, well-tailored – surely, this fellow is a man of means. But he has no coat, no hat, and no scarf. That is because he removed those garments upon entering the domicile he was visiting when he was attacked. He was probably not in his own home because had he let himself in with his own key, which he would have then returned to his pocket, the key would have been at the top of the pocket's contents. Instead, this handkerchief rests on top of the key, suggesting that he has had need of it since he last used his key.

"His hands, though not dirty enough to cause the smears in his pockets, still have evident traces of street grime on them, but no corresponding marks are on his handkerchief, indicating that he hasn't used it in some time. Furthermore, the man clearly suffers from corns and chilblains on his feet, and his shoes look to be a fraction too tight for him.

Unless a man is expecting company, he will remove his dress shoes upon reaching his own house if they cause him discomfort. He has transferred his wedding ring from his left to his right hand, indicating that he is a widower. Given the care with which this button was resewn to his cuff, I think it likely that he keeps a manservant. Now coming back to the handkerchief . . . ."

Holmes unfolded the square of white cloth in front of me with a dramatic flourish. "It bears the initials "*T.M.*" Clearly our guest's initials. His pocket watch . . . ." Holmes pressed the latch and opened it. "Contains a telling inscription: '*To Thaddeus, a wonderful husband and father on our twenty-fifth anniversary. Love, your darling Jewel*'." Jewel is clearly his late wife, and our man is Thaddeus M. We must track down this man's child – or children. If he has been here for several hours, they might be aware of his absence and worried."

"Is there nothing else you can deduce?"

My friend looked the unconscious man up and down a few times, before uttering a quick exclamation of triumph. "Observe! A foreign hair clinging to his own hair. White horsehair that has yellowed. From its length and the curls on it, it comes from a judge's wig! Watson, examine our copy of *Who's Who* – go to the *M*'s – and see if you can find a judge named Thaddeus with a wife named Jewel, though upon further reflection, 'Jewel' may be pet name for his wife."

I obeyed and began scanning pages while Holmes applied his standard level of scrutiny to T.M.'s hands and feet. A few minutes passed, until I finally found an entry that met our specifications. "This could be him, Holmes! Thaddeus Merridew. High Court Judge, his wife Jillian passed away two years ago."

"'Jewel' might feasibly be a *sobriquet* for 'Jill'," Holmes noted. "The usual information on his residence is present?"

"Yes. 2218 Guilders Lane. Not much more information, other than a couple of clubs and the fact that he has a son currently working in Belfast and a married daughter living in India."

"Then we have a solid thread to follow," Holmes replied. "I couldn't find much more of use on his extremities, save for the fact that he was in the habit of carrying a silver-headed walking stick that he needed for a limp in his left leg."

Why fight it? I asked myself. "And how did you deduce that?"

"The scuffing on his left shoe indicates a limp. When a cane is carried to alleviate leg pain or damage, it is generally held in the opposite hand from the afflicted leg. On his right hand, I found traces of silver polish. Clearly, he lost his walking stick soon after the attack. As the cane wasn't merely decorative, he wouldn't have left it at the door along with his coat and hat."

A knock at the door told us that the ambulance had arrived, and the presumed Mr. Merridew, who was just starting to emerge from his stupor, was eased onto a stretcher and carried away to the hospital. At Holmes's suggestion, I continued making my way through the *M*'s just in case there was a second potential name that fit our profile. There was none, and so, once the remaining scones and tea were consumed, we left to investigate.

A knock at the door of Justice Merridew's home brought a ruffled-looking valet to the door. After explaining that his master was not at home, Holmes informed him that we were aware of the fact that his employer had been missing for the last few days and that the judge had been found and was now in the hospital. Our request to be allowed in to ask some questions was accepted. As we entered, Holmes tapped the address plate on the pillar by the door.

"This may explain why Justice Merridew came to our residence and had the fixed impression that it was his house, Watson. He had been wandering the streets of London for some time before he reached our rooms, probably for the better part of a day, given the very slight bit of the dust and dirt of the city on his clothes, and the fact that he wasn't at death's door from dehydration. His brain was damaged, and what remained of his mental faculties was devoted to finding something, anything with a semblance of familiarity to his home. When he saw our address plate for *221B*, he misread it for his own *221B*, and in his impaired mental state he became convinced that he had reached his own dwelling."

The valet was clearly uncertain as to whether he should allow us into the main sitting room, where the judge's guests were welcomed, or if he should lead us into the small back room where he was allowed to meet with his own acquaintances. Holmes, no doubt correctly deducing that the chairs would be far more comfortable in the judge's sitting room, settled into a plush seat, and I followed suit.

"Your name, please?" Holmes asked after introducing ourselves.

"Tenners, sir."

"How long have you been working for Justice Merridew?"

"Just over four years, sir. I started right after Mrs. Merridew fell ill with her long ailment."

"When was the last time you saw him?"

"A few days ago, sir. He had a dinner engagement at The Golden Nectarine, and I prepared his clothes and polished the silver handle his walking stick."

"Can you describe the clothing and cane?"

"An ordinary long black dinner dress coat, a white scarf, and a black top hat. Exactly the same garments worn by thousands of other gentlemen, sir. The walking stick had a handle shaped like a lion's head."

"Do you know who the judge was going to meet for dinner?"

"I do not, sir. My employer is not in the habit of providing me with any details besides what I absolutely need to know for my duties. I was told to expect him back by midnight. I was waiting up until three for him, sir. When he didn't arrive I made some discreet enquiries, but I was waiting to inform the police out of fear of a scandal. The judge wouldn't have liked that at all, sir. He was most reluctant to cross paths with the police unless it was absolutely necessary. He considered it ungentlemanly."

"Do you have any knowledge as to anyone who might want to do the judge harm?"

"None, sir," Tenners answered. "He had no enemies that I know of, but perhaps someone at the Old Bailey might have had a better idea. I dare say a magistrate upset a lot of people with his rulings, but he never shared any details with me."

"No angry or threatening letters?"

"I don't open his mail, sir. I just gather it. He keeps his recent correspondence on that salver there, if you'd care to look."

Holmes examined the stack of envelopes and found nothing of note. Thanking Tenners for his time, we took a hansom to The Golden Nectarine, where we were told that Merridew had a reservation for two that night, but he had never arrived. Another man named Ivers had arrived and asked for Merridew, but after an hour passed with no sign of the judge, Ivers had left. Having learned almost nothing of use, we travelled to the Old Bailey to investigate the judge's chambers.

On our way, we passed two men, a young fellow in his early twenties, and a distinguished-looking man in his mid-sixties wearing a barrister's robe. We wouldn't have given them a second look had we not heard the younger man refer to the elder as "Mr. Ivers". It took only a few moments to introduce ourselves and explain our purpose. Ivers expressed concern and stated that he was happy to do whatever he could to assist us, and his young friend murmured a polite goodbye and slipped away.

"I suspected that something was terribly wrong," Ivers declared. "Thaddeus is never late and he would never miss an appointment. I was certain that *I* had made a mistake of the date, but I was informed at the restaurant that Thaddeus had reserved a table. I was quite certain that something had happened, but I wasn't sure what to do – I didn't have his home address handy, and when I didn't see him around here the last few days, I had a word with his clerk, although he's an elderly fellow and prone

176

to letting things slip his mind. Thaddeus should have forced him into retirement years ago, but they've worked together for most of their professional lives, though Thaddeus has kept his mind sharp as a tack."

Holmes shook his head. "Unfortunately, his mental powers have probably been forever destroyed by the attack." Ivers asked for details, and the lawyer grew horrified as he learned of the damage to his friend's mind.

"Good heavens! How distressing!" Ivers patted his face with a handkerchief. "Is there any hope of a recovery?"

"Unlikely," I said. "In any case, given his overall bad health . . . I don't know if you were aware . . . ."

Ivers nodded. "He was diagnosed with cancer about seven months ago. They said it would be unlikely that he would make it to Christmas. Poor fellow. We'd often talked about what we'd do during our retirements. Thaddeus thought of moving to a warmer climate. And now . . . Would you happen to know to which hospital he was taken? I should like to visit him."

I provided him with the requested information, and Ivers nodded and excused himself, noting that he had to meet with a client. As he walked away from us, Holmes called out to him, "By the way, Mr. Ivers. Did you never think of talking to the police about your missing friend?"

Ivers looked horrified. "Of course not. A gentleman never has anything to do with police if he can help it."

Once Ivers turned around the corner and out of sight, Holmes murmured to me, "He's lying, of course."

"Whatever makes you say that, Holmes?"

"A man like that doesn't just assume that his missing terminally ill friend will be all right and do nothing, no matter how much he dislikes the police. No, there's more to it than that. He's hiding something important."

"Do you think that Ivers harmed his friend?"

"No," Holmes frowned. "I don't. First of all, Ivers is not the sort of man who allows his own hands to get dirty, especially not with blood. I have a feeling that there's a significant link or two or three in the chain that we're missing." He paused and looked reflective. "Watson, do you remember the positioning of the wound? The direction of the thrust of the ice pick?"

I needed a moment to search my memory. "The bit of metal was pointing upwards, wasn't it?"

"It was. And Merridew was a small man. The stab came from beneath. Which means that either his assailant was diminutive, or . . . ."

At first I thought that Holmes was pausing for dramatic effect, but after time passed with no continuation, I realized that my friend was concentrating. After a few people stared at Holmes for acting like a statue,

I gave him a little nudge, prompting him to say, "What I can't understand is, why didn't the assailant follow Merridew to finish the job? Why didn't he strike again with another weapon, or why not restrain him somehow? After all, the odds were likely that his erratic behavior would catch the attention of a police officer. Surely the villain could have caught up with an elderly, injured, seriously ill man. Unless . . . ." Thankfully, Holmes didn't try my patience with too long a pause. "Watson! I have it! The assailant was in a wheelchair!"

I begged him for some explanation.

"It makes perfect sense. Why didn't Merridew's attacker follow him out the door and try to kill him again? Because he couldn't! Whoever did this was too weak in the legs to go after him, though the would-be killer was strong enough to stab him with an ice pick. We must go back to The Golden Nectarine immediately and search the neighborhood.

"For what?"

"For a ramp. A private home with an entrance designed for someone in a wheelchair."

As we began the journey back to The Golden Nectarine, I informed Holmes that I thought that he was making quite a logical leap here, and I was surprised to see that he agreed with me. "Indeed, I may be going beyond the limits of pure logic here. I could be putting two and two together and making five, or even five-million. If I get egg on my face, you have my permission to record my humiliation with total accuracy within your journals. In the meantime, let us see what my deductive leaps produce."

We spent twenty minutes walking around the neighborhood surrounding The Golden Nectarine in a spiral, until Holmes yelped in triumph. "A ramp, Watson! This house has a ramp!"

He noticed the ramp from about twenty yards away. As I struggled to keep up with him, I reminded him that there are many people in London in wheelchairs. "I'm well aware of that," he replied, "but if this doesn't prove to be the domicile in question, then we shall simply have to look elsewhere. If we have beaten the odds and this is indeed the spot for which we're searching, then a young, pretty woman wearing rather too much inexpensive makeup will answer the door for us."

I was too intrigued not to ask, "How on earth did you know that?"

"Didn't you notice the mark on Ivers' neck? Cheap rouge, the kind a young woman of modest background will slather on in an attempt to get the attention she desires. Ivers has a wedding ring, and in any event, a barrister of that standing will have been prudent in his selection of a wife in his youth, but rather more reckless in his selection of a mistress in his later years. A respectable barrister's wife wouldn't coat herself with that sort of cosmetic, nor would Ivers approve of his daughter adorning herself in such a manner."

"Sirs? May I help you?" The front door opened, and a pretty young woman appeared in the entryway. She was tall, with long honey-colored hair and her face was indeed liberally coated with rouge, though I lacked the experience with makeup to tell the cost of this coloring.

Holmes drew himself up with remarkable dignity and replied, "I am here to speak to you, Miss, about your friendship with Mr. Ivers, as well as his friend Justice Merridew."

Even under all of that rouge, it was obvious that the girl had blanched at Ivers' name, though curiously the name of Merridew didn't appear to affect her. Indeed, after displaying clear confusion for a few seconds, she replied, with palpable honesty, "I've never met a Justice Merridew."

"But you *do* know a Mr. Ivers, the barrister," Holmes pounced. "Come, come. There is no point in denying it. You were seen together."

The girl looked troubled. "What do you want from me?"

"Only the truth, young lady, nothing more. And I think that if you would be so kind as to let us inside, and allow us to speak to the resident of this house who uses a wheelchair, we might be able to clear up this entire unfortunate situation."

The girl seemed hesitant to budge, though I cannot say that I blamed her. My friend was playing an excellent bluff, but if she called it, he would be unable to produce any solid evidence to support his theories, nor would he be able to even identify her by her name.

Fortunately, a reedy voice called out from behind her. "Let them in, Millicent. There's no point in dragging this out much longer."

The girl we now knew as Millicent silently stepped backwards and gestured for us to enter. It wasn't a luxurious or even well-maintained home, but it was obviously a place of modest comfort. Millicent led us into a small parlor, where a woman sat in one corner in a wheelchair, sipping a lemon squash. This woman couldn't have been too much older than fifty, but she was clearly in declining health, and if my initial impressions were correct, she was not long for this world. "Cancer," she replied, reading my mind. "It started in my throat and spread throughout my entire body. The doctors give me one to two months. I think that's generous." She sipped her drink. "You're Sherlock Holmes and Dr. Watson. I've seen your pictures in the newspaper. Did the judge's family hire you to find out what happened to him?"

"No, he showed up at our home on his own."

"Is he all right?"

"No, he isn't. His memory has been utterly destroyed."

"So he didn't accuse me?"

179

"He couldn't. He was unaware of his own condition."

"Both the wound I inflicted on him and the cancer?"

"That is correct. You're confessing to stabbing him with the ice pick, then?"

"I might as well. I'll never see the hangman's rope, though perhaps it would be less painful than this. In a way, I might have done him a favor by sparing him some of the knowledge of his own ailment."

"I'm not certain that he would see it that way," Holmes replied with evident disapproval.

"No, he probably wouldn't." The woman took another sip. "My doctor tells me to keep drinking this. It's supposed to soothe my burning throat. It does help, but only if it's nice and cold, so I have to keep adding little chips of ice to it. That's why I had the pick handy a few nights ago. Millicent provides me with a small lump of ice, and I keep breaking off little chunks to put in my drink. Or I did, before I broke the implement." She looked at Holmes searchingly. "Do you even know my name?"

"I do not."

"It's Mattie Allend. Just call me 'Mattie', not 'Mrs. Allend', if you please. I've never been one for formality, and I've never had a husband. I'm just trying to look after my daughter." Mattie pointed at Millicent. "Millie knows nothing until now about what happened, aside from the fact that there was suddenly a hat and coat and scarf and walking stick that she needed to hide away when she came home from babysitting the neighbor's brat. Is that clear? She's totally innocent. Of attempted murder at least. I suppose you've noticed that she's five months in the family way." I had observed that, but I had thought it indelicate to mention it.

"That was my doing, you know. I told her, Millie, you're a very pretty girl, but you're not very clever and husbands are more trouble than they're worth. If you want to be taken care of, you find yourself an older, prosperous career man with a wife and an impeccable reputation, and you get yourself in the family way and make him take care of you and the child. Not a nobleman, though. Those titled yobs are often flat broke, and they've no sense of paternal responsibility. I learned that the hard way with my first child, my son. With Millie, I was more clever. I found a Harley Street physician who liked me and didn't care much for his wife, but couldn't afford a scandal. Luckily for me, Millie is the spitting image of him."

"That was your goal with Mr. Ivers?"

"It was. And a good plan, too. Ivers was besotted with her, and a few nights ago she told him he was about to become a father again. Well, he promised that he'd take care of her, but she had to promise to never let his wife know about her or the baby. That was easy enough. She needs an income, not a scandal. It all would've been all right, but then that judge saw Ivers kissing her on the front steps a few nights ago. The judge stopped his carriage and climbed out, but he was sick and slow. By the time he crossed the street Ivers was long gone, and Millie was on her way to babysit at the neighbor's. He must not have seen her leave, because the judge started pounding on the door, demanding to speak to her. He was making such a fuss that I felt I had to let him in. He hung up his coat and hat, and we had a nice, civilized talk for a while. He didn't approve of me, but I couldn't care less about a judge's opinion of my character unless I'm standing in the dock.

"Then he stated that he was going to Ivers' wife and telling her everything. I told him not to be a woolly-headed fool, that he would ruin everything for Millie, but he insisted. He said Mrs. Ivers was his cousin, and he couldn't keep the news that her husband was going to have a baby out of wedlock from her. We argued, things got a bit heated, and I panicked and struck him with the ice pick. Next thing I know, I'm holding the handle in my hand, and he's stumbled out the door before I can get to him. I expected him to collapse and die right in front of the house. I've no idea how he managed to make his way to your home."

Mattie drained her glass. "Well, that's all, then. Millie came home an hour later and wanted to know what the clothing and cane were doing here, and I told her that at my age, a woman doesn't have to explain or justify her relationships with men. As she was gathering up everything, Ivers came back to the house, saying his friend hadn't come to dinner. When he saw the clothes and cane, I took him aside, and told him for Millie's sake, he mustn't ask too many questions about Merridew. I implied that Millie might be unjustly blamed for his disappearance, so Ivers kept mum and paid the manservant a bit to do the same. So now you know everything. This was all for my daughter. I want to see her taken care of before I die. What'll happen to me now? It seems a waste to pay for a trial. I'm going to a much more final courtroom soon enough."

Holmes gave her a long, penetrating gaze that was not completely devoid of sympathy. "I shall tell the authorities everything, and perhaps they shall be merciful."

They were. After a doctor confirmed that Mattie wasn't long for this world, Scotland Yard decided not to make an arrest, and the unfortunate woman died just over a week later in her own home. Merridew was placed in a convalescent home, and passed away from complications connected to his cancer six months later. To the end, his memory grew more and more abominable, until he finally was unable to finish a sentence more than three words long without losing his train of thought. It was a tragic end to a reportedly brilliant legal mind.

Holmes didn't expect a fee for his efforts, so it was a pleasant surprise when a substantial check arrived in the mail a week later. Its sender, Mr. Ivers, thanked us for finding out what had really happened to his friend, minimizing the fallout of the scandal, and asked us to protect the feelings of his wife and children. Holmes, caring little for the check but understanding the need to protect the innocent members of the Ivers family from embarrassment, agreed. And so I write this account of the case solely for myself. And as soon as I finish, I will take it down to the vaults of Cox and Company and lock it away in a battered tin dispatch-box, where it will rest in peace with dozens of cases that also are better left a secret.

> *"My collection of M's is a fine one. Moriarty himself is enough to make any letter illustrious, and here is Morgan the poisoner, and Merridew of abominable memory . . . ."*

– Sherlock Holmes
"The Empty House"

The Substitute Thief
by Richard Paolinelli

Five months have passed since the death of my friend, Mr. Sherlock Holmes, at Reichenbach Falls. I sit in his rooms on Baker Street haunted by a ghost, wishing that I could once again see him sitting contentedly in his chair and puffing away at his pipe. Or playing his violin, or even hunched over his latest chemistry experiment.

What I would not give to have Lestrade charge in with another puzzle for Holmes to solve, or to have some mysterious new visitor arrive, bearing a new case for Holmes's talents to resolve. But I know that these things will never again come to pass, so I have resolved myself to addressing those cases only mentioned in passing during my previous accounts of Holmes's adventures.

One such case was the Darlington Substitution Scandal referred to briefly during "A Scandal in Bohemia". It referenced a time when Holmes had solved one crime while investigating another . . . .

"A married woman grabs at her baby. An unmarried one reaches for her jewel-box," Holmes had said to me during the Bohemia affair, reminding me of the two previous cases he'd used the trick to solve a case. The first time had been in Darlington, two years earlier.

It had not been Lestrade, or some strange newcomer, that had set Holmes on the trail to Darlington that foggy London night. Rather, it came in the form of a letter.

"It seems, Doctor," he said, holding it up after reading it, "that our assistance is required on a somewhat delicate matter in Darlington," he said.

"Darlington?" I exclaimed. "What could possibly be of such a delicate nature up there?"

"A rare manuscript has been stolen," Holmes replied. "The theft hasn't yet become public knowledge. Lady Lymington – " He waved the note. " – hopes that it can be recovered before news of the theft gets out. Her husband, Lord Lymington, has contacts that are useful to Her Majesty's government.

"I suppose," he added, "it would be most impertinent to turn down such a request. Well, Watson, it has been rather quiet here lately. Do you feel up to a trip north?"

"Of course," I answered without hesitation, and he stood up and retrieved his *Bradshaw*.

We retired early, and the next morning Mrs. Hudson sent us on our way to our waiting train at King's Cross Station with an early breakfast. Shortly after we boarded, the train pulled away on its northeastern trek. As was his custom, Holmes ignored the passing countryside and devoted his attention to a copy of *The Times*, whilst I read the latest *British Medical Journal*.

The train stopped as scheduled three times before pulling into the station at Darlington shortly after midday. We were met by a porter who collected our luggage and led us to the King's Hotel, and we were greeted there by the manager.

"Mr. Holmes, Doctor Watson," the burly man bellowed as he waved the porter upstairs with our luggage. "We've been expecting you. Your rooms have been prepared, and I have a message for you."

He handed us each a key and Holmes a small, plain envelope. The porter dutifully showed us to our rooms and I lingered behind in Holmes's as the porter left. Waiting until we were alone, Holmes opened the envelope and quickly scanned the letter within.

"We are invited to Lymington Hall at three o'clock," Holmes reported. "Once there, the Lady Lymington will answer any and all questions regarding our mission here. If you aren't too fatigued from the journey, I suggest we luncheon and then make our way to our appointment."

Our meal was decent fare and the pub's local patrons seemed absorbed in conversation over a recent football match between Darlington's team and the club from nearby Aukland Town. The game had been played in Darlington a few days earlier and settled by a late goal scored by Aukland's newest player, who was substituting for an injured Aukland man. A rematch was scheduled in Darlington in just two days' time.

After our meal we hired a cab to take us to our appointment, where we were shown in upon presenting ourselves at the door. Lady Lymington didn't keep us waiting overlong in the sitting room.

"Mr. Holmes," she addressed us as she swept into the room. "And you must be Dr. Watson. Thank you both for coming so far on such short notice. Please be seated."

"Lady Lymington," Holmes began. "Your letter provided precious little detail, save for the theft of a manuscript. Pray tell us more about it, why it's of enough value to steal, and how you came to be aware of the theft."

"Certainly, Mr. Holmes," she replied. "The manuscript was the handwritten original of *Sketches in Afghaunistan* by James Atkinson. Mr. Atkinson was born here in Darlington in 1780.

"When my father, Edward Pease, passed away six years ago," she continued, "his will provided for the establishment of a library here in Darlington, as well as directing that many books from his own personal library to be placed there. I oversee the library, and Atkinson's *Sketches* manuscript was among those included in the transfer from my father's collection."

"What is the monetary value of this manuscript?" Holmes asked.

"That is a most puzzling aspect of the crime, Mr. Holmes. I cannot imagine why anyone would steal it. I doubt it would fetch more than a few pounds outside of Durham County."

Holmes pursed his lips in thought. "What would make it of such great value within Durham County to be worth stealing?"

"I have been asking myself that very question since I discovered the theft. There is no other value other than it was written by a native son of Darlington. I cannot fathom why someone would want to steal it – much less substitute it with a forged copy."

"A forged copy?" I exclaimed even as Holmes arched an eyebrow in surprise.

"How can you be certain of forgery?" Holmes asked.

"The color of the book's cover is off slightly," she explained. "And the paper it was written on is newer than the original. To almost anyone else, I suppose the forgery would go unnoticed, but I saw that manuscript on display every day of my life whilst living at Pease Manor. It was one of my father's most prized possessions. I know it almost as well as I know my own hand."

"Is there anything in this manuscript of importance or local interest, aside from the birthplace of its author?" Holmes asked. "Perhaps a member of Atkinson's family wanted the manuscript returned?"

"No, nothing at all. The family gave its blessing for the manuscript to be displayed in the library, and none have shown the slightest interest in it since. In fact, the book is of so little financial value that I would have considered remaining quiet and letting the forgery stand. I doubt any other than myself would spot it. But my concern is this: We have many rare and much more valuable books in our collection. Should this affair come to light, we might lose those books. We might even have to close the library that my father so wanted to leave behind as his legacy."

"When did you discover the forgery?" Holmes asked. "When was the last time you recall seeing the original?"

185

"It was on display the day before the match against Aukland Town," she replied thoughtfully. "I discovered the forgery two days later."

"How many visitors came to the library those two days?"

"It seemed like the entire populace from Aukland was in Darlington the day of the match, and only a very few the day after. I suspect everyone in town passed through our doors at some point during the those two days, Mr. Holmes. One of them must have made the switch then, though how this was accomplished without anyone seeing it escapes me. We have two docents who work at the library. Those two ladies were exhausted by the time the Aukland people left town, but they certainly would have spotted someone stealing the manuscript."

"Makes for a rather large suspect pool, I'm afraid," Holmes remarked. "Would it be possible for me to examine the library tonight – after hours of course? I would also like to ask your docents a few questions, assuming they are aware of the theft."

"They are, Mr. Holmes, and I will arrange for both of them to be there tonight a few minutes after eight. I'll meet you there and let you inside. You'll forgive me for waiting until after the library closes so that curious eyes won't wonder at your presence."

"Of course," Holmes said, rising from his chair. "Watson and I will return to the King's Hotel until our appointment. Good day, Lady Lymington."

We took our leave of Lymington Hall and Holmes remained in silent thought the entire cab ride back to our hotel rooms.

"It is a most curious case, is it not?" Holmes finally broke his silence once we were in his room. "For a thief to go to so much trouble to cover his crime, one would assume there would be great value involved. Yet, the stolen item carries very little, if any, apparent value."

"Someone certainly placed enough value on it to go to the trouble of stealing it," I replied.

"Indeed. Finding the reason why it was stolen will be the key to discovering the identity of our thief. Whomever it is, he is quite clever."

"How so?"

"He picked a time when an extraordinary amount of people would be in town to commit the theft, taking advantage of a mass of confusion to help aid in the theft and replacement, as well as creating the cover of a nearly impossible number of suspects to eliminate should the theft be discovered."

"Where do you begin then?"

"Where we always begin, Watson," he answered with a quick smile. "Where the crime took place."

Uncertain as to how long we would be at the library that night, we dined at the hotel shortly before we were to leave for the library. As at the pub earlier, the conversation in the room was focused upon the recently concluded football match.

"I tell ye," one local opined to the room at large over his meal. "That new man Auckland put out on the pitch was a bloody ringer from London. I'll bet me mother's fine china on that."

"Yer off yer rocker, Horace," another patron scoffed. "Why would anyone tha' good waste 'is time up 'ere? I doubt anyone in Aukland has more'n an extra shilling to spare for necessities, much less payin' off a ringer. They beat us fair'n'square and there's no use cryin' about it. We'll see if that new rabbit of theirs can run as well now that our lads know about him in two days."

"If he has another game like the last," the first man growled. "That Edmund Walker lad had better keep right on runnin' all the way back to Aukland Town. But I still say there be something suspicious about 'im. He certainly didn't play like a lad in his first match, and I've never 'eard of no one by that name playing anywhere else in England. And if I 'aven't 'eard of a player anywhere in the Empire, then they ain't played anywhere of note before."

"My, they certainly seem worked up about that match here," I remarked.

"So it would seem," Holmes agreed with a faraway look before addressing the local football expert. "I beg your pardon, sir. This Edmund Walker – have you ever seen him before? On or off the pitch?"

"Nay, sir, And I travel to Aukland Town once every week. Why, I'd wager there isn't a person named Walker anywhere in the town!"

"Can you describe him?"

"A tall lad," the second man replied. "Surprisingly fast for his height, but as he's as skinny as a rail. I suppose he doesn't have much weight slowing him down. A sandy, mutton chop beard, and quite pale. Like he could stand in the sun all day and not darken a shade beyond alabaster."

"How very interesting," Holmes sat back with an enigmatic smile, and made no further comment as we finished our own meal.

We arrived at the Darlington Library a few minutes after eight that evening and Lady Lymington let us in, locking the doors behind us.

"Where would you like to begin, Mr. Holmes?"

"Let us begin with the forged manuscript, and then I would like to speak with your docents."

She led us to the small glass case which now held the forged manuscript. It rested upon a tall cherry-oak stand with the closed book under the glass cover. Holmes examined the exterior and the stand carefully.

"Can the glass be lifted easily?" he inquired, not seeing any hinges connecting the glass to the base.

"It can be lifted clear and the glass set aside," Lady Lymington reported. "But it isn't an easy operation to perform, nor can it be done swiftly, as the glass is quite heavy."

"Hmm," Holmes replied. "Meaning it was unlikely that one of your visitors could have done so without someone noticing and raising an alarm."

"That seems logical," she agreed.

Holmes lifted the cover, testing the weight of it, before setting it down upon the floor next to the stand. He began examining the manuscript, checking the front cover, several of the pages, and then the back cover and spine.

"Do you have any authentic examples of Atkinson's handwriting available, preferably from around the same time period?"

"We have some of his letters in our collection," she replied. "I'll go see if any are dated from when he wrote this."

Holmes continued examining the manuscript as we waited. Only a few minutes passed before she returned, offering a single document to Holmes, who carefully took it and set it beside the open manuscript. He spent several minutes comparing the letter to several of the pages before straightening up with a satisfied air. He handed Lady Lymington back the original letter, closed the manuscript, and replaced the glass.

"Now then," he said. "I believe it is time for me to speak with your docents."

"They are waiting for us in my office," she pointed the way. "Were you able to discover anything in your examination?"

"Oh, indeed," he assured. "You are quite correct that the manuscript is a forgery. It is a very good forgery, but a flawed one indeed. The paper is not contemporary with the time the original was written, which indicates the forger was not in contact with the original before making the copy. I suspect a printed copy of the book was located, along with a sample of the author's handwriting, to aid in the creation of the forgery. The same can be said of the cover. Someone likely described the cover to the forger, who did the best he or she could to reproduce it.

"It was a valiant attempt," Holmes continued as we walked toward the office. "In fact, in might have succeeded, had someone not intimate with the original been in a position to spot it as you did, Lady Lymington."

"Thank you, Mr. Holmes. Were you able to find any clues as to the identity of forger and the thief?"

"Not yet I fear," he replied. "There is still much data missing for me to do so. But I feel confident that the theft occurred after the celebrated football match and that the original manuscript could remain somewhere in Darlington."

"Really?" I exclaimed. "What leads you to that conclusion? I would think the thief would flee the area once his task was complete – unless you think the thief resides in Darlington."

"I believe the thief does in fact reside in Darlington," he said as we entered Lady Lymington's office. "But as for the task being completed? Let us say for now that I have my doubts as to that."

The two docents were waiting for us when we entered as promised. Both ladies, who each appeared to be in their late twenties, stood up to properly present themselves as soon as the door opened.

"This is Mrs. Olivia Lowe," Lady Lymington introduced the first docent, who offered a slight curtsey. "And this is Miss Virginia Covington. Ladies, this is Mr. Sherlock Holmes and Dr. John Watson. They are investigating the theft of the Atkinson manuscript. I expect you both to give them your fullest cooperation."

"Yes, mum," both docents replied quietly.

"Please be seated," Holmes instructed as he claimed his own seat. "I will try not to keep you too long. I expect you are both eager to return home for supper after a long day."

"I'm sure Mrs. Howard will keep something warm for both of us," Mrs. Lowe replied.

"Mrs. Howard?" Holmes inquired.

"We both board at Mrs. Howard's home, sir," Miss Covington answered. "We've had to stay late at the library from time to time, and she always has something set aside for us on those occasions."

"Does Mr. Lowe also board there?" Holmes asked, puzzled.

"My husband is out of the country on business," Mrs. Lowe explained. "We have a daughter of nearly two years of age. He felt more comfortable with me staying at Mrs. Howard's during his absence, and she enjoys watching little Katherine while I am at library."

"I see," Holmes nodded. "When did you both become aware of the theft?"

"When Lady Lymington brought it to our attention," Mrs. Lowe answered, and Miss Covington nodded in agreement.

"Had either of you noticed anyone paying a particular amount of attention to the manuscript, or inquiring about it in the days leading up to the theft?"

"Not that I saw," Mrs. Lowe responded as Miss Covington shook her head no.

189

"I understand there were an abnormally high amount of patrons at the library on the day of the big match. Were both of you present all day?"

"I began feeling unwell about an hour before closing," Mrs. Lowe reported. "By then most of the crowd had left, and there was only a handful of patrons remaining inside. I left a few minutes before closing."

"Oh? So you were the only person in the library when it closed?" Holmes asked Miss Covington.

"Lady Lymington was in her office, but I did lock up after I made sure that everyone had left. We left the library together about half-past the hour."

Holmes glanced at Lady Lymington who nodded confirmation.

"And you are quite certain that no one remained inside after you departed?"

"Quite certain, Mr. Holmes. We both walked the floors to be sure, as we do every evening."

"Very good," he replied. "I see no reason to detain either of you from your supper any further. Thank you. You have both been very helpful to my investigation."

The docents took their leave as Holmes rose and put on his coat.

"They didn't seem to provide any useful information," Lady Lymington observed.

"On the contrary," Holmes corrected. "They were quite informative. If you will excuse us, Lady Lymington, we will return to our hotel and turn in. I have an early start to the morrow, and Watson will check on a few items of interest here while I'm away at Aukland."

"Aukland?" I asked in surprise. "What do you hope to find there?"

"Data, my dear Watson, as always. Put your mind at ease Lady Lymington. I feel very strongly that by the time your library is flooded with patrons on the day of the next match, your stolen manuscript will be back in its rightful place."

Holmes would say no more about the case to me as we retired for the night. When I awoke at sunrise, I was greeted with a note from him with instructions to spend the day finding out all I could about the Darlington Football Club and the Northern League in which they played, as well as everything I could about the previous matches between Darlington and Aukland, and the particulars surrounding the upcoming match scheduled for the next day.

I spent an enjoyable day watching the Quakers, the nickname for the club, practice, and then chatting with the club's manager about the previous match, as well as the history between the clubs. The last-minute victory had been the first by Aukland over Darlington, accounting for the ferocity of the Darlington fans that something was amiss. That it was on a goal scored by a new man in his first match added to the suspicions, but it had been confirmed that an Edmund Walker was indeed a resident of Aukland, a nephew by marriage of a prominent Aukland family named Harrison, and so no further question could be raised in that matter.

I spent a few hours in the pubs, where the patrons remain convinced some foul deed had been done at Darlington's expense. Revenge would be theirs tomorrow afternoon, they assured me, and young Walker was certain to be a marked man upon the instant he stepped foot upon the pitch.

As informative as these conversations were in matters of football, they served me little purpose toward solving the crime that Holmes and I had come to investigate. The Atkinson family remained in the county, but no one seemed to hold any ill will toward them. Nor could I recover any animosity, or any interest of any kind, toward the late author, James Atkinson.

I was making my way back to the hotel when Holmes called out from behind me. I waited for him and noticed he carried a satisfied air about him.

"How was your excursion to Aukland?"

"Enlightening, very enlightening. I will tell you all about it over dinner. I'm quite famished."

I waited until after we had ordered our meals before filling him in on what I had learned.

"They aren't wrong about young Walker," Holmes remarked when I told him of the lingering suspicions of the new man.

"You mean he is a ringer?"

"After a fashion. There is an Edmund Walker who resides in Aukland, but he is a man of thirty with dark hair and clean shaven. That is not the description we were given of the Edmund Walker who scored the winning goal several days ago."

"No, it is not," I agreed. "But I fail to see how this is connected to the theft."

"Because the ultimate purpose of the substitution of the false Walker for the real one was not to win the match," Holmes explained. "Rather, it was to get the false Walker into Darlington on a day when the town would be filled with strangers. Thus, he would not stand out."

"You believe this false Walker is the thief then?"

"The actual thief?" Holmes replied. "No. But I have no doubt that he is involved. By tonight, we'll know who the actual thief is, and then we'll find out why this manuscript was so valuable."

"Tonight?" I was startled by the claim. "If the false Walker isn't in town, how to you plan to discover the motive for the crime?"

"Because we're going to flush out our thief later tonight. If my suspicions are correct, we'll catch her red-handed with the manuscript in her possession."

"Her?" I exclaimed

"Indeed. I suspect one of the docents is in fact the thief. Tonight, we will discover which one it is."

Our meals arrived and Holmes attacked his with great fervor. It was past nine o'clock by the time we finished. Holmes led us out of the hotel and walked briskly toward a residential area.

"Where are we going?"

"To the boarding house of Mrs. Howard, where we'll meet with Constable Barnes. He's arranging a little diversion that will flush out our thief. Ah, here we are, and there is the constable."

The officer hurried over upon spotting Holmes.

"Everything is set as you ordered, sir" Barnes reported. "I must say, we haven't had an excitement like this in all my years here."

"No doubt," Holmes remarked dryly. "How much longer until we begin?"

"Mrs. Howard runs a tight ship, sir. Lights out by ten. As soon as the last light is doused, my men will light the piles of oil-soaked rags about the house. It shouldn't take long for the smoke to work its way inside and I'll start shouting fire as loud as I can. I imagine everyone in that house will be outside in a shot."

"And carrying those things most precious to them when they do," Holmes replied, then whispered as an aside to me. "At least so I hope. Otherwise this little experiment will prove most embarrassing."

The last light in the house went out. A few minutes later Barnes and his two men lit several small bundles of rags, oily smoke billowing upward and into open windows.

"Fire!" Barnes bellowed as he charged to the front door and began hammering it with his fists. "Fire! Everyone out!"

The occupants inside wasted little time exiting. Mrs. Lowe appeared, clutching her young daughter and carrying nothing else. Miss Covington was the last to exit, and all that she carried was a large jewelry box. The constable collected the shaken occupants together as his men quickly doused the small fires.

"We have caught our thief, Watson," Holmes exclaimed as he walked toward the huddled roomers. "Ladies and gentlemen, it is now safe for all of you to return to your rooms – all excepting you, Miss Covington. That is a lovely box you have there."

"It was my grandmother's," she replied, her voice shaking and her eyes wide. "I use it to keep my valuables in."

"Including the Atkinson manuscript that you stole from the library? That box is the perfect size to hold the missing manuscript, is it not?"

The young woman's eyes went even wider, darting back and forth. Her mouth opened and closed, but she failed to utter a single word of protest. Holmes reached out and took hold of the box. At first she resisted, but eventually she yielded to the inevitable and turned loose her grip upon it.

Holmes studied the bottom of the box for a moment and then manipulated something at each of the corners. The bottom sprang open and Holmes gently slid out the missing manuscript. The young woman merely hung her head, and tears began trickling down her cheeks.

"Mr. Holmes," the constable stepped in. "The telegram I received from the Home Secretary stated I was to give you my fullest cooperation. But if there has been a theft in my jurisdiction . . . ."

"For reasons I am not at liberty to divulge, Constable, any decision to file charges in this matter will be made at a later time. For now, I must ask you not to divulge anything you've seen or heard here tonight."

"That is most irregular, sir, but I suppose the Home Secretary knows what he is doing."

"Thank you, Constable."

"What is to become of me?" Miss Covington asked quietly.

"First, you will accompany us to the Library, where Lady Lymington is waiting for us to report on the outcome of our trap," Holmes replied. "Once there, you will make a full confession as to why you stole this manuscript and to whom you were going to deliver it."

She merely shook her head, tears streaking down her cheeks.

"His name is Edward *Waller*, isn't it?"

She declined to answer, but her head dropped even further, all but confirming his accusation.

"Come along now," Holmes said, not unkindly. "We will sort out the rest of this affair after we've returned this manuscript to its rightful place."

She offered no further protest or explanation as we journeyed back to the library. Fortunately, the young woman hadn't yet undressed for bed, so she was spared the embarrassment of being escorted among the streets of Darlington in her nightgown and robe.

We were admitted into the library by Lady Lymington, who joyfully took possession of the manuscript Holmes offered her.

"Yes, this is the original manuscript," she confirmed after a quick examination before turning her ire upon her docent. "How could you, Virginia? How could you do such a thing?"

The lady clutched the manuscript to her bosom, as if she feared her subordinate would attempt to steal it once again.

193

"If you are to have any hope for clemency, my dear," I prodded. "A full confession is possibly your only chance."

"We already know of your involvement and the name of your accomplice," Holmes added. "I assume he brought you the forgery the day of the match and you made the switch later that night, before closing the library. The members of the Aukland team returned home immediately after the match, so there was no time to deliver the stolen manuscript. That was to be accomplished tomorrow, when the Aukland team returns for the rematch and what in all likelihood would be the false Walker's final game in Aukland colors.

"As we have established the real name of your accomplice as Edward *Waller*," Holmes continued. "a known petty criminal in London who specializes in matters of forgery and who has some athletic talent. All that remains to be discovered is why Waller wanted the manuscript and how he came to recruit you into the theft."

"I met him a month ago here in Darlington," she finally confessed. "He said he knew that I worked at the library and wanted me to help him. The manuscript, he said, held an important secret for a family he knew in Auckland. They knew there was no possibility of getting the manuscript from the library legally, so they asked him to help them get it.

"He said they had a copy of the manuscript to replace with the original," she continued. "No one would ever know the switch had occurred. The family was willing to pay him handsomely for his help in recovering it. He said it was a lot of money, and he promised to take me away from here with him when he left. That manuscript was my ticket out of here."

"Which is why you grabbed the jewelry box that you'd concealed it in when you thought the house was on fire," Holmes observed. "Just like Mrs. Lowe collected the only thing within those walls that mattered to her – her child."

"Yes."

"What do you know of this family that your lover was helping? Why did they need the original so badly when they already had a copy?"

"That I do not know, Mr. Holmes, I swear. Only Eddie knows that."

"When and where were you to meet to hand him the original?"

"I was to hire a cab and wait for the end of the match," she replied. "He would join me and we would return to Aukland together with the manuscript. I was packing my bags when the fire started tonight."

"Watson, if you would be so kind and to keep close watch on Miss Covington while I examine the original manuscript?"

I stood guard as Holmes regained possession of the manuscript and carefully pored over it from cover to cover. He paused for a long time over the back binding, then looked up at Lady Lymington.

"If I am wrong, I will profusely apologize," he said before withdrawing a small, slim knife from his pocket and carefully separated the paper covering the inside of the back cover.

"Mr. Holmes, whatever are you doing?" Lady Lymington exclaimed sharply.

Holmes said nothing as he completed a pass of his knife from one end to the other. He then slipped a finger into the gap and withdrew it and another sheet of paper that had been concealed within.

"What on earth is that?" she asked as Holmes read the document.

"When your father's estate was settled," Holmes asked. "Was there any mention of property owned by him in Aukland?"

"Why, no," she answered in surprise. "As far as I know, he did no business anywhere near there in his entire life."

"Then it is my happy duty to inform you," Holmes replied as he handed her the document. "That your father's estate is the owner of five-hundred acres of land just outside of Aukland. This is a deed to said land, signed over to your father by one Bernard Harrison against a loan of one-thousand pounds in 1872.

"That's the same Bernard Harrison, I suspect, that owns the Auckland Club team that is coming to Darlington tomorrow." Holmes continued. "For some unknown reason, Mr. Harrison was in need of financial aid and offered the land as collateral to your father to secure the loan. Obviously, the loan was never repaid. Since the matter never came up in the settling of the estate, Harrison must have felt he was in the clear. However, he couldn't risk this document ever being discovered and made public."

"But how could he know where to find it?" I asked.

"That is something we will have to discover, should we confront Mr. Harrison," Holmes replied.

"Should? Why wouldn't we?"

"Because there is the matter of discretion to consider," Holmes answered looking at Lady Lymington. "Should young Waller be arrested and Harrison confronted, the theft from the library would become public knowledge. Is this what you want?"

"No, Mr. Holmes, it most certainly is not."

"Then I suggest a note to Mr. Harrison explaining that you are in possession of the document and are aware of his attempts to obtain it, after you have filed your claim upon the land in question. I will deliver it upon his arrival tomorrow. That should put an end to that aspect of this affair."

"As for young Waller," Holmes continued. "I will also meet him tomorrow and suggest that he take the very next train out of town, without the manuscript or Miss Covington, and never return to Durham County. I am sure the people of Darlington will not be unhappy to see Aukland missing that particular man in tomorrow's match."

"And what's to become of me, Mr. Holmes?" Miss Covington asked, her voice a hoarse whisper.

"That is entirely up to Lady Lymington," Holmes answered.

Lady Lymington looked at her docent for a very long time in silence. She turned her back on her, walked to her desk and withdrew a chequebook. She scratched out an amount and signed it then walked over and gave it to her docent.

"You have betrayed my trust," the Lady began, "and for a very foolish reason. I cannot trust you ever again, but I will not see you destroyed by one lapse of judgment. You will take this and take your leave of this County. You may accompany your lover if you wish or go in another direction. But after tonight, I do not ever want to lay eyes upon you again."

The young woman nodded, took the cheque in trembling hands, and mumbled her thanks. Then she turned and fled the library before the lady changed her mind.

"Are you quite certain, my Lady," I asked. "It seems no one is to be punished for this crime."

"It is just, Doctor," she replied. "Harrison will lose the land that would never have been lost had he not tried to steal the manuscript. This Walker or Waller or whatever his name really is will meet his justice elsewhere. As for her, she will live with the shame of what she has done for the rest of her life.

"In the meantime," she continued. "The manuscript is safe and will be restored to its rightful place, and the library will remain open with no one the wiser. Thank you Mr. Holmes and you as well, Doctor."

"Most kind, my lady," Holmes said with a slight bow. "May I make one request?"

"Name it, Mr. Holmes."

"May I take the forged copy back to London with me?"

"I was planning on burning it," she replied with a slight laugh. "But by all means, take it away with you."

Holmes collected his prize and we took our leave. The next morning, Holmes confronted the false Walker as promised, who promptly boarded a waiting train for Scotland. Months later we received word that he'd been arrested in Glasgow and sentenced to prison for ten years. We never saw nor heard from Miss Covington ever again.

Harrison provided confirmation of Holmes's theory when we delivered Lady Lymington's note to him as he stepped off the train. He had in fact taken a loan from Pease, using the land as collateral, and never repaid the loan.

"When Pease died and the document was never raised in probating his estate, I was relieved," Harrison confessed. "But in time I began to worry what would happen if it were to be discovered. It clearly hadn't been among his papers, and I made several trips to the library here to search those books of his in case he'd placed it within one of those volumes.

"I had almost given up on it entirely until I passed that case with the Atkinson manuscript," Harrison continued. "Pease had been replacing the old binding on it on the day I signed over that land to him. Suddenly, I knew exactly where that document was. I just didn't know how to obtain it without drawing attention to it.

"An associate of mine in London spoke of a young man named Waller who was quite handy in such matters," Harrison said. "Since he had some talent at football and I owned the club, it seemed having him present himself as my wife's nephew – who never appears in public in Aukland – was the perfect way to get that manuscript out of the library and save my land."

"And it very nearly worked," Holmes replied. "However, it has in fact failed. You are fortunate not to face official charges for your crime. While no further action will be taken against you, Mr. Harrison, you must not make any further attempts to recover that document, save the paying off of the original loan with suitable interest. Assuming Lady Lymington should be inclined to accept such a payment after this affair."

The color drained from Harrison's face as he realized the depth of his error. He slowly walked away, defeated. Holmes and I departed Darlington for London later that day.

A few months later, Holmes showed me a press clipping from Durham County sent to him by the Lady Lymington. One Bernard Harrison paid Lady Lymington the sum of ten-thousand pounds in exchange for a parcel of five-hundred acres of land near Aukland, owned by her father's estate.

As for that vaunted rematch between Durham and Aukland that day after Holmes recovered the manuscript? Without young Edmund Walker, who had reportedly severely sprained his ankle earlier that morning and was unable to play, Aukland was overwhelmed on the pitch by the Darlington Quakers by a score of five-nil.

As I look back upon this affair all these months later, I realize that justice was very much served that night in the Darlington Library, and all thanks to my good friend, Mr. Sherlock Holmes, solving one crime whilst investigating another when "an unmarried woman grabbed her jewel-box".

"It was all-important. When a woman thinks that her house is on fire, her instinct is at once to rush to the thing which she values most. It is a perfectly overpowering impulse, and I have more than once taken advantage of it. In the case of the Darlington substitution scandal it was of use to me, and also in the Arnsworth Castle business. A married woman grabs at her baby; an unmarried one reaches for her jewel-box."

– Sherlock Holmes
"A Scandal in Bohemia"

The Whole Story
Concerning the Politician,
the Lighthouse, and
the Trained Cormorant
by Derrick Belanger

Readers: As you are aware, Sherlock Holmes often complains of my retelling of his adventures. He believes that my adding-in of florid details changes the tone of the actual case and makes what should be a cold and scientific account into more of a thrilling narrative. With this particular tale, however, I have Holmes's blessing to make significant changes to the events which transpired.

This story is a somewhat fictionalized account of a case earlier in the career of Mr. Sherlock Holmes. While Holmes would say that all of my accounts of his casebook are somewhat fictionalized, this story is even more so, for Holmes and I swore we would keep the truth behind this memoir hidden from public knowledge. We would reveal nothing unless one particular individual violated a certain agreement. If that occurred then we would be free to reveal the whole truth. Said individual has not violated said agreement just yet, but there are rumors that he has stepped up to the line that agreed not to cross and his foot is currently lifted over the other side, dangling inches from the ground. If said foot touches down, rest assured a very different version of this story will be published.

To said individual: You have been warned. Do not take the warning lightly.

The story begins in late summer of 1886 when Holmes and I were visiting the northern coastal town of Port. It is small, appearing on few maps, but it contains an exceptional private library where Holmes wanted to spend some time conducting research on a shadowy figure purported to have assisted Charlemagne.

"He is a difficult figure to uncover," Holmes explained to me. "Like me, he helped untangle webs but saw no need to take any credit for his work. If not for this man, Charlemagne might never have united Europe. The Lombards would have continued to rule Italy's northern region for many decades and the Muslims might still have a grip in Spain. Yet I cannot find much about this man. How I wish that he had a Boswell such as you to tell his story."

The Jacoby Library in Port had an extensive collection of writings about Charlegmagne, as well as coins, armor, and other pieces from the time period. Holmes had been granted permission to study the work, and so we took a brief sojourn away from London. I was pleased, as the cases on which Holmes was working in London had been rather dull and simple. He was more restless and moody, and I worried that he would go into one of his dark spells if something didn't stimulate his brain soon. I was happy when he told me of the library and how it contained information that he'd always wanted to study. This elusive consultant to Charlemagne was the perfect distraction to occupy my friend's mind until a more intriguing case was brought to his attention.

One fine day, we were walking along the pier when we saw a group of cheering children surrounding a fisherman who was pointing to something standing on the ground before him. Holmes and I made our way over to the group to see what the excitement was all about. The young boys and girls were jumping jubilantly and calling out, "More!", "Bravo!", and "Send Cora out again!"

Holmes asked a dainty boy whose trousers would surely have slipped off him if it weren't for the red suspenders holding them up what all the excitement was. "It's Mr. Paterson and Cora. Cora's a cormorant who can catch any fish in the sea. She's magnificent!"

"Magnificent, eh?" Holmes asked.

The boy looked like he might burst if he tried to contain his jubilation. "Stupendous! She can catch anything. Just watch, he'll send her into the water, and she'll come back with a huge fish – maybe even a sturgeon."

Holmes thanked the lad and we both smiled at his exuberance. "Shall we?" Holmes asked, motioning for me to move up through the crowd so that we could see the bird which was causing so much joy.

When we moved to the front, we saw a soap box with a slick, black feathered bird, its almost bat-shaped wings outstretched in a way made it look like some of the prehistoric flying lizards from the past. Its head bobbed up and down at the children as though it were inspecting an army, and this made them clap and call out even louder. Standing next to the bird was a swarthy, red-haired Scotsman with a curled mustache. He wore thick cotton trousers, a brown plaid shirt, and a dumpy oilskin hat to stay warm after being out on the water all day.

Next to the man was a large net filled with mackerel, flounder, and whiting.

"Well, lads, let's have one of the ladies take a turn, shall we?" the man asked cheerily.

Some of the boys pouted and let out an "Aww!" while the girls squealed with delight.

Paterson asked, "What'll it be? Saithe or mackerel?" Both fish names were shouted by different girls, but saithe won out.

The Scotsman turned to his bird, held up three fingers in front of the cormorant, and said, "Get me a saithe, Cora." The bird nodded its head in approval, flapped its wings, and flew up over the ocean. We watch it soar for a moment before diving down below the waves.

Cora came up and dived into the water several times, moving almost like an eel, and then suddenly she took to the sky, made a loop above our heads, and landed back down on her soapbox. She nodded, opened her mouth, and spit out a nice sized saithe which flopped around on the boardwalk. The children erupted in applause and cheers, and I admit I found myself joining them. Holmes looked on – the careful observer, learning the tricks of cormorant fishing.

One young freckle-faced girl in pigtails standing beside me called out, "How about a ring, Mr. Paterson?"

Paterson chuckled like Father Christmas at the request. "Now, now, Miss Marley. You know I can't guarantee that Cora will find a sparkly."

"But she has for the last three days," said one of the lads, followed by shouts of "Yes!", "She can do it!", and "Please try!" from the others.

"All right, all right," Paterson assured them. He turned to Cora, and put his pointer fingers and thumbs together to make a diamond shape with his hands. He told the bird, "Sparkly!"

Cora gave three nods of her head and then took to the air. It did not take long for the sea bird to dive into the water and come back with a gold ring held in her beak. Paterson took the ring from the bird's mouth, held it up to the light for a moment, and then handed it over to the girl who boisterously thanked him.

"All right, now. My net is full, and I'm done for the day." The children complained and asked for more, but Paterson wouldn't hear of it. "Cora and I need a rest, but we'll be back tomorrow." The children cheered and danced around the man and his bird before starting off in different directions.

I walked up to the man and told him how impressed I was with his trained cormorant. "Thank you, sir," he said to me in a strong brogue. "I've been a cormorant fisherman for many years now, and have had a number of birds, but Cora's special. She's the smartest of the lot. Every other one I've owned had to wear a snare around the throat to prevent it from swallowing fish. It didn't hurt the birds, but if I hadn't, they would have eaten all of the fish. Not my Cora, though. She'll eat her fill and still come up and provide me with my day's catch. Truly remarkable creature."

I asked a question about how he'd trained her, and Paterson explained his methods – how the combination of the command word and the symbol

201

he made with his hands worked to direct Cora to get the specific catch that he was requesting. His answer was polite, but I could tell he was tired after working all morning, and he really did want to go back to his home and rest. He said his goodbye and started walking away with his bird and his catch, but his attention was drawn behind me, and he asked me, "What's your friend up to?"

I turned to see Holmes standing with the girl who had been given the ring found by Cora. Holmes was inspecting the piece, and then he gave it back to the girl and sent her on her way.

There was an energy in Holmes, as though the ring acted as the lightning strike awakening Shelley's modern Prometheus. Gone was the dull distance that had started overtaking him. His eyes were sharp, maybe even a touch wild.

"Tell me," Holmes said to Paterson, "how many of those rings have you found?"

"There's no money in it," Paterson responded. "They may have a touch of gold in them, but they're cheap, probably worth no more than a farthing."

"I'm sure," Holmes agreed with the man. "But have you always found those rings?"

"No, no. Just this week. Cora came up with one in her bill. I checked it over and found it was a crude ring, probably made for a poor man to show to a girl he is sweet on, but nothing of value. Then, Cora found a couple more, and I started handing them out to the children. The rings may not be worth much, but the delight it brings to the young ones is priceless."

Holmes nodded his head and then asked. "Could you have Cora get me one of the rings?" Before Paterson could object, Holmes added, "There's tuppence in it for you. Get Cora a treat for her work."

"Keep your money, Mister – "

" – Holmes," he replied. "And this is Dr. Watson. We are on a brief sojourn, visiting from London."

"I see," Paterson sighed. I could see any suspicion he had as to why Holmes might want the ring evaporated. He saw Holmes as a city tourist wanting a souvenir from our travels.

Paterson put down the soapbox and had Cora jump back on. He made the diamond symbol and said "Sparkly." Cora nodded her head three times, spread her wings, and took to the air.

"Now I can't guarantee she'll come back with a ring," Paterson warned Holmes so as not to get his hopes up. However, in a few moments, the bird returned with a ring in its bill.

"There you are," Paterson said to Holmes as he gave the ring over to him. "There must be a whole crate of those rings down there. Now gentlemen, if you'll excuse me, I need to get my catch home and cleaned up. There's still plenty of work ahead for me today."

Holmes thanked the man and we said our goodbyes. I watched him wander away with his catch slung over his shoulder, his hands carrying the soapbox, and Cora waddling beside him.

"What a fascinating creature," I said to Holmes.

He wryly asked, "The bird or the man?"

"The bird, of course, though Mr. Paterson is a fine fellow, particularly for entertaining the local children. It was also rather nice to have Cora fetch you that ring."

"Mmm, it was. Have a look at it, Watson, and tell me what you think."

Holmes handed me what I thought at first was a nondescript gold band. "Nothing too interesting," I told him. I pressed hard and could tell the ring was of a cheap material. "The ring has a green hue on the interior, showing its poor composition. It looks to have some actual gold in it, but certainly not pure."

"Indeed," he agreed. "What else?"

"Well . . . wait, what's this?" I looked closely and noted a carving on the side of the ring. It looked to be an emblem of sorts. There was a striped shield with two birds on its side. "Why, there's a shield with cormorants on the side."

Holmes chuckled at this. "I believe you're too enamored with Cora, Watson. Those are not cormorants, but ravens."

"What an odd thing to put on a cheap ring," I said. "Is it for a theatrical performance?"

"Very good. But, no, a theatre may have a couple of copies of this ring, but there is no reason for them to have a half-dozen or more."

"Well, I'm stumped. I don't know what this coat-of-arms means, and so I can't say anymore. I would need to know what that symbol stands for. Perhaps it's of some local group similar to a Masonic Lodge." I stopped there, knowing I had crossed into speculation.

"Excellent, my friend," Holmes agreed. "More research is necessary before drawing any conclusions. However, I do know the meaning of the symbol."

I was surprised that Holmes hadn't revealed this to me and told him so.

"Ah, I was curious to see what information you could glean without any help from me. You did quite well, I must say. Perhaps in another few years, the Yard will be coming to you for advice."

I must have blushed slightly at such a statement, but then I noticed the look on Holmes's face and saw that he was having a little joke at my expense. "What does the symbol mean?" I grumbled.

"It is the fourteenth century coat of arms for the Kingdom of Sicily under the House of Aragon. The birds you see on the side are ravens and the stripes, if accurate, would be colored red and gold."

"Why would someone make rings with that symbol on it?"

"Why indeed?"

"I assume we will need to wait until our return to Baker Street before finding out more."

"Nonsense. There is an excellent research library here. Come. We shall make our way to the Jacoby Library."

I expected the Library to be a large private collection as part of a large manor house. I did not expect to find a two-story building the size of a small museum, situated about a mile inland from the coast. The brick structure, hidden away below billowing trees and thick strands of ivy, almost looked like it belonged on the campus of Cambridge University. Yet the building was missing those fine fixtures which would make it look distinguished. There were no fountains, no Grecian statues, no carved marble lions between the entryways. This building was designed to look respectable, but not garish in any way. The library was meant to remain private. I guessed that few in the town knew of its existence.

When we knocked on the door, it was a few minutes before it was answered. A stern-looking elderly man opened the top half of a two-piece locking door, made so that he could check on visitors but prevent them from entering the establishment. He had time-worn scuffed spectacles on his beak of a nose. His creased blue eyes stared at me from under his bushy white eyebrows, and his lips reached outward in a sour pucker. "Appointment," the man declared. I wasn't sure if he was asking if I had an appointment or telling me that I needed one.

"Mr. Barnes," Holmes said to the fellow.

Barne's eyes shifted over to Holmes and when he saw Holmes, recognition appeared on his face, though his rotten expression did not change. "I thought you were through in your endeavors, Mr. Holmes."

"As did I, Mr. Barnes, but alas, a different matter has been brought to my attention, and I must insist on seeing Mr. Winter."

Barnes scoffed. "You know the rules, Mr. Holmes. An appointment must be made at least three days in advance of being allowed in to see the collection."

"I can assure you Mr. Barnes that this is a matter of urgency. I believe Mr. Winter would understand my need to interrupt his work."

Barnes's eyes shifted between Holmes and me for a moment. I could see him considering the request and trying to decide whether anything was worth breaking the rules of the establishment. Finally, he reached a decision. "This is highly unusual, Mr. Holmes, and . . . ."

I was waiting for the librarian to finish his sentence then I realized he was waiting for me to provide my name. "Dr. Watson," I provided.

"Doctor," Barnes said and for the first time I detected him to show pleasantness. "In what field?"

"Why, I'm a medical doctor."

Barnes practically sneered at me. "Oh, *that* kind of doctor," he said. "Wait here, and I shall see if Mr. Winter can spare a moment or two for you, Mr. Holmes and *Doctor*."

"Whatever was that about?" I asked Holmes while we waited.

"Librarians tend to be planets orbiting their specialized field of study. Had you been a historian or anthropologist, we probably would have been invited inside immediately."

I wondered if I should feel insulted. Then, I thought of who was doing the insulting and decided that it really didn't matter to me. I had survived the worst situations in Afghanistan. I could tolerate this librarian's doctoral caste system.

Soon the door opened again, and Mr. Barnes was joined by another ancient fellow whom I assumed was Mr. Winter. He had large circular glasses, a curled nose, and thin lips. If he looked any more like an owl, I believe that he would have hooted.

Echoing Mr. Barnes, Mr. Winter greeted us not with an introduction but simply, "This is most irregular. No appointment, and you requested to see me."

"I did, Mr. Winter. I need to show you something."

"All right, go on then," he said, his voice squeaking a little, like a bicycle needing to be oiled.

Holmes took the ring from his pocket and showed it to the librarians. They both squinted slightly and then suddenly there was chaos as Winter's arms flailed and he shouted. "Impossible! How did you . . . where?"

"Would you believe from the bill of a cormorant?" Holmes answered. "And there are at least six others like it."

"Six!" Winter flung the bottom half of the door open, grabbed Holmes by the arm, and pulled him into the library, almost knocking over Mr. Barnes in the process.

I followed, and soon we were all four sitting around a work table while Mr. Winter used a magnifying glass to inspect the ring. "You say that it was found in the water by the boardwalk?" Winter enquired.

"Yes, but off the shore. The trained cormorant is the one who is retrieving the rings. I'm sure there are even more there, and if you'd like, you could join us tomorrow, and Mr. Paterson could have Cora fetch you one." Holmes had given the two librarians a brief explanation of how the ring came into our possession. Then he added, "I'm assuming that you have a similar authentic piece in your collection."

"Not just similar. Identical," squeaked Winter excitedly. "It is uncanny how close the two pieces are, and yet, I can't fathom how a copy of the ring could have been obtained. Very few people know about the piece. It's on loan from the Spanish Royal Family."

"Is it still in your collection?" Holmes asked. "I hate to suggest it, but could someone have swapped the real ring for one of these forgeries?"

Winter motioned his head, and Barnes got up from the table. He excused himself and returned five minutes later with the original ring from the collection. Winter inspected it carefully to ensure it was authentic. "This is the original ring. Notice it doesn't tarnish, and there are a few scratches at the base which occurred over time and are missing from the imitation."

Holmes looked rather disappointed when this information was revealed. "Tell me, what security do you have for this building?"

"We have a system of locks to keep out any intruders."

"I see. And are there any other employees besides you two?"

"There's Miss Odger who cleans the library once each week, but Mr. Barnes and I are here when she works. She's never allowed in the vault with our most precious pieces."

"Does anyone else have access?"

"Only our visitors."

"May I see your guestbook?"

Winter looked horrified at the suggestion. "Certainly not. That is confidential. Besides, no one has asked for or been granted access to the vault containing the Sicilian ring."

"Thank you. I believe that will be all."

"Should we contact the police?" Winter asked meekly.

"I see no point in doing so. No crime has been committed – at least none that we know about. No law says someone can't make a low-quality, imitation ring."

"What should I do, then?" the librarian asked, practically begging for an answer.

"Make sure all of your locks are fastened. I shall be in touch with you tomorrow afternoon with more information. Until then, good day."

After we left the library, Holmes sent me to fetch some dinner and meet him at the rooms we were renting. "Do you really think that you'll have this puzzled out by tomorrow?" I asked when we were back, sitting at our dinner table and eating Cod pie.

206

"I do. This is a small community, with limited possibilities as to the meaning behind the copies of the rings." Holmes answered as he reached for my glass and refilled it with a fine Merlot we were sharing.

"Thank you. Do you have any leads at all?"

"I know that someone is breaking into the library and making copies of several pieces in the vault. When you left, I went around to a side window of the place. The locks are in excellent shape, and I noted no signs of a break-in. Most likely that means either an employee or a visitor to the library is responsible for making a copy of the ring."

"So someone connected to the library is making shoddy copies of one of their pieces of jewelry. I don't understand why. Could it just be someone who wants a copy for his or her own collection? Show it off to friends but not let them look too closely at the poor copy?"

"I don't have the answers quite yet, but I shall soon, and the perpetrator or an associate will come visit us tomorrow morning."

"The thief will come here?"

"Not a thief. Remember, they haven't stolen anything as of yet, but yes, they shall come here. I've placed an advertisement in the local newspaper saying that we've found a lost ring with the description of the insignia. I made it sound as if I believed it to be a family heirloom. Whomever made the ring will want that copy back. I'm certain that the loss of the duplicate rings was an accident. Whatever their purpose, we shall have a better understanding soon enough."

Holmes was correct in his assertion, for the next morning, after I awakened and dressed, I came in to find him in the sitting room in his lounge chair, smoking his clay pipe, and looking out at the beach through our bay window. Like our rooms in Baker Street, we were on the first floor, overlooking the entryway.

"Are you going to wait by the window all morning?" I asked after a yawn and a stretch.

"No need, for he has already arrived."

I went to the window and looked out as Holmes pointed to a large, fair-haired man, puffing away at a cigarette and pacing back and forth in a small little line. I noted the remains of several cigarettes at his feet.

"How long has he been there?" I inquired.

"For half-of-an-hour. He must have come soon after reading the paper. He is troubled, and he's trying to decide his best course of action. Should he approach us with some concocted story, or should he wait for us to leave our abode and try to steal the ring while we are away? He's nervous, and not very good at this. What, ho! Look Watson – he has decided not to do either. He is leaving. We shall follow."

"Amateur" would be a polite way to describe our target, for the man did nothing to hide his tracks and led us straight to a boat repair shop on one of the south piers. He knocked at the door and was met by a large bull of a man. His dark, wild curly beard and tufts of unkempt hair made him resemble the Minotaur from Greek mythology.

Holmes and I stayed on the boardwalk and paused, pretending to look out over the ocean. The gruff man let in our fair-haired prey and closed the door behind him. So poor were these two in their planning that they didn't bother to close the windows to the shop, and Holmes and I easily approached one unseen and, crouching down, listened to their conversation.

The first part of the conversation came from the man whom we had followed. He said, "I tell you it should be easy enough. They'll leave at some point this afternoon. You can go inside and take the ring, or you can go in uniform while they're home and say that the piece has been reported stolen. There's no reason why they'd be suspicious, and the chief doesn't even need to know about it."

"It had better be easy. When his Lordship sees the paper – " Here Holmes and I exchanged startled looks. A Lord was involved in this unusual case? " – he'll have both our heads on pikes."

"I wasn't the one who lost the trunk. That was you!" the fair-haired man snapped at his burly partner. "Why I let you use my boat, I'll never know, you clumsy oaf!"

"Clumsy, eh!" We heard a brief struggle followed by the brutish man snarling. "If you ever call me an oaf again, I'll wrap you in irons and toss you into the sea, understand? I'm the one who got us into the library. I'll be the one getting us back in tonight. We wouldn't have the jewelry if it wasn't for me!"

There was a choking noise, and I assumed that it was the blonde man gasping a yes, and then the struggle was over. "All right," the blonde gasped. "I was upset is all, and I lost my temper. Remember, we are almost through. We'll smash a few things tonight and then we can wash our hands of it. For now, just get the ring back while I take the next load. They're at home now. Get dressed and head over. Your shift doesn't start for another hour. You have plenty of time."

The brutish man grumbled at his friend's reasoning, but he agreed. Holmes and I stepped away and went back to the pavement.

"Watson, I shall go and wait for the oaf to come for the ring. I need you to keep watch and let me know where that boat goes. It's imperative that you find out where it docks."

I told Holmes I would. I knew of a place nearby to rent a rowboat and fishing pole. No one would suspect me if I was casting a line out on the water. I just had to get out to sea ahead of my target. Fortunately, it was a slow day on the docks and by paying an extra shilling for expediency, I was able to have my boat, line, and lure in no time at all. I was even able to make my way out some distance before I saw the fair-haired man rowing out from his dock. He was faster than me, but it didn't matter. I saw that he was rowing out to the lighthouse not too far out from the shoreline.

The lighthouse was on a short, jagged peninsula connected to the mainland. While it would be possible to get a wagon across to it, using the boats to transport the counterfeit jewelry was a much easier and more direct way from there to the town.

I rowed as close as I could to the rocky shore before anchoring and casting out a line. It was a shorter lighthouse, three stories in height, connected to a small building for the keeper's quarters. As I sat facing it, I could make out three distinct figures unloading several crates. Then the three men went into the lighthouse and all was quiet on the shore. I wrestled with my curiosity and internally debated about whether to go ashore and try to catch a glimpse of what was going on inside, but I knew that it was too risky. Even if I gave them an excuse, such as I wanted to try fishing from there, the men could be dangerous, and I could find myself at the bottom of the sea. My mission was to find out where the boat had gone, and I'd accomplished it. I decided to spend a little more time out on the water. I didn't want to immediately return the boat, as that could arouse suspicion. I took time to enjoy fishing and even got a few bites on my line. I realized it would be much easier to fish if I had a bird like Cora.

I thought fondly of that talented feathered friend and imagined her getting into all sorts of mischief – taking the keys to a seafood restaurant out of the chef's pocket, retrieving lost treasure hidden away in a cave, finding a lost needle in a haystack. My mind thought of how I might be able to use Cora in a series of books, especially if I decided to expand my writing beyond my notes on the cases of Sherlock Holmes.

My mind was snapped out of my daydreaming when I saw movement again on the lighthouse shore. Two men were carrying much smaller boxes out to the row boat. I watched them load it with several of them before dragging the boat back out onto the water.

I followed my quarry back to shore and watched as he tied the boat to the dock next to the repair shop and then went back inside. I waited for a quarter-of-an-hour before I saw him exit the premises and walk away toward town. I couldn't believe that this man was so nonchalant with the crates. He simply left them under a tarp in his boat where anyone might take them. While it was dangerous to consider landing my boat and exploring the lighthouse shore, there was nothing dangerous about inspecting the cargo he'd left alone. I decided to have a look, and I thought that I'd have much to report back to Holmes when we rendezvoused at our rental.

"You have done exceptionally well, Watson," Holmes told me. We were sipping tea and eating scones for our elevenses. I had explained all to Holmes about what I'd witnessed, and I showed him a handful of different pieces of jewelry I had taken from one of the boxes. I had rifled through them, and they all contained the same items. One was an exquisite copy of the Sicilian ring. Another was a gold necklace containing a charm with the Sicilian crest. There were others too. Holmes explained some pieces were from France and Germany, and all from royal families.

"The library has a highly regarded reputation," Holmes told me. "These pieces are on loan. At least, the originals are." Holmes smiled. He was enjoying himself with this little matter. "Well, I believe we've almost all the pieces to this little puzzle. The matter shall end tonight. After we finish our meal, we shall pay a visit to Mr. Winter, a bit earlier than I expected."

Holmes regaled me with his story of what he'd accomplished while I was watching the lighthouse. He had followed the burly man back to his home where he changed into his police uniform. "His name is Hodgson. He's a low-ranking constable and has been for a number of years. The reason is partly because in a small town such as this, there is very little room for advancement. The other reason is that he's incompetent. Someone of his skill level would have never lasted a month in London. Out here, where crime is low and police mainly walk a beat to ensure people that they exist in case of an actual crime, a policeman of his skills does just fine."

I thought that was saying much, considering the mistakes the inspectors of the Yard made which Holmes had to clean up. "How did you learn this?" I asked.

Holmes gave one of his odd silent chuckles. "Oh, Watson, this town is an open book. Most people leave their doors and windows unlocked. It's why Mr. Facer – yes, that is the name of the man you were following – had no concern in leaving boxes of jewelry in an open boat.

"After Constable Hodgson dressed into his uniform, he came back here and said that the ring was reported stolen. So poor was he at his job that he never asked me how I came into possession of the ring to see if I was the thief or knew the thief. He simply asked for the ring, which I supplied to him and sent him on his way.

"Once the constable left, I changed into a sailor's outfit and went to a few of the local taverns. They were less busy at breakfast time, but even at mid-morning, a few locals were eating after catching their fill for the

210

day. It's through talking with them that I learned of Constable Hodgson, who has such an ill reputation that most either scoffed at or laughed at him. I also learned that his superior, Chief Inspector Quinn, is an upstanding individual. He caught two of his officers taking bribes and he fired them immediately. Though I can't say for certain without meeting the man, he sounds trustworthy, and we'll need an honest officer of the law to work with us tonight."

We finished eating, and Holmes instructed me to gather the jewels that I'd confiscated. We then departed for The Jacoby Library.

"Inconceivable!" Mr. Winter sounded like an unoiled door hinge as he looked from one piece to the next. His wide eyes flitted back and forth as his brain reeled from considering what he thought was not possible. We were sitting around his work table, along with Mr. Barnes, who was chewing his fingernails as he watched Winter flit from one piece of jewelry to the next. "The Flag of Moyette! Bah, how?" he stammered as he looked at a necklace with the French emblem. "The German *Reichsadler*!" He said looking at another ring. "This one is from the fourteenth century! How could this have been done? *How?*"

"Excellent questions, and I assure you that I shall provide you the answers. But first, I believe it's time to notify the police and report that you have been robbed," Holmes calmly suggested. This caused both the librarians to flail their arms in the air like the tentacles of an octopus. It took Holmes a moment to calm the two down and for him to explain his recommendation.

"But you said that we weren't robbed – that nothing was stolen," Mr. Barnes screeched.

"Correction," Holmes explained, still keeping his cool demeanor. "I said that, at the time, there was no evidence that you had been robbed. I believe if you go and find the originals of these pieces, you will find at least one which has been replaced with a poor copy."

Both librarians bolted from the table and, in a whirlwind of motion, were back with the pieces in no time. Winter went through them one by one, nodding his head, and looking relieved as each appeared authentic – that is, until he came to the brooch with the Flag of Moyette.

"A terrible forgery," he squeaked. I thought he was going to go into a nervous fits. Instead, his eyes shifted to Holmes and he inquired. "But Mr. Holmes, I'm even more confused now than before. Why is there only one fake?"

"Because at one point they were *all* fakes, just not at the same time." At Holmes's words, Mr. Barnes, Mr. Winter, and I all exchanged puzzled looks. Before we could ask about what he meant, Holmes continued with his explanation.

"This is a rather clever little scheme," he started. "The criminals have made copies of very specific pieces in your collection. These are rather simple objects made of gold and containing an engraving – not covered in diamonds and other jewels which would be much more difficult to forge.

"The criminals have made both poor and excellent copies of the jewelry. They have entered the library at night when no one was here and taken the pieces from your collection. They've used cheap replacements, betting that no one would come looking at the gold pieces, since the few visitors that you have are focused, like myself, on your Charlemagne collection."

"But how did they break in?" Mr. Barnes stammered. "We have seen no signs of a forced entry."

"That is because the door was not forced. Your locks are secure. However, one only needs to make a wax copy of the front door lock to get a key. If these forgers can easily make a duplicate ring, a fake key is a simple task for them."

"Who are these men?" Mr. Winter growled. His nerves had given way to ire, and his face was now flushed with fury.

"Watson and I can identify two of them. Neither is, as the expression goes, the ring leader, but it will be easy enough to catch them and use them to bring us to the man behind this operation."

"Let's contact the police at once!" snarled Mr. Winter.

"We have to be careful there. I'm afraid that an officer of the law is one of the villains behind this charade."

"A police officer!" Winter and Barnes snapped, their arms returning to their wild gesturing.

"Yes, and I'm not sure if he has additional allies on the force. It's best to summon a man whom we know that we can trust. I've heard that Chief Inspector Quinn is one such man."

I could tell that Winter was unfamiliar with the name, surprising for a resident of a small town, but Barnes cautiously nodded his head. "He has an impeccable reputation," he agreed. "I shall call on him, personally."

"Do you know him well?" I asked.

"Not well, but he is married to my cousin. If I send a message to him requesting that he come, he shall do so."

"Excellent," agreed Holmes.

"There is one thing, more," added Winter. "What is their end game here?"

I told them that I was wondering the same thing myself.

"Tonight," Holmes explained, "the criminals shall forcibly break into the library causing much damage. They shall also replace the brooch with the correct one, covering their tracks. The newspapers will report that the Jacoby Library had a break in and was vandalized. However, no pieces were damaged or taken."

"That seems pointless," I surmised. "Why make copies if you can't sell them? Stealing the jewels seems to be a more straightforward method."

"There are brains behind this scheme, my dear Watson. Once the news is out of the break in, they will start rumors that pieces from the collection *were* stolen and were replaced with cheap imitations so as to not anger the royal families of several countries. Some of the cheap pieces like the ones our feathered friend uncovered will be allowed to slip out in the market, adding validity to this assertion.

"Once collectors believe that the pieces were stolen, the thieves can start selling their higher-quality forgeries. Buyers will keep these pieces in their private collections, and it will be unlikely that they will ever get rid of them. The thieves will be able to sell these gold copies, made relatively cheaply, for twenty times their expense. They will make a fortune from this scheme and will have violated only minor laws. It will appear as though no pieces of jewelry from the museum were ever stolen. Most likely, the worst charge the criminals might get would be for vandalism."

"That is quite the scheme," Winter said.

"It is, Mr. Winter, and I look forward to meeting the mind behind it."

The depiction of Chief Inspector Quinn being an upstanding individual proved to be true. He met us at the library. Straight backed, broad shouldered, perfect posture – at the sight of the man, I knew that he was former military. His square jaw and handsome face were almost perfect, except for a scar running down his left cheek that I was later to learn he received at Majuba Hill.

The man sat back while hearing our story, his hands tapping on his knees as he listened intently. He would occasionally interrupt Holmes – for it was he doing most of the talking – to ask a clarifying question.

After Holmes had finished our tale, Quinn sat still, pondering it all. Mr. Winter lost his patience and scolded, "Don't just sit there. Do something! Arrest this Hodgson fellow before he breaks in."

Quinn remained silent for another minute before responding. "No."

"No? No?" Winter blurted. "No what?"

"No, I shall not arrest Hodgson, not until tonight. We have no hard evidence against him. We would do better to catch him breaking and entering and hold that over him and Facer."

"Ah, you are familiar with Constable Hodgson's associate," Holmes noted.

"Yes, he was also a constable. A drunkard with a reputation for starting fights, he was fired for missing his shifts. He and Hodgson were friends, so I'm not surprised that they're working together. No one liked them, so they stayed together, even though they were known to go to blows on occasion.

Quinn looked directly into Holmes's grey eyes when he addressed one of his greatest concerns. "You don't need to worry about a conspiracy in my station. The constables are good men. I trust them all with my life – well, all but this one. I suppose even a near-perfect peck of plums will have one rotten piece of fruit in it."

"That is all I needed to know to put my plan into play," said Holmes.

"And what plan might that be?" asked Quinn.

"One that ensures that all the villains behind this operation shall suffer."

Holmes's plan worked as he expected. When Hodgson and Facer broke into the Jacoby Library, Quinn and a small team of officers were ready to arrest them. Hodgson took a swing at Quinn, but the Chief Inspector easily dodged it, and it instead connected with the jaw of Facer who was standing by the inspector, not sure which direction to run. After Facer collapsed in a daze, two constables jumped Hodgson and brought him to the ground. It did not take long before the two bumbling fools were in irons.

"You've made a big mistake, Quinn!" Hodgson roared. "I'll be free in under an hour!" He paused and looked down at his associate who was still unconscious from the unexpected hit to his jaw. "We'll both be free."

"That is highly unlikely," Holmes said. "You and your associate were witnessed breaking and entering into a library where you smashed a lamp before being apprehended."

"Heh, I was just minding my own business, walking by with my friend when I heard a commotion coming from inside the library. I'm an officer of the law and had to make sure that everything was fine. When I entered, I accidentally knocked over a lamp, and Facer accidentally knocked over a chair. I apologize if anything was broken."

"Then how do you explain this?" asked one of the constables who had taken Hodgson. He held up a copy of the door key that he removed from Hodgson's pocket.

"I don't know how that got in my pocket. The door was unlocked. Maybe somebody else broke in."

I was disgusted with the man and sharply said, "That story will never hold up."

"Oh, it will," Hodgson chortled. "I have friends in high places."

"You mean his Lordship," Holmes said firmly.

This surprised the corrupt constable, and he actually said, "You know about Lord Cecily?"

The constables gasped. Chief Inspector Quinn remained calm, but raised his brows at this. Holmes remained stoic.

"A member of Parliament is behind all of this," Holmes stated matter-of-factly.

"That's right," boasted Hodgson, trying to turn this revelation into a positive. "And when he finds out that you have us, he'll make sure that we're set free."

"We shall see," Quinn responded coolly, and then he had his men take Hodgson and Facer away.

Once they'd left, Quinn told Holmes, "He may be right. This isn't London. I only have so much power. If his Lordship is behind this, this operation may crumble."

"Tell me, Chief Inspector," said Holmes, "did you do as I asked?"

"Yes, though I haven't heard word yet, but I assume everything went as planned." Almost as though he were an actor cued from the stage, a constable came running in with a message for the chief inspector.

"There you have it, Holmes," said Quinn. "The arrests have been made, and the shipments will soon be on their way to London."

Holmes lit up at this news. "Excellent. I believe you'll see that he'll offer you no trouble."

Packwood Hall, Lord Cecily's home, was a sprawling estate on the outskirts of the village. After a footman took our carriage, we were met at the door by a Mr. Jeffries, the head footman, who took our card and ushered us into the sitting room. Before long, he came to retrieve and take us into Lord Cecily's study where the man was sitting with his feet up on the desktop, laying back in a recliner, reading *The Times* and puffing away on a cigar. He was a thin wisp of a man, bald at the top with a few strands of hair at his sides, combed over to do his best to cover up what he could of his dome.

"Chief Inspector, eh?" said the Lord who swung his feet down, sloppily tossed the paper on his desk, and stood to greet us.

"Yes, my Lord," said Quinn. His tone was that of an official, and I admired him for not kow-towing to the man before him. "May I present to you Mr. Sherlock Holmes, a London detective, and his associate, Dr. Watson."

215

His Lordship greeted us kindly and invited us to sit. The chairs, like the manor, were comfortable and opulent. The soft-cushioned seat reflected the warmth of the yellow-and-orange color tones of the house, and the ornate carved patterns showed the glory of the wealth and power of our host, which was reflected in the size and condition of the estate.

"Tell me, please, what brings you here," his Lordship invited.

"There was a break in at the Jacoby Library last night," the chief inspector explained. "The perpetrator, I am ashamed to say, was one of my constables."

"How awful. I assume that you've apprehended this man."

"Yes, he and his associate were arrested."

His Lordship nodded approvingly. "That's very good. Now, what does this have to do with me?"

"According to Constable Hodgson, he broke into the library on your authority."

Lord Cecily chuckled deeply at the accusation. "Really, Chief Inspector, that sounds like a desperate man trying to claim he has – how does the saying go – *friends in high places*. It wouldn't be the first time a criminal has tried to associate himself with a reputable man to gain leniency."

"True, my Lord," said Holmes. "So there is no connection between yourself and the constable?"

"None whatsoever."

Holmes leaned back in his chair looking fully relieved. "I don't think we need to bother his Lordship any further, gentlemen."

Quinn and I nodded in agreement. Lord Cecily went to stand to bid us *adieu*, but Holmes stopped him.

"My Lord, since you are a member of the House of Lords, I think you should be informed of the constable's connection to a crime syndicate working here in Port."

Lord Cecily raised his eyebrows at this. He took a puff from his cigar, tapped some ash into his tray, and said, "Go on."

"It appears that there was a criminal organization working out of the old lighthouse off the shore near the piers. You know it?"

"Of course, I do," Lord Cecily said. His voice was level, but I noted beads of sweat had begun to show on his forehead.

"Very good. Inside this lighthouse, believe it or not, was a jewelry forgery business. They were making copies of jewelry contained in the Jacoby Library – the pieces on loan from foreign governments and royal families. Fortunately, the chief inspector here was able to round up all of the workers behind the operation and confiscate all the gold they were using in this scheme."

"Humph," said his Lordship. "Well done, Chief Inspector."

"Yes. Several more members of the operation also implicated you, your Lordship, as the mastermind behind the forgeries."

The Lord chuckled again at the accusation, but he now had to take out a handkerchief and wipe the sweat from his forehead. I also noted that his coloring had gone pale. "Gentlemen, I assure you that I was not the brains behind this operation."

"No," Holmes agreed. "I thought not. Though, could it be possible," Holmes speculated, "that the man behind this operation meant for you to reap the rewards? Could it be that he intended to give you the money raised from these forged jewels in violation of corruption laws?"

"I am a Lord, Mr. Holmes, and I am not elected," he scolded. "You should know that."

"I agree, but interestingly enough, some of the criminals we arrested said that the plan was for you to use the money to influence the election of certain members of the House of Commons. That would be in violation of the Corrupt and Illegal Practices Act, would it not?"

"Well, if this were true, I suppose – "

" – It is good that it is not," Holmes interrupted Lord Cecily to continue. "It is also good that we were able to stop these criminals before they caused any significant damage. We sent all the confiscated gold by train to London."

"You what?" Lord Cecily's eyes were wide and his mouth dropped.

"Yes. You see, your Lordship, I, too, have friends in high places, and with this matter involving Continental issues, we made certain that the gold was sent to senior authorities in the British government. Have no fear – all of the gold and jewels will be retained as the investigation continues."

"But that's a fortune. The loss will ruin – "

" – the loss will ruin those who owned the gold or who purchased the gold. Anyway, it matters not, for it doesn't concern you," said Holmes with a harsh gravity to his voice.

His Lordship looked stunned at this news. He stood with his jaw slacked for thirty seconds and only snapped to attention when some hot ash from his cigar fell upon the leg of his trousers. Lord Cecily jumped up and wiped it away before it could burn him.

"Gentlemen, it sounds like you've done good work. I can assure you that I have no association with these men whatsoever."

"Very good, my Lord," said Holmes agreeably. "We take you at your word." At this we stood and thanked his Lordship for his time. The chief inspector and I left the room. As Holmes stepped out of the room, he turned back to address his Lordship.

"Oh, there is one more matter, my Lord," Holmes said.

217

"Go on," Lord Cecilly invited.

"Should any word of this operation make the press, it would cause an international crisis. France and Germany would be furious if it came out that some of their precious treasures were allowed to be taken and copied. With the accusation of you planning on bribing members of the House of Commons – well, the public would be furious. There would be an investigation, a scandal, and no matter who was innocent, there would most definitely be ruin."

"Are you threatening me, Mr. Holmes?" his Lordship scoffed.

"I can't threaten an innocent man, now can I? But let me make this point clear: Should your name come up again in any illicit activity, then this story will be made public, and I believe you know that no matter if it is public now or fifty years from now, there will still be great damage to the reputation of those involved. Good day, my Lord."

"Do you really believe that this is over, Holmes?" I asked. We were back at the pier, this time with Chief Inspector Quinn, watching Cora, the talented cormorant, fetch a gar for the delight of the children. It was our last morning in Port, and we wanted to see Cora one final time before venturing back to Baker Street. We invited the chief inspector along so he could see the bird which started us off on the case.

"For now, yes. We have dealt a serious blow to his Lordship's finances, so he doesn't heave the current means to cause any mischief in any upcoming elections."

"But you said that he wasn't the man behind the operation?"

"Not solely, no. Some of the gold belonged to him. The other man behind the operation, the true mastermind, of him, I admit, I know little, but he has also been hurt by our unraveling of their little operation. Even if he has the financial means, Lord Cecily has been checked and will not participate in distributing any bribes, quite possibly for the rest of his career. If he does, I will make certain that this story and his part in it reaches the light of day."

Holmes paused when the children burst into a thunderous round of applause as Cora returned to her soapbox and spit up the catch before them.

"Perhaps," I confided in Holmes, "I may take a stab at writing up a version of this adventure."

Quinn looked surprised. "Really, Doctor? I didn't take you for a writer."

I deprecate, however, in the strongest way the attempts which have been made lately to get at and to destroy these papers. The source of these outrages is known, and if they are repeated I have Mr. Holmes's authority for saying that the whole story concerning the politician, the lighthouse, and the trained cormorant will be given to the public. There is at least one reader who will understand.

– Dr. John H. Watson
"The Adventure of the Veiled Lodger"

A Child's Reward
by Stephen Mason

As I approached our rooms in Baker Street after a long day of visiting patients, I noticed that the sun was considering once again placing itself into the arms of Morpheus. Late in autumn, the days were becoming noticeably shorter, with a crispness in the air each evening. As I reached the steps outside the front door, it was comforting to see the usual ornaments – the gas lights paired on either side, the fire insurance company emblem from a bygone period, and the hook-rug mat for cleaning one's shoes before entering the domicile. Mrs. Hudson greeted me in the hallway, indicating supper, consisting of soup, beef, and potatoes, would be served in approximately thirty minutes.

Climbing the stairs and crossing the threshold into our sitting room, I found my flatmate sitting in his favorite chair near the fire. A quick glance indicated he had removed several of the sheets stuck to the mantelpiece by the jack-knife, clearing away some of the backlog of requests for his attention.

"Welcome home, Watson. Pull up a chair and tell me about your day."

I hesitated, wondering if I had just stepped into a dream. Never before had he shown much – or for that matter any – interest in my professional duties.

"I would be happy to, but I must admit you've taken me by surprise. You seem to be in an unusually humorous mood. Do you have an explanation for this attitude?"

"I have taken to heart your constant scolding, and have attempted to lessen the load held down by my unique paper weight. I must tell you, many of these missives aren't so much a request to solve a mystery as they're a personal unburdening of one's soul. For example, this particular note is from a respected banker in Nottingham who has been slowly embezzling funds from his institution to support a mistress. He is asking if I believe that he should turn himself to the police, or simply try to pay back the funds over a period of time, now that the tryst has ended."

"Surely at least one of the notes provide a hint at future work?"

"Nothing intriguing enough to whet my appetite."

"Well, Mrs. Hudson gave me notice that our meal will be arriving soon.

"Good," he replied. "Since we have a few minutes, I would like to discuss a matter with you, Please, take a seat."

I did so, puzzled, and he continued. "As you recall, yesterday morning before leaving the house, you asked for your cheque book, as you were planning on purchasing some new equipment to replace those holdovers from your army days – a new medical bag and stethoscope, for instance. As I left before you, I didn't notice until the early afternoon that you had replaced the book on my desk. While I would never consciously impose on your privacy, it was easy to discern you hadn't removed a cheque from the book. Yesterday evening, it was apparent on several occasions you were considering to start a discussion, but each time held your tongue. I felt it best to allow you to choose when the time was ripe for a conversation."

As I positioned myself in my comfortable armchair, I pondered where he was headed. Before I could speak, he continued.

"However, I have since decided instead to force the issue. As we have been in association now for a while, I believe we should discuss our financial positions. I'm aware of your paltry wound pension of approximately two-hundred-pounds-per-year. Your medical services working at Barts and as a *locum* don't add substantially significant funds to your account. I can see how an individual of your standing can sometimes struggle to get by on such a balance."

I was a bit embarrassed, and defensive. "As you know, I have been in discussions to add another source of income – namely monies to be earned from chronicling your cases. I'm hoping to negotiate a solid return for each of those 'stories'."

"I hope that you have made a suitable and profitable arrangement."

"Interestingly enough, I left the bargaining part of the deal to Doyle – he's acting as my literary agent. While I'm not quite aware of the specific amounts that's he's hoping to arrange for each of the stories, which we hope will be soon appearing on the newsstands, it seems as if he'll get the larger percentage of the income for his efforts."

"Hmm. Have you considered finding a new agent?"

"As you know, he is also a medical practitioner, but writing appears to be his true calling, and I'd like to help him to get more firmly established in the field. And to this point, he seems pleased to be involved in bringing your cases to the public. They seem to be a nice diversion from his more serious literary efforts."

Holmes nodded. "Which brings us around to my reason for initiating this discussion. From our early association, our arrangement was that you would share in my fees on those cases where you acted as a consultant – there was no reason that you, as a professional, shouldn't be treated as such. After all, you are often called upon to provide medical services. You regularly do substantial leg work on my behalf, often putting your life and health at risk – not to mention the lack of sleep from my eccentric late-night habits. As my little practice has grown and achieved greater success, I would propose that you deserve a greater portion of that."

I swallowed, not quite sure how to react. "And what," I said, "would you consider to be a fair amount to compensate you for my services?"

"Oh, I'm not prepared to discuss specifics – at least not yet. I simply wanted to broach the subject to determine how you would react to my proposal."

Before I could respond further, both of us noticed footsteps on the landing outside our door, succeeded by knocking.

"It appears that Mrs. Hudson has brought up a visitor, and based on the lightness of the steps, I wouldn't be surprised to find that it's one of the Irregulars to provide an update on a small matter in which I've asked their for assistance. You may enter, Mrs. Hudson."

In stepped our landlady, and as Holmes had correctly predicted, a youngster followed right behind her. But to our surprise, the expected lad turned out to be a lass.

"Mr. Holmes, apparently this young lady has requested an audience."

"Fascinating. It appears that our Wiggins has expanded his pool of helpers. Or else someone has decided to pull a practical prank on me."

"Actually, I believe that she would like to discuss your services as a detective."

"I'm not sure what assistance I could possibly offer her, but as this may be a novel experience, I suggest she come in and take a seat. Mrs. Hudson, would you please send up appropriate refreshments for our young guest."

"Mr. Holmes," said the girl, "I'm your *client* . . . ."

"That is yet to be determined."

"I don't know if I should have anything to eat. It might ruin my dinner, as my mother always tells me."

"I think we can risk a glass of milk. Why don't you sit on the edge of the cane-backed chair and explain why you're here talking to us, in lieu of doing chores or schoolwork."

"I don't have much time, as I'm supposed to be out of the house for only fifteen minutes, visiting my friend, Katie."

"As time is a premium, then, let's start at the beginning, Miss – "

"I'm Elenora Darlington, but my friends call me 'Ellie'. I'm here to hire you to help me with a very troubling case."

222

"While I'm sure you're sincere in your request, I'm not too sure that can help you to find a lost puppy or repair a broken toy."

"Mr. Holmes, that seems to be a little on the patronizing side," she said, surprising and amusing us both. "I assure you that my request is much more serious, and will test your skills as an investigator."

"Miss Darlington, I apologize for taking your young age for granted. I am curious: How old are you?

The young lady held up both hands, with four fingers extended on each hand.

"So, eight years old."

"Yes. I was confirming you can count." She giggled, and then flashed a huge smile toward Holmes, which then quickly changed to a frown. "I'm sorry. My father says that I'm bright for my age, and that it will get me into trouble. I need your help finding out what has happened to my mother."

I reacted quickly. "Is she missing, or worse?"

"No, she is still with us. But she's not."

Holmes gave me that look which meant to allow time for the client to tell her story. "I don't quite follow," he said. "Start at the beginning, and explain in as much detail as you can."

Mrs. Hudson stepped into the room just then with a small glass of milk, which she handed to our petite visitor. "Mr. Holmes, do you think it prudent for me to stay, lest the girl need something else?"

"Normally I like to interview my clients in private, but in this instance, I believe your presence to be welcomed. Now, young lady, you were saying . . . ?"

"I'm not too sure where to start."

"Let us follow a series of questions and answers that may help you arrange your thoughts better. To begin, what is your father called?"

"Daddy!"

"Actually, Ellie, I meant, do you know your father's first name?"

"Yes, it's Nathaniel. Most of my family call him 'Nate'."

"Including your mother?"

"She . . . used to . . . ."

"And what does your father do?"

"Normally whatever mother and grandmother tells him to do."

"I meant, does your father work at a job?"

"Yes. He's is a teller at a bank several blocks from here. He says that we'll never be rich, but it pays the bills."

"Who else lives in your house? Do you have any brother or sisters?"

"No, it's just mother, father, my grandmother, and our new housekeeper, Mrs. Wiggleston. Mother says that Mrs. Wiggleston helped to bring her into the world."

"Earlier, you said your mother was here, but wasn't. Can you please explain what you mean by that?"

"It's very confusing to me. My Mother, Norah, has always been, as my daddy calls it, a little 'flighty'. But lately, it's been much worse."

"In what manner?"

"She's extremely forgetful. She can't remember where she put things, or events that occurred in the past, and even names of pets that we've had. And doesn't even call me 'Ellie' anymore. It's now 'Elenora'. The same with daddy – 'Nathaniel', and not 'Nate.'"

"Do you believe that your father has noticed these differences?"

"Oh yes. He and I have talked about it. He thinks mother is just upset about something."

It was my turn to join the questioning. "Ellie, while all of that may seem strange, you must understand that when parents come under unusual stresses, it can show itself in different ways. There might temporary loss of memory."

"Oh, it isn't just forgetting things. She acts differently too. Lately she seems to be much more distant to grandmother, who is usually sick in bed, and doesn't have many good days, while being much friendlier to Mrs. Wiggleston."

Here she paused, and a tear began to form in her right eye.

"I don't think she loves me anymore, either."

As Holmes and I sat there, not sure on how to react, Mrs. Hudson saved the day by stepping forward and gently hugging the child, stroking her hair until she had composed herself.

"Miss Darlington," said Holmes, "I'm not sure what Dr. Watson and I can do to solve your mystery, but believe me when I state we won't rest until your fractured world is made whole again, even if we must use all the glue and paste in the universe."

While I may never be blessed with a child of my own, if ever so fortunate, I hope each night to see the same smile which came across this little girl's face. Her entire countenance lit up – but then a serious look once again appeared.

"I'm afraid that I may not have enough money to pay you. But I'll give you every penny that I have."

"Which is how much?"

"Twelve pennies."

"What a coincidence! That just happens to be my fee." With a smile my way, "Watson, per our previous discussion, I feel comfortable splitting it evenly with you."

"I think that I'll waive my percentage for this one, thank you very much."

"Ellie, can you estimate how long this change in behaviour has affected your mother?"

"It started a couple of weeks ago."

"Did anything else happen around that same time?"

"Not exactly, but it was just a few weeks after Mrs. Wiggleston started working in our home." She wiggled forward, now much less upset than before. "So what is our next step?"

"*Your* next step is to get yourself home before you get into trouble with your parents. I have the beginnings of a plan already formulated in my mind. Dr. Watson and I will drop by your house tomorrow afternoon to meet your mother. I'll need you to be a detective-in-training to aid us in solving this case. Can you play-act when we appear, and simply follow along with whatever I say?"

"Oh yes. My daddy thinks that I'll be a stage actress when I grow up, so I can definitely help you."

"Young lady, please leave your address with Mrs. Hudson as you exit downstairs. By the way, how far do you live from here?"

"Three blocks or so, though it seemed much longer when I was walking. I have such short legs. And of course, I'm not allowed to cross the street by myself, so a very friendly woman took my hand at each of the corners."

After Mrs. Hudson had escorted our young client out the door and down the stairs, I smiled over at Holmes.

"I have no idea what is in your mind, but I just can't imagine that there's much of a mystery here to solve."

"You may be correct, but it's just possible there's more to the story than we just gleamed from her statement. Let us have our supper, after which I'll focus on the task at hand. You'll have a part to play in this drama, which I will outline before we sally forth after lunch tomorrow."

Approximately one-thirty on the next day found Holmes and me on a pleasant walk from our lodgings to Miss Darlington's residence. While Holmes is much more familiar with London geography, I was less knowledgable about these nearby blocks, in spite of their nearness to Baker Street. The homes were similar to Mrs. Hudson's structure at 221, but these domiciles appeared to have more families with children located within. We reached the address provided, with Holmes surveying the house for a few minutes before approaching the front door and using the attached knocker.

A middle-aged woman, average in height and appearance, opened the door with a look that I can only imagine was reserved for salesmen and tax collectors.

"State your business and don't tarry, as if I have enough to take care of without listening to your fast talk of gadgets that I neither need nor desire."

Holmes tipped his hat, "Madam, I can understand your feelings toward those of the soliciting profession. I tend to hold the same opinion of many of them. However, our business is with Mrs. Darlington, the woman of the house. I believe that she'll be grateful to see us, once we've stated our intent."

"Please step in – minding that you wipe your feet first. I'm not going to re-clean the foyer because of your carelessness."

The domestic left us the hallway, and two doors opening and closing deeper within the house were soon heard. In the few minutes that we were left to ourselves within the front entry, Holmes observed every object, including the small statuary on the end tables, and a few photographs hanging on the walls. His focus seemed to linger particularly on a family portrait

"Gentlemen, I believe that you requested time with me. May I have your names and purpose of this visit?"

The question was issued by a woman of medium height and build, with brunette hair and a disposition that indicated our presence was a bit bothering. The similarities in facial features made it easy enough to see Elenora Darlington was her offspring. Holmes stepped forward, withdrew from his pocket two visiting cards, one light blue and one teal in color, and waited while Mrs. Darlington reviewed both of them.

"So which one of you is Mr. Jonathan Franklin?"

Holmes slightly nodded his head. "That would indeed be me, my lady. However before we continue introductions and purposes, may I request that you invite your daughter to join us? The impetus of our appearing at your doorstep includes her."

It was apparent Mrs. Darlington was slightly confused by the request, but turned to the servant, who had been slouching against the doorframe to the hallway. "Mrs. Wiggleston, would you fetch Elenora? And please bring tea and biscuits for our visitors. Gentlemen, please take a seat while we await my daughter."

Within a few minutes, our little client sprinted through the doorway, breaking out into a wide grin as she spotted Holmes. However, a slight shaking of his head, which only the daughter could see, was enough to quell her enthusiasm.

"Mrs. Darlington, as the cards indicate, my name is Jonathan Franklin, a sales representative for Kirby Housewares. My line of business doesn't have an impact on our visit. However, my friend here is Asa Billings, and his vocation is important to our task. As his card indicates, he makes his living by his talents for telling a story – thus as a writer for *The Evening News*. I know that your time is valuable, so I'll make my explanation both clear and concise.

"I have a daughter of similar age to your dear Elenora here. I love my little girl to death, but she would leave her head on a park bench if it wasn't attached to her body. Yesterday afternoon, the latest of more times than I can count, she left the front door open after returning from a romp in the park. Of course, our small terrier, Benji, made a break for it, escaping down the street. It would have only been a matter of minutes before he would have become the unfortunate stepping-stone of one of the thousands of horses on our busy city thoroughfare. Miraculously, your daughter happened to see our wandering family member racing down the pavement, and with no thought of her own safety, grabbed our little darling just before she ran out into the street, facing certain peril, if not death."

"Elenora," said Mrs. Darlington with a frown, "when did this feat of bravery happen?"

Ellie spoke without hesitation, immediately playing her part to perfection. "It was yesterday afternoon, Mother, as I was returning from Katie's house."

"To finish the tale of heroism," continued Holmes, "as I was pursuing our adorable little mutt, I soon encountered Benji in the loving arms of your daughter. I offered her a cash reward, which she humbly refused." Mrs. Darlington glanced strangely at Ellie again at that bit of information. "But I decided the story of your daughter's selfless act needed to be told to the residents of London. So this morning, I contacted my good friend, Mr. Billings here, who has offered to write up the story for the next edition of his periodical. And there you have it."

"That is an amazing story. Elenora. Why didn't you tell me about this adventure when you returned home yesterday?"

"Umm . . . if you remember, you and father were in the middle of an argument – "

" – Lively discussion – "

" – and it simply slipped my mind by the time we gathered for supper."

Holmes stepped back into the conversation. "Mrs. Darlington, I believe that this story will tug at the heartstrings of citizens far and wide.

Do we have your approval to have the narrative placed in the newspaper tomorrow evening?"

"Yes, I suppose that would be all right."

"Mr. Billings, do you have everything that you need for the story?"

"I have all the details that you provided to me earlier today concerning the actual events, but Mrs. Darlington may be able to fill in some background information concerning the family – particularly of young Miss Elenora."

Mrs. Darlington interrupted, "Oh. I'm so sorry, Mr. Billings, but Elenora and I are overdue for an appointment that we must not miss. I'm afraid that you must rely on Mr. Franklin's statement for the basis of the story. I'm sure that would be sufficient."

Holmes answered, "That it will. However, I do know that Mr. Billings could use a photograph of Elenora to assist in preparing an artist's rendition for the article. May we borrow this one hanging on the wall, as it appears to be a very recent one? I promise to return it within a day or two."

"That should be alright. I'm not one to be too overly attached to such objects of sentimentality. And now, gentlemen, my daughter and I must get ready for our appointment . . . ."

"Certainly," agreed Holmes. "I believe that we have sufficient to our needs. Elenora, again thank you so much for your assistance in the matter."

"You know Mr. . . . . Franklin," she said with a twinkle in her eye, "I have had time to think about it, and I believe I will accept that reward you offered me yesterday."

Mrs. Darlington showed her surprise, "Elenora! That is being just a little impudent, don't you think?"

Holmes replied, "Not in the least! It shows that Elenora has spunk – she might even make a good sales lady in future years."

Holmes fished a coin out of his trouser pocket and handed it to the young lass. "Here is a sovereign for you to keep. I would suggest that once you're older, you always keep a sovereign with you, as you never know when you might need it to repay a bet or as a debt of gratitude."

Mrs. Wiggleston led us to the front door, where in my role as a reporter, I asked, "Before we leave, may I ask you one or two questions?"

Looking like a very nervous fox on the morning of a hunt, the lady nonetheless relented.

"How long have you known this lovely family?"

"I have worked as their housekeeper for two months. But I've been informally part of the family for years. I had the wonderful experience of bringing Mrs. Darlington into this world. I worked for Mrs. Darlington's mother then, twenty-seven years ago, was so taken by such a sweet baby I stayed on with the family, acting as both nanny and nursery-maid. I only left their employment once young Mrs. Darlington went off to boarding school. With no other family of my own, I sought out the possibility of once again joining the family to look out for Elenora in the same manner as before."

Holmes didn't seem to have any further questions, and with that, we tendered our thanks and left the Darlington residence, walking briskly back to our Baker Street quarters.

I settled back into my favored chair, but Holmes paced back in forth in front of the fire, occasionally taking a puff on a cigarette, but letting most of it burn down on its own. The picture he'd borrowed was propped nearby.

"Holmes, where do we turn now? I simply don't see a mystery here to solve. Again, I believe that Mrs. Darlington's forgetfulness is due to some stress that we may not have witnessed. Am I missing something?"

"Yes you are. Within five minutes of being at the house, I had observed the key to unlocking this mystery. I now have to determine the best way of resolving it, without having anyone physically harmed."

"You suspect there may be foul play?"

"I suspect that is a possibility, but it hasn't occurred yet. I'm concerned that our little ruse this afternoon may be discovered by the parties involved before I'm ready to move against them. Therefore, time is of essence. I'm off to visit someone whom I've been able to assist in a couple of small issues – in return, he is often willing to help me in my investigations. I believe that the final piece to this puzzle may reside in the general census and birth certificate records."

By the time that I'd retired for the evening, Holmes still hadn't yet returned, which I assumed meant that he might have found another clue to chase, or that he might be pursuing leads for another case of which I wasn't yet aware.

The next morning over breakfast, Holmes gave me a short *précis* of his activities the previous afternoon, and not long after, I found myself standing with him, alongside Inspector Lestrade, outside of the Darlington residence. Holmes had spoken to him yesterday after the direction of his research began to make clear what was going on there.

"Mr. Holmes, once again, I'm in your debt for unweaving this tangle, but I'm perplexed as to why we're taking this route to close out the case."

"Watson will tell you that while I focus on the details of the case and the smallest of trifles, I cannot resist allowing just a little drama. Please knock on the door, and remember to play out your parts."

Response to the summons took longer than expected, with a gentleman that I could only assume was Mr. Darlington opening the door and staring out at the three of us with a questioning look. His dress indicated that he was likely preparing to venture off to work.

"You must forgive my tardiness in answering the door. Evidently our housekeeper hasn't yet arrived for her daily duties. May I help you three gentlemen?"

"Yes, I'm Inspector Lestrade of Scotland Yard. We've had a series of serious crimes on this block in the past two days, including robbery, burglary, assault, and even an attempted murder." The crisp way that he listed the offenses almost convinced me that it was true. "I would like to ask you and your wife a few questions to see if you might be of any help in my investigations."

The man looked surprised. "We would be happy to assist in you in any manner possible, but I can assure you neither of us will have any pertinent information that you might be able to use."

Interestingly, and thankfully, Mr. Darlington didn't question purpose of either Holmes or me being with Lestrade.

We were led through the main hallway to a pair of sliding glass doors at the left of the stairway, revealing a library. "Wait here while I summon my wife."

"And your daughter," added Holmes.

Darlington looked puzzled, but he nodded in agreement and left us.

Many of the room's shelves were sparsely filled with books, but instead were cluttered with frames containing coins of various denominations and origins. Darlington returned and said that his wife would join us momentarily. Then, noticing my interest in the collection, he stated, "I'm the head teller at one of the branches of the Capital and Counties Bank. As you can guess, I regularly come into contact with coins of all ages and from numerous countries on a daily basis. Though my annual salary limits my ability to purchase the most valuable of coins, I'm able to obtain those which catch my collecting fancy before they're turned back into circulation.

"For example, take this frame here," pulling one down from the second shelf from the top. "While none of these coins would be considered extremely valuable by any reputable numismatist, I fell in love with them because of their unusual toning. Most silver and copper coins will turn to various tints over time, while gold coins are the most resistant to this transition. Once the coin turns black or brown, they lose their draw to me, but the various shades of magenta, blue, orange, and even green, have always caught my eye."

Once the frame had been passed to each of us, with Holmes and Lestrade showing polite interest, it was returned to its original resting place. Then Darlington turned back to Lestrade. "Now, how do you believe we can support you in this investigation? As an officer of a bank, is there any chance that my help in solving a crime may ultimately benefit my own employer?"

"So that I don't have to repeat myself," countered Lestrade brusquely, "we'll wait for your wife and child to be present. They may be able to provide valuable input into this inquiry."

We stood in awkward silence while Darlington took a spot behind his desk. Within a few moments, we were joined by Ellie and the woman whom we had met yesterday afternoon. They went to stand with Darlington.

Immediately upon seeing us, Mrs. Darlington expressed surprise. "Mr. Franklin – Mr. Billings! What an unexpected – ! I honestly didn't expect to see you again."

In his element, Holmes then took charge of the discussion.

"Mrs. Darlington, I'm afraid that our visit yesterday was a bit of a charade. In reality, my name is Sherlock Holmes. I'm a consulting detective, occasionally called in by Scotland Yard to consult upon difficult investigations. This is Dr. John Watson, my associate. Your husband has already been introduced to Inspector Lestrade, representing the Yard."

Mrs. Darlington inquired, "Why did you lie to me when you were here yesterday? I'm at a complete loss to what is occurring here."

"Until we had a better grasp of what was happening within a few houses of your residence," replied Holmes, his tone grim, "we didn't want to unduly frighten you or your daughter."

Holmes then glanced over to young Elenora, who had been standing close to the library doors, away from her mother and father. A quick wink that only the young lass and I could witness seemed to give her comfort. He then turned his attention back to the mother.

"I'm afraid that your daughter may be unwittingly involved in a sequence of crimes that could put her life in jeopardy," he lied. "The dog that she rescued yesterday didn't escape from my house, as I fictitiously told you. Instead, it escaped from the clutches of the leader of a major criminal syndicate which operates just a few blocks from here. This villain had paid a substantial fee to import a very exotic breed from the United States as a gift to his wife, and was desperate to recover the pet.

"A source of mine, who is buried deeply within this man's organization, happened to mention last night that the principal of the group has discovered that your daughter was in possession of the canine, and will stop at nothing to regain it."

231

Holmes spun the tale that we had rehearsed, but even though I knew it to be false, it still gave rise to feelings of concern. I was impressed that Ellie, who knew that she had never recovered a dog – either for Holmes or a criminal – showed no indication that the story was entirely false.

"Why not simply come to our door and ask for the dog's return?" asked Mr. Darlington, looking confused. "And by the way, who does have the dog?"

"He has been turned over to the local authorities for safekeeping," replied Holmes. "Unfortunately, your question doesn't have a simple answer. This particular person is simply evil, through and through. He believes that your daughter intentionally took the dog, and has no intention of ever returning it to the rightful owner. It's my belief that the term 'rightful' is being very generous, as there is evidence this man may himself have had the dog stolen from a wealthy land owner before having it shipped to England.

"While it may seem incredibly cruel to you, this monster has been known to punish those that he believes have 'wronged' him – in very unspeakable ways. It's also entirely possible that not only will he attempt to vindicate his loss upon your daughter, but your entire family. We believe he has also learned of your occupation, Mr. Darlington, which may give him impetus to attempt a kidnapping for ransom."

At this point, Mr. Darlington laughed quietly, but then asked with a very muted voice, "This is simply too amazing of a story for me to believe. What game are you gentlemen really playing?" The tone in which the question was asked indicated that he hoped he was correct in this assumption.

Lestrade responded, "Sir, do you really believe that the three of us have nothing better to do than to waste your time, or to make up such a fantastic story for no purpose?"

"I suppose not," was the man's nervous reply.

"As a matter of fact," continued the inspector, "we have received information, believed to be credible, that the organization we're discussing has planned on moving against your family and this residence as early as this morning. I've posted another inspector outside – inconspicuous of course – to provide further protection for you. I just hope that four of us here in the house may be enough to blunt any type of offensive attack."

"Mr. Darlington," Holmes said, "should the unthinkable occur, and an assault be attempted on this house, what would you consider to be the most defensible room?"

"Good heavens, man! We're not at war here!"

"Trust me, I wouldn't be asking this if I didn't think of this conflict to be most serious. Again – which room would you feel that we could secure?"

"I would assume the basement cellar."

"Where is the entrance?"

"Toward the back of the house, just adjacent to the kitchen."

"Is there more than one exit from below?"

"No, just the interior stairway."

"That wouldn't be safe, then, as they could easily block our sole way to exit. A fire would then seal our fates." Holmes was painting quite a forbidding picture.

"I suppose that the next best choice would be the dining room, which is adjacent to the kitchen. There are two entrances, but both could easily be blocked with the table, the hutch, or the sideboard. There are no windows within that room."

Lestrade stated, "I think that we're safe for a while longer, but I do think that we'll need to consider what we need in terms of supplies, arms, and other items if we're required to make a defense within the dining room."

As one can imagine, by this time both parents looked extremely frightened. Holmes, again only seen by Elenora and myself, gestured for the young girl to move closer to her mother, standing between the desk and hall door. Holmes himself moved over to the one window looking out onto the street, and very gently pulled back the drape so that he could cautiously peer out.

Just then, two shots rang outside on the street. While I was prepared for some type of disturbance, the volume of noise even made me nervously jump. Both Holmes and Lestrade immediately took up position next to each of the library doors.

Mr. Darlington ducked behind his desk, but within seconds, circled around, grabbed his daughter, and pulled her to safety behind the solid piece of oak furniture. After what seemed to be a long minute, but couldn't have been more than a few additional seconds, he glanced over the top and inquired, "Where is my wife? She isn't here."

Holmes was able to provide a response, "As soon as the shots occurred, she bolted out through the doors, down the hallway, and – I must assume – has now sheltered herself in the dining room, as we discussed. It's now time to pull down the last curtain to this little drama.

"Lestrade, if you will be so kind as to recover Mrs. Darlington from her hiding spot, while Watson invites Gregson into the library."

The library had become slightly crowded, with Holmes, myself, Inspectors Lestrade and Gregson (who had waited outside), Mr. and Mrs. Darlington, and Elenora all present. As might be expected, Mr. Darlington was exasperated and more than slightly irritated.

"I demand some answers to what has been going on right under my nose. I'll be damned if I have a clue to what has transpired."

Holmes patted the father on the sleeve. "Mr. Darlington, I know all of this must have been extremely trying to you. But I hope our little charade just now will make everything clear. The explanation to this tale will take a few minutes, so please feel free to get comfortable."

As he spoke, I kept an eye on Mrs. Darlington, who looked as if she would bolt from the room if a path presented itself.

"We start with a visit by your very bright and innovative daughter the day before yesterday. Ellie was very concerned with your wife's behaviour of late, and wished for me to look into the matter to see if I could discover a cause."

Mrs. Darlington opened her mouth as if to chide the child for her impertinent deportment, but Holmes hushed her before a word could be uttered.

"Madam, I would suggest you stay quiet and let the full story be told without any interruptions on your part. To continue, by the end of Elenora's visit, I was still unclear on what was going on within the confines of this residence, but I believed the sincerity of Ellie, and that her instincts were correct that something was amiss.

"Yesterday, Dr. Watson and I visited your residence with a story about a lost dog, concocted to simply get a feel for the mood of the house, and to talk to your wife firsthand. And now, before I continue, Mr. Darlington, I would strongly suggest you take a seat."

"I believe I will remain standing, as I still am undecided on whether one or all of you deserve a rain of my fists for this shocking conduct."

"Such is your choice." Holmes then turned to the library doors, and with raised voiced, called out, "Constable, would you please bring in the other women?"

Though I was prepared, it was still a shock to see Mrs. Darlington walk into the room, standing where she could stare balefully at – Mrs. Darlington. Holmes reached out to steady the father, as it was apparent his knees had just buckled and his eyes gave every appearance of fainting at any moment.

Next to enter was Mrs. Wiggleston, her arm in the grip of a constable. "Watson," asked Holmes, "would you please pour some liquid strength for Mr. Darlington from the decanter on the back shelf? Here, drink this, and now take that seat I offered just a few minutes ago."

Now mild as a kitten, Darlington acceded to Holmes suggestion, staring quietly at both women with a look of complete confusion. In the meantime, Mrs. Darlington – the newly arrived Mrs. Darlington – quickly crossed the room and stood with her husband and daughter.

"Mr. Darlington, yesterday while Watson and I were waiting for your wife and daughter within the front room, I took notice of the family portrait hanging on the wall."

"That was taken just a couple of months ago," said the confused man.

"Yes. A few minutes later, I noticed that your daughter was wearing the same dress as the one in the photograph. Now, as girls of her age tend to sprout up faster than a plant in the spring, I assumed that the picture must have been recently made.

"More importantly, I saw a couple of other interesting items – things that I have trained myself to observe. First, as your daughter was standing next to her mother, it was obvious that she seemed to be a good inch or so shorter than she was in the photograph. Now, one can put that down to the fact that possibly one or the other wearing raised shoes, but since the photograph was a full-length, I could tell that everyone concerned was wearing low heels – as were both mother and daughter yesterday. Their heights then should have been the same in both photograph and here yesterday – or Ellie should have been taller. But somehow daughter had instead shrunk instead of growing in the few months. I also noticed that the Mrs. Darlington that I met yesterday was slightly heavier than the subject in the photo – not significantly, but at least six or seven pounds, I think. Now it's not impossible for someone to gain a bit of weight in that amount of time, but there was a noticeable change.

"With these items, along with your daughter's suggestion at forgetfulness, not using pet names for you or her, and her apparent affection for Mrs. Wiggleston – preferring this woman from her long-ago past over her own invalid mother upstairs, with whom she had markedly decreased her level of contact – a very strange idea began to ferment in my mind. After we left here, I was able to make my way to offices housing the various birth records, where I have friend who is willing to support my vocation with information as I may need.

"Imagine my surprise, Mr. Darlington – actually, I'm sorry. I wasn't surprised – to find that Mrs. Wiggleston here is the proud mother of an adult daughter, who just happened to have been born on the exact same day as your wife."

With a shake of the head, Darlington responded, "That's not possible. I've heard the story over and over again. She delivered my wife on the second of May, 1859, according to both her and Grandmother. How

235

could she have given birth to her own child on the same day when she was assisting in that birth? Wait – "

Suddenly he glanced quickly around the room. "Where is Grandmother? How could we have forgotten her through this whole ordeal?"

Ellie answered, "When I came downstairs with . . . Mother – " She glanced nervously at the woman who had accompanied her just a few minutes earlier. " – Grandmother was knitting in her bedroom. I assume that she's still up there. Should I go ask her to come down and hear all of this?"

"No," said her father. "I think that the shock would be too much for her – it may still be too much for me."

Holmes continued, "I believe that is wise. She'll have plenty of time later to digest these proceedings. Nonetheless, trust me, Mr. Darlington, when I say that I personally observed the birth certificate which indicates that Mrs. Wiggleston, recently widowed, gave birth to a baby girl named Sheila Wiggleston on the exact same date that your wife was born. I would ask Mrs. Wiggleston to explain this seeming contradiction, but it appears from her flushed colour that discussing this issue would be very difficult for her right now." All the servant could do was gently nod her head up and down.

"I suspect that it's really is quite simple, if not a little sordid, of an explanation," said Holmes. "It seems – " He addressed the woman who had rushed across the room and was still gripping the hands of her husband and daughter. " – that Mrs. Darlington's mother actually gave birth to *twins* on that day twenty-eight years or so ago. Unfortunately, she was led by Mrs. Wiggleston to believe one of the girls had been still-born, and so, while tending to the needs of the remaining live birth, she managed to somehow bundle the other baby out of the room and then the house in order to make the necessary arrangements to keep her."

"It wasn't like that," interrupted Mrs. Wiggleston.

"Indeed. Then how was it?"

"We truly thought that the second baby was dead. It was only later, as I was carrying the poor thing away so that the mother wouldn't be upset, that I saw her breathing."

"Then," said Holmes, "the prudent thing to do would have been to immediately retrace your steps and present the matching baby back to her mother. But sadly, you yourself had lost a child the year before – the records confirm this as well – and earlier that year your husband had passed away from a bout of influenza. Giving you as much benefit of the doubt as possible, you simply walked away, cradling the baby next to your bosom."

236

"Once I arrived at home," explained Mrs. Wiggleston, "I was obviously not in my right mind. I had decided to raise her as my own, but I had no plan beyond that." She looked toward the real Mrs. Darlington. "I suppose that I felt that if also remained part of your life as your nanny, my dear, that it would somehow remove some of the guilt that I felt for depriving you of your twin sister."

"And so things have remained for the past twenty-eight years," said Holmes. "At some point, Mrs. Wiggleston left your mother's employee, Mrs. Darlington, when her services were no longer required, having some kept the existence of her own 'daughter' a secret through those years. Then, a few months ago, you and Mrs. Wiggleston became reacquainted, and she was hired to work as Ellie's nanny, as well as the housekeeper of the house. She saw the life that you had – a loving husband, and a fine child – and thought that her daughter was being unfairly deprived."

"No!" cried Mrs. Wiggleston. "It wasn't like that!"

"How can you say that?" cried Mrs. Darlington, rising to her feet. Then she turned and looked at her husband. "She lured me to her house one weekend while you were out of town, visiting your parents, and then – ever since, I've been her prisoner! While my . . . while my *sister* was here, trying to take my place." Then she scowled. "And neither of you even noticed the difference!"

"That isn't true," countered Holmes. "Both Ellie and her father had discussed how unusual you were acting, and Ellie took the initiative to hire me to investigate. And you must remember that Mrs. Wiggletson had been careful to coach her daughter in your various behaviors, so that she could fit in as easily as possible. Even so, her performance was far from perfect."

Throughout, Sheila Wiggleston had simply looked toward the floor, offering no comment or response. Holmes glanced at her, and then toward Lestrade and Gregson. "Inspectors? I believe that the rest is up to you."

Gregson moved to speak, but he was interrupted by Mrs. Darlington. "Wait!" she cried. Then, looking toward Holmes, she asked, "What will happen to them?"

"They committed a crime," said Holmes simply. "They will be charged with kidnapping you, plus whatever else that seems appropriate."

The room was charged with silence for a long moment while the lady chewed at her lip. Finally, she shook her head. "If I don't press charges, will they still be arrested?"

"No, ma'am," said Lestrade. "But the charges are serious – not to mention if we can still make anything stick related to that long-ago kidnapping of your newborn sister. I urge you to – "

"No!" interrupted Mrs. Darlington. "No – I want a chance to know my sister. What they did was wrong. I've – I was kept prisoner by Mrs.

Wiggleston, it's true, but she was not unkind to me. I missed my family here terribly, and I could only imagine – " She paused and swallowed. Then, "And . . . and I don't know how this would have ended if . . . if Sheila had been able to successfully replace me. But she is my sister, after all, and I want to know her better. And my mother upstairs deserves to know that she has another daughter as well."

Gregson frowned, and Lestrade threw up his hands in frustration. "Well, then, I suppose that there's nothing for us here." Then he looked at Holmes, with something like a twinkle in his eyes. "Thank you, however, Mr. Holmes, for a most interesting morning. Rather like something from *The Prince and the Pauper*."

When the police had departed, and we were left with the Darlington family, as well as Mrs. Wiggleston and Sheila, Darlington stood, his hand reaching again for that of his wife. If she had been angry at him a moment earlier, it had dissipated.

"Why, then," he asked of Holmes, "all of this drama?" He waved his free hand. "Why not just free my wife and arrest these women?" He glared at Mrs. Wiggleston and her adopted daughter.

"It was in the way of a demonstration – to you and Ellie, as well as to Sheila Wiggleston herself. She needed to understand that she isn't a true mother – at least not yet – and that she had no business trying to take on that role without earning it honestly.

"As you have probably guessed by now," he continued, "the entire story that we told you after our arrival – a criminal with a missing dog seeking vengeance – was complete fantasy, designed to solicit a suggestive response from Sheila when the proper time arrived. That's when I looked out the window, to give a signal to Inspector Gregson, waiting outside. The shots that you heard were courtesy of him, firing his service revolver into a couple bales of hay that we'd placed nearby.

"Sheila," he said, turning to the young woman who looked so much like Mrs. Darlington, "it's my belief that a mother, when she believes danger is about to reach her family, will seek to protect her most valuable and cherished asset: Her children. You, unfortunately, reacted totally differently, running *away* from the danger, only thinking of your own safety. That isn't the appropriate response to take in a moment of crisis for a mother."

Sheila looked up then and nodded before again lowering her eyes.

"But Mr. Holmes," said Mrs. Wiggleston, puzzled. "Why go to that trouble – to give us such a scare, and to let Sheila have the opportunity to learn such a lesson? You must have known that she wouldn't be going to prison. What gave you that idea?"

"Why, from Mrs. Darlington herself." All eyes turned to Ellie's mother. "Yesterday afternoon, while you were here, Mrs. Wiggleston, I reconnoitered your little dwelling in Orde House Street, just around the corner from the Hospital for Sick Children. I have some skill with entries through locked doors, and I found Mrs. Darlington inside, as I thought that I might. I arrived prepared to take her away with me, but immediately after identifying myself, she began to ask me what she had missed. She assured me that she'd been well-treated – but that without a doubt she was a prisoner. I told her why I was involved, and what I'd learned from the birth and death records. She confirmed much of the same from what you'd told her during the two weeks that she was kept locked up, unable to escape, and unheard by the neighbors when she would call out.

"And yet, she has some sympathy for her newly discovered sister, and through our conversation yesterday afternoon, we conceived of this little idea together. I involved the police because their presence leant veracity to the endeavor, but Mrs. Darlington never intended to actually press charges."

With that, the lady herself released herself from her husband's grip and walked across the room to her sister. The similarity between the two was striking. "I wish that we had met under different circumstances, but I would rather know you this way then not at all." She reached out, and after a moment Sheila took her hand with a smile. "Would you like to come upstairs and meet our mother?"

Sheila nodded, and Mrs. Wiggleston gave a small sob – I couldn't tell if it was from happiness, perhaps at the punishment they'd narrowly avoided, or possibly that she was about to irretrievably lose some aspect of the relationship to the girl that she had raised as a daughter. In any case, the Darlingtons, along with Sheila and Mrs. Wiggleston, all left the room together, with only Ellie remembering to look back in our direction, giving each of us a sweet smile.

I'm happy to report that a few weeks ago young Elenora Darlington visited our Baker Street sitting room, accompanied by her newly found Aunt Sheila. It turned out that her grandmother is a woman of stronger constitution than anyone had thought, and once the initial shock wore off, she had gratefully accepted having a second daughter.

And more importantly, Ellie seemed to relish having something of a second mother.

"It was all-important. When a woman thinks that her house is on fire, her instinct is at once to rush to the thing which she values most.

It is a perfectly overpowering impulse, and I have more than once taken advantage of it. In the case of the Darlington substitution scandal it was of use to me . . . ."

– Sherlock Holmes
"A Scandal in Bohemia

The Case of the
Elusive Umbrella
by Leslie Charteris and Denis Green

Sherlock Holmes and The Saint
An Introduction by Ian Dickerson

Everyone has a story to tell about how they first met Sherlock Holmes. For me it was a Penguin paperback reprint my brother introduced me to in my pre-teen years. I read it, and went on to read all the original stories, but it didn't appeal to me in the way it appealed to others. This is probably because I discovered the adventures of The Saint long before I discovered Sherlock Holmes.

The Saint, for those readers who may need a little more education, was also known as Simon Templar and was a modern day Robin Hood who first appeared in 1928. Not unlike Holmes, he has appeared in books, films, TV shows, and comics. He was created by Leslie Charteris, a young man born in Singapore to a Chinese father and an English mother, who was just twenty years old when he wrote that first Saint adventure. He'd always wanted to be a writer – his first piece was published when he was just nine years of age – and he followed that Saint story, his third novel, with two further books, neither of which featured Simon Templar.

However, there's a notable similarity between the heroes of his early novels, and Charteris, recognising this, and being somewhat fed up of creating variations on the same theme, returned to writing adventures for The Saint. Short stories for a weekly magazine, *The Thriller*, and a change of publisher to the mainstream Hodder & Stoughton, helped him on his way to becoming a best-seller and something of a pop culture sensation in Great Britain.

But he was ambitious. Always fond of the USA, he started to spend more time over there, and it was the 1935 novel – and fifteenth Saint book – *The Saint in New York*, that made him a transatlantic success. He spent some time in Hollywood, writing for the movies and keeping an eye on The Saint films that were then in production at RKO studios. Whilst there, he struck up what would become a lifelong friendship with Denis Green, a British actor and writer, and his new wife, Mary.

Fast forward a couple of years . . . . Leslie was on the west coast of the States, still writing Saint stories to pay the bills, writing the occasional non-Saint piece for magazines, and getting increasingly frustrated with RKO who, he felt, weren't doing him, or his creation, justice. Denis Green, meanwhile, had established himself as a stage actor, and had embarked on a promising radio career both in front of and behind the microphone.

Charteris was also interested in radio. He had a belief that his creation could be adapted for every medium and was determined to try and prove it. In 1940, he

241

commissioned a pilot programme to show how The Saint would work on radio, casting his friend Denis Green as Simon Templar. Unfortunately, it didn't sell, but just three years later, he tried again, commissioning a number of writers – including Green – to create or adapt Saint adventures for radio.

They also didn't sell, and after struggling to find a network or sponsor for The Saint on the radio, he handed the problem over to established radio show packager and producer, James L. Saphier. Charteris was able to solve one problem, however: At the behest of advertising agency Young & Rubicam, who represented the show's sponsors, Petri Wine, Denis Green had been sounded out about writing for *The New Adventures of Sherlock Holmes*, a weekly radio series that was then broadcasting on the Mutual Network.

Green confessed to his friend that, whilst he could write good radio dialogue, he simply hadn't a clue about plotting. He was, as his wife would later recall, a reluctant writer: "He didn't really like to write. He would wait until the last minute. He would put it off as long as possible by scrubbing the kitchen stove or wash the bathroom – anything before he sat down at the typewriter. I had a very clean house." Charteris offered a solution: They would go into partnership, with him creating the stories and Green writing the dialogue.

But there was another problem: *The New Adventures of Sherlock Holmes* aired on one of the radio networks that Leslie hoped might be interested in the adventures of The Saint, and it would not look good, he thought, for him to be involved with a rival production. Leslie adopted the pseudonym of *Bruce Taylor*, (as you will see at the end of the following script,) taking inspiration taking inspiration from the surname of the show's producer Glenhall Taylor and that of Rathbone's co-star, Nigel Bruce.

The Taylor/Green partnership was initiated with "The Strange Case of the Aluminum Crutch", which aired on July 24th, 1944, and would ultimately run until the following March, with *Bruce Taylor*'s final contribution to the Holmes Canon being "The Secret of Stonehenge", which aired on March 19th, 1945 – thirty-five episodes in all.

Bruce Taylor's short radio career came to an end in short because Charteris shifted his focus elsewhere. Thanks to Saphier, The Saint found a home on the NBC airwaves, and aside from the constant demand for literary Saint adventures, he was exploring the possibilities of launching a Saint magazine. He was replaced by noted writer and critic Anthony Boucher, who would establish a very successful writing partnership with Denis Green.

Fast forward quite a few more years – to 1988 to be precise: A young chap called Dickerson, a long standing member of *The Saint Club*, discovers a new TV series of The Saint is going into production. Suitably inspired, he writes to the then-secretary of the Club, suggesting that it was time the world was reminded of The Saint, and The Saint Club in particular. Unbeknownst to him, the secretary passes his letter on to Leslie Charteris himself. The teenaged Dickerson and the aging author struck up a friendship which involved, amongst other things, many fine lunches, followed by lazy chats over various libations. Some of those conversations featured the words "Sherlock" and "Holmes".

It was when Leslie died, in 1993, that I really got to know his widow, Audrey. We often spoke at length about many things, and from time to time discussed Leslie and the Holmes scripts, as well as her own career as an actress.

When she died in 2014, Leslie's family asked me to go through their flat in Dublin. Pretty much the first thing I found was a stack of radio scripts, many of which had been written by *Bruce Taylor* and Denis Green.

I was, needless to say, rather delighted. More so when his family gave me permission to get them into print. Back in the 1940's, no one foresaw an afterlife for shows such as this, and no recordings exist of this particular Sherlock Holmes adventure. So here you have the only documentation around of Charteris and Green's "The Case of the Elusive Umbrella" . . . .

Ian Dickerson

Constant readers will be aware almost immediately that this narrative, a version of that famous Untold Case regarding the mysterious disappearance of James Phillimore, doesn't actually have James Phillimore in it. It does, however, have the other important elements: An umbrella, and a house, into which a man steps and vanishes.

I'm usually quite strict about these things – stories have to be Canonical. Holmes and Watson have to be portrayed correctly, and there can be no aspects of parody, or actual supernatural encounters, or elements of anachronism. And when a book has a theme, I actually hold the contributors within those guidelines. I've rejected stories for this collection that didn't fit – they were previously untold, but not "Untold Cases". But this time . . . .

In 2017 and 2018, Ian Dickerson edited and published two collections of "lost" Holmes radio scripts by Leslie Charteris and Denis Green, all from the 1944-1945 season which had starred Basil Rathbone and Nigel Bruce. Between them, these two excellent volumes – Sherlock Holmes: The Lost Radio Scripts *and* Sherlock Holmes: More Lost Radio Scripts *– collected twenty-three full scripts and three that were incomplete. As a fan who was thrilled to be able to finally read these adventures – long thought to be lost – I reached out to Ian to express my joy. We soon worked it out that one of the still-unpublished scripts in his possession, as obtained from The Estate of Leslie Charteris, could appear in an MX anthology. Thus, it was my pleasure to be able to introduce a Holmes adventure, via Rathbone and Bruce (and Charteris and Green), that had never been seen before by modern generations.*

Alas, it turned out that there weren't enough of them left after Ian's two collections to make up another full-sized book, and a third volume wasn't planned by the publisher. It seemed that those other rediscovered treasures would remain unseen by most of us. But Ian has since been gracious enough to allow further scripts to be published in these MX anthologies – four others so far, besides this one. There are still five from that season, when Charteris and Green co-wrote them, that are left unpublished, and I very much hope that they'll appear here in future MX volumes. (Ian: Hint hint . . . .)

And as for this story, which is an Untold Case and almost about James Phillimore if one squints just a bit: Well, with the chance to publish another lost script from the 1940's by Charteris and Green, and also being able to bring a bit of unknown Rathbone and Bruce to a modern audience, I wasn't going to turn this one down just because of a mere technicality. After all, Watson surely changed names –obfuscated, shall we say – when writing up his narratives, so the reader can simply swap "Phillimore" for "Rush" when reading it. (I considered – for about a second – making the change in the text from "Rush" to "Phillimore" as an editorial decision, but that would have been a terrible thing to do.)

Why – with this tale's clear connection to the peculiar disappearance of James Phillimore – did Charteris and Green change the name? We'll never know, but I suspect that it was because just about a year before, on January 3rd, 1944, Rathbone and Bruce had performed in another radio version of this Untold Case entitled "The Incredible Mystery of Mr. James Phillimore", as written by Edith Meiser, who had created the Holmes radio show way back in 1930, and had been the sole writer for the series for the entire run, until Charteris and Green took over on July 24th, 1944. (Unlike this Charteris and Green version, Meiser's script is lost and hasn't been found.) Perhaps the idea of two versions of Mr. Phillimore (broadcast within a year of each other) was considered too confusing for the 1940's audience. Modern Sherlockians are more sophisticated, and can handle multiple versions of Untold Cases.

Now turn up your radio, and find that long-misplaced bottle of Petri Wine, and join us for another New Adventure of Sherlock Holmes, starring Basil Rathbone and Nigel Bruce . . . .

D.M.

The Case of the Elusive Umbrella

Originally Broadcast on January 22nd, 1945

<u>CHARACTERS</u>
- SHERLOCK HOLMES
- DR. JOHN H. WATSON
- INSPECTOR LESTRADE
- ISABEL RUSH
- STANLEY RUSH
- NATHAN BLACK
- TAYLOR

BILL FORMAN (ANNOUNCER): Petri Wine brings you –

<u>MUSIC: THEME (FADE ON CUE)</u>

FORMAN: Basil Rathbone and Nigel Bruce in *The New Adventures of Sherlock Holmes.*

<u>MUSIC: THEME – FULL FINISH</u>

<u>OPENING COMMERCIAL</u>

FORMAN: The Petri family – the family that took time to bring you good wine – invites you to listen to Doctor Watson tell us about another exciting adventure he shared with his old friend – that master detective – Sherlock Holmes. I'm all set for a good story tonight – because I had a swell dinner this evening. My family had chicken – fried chicken – and with that chicken, naturally, we had Petri California Sauterne. You know, what with rationing tightening up and chicken being ration free, we're having chicken more often than I suppose we ought too. But when you can have chicken and Petri Sauterne – boy, you're really eating! That Petri Sauterne is a wine that can make any meal taste better. Petri Sauterne has a beautiful golden color that brings sparkle and cheer to your table . . . it makes even a simple wartime meal look fancy. And when it comes to flavor – well, that Petri Sauterne has a flavor right from the heart of luscious, hand-picked, California grapes, a flavor that's subtle . . . delicate and intriguing. Try Petri Sauterne the next time you have chicken. Share Petri Sauterne with your friends – Yes, and serve it proudly, because

246

the name "Petri" is the proudest name in the history of American Wines!

MUSIC: *SCOTCH POEM*

FORMAN: And now for our weekly visit with the good Doctor Watson. Evening, Doctor.

WATSON: Good evening, Mr. Forman, Quite foggy out tonight, isn't it, my boy?

FORMAN: It certainly is, Doctor. I wasn't sure if I'd be able to get here.

WATSON: You should have seen the fogs we used to get in London in the old days.

FORMAN: Pea-soupers, I believe you used to call them, didn't you? Does tonight's story take place in one by any chance, Doctor?

WATSON: No as a matter of fact, it doesn't. Although a slight drizzle of rain, which out here you call "precipitation", was the start of all the trouble. Draw up your chair and make yourself comfortable. Smoke?

FORMAN: Thanks. I rather think I will. I – I've brought my own cigarettes, you see.

WATSON: Very thoughtful of you, my boy. On looking back over the years, I'm inclined to think it was one of the oddest problems Sherlock Holmes ever solved. It began when a man went back into his house to get his umbrella – and proceeded to vanish off the face of the earth!

FORMAN: That sounds exciting!

WATSON: It started conventionally enough. Holmes and I had been to the St. James Hall to hear a noted Italian violinist, and after the concert, we returned to Baker Street to find Inspector Lestrade waiting for us. As we came up the stairs and opened the door – there he was (FADING) pacing up and down our room . . . .

SOUND EFFECT: FOOTSTEPS. DOOR OPEN AND CLOSE.

LESTRADE: (FADING IN) . . . Mr. Holmes, I'm certainly glad to see you! Evenin', Doctor Watson.

WATSON: Hello, Lestrade.

HOLMES: Lestrade, my dear fellow, you seem very agitated. I shall presume, therefore, that this is not entirely a social call.

LESTRADE: It isn't, Mr. Holmes. I'm onto one of the most puzzling cases I've ever had – and that's a fact.

HOLMES: And you want my help in the matter?

LESTRADE: I certainly do, sir.

HOLMES: Splendid. Sit down and tell me all about it.

LESTRADE: Well, Mr. Holmes, it sounds like one of those tricks Maskelyne and Devant do on the music halls. Yesterday afternoon, a man by the name of William Rush left his house in Onslow Square, and went out to a carriage with his partner – a man by the name of Nathan Black. As he reached the carriage, it started to rain, so he said he'd go back to the house for his umbrella. Black saw him open the front door and go in – but he didn't come out again. After a little while, Mr. Black got worried and went after him, but not only was there no sign of the man, but his wife and brother who were inside the house swore he never did come back.

WATSON: What an amazing story!

HOLMES: You searched the house thoroughly, of course.

LESTRADE: I've searched, and examined, and questioned until I'm blue in the face, Mr. Holmes, an' I can't find no trace of him.

HOLMES: Hmm. Was anyone able to verify Mr. Black's story?

LESTRADE: Yes, Mr. Holmes – Mr. Black's coachman. He swore on oath that he saw Rush go back into the house.

HOLMES: And the couple inside the house swore he didn't come back, eh, Lestrade?

LESTRADE: That's right, sir.

WATSON: But people just don't vanish in thin air, y' know.

HOLMES; A very intriguing problem, Lestrade. The couple outside swear the man went back – the couple inside swear that he didn't. If neither couple is lying, one might think that somewhere within the thickness of a front door a man has vanished!

WATSON: That's what it looks like, Holmes. That are you going to do about it?

HOLMES: Do, old chap? I'm going to do the obvious thing. I'm going to pay a visit to Onslow Square.

MUSIC: BRIDGE

LESTRADE: Well, I hope you're satisfied, Mr. Holmes. You must have searched every inch of the house.

HOLMES: I am, thank you. And now, Lestrade, I'd like to talk to Mrs. Rush and her brother-in-law.

LESTRADE: They're waiting for you in the library. I'll take you in.

SOUND; FOOTSTEPS ON WOOD. FOOTSTEPS STOP. KNOCK ON DOOR

ISABEL: (OFF) Come in.

SOUND EFFECT: DOOR OPEN. FOOTSTEPS

LESTRADE: Mrs. Rush . . , this is Mr. Sherlock Holmes and Doctor Watson. They're working with me on the case.

ISABEL: Good evening, Mr. Holmes. Dr. Watson.

WATSON: How d'you do, Mrs. Rush.

HOLMES: Good evening, madam.

LESTRADE: And this is her husband's brother, Captain Stanley Rush.

HOLMES: How are you, sir?

WATSON: How do you do, Captain Rush.

STANLEY: (ABOUT FORTY – GRUFF, UNPLEASANT) How d'you do.

LESTRADE: And now, if you'll excuse me, I have to go back to the Yard and make a report. (FADING) Good evening. See you later, Mr: Holmes.

SOUND EFFECT: DOOR CLOSE

ISABEL: Sit down, won't you? And tell me what I can do to help you.

HOLMES: (AFTER A MOMENT) Thank you, Mrs. Rush. I just want to ask you a few questions.

ISABEL: Ask me anything you want to, Mr. Holmes.

HOLMES: First, are you convinced – beyond any shadow of a doubt – that your husband did not re-enter the front door after he left here yesterday afternoon?

ISABEL: I'm . . . positive.

HOLMES: Then please tell me exactly what happened, Mrs. Rush.

ISABEL: After my husband and Nathan Black had gone, Stanley and I came back here into this room. I'd left this door open as I intended going out myself soon, and was about to go upstairs to change my dress. After a few moments, I started to leave the room, and as I passed the window I noticed that the carriage was still waiting (FADING) in the street outside . . . .

ISABEL: Stanley? Whatever's holding them up out there? The carriage hasn't moved.

STANLEY: (FADING IN) I don't know. Let's find out. I'll yell at 'em from the window.

250

STANLEY: Hello – it's started to rain. (RAISING HIS VOICE) What's keeping you, Nathan?

BLACK: (OFF CALLING – ABOUT FIFTY) We're waiting for Bill.

STANLEY: But he came out with you.

BLACK: He went back – for his umbrella.

STANLEY: He couldn't have done. We'd have seen him.

BLACK: Yes he did, Stanley, I saw him go in the front door.

STANLEY: (CALLING) Better come back here, Nathan. (TO ISABEL) I don't know what he's talking about. He says that Bill came back for his umbrella.

ISABEL: This doesn't make sense. Let's go and find out what Nathan's talking about.

SOUND EFFECT: FOOTSTEPS. AFTER A MOMENT, DOOR OPENS

BLACK: (FADING IN – LAUGHING) Well, d'you believe me? Where is he?

STANLEY: I tell you Bill didn't come back here.

BLACK: And I tell you I saw him unlock the front door!

STANLEY: That's ridiculous: Isabel and I were just inside the library here. We'd have seen him.

BLACK: Yes, you would. But the fact remains I saw him enter and close the front door behind him – and so did the coachman!

ISABEL: (STARTING TO PANIC) Something's happened to him!

STANLEY: Now Isabel – what could have happened between the carriage and here?

251

ISABEL: I don't know – but something has!

STANLEY: This is utterly ridiculous. (FADING) A man can't just dissolve –

ISABEL: (FADE IN) We searched the house from top to bottom, Mr. Holmes, and we found no trace of William, so I got in touch with Scotland Yard.

HOLMES: Before your husband and his partner, Mr. Black, left yesterday afternoon, had you been discussing anything of a significant nature – or was it just a social gathering?

ISABEL: Not, it was a conference about the business.

STANLEY: And my brother also told us the terms of his will.

WATSON: What *were* those terms, may I ask, Captain Rush?

STANLEY: He left everything to Isabel, and named me as executor.

HOLMES: Was this a new will?

ISABEL: Yes, it was.

HOLMES: Signed?

STANLEY: No. Bill wanted to discuss it with us first.

HOLMES: What were the terms of the previous will?

STANLEY: Isabel was to get three-quarters of the estate, and I was to get one-quarter.

HOLMES: So that the new will – had your brother signed it – would have cut you, Captain Rush, out of any benefits?

STANLEY: (ANGRILY) Are you suggesting that I tried to get rid of my own brother to prevent him signing the will?

HOLMES: Captain Rush, you seem remarkably touchy. I'm only asking some obvious questions. I'm not *suggesting* anything.

STANLEY: I'm sorry.

HOLMES: This business conference – was it entirely an amicable one?

ISABEL: (HESITANTLY) Well . . . .

STANLEY: Might as well tell the truth, darling.

WATSON: Yes, indeed, madam. We can't possibly help you unless you tell us everything.

ISABEL: My husband had quite a heated argument with Nathan Black. Nathan handles the financial side of the business, you see, and he got very angry when William said he was going to get a certified accountant in to go over the books and figures.

HOLMES: Did your husband accuse Mr. Black of dishonesty?

ISABEL: No, but he implied it. However, by the time they left, it had all blown over and they seemed on the best of terms,

WATSON: May I ask, madam, what is your personal opinion of Mr. Black?

ISABEL: I dislike – and distrust him.

HOLMES: That's concise. And you, Captain Rush?

STANLEY: I've always disliked him, but I haven't distrusted him until a few weeks ago.

HOLMES: Was there something that caused you to change your opinion as to his honesty?

STANLEY: Last month, Bill and I were going through some of my father's papers, and we came across an old diary that he'd been writing in just before his death. We found some entries concerning a copper mine in South America, and also some references to buying shares in a silk house in Paris. Now Nathan was executor of my father's estate, and as we'd never heard of these interests until we read the diary. . . naturally we questioned him. After all, he'd been my father's partner for sixteen years.

HOLMES: And what did he say?

STANLEY: That he knew nothing about it. Of course we didn't believe him. And that started Bill looking into the current business affairs a little more closely.

HOLMES: When did your father die, Captain Rush?

STANLEY: Three years ago – in a yachting accident. And that's another thing – the only other person on the boat was Nathan. He tells a story of how he tried to save Father and nearly drowned himself in doing it. But I'd lay you hundred guineas to one he murdered him and then capsized the boat to make it look like an accident.

HOLMES: Did your brother believe that, too?

STANLEY: Yes, he did.

WATSON: And yet you've both said that when your brother an' Mr. Black left here yesterday, they were on the best of terms. Seems a little incongruous, under the circumstances.

STANLEY: (FLUSTERED) Perhaps Bill didn't feel it as strongly as I did. But he definitely distrusted him.

HOLMES: Hmm. Where d'you suppose we might find Mr. Nathan Black at this time of night?

STANLEY: That's easy to answer, Nathan is a man of habit. He always dines at the Criterion Restaurant – when he's in London. It's only eight-thirty. I imagine you'll still find him there.

HOLMES: Thank you, Captain Rush. And many thanks to you both for your help and cooperation. Come along, Watson.

ISABEL: Mr. Holmes – Do you think you're going to be able to find out what's happened to William?

254

HOLMES: I hope so, Mrs. Rush. I hope so sincerely.

MUSIC: BRIDGE (STRAUSS WALTZ THEME). ORCHESTRA CONTINUES PLAYING STRAUSS WALTZ

HOLMES: (AFTER A MOMENT) Mr. Nathan Black?

BLACK: (FADING TN) Yes, gentlemen. What can I do for you?

HOLMES: My name is Sherlock Holmes, and this is my friend, Doctor Watson.

(AD LIB "HOW DO YOU DO'S")

HOLMES: We're investigating the disappearance of your partner, Mr. Rush.

BLACK: Sit down, Mr. Holmes, won't you? And Doctor – ? I'm very glad to meet you.

SOUND EFFECT: CHAIRS BEING MOVED

BLACK: A dreadful business. Have there been any new developments?

HOLMES: I'm afraid not. You don't mind if I ask you a few personal questions do you, Mr. black?

BLACK: Of course not. Fire away.

HOLMES: Mr. Black, wasn't there some little difference of opinion between you and your partner regarding a diary that was recently discovered?

BLACK: (LAUGHING) I see that Stanley Rush has been talking to you! All I can tell you, gentlemen, is that if their father had any interest in copper in South America, or silk in France, that it's the first I ever heard of it.

WATSON: Then may I ask, sir, how you account for those entries in the diary?

BLACK: I could answer that question a little better if I'd seen this supposed entry in the diary. Personally, I don't think it exists – except in Stanley's imagination.

HOLMES: Mr. Black, despite this argument you indulged in with the missing man yesterday, I understand you left the house together on the best of terms?

BLACK: Oh yes. We've had disagreements before, but they always blew over – as this one did. I'm much too fond of William to stay angry with him for very long.

HOLMES: You're *convinced*, aren't you, that your partner went back into the house for his umbrella yesterday afternoon?

BLACK: Of course I am – because I saw it with my own eyes. If you need any corroboration, you can ask my coachman.

HOLMES: I *should* like to hear his version – purely as a matter of routine.

BLACK: He's waiting for me outside now. Why not question him at once?

HOLMES: An excellent idea. And many thanks for your courtesy, Mr. Black.

MUSIC: BRIDGE

SOUND EFFECT: STREET NOISES

BLACK: (AFTER A FEW MOMENTS) Here's my carriage, Mr. Holmes . . . (CALLING) Taylor come down here a minute, will you?

TAYLOR: (FADING IN – MIDDLE-AGED COCKNEY) Right y'are, Mr. Black.

BLACK: This gentleman would like to ask you a few questions. Go ahead, Mr. Holmes.

HOLMES: Taylor. . .you were standing outside when Mr. Rush and your employer came out yesterday, weren't you?

TAYLOR: That's right, guv'nor.

256

HOLMES: Will you give your own version of what happened, please.

TAYLOR: They come out to the carriage. I hops down and opens the door for 'em. As they start to step in, it begins to drizzle wiv' rain, an' Mr. Rush says he's goin' back to get his umbrella. He climbs up the steps again, unlocks the front door wiv' 'is latchkey, and goes in an' closes the door behind 'im . . . and that's the last I sees of him. After a few minutes, Captain Rush comes to the window and asks us why we're waiting and that's when all the how-d'-you-do starts.

HOLMES: Thank you, Taylor.

BLACK: Satisfied, Mr. Holmes?

HOLMES: Yes, but puzzled, Mr. Black. Very puzzled. In fact, I think I'd better return to Baker Street. I'm very much afraid this is at least a three-pipe problem.

MUSIC: BRIDGE

WATSON: (SLEEPILY) Holmes, it's nearly two o'clock in the morning, you're smoking your fifth pipe – and yet you said it was only a three-pipe problem.

HOLMES: Obviously, therefore, old chap, I underestimated the problem.

WATSON: I've been puzzling about the case, and I have a couple of theories.

HOLMES: Good. Let's hear them.

WATSON: Well, I was reading a book the other day – I think it was by Henry James – in which a man had the ability to slip back through time and come out in another century, maybe two- or three-hundred years ago.

HOLMES: (CHUCKLING) Watson, dear fellow, you're most refreshing. You mean that you think that Mr. Rush stepped through that front door yesterday – and into another century?

257

WATSON: It's rather a wild theory, I must admit, but it seems to me this whole case can only have a supernatural explanation.

HOLMES: Let us leave the supernatural explanations until we have disposed of the natural ones. Four witnesses have testified to the impossible. Therefore two of them must be at least mistaken. The question is – which two?

WATSON: My other theory was connected with hypnotism. Supposing Rush wanted to disappear for some reason, and so he hypnotised the witnesses. Now you know as well as I do that hypnotism is a perfectly –

HOLMES: (INTERRUPTING EXCITEDLY) Idiot! Numbskull!

WATSON: (HURT) Well, that's very rude, Holmes. I'm not pretending they're very sound theories.

HOLMES: No, old chap. *I'm* the idiot!

WATSON: What d'you mean?

HOLMES: The umbrella – That's the clue! William Rush returned for his umbrella. If it's still there, he might have gone back for it. If it's not, then perhaps he had it all the time. Get your hat and coat, Watson!

WATSON: You mean we're going to the house at this time of the night?

HOLMES: Certainly.

WATSON: But you can't rout people out of bed at two in the morning.

HOLMES: I don't propose to. I have skeleton keys, and anyway, I don't want to draw attention to our visit. Our enemy – whoever he may be – could think of the same thing at any moment. We must hope that we get there before him!

MUSIC: UP STRONG

FORMAN: We'll bring you the rest of Doctor Watson's story in just a few seconds, which gives me plenty of time to mention a wine that can make even a sandwich taste like a feast – That wine is Petri California

258

Burgundy. Petri Burgundy is the best friend a good meal ever had, and it's a friend indeed to simple, war-time meals. A rich deep red in color and hearty, full and delicious in flavor – Petri Burgundy is the perfect companion for all your old standby dishes. Petri Burgundy is great with hamburger sandwiches . . . it's just about the last word when you have good old-fashioned spaghetti. And if you're planning a piping hot pot roast or your favorite beef stew – well, you just can't forget Petri Burgundy. Believe me, with food, nothing can take the place of that good Petri Wine!

MUSIC: *SCOTCH POEM*

FORMAN: And now, back to tonight's new Sherlock Holmes adventure. William Rush, wealthy business man, stepping back into his house for his umbrella, has apparently vanished from the face of the earth, and Sherlock Holmes and Doctor Watson are investigating the strange mystery. As we rejoin our story, it is two-thirty in the morning and the famous pair are engaged in breaking into the missing (FADING) man's house.

SOUND EFFECT: SCRATCHING OF KEY IN LOCK

WATSON: (WHISPERING) I don't like this, Holmes – breaking into people's houses in the middle of the night.

HOLMES: Hold the lantern a little higher, will you, old chap – that's it. There we are.

SOUND EFFECT: DOOR OPENING AND CLOSING SOFTLY. STEALTHY FOOTSTEPS

HOLMES: (AFTER AN APPRECIABLE PAUSE) The umbrella stand. Now what do we find?

WATSON: Several parasols . . . obviously Mrs. Rush's.

HOLMES: One very shabby umbrella. And – what have we here – this looks more like it.

WATSON: By Jove, yes. A neatly rolled one with a gold band on it.

HOLMES: Yes, but unfortunately for our purposes, it has the initials "*S.R.*" on the band. Obviously, it belongs to Captain Stanley Rush. And that completes the collection.

WATSON: Then William Rush's umbrella isn't here, and that means he had it with him all the time – and that he didn't come back.

HOLMES: That would appear to be what happened, my dear Watson. On the other hand, someone might have assumed we would reason along those lines, and in consequence have hidden or destroyed the umbrella.

WATSON: That's true. I wonder where they might have hidden it?

HOLMES: I'd suggest the cellar as being a likely place. Also, it has the advantage of having a most convenient furnace down there. Come on . . . through the kitchen.

<u>SOUND EFFECT: STEALTHY FOOTSTEPS. AFTER A MOMENT, DOOR OPENING</u>

HOLMES: And now, down these stairs . . . watch your head.

WATSON: Holmes, you don't need to tell me to – (EXCLAIMING) Ouch! Confound it! Why do they design staircases for midgets?

HOLMES: Shh, old fellow. We don't want to wake the whole house.

<u>SOUND EFFECT: STEALTHY FOOTSTEPS DECENDING STAIRS</u>

(NOTE: VOICES IN ENSUING SCENE ON ECHO)

HOLMES: (AFTER A FEW MOMENTS) Well, here we are.

<u>SOUND EFFECT: FOOTSTEPS ON LEVEL</u>

WATSON: (SUDDENLY) Hello! That furnace is burning very brightly!

HOLMES: Yes. Surely no one's been stoking it at this hour of the morning.

<u>SOUND EFFECT: FOOTSTEPS STOP</u>

HOLMES: Let's see what's burning.

SOUND EFFECT: FURNACE DOOR BEING OPENED

WATSON: (EXCITEDLY) By George, Holmes! It's a burning umbrella!

HOLMES: Give me that poker . . . That's it . . . Now let's see if I can get it out again . . . .

SOUND EFFECT: RATTLING OF POKER AGAINST FURNACE

WATSON: Good work, Holmes! You've got it!

SOUND EFFECT: STAMPING OF FEET

HOLMES: (GRUNTING) First of all, we'll put out the flames.

SOUND EFFECT: MORE STAMPING OF FEET.

HOLMES: There we are.

WATSON: Not much left of it. Just a twisted metal frame.

HOLMES: But enough to give us a clue. Look here –

WATSON: A gold band!

HOLMES: Exactly, and on it the initials "*W.R.*"

WATSON: William Rush! The missing man's umbrella! And it must have been put in the furnace only a few minutes ago. The fabric was still flaring as we came down here.

HOLMES: Obviously someone was trying to dispose of very incriminating evidence.

WATSON: But who'd be here at this time of the night except –

STANLEY: (FADING IN – AGGRESSIVELY) Who's down here? I've got a revolver, so don't try any tricks!

HOLMES: Captain Rush –

STANLEY: Mr. Sherlock Holmes! What in blazes d' you think you're doing in the basement at three o'clock in the morning?

WATSON: We're searching for evidence – and we've found some.

STANLEY: How did you get in?

HOLMES: I . . . er . . . took the liberty of using a skeleton key. I didn't want to disturb anyone.

STANLEY: You're just a couple of house-breakers! I'm going to send for the police! Go on move up those stairs!

WATSON: But this is ridiculous! My friend was asked to investigate the case!

STANLEY: I didn't ask him. Go on – get moving!

WATSON: But –

HOLMES: I suggest you do as the Captain orders, Watson. He still has a revolver pointing at you, you know.

SOUND EFFECT: FOOTSTEPS ON STAIRS

WATON: Outrageous – treating us like a couple of criminals.

STANLEY: I never wanted you brought in on this case. The police are perfectly capable of handling the matter, and that's what I'll tell Lestrade when he gets here.

HOLMES: If you're sending for Lestrade, I wonder if you'd mind asking him to bring Nathan Black with him. If you insist on having a party, I feel that we should have all sides of the case equally represented.

MUSIC: BRIDGE

LESTRADE: (REPROACHFULLY) What's this Captain Rush has been telling me, Mr. Holmes? Breaking into people's houses at three in the morning? You and Doctor Watson ought to know better than that, y'know.

HOLMES: I had excellent reasons. Good evening, Mr. Black.

BLACK: What's good about it? Dragging people out of bed at this hour –

STANLEY: Yes, Mr. Holmes, I think you'd better explain what the devil you think you're up to.

HOLMES: Gentlemen, I am trying to discover what became of William Rush. Doctor Watson and I came here tonight in search of evidence. Here it is . . . this twisted umbrella frame.

BLACK: That's William's umbrellas –

HOLMES: You have remarkable eyesight, Mr. Black. The only thing that identifies it are the initials on the gold band. But you're right – it is William Rush's umbrella.

LESTRADE: Where did you find it, Mr. Holmes?

HOLMES: In the furnace.

BLACK: I see it now, Stanley! You murdered William because you were in love with Isabel. You disposed of his body and tonight you were trying to dispose of the rest of the evidence, you scoundrel!

STANLEY: (MENACINGLY) I murdered Bill? Why Nathan, you low-down –

BLACK: D'you deny that you're in love with Isabel?

STANLEY: Keep her out of this!

HOLMES: I'm afraid we can't, Captain Rush. That's a pertinent question and I think you should answer it.

LESTRADE: So do I, Mr. Holmes. Now Captain Rush – were you in love with your sister-in-law?

263

STANLEY: Yes. But Bill didn't know – and I'd never have broken his heart by telling him.

BLACK: No, you wouldn't break his heart – you'd just murder him!

STANLEY: (CURIOUSLY) You killed him yourself. Just as you murdered my father!

SOUND EFFECT: SCUFFLE

LESTRADE: Here here, gentlemen. Take it easy.

WATSON: Yes, indeed, you'll settle nothing by murdering each other.

HOLMES: Since you each accuse the other, there's one very simple way of solving this matter.

WATSON: What's that, Holmes?

HOLMES: I want each of you to sign a confession that you did away with William, and then lied about what happened.

STANTLEY: But that's ridiculous!

BLACK: Of course it is.

HOLMES: No it isn't. You have nothing to lose gentlemen, either of you, because since both these confessions can't be true, only one can be damaging – it's corroborated.

STANLEY: But to sign a confession – that's an admission of guilt!

HOLMES: Only if you are guilty, Captain Rush.

WATSON: Both the confessions can't be valid, y'know.

BLACK: What are you going to do with two confessions?

HOLMES: That I shall demonstrate to you after I have the confessions. Now, I see pen and papers on the writing desk over there. If you'll write what I dictate, please: "*I hereby confess that I murdered*

William Rush and lied about what happened to him." And now sign it, please.

BLACK: (OFF A LITTLE) I must say, Mr. Holmes, this seems the most arrant nonsense, (FADING IN) Here you are.

HOLMES: Thank you.

STANLEY: I hope you know what you're doing. (FADING IN) Here.

HOLMES: I shall confront your separate partners with these confessions and see what they say – In Captain Rush's case, it will be Mrs. Rush, and in Mrs. Black's case, it will be Taylor, his coachman. Lestrade, will you go upstairs and ask Mrs. Rush to come down here, please?

LESTRADE: (FADING) Certainly, Mr. Holmes.

HOLMES: Mr. Black, I presume your coachman, Taylor, is waiting for you?

BLACK: Yes, he's outside. I'll fetch him.

HOLMES: Thank you. I prefer to fetch him myself.

SOUND EFFECT: DOOR OPEN. FOOTSTEPS DOWN STEPS

HOLMES: (CALLING) Taylor! Taylor!

TAYLOR: (FADING IN. SLEEPILY) Yes guv'nor – Aow! It's you!

HOLMES: Yes. It's me. I want you to read this very simple document just written by your employer. You can read it in the light of your cab lamp.

TAYLOR: (STARTING TO READ WITH DIFFICULTY) *"I hereby . . . confess . . . I murdered –"* 'Ere! Wot's 'e think – ?

BLACK: (FADING IN. SMOOTHLY) Oh no, Mr. Sherlock Holmes. You don't really think I'm such a fool, do you? Feel this gun against your ribs? Don't think of turning round, will you?

265

HOLMES: I have no intention of – (WITH A SUDDEN GRUNT OF EXERTION) – turning round!

SOUND EFFECT: SCUFFLE. REVOLVER SHOT

HOLMES: Rather a neat trick, don't you think? It was taught to me by a Japanese wrestler. Now that you've dropped your revolver, I'll borrow it if you don't mind. I suggest that you both stand under the gaslight where I can keep my eyes on you. Thank you. By the way, Taylor – give me back that confession, will you? I think Inspector Lestrade will find it interesting evidence.

WATSON: (FADING IN EXCITEDLY) Holmes! Are you all right?

HOLMES: Perfectly, thank you, old chap.

WATSON: But that shot?

HOLMES: I'm afraid I spoiled Mr. Black's aim.

STANLEY: (FADING IN) What's going on, Mr. Holmes?

HOLMES: There, Captain Rush, are the two men who can tell you the true story of your brother's fate. Will you tell him, Mr. Black?

BLACK: I refuse to talk without a lawyer present.

HOLMES: Then let me reconstruct the case. Obviously, William never went back to the house. Nathan Black and Taylor silenced him as he got into the carriage and, after a suitable pause, went in and produced the false story that he had returned for his umbrella.

WATSON: Then why did we discover the burning umbrella in the furnace earlier on?

HOLMES: Undoubtedly Mr. Black or his servant Taylor brought it back in the hopes the burning remnants would incriminate Captain Rush. In fact, if we hadn't interrupted them earlier, I'm pretty well certain Mr. Black planned to be 'round in the morning, suggesting that we search the furnace.

STANLEY: I don't care about all that. What I want to know is what's happened to Bill!

HOLMES: Tell him, Taylor.

BLACK: Keep your mouth shut!

TAYLOR: Naow! I won't. You think becos' you pay me ten quid you can shove the blame off on me. Well, you can't, see? 'Eres what 'appened, gents. The bloke gets in the carriage and Mr. Black slips this pad wiv' chloroform on his face, an' he goes to sleep, an' we hide him under the rugs. Later on we drives out to Putney. On the ways I hears a shot in the carriage, and when we gets to a quiet spot just below the bridge . . . we stops and throws the poor bloke in the river.

STANLEY: (VIOLENTLY) Why, Nathan you –

SOUND EFFECT: CRACK OF FIST ON JAW. GROAN, FALLING BODY

HOLMES: I can't say I blame you, Captain Rush. But I suggest you leave this pair to us while you go back and break the news to Mrs. Rush.

STANLEY: Very well Mr, Holmes . . . (FADING) I'll do that.

LESTRADE: (FADING IN EXCITEDLY) Mr. Holmes – what's going on?

HOLMES: Ah, Scotland Yard – late as usual. The case is solved, Lestrade,

LESTRADE: Solved? But who –

HOLMES: The dormant Mr. Black is your murderer, and that cringing apology of a man Taylor is an accessory.

LESTRADE: But why –

HOLMES: Come now, Lestrade. I can't provide you with both the criminals and the motive at this time of the morning. Here is the confession. I suggest that you have Taylor drive you and your evidence over to Scotland Yard.

WATSON: Good idea, Holmes. Here, Lestrade. I'll give you a hand with getting Mr. Black into the carriage . . . .

WATSON: There we are . . . .

LESTRADE: Thank you, Doctor. And thank you, Mr. Holmes. Once again you've helped me out of a very tight place.

HOLMES: Not at all, dear fellow. I'm glad to have been of service. I'll be round at the Yard in the morning.

LESTRADE: (FADING) Good night, gentlemen.

HOLMES and WATSON: Good night.

LESTRADE: (OFF A LITTLE) All right, Taylor. Off you go . . . and no funny tricks. I've got a revolver, remember.

HOLMES: Oh, Lestrade –

LESTRADE: (OFF) Yes, Mr. Holmes?

HOLMES: Sure you don't want to take us with you?

LESTRADE: How d'you mean, sir?

HOLMES: After all . . . technically we're criminals. We're guilty of housebreaking, you know.

LESTRADE: (LAUGHING) That's all right, Mr. Holmes. Just this once I think we can overlook that!

FORMAN: Well, Doctor, that was an unusual story. And I must say I was a bit surprised at the outcome.

268

WATSON: Surprised – in what respect?

FORMAN: Well – to tell the truth, I thought Stanley Rush was guilty – not Nathan Black.

WATSON: Why did you think that?

FORMAN: Well – Stanley looked so rough and uncouth, while Black looked every bit the gentleman.

WATSON: (LAUGHS) I'm afraid you're as bad a detective as I am. You know, determining a man's character is like determining the character of a wine. You don't judge a man by the clothes he wears any more than you judge a wine by the glass it's served in,

FORMAN: Well – get him! Dr. Watson, the philosopher. (LAUGHS) But you've got something there, Doctor. A good wine does taste good in any kind of glass, and that's particularly true about Petri California Wine. You can serve Petri wine in water tumblers or even tea cups and it will still be clear, fragrant and delicious. That's because the Petri family really knows how to make good wine. They've been making wine for generations – ever since they first started the Petri business way back in the eighteen-hundreds, And because their business has always been a family affair – well they've been able to hand on down in the family – from father to son, from father to son – everything they've ever learned about the art of making fine wine. Yes sir – the Petri family knows all there is to know about turning plump, hand-picked grapes into wonderful wine. That's why you can't go wrong with a Petri wine . . . because Petri took time to bring you good wine! And now, Doctor Watson, how's about a clue to next week's story?

WATSON: Next week, Mr. Forman, I'm going to tell you about a strange and terrifying adventure that Sherlock Holmes and I had on the rocky coasts of Cornwall. It concerns a most unusual house, two brothers – and a *werewolf*!

MUSIC: *SCOTCH POEM*

FORMAN: Tonight's Sherlock Holmes adventure is written by Denis Green and Bruce Taylor and is based on an incident in the Sir Arthur Conan Doyle story, "The Adventure of the Empty House" *[sic]*. Mr.

269

Rathbone appears through the courtesy of Metro-Goldwyn-Mayer and Mr. Bruce through the courtesy of Universal Pictures, where they are now starring in the Sherlock Holmes series.

MUSIC: THEME UP AND DOWN UNDER

FORMAN: The Petri Wine Company of San Francisco, California invites you to tune in again next, week, same time, same station.

MUSIC: HIT JINGLE

SINGERS: *Oh, the Petri family took the time, to bring you such good wine, so when you eat and when you cook, Remember Petri Wine!*

FORMAN: Yes, Petri Wine made by the Petri Vine Company, San Francisco, California.

SINGERS: *Pet – Pet – Petri . . . Wine.*

FORMAN: This is Bill Forman saying goodnight for the Petri family. *Sherlock Holmes* comes to you from the Don Lee studios in Hollywood. This is the Mutual Broadcasting Network!

> *Somewhere in the vaults of the bank of Cox and Company, at Charing Cross, there is a travel-worn and battered tin dispatch-box with my name,* John H. Watson, M.D., Late Indian Army, *painted upon the lid. It is crammed with papers, nearly all of which are records of cases to illustrate the curious problems which Mr. Sherlock Holmes had at various times to examine. Some, and not the least interesting, were complete failures, and as such will hardly bear narrating, since no final explanation is forthcoming. A problem without a solution may interest the student, but can hardly fail to annoy the casual reader. Among these unfinished tales is that of Mr. James Phillimore, who, stepping back into his own house to get his umbrella, was never more seen in this world.*
>
> – Dr. John H. Watson
> "The Problem of Thor Bridge"

270

The Strange Death
of an Art Dealer
by Tim Symonds

Chapter I
The King of Scandinavia Makes an Unexpected Visit

Continuous showers throughout the capital that day had caused pedestrians to leap aboard every conveyance, myself among them. Eventually I reached Baker Street and crossed the pavement to the safety of our door. As I entered the hallway, and without the slightest warning, my frame was suddenly shoved violently to one side, spinning me like a coracle in the wake of a twelve-thousand-tonne Cunarder. I looked up in time to see a figure flying past me and up the stairs, his blue cloak flapped open like the wings of a giant Urvogel. With an immense final bound, the intruder reached our quarters and barged in without a knock. I rushed up after him, my heart thumping.

In the sitting room, the man who had treated my presence downstairs with such hauteur stood towering over Holmes. One huge hand was wielding a large photograph like a sword of Damocles, the other clutched a pink envelope.

"Come, Watson," Holmes called out, with the easy air of geniality he could so readily assume, "I believe you know our guest?"

I had recognised him at once – the King of Scandinavia. Swinging his cloak from his shoulders, he said, "Apologies for brushing you aside, Dr. Watson, I was in a hurry. Yet again I have travelled all this way for the sole purpose of consulting the keenest mind in Europe."

At our last encounter, two years earlier, our visitor had been the Crown Prince of Scandinavia. Then as now, the dark rings under our visitor's eyes were those of a man weighed down with some great anxiety. Since then, he had inherited the throne. He was now the King.

"Perfectly understandable, Your Majesty," I countered. "It's good to see you again."

"Gentlemen," Holmes remarked, "shall we all take our seats? Your Majesty, Watson and I will be interested indeed in discovering the reason that you've obliged us with a second visit. Are we to take it your reputation is once more in jeopardy?" Looking upwards with a slight smile Holmes added, "and that it may have something to do with the items in your hands?"

271

"It is, and it does," came the terse reply, the monarch's expression one of deep distress, "both occasioned as before by the cruellest of adventuresses, my former paramour, Enid Westburton."

He thrust the photograph into Holmes's hand. "Once more she is blackmailing me with another of these!"

The King pushed a pink envelope into Holmes's other hand. "And with this."

Holmes placed the picture on a small table in front of him and extracted the letter from the envelope.

"Your Majesty, I assume that we are about to hear why, in view of this note, you haven't yet handed over a sufficiency of your great wealth to satisfy the demand spelt out in this letter, thereby being done with the matter."

"Sir," came the King's piteous cry, "I believed that this affair was finished two years ago. I trusted that would be the end of it. But apparently she holds a number of other photographs, any one of which would serve as proof of my youthful indiscretions. The she-devil may have kept a hundred of my letters and ten – even twenty – such photographs taken during our time together. She can blight my life for years to come."

His face reddened. Tears welled up in his eyes. "To think she gave her solemn word she would never besmirch me again with such evidence of our affair, and yet here she is – "

His voice trailed away.

I expected to see Sherlock Holmes's patience crumble under the rambling narrative. On the contrary, he listened with the greatest concentration of attention. Once read for a second time, the letter was folded and returned to its envelope.

"Rest assured, Your Majesty," Holmes said soothingly, "Watson and I are ready again to assist you in any way we can. Please continue."

Holmes pointed to the photograph. "Now, Your Majesty, we may continue. Take a last look at this before you leave it in our safe hands."

"If I must!" the King cried. He gave the most cursory peek at the image before flinging it back.

Holmes passed the photograph to me. Two people were portrayed in an elaborately decorated setting. The then-Crown Prince, in the full dress uniform of his House, replete with insignia, sash, belt, and lapels, was seated on a bench of Ceylon ebony. He held the head of a sword in his left hand and a hat with plumes in his right. The picture was exactly as I remembered him from when we met several years earlier, before the cares of his position had aged him. It was the other figure which caused my sharp intake of breath. A woman lay full-length before him on a rich carpet looking up at the Prince in an adoring fashion. With the exception of jewellery and a pair of oriental slippers on her feet, the voluptuous body was completely nude.

"You see what I mean, Dr. Watson," the King growled. "The vixen has broken her word."

"You, sir, we recognise at once," Holmes broke in, "but be so kind as to confirm for us the woman stretched out along the floor is Enid Westburton, *née* Bainbridge."

"Who else!" came the mournful reply. "That profile! The hair adorned with a simple gardenia. The Gypsy ring in her ear. Who else could it be? You see her right arm. I gave her that bracelet at the very height of my unreasoned passion. The gift was made to my design by the Royal jeweler – fiery-red pryopes of the finest quality sourced from the mines of Meronitz, the emeralds from South America at a price even beyond the normal reach of princes. For three years I showered her with such evidence of my infatuation – parcels of precious jewels, the finest silks and furs. Even – " He groaned in unexpected self-mockery. " – a dressing-table made of Purple Heart wood from the island of Trinidad, equipped with a secret compartment to hold the rings and bracelets and intimate items such as that . . . that . . . ." He spluttered, pointing at the photograph. "I tell you, gentlemen, she could make Verdi's Lady Macbeth her very own. There must be something devilish in her, something I completely failed to see at the time, something stifled and dark."

"The letter," Holmes interrupted. "Have you read it in its entirety?"

With a sullen look the King replied, "In its entirety, no. You can see she made herself clear quickly enough. I was so shaken I ordered my coach to bring me here at once. Thus you see me before you."

Holmes moved across to a cabinet and, after searching through various documents, pulled out a letter. "This is one of the notes that she sent to you several years ago, and which you provided to us at the time.

"Watson," Holmes called, "both of these letters are written on fine-quality pink notepaper, with the same watermark and in the same swashbuckling black ink."

My friend returned to the photograph. Eventually he looked up and asked, "Your Majesty, does anything about her stand out in any way?"

"I remember her being a little less buxom," came the reply, "but perhaps, with the passage of time, one's memory . . . ."

He paused and sighed. Then, "Oh my God!" he exclaimed despairingly. "It could be a catastrophe! I beseech you, Holmes, sort this whole thing out. I can neither think nor sleep nor attend to any matter of State. It's enough to unseat my reason."

Holmes stood up.

"Your Majesty, let us know where we can reach you. From this moment on, the weight of the matter rests upon mine and Dr. Watson's shoulders."

The King reached into a pocket and withdrew a small gold box.

"Mr. Holmes, this time, I shall insist on conferring upon you the freedom of my capital city which comes with this gold box, ready to be inscribed to record the occasion. If that is insufficient, you may ask for an entire Province of my Kingdom."

Holmes replied in a business-like tone, ""Before that, sir, comes the case, and before that, the little matter of our expenses."

The King took a heavy chamois leather bag from under his cloak and dropped it on the table. "Shall we say a deposit of one-thousand pounds?"

He swung round to the hat-stand and retrieved his cloak.

"Gentlemen," he intoned, "I'm staying at the Langham Hotel. You have *carte blanche*. Do whatever is necessary." In a change of tone he added, "You must succeed. I was been prone on the previous occasion to let the better side of my nature prevail. Now too much is at stake. I have a dynasty to protect. My throne may not withstand this. Republicanism runs deep in Scandinavia."

He paused for a moment, glancing in my direction. "The Lands of the Scandinavian Crown, Dr. Watson, may not equal in wealth and extent the India of your familiarity, but for me they encompass my whole world. From here on in, the velvet glove must be ready to give way to the . . . ." He paused, trying to think of the word in English but failed, concluding with "*Eisenfaust*."

With a wry, "I believe that I know the way out," he turned toward the stairway. Holmes called after him, "The letter asks for a large sum in *kruna* and several pouches of perfectly transparent diamonds with no hue or colour, each gem within a given range. Did you read that far? If so, have your brought them with you? I may need them at the ready if I'm to act as intermediary."

"I have them here, Mr. Holmes," growled the King of Scandinavia. "They are in the safe at The Langham, just in case . . . ."

Holmes went with him to the top of the stairs. "If the author of the letter is within the grasp of England's Law, we already have enough evidence to go to the police."

"My dear Mr. Holmes," the King replied reproachfully, "I could certainly go to the law. However you must explain to me how would I profit if the author of that blackmail note was sentenced to a few months imprisonment while my own ruin must immediately follow from the publicity?"

From the window we watched the King clamber into a stately Canoe Landau. The wheels of the carriage rolled away down the street.

I had held my tongue, having long-ago learned to let Holmes take the lead on such matters. "You do know," I said, "that . . . Enid Westburton and her husband are . . . dead. They died within a few months of their marriage. Their yacht sank in a terrible storm off the tip of South America and they drowned. It's that which makes this case so utterly inexplicable. A shiver went up my spine when the King waved the new extortion note at you. She couldn't possibly . . . ."

Holmes nodded and stepped to his files, pulling a box of newspaper clippings off the shelf. "Here is a cutting from *The Times* dated December 1884. '*Couple Lost at Sea*'. '*From our Buenos Aires Correspondent*'. It goes on: '*A tragedy is reported to have taken place. Mr. William Westburton, a barrister of the Inner Temple, and his wife are reported missing off Cape Horn, believed lost in a storm while heading for Valparaíso aboard their yacht, the* Santa Margherita'.

"A footnote by *The Times*'s legal correspondent goes on to state that unless their bones are brought up in a fisherman's net, their fate remains in limbo until declared dead *in absentia*. According to friends conversant with English Law, it's generally assumed a person is dead after seven years if there's been no evidence to the contrary."

He returned the cutting to the box. adding, "Nothing's been heard of Mr. and Mrs. William Westburton since then. I suggest it's a case of *Defuncti sunt*."

"But how – " I began.

Holmes interrupted, reaching for his coat. "Watson, our client displays scant consideration as to how little we have to work with – no footprints on the floor, no codes or ciphers, no cigarette ash, no dogs, no corpses, no bloodstains. Just one jot – the letter – and one tittle – the photograph. A stroll would help clear the mind. I suggest we forego Mrs. Hudson's wonderful Scottish fare and lunch out today at the King of Scandinavia's expense."

"Excellent suggestion!" I replied. "Will it be off silver at Simpson's? I dream of their joint of beef."

"Nothing quite so exotic," came Holmes's cheery reply. "More like steak-and-kidney pudding off tin at Ye Old Cheshire Cheese on Wine Office Court. Bring the photograph. After lunch, hurry it over to Gregson at the Yard. Ask him what he makes of it. I suspect he might have an idea . . . ."

Chapter II
I Take the Blackmail Photograph to Scotland Yard

Holmes and I maintained a reflective silence during the walk to Wine Office Court. My mind went back two years to the rather straightforward events concerning the earlier attempt to blackmail the then-Prince. Perhaps we should have known that the affair wasn't truly finished.

Holmes and I parted company after a veritable feast of diced beef and kidney, fried onion, and brown gravy. Later, at Scotland Yard, I swore the admirable Inspector Gregson to secrecy and handed him the photograph. On my return a few hours later, Holmes was at the dining table, the two pink letters in front of him, held down against gusts of air from the open window by the gasogene bottle.

I opened my mouth to speak, but Holmes's hand rose swiftly. "Watson, this is a time for observation, not for talk. Take another look at these. This first is unquestionably written by Enid Westburton."

"What am I to look at?" I asked.

"At the way it's signed off," Holmes requested.

"'*Enid Westburton, née Bainbridge*'," I read out.

"Now," Holmes went on, "how does the extortion letter end?"

"With "*I have the honour to be Sir Yours obediently, Enid*"," I replied.

"Exactly! Doesn't that seem peculiar? She uses a magnanimous '*Yours obediently*'. Now take this second extortion note. It's for the King's eyes only, someone she knew intimately, but it ends with a salutation as stiff as if the letter-writer were addressing His Royal Highness Albert Edward, the future King of Great Britain. Why?"

I had no answer.

I spent the evening flicking through articles in *The Journal of the American Medical Association*. A heart specialist, Professor Robert H. Babcock, recommended prolonged physical repose in cases of valvular disease. My experience with such patients was quite the contrary. The striated cardiac muscle degenerates under prolonged rest. I resolved to contradict the Professor's conclusions in a Letter to the Editor. I threw the journal down. The chimes from our landlady's spring-driven regulator wall clock told me it was a quarter-to-midnight.

"Time for me to turn in," I said.

Holmes was bent over his Powell and Lealand No. 1 microscope, tucked among an array of Bunsen-burners, glass tubes, and pipettes at the chemical bench. A thought occurred to me.

276

"Holmes," I said. "You do know that . . . Enid Westburton and her husband are . . . dead."

"*Defuncti sunt*," Holmes said, shaking his head while repeating his comment of earlier that day and looking pensively across to the extortion letter. "Thank you, Watson. Now may I wish you good-night."

I lay awake well into the early hours. I could see the possibility – probability even – that the King himself, tucked away in Scandinavia, might have had no knowledge of the tragedy. No courtier or Scandinavian newspaper would mention the obscure names of William and Enid Westburton. But what was going on in Holmes's mind? He seemed to deliberately ignore the information about the sinking of the *Santa Margherita*. If so, why? What good reason could he have had to do so? Why had he repeated the words *defuncti sunt* in so dubious a tone? *They are dead.* Was my Latin at fault – or my assumption of their deaths? Why had he made so much of the way that the two Westburton letters had been signed? I vowed to have it out with him over breakfast.

I awoke with the dawn and washed and dressed immediately. Holmes was already eating breakfast. He greeted me with an air of geniality.

"I have a question for you," he began. "Shall we agree you are more of an expert on wedding procedures than I?"

"We can agree on that."

Holmes continued. "Then tell me, what first steps are required which lead eventually to the Altar?"

I filled a plate with our landlady's devilled kidneys and kedgeree.

"My friend," I replied, "if you are for some reason referring to the marriage of the late Enid Bainbridge and the late William Westburton, which occurred shortly after the lady's first attempt to blackmail the King, matters would have typically commenced through an exchange of formal letters between the groom and the vicar."

"Let us say that I am indeed referring to that marriage." Holmes responded. "Where do you suppose that correspondence related to it would be held? Tucked away in a tin box in a crypt?"

"Almost certainly in a file in the vicar's study," I replied.

"Then I'm in need of your help, Watson. It's imperative to get into the vicarage of the church where the two of them were married and examine one of Westburton's formal letters. The solution to the case may depend upon it."

A cab discharged me at the vicarage of St. Catherine's Church, a double carriage-sweep leading through lawns and past an immense Cedar of Lebanon at the entrance. A slightly plump house maid showed me to the study. The vicar stood up, stretching out a hand.

"You must be Austin Bidwell," he said, "I'm William Barker."

The vicar withdrew a letter from an overflowing file. "I have your letter here. You indicated wish to get married in St. Catherine's and you are a resident of this parish."

"Correct, Vicar," I lied, "even as we speak, my fiancée is choosing the month and day of our wedding."

"Not in May, I hope!" the vicar joked. "Remember, "Marry in May and rue the day"."

"Then certainly not May – " I began.

Our conversation was cut short by a loud hub-bub between the house maid and someone at the front door. The vicar jumped to his feet.

"Do excuse me, Mr. Bidwell, it seems I must intervene on Miss Nightingale's side. Probably beggars again. I shan't be a moment."

Virtually in step, I followed him as far as the study door and eased it shut behind him. The vicarage's front entrance was visible from the study window. Gesticulating dramatically, almost nose-to-nose with the Reverend Barker, was a figure in clerical garb replete with broad black hat, baggy trousers, and white tie – a disguise that Holmes particularly favored. He was the very model of the amiable and simple-minded Nonconformist clergyman from the village of Rollesby on the Trinity Broads, except that now there was a difference: The amiability was completely absent. His facial expression had changed utterly from one of benevolent curiosity to one expressing utmost scorn. I heard him shout, "My dear Vicar, yes you are! Don't deny it! I have myself just returned from Cape Colony. I have no doubt that you are tolerant of Zulu polygamy! Clearly you are a heretical follower of Bishop Colenso!"

"I am most certainly not!" the vicar was protesting loudly.

"Yes, you are!" insisted the newcomer, "I would wager half of my stipend that you have the Bishop's confounded work *The Pentateuch and the Book of Joshua Critically Examined* on your shelves! Let me in to see if I'm right, sir!"

"I am not, and I do not, sir!" the vicar shouted back. "And I shan't! You are a lunatic! You may leave my door immediately, never to darken it again, d'you hear?"

"I shall not move one foot from here, sir," came the angry response, "until you confess!"

I hastened to the vicar's desk. The sounds of two people pushing furiously at each other continued, their voices combining with Miss Nightingale's, all three rising ever-higher. At *W* under "*Marriages*" I found correspondence from William Westburton dated two years before.

It had been signed off with *"I have the honour to be Sir Yours obediently . . . ."*

I made for the door. The Nonconformist clergyman had beaten a retreat. I promised the badly-upset vicar I would be back in touch with dates for the wedding (other than May) and hurried to catch up with Holmes at the Cedar of Lebanon.

Chapter III
We Meet Inspector Gregson at Simpson's in the Strand

On the morrow I was awaked by a familiar rat-tat-tat on my bedroom door. It was flung open to reveal Holmes waving a telegram. "Our Scotland Yard inspector has some information for us. I've arranged a quiet table at your favourite temple of food, Simpson's."

A few hours later, Holmes and I met the tow-headed Gregson in the foyer, his hat in one hand, a package the exact size of the photograph in the other. He was in mufti, his pea-jacket and cravat giving him a decidedly nautical appearance. He looked pleased with himself.

"Well, Gregson," I asked, "what have you got for us? Can you confirm the woman lying on the carpet is Enid Westburton?"

"I've no idea if Mrs. Westburton ever allowed herself to be captured *au naturel* like that," came the unexpected reply.

Frowning, I pointed at the package containing the photograph. "Surely that's proof enough!"

"I'm afraid not," Gregson responded.

We were shown to a corner table.

"I can confirm the woman's head with the ear-ring is Enid Westburton's," Gregson resumed. "Equally I can confirm the arm with the bangle is hers as well. But I cannot confirm," he tapped the package "that the torso is Enid Westburton's."

Holmes broke in, "That could explain why our client reported her 'rather more buxom' than he remembered."

The table fell silent at the approach of the *maître d'hôtel.*

Gregson chose the roast beef, Holmes the woodcock. I opted for the smoked salmon and my favourite dessert, the treacle sponge with a dressing of Madagascan vanilla custard. The *maître d'hôtel* retreated to the kitchen with our orders.

Gregson continued, "We did exactly what you asked, Mr. Holmes. The Yard has developed twenty forensic techniques. Only if all twenty, from the packaging to the shadows, are completely consistent will we declare the photograph real, but in this case, Mr. Holmes . . . ." He glanced my way. "May I have the momentary loan of the ten-power magnifying glass you always have with you? Thank you. Dr. Watson, do me the kindness of looking at the woman's hair."

Through the glass, I examined the luxuriant dark hair spilling on to the shoulders.

"What am I to look for?" I asked.

"The reflection of the light on her hair and the ear-ring," came Gregson's reply. "Specifically the source of the light."

"I would suggest that it was sunlight through a window this side of where she's lying," I replied.

"Good!" Gregson exclaimed. "And now the bracelet. The light scattering off the brilliants. The source of the light – still the same window?"

"It can't be," I responded. "It's coming from the other side."

"Bravo, Doctor! Now if we take the light reflected from the skin of the legs and buttocks and back, you'll see it's coming from yet a third direction – from above. Very likely a skylight. This print cannot be from a single photograph. What we have here, gentlemen, is an ingenious example of combination printing. The head and right arm are from one plate, but they've been added to a torso and legs from a separate plate – the latter a work we have identified as '*Reclining Female Nude Artists, Study, Dorsal*' by the artist-photographer Oscar Rejlander."

"So all Holmes and I have to do – " I began.

Gregson interrupted, his face creasing into a grin " – is to confront Rejlander and ask who bought the nude artists' study plate. Confronting a suspect is always a good idea, Doctor, a splendid idea. Alas, Rejlander died not long after making that study. His body lies in an unmarked grave in Kensal Green Cemetery, near Isambard Kingdom Brunel."

"Then who made this brilliant fake?" I asked.

"One living artist-photographer possesses the skill," he replied. "We believe that he may also be the owner of the plate. When Rejlander died, he left little money, not even enough for a tombstone. His widow was obliged to put his earlier works up for auction. A job-lot of plates was bought by a certain society photographer – but there's a problem in assuming he's the perpetrator of a fake of this order. You'll see why in a minute, when I come to his name.

"As I am singing for my dinner, gentlemen," he went on, "I've another fact of relevance to your case – the camera used by the draughtsman. The camera that created this photograph – or so my experts tell me – held a twenty-by-twenty-four-inch plate. That size is both rare and expensive. We think it could only have been an Eastman Interchangeable View camera brought over from America. Even without a Beck lens or Laverne shutter, it would come with a heavy price tag. At least one-hundred dollars." Gregson looked longingly at the slices of beef on the dish being placed in front of him. "Only one or two photographer-artists in the whole of England could afford that equipment and have the right skills to produce the work in question – one of them being the photographer of impeccable standing to whom I referred."

"Watson and I shall be very much obliged to you, Gregson," Holmes remarked, with a hint of impatience. "If you will now give us the photographer's name, you may then pick up your knife and fork and carry on with your lunch."

The inspector leant forward. "Alexander Berlusconi," he whispered. "It was he who purchased the Rejlander collection, though why in heaven's name he would associate himself with criminal activity of the sort you describe is beyond my comprehension. The walls of his premises are covered with studies of England's rich and powerful – aristocrats, Prime Ministers, leading names from the military, sciences, and arts. Even our Great Queen herself."

Dessert behind us, we left the restaurant. Gregson bowed solemnly and strode off into the dense fog that had settled over the city. Back at 221b, I picked a red-covered volume from a line of books of reference beside the mantelpiece. Over the years my collection of the biographies of men of affairs, living or dead, had become so comprehensive that it would have been difficult to name a subject or person on which I couldn't at once furnish information. Squeezed between Bell and Blackborough was an advertisement clipped from a national newspaper:

Old Photographs Enlarged

Old or faded carte de visite *or cabinet photographs may be enlarged and changed into valuable portraits, suitable when framed, to hang or stand in the drawing room.*

Photographs entrusted to Messrs. Berlusconi for this purpose are finished in black-and-white or watercolours.

"A faithful yet improved reproduction of a cherished original." – Vide the Press.

Specimens on view at Messrs. Berlusconi, 25 Old Bond Street, and 42 Pall Mall, S.W.

281

Chapter IV
Holmes Confronts the Society Photographer

The cab dropped us at the Messrs. Berlusconi Old Bond Street entrance. The studios were spread over three floors, joined by a broad staircase. There were reception rooms and dressing rooms, and two main day-lit studios equipped with good-quality furniture and props. Berlusconi was waiting for us in a small room at the top. He appeared nervous.

"Gentlemen, please have a seat. I look forward to taking your photograph. I presume that you are here for that reason? Am I to get a 'first' – namely the famous Consulting Detective together with his faithful friend, Dr. John Watson?"

Holmes shook his head, his expression cold.

"I'm afraid not, Mr. Berlusconi. Dr. Watson and I are here on a rather more serious matter. It seems you have recently used your very considerable skills to create an entirely spurious scene. Even as we speak, it is being used by a blackmailer to extort a large sum of money and precious gems from an eminent Central European personality."

The famous photographer blanched.

"Mr. Holmes!" he protested. "I am outraged! You come here to my premises to accuse me of a serious crime, one which would disgrace me both personally and professionally? Why, you only have to look to my reputation . . . ." He gestured towards a large framed photograph deliberately placed on the wall behind his chair. It was of Queen Victoria in a black bombazine and silk dress. A large satin bag at her side was embroidered with a poodle in gold. Beneath, the Queen-Empress had penned, *"To Mr. Berlusconi, for this study of me and its honesty, total want of flattery, and appreciation of character"*.

"We appreciate your standing with the House of Hanover," Holmes responded, staring at the hapless man in a markedly unpleasant fashion, "which is why Dr. Watson and I are here rather than already at Scotland Yard. We offer you a chance to stay in Her Majesty's good books by confessing all and providing us with an explanation of your conduct. Then nothing will go outside this room."

Holmes turned to me. "Watson, how much time do we have before we solicit an appointment with Inspector Gregson?"

I pulled out my pocket-watch and gave it an exaggerated inspection. "It's now half-past ten," I replied, going along with the charade. "If we leave now we should be at the Yard in half-an-hour."

"Stop!" the agitated figure shouted. "All right – I confess. I was put under terrible duress. I had no idea of the man's intentions. I made a photomontage of a Teutonic-looking fellow covered in medals and

282

epaulettes seated on a bench, with a nude woman lying on a carpet in front of him."

"And the name of the person who pressed you to do this?" Holmes asked, his voice deep with menace.

"The art dealer, Charles Augustus Howell," came the whispered reply. "I repeat, Mr. Holmes, I have no knowledge of the uniformed man in the photograph which he supplied, nor to whom the woman's head and arm belong."

He gave a shudder. Beads of fear appeared on the trembling upper lip.

"Howell glared at me with his cold, baleful eyes. It gave me a feeling of uncontrollable anxiety – the same sensation as if I were standing before the giant bird-eating spiders in the Regent's Park Zoo. On his instruction, I went through my rarest plates for a suitable nude."

He gestured towards a cabinet. "I came across a study made many years ago by Rejlander. All I did was leave the fellow on the bench and place the nude torso with a new head and right arm on the floor before him. After I completed the task, I told Howell to leave and never to darken my door again."

"Before we go, Mr. Berlusconi," Holmes ordered, "tell us precisely why this man was able to persuade you to become involved in a criminal enterprise."

"Howell had been sold some information about my father," came the reply, "something so scandalous that if it came to light it would place a permanent slur on my family's reputation and endanger my standing in London society."

He pointed in the direction of Buckingham Palace. "Especially with Her Imperial Majesty. If you wish to move in Royal Society, you must make a great show of gentility. If you harbour any hint of a shocking or sordid secret about your personal life, or that of a member of your family, you quiver in fear at the thought it may one day become public."

"And the Rejlander plate?" I asked. "Where is it now?"

"I destroyed it in the hope of avoiding detection," came the reply.

"Enough," Holmes commanded, getting to his feet. "Come, Watson. A telegram to this Howell requesting an appointment is in order, I think."

A knock came at the front door of 221 Baker Street, followed by the sounds of our landlady climbing the stairs. She came into the room with a card on a silver tray. It read *"You may call at 6:30 tomorrow evening – No. 6 Tilney Street, W1. C.M."*

"Charles Howell lives at No. 6 Tilney Street?" I exclaimed. "He must be doing extraordinarily well. Wasn't that once the home of the famous Georgian courtesan, Maria Fitzherbert?"

"The very same," came my friend's reply. He searched through his papers before finding a brochure. "In the event that we need to burgle the premises, let me read you a description of the house the last time it came up for sale: '*The grand suite embraces five drawing rooms, lofty and of the best proportions, all* en-suite, *and terminating with a conservatory, which entirely overlooks the Park. On the ground floor as the* salon à manger, *library, and breakfast parlour – nothing is wanting to render it an abode especially adapted to a family of consequence. There is an abundance of stabling, two double coach-houses, with servants' rooms'*."

Holmes stood up. His face wore the inexorable look he usually reserved for hunting down murderers. "I tell you, Watson, I've already developed a total revulsion for this fellow. Just to be completely safe, put a revolver in your jacket pocket. The Adams Mk III in .450 calibre will do nicely. We may not require it, but on both sides the stakes are high."

Chapter V
Our Encounter with a Blackmailer

Shortly after six o'clock the following day, we set off for Tilney Street. The weather remained foul. After our meeting, I planned to go on to a performance of *The Sleeping Beauty*, and on our way out of the house I knocked on Mrs. Hudson's door to borrow her opera glasses. The doors at No. 6 Tilney Street were pulled open as we leapt from the cab. We hurried in past the valet, keen to escape the squalls of driving rain. The butler came forward to take our coats and hats.

"Gentlemen, you are earlier than the Master suggested," he pointed out. "He may be engaged for a while. Please follow me."

We were led up a fine staircase via a succession of ornate rooms to the conservatory. I crossed to windows looking toward Hyde Park. In a direct line of sight across Park Lane was the eighteen-foot statue of Achilles, commissioned by the Ladies of England – a patriotic, upper-class society, in honour of the Duke of Wellington's victories against Napoleon. The sculpture was made from melted-down enemy cannon, the head modelled on the Duke himself, the body on a Roman figure on Italy's Monte Cavallo. I raised Mrs. Hudson's opera glasses. Some twenty yards from the statue a bedraggled figure with a camera on a bi-pod battled the heavy downpour and gusts of wind, his cape flapping wildly around his head.

"What do you see out there?" I heard Holmes ask.

"There's a hapless fellow trying to take photographs of the Achilles statue in the drenching rain," I replied. I passed over the opera glasses. "Here, take a look."

As he did so, our host entered. Despite a commanding role in the world of Fine Art, Charles Augustus Howell was only in his mid-forties, with a large, intellectual head, a round, plump, hairless face, and alert grey eyes behind gold-rimmed glasses. He advanced towards us, expressing regret at keeping us waiting. Holmes disregarded the outstretched hand, looking at him with a face of granite. Howell's smile broadened. He shrugged his shoulders. With a practiced dance-like step, he turned to take a seat. As he did so, the butt of a large revolver momentarily projected from an inside pocket.

"What brings you to my humble abode, gentlemen?" he asked. "Have you come to buy a Rembrandt? One of his self-portraits? Or are you hoping to view the Gainsborough, the *'Duchess of Devonshire'*?" at which he broke into a chortle. "If the latter, I'm afraid I can't be of help. I'm told the Duchess may as easily be in Chicago as here in Mayfair."

He spoke in a jesting tone, but there was no jest in his eyes as he looked at Holmes.

"No, we're not here in pursuit of a Rembrandt or the stolen Gainsborough," Holmes rejoined sternly.

"Then why are you here?" Howell retorted, almost insolently.

Holmes withdrew the pink envelope from an inside pocket and read aloud from the letter: "*My dearest Sigismond, I believe you will recognise this photograph and the happy memories it evokes in me of our time together. I keep the picture in my dressing room. I never choose my evening's attire without stopping to look at it – and yet, curiously, when you were present with me, I scarce ever cast my eyes upon it . . . .*'"

Holmes lowered the letter.

"Should I go on?" he asked with a cold look, "even though the words must be perfectly familiar to you?"

"Please, do go on, Mr. Holmes!" came the energetic response. "I'm finding this of extraordinary interest. I shall be especially keen to know who wrote it and for what purpose!"

Holmes continued, "*Time has been good to you but unkind to me. My husband struggles to provide me with the small things which make life attractive. In return for the photograph, I ask only for a small part of what you have in abundance – wealth – but which I am sorely lacking (and am enduring penury as a result). Your assent or otherwise to my terms should be addressed to me at the Leadenhall Street Post Office, to be left until called for.*"

Holmes put the letter down. "Does it strike a chord now, Howell?"

"Sir," came the hurt reply, "it does not!"

He snatched off the gold-rimmed glasses. "Mr. Holmes, you astound me! I counsel you to inform the police at once! Surely you're not accusing me of some involvement – " He waved a hand at the table. " – with *that*?"

Holmes ignored the outburst. He retrieved the letter and recommenced: "'*I suggest 100,000 kronas and four or five of those delightful chamois pouches of colourless diamonds of yours. Each must be in the 80- to 120-carat range. Each must be uncut and unpolished, and not altered in any way after they were mined. A few uncut emeralds would be nice too. On receipt of the above, I shall destroy the photographic plate and have no further communication. You may rest in peace without hindrance.*'"

Holmes looked up. His eyes fixed on the art-dealer. "Howell, we know you were the appointed go-between."

"I assure you," our host sang out, "you have the wrong person. I deal in *Art* – Caravaggios, Mantegnas, occasionally even a Poussin. I know absolutely nothing about this. Besides, you haven't revealed who wrote that letter. Perhaps the name is familiar to me?"

"The letter is signed '*I have the honour to be, Sir, Yours obediently, Enid*' – " Holmes replied, "– namely Enid Westburton, formerly Bainbridge, wife of William Westburton."

An exaggerated look of incredulity crossed our host's pudgy face.

"My dear fellow!" he exclaimed, "do you have a temperature? Are you at death's door with brain-fever? William and Enid Westburton were reported dead years ago, lost off Homos Island! I remember reading about it in the – "

Holmes interrupted savagely. "Enough, Howell! The game's up, as Watson can tell you." Holmes turned to me. "Can't you, Watson!"

Before I could compose an answer, Holmes continued addressing me. "That fellow in the Park, the one you observed just now – lurking at the statue pretending to be taking photographs of Achilles in the rain. Would you say he was in his late-thirties, approximately of my height, about six feet tall?"

"Holmes, to tell you the . . . ." I began. Then observing the warning glint in the deep-set eyes I stammered, "Why, certainly . . . ." I patted our landlady's opera glasses hanging from my neck. "Yes, I'd say late-thirties, about six-feet tall."

"Good-looking in a dark, aquiline way?" Holmes prompted.

"Yes," I replied.

"And moustached? I'm sure that you observed the moustache?"

"Definitely moustached," I agreed.

Holmes turned back to our host. "You see, Howell, the man taking a soaking in a thunderstorm hardly a hundred yards from here – the man no doubt waiting to rush in the moment he sees us depart – that man is none other than the erstwhile Honourable Member of the Inner Temple, William Westburton, husband of Enid Westburton. He is the man who, only a week or so ago, provided you with the bogus document that I have in my hands. You may or may not know that it was he who forged it. The ostensible author, Enid Westburton, has nothing to do with this criminal affair."

"My dear fellow!" Howell exclaimed, the tone markedly less bombastic, "they do say ghosts wander around Hyde Park, but not usually in the rain! Must I repeat, the pair were lost off Cape Horn years ago. You must have seen it in *The Times*. They haven't been heard of since."

Holmes got to his feet. "We must go," he said to me. To Howell he said, "Enough of your banter. The King of Scandinavia has made my task eminently clear – find whomever organised the delivery of this letter, so that man will then regret his criminal involvement for every minute of every hour of every day for the rest of his miserable life. The King's much-feared 'Iron Fist' will be released from its velvet glove. Your career as a blackmailer is coming to an abrupt and well-deserved end. It may well mean five years in one of Her Majesty's gaols. If you continue to deny the fact of your involvement, Watson and I will now resume our journey to our friends at Scotland Yard and hand the matter over to them."

The threat had no effect. "Then gentlemen," demurred our host, "the butler must bring you your coats and hats. I must not keep you a minute longer!"

The insolent tone grew in confidence. "Do please give my compliments to Inspectors Lestrade, Gregson, *et alia*, won't you?" he begged. "Tell them I'm sorry I can't be of more help in this very distressing matter, but there we are!"

At this he rose as though to see us to the door. Holmes waved a hand towards the luxurious reception rooms. "Watson, just think: The Howell that we see before us, the Howell of open manner and exhaustless amusing talk, friend of Ruskin and Rosetti, is also Howell the master extortioner. Sculpture and Painting are his camouflage. It's as good a tale of villainy as has ever been recorded. Before we go to Scotland Yard we have another civic duty to perform. Scandal rags abound, brim-full with the latest assaults, outrages, tragedies, murders, and blackmailings, all delightfully described in lurid detail with illustrations to match. What a backdrop No. 6 Tilney Street will provide to whomever is asked to do the illustrations! Let's think, we can readily break our journey to the Victoria Embankment. We must first drop by *Tit-Bits* and a few other sensational rags, followed by *The Illustrated Police News*."

The words "scandal rags" transformed the expression on our host's face. Smugness changed to alarm.

"Now don't be so hasty, Mr. Holmes!" he gasped, rubbing a handkerchief across his gold-rimmed glasses. "All right. I shall own up – after all, I was merely the messenger in the prank – but in return you must promise me confidentiality. I know from first-hand experience a thing or two about the damage adverse publicity does to reputations. Yes, I knew Westburton during his days at the Inner Temple. I had believed him dead, so you will understand that when I came into this conservatory about three weeks ago, I nearly had a heart attack to find him sitting exactly where you are.

"Westburton was desperate. He forcibly pointed out how indebted I was to him. When he was at the London Bar, he managed to suppress very damaging evidence against me. Even now, if that evidence were to leak out, I could be brought before the Old Bailey on a charge that – well, I prefer not to go into it. More to the point, he promised me a choice of uncut gems if the enterprise succeeded. He told me that Enid was alive but desperate for money. He explained she had grown to regret her earlier leniency over certain photographs retained from her liaison with the then Crown Prince of Scandinavia. She regretted not asking for more – a large sum in money, for instance, and especially a pouch or two of fine raw diamonds and an assortment of Musgravite, Alexandrite, Red Beryl, and Padparadscha sapphires which the Crown Prince had in abundance.

"Westburton gave me specific instructions on the type of photograph that he wished to be prepared – he believed that I had the knowledge and contacts to accomplish this – and he added that a pink envelope would be put through my front door that same night containing a letter that she had composed. It wasn't to be opened by anyone before it and the photograph were placed into the hands of the King, who has been staying in London for an extended period. Westburton's own involvement was to be kept secret. I swear that's all I did. Now that I think about it, I wasn't even the messenger. I was the delivery-boy."

As we went down the wide stairs to the atrium, Howell's voice followed us. "You take me by surprise in one respect, Mr. Holmes. I had no idea the letter was a forgery and that Westburton the author."

The large entrance doors of No. 6 Tilney Street shut behind us. Holmes declared, "We have stopped the plot in its tracks, Watson. Our case is almost done, but – " He then gestured towards the statue of Achilles. " – to quote the Iron Duke after the Battle of Waterloo, it was the nearest-run thing you ever saw in your life. If our blackmailer friend had held his nerve back there, we would have suffered a defeat. Our august

288

client would have been given the choice of paying up multiple times over the years, or suffering excruciating loss of standing across the whole of Europe, possibly even his throne."

I pointed to the towering statue of Achilles. "How you identified the person with the camera as Westburton when I and the whole world thought him dead is unfathomable! Not once did the fellow have his face towards us."

"That's what I meant about the nearest-run thing, Watson," Holmes chuckled. "I haven't the faintest idea who the man with the camera was, any more than you do."

After a moment of stunned silence I asked, "Then how did you know Westburton was still alive?"

"I realised it moments after the King handed me the letter," Holmes replied. "The instant I saw the way it ended. That's why I needed to silence you. For Enid Westburton to sign off to someone with whom she had had an intense and deeply affectionate romance with '*Yours obediently*' was utterly out of custom. Even our Royal client would have smelt a rat if he had read the letter through to the end. If she'd composed it herself, the concluding words would have been quite different. Therefore, if she did not write it, certain deductions follow: Either she did die in a terrible storm off Cape Horn and the letter was forged *post mortem*, or she is alive but played no part in the plot. So I asked myself, who was the author? Who was close enough to Enid Westburton to have knowledge of her writing style? Who spent time in the formal world in which that letter was composed – for example, that of lawyers and the Inns of Court?"

"Of course!" I exclaimed. "Westburton himself!"

"Just so," Holmes continued. "The letter is dated the tenth instant. Clearly newspaper reports concerning his death were extremely premature. At this very moment, I'll wager that Howell is apprising him of our meeting, and how – of course without the slightest cooperation from Howell! – Sherlock Holmes and Dr. Watson are closing in upon him. I'll wager there'll soon be a desperate hammering at our door. Be a good chap, Watson, and wave down a hansom. Let's make our way with all due speed through this wet Mayfair traffic to Baker Street. I'm overcome with curiosity on one point in particular: The letter itself was utterly compelling, but why, if Westburton forged the letter in his wife's name and style, did he end it in such a formal way? That blunder and that alone gave the game away."

Chapter VI
Westburton Returns from the Dead and Tells His Story

Holmes's surmise proved correct. Within minutes of our return to Baker Street, steaming horses pulled a cab to a halt at the front door. A frantic clanging of the bell followed. Mrs. Hudson let in the visitor. Upon Holmes's shout of "Enter, Mr. Westburton!" he rushed in.

"Mr. Holmes! Dr. Watson!" he cried out. "I am here to beg you to hear me out and not – "

"Pray, sir, take a chair by the fire," Holmes interrupted, casually lighting a cigarette and throwing himself down into his own armchair. "Start at the beginning. I hardly need to inform a member of the Bar, even a drowned one, that he will have to offer up the most convincing explanation if my colleague here isn't to summon Scotland Yard to come and arrest 'the corpse' on the spot. You won't be the first extortioner dragged from this room to the Old Bailey."

Westburton took my seat and, for the next twenty minutes, he poured out a story of extraordinary human emotion and fallibility.

"When I first met my wife-to-be, Enid Bainbridge, here in London," he began, "she was living rather quietly, far from the life she had pursued just a year or so earlier on the Continent. I too led a prosaic if moderately successful life – living with my mother in Onslow Square, with chambers at No. 2 Buck Court. Then something utterly unexpected took place. Some weeks after Enid came to consult me on a private matter, I began to sense that I had a chance of gaining her hand in marriage. At first it seemed a fantasy – an impossibility – yet as the days passed, her early affection appeared to turn into something stronger."

My impatience and curiosity at the slow pace of Westburton's narrative overcame me. Risking Holmes's disapproval I intervened. "Mr. Westburton, like my friend Holmes here I am agog to hear the story of your marriage, but first I have a question which needs clearing up. The world thinks that you and your wife are long dead. Can you explain how notices generating that belief sprang up in *The Times* and *The Daily Telegraph*, hardly a year after your marriage?"

Westburton's face broke into a sheepish smile. "I can, Doctor. At your instance, I shall go into that now. During our brief courtship, Enid confided she had had enough of fame. She said it was nothing but an illusion. If – and it was then the word 'married' itself first came to her lips – if we were to get married, we should seek a life of the utmost privacy. She told me she had long wanted to visit the very tip of South America – she had read of the Tehuelche Indians of southern Patagonia and the

290

flourishing society in the capitals of the Argentine and Uruguay and Chile and Peru. I said surely her fame was such that the very name Enid Bainbridge – even if changed to Westburton – would be known even in such a remote corner of the world. She convinced me otherwise – that she could disappear into a peaceful life of obscurity, which was her greatest desire.

"So desperately had I fallen for her beauty and intelligence that I, regardless of the likely effect this exile would have on my own career, agreed. I went further. I told her, if you want the greatest anonymity possible and for it to last forever, we must disappear so completely that no one will ever come out to search for us. In short, we must fake our own deaths by combining our disappearance with her dream of a new life in South America.

"Over the years I had done a great deal of sailing in the dangerous waters around Cherbourg and the Channel Islands. It seemed to follow naturally that we should look for a yacht in St. Peter's Port and sail her down to the South Atlantic. We put our affairs in order before taking a ferry to Guernsey, where we purchased a caique already fitted out for a lengthy voyage. Enid renamed it after the church of Santa Margherita, said to be where Dante married Gemma Donati in the thirteenth century. We loaded the *Santa Margherita* with all our keepsakes.

"Months later, we made landfall at Cape Tres Puntas, where we discharged the crew taken on for the crossing. Within days, to the fanfare of a brass-band at the dock, the two of us set off again. It was to become the last leg of our life as William and Enid Westburton. Soon we engineered the belief the *Santa Margherita* had gone down attempting a reckless journey around the Horn in weather of the worst kind. Under changed names for the yacht and ourselves, we sailed into El Callao, a stone's throw from Lima, but to the world we had been lost at sea."

The recollection overcame him. Tears welled up in his eyes. Westburton sprang from his chair and paced up and down the room in uncontrollable agitation.

"From then on things did not go well," he continued. "You can have no idea of the transformation that came over my wife shortly after our arrival in Peru. It was as though she had changed not just her name but her personality. It gradually became evident she couldn't have been leading the modest life here in London I'd assumed. I expected us to settle into a quiet life – the quiet life that she'd insisted that she wanted! – where I would build a practice, but within weeks she became restless. Our money was at a premium, yet Enid began spending frivolously, eating into what limited resources we had. She repeatedly asked why I wasn't bringing in the money that she was used to. During one flare-up, she rushed to her

291

things and withdrew an exquisite gold-enamelled-and-diamond ink stand in the form of a state barge which the King had presented to her so that she could write her love letters to him. This was followed by a pair of ornate fly swatters studded with jewels which Ram Singh II, Maharaja of Jaipur, had bestowed on the Crown Prince, and he in turn on her.

"She accused me of gaining her hand in marriage under false pretences. Hadn't I taken into account her standard of living, her expectations of at least 'adequate' money, when I forced myself upon her happy spinsterhood and lured her into marriage? Out came a heavily-jewelled ring which she flung at me with 'Why don't you go and sell this if you can't find the money elsewhere!'."

He paused, shaking his head at the memory. "Well, what a ring! Shakiso emeralds. Slightly bluish-green with vivid saturation. 'Glowing' would be the word. The ring had been given to the Crown Prince by the Ethiopian Monarch Sahle Miriam Menilek II. As I inspected it, my wife was shouting 'That's the sort of gift I'm accustomed to being given!'

Westburton lowered his head towards me, his face agonised. After a short pause he resumed. "The recriminations became a torrent. 'I remember when the Archduke gave me this, and when the Crown Prince awarded me that, and when His Royal Highness presented me with this!' *etcetera*. Finally a kind of madness came upon me. I felt driven to prove that, come what may, I too was capable of giving her a bejewelled Indian this and an ivory Japanese that. But how was I to accomplish this? Even in a fit of insane rivalry with her past lover, the Royal personage, how could I promise her anything of the sort?

"To have once imagined my stuttering law practice could bring in the money necessary is beyond my present comprehension. I was still in the throes of adapting to an entirely different legal system – Peruvian law is based on the Napoleonic Code. Simultaneously, I had to learn not only Spanish but the Quechua and Aymara languages. Out of the blue, deliverance seemed to come like manna from Heaven. It started when one day I left my house for the Lima law courts. An anonymous note – in English – was pushed into my hand."

Westburton reached into an inside pocket and withdrew a scrap of paper. "Here it is, Mr. Holmes."

Holmes took it and for my benefit read aloud, "'*Your Excellency, if you are desirous of owning the largest emerald jewel in Peru, perhaps in the whole world, in three days' time go alone to the ruins of an ancient temple one hour's walk north-east of the village of Pachacamac in the Valley of the Lurín River. You will be met at mid-day, where the gem will be shown to you. It weighs more than two kilos. It is the lost sacred emerald of the Incas, the flawless Umina.*'"

"The largest emerald jewel in Peru – perhaps in the entire world!" Westburton repeated, his eyes burning with recollected excitement. "It was Kismet! My darling Enid and I were destined to stay together. If only I could obtain this emerald for a satisfactory price and bring it back to London, I could sell it anonymously – perhaps to an emissary of the Russian Czar . . . ."

Early in the morning three days later, Westburton had set off for Pachacamac. He was met there by an old man dressed as the priest of a temple. "We sat at the foot of a gigantic kapok tree hundreds of years old. The 'priest' told me that Umina dropped from the sky in the body of a meteorite. For many years, the jewel was worshipped and kept in its own temple under the protection of the priests. Umina reinforced the Incas' belief their gems were not just ornaments but precious gifts from the gods. Then the Conquistadors arrived, with nothing but contempt for religions other than Catholicism. When the priests saw how the Spaniards lusted after emerald crystals, they spirited Umina away, just in time. The Spanish soldiers came and razed the Temple to the ground. For centuries the whereabouts of the sacred emerald remained a mystery, until this elderly priest himself stumbled across it.

"'Show it to me!' I begged. He brought out a jewel the size of an ostrich egg, carved in the shape of a human torso. He said his greatest wish was to rebuild the temple before he died. He would rather sell the Umina emerald to a rich foreigner and use the money for that purpose than tell the Peruvian Government how he had discovered it in a special cavity built into the foundations of the ruined temple. He was certain government officials would sequester it and offer a pittance in compensation."

Westburton paused and looked at us. "Mr. Holmes, Dr. Watson, what I would give if every client I placed in the witness box was so skilled in deceit! The story was utterly plausible. The cost of rebuilding the temple would be the price I had to pay, but it would nowhere near approximate the fortune I could obtain for the jewel. He even suggested I should first take it to Jaipur, the historic pink city of palaces and forts where craftsmen could cut Umina into matching emeralds and separate them into dozens and dozens of anonymous parcels. That such a suggestion came from a priest should have rung alarm bells, but I was too enraptured with gaining possession of such a jewel. I knew nothing about emeralds. Since then I have learned that many gemstones in the possession of the best-endowed museums or the richest collectors like Czar Nicholas or the Rockefellers are in reality fake. Suffice to say, I went to every point of the compass to raise the money. I even sold the yacht which had brought us all the way to our new life in South America. I told Enid that the boat had been stolen. At the 'priest's' insistence I assembled the payment in untraceable five-

peseta silver coins. I pretended that word had come of my mother's death, so I would need to return to England *incognito* to visit her grave. And that's how I managed to get away, bringing Umina with me."

Holmes and I watched in silence while Westburton took time to gather his thoughts.

"Then came the most bitter disappointment of my life," he resumed. "I arrived at the London docks. I hurried straight away to Bonham's auction house. In front of their gem specialist I unwrapped the emerald from its hiding place in the hollowed-out husk of the Copuazú fruit. He was barely able to suppress a smirk. Had I purchased it in Lima? he asked at once. He informed me I was at the very least the tenth foreign visitor to Lima to fall for this trick. Far from being an emerald crashing to Earth from the skies or transported through jungles centuries before from the renowned mines of Ecuador or Columbia, Umina was chrysolite, probably quarried in Brazil, not even of gem quality. The specialist proved it to me with the "fog test". Breathing on an emerald for one second will produce a mist on the stone which – if the stone is genuine – will evaporate in almost exactly two seconds. By contrast, the mist on a fake emerald will take at least five seconds to begin to dissipate.

"Gentlemen, I don't need to tell you how long the fog lasted on 'the sacred emerald of the Incas', nor that I, like every one of those deceived before me, did not want the fraud brought to public attention. I was in a state of shock. I asked Bonham's to call me a cab. An hour earlier I had arrived at the auction house in a neat little landau. For my departure they ordered a spavined one-horse hansom driven by a brown-whiskered, no-coated cabman in a battered billycock. This modest transport befitted my dashed hopes of great wealth.

"Hardly able to contain his mirth, Bonham's doorman passed Umina up to me, shoved back into the fuzzy skin of the Copuazú. I yelled at the cabbie to get me away as fast as he could oblige his horse, in whichever direction took its or his fancy. The nag made a great show of movement, but little progress. After a passage of who knows how long, a flash a solution to all my woes came to me. It rested squarely with the King of Scandinavia. A particular feature of my legal career and regular appearances at the Old Bailey was that I had accumulated all the resources for a great criminal enterprise. Among my clients were courtiers, politicians, adventurers, and Fellows from my old Trinity College. Among the legal fraternity were members of the Bar and masters of the High Court. In addition, there was a blackmailer over whom I had a hold."

Westburton turned his head to stare at the pink envelope. "Best of all, for my purposes, there was a former *confrère*, a barrister's clerk, whose skill in writing documents in my or any other hand was matchless. Many a time in my absence and for my convenience he composed and signed off legal letters in a hand so identical that I couldn't later be sure which was his and which mine. I had a hold on him too. I knew that he had built a lucrative side-career forging historical documents to sell to the British Museum Library, using writing materials and self-made inks from the appropriate period. His most profitable line was in letters purportedly written by Oliver Cromwell in the summer of 1647."

Westburton pointed towards the envelope. "Over the next day or so I put the wording together, demanding 100,000 silver kronas and five pouches of uncut gems of the finest quality. I knew which stationer's supplied Enid's hallmark distinctive black ink and pink stationery. I even went to Regent's Street to purchase a small bottle of her favourite scent for the clerk to spray on the paper. After that, it was simply a matter of a brief exchange of carefully-worded telegrams to set a meeting with the final link, the professional art dealer and blackmailer Charles Augustus Howell. Thus I have been brought to this pitiable pass."

I asked, having the prospect in mind of writing up the story one day, "The King was ordered to respond in writing *poste restante* to Mrs. Westburton at the Leadenhall Post Office. How would you have retrieved it?"

Westburton patted his jacket pocket.

"The fear that Enid might disappear without a trace before I return home drove me to bring her passport with me."

Up to this point, William Westburton had been staring into the embers. Now he looked up. "Tell me, Mr. Holmes, what gave you the clue that the letter wasn't from Enid herself? Was the clerk's calligraphy less than perfect?"

"The script was perfect," Holmes replied. "Even when I compared it to the writing style from your wife at the time of your marriage I could find nothing suspicious."

"Then please enlighten me. How did you – ?"

"A blackmail letter is a most intimate form of communication, penned for the victim's eyes only," Holmes responded. "'*I have the honour to be, Sir, Yours obediently*' is hardly the signature of a courtesan to a former Royal lover." He then explained how we had obtained a look at a sample of one of his letters – that in the vicarage at St. Catherine's.

Holmes then passed the extortion letter across to our visitor. "I haven't set eyes on this letter until this very minute," Westburton murmured. He replaced the letter in its envelope. "I now see that the clerk simply wrote the style of ending he knew from fashioning so many of my more formal letters." His voice was weary. "A blunder indeed. I should have checked the letter before it was sent, but rather than risk delay, I ordered the clerk to complete the missive and take it straight to Tilney Street. Time – or rather, the lack of it! – was of the essence. I was obsessed with hiding my presence in London. The longer I stayed, the greater the chance that I'd be unmasked. Howell assured me he would engage a courier as soon as the photograph was complete to expedite it and the letter to the King."

Holmes nodded. "What happened to the original photograph, the one which caused the Crown Prince so much panic?"

Westburton grimaced. "It was very much like the one which I had reproduced. I missed the opportunity to lay my hands on it. One afternoon I came back to our house in Lima to find that my wife had gone out. I was gripped by the greatest fear that she was preparing to leave me. Remembering where she'd hidden the Emperor of Ethiopia's emerald ring, I searched her things. Finally, before my disbelieving eyes, was the infamous photograph. I hardly had time to steal a glance at it when the sound of footsteps came from the stairs. Hurriedly I hid it again and flung myself on the bed as though asleep. When I had a chance to look for it again, it was gone. I never saw it again. When I needed to provide a photograph to Howell, the only one of Enid that I had was a perfectly demure picture that she had left at my quarters in the Inner Temple early-on in our courtship. She was in evening dress, seated on a bench, wearing the ear-rings and a bracelet given to her by the Crown Prince."

Holmes murmured, "Which Howell took to Berlusconi to be altered."

Westburton nodded. "That was the photograph that I handed over to Berlusconi."

I broke in. "What made you take it for granted the King would still be willing to pay a fortune for it? He had long since married. Why do you suppose he isn't calm and reflective – sanguine even – these days?"

Westburton smiled. "I ask you, Doctor, how calm and reflective he would be, knowing as well as you or I that the Chusseau-Flaviens Agency would eagerly distribute such a photograph to every newspaper across Europe, the Orient, the United States, and elsewhere. You yourselves might have come across it in *The Illustrated London News*. Yes, I do believe he'd have paid almost anything, Doctor – and would have if Mr. Holmes here hadn't intervened.

"The Crown Prince is now King, and now married. He and his Queen have produced a child. He would wish to protect them from a scandal which would rock society if the photograph were to become common currency in the newspapers. Besides, the King is richer than ever. His new family owns eleven castles and palaces, every one of them set in immense and fertile estates. They are the wealthiest and most glamorous Royals of them all. Not even the Romanovs compare."

A long silence followed. Holmes puffed at a cigarette and gazed down into the fire. The silence was finally broken by the creaking of his chair as he leaned forward, pushing the pink envelope towards me.

"Alarums, Watson," he murmured, "but no lasting harm."

He pointed at the flames flickering in the grate.

"Westburton, no doubt Dr. Watson has your permission?"

"He does, Mr. Holmes!" Westburton exclaimed, his eyes shining with relief. "I shall be glad to see the last of it."

The envelope caught fire at the edges. Within seconds the coals had consumed the missive. Only the faintest sniff of Enid Westburton's favourite perfume lingered on in the sitting room air.

Chapter VII
The Hereditary King of Scandinavia is Given the News

The following morning I came down to breakfast to find Holmes in buoyant mood. I greeted him with a concern which had pressed in on me during the night. What did he intend to do about William Westburton? "After all," I said, "here's a man sworn to uphold the laws of England. A Member of the Bar, an Honourable Member of the Inner Court. Yet we have now burnt the most significant piece of evidence that Scotland Yard would need to – "

"It was a three-pipe problem," Holmes broke in. "I have decided Westburton's fate. However, that leaves a larger concern: What's to be done about Howell? He's equally complicit, yet he remains untouched – a deadly virus at the heart of London Society. You saw it was a matter of complete indifference to him when we threatened him with Scotland Yard. He's perfectly aware that blackmail remains outside the ambit of the criminal law."

"Holmes, your knowledge of the Law is greater than mine. Isn't there any kind of charge which might succeed against him?"

"Larceny by Extortion, perhaps," Holmes replied, "but he would plead that he was merely offering the King an item of great sentimental value in the hope of the suggested reward."

Holmes reached for his tobacco pouch and blackened briar. "By contrast, Westburton's fate lies entirely in our hands," he continued. "We must distinguish between his motive and that of a professional blackmailer. Howell is driven by an evil and merciless love of money and power. Westburton more despises money than craves it. As to gaining power over someone, rather than mastery he is seeking a form of servitude to Enid Westburton. I have never loved, but if I did, Watson, and if the woman I loved underwent a metamorphosis of the order Westburton

297

swears Enid Westburton has undergone in Peru, I might act even as our lawless barrister has. Men have been driven to distraction by far lesser souls. Think how the Achaeans waged war against Troy when Paris stole Helen from Menelaus, King of Sparta. One day we might even see a King forsake the throne of England for such an *inamorata*."

Holmes leaned back on the settee, blowing little wavering rings of smoke up to the ceiling before continuing. "I expect His Majesty to arrive here at any minute. Half-an-hour ago I sent word to him at the Langham, absolving Westburton of any involvement. I assured him that he can empty the hotel safe of his fortune in uncut white diamonds and the assorted Columbian emeralds and return home."

"Holmes," I returned impatiently, "make yourself plain. Do you plan to let Westburton go scot-free?"

"Not quite," came the response. "In any case, the decision must appear to be our client's idea."

He tapped his jacket pocket. "I have Westburton's confession in writing, plus his sworn word that he'll leave our shores for good and settle in a land where he has every prospect of making the income he believes he needs to keep Enid Westburton at his side."

"Which is where?" I asked.

"Where else," came the reply, "but in the most litigious country on Earth – America – and in its most litigious city – Chicago. He'll try to wean 'Liana Monte' off her extravagant expectations and persuade her to join him, magically returned to life from the vasty deep."

"Starting anew in America?" I asked, astonished. "How can Westburton afford it?"

The reply came with an airy wave of the old briar. "Inspector Gregson persuaded Bonham's to offer our barrister friend a very substantial sum for Umina. It'll be donated for permanent display in Scotland Yard's Black Museum, alongside the various other items used for giving police officers practical instruction on how to detect and prevent crime."

At the words "Black Museum", the rumble of a carriage drawing up outside our lodgings came through the open window.

It took twenty minutes and a pot of Mrs. Hudson's hearty black tea for Holmes to explain every detail to a rapt King. Our Royal visitor's eyes sparkled. He sent up a blue triumphant cloud from his cigarette and gave Holmes a penetrating stare. "*Was ist zu tun mit* Westburton?"

"Your Majesty," Holmes replied gravely, "his fate lies entirely in your hands. He waits trembling at his temporary lodgings for news of your decision. He knows that we have sufficient evidence to strip him of membership in the Bar and the Honourable Society of the Inner Temple, and to put him on trial where he, for a change, must take the stand."

The King's brow clouded. "A public trial before a gallery packed to the brim by reporters from the sensational press," he muttered. "That could have unfortunate consequences for me."

Holmes responded, "Perhaps you might offer Westburton a way out instead? You can oblige him to sign a confession and promise to leave England at once, never to return."

"I agree," the King accepted hastily. "Yes, that's it! Gentlemen, let him know I will take nothing less than a full confession and a solemn promise to leave England, never to return. That will do. It's punishment enough. Once you have obtained both, I'm inclined to show magnanimity – even to get a regular remittance to him. In fact, from the very start I considered this attempt at extortion quite entertaining."

Sotto voce, Holmes muttered, "So much for the 'Iron Fist'."

To the King he said, "A wise and generous offer, Your Majesty. Westburton will be grateful. I'm sure he'll accept those terms and abide by them. There's no more to be done in the matter except for a settlement of our expenses and my fee, after which Watson and I shall have the honour to wish you a very good journey home."

"But what of Howell?" the King asked suddenly.

"I'm afraid there's nothing we can do about him within the Law, Your Majesty," Holmes responded. "Howell will be getting away scot-free. *Latet anguis in herba*. A snake lies in the grass."

Our visitor rose. The hang-dog look of recent days had vanished into thin air. He strode across to the hat stand. From his cloak he took a bulging pouch. It tinkled merrily as he dropped it on the breakfast table.

"Gentlemen," he said, with a bow, "you may gather from the sum in gold in this purse precisely how appreciative I am."

At this he turned to Holmes and grasped him by the shoulders. "Mr. Holmes, there is one last ceremony I wish to perform." The King reached into a second pocket and extricated the small gold box. "We shall have it engraved right away on Regent's Street."

As he spoke, the screech of a carriage wheel scraping the kerb rose from the street, followed by the thumping of feet coming up the stairs two or three at a time. The door crashed open. Inspector Gregson rushed into the room.

"Mr. Holmes," he called out breathlessly, "what is it? Why the urgent summons? Has someone been murdered – ?" The police officer caught sight of our guest. "Your Majesty," Gregson exclaimed, throwing a sideways look at Holmes with a questioning and rather startled gaze, uncertain whether he should suppress any mention of his own involvement in the case, "I had no idea – "

"Of course you didn't, Gregson," Holmes assured him cheerily. "It's all highly confidential. His Majesty is here solely because he has an official duty to perform before he returns to his throne. For special services, His Majesty insists on conferring upon you, Tobias Gregson, Scotland Yard Inspector, the Freedom of the City of Prague!"

Epilogue

Throughout time, blackmail has been high on the list of the foulest of crimes – cold-blooded in its premeditation and repeated in its torture of the victim. Not one woman or man in a thousand will march off to the Chief Magistrate at Bow Street to make a sworn statement detailing all that they know about the extortioner. Howell's access to the closed and privileged *milieu* of Aristocracy continued, with scandalous gossip its everyday currency. It was of some small satisfaction to us that Howell's involvement in this matter failed to gain him even one krona, let alone a share of raw diamonds or the uncut emeralds that the extortion letter had demanded. Nevertheless, the king of blackmailers continued to be known as the pit-viper *fer-de-lance* because more than half of the victims that he sank his fangs into ended up killing themselves while he waxed richer and richer.

One night in April 1890 his nemesis struck. A piece appeared in the weekly magazine *Tit-Bits* announcing his death in circumstances as strange as any Poe or Ainsworth novel. The butler at Tilney Street reported that his master had failed to return home. A corpse identified as Charles Augustus Howell, fine art dealer, was found near a Chelsea public house, an area known for ribaldry and flaunting vice. At first it was assumed that he was the victim of a common street robbery, except that the pavement was curiously lacking in pools of blood, indicating that death took place elsewhere. A *post mortem* examination found the throat had been slit posthumously, slashed with such venom that the windpipe was sliced right through and the head nearly severed. The presence of a half-sovereign coin left with the victim's body was known to be a criticism of those guilty of slander. In this instance, what went unreported was that there was also, jutting from the oozing wound, a curious addition to the gold coin – a gilded bronze key, the splendid rank-insignia of the Grand Chamberlain of The Councils of Scandinavia.

Knowing Holmes's general commitment to due process, no matter how disgraceful the crime, I tried to draw my comrade-in-arms into expressing a view on such extreme savagery inflicted without legal proceeding. Holmes declined to answer, though for several days he seemed unusually at peace with the world.

> *"A most painful matter to me, as you can most readily imagine, Mr. Holmes. I have been cut to the quick. I understand that you have already managed several delicate cases of this sort, sir, though I presume that they were hardly from the same class of society."*
>
> *"No, I am descending."*
>
> *"I beg pardon."*
>
> *"My last client of the sort was a king."*
>
> *"Oh, really! I had no idea. And which king?"*
>
> *"The King of Scandinavia."*
>
> *"What! Had he lost his wife?"*
>
> *"You can understand,"* said Holmes suavely, *"that I extend to the affairs of my other clients the same secrecy which I promise to you in yours."*

> – Lord St. Simon and Sherlock Holmes
> "The Adventure of the Noble Bachelor"

NOTE

Holmes and Watson's Use of Surnames: In the twenty-first century, it seems strange that very good friends in past times used each other's family names just in the way we now tend to use a first name. No character in the original Sherlock Holmes stories, except Holmes's older brother Mycroft, called him "Sherlock", nor did anyone call Watson "John", (except presumably his wives – except for that one curious incident when Mary Watson called him "James" in "The Man With the Twisted Lip", which leads to a completely new discussion). The use of the surname/family name was considered both civilised and friendly.

GLOSSARY

The Black Museum: Officially "The Crime Museum". A collection of criminal memorabilia kept at Scotland Yard, headquarters of the Metropolitan Police Service in London. The museum came into existence sometime in 1874.

Blackmail: Amazingly, blackmail did not become a criminal offence in England until the Theft Act of 1968. Blackmail is defined under English criminal law as an unwarranted demand with menaces, with a view to making a gain or causing a loss. Menaces can include a threat of physical violence, but other forms – such as a threat to expose a secret – can constitute blackmail.

Defuncti sunt: "They are dead." Watson's Latin was competent from his schooling and medical training.

Eisenfaust: The Iron Fist. The King knows that Holmes speaks fluent German.

Elysian: From the idyllic Greek mythological place called Elysian Fields.

Fer-de-Lance: Pit-viper. One of the world's most deadly snakes. Its haemotoxic venom spreads through cells and blood vessels, causing swelling and blisters and destroying tissue. In the lowlands of Central America, it can reach lengths of up to six feet and is responsible for more than half of all venomous bites.

Gasogene Bottle: Late Victorian device for producing carbonated water.

Latet anguis in herba: "*The snake lurks in the grass*". A treacherous person. First known use by the poet Virgil. Holmes showing that he too knew Latin phrases.

Urvogel: "*First bird*". Watson refers to *Archaeopteryx* (*A. lithographica*), the fossils of which are synonymous with the Solnhofen quarries and dug up in 1861. Watson must have been reading about it. However, *Archaeopteryx* was probably not the first bird to evolve.

Watch Him Fall
by Liese Sherwood-Fabre

The regularity of some occurrences provides a certainty to life. The changing of the seasons, for example. Another, the arrival of Mrs. Hudson each morning with our breakfast. When, one rather blustery winter day in 1887, she had failed to appear with our coffee and eggs, I was taken aback. Not only had she not brought up a tray, but the remains of our dinner still lay as we had left it the night before. Never had such a deficiency appeared previously, and I felt my whole world tilt as a result. Would the sun not rise tomorrow?

"Holmes," I said, staring at the congealed fat adorning a serving bowl and spoon, "something's happened to Mrs. Hudson."

My friend and colleague shifted his attention from some chemical analysis on the other side of the room to glance first at me and then at the table. "What time is it?"

"A little past seven," I said after consulting the clock on the mantel.

He put down the beaker into which he been measuring some liquid and scratched his chin. "Why don't you check on her? I'm in the middle of an experiment. If something physical has befallen her, you're a better choice than I."

My gaze shifted from the table to Holmes and back before moving to the door. When he was in such a state, I knew drawing him out would only lead to bad humor and an irritation that I preferred to meet on a full stomach.

At the bottom of the stairs, I knocked on Mrs. Hudson's door and called out to her. I held my breath, uncertain whether I would have to break it down and what I would find on the other side. To my relief, I heard a shuffling of footsteps, a click of a key, and our landlady opened the door enough to peer through the crack at me.

I couldn't make out much of the woman, but what I did see distressed me to no end: A blood-shot eye, usually well-groomed hair hanging limp over her face, and a crimson-tinted nose. Had I not known better, I would have considered her in her cups, but I detected no scent of gin or other spirits wafting through the opening.

"My dear," I said, trying to remain calm while various causes for her current appearance ran through my mind, "are you all right?"

She only croaked out a strangled "Oh," shoved a handkerchief she held in her hand to her mouth, and shut the door in my face.

Despite my earlier reservations, I was able to garner Holmes's aid to coax the woman from her apartment. Seating her in Holmes's chair by the fireplace, I handed her a bit of brandy, which she gulped down in one swallow. She set the glass down on the table next to her and I took her hand. My friend stood to one side of the fire, elbow resting on the mantel, and listened as she began her tale.

"I've been a fool," she said and hiccupped, "and now I'm ruined."

I swallowed hard and forced myself not to glance in Holmes's direction. While I had always had the utmost respect for our landlady – few would have tolerated a tenant who played the violin at all times of the day and night or stunk up the place with his chemical experiments – I realized that I had never taken the time to truly learn much about her background, which she claimed was now in tatters. At the same time, the woman, having been married and no naïve maid, wouldn't have been easily duped by some Lothario. My outrage that one might have done so to such an upright woman pushed me to give voice to my concerns.

"You tell me the name of this scoundrel, and we'll take him to court. If it is a breach of promise – "

Her eyes widened, and she stared at me. "You can't take him to court. I can't have the world learning that he – he – "

A sob cut off the rest of her thought.

I glanced at Holmes. His mouth was turned down into a most intense scowl, and I feared that he would toss the poor woman out if she didn't get her story out soon. I carried her glass to the sideboard to pour her another brandy.

Before I could return, he asked, "How much did Mr. Innes swindle from you?"

That question brought both me and Mrs. Hudson up short. She raised her tear-stained face to my friend, and I stared at him from halfway across the room.

"How did you know his name?" she whispered.

Holmes pulled the jack-knife from the stack of correspondence on the mantel and handed her the top document. "It was delivered here while you were out, and I hadn't a chance to pass it to you yet."

Returning with the brandy, I read the missive over her shoulder as, this time, she sipped the medicinal draught. Directed to *the many victims of Mr. Innes*", the note requested attendance at a meeting at the Queens Arms in Camberwell to discuss getting back their investments.

"Investments?" I asked. "In what?"

"Gold. In Australia," Holmes said and handed me the evening newspaper. A short article he pointed out to me discussed the disappearance of a Mr. James Innes of the Tasmanian Gold Mining

Company. "I'd planned to ask Mrs. Hudson about it when she collected the dinner dishes. Which she never did."

"I – I couldn't do anything but think about how I'd been duped," she said with a sniffle and another gulp of brandy. "I didn't need the note. Someone called on me right after I brought up the dinner tray. Said he was Innes' secretary and gotten my name from his list of investors. That he'd learned how the man was fleecing us all and that we had to stop him before he left with our money."

"You have his card?" Holmes asked.

She nodded. "In my kitchen."

I headed to the door to retrieve it. "This is a matter for the police. This man must know where the scoundrel is."

Our landlady's wail stopped me in my tracks. "No! No police. If he's arrested, we might never find any of the money. You don't understand. I borrowed against this house. If I don't get my money back, we'll all be on the streets."

I turned back around, my stomach roiling, and not just from hunger. Glancing about the room, a sort of panic possessed me. I'd spent over six years here and with neither kith nor kin – other than for my friend Holmes. I couldn't imagine where I'd go. And Holmes? Would it be even possible to find another place? With someone as tolerable to his ways as our dear Mrs. Hudson?

"What should we do?" I asked after a swallow to force down the bile threatening to rise.

"Start at the beginning by paying a call on Mr. Innes' office." Holmes turned to Mrs. Hudson. "I need the card from the secretary and any papers provided to you about the Tazmanian Gold Mining Company."

In the carriage toward Camberwell where Mr. Innes had his office, Holmes studied what Mrs. Hudson had shared with him. "According to these documents, she has purchased at first about one percent of a mining company in Australia. Later on, another two percent with the proceeds from the first portion, and then two more with dividends of the first two for a total of five percent, representing four-hundred pounds."

"If it's been paying well, why, then does she think she's ruined?"

"I'm hoping the secretary will be able to shed some light on it."

The offices of the Tazmanian Gold Mining Company were on the third floor of a building in the southern part of Camberwell. While the northern part held large manor houses on top of a hill, this area involved rows of homes cheek-to-jowl built for the lower middle-classes. Interspersed along the street were shops and tradesmen's offices with their garish signs advertising their efforts as shoe cobblers or tailors.

The person who responded to our knock did not fit my conception of a secretary at all. The man was tall, muscular, and with a large moustache that reminded me more of a boxer than someone who copied letters for a businessman.

"Mr. . . . ?" Holmes checked the card in his hand. "Armaund? I'm here on behalf of Mrs. Hudson, our friend and landlady."

His identification of Mrs. Hudson as a "friend" caused me to glance at him. In reviewing my own sentiments toward the woman, I would have used the term, but found it quite revealing Holmes had done so as well. She was certainly more than just our landlady, and it saddened me a bit to think a crisis like this had to occur to make me realize it.

Armaund studied first me and then Holmes and pulled open the door. "You're Sherlock Holmes, aren't you? I figured if I spoke to Mrs. Hudson, you'd be here. I need your protection."

"I'm afraid, sir, you are mistaken. We came here – "

"To get her money back. I know. I visited her and all the investors to let them know what Innes had done. I thought we could catch him before he got away, but – "

The man held out his hands in a sign of resignation.

Holmes completed the thought for him. "He disappeared yesterday. And I assume the money has vanished with him?"

The man nodded, a frown creasing his forehead.

"When did you last see him?"

"Very early yesterday." The man stepped back and allowed us to enter the office proper. He swung his arm to the right to indicate a desk covered in papers. "He was sitting at this desk, reviewing the current list of investors with me. That's when I determined he was not what he appeared."

Holmes moved to the desk and picked up one paper and then another, studying each. As he did so, he spoke, without raising his gaze from whatever he held in his hand. "Have you known Mr. Innes long?"

"I used to be a prizefighter. Mr. Innes was my backer."

Holmes turned to him. "Not Armaund the Anvil?"

"The one and the same," the man said, puffing out his chest.

"There was a tragedy in the ring, I believe," Holmes said, rubbing his chin. "About four years ago, your opponent, Bernie the Bruiser, dropped dead in the final round."

The man's gaze shifted to the ground. "Must've had a glass jaw. I didn't hit him that hard. I couldn't go into the ring again after that. But Mr. Innes, he said he could always use a strong man like me to help him out. Hired me to keep his records. I was copying them fresh into a ledger for this project when I saw it."

306

"That he had sold more than one-hundred percent of his shares to his investors."

"How did you know?"

"From what I'm seeing on his desk. Here's a certificate for five-percent," he said and held up an official-looking piece of paper. "Another for ten-percent." He displayed another. "I would guess that if we added up these percentages – "

"It's three-hundred percent. He sold the company three-times over," he said, with a shake of his head.

"I don't understand," I said after I recovered from the shock of such a blatant act of thievery. "Why didn't people see what he was doing?"

"He did it gradual-like. Someone would give him money for say, three months, and he would give them it back – and more – with money he took in from some other investor. And they'd be so happy, they'd give it back to him and more to increase their share. He'd take that money and give it to another. Mind you, I wasn't privy to all this at the beginning, but he'd bring in all this money, have me count it out, and put it in a big bag hidden under the floorboards.

"And this morning, I was making the new ledger as I told you and I asked him about how there can be that many shares to the company. He told me I didn't understand financing, but I do. When I was a boxer, I had backers who bought a piece of my earnings same as his investors get a piece of the gold mine. That's when I took the ledger and went to visit all he took money from."

"And the big bag under the floorboards?" Holmes asked.

He pointed to the desk. Holmes rounded it and disappeared from view as he crawled underneath.

"When did you return to the office?" Holmes asked, straightening himself after crawling out from under the desk.

"I was out most of the day. There were a lot of investors," he said with a frown. "Did you find anything in the hole?"

"It could be nothing, but my rule is never to overlook a trifle." He glanced about the room once again and asked, "Can you provide me with the list of the investors? I'd like to see how many actually make it to the meeting tonight."

Armaund shuffled papers on his desk and pulled out a ledger. "This is the one I was copying all the information into. Has all the names, addresses, and amounts."

"Thank you," Holmes said and tucked it under his arm. "I appreciate your time. Until this evening."

Back on the street, we hailed another cab, and once seated he handed me the ledger.

"Do you want me to study the names?" I asked. "See if I recognize anyone?"

"There might be something there," he said. "I'm much more interested in what I found in the hole. I need to examine this further with my laboratory equipment." He called up to the cab driver behind us. "I need to stop at the nearest telegraph office. After that, I'll double your price if you can make it to Baker Street in under an hour."

When the cab jerked and threw us against the back, I knew the driver would do all he could to earn his extra fare. More importantly I knew my friend suddenly had some insight that he felt the need for more urgency.

"What has occurred to you that you need the extra hour at home?" I asked.

He grabbed the edge of the cab to keep himself from being flung out of the conveyance when we hit some sort of dip on his side. Once righted, he said, "I was reviewing the events as Mr. Armaund described them, and I think I've discovered a discrepancy. Should I be correct, we must act quickly before he slips away."

When we arrived, we found the remains of our dinner finally cleared away, replaced with a plate of cold meats and fruit for a repast. Without a glance, Holmes passed it to his chemistry bench in the corner. He went straight away into preparing some sort of examination of the contents that he'd stored in a handkerchief he pulled from his pocket. I, however, having skipped breakfast, filled a plate. Munching on the items, I was debating whether I should bother Mrs. Hudson with water for tea when she appeared with a fresh pot.

Of course, I didn't need my colleague's penchant for observation to know she had used the water as a pretext for gaining more information.

"Did you find Mr. Innes?" she asked as she set down the pot.

When Holmes didn't respond, I felt obligated to at least share some news with her. "We spoke with his secretary, Mr. Armaund. Nice man. Very concerned about all the investors."

"Yes," she said and sniffed. "Do you think you'll get my money back?"

I shifted on my feet and glanced at Holmes, who was now titrating something into a beaker. I knew the money that Innes had collected had disappeared with him but wasn't certain both might not be recovered. Then again, providing false hope would have been cruel. I'd taken an oath to do no harm and felt it prudent to follow this directive in this situation. In the end, I said, "We'll try."

"Do you think I should go?" she asked. "To the meeting tonight?"

"It would be a complete waste of time," Holmes said from the corner. We both spun to face him. He swirled whatever was in the beaker and held

308

the muddy concoction to the light coming through the window as it slowly changed to dark blue. "I am certain that Mr. Innes will not be there, and your presence will not make him appear."

Mrs. Hudson let out another of her wails and pulled her apron up to her face. "I'm ruined. I just know it."

He raised his gaze to the ceiling and blew out through his lips. "I never said that. I just said attendance at the meeting would not benefit you."

"As a physician, Mrs. Hudson, I am going to provide you with something to calm your nerves." Placing an arm about her shoulders, I led her to the door. "I'll be down in a minute with the restorative."

Once the door closed behind her, I prepared a mild nerve tonic. "Did you truly have to be so harsh on her? Her nerves are frayed. A little gentleness – "

" – Won't bring back her funds. I have a plan, Watson, to ensure a return of all that she invested. At the same time, she needs to learn an offer too good to be true most likely is. If this becomes too easy for her, she most certainly will be fooled again in the future."

"I suppose so," I said, adding water to the powder I'd poured into a glass and stirring it. He was watching me now, and I had to give a little smile. "We're both with our potions at the moment, aren't we?"

"Yes," he said, drawing out the vowel. "But yours won't make several thousand pounds reappear."

"Is that blue muck some sort of magic that will conjure a bagful of money onto this table?" I asked, trying to decide whether to be offended or simply annoyed at his attitude.

He set down the beaker and turned to me. "As you know, I'm quite familiar with the various soils in and about London, and I found some rather interesting samples in that hole. This little analysis has now definitively identified them. I think I shall now enjoy some of the lunch Mrs. Hudson has left. I also have one item I must consult in my files prior to the meeting."

Before I could return up the stairs after ensuring our landlady's nerves were sufficiently calmed, a knock at the front door produced a telegram addressed to my friend.

"Excellent," Holmes said as he accepted the missive from me. His face, however, soon shifted into a frown as he read.

"Bad news, I take it," I said when he stuffed it into his pocket.

"Possibly," he said. "I need more information before I can confirm that." He glanced at the clock on the mantel. "We will need to be leaving shortly if we are to make it to the meeting at the tavern on time."

He stepped to his desk and retrieved his revolver. After securing it in his pocket, he said, "Better bring yours along as well."

"Do you truly think things will become violent?"

"We're dealing with a group who has been swindled of their hard-earned money, my friend. They are angry and frustrated – easily turned into a mob seeking revenge on whomever they think might be guilty."

On the cab ride back over the river, Holmes held out his hand. "Let me see the ledger now, Watson. It might prove useful to become acquainted with some of those sharpening their axes for Innes' neck."

"I didn't have a chance to examine it," I said, "what with Mrs. Hudson becoming so emotional again."

"Yes," he said, dragging out that vowel again and warning me I'd lost him to the pages of names Armaund had so carefully detailed.

After reviewing the whole list once, he then ran his finger over the column of names one more time. Stopping about three-quarters of the way through, he tapped one line and stated a single-word observation: "Interesting."

Holmes hadn't been wrong about the crowd's mood at the tavern. They'd taken over the main room at the Queens Arms. I quickly spotted Armaund. He stood on a bench next to a red-faced fellow who was shaking his fist at the angry investors below.

"I say we search every inch of Camberwell until we find this swindler and our money!" said the man.

Those around him shouted in agreement. Studying the mob, I came to understand the type of people Innes had targeted. From their dress and manners, they were not unlike Mrs. Hudson – hard-working, trusting folk who had lost whatever nest egg they'd managed to save over the years. My own anger boiled at the injustice as much as theirs.

"Come along, Watson," Holmes said, shouting into my ear.

Unable to reply over the din, I could only follow as he shoved his way to the front. By the time I reached him, Armaund had already pulled Holmes up onto the bench, where he stepped to the center and raised his arms.

"Ladies and gentlemen!" Holmes said in a loud voice.

The crowd jeered at him and shook their fists. They appeared not to want speeches or to be suggested that they were "gentle". When the cacophony grew, making it difficult for him to repeat himself, he drew his revolver and gave a single shot into the ceiling. Silence reigned, except for the ringing in my ears. As the scent of gunpowder drifted over the crowd, most stared slack-jawed at the man now addressing them.

"As I was saying," he paused to slip his revolver back into his coat pocket, "I am Mr. Sherlock Holmes, the friend of one of your number. I, too, would like to have a word with Mr. Innes, but unlike the rest of you, I know where he is."

That announcement renewed the crowd's shouts, this time with some insults and threats directed at the speaker. They calmed, however, when he drew his pistol out again and pointed it upward.

"I will help you apprehend and bring this man to justice, but I have a price. Exactly four-hundred pounds." The entire audience drew in their breath, including me – although for a very different reason. I recognized it as the amount Mrs. Hudson had paid to Mr. Innes. "Should I recover any of the monies that Mr. Innes took from you, I will return it to Mr. Armaund – minus the four-hundred pounds – for his equitable distribution to you, the investors. I cannot promise full restitution, but as much compensation as possible to each of you."

"Tell us where he is – " the red-faced man on the bench shouted at him, " – and we'll take care of our 'compensation' ourselves."

"I refuse to hand the man over to a mob. He will be dealt with by those in authority, or I will remain silent. I am convinced that he has a plan to leave the country, and if you don't accept my terms, you will never see him or any of your money again."

The mob's leader surveyed the crowd's upturned faces and then glanced at Holmes, pistol still in hand. "You say you can get us back our money?"

"All that Innes has not spent, minus my fee of four-hundred pounds."

The leader scratched his head, his face losing some of its florid hue. "We'll put it to a vote. All those in favor of lettin' Mr. Sherlock Holmes find what's left of our money, say 'Aye'."

The room rang with the crowd's voice. "Aye!"

"Any what say 'Nay'?"

A general shuffling of feet suggested the presence of some who might not be in agreement but were, nonetheless, not prepared to announce their objection out loud.

The man turned to my friend. "All right. You have twenty-four hours to produce our money." Facing the room, he added. "We'll meet here tomorrow, same time, for Mr. Holmes here to bring us our money."

Holmes jumped down and stood next to me, as the crowd, grumbling in a manner that suggested not all were convinced of his abilities, moved out the door. Once emptied, the ringleader stepped off the bench and said, "Where we goin', gents?"

"*You* are going home," Holmes said. "Dr. Watson, Mr. Armaund, and I will be seeking out Mr. Innes and your funds."

We put on our hats and escorted the man from the pub.

311

After the ringleader had disappeared around the corner, Holmes faced Armaund. "Are you going to show us which hotel or rooming house Mr. Innes is staying at near the Grand Surrey Canal timber lots, or will we have to inquire at each? There shouldn't be too many."

"Armaund's known all along?" I asked. My face grew hot, and I feared I didn't appear much different than the ringleader had when first addressing the crowd. "Holmes, why didn't you – "

"Because you saw that mob," he said, pointing to the tavern. "I feared what they might have done to both Armaund as well as Innes."

"I understand your identification of the Surrey Canal from the soil, but the timber lots?"

"In addition to the mud from the canal area, the sample I retrieved also contained ash from wood scraps such as those burned to heat creosote. Before rising on the bench, I had an opportunity to observe Mr. Armaund's pant legs. They currently have similar splashes of mud – something which he didn't have earlier in the day.

The secretary sighed. "I'll take you to him, but what makes you think he hasn't left already? He wasn't there the last time I checked."

"Because I checked with the harbor authorities to determine when the next international passenger ships were leaving. The earliest one is tomorrow afternoon. In addition, the Surrey Canal authority provided me with information on the barges with some covered space where a person might hide while heading to the port. Again, none until tomorrow."

Armaund's shoulders rounded, a defeated fighter, while Holmes pulled himself straighter, his deductions confirmed. I took up the stride behind the two during our trek to Innes' hotel, reviewing how my judgement of people had been misled. Armaund had seemed a decent fellow, intent on helping those swindled. Had it been an act I didn't see through? If that was the case, how could I ever trust my own instincts again?

The hotel turned out to be a rooming house, next to a timber yard, as Holmes had determined. Its occupants, for the most part, were laborers working the barges up and down the canal – rough, strong men who put in a hard day's efforts. The owner appeared to be retired from the same pool of laborers.

He greeted Armaund as we entered. "If you're lookin' for your boss, you missed him. Left about an hour ago with that big bag of his. Must have been pretty heavy. Had a hard time carryin' it with one hand."

The three of us exchanged glances. Armaund's eyes rounded, as I was certain mine did as well. Holmes, however, only squinted at the owner. "You saw him then?"

"Plain as the nose on my face. Wearin' that big coat of his, cap down low, and carryin' that big bag."

"Did he have any visitors before that?"

"Not a one what doesn't live here been up these stairs today."

"Would you mind if we checked out the room? Perhaps he left something to indicate his intentions."

"Cleanin' lady don't come 'til in the mornin'," he said, handing over a key. "Lock it when you leave."

The room occupied a corner overlooking the street and was sparsely furnished with a bed, nightstand, dresser, and a table and chair. It was also in use. A man lay under the bedcovers, as if asleep. As a physician, however, I knew immediately, he wasn't breathing. Rushing to the bedside, I put my fingers around his wrist. No pulse.

"This man is dead." I glanced at the other two. "Do we know who he is?"

"That," Holmes said, "is Mr. James Innes."

"Then who was it who left with the money? And where did he go?" I asked.

"Let's hope that he left something to point us that way."

Armaund slid his hat from his head and stared at his feet, as if in prayer, and I followed suit. I didn't know the man, but still, one must show some respect for the dead. Holmes, however, was moving about the room, checking in the drawers and under the bed. After a brief pause, I bent over the bed to examine the man lying in his final repose.

"He's still warm," I said and lifted his arm. Flexing it, I found it difficult to bend. "*Rigor* setting in. More than three hours since he passed."

Armaund shook his head. "People were shouting for his death, and he already was. I'll go for the police."

"If you would be so kind," Holmes said. "Watson and I will remain here until you do – to ensure nothing is disturbed."

Armaund gave a little bow and left. Once the man had gone, Holmes truly went to work about the room, studying the few items on the little table next to him. "A set of keys, some coins, and his watch," Holmes said more to himself than to me. He compared the time on the watch with that of his own. "Well-maintained, I can see. The time matches my own – half-past-eight."

After examining both the front and back, he thoughtfully wound it and put it in his pocket.

I pulled out the single chair next to the table and sat down. The remains of Innes' meager dinner were still there, next to a water pitcher and basin. Some sort of gruel, crusts of toast, and an empty teacup.

"Poor looking fare for his last meal. It appears he was ill. He may have succumbed to some sort of heart or stomach problem," I said glancing over my shoulder. "Should it be saved to be checked for poison?"

"We can leave those items to Scotland Yard, but he wasn't poisoned – at least by anything hidden in his food. Consider how neat his bedclothes. Strychnine and arsenic – the usual poisons of choice – cause convulsions. Whatever killed him wasn't that conventional."

After glancing around the room as if taking a final inventory, he said, "I'm going to interview some of the other roomers on this floor and talk to the landlord again. Also, I'll check on what's taking Armaund and the police so long. Please keep any curiosity seekers out until I return."

Once Holmes had secured the door, I studied the scene out the window. The timber lots Holmes had identified from the mud splatters were visible from this corner. A gaslight illuminated the scene below and danced off the murky canal water beyond. I found the whole scene quite peaceful. Soon my eyelids drooped, then closed completely.

After only what seemed seconds, I was roughly shaken awake. Holmes called my name over and over, followed by the sound of a door or window slamming. Four hands grabbed my shoulders and forearms to force me through some opening. Several slaps on my back caused me to cough and pull in lungfuls of air. I opened my eyes and focused once again on the canal and timber lot – only this time, I was staring straight down at them. My feet slipped along the wood floor as I struggled against the hands on me to pull myself back through the open window. Turning about, the frowning faces of the landlord, Lestrade, and Holmes sharpened into view.

"Watson," Holmes said with a sharp bark. "Who am I?"

I coughed, and a sharp pain split across my skull. Rubbing my forehead, I peered through my fingers at the man speaking. "What do you mean, 'Who am I?' You're Sherlock Holmes, of course. Did you forget?"

He placed his hands on my shoulders and moved his face close to mine. "Listen to me, Watson. You've been poisoned. Carbon monoxide."

After blinking at him several times – that headache had to be the worst I'd ever experienced – I catalogued my own symptoms. In addition to the deep sleep, there was the headache, and . . . .

"Excuse me," I said, pushing away Holmes's hands and rushing to the basin on the table. After vomiting into it, I added the last symptom. "Nausea."

Straightening from the table, I took in once again the three gentlemen in the room, then to the corpse on the bed. With a careful gait, I moved to the deceased and attempted to lift his arm. Now completely stiff, it wouldn't raise unless I broke the *rigor*. Instead, I focused on his hands.

314

The bright pink tell-tale signs of carbon monoxide poisoning were there on his fingers.

"Why didn't I notice it earlier?"

Holmes stepped next to me. "I didn't either – at first. You gave me the first clue, when you noticed his dinner – that of someone ill. When I went to see what was taking Armaund so long, I found out he'd left without a word to anyone. The landlord shared with me that Innes had complained about feeling ill since arriving and had requested only gruel this evening.

"After sending the landlord for the police, I returned to this floor to interview the others living here. Given the hour, most were in and not quite happy with me disturbing their evening. One, however, was conspicuously absent. The one sharing the wall with Mr. Innes. The wall where the stovepipe passes."

"This room used to be a suite with the room next door bein' the sittin' area," explained the landlord. "Nobody interested in such a big room. Better to fill in the door and collect for two."

"What can you tell me about the one who rented the smaller room?" asked Holmes.

"Mr. Jones?" The landlord scratched his head. "Hardly saw him. Come in a week ago. Quiet man. No visitors."

"And this corner room. How did Mr. Innes rent it?"

"Mr. Armaund arranged it. Said it was for his boss."

"Armaund told us as much," I said. "And he was with the investors when Innes was asphyxiated. Almost four hours ago now."

"How long does it take for someone to die from carbon monoxide?" Lestrade asked, pulling out his notebook.

Despite the throbbing in my head, I forced myself to consider how fast I had dropped off in the room. "It depends on the concentration, of course," I said. "Can be as little as a few minutes. Based on what happened to me, it'd be longer than the time Holmes left me in the room. That and the *rigor*, I'd say, indicate that he succumbed about half-past-five or so."

"I'm afraid, Watson, you are wrong," my friend said.

Accustomed as I was to Holmes's corrections of the observations by those in law enforcement, I found his assessment of my medical conclusion more than I could take. My face grew warm, and I found it difficult to keep a civil tone in my response. "I didn't know you had that much experience with the aspects of clinical death."

"Really, Watson, I don't understand your indignation. I have read any number of treatises on the subject, including one by a John Davey who discovered that high temperatures accelerate the onset of *rigor*. This room gets more than its share of sun. Add to it the fire in the wood stove, and *rigor* will be duly hastened. More important is his watch."

315

He pulled the item from his pocket, checked the time, and wound it once again. "When we arrived, I rewound the watch, counting the revolutions. Just now – about an hour from our arrival, I wound it again. While not completely accurate, I can tell you that it was about half of that I found at the first count. In other words, he was alive enough to wind it a little more than two hours before we arrived. We also know that this Mr. Jones left about an hour after that. He had to wait until the man died to be able to retrieve the bag with the money, as well as Innes' hat and coat. I am certain Armaund has gone to join up with Jones, and we must work quickly if we are to catch them both."

Both Lestrade and I stared at my friend. The inspector had to be thinking just as I was that Holmes was joking. Find a man named Jones in this city? Easier to find the proverbial needle in a haystack.

The inspector voiced this concern out loud first, "And just where do you suggest we seek out this Mr. Jones?"

"I have the address right here in the ledger," Holmes said and opened the book that Armaund had given us earlier. "I'll explain it all in the carriage to the Borough."

Lestrade pulled back his chin at the mention of that quite disreputable area. "Are you saying that Jones lives in the Borough?"

"I am, and he has more than a three-hour head start on us."

Following the two men out of the room, I found myself moving rather slowly. Holmes returned and placed a hand on my arm as we descended the stairs. "Still recovering, eh? Let's make sure we don't lose you now because of a loose step."

Upon reaching the Black Maria police van waiting in the street, Holmes shouted an address to the driver, and as soon as the back door shut, we were off. Given the hour, the horse kept up a steady pace that suggested we'd arrive in good time. Every instance in which we hit a bump or hole, my head would ring from the wheel's impact, and I was soon feeling something akin to seasickness.

"Watson, I believe you're looking a little green about the gills," Holmes said. "Stick your head by the window there and take some deep breaths of the night air while I tell you a bit about this mysterious Mr. Jones to take your mind off the ride."

"I'm not sure I can concentrate on all the facts, but you can try," I managed to say, although more than words wanted to accompany the sentence when the carriage gave a rather ominous sway.

After a few gulps of the cold winter air, I did feel somewhat less queasy and decided to continue the therapeutic breaths.

"A review of the list of investors included a name I recognized, but I had to consult my files to confirm. You recall that Armaund had once been a fighter. Armaund the Anvil. I mentioned that he had a rather famous bout with Bernie the Bruiser, in which Bernie had been knocked out in the last round and died shortly after."

Lestrade drew in a breath. "I remember that fight. There was talk, if I recall – "

Holmes said. "Do you recall Bernie's full name?"

"It was something odd," Lestrade said. "Something foreign . . . ."

I pulled my head in. My face felt slightly numb from the cold and my teeth chattered slightly as I said, "Bervins."

"The night air must be quite bracing. Your cheeks have gone from pale to crimson," Holmes said to me and then continued with his tale. "A Latvian by ancestry. His actual name was Bernhards Bervins – Bernie the Bruiser. His obituary mentioned a wife, Liena, two children, and a brother-in-law, Patriks Johnsone. The brother-in-law appears on the investor list, along with his address in the Borough."

"And you think this Patriks Johnsone is our Mr. Jones?" Lestrade asked.

When Holmes nodded, I shook my head. "Armaund had this planned from the beginning. He set up the meeting to give himself an alibi while Jones or Johnsone murdered the man."

Holmes, however, didn't respond to my observation. Instead, he said, "The driver's slowing. I suppose we're near the address I gave him."

I had accompanied Holmes to many parts of the city – above and below ground, to opium dens, and down the Thames – but I had never found myself so deep among London's less-fortunate than I did that night. When the driver pulled to a stop, we stepped onto a muddy street piled with garbage and a cess-trough running through the middle of the lane. One whiff of the miasma circulating about us almost led me to contribute to the trough's contents.

Lestrade put a handkerchief to his face, but Holmes seemed unaffected by the stench and misery about us. Taking a cue from him and my military training, I stiffened my spine and immobilized my expression.

Holmes entered one of the tenement buildings lining the street, and we followed into a new hell of dark corridors, shouts, and cries behind different doors, and an overpowering reek of rotting food, bodies, and minds. I gave a little prayer of thanksgiving that we didn't have to ascend the stairs, blocked halfway up by a man passed out across the steps. Instead, he glanced around and then nodded down the hallway. We proceeded to a door toward the back of the building.

Holmes rapped sharply on the door and shouted to the inhabitants. "Mr. Johnsone, unlock the door."

317

A small child blinked at us when it opened. Lestrade pushed Holmes out of the way and bent low. "Hello there, Poppin. Any chance your da or ma is at home?"

"Let them in, Brigita," Armaund called from inside.

The door swung back, and we stepped into a mean little room that made Innes' final resting place seem like a palace. A threadbare quilt on a rickety bed, occupied by two more children, an unpainted cabinet serving as both larder and cupboard – judging from its contents – and a table with four spindly chairs. Beside the door was a series of pegs holding what had to be the inhabitants' entire wardrobe. Despite the poverty, the room and its occupants showed no grime or dust – but were scrubbed clean.

We approached the table covered in stacks of bills and coins where Armaund and a one-armed man, who I assumed was Mr. Jones, were seated.

Armaund met Holmes's gaze. "We're just about finished counting it. I set your four-hundred pounds over here." He pushed a stack of bills toward Holmes. "I assume that's for Mrs. Hudson."

Holmes studied the piles on the table. "And I assume the rest is for Mrs. Bervins."

"I don't want it," a small woman with a flowered scarf around her shoulders spoke from a corner and said in a slight accent. "It's blood money."

The other man at the table spoke for the first time. "Let Mr. Armaund go. I'll confess to all, if you do."

"No, Patriks, I can't let you do that," Armaund said, placing a hand on Johnsone's arm. "What happened to Innes was an accident. It wasn't supposed to end this way."

"What I see," Lestrade said, putting his hands behind his back and rocking on his heels, "is the money stolen from the investors and the two men who stole it after murdering the owner."

Holmes raised a hand to stay the inspector. "Perhaps we should let them explain what happened and how it was an . . . accident."

"You know I used to be a fighter and Innes was one of my backers," Armaund said with a sigh, glancing at the three of us. Holmes nodded, urging him to continue. "What you don't know – no one does – was that he'd worked out a plan with Bernie's backers that I would win. They all placed bets against Bernie and gave him something that was supposed to make him pass out by the last round. Only it didn't just make him pass out – it killed him."

"But you didn't know that at the time. You thought *you'd* killed him," Holmes said. "That's why you left boxing."

"I couldn't believe I killed a man with my fists. When I went to see Bernie's family to tell them how sorry I was, I found out what it meant for them to lose him. You can see where it left them. Patriks tries, but with only one arm . . . ." he said with a shrug. "I also learned that Innes had told him to let me win, but Bernie refused. I'm not sure why Innes hired me as his secretary – maybe to keep me close and make sure I didn't go to the authorities. I passed every penny I could to Bernie's family, but you can see they needed more."

"Innes came to me one day," Patriks said, taking up the story from the former boxer. "Said there was this great opportunity for investment. Seen how other investors were gettin' rich. Puttin' in a little money and gettin' back a whole lot more. We scraped together all we could and put in Innes' company."

"Only you found out it wasn't what it appeared," I said.

"Innes thought I wasn't very smart," said Armaund. "Big and dumb, he called me once. Said I didn't understand high finance when I showed him how he'd sold more of the company than existed. The ones who invested early they got their money back and more. The ones that came later – "

"Like Bernie's family," Holmes said.

"They lost it all. Kept telling them they needed to be patient until more diamonds were found."

"That's when we came up with the idea of takin' the money," Patriks said. "Armaund came to me last week. Said Innes was plannin' to run away with the money he'd collected. From us and all the others."

"First, I contacted the other investors on the sly," Armaund said, his voice picking up speed as if he were proud of the plan's details. "Told them how Innes was lying. As I guessed, no one wanted to go to the police and admit to being hoodwinked. But some did go to Innes and demand their money. That's how I got him to go into hiding."

"I found the rooming house. Thought I'd just stay next door to keep an eye on him and take the money when he went out. Only Innes never went out and kept the money bag in bed with him. Then I saw that the stovepipe to his room passed through mine," Johnsone said. "I had the idea of just putting him out and taking the money. He was a light sleeper, and I could never get him passed out enough to get in to steal the bag."

"So the night of the meeting," Holmes said, "you decided to stuff the pipe completely while Armaund was with us and would have an alibi."

"It might have worked if he hadn't gotten Mrs. Hudson involved," Armaund said with a sigh. "He never knew she was Sherlock Holmes's landlady. He might have run even sooner if he had."

Lestrade let a studied gaze pass over the table. "How much of the investments is left?"

Armaund held up a ledger similar to the one he passed to Holmes earlier. "Enough to cover almost three-quarters of each investment – less Mr. Holmes's fee."

Lestrade faced Holmes. "You're still going to take the fee?"

"It's not for me," Holmes said, reaching for the pile Armaund had indicated earlier. "It's to save Mrs. Hudson from ruin. Without it, she can't pay back the loan she took on her house." He turned to Armaund. "I assume the three-quarters payments includes Mr. Bervins' family?"

Armaund nodded.

"Leave that on the table, then," Lestrade said. "Gather up the rest and give it and the ledger to Mr. Holmes. I have to bring you two in for murder. Perhaps a judge will see how your actions were well-meaning and the death an accident."

We watched the men put the funds in the bag, leaving a very small pile on the table. Holmes pulled the pocket watch we'd found in Innes' room and placed it on top of the pile. "A small contribution from your husband's killer," he said to the silent Mrs. Bervins.

She'd watched the scene with tears in her eyes. With that gesture, they spilled over and coursed down her cheeks. Her mouth opened as if to speak, but she turned her back to us instead, as if unable to watch her brother be led away by Lestrade.

Outside on the street, the two foreigners climbed into the back of the police van while the three of us sat up with the driver. When they let us off in front of 221b, the wind had whipped up into a wintry blast.

After watching the van pull away, Holmes turned to me. "Beyond establishing the time of death by winding a watch, there's nothing to this Camberwell poisoning case that would be of interest to your readers, Watson. Simply a tragedy that began four years ago and ended with the ruin of a man who had tried to do right with terrible consequences. Not to mention poor Mrs. Hudson's involvement. Best your notes remain in your dispatch box."

The year '87 furnished us with a long series of cases of greater or less interest, of which I retain the records. Among my headings under this one twelve months, I find an account . . . of the Camberwell poisoning case. In the latter, as may be remembered, Sherlock Holmes was able, by winding up the dead man's watch, to prove that it had been wound up two hours before, and that therefore the deceased had gone to bed within that time – a deduction which was of the greatest importance in clearing up the case.

The Adventure of
the Transatlantic Gila
by Ian Ableson

The encyclopedic knowledge of my friend Sherlock Holmes, while vast and varied to a degree rarely seen in this world, has nonetheless always been biased towards those realms of knowledge which are most likely to be of use in his chosen profession. While I have mentioned before his deficiencies in several areas – his lack of knowledge or any enthusiasm regarding astronomy in particular irks me to no end – one consequence of this method of prioritization is that the level of detail that he can reach on most topics decreases the further one gets from London. For example, while Holmes can easily determine any Londoner's daily commute by analyzing the mud on his boots, this same skill would not easily transfer to an adventure in France.

This discrepancy has perhaps never been more fully on display than the curious case that was brought to us by a gentleman by the name of Mr. Isaac Huxley on one fine autumn evening regarding a particular reptile from the American Southwest, an area far outside Holmes's normal territory. Indeed, Holmes has often referred to this one as one of "my" cases – that is, a case in which I was more involved in the uncovering of a crucial piece of information, a designation with which I'm not entirely sure I agree. Mr. Huxley appeared before us that evening in a state of minor dishevelment and no small amount of consternation, having just been ushered up the stairs by Mrs. Hudson.

"You are Mr. Sherlock Holmes?" he asked. He was a well-dressed man, perhaps in his upper fifties, and he boasted several small fineries that distinctly marked him as a man of means. "My name is Isaac Huxley. I come before you perplexed, but also in great fear for my life. I intended to be here earlier, but the evacuation of my family and my household took some time."

"Well, you've certainly caught my interest with such an introduction," said Holmes lightly. "Please, have a seat and continue."

"Thank you. In order to understand both my fear and my confusion, it is necessary that you know something of my history. I come before you as an extremely fortunate man, in both senses of the word. In the material sense, I have not been wanting for several decades, thanks to some wise investments of my initial wealth. However, the means by which I came by the aforementioned initial fortune involved a large amount of luck, as well as some persistence on my part.

"I was twenty years old when first I heard word of the discovery of untapped gold veins in the American state of California. At the time I was a poor young man. My parents had done their best to ensure that I was both educated and literate, but when they passed of a pestilence, their incurred debts meant that I inherited very little. To a young man of such meager means, with no family and few prospects, a wealth of unclaimed gold sounded like a blessing from God himself. My father was a seaman in his youth, and he taught me enough for me to be able to find work aboard a transatlantic ship in exchange for passage to America. The road from England to California is not an easy one in our modern age, and it was even less so then, but after some time I made my way to the Sierra Nevada.

"I won't trouble you with all of my trials and tribulations during my first year in California, nor shall I bother with an explanation of the fervor with which those involved hunted for their future fortunes. I suspect you know the basics, and for this tale that should be enough. However, in the interest of completeness I will outline the basics of how I became one of the lucky few to actually acquire the fortune that we all so desperately sought.

"While I had struck out for California alone, I eventually allied myself with two other treasure hunters. These sorts of partnerships were common in those days, both for a wider range of hunting – three sets of eyes could see much more than one, after all – and for safety as well. Both of my partners were American, as were the majority of Forty-niners in the early days of the Rush. One of them, George Rothfuss by name, was a New Englander, native to Rhode Island. He was about forty years or so in age. A bookseller before the Rush, but unfortunately a few poor business decisions and a weakness for gambling forced him to close his shop and left him teetering on the edge of destitution. He was rather small in stature for a treasure hunter, thin-faced, with a pair of reading glasses that never left his side, but his analytical mind proved surprisingly suited towards identifying likely gold deposits. He had read every book on geology and mineralogy he could get his hands on during his travels west, and he managed to gather a bounty of regional maps that served us equally well.

"My other associate could hardly have been more opposite the New England bookseller. Roy Smith was a Californian native. Young, brash, illiterate, an avid outdoorsman, and of a distinctly working-class disposition, he was nevertheless a jolly soul with a rather magnetic personality, and he and I struck up a decent friendship due to our similar ages. Perhaps one reason for his good cheer was that he lacked the faint air of desperation that clung to most hunters. He had barely even had to travel to participate in the Rush – he'd grown up not thirty miles from the boom town where the three of us first met and agreed to join forces – and so for him the Rush was consequently far less of a last-ditch effort to avoid destitution and more a novel opportunity to give him a few more stories to tell the lads back home. But he was a large man, and very strong – he could move a truly staggering amount of earth when he put his mind to it. And so the three of us made for an unusual but – as I've already mentioned – surprisingly beneficial partnership.

"The day we first struck gold, we found a few scattered nuggets and nothing more – enough to cover our lodgings and food for a fortnight or so, but nothing to brag about. But Rothfuss was convinced that these few nuggets were but a hint of what the surrounding basin contained, and so over the next few days we systematically dug and panned our way in a circle around those first nuggets. Tensions ran over the following four days as we found nothing but dirt, and I think we all exchanged some words that we later came to regret. But to our astonishment and overwhelming joy, on the fifth day I saw the telltale glint of gold sparkling mischievously from Smith's shovel. All three of us concentrated our efforts on the fifty or so square feet around him, and in a matter of hours we had pulled more wealth from the earth than any of us had ever seen in our lives.

"Suffice to say, gentleman, that we were all three absolutely beside ourselves with ecstasy. We dug through the night, ignorant of the movement of the sun, and then we dug for four days straight, equally ignorant of the calendar, until we were absolutely certain that we had completely exhausted the vein that we'd found. Perhaps one of the larger companies that eventually developed could have used their heavy machinery to extract the ore from deeper in the earth – indeed, perhaps at some later point one of them did – but after the fourth day we knew we had done all that we could, and we also knew that in the span of four days we had achieved the dream of every Forty-niner.

"But we were also savvy enough to understand the precariousness of our situation. If we took the gold back to the boom towns of California where we were lodged, we risked trickery, theft, and perhaps even violence for the sake of our newfound wealth. Instead, we hatched a plan to take naught but our donkeys and the clothes on our backs and leave immediately for Arizona, where gold fever held far less sway. There we could meet with a banking friend of Roy Smith's, divide the wealth evenly amongst us, and make our way to our respective homes, successful Forty-niners all.

"I thank you all for indulging me in my preamble, but I think you'll understand that it's important to my current predicament. You see, during our travels through Arizona, Smith and Rothfuss warned me, the ignorant

Englishman, to be on the lookout for a monster, one particular beast that was unique to Arizona and Mexico – the terrible, dreaded Gila Monster. Fast, aggressive, and horrifyingly venomous, it was said that many a native Arizonan's last sight on this Earth was that of the black-and-orange scales that adorn the lizard's body. I have no shame in admitting that I hardly slept during our travels for fear of them. To come so close to unimaginable wealth, only to have it ripped away from me at the fangs of a venomous monster was a nightmare too dreadful to imagine. Indeed, I must admit that even in my later years I've never truly shaken my phobia of them, and I tend to avoid lizards of all kinds.

"This morning, decades after returning to England a wealthy man, I awoke to find that my nightmare had become reality. When I roused myself to seek my breakfast this morning, there was a Gila Monster in my room, sitting atop my desk, staring straight at me, orange-and-black glinting in the morning sunlight. I screamed – loudly, I might add – and uttered several words which have never passed my lips before. My poor wife was very startled, but thankfully she kept her head on straighter than I. One look at the monster and she rushed me out of the room, closed the door, and locked it tight. We evacuated the rest of the household, took a room nearby, and I came here as soon as I was able."

"And the lizard?" asked Holmes.

"Still in the room, presumably. I dare not approach it. Smith and Rothfuss warned me that its venom was powerful enough to kill a man long before any medical aid could possibly be administered. I thank the heavens that I happened to waken before the beast killed us both in our sleep. I come to you with what I suppose I must consider an attempt on my life, but one that was clearly carried out by someone who knew me personally. I haven't been shy in telling the story of my time in the Americas, much the way I've told you now, although often with much more elaboration – or perhaps theatrics would be the better word. Every good story needs a villain, Mr. Holmes, and the Gila Monster has played the role splendidly in mine. Nevertheless, the amount of effort that I imagine would be required to get one of those beasts here is astronomical, considering both the distance traveled and danger involved in handling the beast, and I struggle to imagine who would spend such a sum just to visit this nightmare upon me."

"Yes," said Holmes, contemplatively. "All for, as you say, what we must consider an attempt on your life – a poetic one, perhaps, but very inefficient. And, it would seem, equally ineffective." He stood. "Mr. Huxley, your story intrigues me greatly, but the amount of data that I have at present is insufficient for even the slightest conjecture. If there is still a cab waiting for you outside, I think we'd best make our way to your house and see the beast in question."

Over the course of the cab ride, Holmes plied Mr. Huxley with questions regarding his social life, especially regarding any potential suspects – any associates, recent or otherwise, who might feel a newfound antagonism towards him, including his small household, which consisted only of himself, his wife, a maid, and a cook. He also tried questioning Huxley about who might have heard of the story of the Gila Monster, but he soon abandoned this line in frustration. It quickly became clear that regaling friends and business contacts with stories of the dreaded Gila was a favorite pastime of Huxley's, and any attempt to narrow down the suspects based on who had heard the tale would be a fruitless endeavor.

Huxley's home was a massive one, an incredible achievement for one with such a poverty-stricken background as he. When Holmes politely mentioned this fact, Huxley did little to disguise the pride on his face.

"Forgive me, gentlemen, but I must admit that it brings me some contentment to reflect upon my past accomplishments. I had little in the way of wisdom as a youth, but still I managed to resist the temptation upon my return to England to spend my newfound gold on frivolous pursuits, and I spent my money carefully and wisely. Many British manufactured goods were in high demand during the economic boom in the Western Americas, and as a Forty-niner myself I knew all too well which were the most valuable. I invested in one or two burgeoning companies that had developed in response to the demand, connected them with contacts I had met during my travels, and the home that you see before you is one of the results."

His countenance darkened. "And yet it would seem that someone has seen fit to invade it. Before we enter, gentlemen, I must express my concern for all of our sakes. I am hopeful that the beast is still in the bedroom, for the window was shut and with the door closed there is no exit from the room, but we must be on high alert regardless. I heartily recommend against any attempt to capture the beast, Mr. Holmes, for they have a reputation as fast, wily – and I must stress again, exceedingly deadly."

"I appreciate your concern," Holmes said, grimly, "yet I feel that there is no alternative. Your house holds the only clues that we have in this case, and it is imperative that I have a chance to examine it if we are to have any hopes of finding answers. I will trust you and Dr. Watson to keep watch."

"Very well," said Mr. Huxley after some time. "Let it never be said that Isaac Huxley refused to face his fears." With that he unlocked the front door and the three of us entered the house.

The house's interior matched its exterior in terms of presentation, beautifully furnished and carefully kept. All about, however, there were signs of the household's hasty exit from the premises – a dropped glove, an upturned corner of rug, a coat knocked to the floor – each of which Holmes examined briefly as Huxley and I watched for movement. Finding little of note, we moved swiftly, if cautiously, up to the bedroom door, where Mr. Huxley's agitation reached its peak.

"Mr. Holmes!" he said. "I cannot, in good conscious, let you enter that room. I brought this case to you out of sheer desperation, but I refuse to let you risk your life for its sake."

"Perhaps we can compromise. I will stay in the entranceway and examine the room from here. Watson, if you would kindly keep hold of the door and prepare yourself to close it at the first hint of a wandering reptile, I think that we can be reasonably assured of our safety."

To this Mr. Huxley reluctantly agreed. I took hold of the door and swung it outwards, peering anxiously inside with Holmes next to me.

In truth I remember very little of the room itself, for the image of the reptile claimed my attention immediately. It was a striking creature, orange patterns splashed across a black body as though splattered by an unseen brush. It sat basking in a pool of sunlight that streamed in from the neighboring window, small beady eyes watching us cautiously. Remembering Huxley's warnings regarding the creature's speed, I slammed the door closed again immediately.

"Thank you," said Holmes, unshaken. "That was most informative. If you'll come with me, gentlemen, I believe we can leave our scaly assassin where he is for the time being and examine the grounds."

"Mr. Holmes," said Huxley in shock, "I'm familiar with your talents, else I wouldn't have turned to you in this time of need. But that door cannot have been open for more than three seconds, and I find it unfathomable that you could have gathered all the information you needed in that amount of time."

"All the information, no," Holmes admitted. "However, I have now ruled out several possibilities. Firstly, I think we can confirm for certain that this is a genuine Gila Monster. The expense and pains required to transport such a deadly animal from the American Southwest made it more likely, in my mind, that our unknown criminal disguised some native lizard as a Gila. I am no expert in reptilian features, and I have only heard of the Gila Monster itself in passing before today, but I saw no sign that the coloring was artificial in any manner – either by shape of the pattern or by

327

quality of the coloration, and in shape and anatomy it certainly did not resemble anything that I would expect to find on the British Isles. Secondly, I must confess that I have been suspecting that a member of your household, either family or servant, must be in league with the perpetrator for the reptile to have been placed into the room without your noticing. Now, however, I see that there is a very different, and in some ways much simpler, solution. If you will kindly come with me, gentleman, the answer will be much easier to see from the grounds."

Holmes led us to the backyard, where he pointed out an overlooking window that clearly led straight into the bedroom. "While I realize that the past day has already been trying for you, Mr. Huxley, I regret to add a small termite problem to your list. It seems that they've been eating away at the windowsill around your bedroom window. I would think that, assuming our criminal is not intimately familiar with your bedroom, he or she planned to break the window in the night, place the beast within, and make a quick getaway before you recovered your senses. This person must have spotted the rotting window frame and realized its potential in a moment of happy opportunism. You can see how it was pulled away what remained of the eastern side of the windowsill, discarding the scattered pieces on the ground here. Not enough to fit a person into, but plenty of room to slip in a lizard. And, I must add, much quieter than breaking a window."

"My woes multiply by the minute!" said Huxley. "But I am glad we needn't go further into the room. Alas, we seem no closer to identifying the culprit."

"Oh, I think we have some leads yet. For a while, however, I think that Watson and I can do well enough on our own. Allow me some time for a quick sweep of the grounds, and then I feel it is best that we return you to your family, Mr. Huxley, with the understanding that we will come and get you as soon as we have more information. And until we understand more about this enemy of yours, I think we had best arrange for the police to watch over you and your family as well."

"As I see it," said Holmes after we'd dropped off Mr. Huxley at his hotel and notified Inspector Lestrade, "there are two primary channels through which we could gather data for this case. The inspector had promised to have one of his men stay close to the Huxley's family's hotel for the afternoon and evening and keep an eye out for suspicious behavior. "The first is to learn more about the Gila Monster itself. Perhaps there are methods for soothing or capturing the beast with which Mr. Huxley is unfamiliar. Even better, perhaps there are regional differences between varieties of the reptile that would allow us to more accurately pinpoint its origin were we to see it again. An overly optimistic scenario, perhaps, but increasing our levels of data about the creature can only help in future deductions."

"That sounds reasonable," I said.

"The second," Holmes continued, "is to learn how the reptile arrived in Great Britain. I will reiterate, to travel with such a dangerous beast cannot have been an easy task. I imagine the possibility of losing the reptile, or to have it escape and kill the wrong person, must have weighed heavily on the assassin's mind. Therefore, I believe the other way to pursue this case is to make our way to the docks. The dockhands of London have a knack for noticing the unusual, and with proper persuasion – usually monetary in nature, although I've found that on occasion a swig of brandy is enough to do the trick – they can often be convinced to share their discoveries. Of course, there is a flaw in this line of logic as well. If Mr. Huxley's enemy transported the lizard into the city by land rather than sea, then we will gain nothing from questioning dockhands apart from a lighter purse. Overall, however, I still feel this method to be more likely to gain us relevant data."

"Shall we make our way to the docks then, or do you wish to wait for the evening? Or are you planning on approaching them in disguise?"

Holmes smiled at me. "I will be using a disguise, but that is beside the point for the moment. For you see, I find myself immeasurably fortunate in this case, as with many others, that I need not rely on only myself to solve it. Tell me, Watson, is your friend Mr. Brandt still a zoologist at the Natural History Museum?"

"Brandt? Why yes, he is! I can't believe I didn't think of him already. He was something of a specialist in reptiles before earning his place at the museum. He may indeed be able to shed some light on this matter. But how did you know about Brandt? I don't believe I've ever had the opportunity to introduce you."

"You mentioned him once, perhaps two or three years ago, while we were debating the theoretical merits and ethics of using my specialized brand of deduction to bet on horse and greyhound races. I believe you were making the point that his superior knowledge of animal anatomy would provide him a similar advantage were he a gambling man."

I shook my head in astonishment. "One name, mentioned in passing two years ago, and you've retained it long enough to retrieve it again for this very instant where it could prove invaluable. You truly possess a remarkable mind, my friend."

Holmes's smile may have widened ever so slightly, but he remained silent.

Ferdinand Brandt was an undeniably eccentric character, but he is one that I have happily thought of as a friend ever since our chance meeting soon after my return from Afghanistan. Indeed, he was one of the first friends I made upon my return to England, and we had since made it a point to meet for tea or a drink when we could. He did not mask his excitement at my appearance outside his office door that fine afternoon, and quickly ushered me inside.

"Watson!" he boomed, the smallest remaining hint of a German accent revealing itself only in the "*V*" sound that replaced the "*W*" at the beginning of my name. "This is a fine surprise! I have been in the middle of some unimaginably dull cataloguing of our newest donation of Cornish seashells, and your presence is a most welcome distraction. Come, would you care for a drink? I find that a hint of brandy makes the seashells much more tolerable."

I graciously accepted the drink and sat carefully in one of the only two chairs in the room that wasn't covered in the aforementioned shells, which covered an impressive array of sizes, shapes, color, and patterns. Boxes of the things sat on his desk, his bookshelf, and most open sections of the floor, leaving only the smallest pathways of walkable space.

"Look at all these!" said Brandt, helplessly waving his hands at the state of the room. "Here I sit at an illustrious institution, an expert of ornithology and herpetology, with some passing knowledge of mammalogy and ichthyology, and yet the moment that my colleagues in the invertebrate zoology collections – an area in which I know comparatively little – are overwhelmed by one little donation from the collections of some wealthy old Cornishman, they expect me leap into the action right along with them! Ah, but I can't complain, not really. It is worth it for the chance to work in such a wonderful establishment. And one day, when I've been presented with some equally large pile of unidentifiable vertebrae or teeth, I will have plenty of favors to call in." He sat in the room's other chair, seizing his glass of brandy from its designated spot amongst the shells on his desk and taking a sizable swig. He sighed contentedly. "But I am sure you did not come to hear me recount my malacological woes. What can I do for you, my friend?"

"Perhaps not, but I am searching for your professional opinion on a matter. You remember, I'm sure, my friendship with Sherlock Holmes?"

"But of course!"

"We've come across something of a stumbling block in the midst of a case, and any help you could give would be invaluable. Are you familiar with the Gila Monster of the American Southwest?"

"*Ja*, my friend! There are so few venomous lizards in this world, I would be a poor herpetologist indeed if I were to be ignorant of one. While

330

I have not had the pleasure of interacting with a live specimen, I have examined one or two after they'd already been pickled in formaldehyde."

"What would you say if I told you that I saw a live one in London just this morning?"

"I would ensure that you've not been indulging in your own medications, Doctor, and perhaps misidentifying some poor stray cat. A Gila Monster in London? Why, you must take me to see it!"

"In truth, I barely saw it myself," I confessed. "But Holmes is positive as to its identity, and the creature itself may prove key to cracking this case. But we are hesitant to approach the creature for fear of being bitten. I suppose there is no antivenin that you may know of?"

Brandt shrugged. "In truth, Doctor, I doubt anyone would bother. We have not developed an antivenin for the bee sting either, have we?"

"Well, no," I conceded. "Still, I would feel much more comfortable approaching the beast with a medical solution of some sort in hand, even an untested one. What is the cause of death after the bite? Are the effects respiratory? Neurological? Perhaps muscular?"

Brandt looked at me in consternation. "Death? Doctor, unless you are some small rodent or rabbit, no bite from a Gila Monster will cause you more than temporary inconvenience. It is painful, yes, but for a hale and hearty man such as yourself . . . Well, I imagine it cannot be worse than the wounds you received in Afghanistan. Why, my colleague, Dr. George Goodfellow of Tombstone, Arizona, has allowed them to bite his finger just to study the effects of the venom! And on top of that, as with many such lizards, they are so sluggish and slow that you would have little to fear unless you were to approach the beast."

"Nonlethal?" I asked, astonished.

"A mild neurotoxin only."

"But this changes the case entirely!" I cried. "We have been treating this as an assassination attempt! But if the Gila Monster is as relatively harmless as you say, then we are dealing with a very different set of circumstances. What then? A jest? Or was the lizard placed by one who was equally unfamiliar with the mildness of the venom?" My thoughts swirled as I considered the new possibilities brought on by this revelation.

"Hmm," said Brandt thoughtfully, a wide grin starting to play on his lips. "You know, it has been quite a long time since I have done any good honest fieldwork. And a Gila Monster in London! It's not an opportunity that is likely to present itself again. And truly, shouldn't a representative of the museum be present to examine such an oddity? Come, my friend! If you will allow me a few minutes to gather some supplies and perhaps a thick pair of gloves, then I will guarantee you and Mr. Holmes a very close examination of our misplaced reptile indeed."

331

And so it was that the evening found Holmes (who had discovered nothing of importance at the dock), Huxley, and me all gathered once again outside of Huxley's master bedroom, this time with Ferdinand Brandt in our company as well. The former three of us were thoroughly shamed when Brandt, with minimal hesitation and no small amount of excitement, strolled forward, grasped the Gila Monster firmly with one hand on the hind legs and the other gripping the back of the head, and placed it inside a wooden box that he'd brought with him. Although startled initially, the creature soon settled down and seemed content to rest in the box as we examined it, especially once Brandt moved it into the sun to bask.

"Mr. Brandt, you have saved me a great deal of difficulty!" Huxley exclaimed. "Although I feel that I have been rather unjust to this creature for many decades, now that I stand but a foot away and it seems no more interested in me than it would be in a large rock. Upon close inspection, it is a rather handsome beast. The orange is very striking when compared to the coloration of our native lizards." He sighed ruefully. "In truth, it makes a poor villain. I am sorry to have cast it as one."

Brandt laughed merrily, energized by the opportunity to see and handle the Gila in person. "There is no fault to be had, sir. The revelation that the Gila is less dangerous than the old tales would have us believe is relatively new to science. Word has spread amongst the local communities of the American Southwest, but such information is much slower to travel overseas. Indeed, were it not for my friendship with Dr. Goodfellow in Tombstone, I may not even know myself."

Holmes, who had begun searching the room the moment that the reptile was caught, gave a cry of triumph. "It would seem that our lizard was not an assassin, but a messenger," he said, lifting a small, crumpled piece of paper attached to a loop of string. "This note seems to have been tied around the lizard's tail, shaken free sometime over the course of the day." The three of us gathered eagerly around as he read the note.

"It's rather short," he said. "It reads: *'Isaac Huxley, your fortune is crafted on a lie. You will meet me at the Chelsea Harbor Inn tonight at eight o'clock to make right your infraction.'* There is no signature, unfortunately. Mr. Huxley, do you have any idea to what infraction this may refer? I must ask you to think carefully. Even unintentional injustice can beget an impressive grudge."

"None whatsoever," said Huxley, looking bewildered. "And furthermore, I can think of no associates who would send me the message in such a bizarre manner."

332

"Hmm. Perhaps we can narrow it down. First of all, our messenger is clearly an American – he or she has left out the '*u*' in the name of the Chelsea Harbour Inn. Does this bring any names to mind?"

"None. I have known very few Americans since my return to England. And even fewer whom I may have treated unjustly – even unintentionally."

Holmes was silent for a long time, lost in thought. Recognizing this behavior from many previous cases, I made small talk with Huxley and Brandt as Holmes analyzed, aware that he would need as few distractions as possible until his deductions were complete.

"Tell me, Mr. Huxley," he said when he emerged from his fugue, "when you arrived in Arizona with the gold in hand, who worked with the banker to weigh and divide it?"

"Why, that would have been George Rothfuss. His history as a bookseller made him the most qualified to handle the business end of the transaction."

"Ah," said Holmes. "In that case, I think it is time that we go to the Chelsea Harbour Inn. I suspect we will find your old business partner Roy Smith awaiting us there."

Holmes, Huxley, and I found Roy Smith seated at the end of the bar in the Chelsea Harbour Inn late that evening, nursing a pint of beer. Brandt had taken the Gila Monster with him to the museum, although not before urging me to visit again soon so that he might learn the ending of this peculiar tale.

Roy Smith was a large man, thickset, with a thick black beard streaked with grey. His clothing was simple, similar to a dockhand's attire, and the hands that gripped the beer glass were rough from years of work. While Holmes had advised caution before we met with him, a single look at the man was enough to assuage any fears that this meeting may turn to violence. There was no anger in Roy Smith's body language, only a sort of weary resignation as he sipped slowly at his beer, his eyes distant.

"Isaac Huxley," he said, raising his pint glass in greeting. "I'm glad you came, and it was smart of you to bring associates with you. If I'd run into you two days ago, you may have needed them. But I've done a lot of thinkin' today, and I seem to have thought myself out of my anger."

"Roy Smith," said Huxley, incredulous, "I truly wish this was a more pleasant meeting. But I'm afraid you have the advantage of me. In my memories of our time together, I know of no reason for you to hold me in any ill will."

"You don't?" Smith asked sharply, and he gave Huxley a long, piercing gaze, eventually shaking his head in disbelief. "You truly don't, do you? Now I'm even more ashamed than I was before. I guess I should've known it, though. You always were an honest fellow, even back then." He took a long swig from his glass, then set it on the bar, and turned to us. "Take a seat, gentlemen. My story isn't a very long one, but so long as you've already come here to find me, I suppose I may as well tell it you anyway.

"About four months ago my friend Joseph Leach passed away. Now I don't expect you to recognize the name, Huxley, not after all these many years, but he was the banker who helped us divide our prize. He was in a bad way by the end, half-delirious with fever, but nevertheless he asked to see me, by name, not two hours before he passed from this world. At first I thought it were just a part of his ramblings, but when I walked into the room it was just him and the priest, and his eyes looked as sharp as I'd ever seen them. He was confessing his sins, you see, and there was one he wanted to confess to me.

"He told me that on the day that I appeared before him with two strangers and a load of gold, he did me a great disservice. While working with Rothfuss to divide our earnings, he allowed Rothfuss to coax him into a deal, said that Rothfuss spoke with a silver tongue that would've shamed the Devil himself. He and Rothfuss came to an arrangement to split the payouts unevenly: Larger percentages of the gold to himself and to you, Huxley, while giving me three-quarters of the even third that I was owed. Then Rothfuss paid Leach some portion of the remainder for his part in fiddling with the numbers, and as a reward for keeping quiet about the deal.

"I forgave him, of course, because you don't let your fury show to a dying friend on his deathbed. But fury there was, Huxley – hot rage that coursed through my veins, and that I reckon has singlehandedly guided my actions over the past four months. Since I couldn't be furious at Joseph Leach, I got furious at you and Rothfuss. I'm a good outdoorsman and a good traveler, so it didn't take me long to get to New England, and tracking down a Rothfuss wasn't hard since I remembered the name of old George's hometown. Met his nephew, but it turns out that George Rothfuss is dead near a decade now, so I didn't have any choice but to turn my anger onto you.

"See, I figured there was no way that you weren't in on it. Even if Leach only mentioned Rothfuss, I figured it must have been a conspiracy between all three of you. But now I think I see my error. None of us really knew how much all that gold was worth – that's what we needed a banker for in the first place. But you had something I didn't, Mr. Huxley. You could read, and even if mathematics wasn't your strong suit, you were still a sight better at it than me. Rothfuss must've figured that you'd see

334

through the deception if your sum came up short when we got the cash, so he only shorted me.

"Well, I wasn't thinking about any of that when I found work on a ship to England to get myself over the sea. Wasn't thinking much at all, apart from the anger. But I had enough clear thinking to remember your terror at the Gila Monsters. I've got something of a knack for dealing with them now – folks'll hire me to take them off their property, and it's some of the easiest money a man can make once he knows what he's doing – so it wasn't hard to catch and care for the beastie while we traveled, even overseas. It was a vindictive move, to be sure, and not a smart one – I didn't even know if you were alive! – but I wanted to scare you, to make sure that you knew I was serious, and to bring back a nightmare from your past was the best way I could think of."

"So you wished only to scare me? Not to kill?" asked Huxley. He hadn't moved since Smith started speaking.

Smith shook his head emphatically. "Course not. Not in the deepest depths of my anger did I want you dead. But I did intend to blackmail you – to make you pay the cash that I felt was owed to me. Maybe a little roughing up, depending on how it went. But then, after the deed was done and I ran from your well-kept house, framed by your beautiful gardens, and cleared that iron fence, something happened. All the anger drained from me, like a drunken man struck by a sudden moment of sobriety. Because in that moment I looked at what you'd *done* with the fortune we'd made, the life you'd built, and it made me reflect on what I did with my share of that gold. Oh, I had maybe three years of high living, all right, but after those three years I was a working man again. And here you were, living good decades later, and when we met you were as poor as I was. It got me thinking, you see. Even if I'd gotten that money, where would it be now? I can guarantee you I wouldn't be living any better than I am now. So you have my apologies many times over, Isaac Huxley, and I hope you can one day forgive a greedy old fool."

Huxley was silent for a long time, staring into the distance, a man in deep consideration, perhaps examining decades of memories. Roy Smith twisted and fidgeted in his seat.

"You are," Huxley said slowly after some time, "still fairly handy, I imagine?"

"Well, sure."

"Hmm. That's good. You see, I seem to be in need of someone to fix some damage to my window frame. It won't be a difficult job, but I imagine it will pay quite well. For now, however, I have had a rather long day, and I think an ale would help me end it a tad more relaxed than I started it. Seeing as your glass is empty, I think I may as well ask the innkeeper to bring us two."

Holmes and I left fairly soon after that.

"Roy Smith was by no means the only person who could have been sitting at that bar at the Chelsea Harbour Inn," said Holmes sometime later, when both of us were seated in our respective armchairs, "but overall, I felt him to be the most likely candidate based on two factors. One, as we mentioned, was the spelling on the note that identified the writer as an American. The second, which I failed to mention at the time, was this." He pulled the note from the pocket and handed it to me. "If you'll look at the cord that was used to attach the note to the Gila Monster's tail, you'll notice it's no ordinary twine. That is braided fishing line – a peculiar choice for many possible suspects, but certainly something that an American outdoorsman like Mr. Smith might regularly keep in his pockets."

"Marvelous," I said, chuckling lightly. "If you've no pressing engagements tomorrow, Holmes, I do hope you'll join me for a visit to the natural history museum tomorrow. I promised Mr. Brandt I would inform him how the case resolved itself, and I think it may take both of us to convince him that the Gila Monster should be returned to the American Southwest at the earliest opportunity."

"Yes, I suppose it should. Although," said Holmes, an impish smile playing at his lips. "Then again, should travel arrangements prove difficult, perhaps Mrs. Hudson could use a scaly companion."

I leaned back and took down the great index volume to which he referred. Holmes balanced it on his knee, and his eyes moved slowly and lovingly over the record of old cases, mixed with the accumulated information of a lifetime.

"Voyage of the Gloria Scott*," he read. "That was a bad business. I have some recollection that you made a record of it, Watson, though I was unable to congratulate you upon the result. Victor Lynch, the forger. Venomous lizard or gila. Remarkable case, that! Vittoria, the circus belle. Vanderbilt and the Yeggman. Vipers. Vigor, the Hammersmith wonder. Hullo! Hullo! Good old index. You can't beat it*

– Dr. John H. Watson and Sherlock Holmes
"The Adventure of the Sussex Vampire"

Intruders at Baker Street
by Chris Chan

It is with some surprise and a bit of pleasure that I acknowledge that 221b Baker Street has become inextricably linked in the popular imagination with my friend Sherlock Holmes and myself. With the exception of certain politicians and members of the Royal Family, is there anyone else in England whose address is so well-known and iconic?

Recently, I realized that I had no idea who the inhabitants of 221 were before Holmes and I moved there. We never received mail in any of their names, and Mrs. Hudson never mentioned them. I thought of asking our dear landlady about them, and then realized that I really had no interest in Baker Street B.H. – *Before Holmes*. There was one case, however, when I was to discover who was living in 221b *Instead of Holmes*.

It was late January of 1887. After my marriage and my moving out of 221b, my visits to Holmes and the old homestead were far more infrequent than I would have liked. It was with great pleasure and some confusion that I received a note from Holmes one evening, telling me:

Come to 221b this evening – Cancel all other plans.

S.H.

If there was any trace of resentment in me at being ordered about by my friend, it was far overshadowed by my excitement at the prospect of another adventure with Sherlock Holmes. And so, after informing my wife that I wouldn't be home for dinner and assisting a rather querulous old woman with her chilblains, I made my way to 221b to see my friend.

As I knocked on the door, I expected to see the familiar face of Mrs. Hudson greeting me. Instead, a much younger, taller, and lankier woman answered, speaking in a high-pitched Cockney voice that was utterly unlike anything that ever came out of Mrs. Hudson's.

"What're ya doing 'ere?" Mrs. Hudson would never have addressed a caller in such a manner.

"I'm here to see Sherlock Holmes," I informed her, wondering if Mrs. Hudson was ill and had recruited this person to handle her duties until she had recovered.

"'Oo's that?"

"Sherlock Holmes. The detective."

"Never 'eard h'of 'im. 'Oo're you?"

"I'm Doctor Watson."

"We don't need ya. No h'one's sick 'ere."

I was beginning to detect a touch of asperity creeping into my voice. "Now see here, I lived here for a number of years, and – "

"Well, 'ow h'am h'I supposed t'know that? Hi've only been 'ere since this mornin', 'aven't h'I?"

My initial suspicions appeared to be confirmed. "Where is Mrs. Hudson?"

"Never 'eard h'of 'er."

"But this is her house. She's the landlady here."

"H'I don't know wot to tell you, Doc, but I never met a Mrs. 'Udson. No h'one mentioned 'er name h'all day. The Darlingtons 'ired me. This h'is their 'ouse."

I was completely blindsided. Could Mrs. Hudson have relinquished the lease to 221 without my knowledge? Who were the Darlingtons?

"Young lady, I realize that you cannot be aware of the history of a house where you have just become employed, but I can assure that that Mrs. Hudson has held the lease of this building for years, and Mr. Sherlock Holmes is the well-known resident of these rooms. I should like to speak to him."

"'Oo can't. There's no wot's-'is-name 'ere. Just Mr. and Mrs. Darlington and 'is brother. And they've left orders not to be disturbed."

My patience with this woman had just reached its limit. "What is your name?"

"Hi'm Mrs. Turner. Least, h'I think h'I still h'am. 'Aven't seen him h'in h'a long, long time, but that don't mean my name changes back, does h'it?"

I was fairly certain that abandonment didn't necessitate a return to a woman's maiden name, but I was in no mood to ponder the intricacies of marriage law and customs. "Mrs. Turner, it is of the utmost importance that I should be allowed into this building. Please allow me to come in. I shall make sure that you are not blamed for anything."

Mrs. Turner pursed her thin lips. "Well . . . h'I don't know . . . ." Frustration started to seep into every fiber of my being, until I noticed that Mrs. Turner's right hand, dangling at her waist, was clenching and unclenching. Picking up on the hint, I rummaged in my coat pocket, extracted a few shiny coins, and slipped them into her outstretched fingers. With a triumphant smirk, she stepped to one side, saying, "H'if h'anybody h'asks, you pushed past me."

"Fair enough." I took the stairs two at a time, and when I reached the door to the sitting room, I knocked on it. When no one answered after several seconds, I seized the knob and entered. What I saw astounded me.

Three strangers, two men and a woman, were seated around the fire, surrounded by papers. Few of Holmes's possessions remained in their normal places, as the entire room looked as if it had been well rifled-through, though nothing was broken. The coal-scuttle had been dragged out to between the chairs, and all three invaders were smoking the cigars Holmes habitually kept there. From the large quantity of butts and ash littering some glass dishes that Holmes used for scientific experiments, and the emptied Persian slipper thrown into one corner of the room, they had nearly gone through Holmes's supply of tobacco.

"What are you doing here?" I asked.

At first, all three appeared unsettled. Then the larger of the two men stood up, attempting to appear calm and controlled. "I'm Roger Darlington. This is my home."

"It most certainly is not. This is Mr. Sherlock Holmes's home. I know this for a fact. You have no business being here."

"Nonsense! We've lived here for months!" This high-pitched declaration came from the woman, who was presumably Mrs. Darlington.

As I was aware that there was absolutely no truth to this statement, I knew at once that the three were liars. I was about to step forward and demand answers when I abruptly realized that Holmes and Mrs. Hudson were very likely in danger. I immediately stepped out of the room and called down to the substitute housekeeper. "Mrs. Turner! Please go out and fetch the nearest policeman. We need the authorities immediately." At first Mrs. Turner looked disinclined to leave, but I dipped into my pocket, selected the largest coin I could find, and tossed it down to her. Mrs. Turner sprinted out of the house the second the money touched her palm.

I whirled around to confront the interlopers, only to see a very large revolver pointed directly at me. The other man, not Roger Darlington, was pointing it at me. "Come back in here and don't make a sound," he snarled.

I had no choice but to reenter the room and sit down when the man gestured me into a chair.

"Who are you?" he asked.

"I'm Doctor John Watson. I'm a close friend of Sherlock Holmes, and I lived here for many years. I know that this is his home, I know that you have no business here, and now I wish to know who you are and what you're doing here." I was in no position to make demands, but I wasn't in the mood to cower in front of these people.

The man with the gun made the most unpleasant smile I've ever seen. "You can call me Jack Darlington. You met Roger, and that's Eva there. And what we're doing here is none of your business."

I wasn't about to be silenced, even if he was holding a gun. "Where are Holmes and Mrs. Hudson? Are they all right?"

"They're fine for now."

"Jack! Don't tell him any more!" Roger Darlington crossed the room. "We'll tie him up, and as soon as we can we'll put him with the others."

"Don't bother with that! Just take care of him!" If this was representative of Eva Darlington's character, I did not envy Roger for having this vicious creature as his wife.

"That would be most unwise," I informed them. "The walls here are definitely not soundproof. Do you see those bullet-holes in the wall there? Mr. Holmes is in the habit of practicing his pistol-shooting in this very room. Every time he has done so, he has drawn a great deal of unwanted attention. Pull that trigger, and a hundred angry neighbors will come rushing to complain. Can you fend off all of those people, with at most five bullets left in that gun? I should remind you, they all know who Holmes is, and they'll be wondering why you're here instead of him." This was a bluff. The neighbors have grown used to Holmes's pistol-shooting, and they stopped complaining about the noise years ago. Gunshots had long ceased to raise eyebrows in that neighborhood. But the Darlingtons didn't know that, and they appeared unsettled.

Presently, we heard the front door slamming. "That's the police," I informed them. "Can you really afford to risk a constable coming in and seeing you holding a gun?"

Roger tugged at Jack's elbow. "Go into the bedroom. We'll handle this." Jack obeyed, and disappeared into Holmes's bedroom just as Mrs. Turner and a policeman appeared in the doorway.

"Hello!" Roger said. "What are you doing here?"

"This woman here says you needed a policeman," the officer of the law replied. He was new – we didn't know one another.

I didn't want to waste any time. "Officer, these people are criminals. This is the home of Mr. Sherlock Holmes, and they have kidnapped him and his landlady. I don't know what they're doing here, but there is a third member of this gang of crooks in the bedroom there, and he has a gun. Mrs. Turner, please run out and get as many policemen as you can! I will pay you for your efforts later."

Mrs. Turner turned to go, but the policeman stopped her. "Just a minute. Stay where you are while I ask a few questions. What's going on here?"

Roger Darlington affected a worried air. "I'm so glad you've come here. This man is clearly deranged. He burst into our home half-an-hour ago, rummaged through our things, and he refuses to leave."

Mrs. Darlington started sniffling. "He tried to take advantage of me! Fortunately my husband fought him off!"

"Did he now?" The policeman started growling at me.

"Sir, they are lying to you!"

"Are you calling that lady a liar?"

She's no lady, I thought to myself. I was starting to feel some trepidation. Perhaps something about the Darlingtons was more convincing to this policeman than I was, and I feared that unless I could completely win over this fellow, it was more likely than not that I would be dragged to the police station and kept there until I could prove that I was telling the truth. And in the meantime, what of Holmes and Mrs. Hudson? It might be hours before I could vindicate myself, and for all I knew, my friends could be in mortal peril.

I decided to prove my story quickly. "I have worked with the inspectors of Scotland Yard – Lestrade for instance – on many occasions. He can verify the fact that this is truly Sherlock Holmes's residence."

There was a flicker of a response in the policeman's face, but it only lasted a moment. "I'm not familiar with him, but it seems to me that this is a well-dressed couple. They don't look like burglars."

"Don't you see the mess in here? They've been searching this place!"

"That's true," Eva Darlington answered. "We're looking for . . . a little diamond that fell out of one of my rings. I know it must be somewhere in our home, but we don't know where. I don't want a precious gemstone to be thrown out or lost forever, so we're performing a careful and methodical search. I admit things are a bit messy, but we'll straighten everything out once we find my diamond."

I couldn't believe it. That mutton-headed oaf in a helmet was nodding. "That sounds reasonable to me."

"Don't you see they changed their story? First they said that *I* rummaged through their things, and then they said they're looking for a mythical diamond. They're clearly lying!" If the young bobby heard a word I said, he didn't show any signs of having done so.

Roger Darlington seized the opportunity. "This man is clearly not in his right mind. He's been blathering on and on about his imaginary friend and we cannot get him to leave, and he's threatened my wife. I'd be very grateful if you could be kind enough to take him with you."

"I'll do that, sir. Sorry that you've been troubled by this man." The fool put his hand on my arm. "If you'll come with me, mister!"

341

"Just a minute!" I whipped Holmes's letter out of my pocket. "Look at the return address on this envelope! Sherlock Holmes! 221b Baker Street!"

This stopped him. He stared at the envelope for a moment, and for the first time in a while I had hope that I might be able to convince him that I was in the right.

"He probably wrote that himself," Eva Darlington scoffed.

I have never felt such feelings of loathing towards a woman as I did at that moment towards Eva Darlington.

"Yes, he probably did, didn't he?" The moron's face actually brightened.

I was reminding myself that it would be unwise to descend to the use of physical violence to extract myself from this situation when inspiration struck me. "Look here – the Darlingtons claim to have lived here for years. Can they produce a single piece of mail with their names on it that was delivered to this address?"

The look of horror on the Darlingtons' faces told me that the tide was turning in my favor. My eye wandered over to the fireplace, and I spotted my salvation. Turning back to the policeman, I confidently informed him, "These frauds claim they've never heard of Sherlock Holmes and that I've only been here a short while. Take a look at the center of the wooden mantelpiece. You see that jack-knife sticking out of it? Look at all of the envelopes that have been pierced with that blade. Take a good look at them, and see who they're addressed to. And if you still doubt me, check the postmarks. You'll see that they were delivered at least a couple of days ago, long before the Darlingtons claimed that I first darkened their doorstep."

The policeman shuffled over to the fireplace, extracted the jack-knife with some difficulty, and peered down at the name written on the envelopes in the addressee section. "'*Mr. Sherlock Holmes*'," he muttered with a look of pure incredulity on his face.

Before I could cry out a warning, Roger Darlington seized the fireplace poker and swung it through the air, striking the policeman on the back of the neck.

It looked to me as if he'd moderated the force of his blow, just enough to knock the man out, but not enough to kill. Mrs. Turner started screaming, and I moved towards her, but Eva Darlington practically flew across the room and knocked Mrs. Turner to the floor, ripping the cap of Mrs. Turner's head and stuffing it into her mouth.

I made a very quick decision. I could try to disarm Roger Darlington, or I could try to save Mrs. Turner from Eva Darlington. But whichever Darlington I attacked (and my sense of honor reeled at the thought of fighting a woman), there was another factor in play: The third Darlington, Jack. At any moment, he could burst out of Holmes's room with a loaded gun.

I chafed at the prospect of retreating, but I realized that I had no choice but to flee and gather reinforcements as soon as possible to rescue the policeman and Mrs. Turner. I rushed out the door as fast as I could, realizing that Roger Darlington was running after me, brandishing the poker.

Practically flying down the stairs, I sailed out the front door and down the street. After sprinting another hundred yards, I became aware that Roger Darlington was no longer chasing me. I sought out familiar faces and competent representatives of law enforcement as quickly as I could, and in less than five minutes I returned to 221b with a passel of allies in tow.

The policeman was still lying in front of the fireplace and I confirmed that he was merely unconscious and not in mortal danger. There was a nasty lump on Mrs. Turner's forehead, almost certainly inflicted by the brutish Roger Darlington's poker. She wasn't badly injured, and as I examined her, one of her eyes fluttered open and she muttered, "'Oo wouldn't be thinkin' about taking your coins back from me while hi'm h'out cold, would'oo?"

I smiled. Despite my initial misgivings, I was starting to like Mrs. Turner.

The policemen, far more competent than their unconscious colleague, searched Holmes's adjacent bedroom, and then the rest of the building. There was no trace of any of the Darlingtons. Holmes and Mrs. Hudson were nowhere to be found, either.

The injured policeman and Mrs. Turner were taken to the hospital for observation, and I started searching for some clue as to why the Darlingtons had installed themselves there, and what they might have done with my friends. As I sorted through the papers that had been strewn about, I realized that they had completely torn apart Holmes's index of assorted people and subjects. The index was so vast and comprehensive that it was impossible for me, who had only had a brief glimpse of its contents now and then, to identify what, if anything, was missing.

The police officers had departed, confident that I was safe on my own. I spent the better part of an hour poring through the sitting room, not knowing exactly what I was looking for, but hoping for the best. Finally, I thought to look inside the wastepaper basket and discovered a small paper bag with the name *"Bunder's Bonbons"* stamped on it. Inside were a few fragments of a sickly floral-smelling hard candy. I had never known

Holmes to partake in that sort of sweet, and after a minute's reflection, decided that it was the closest thing to a clue that I had.

A few inquiries, and I had the address of Bunder's Bonbons. I decided not to inform the police, as I had no solid proof that this was anything more than a scrap of litter that had inadvertently blown into the house, where Holmes had disposed of it. Still, if there was any chance at all that it might lead me to my missing friends . . . .

I hired a cab and asked the driver to speed as fast as humanly possible to my home, where I informed my wife of my destination and instructed her to call the police if I didn't get in touch with her within three hours. After making sure that my service revolver was fully loaded and securely in my pocket with a supply of additional ammunition, I returned to my carriage and requested that the driver travel more quickly than ever before in his life.

In half-an-hour I had reached Bunder's Bonbons, a seedy little shop in a run-down part of London. After instructing the carriage-driver to wait for me, I stepped inside, where an acne-scarred young man slouched behind the counter.

"Can I get anything for you, sir?"

I sized him up and decided to confront him with a blunt question. "Do you know anybody by the name of Darlington?"

"Certainly. They rent part of our basement. Why do you ask?"

I was astounded. Part of me expected this young man to be in league with the Darlingtons, and I hadn't thought that he would be so obliging with his information. Wary of a trap, I asked him to describe the Darlingtons. His words exactly matched the three people I'd seen. When I inquired as to why they rented rooms in their basement, he shrugged and replied, "They say they need the space to house some things of theirs. We've got more room than we can use, and we need the money, so it's a good deal for us. Would you be interested in renting some space down there? I can give you a good price."

I expressed an interest and asked to be shown down there. I made that sure the young man went first. He seemed harmless enough, but I was prepared for a sudden attack, so as we made our way down the rickety, dark stairs into the moldy basement, I kept my hand on my revolver, just in case I was being led into an ambush.

The passageway was quite narrow, and I was trying to keep my coat from brushing against the stone walls, which I could see in the dim lantern light were covered with dust and grit and cobwebs. A few doors were spaced out on either side, but my guide led me to the very end of the corridor, to the only one that was fastened shut with a lock.

"I don't have the key," he informed me. "But this is the Darlingtons' storage room. Can I show you one of the other empty rooms?"

Before I could answer, I heard a couple of thumps behind the door. "What was that?"

"Couldn't tell you. Maybe it's rats. There were a couple of big ones a couple of months ago that got into the peppermint rock. I thought I got rid of 'em, but you never know with rats, now do you?"

My instincts told me that the noise in question wasn't being made by rodents. I pushed past the young man and rapped on the door. I heard more thumps in reply, and despite the fact that I used none of Holmes's famous methods of deduction, I was quite certain that I knew what was behind that door.

"Holmes! Mrs. Hudson! Get away from the door if you can!" I withdrew my service revolver, advised my young colleague to cover his ears, positioned the gun, and shot open the lock. The door remained slightly stuck, so I planted my feet, delivered a mighty kick to door, and sent it swinging backwards. Behind me I heard the young man headed up the stairs in a hurry.

A pair of muffled voices came out of the darkness. Taking the lantern, I inched into the room, and found Holmes and Mrs. Hudson lying on the floor, separately bound and gagged. The knots were a challenge, but fortunately my young associate lent me the use of his pocket-knife. I cut Mrs. Hudson free first, and it only took a few more moments to release Holmes.

My friends were unharmed, but sore and dirty, and it took a bit to get the blood flowing back into their legs, allowing them to rise to their feet. We all made our way upstairs, where there was no sign of the clerk. After Holmes and Mrs. Hudson had cleaned themselves up a bit, I started to recount my experiences that evening to them. After just a few minutes, Mrs. Hudson was shocked at hearing of strangers in her house, and highly suspicious of Mrs. Turner, so she insisted on returning home immediately in order to examine how much damage the Darlingtons had done. I placed her in the cab and sent her back, while Holmes and I made our way to a nearby public house for some refreshment.

Holmes helped himself to a plate of dark brown bread and very pale cheese with rather more delight than I felt this simple fare deserved, though I could understand his hunger. I explained my experiences in more detail as he ate and we both drank, and by the time I finished, not a crumb of bread or a speck of cheese remained on the plate.

"I must congratulate you," Holmes told me right after he downed the remaining contents of his glass. "You have performed admirably tonight. I freely admit that you have distinguished yourself far better than I have."

345

"Holmes, what happened to you? Who are the Darlingtons and why did they take over your rooms?

"This will take a bit of time. I suggest that you take a moment to write out a note informing your wife that you have found us and everybody is quite all right, and that she shouldn't worry if you don't come home tonight until quite late. I believe I see an old acquaintance of mine in that corner over there who will be happy to serve as a messenger in exchange for a few shillings."

Realizing this was a good idea, I followed Holmes's suggestion and noticed that he was scribbling a note of his own. I was about to ask him what he was writing, but I reasoned that he would tell me as soon as he was prepared to do so. As soon as the messages were written and sent on their ways, Holmes returned to the table with another pair of drinks and leaned back in his chair. "I shall begin by answering your second question first. The Darlingtons are a family of con artists, two brothers and one brother's wife. I'm quite certain that Darlington is not their real name, and the first names Roger, Eva, and Jack are just as likely to be spurious, but that doesn't matter at present. For the moment, we can use those titles. The Darlingtons specialize in a very specific branch of fraud. They are professional substitutes."

"What on earth are 'professional substitutes'?"

"The word 'imposters' would be just as apt a term, I suppose. The Darlington collect their ill-gotten gains by pretending to be other people, and they insert themselves into unsuspecting people's lives in order to obtain themselves at others' expense. They learn of prominent people whose faces aren't very well-known, and assume their identities in order to get ahold of as much money as possible. They like to specialize in titled individuals living abroad, for instance. Lord and Lady Eggmere lived in India or nearly twenty years, and the Darlingtons posed as the Eggmeres for just a few days, claiming that they were back for a brief visit to take care of business matters. They wound up cleaning out one of the Eggmere's bank accounts, and obtained several enormous loans from both respectable financial institutions and shady dealers in the Eggmere's names. As soon as suspicions started being raised, they went into hiding. In another case, a Mr. and Mrs. Totnurse left some valuable heirlooms at a jeweler's to be reset while they were off for a month-long holiday in Paris. A couple of days before the real Totnurses returned, the Darlingtons arrived at the jeweler's, disguised as the Totnurses, and collected all the necklaces and rings. They have been in this business for over three years, and they are very careful to space out their crimes with four to six-month breaks between them, so as to avoid suspicion. I believe they have accumulated a considerable fortune by now."

"How did you learn about them?"

"One of their victims is a member of an extremely prominent family, who was temporarily exiled to Kenya for some potentially embarrassing indiscretions. It was hoped that after a couple of years of managing a coffee farm, this reckless young man might be allowed back into polite London society. However, one of the Darlingtons pretended to be him and visited some of the most infamous moneylenders around, taking out loans that ran into tens-of-thousands of pounds. The family, who for reasons I am sure you will understand I will not name even to you, worried that even though their prodigal son was completely innocent in this matter, any sort of scandal attaching to his name might lead to an extended delay in the errant young man's return to England, or that he would be unable to make a prudent marriage to some well-off young woman. The family in question, though very respectable, is in somewhat limited financial circumstances, and they lack the liquid assets to pay off the debts recently acquired by the Darlingtons."

"Surely the family wouldn't plunge themselves into bankruptcy in order to pay off loans taken out by criminals under false pretenses."

"You forget the delicate reputations of high society, Watson. In these circles, the slightest connection to a crime is a most fearful scandal, even if one is called into court solely as a witness. The merest connection with wrongdoing is to be avoided at all costs. If false loans were taken out in the errant scion's name, it might potentially affect the family's credit, and they currently need to take out a perfectly respectable bank loan in order to pay for the repairs to the roof of their family estate. Not only that, but the lenders do not care one whit for the fact that the person who borrowed money in the young man's name was an impostor. The loans were taken out four months ago, and they are accumulating interest by the week. The moneylenders want to be paid back immediately, and they're willing to make quite the fuss if they don't get recompensed sooner rather than later."

"That hardly seems fair."

"It isn't. That is why the eldest daughter of the family in question came to me, asking me to help them track down the criminals and retrieve the money if possible. That way, the ill-gotten funds could go back to the moneylenders, and the family would be willing to swallow the costs of the additional interest payments."

"So what happened?"

"I interviewed a handful of the lenders, and they managed to provide me with some useful information from snippets of small talk that the imposter had made with them. He'd mentioned lunching at the Savoy, and when I spoke to the *maître d'* and gave him a description of the man and his clothing, he told me that the man dined there regularly. I frequented the Savoy for a few days, until the *maître d'* pointed out that the man in question had returned. After he had finished his meal, I followed him to the house he shared with his brother and sister-in-law. I wondered if they kept their ill-gotten gains at their home – after all, they couldn't deposit their stolen funds into a bank without drawing unwanted attention, so I fancied that I would try to make them retrieve their hidden cache of loot through a ruse.

"I wrote a quick note and sent it to you, thinking that I might need your help later in the evening. After surreptitiously looking in the window and finding all three of the Darlingtons there, I decided to climb up to the roof and block the top of their chimney. It didn't take long for the house to fill with smoke, but my hopes of seeing the three of them run out of the building carrying enormous sacks of stolen cash were dashed. I did notice that Mrs. Darlington was clasping her jewel-box close to her heart. I suspect that the box was filled with illicitly-obtained jewelry. The larger of the Darlingtons noticed the plank of wood I'd placed over their chimney, and immediately started climbing up the roof to remove it.

"While he was up there, he must have seen me crouched in the hiding place that was not as secure as I'd hoped. When he climbed down, he slowly ambled in my direction, calling out something about buying some cigarettes, and then lunged at where I was hiding, catching me off guard and pinioning me. I might have been able to fight him off, but before I could do anything the other two Darlingtons surrounded me. Mrs. Darlington identified me at once – how she recognized me I'm not sure, but I suspect that she read of me in a newspaper account.

"They knew that I was after them, and when Mrs. Darlington asked what they were going to do with me, one of the brothers growled "This!" and struck me firmly on the back of the neck. When I regained consciousness, I was hopelessly tied up in a room with no light and no way of figuring out where I was. After an hour or so, the door opened and the infernal family threw a similarly bound-and-gagged Mrs. Hudson into the room with me. With the light that the Darlingtons brought, I could see that the room was filled with several large steamer trunks. From the way the Darlingtons handled some of them, I suspect that some were filled with cash, and others were filled with heavier items. At a guess, I'd say that another of them held the equipment that they used to create the false identification papers that are used in their impostures, and others contained jewelry and other valuable items they'd stolen over the years. They said nothing to us, and I had no idea if they intended to have someone come to rescue us as some point, or if they simply decided to leave us there and let us die of starvation. I spent hours trying to free myself, gaining nothing but a few rope burns in the process. Then you came by and saved the day, my dear fellow, and for that you have my eternal gratitude. Thank you."

I savored the complement for a moment. Eventually, my curiosity triumphed over my need to bask in this rare bit of praise. "But why did they move into 221? What did they hope to accomplish by that? And why did they hire Mrs. Turner?"

"They must have somehow learned the address – it's no secret, you know – and they may have thought it wise to look through my belongings to see if I'd left some notes to tell them just how much I knew about their crimes, and how safe it would be for them to remain in England. They are sufficiently inured to violence to knock out innocent people and to threaten them with firearms, but to the best of my knowledge and belief, they have never actually killed anyone, and they may not have the stomachs to torture someone for information, either. They probably figured it was easier and more effective to search my rooms than to interrogate me. As you told me, Watson, they were rummaging through the contents of my comprehensive index. When they discovered it, they likely realized that it could potentially be a gold mine of information for them, as it contained valuable information on many people, including new victims for them to impersonate.

"In any case, they didn't know if I'd told anybody about the location of their home, so they must have decided it wasn't safe for them to return there. At some point, Mrs. Hudson caught them and knew they were up to no good, so they incapacitated her and smuggled her to their hideout. I dare say they selected the basement of the candy store to hold their ill-gotten gains because it was cheap to rent, the owners aren't inquisitive, there's a back door leading to an alley that they could use to sneak in and out, and the basement of a sweet shop is the last place the police would look for a fortune in ill-gotten gains. The Darlingtons knew that they needed a little peace and quiet to sort through my index, so they quickly found a housekeeper who would turn away anybody coming to consult with me, and bring them some refreshment as they needed it."

"So now what will happen?"

"As you saw, I wrote a note that my acquaintance will deliver to Lestrade. They know that their home, their hideaway, and 221 are no longer secure for them. They retrieved several large trunks, and they cannot simply carry them around. Unless they have another hiding-place, which I think is unlikely, they'll head for a port and set sail overseas, probably to Canada or the United States, though I cannot rule out some other location. Scotland Yard is best equipped to track them down, though we should make ourselves available to the authorities in case they need us to identify the Darlingtons."

349

Holmes was completely correct. Within two hours, Lestrade's men had caught the Darlingtons aboard a ship scheduled to set sail for Nova Scotia in the morning. In addition to the trunks filled with money and valuables, they found Holmes's notes from his index. They were clearly planning to continue their schemes by exploiting some prominent Canadians. Though they'd spent a fair portion of the stolen cash, the victims of the impostures all received the lion's share of their stolen goods back, and Holmes was able to prevent a scandal from impugning the good name of a prominent family.

Holmes and Mrs. Hudson suffered no lasting ill-effects from their confinement, and after interviewing Mrs. Turner, Holmes took a liking to her. Over the coming years, Mrs. Hudson routinely hired Mrs. Turner to take over her duties when she was out of town visiting relatives.

The young policeman who'd nearly sided with the Darlingtons over me spent a few days under observation in the hospital, but suffered no ill-effects. He had little talent for his profession, but he had influential relatives, so he was swiftly promoted to a supervisory position where he could do little harm.

I spent much of the next day helping Holmes straighten up his rooms and, after several hours of tidying, sorting, and re-alphabetizing his index, the sitting room looked exactly as it did before the Darlingtons took over the place. As I looked around, I realized that not only could I not imagine anybody else living in this place, I never wanted anyone other than Holmes to live there either.

"When a woman thinks that her house is on fire, her instinct is at once to rush to the thing which she values most. It is a perfectly overpowering impulse, and I have more than once taken advantage of it. In the case of the Darlington substitution scandal it was of use to me, and also in the Arnsworth Castle business. A married woman grabs at her baby; an unmarried one reaches for her jewel-box."

– Sherlock Holmes
"A Scandal in Bohemia"

The Paradol Chamber
by Mark Mower

I have often reflected on the myriad of colourful characters that ascended the seventeen stairs to our Baker Street apartment. The footfall on those well-trodden steps truly represented all walks of life and the rich variety of our human species. So it was that when Mr. Anthony Kildare was ushered into our quarters in the late-February of 1887, neither Holmes nor I raised so much as an eyebrow as he flounced in with a distinctly cavalier attitude and a flamboyant wardrobe to match.

Without waiting for an invitation to sit, he made straight for the nearest armchair and began to divest himself of his outer garments – a wide-brimmed purple hat, an orange knitted scarf with matching mittens, and a vibrant blue tartan cape. In age, I guessed him to be in his late-fifties and the greying strands, rooted in his long, distinctly unkempt brown hair, provided further assurance that he was no younger. It was also immediately apparent that he suffered from acute myopia, for I had never seen eyeglasses with thicker lenses.

"You, fellow!" he bellowed, addressing Holmes abruptly. "Am I to take it you are the detective chap that my personal secretary has told me so much about?" He cast a glance in my direction but seemed content to otherwise ignore my presence.

Holmes coughed and stifled what appeared to be a laugh. "Indeed I am. And this is my colleague, Dr. John Watson. Now, Mr. Kildare, you have travelled with some haste from your quarters in Belgravia where your light breakfast of coffee and croissants was interrupted by the arrival of a significant letter in the first post – a missive on which you are now seeking my professional view. I already have something of a busy schedule today, so would be grateful if you could lift the veil on the nature of this particular correspondence."

The sarcasm was lost on our visitor who was momentarily stuck for words, something to which I imagined he was rarely susceptible. When at last he managed to voice the concern he had been pondering, his tone was a little more conciliatory. "Sir, I apologise for my abrupt entrance, but how the deuce did you know all that?"

Holmes smiled and took to his favourite chair, nodding for me to do likewise. "The enamel badge on your cape proclaims you to be the President of the Prévost-Paradol Society, a social, literary, and debating club set up to honour the French journalist and essayist Lucien-Anatole

Prévost-Paradol – a talented man who advocated for greater liberalism across Europe and took his own life in Washington in 1870, having been appointed as an envoy to the United States. While I never met the man myself, I have read some of his essays. I know the Society's headquarters are close to Grosvenor Gardens, and the fact that your cab pulled up opposite 221b and had, therefore, been travelling south to north, suggests that you came directly from your accommodation there. The small, flaky remnants of a croissant still adhere to your expensively-tailored cape, lending weight to my theory that your breakfast was cut short and you finished what remained of the pastry while in a hastily hailed cab. The odour of strong coffee on your breath is a final, telling indicator that your meal was concluded only a short time ago. As for the letter, it is protruding from the left pocket of your frockcoat, which gives me both your name and a final confirmation of your address in Belgravia."

It was my turn to suppress a chuckle, for Mr. Kildare looked completely befuddled and merely removed the crumpled envelope from his pocket and passed it across to me, so that I might place it in Holmes's hands. Only when I had done so did he seem to come to his senses with a quietly voiced, "Thank you, Dr. Watson."

Holmes began to study the envelope and letter with characteristic zeal and customary precision. All of his senses were alert to the potential for additional information beyond that openly presented in the missive. He sniffed at the paper, felt the thickness of the stationery, held the correspondence up to the light, and scanned every inch with his powerful magnifying lens. Our visitor was mesmerized and held his tongue for some minutes until my colleague addressed him directly, "Mr. Kildare, this is a most interesting communication, and I am grateful to you for bringing it to me. Without doubt, there is some skulduggery at play here. But what were your thoughts when you first read it?" Holmes's eyes were now focused attentively on Kildare as he passed the letter back to me.

"I did not know how to take it, Mr. Holmes. Clearly it contains a threat, both to me and other prominent members of the Society, but beyond that I cannot fathom its rationale or intent. If it is designed merely to promote fear, I can confirm that it has already had the desired effect. There is something in the nature of it which terrifies me and makes me believe that there is genuine menace behind it."

Holmes did not disabuse him of the thought. "Indeed, there is clear intent behind this. I will gladly take your case, and have high hopes that we will be able to make some progress very quickly. A few basic facts, if you will. Please tell us a little more about the Society and, in particular, the identities of the other members of the 'Paradol Chamber' referred to in the letter? Doctor Watson will note down the salient facts."

Kildare seemed eager to oblige as I reached quickly for a notepad and pen. "Certainly. The Prévost-Paradol Society has over a thousand male members who pay an annual subscription to enable them to enjoy the various events and activities which we organise. In short, these comprise dinners in our building – Wellington House – and talks by authors and journalists who share our liberal views, alongside a wide variety of *soirees* and get-togethers to honour Lucien-Anatole. The main committee of the Society – which we refer to as our 'Paradol Chamber' – is drawn from the wider membership. Elections take place every six years, the latter being the effective tenure of those chosen by the membership to provide stewardship and oversight of the Society. The elected chamber then selects its own President for the same period of office, a position which I have been privileged to occupy for some six months now. As well as receiving a small stipend, the President is offered the occupancy of an apartment on the top floor of Wellington House and takes charge of the household staff: A concierge, housekeeper, bookkeeper, chef, maid, and personal secretary.

"The other five members of the Paradol Chamber are not paid for their work, but can be reimbursed for any expenses they incur in promoting the interests and influence of the Society. The chamber meets in Belgravia four times a year, each meeting taking place on the first day of the month in which they occur – this being March, June, September and December. The current chamber contains a mixture of talented and capable men who work hard to maintain the profile and reputation of the Society. My own background is in the arts, where I was previously the curator of a major art gallery in Paris. Alongside me, there is Sir Peter Daines, a former British ambassador to France, Claude Ponelle, a journalist from Nice, Nicholas Lamboray, an international banker, Austin Cantwell, an American cattle rancher, and Damian Gastineau, an antiquarian book dealer who ordinarily resides in Berlin. I can happily provide you with further information, if that would assist you."

Holmes dismissed the offer with a somewhat nonchalant wave of his hand. "Thank you, Mr. Kildare. For the moment, that is quite sufficient. Now, I suggest you return to Belgravia and ensure that you remain vigilant in the coming hours. I do not believe you to be in any immediate danger, but cannot be certain. And for the moment, I would be grateful if you did not mention the letter to any of your chamber colleagues or household staff. Watson and I will call upon you at nine o'clock tomorrow morning, when I will appraise you of our progress. Good morning to you."

Kildare seemed content with Holmes's plan of action and, having expressed his gratitude, then donned his cape, hat, scarf, and mittens, and made for the door. A few minutes later we were alone in the sitting room.

I was finally able to scrutinise the envelope and letter which had prompted our client's visit. The typed note ran as follows:

The Prévost-Paradol Society
Wellington House
Grosvenor Gardens
Belgravia
London

Wednesday, 23rd February 1887

To whom it should concern,

> *You will pay for what you have done. The Paradol Chamber is no sanctuary for your kind – expect swift retribution. And reflect on my name:*
>
> > *I start with the sixth, so easy to discern,*
> > *Find gold in a table, a symbol to learn.*
> > *Derived from the gimel, in temperature and time,*
> > *With almost a single, to finish my rhyme.*

Vengeance is in my hands,
Anon

"Well, it's certainly cryptic," I said, having read through it three or four times. "What do you make of it?"

Holmes gave me a tell-tale look. "It is most revealing, Watson. The postmark tells us that the letter was posted yesterday in central London. The paper is of a superior quality and matches that of the envelope – stationery from a gentleman's writing set no doubt. And yet the missive is typed, without any obvious errors, so our writer is either an excellent typist or has made use of someone who is. The timing of the letter is also significant."

"Yes, that I had spotted. From what Kildare told us, the Paradol Chamber will next meet on Tuesday. The clear intent is that this 'swift retribution' will occur when the members are next together."

"Indeed. And it seems as if the action is likely to take place at the meeting itself, perpetrated by the writer of this letter – hence the reference to the chamber being 'no sanctuary' and 'vengeance' being in his own hands. The wording also suggests that there is one intended target, although I cannot be certain of that yet. Mark my words, our man intends to act and is brazenly announcing his intention to do so."

"Then he must be one of the chamber members, or possibly one of the household staff. An outsider would have no obvious access to the meeting."

"That is my working hypothesis. The fact that he refers specifically to 'The Paradol Chamber' suggests some knowledge of the inner workings of the Society. Perhaps that is why the letter was typed – our man being fearful that his handwriting might be recognised."

"How do you think he intends to act?" I then asked.

Holmes reached for his briar pipe and matches. "That is the crucial question. But I have no doubt he has a canny scheme in mind. The perpetrator sees this as a deadly serious game, and has even given us a clue which may help to identify him."

"Yes, that bit I couldn't fathom. The verse meant nothing to me. Why would he risk revealing his name?"

My colleague had succeeded in lighting the pipe and took two or three rapid puffs from it, sending a thick plume of aromatic smoke into the air. "Because, like so many of the colourful characters that we encounter in our work, he believes himself to be cleverer than everyone else. That, of course, will be his downfall, his *hubris* or fatal pride."

"Does the verse reveal his name?"

"Possibly. I know what it says, if that is what you're asking. But I suspect it may be something of a smokescreen."

To my frustration, Holmes refused to be drawn further and announced suddenly that he intended to go into town. He took with him my notebook, containing the information I had gleaned from Kildare. I had little doubt that he intended to find out more about the Society and its enigmatic Paradol Chamber.

It was just beyond seven o'clock that evening when I heard him return. Mrs. Hudson had already indicated that she had prepared a large shepherd's pie for our supper. I knew she would be relieved that Holmes had returned in good time. Some ten minutes later we were tucking into the delicious dish which the landlady had served, together with a warming glass of cabernet sauvignon.

"A fruitful day, Watson. How did you spend your time?" Holmes asked.

"I attended to a new patient – a Mr. Harold Semper. He has a most interesting case of cretinism."

"That would explain the faint smell of iodine I detect about you. I could not be certain that you had used it to treat someone with thyroid

355

problems – for I know that iodine has many medical uses – but if pushed, that would have been my supposition."

"And your progress?"

"A most productive day. I made a few enquiries relating to the Bassey-Fisher abduction case, but also found time to visit the British Library and countless government buildings to gather relevant information on the Kildare mystery. I now have a much clearer understanding of the nature of the Prévost-Paradol Society, and I have to say it is not what I expected."

I looked across at him, my fork balanced before me with a steaming mouthful of creamy mashed potato. "Really? You surprise me. I imagined it to be a pukka gentlemen's club."

"No. In fact, it has run into difficulties in recent years and there have even been rumours of fraud among earlier members of the Paradol Chamber. While the Society was set up to honour the intellect and democratic ideals of Lucien-Anatole Prévost-Paradol, it has descended into something of a Hellfire Club. Members are carefully vetted before they are permitted to join and then pay a sizeable fee each year to partake of an annual programme of events largely designed to cater for their salacious desires and appetites. Still, perhaps they see Lucien-Anatole's early history as the perfect metaphor for their dubious activities. He was, after all, conceived as a result of an irregular liaison between the renowned opera singer Lucinde Paradol and the writer Léon Halévy."

I could not help but smile at my friend's pejorative stance, but let the matter rest. "So given the nature of the Society, I imagine that elevation to the Paradol Chamber is seen by many to be a coveted position. Its members effectively control both the Society's finances and its social activities."

"You are not wrong. Even being shortlisted for consideration as an election candidate is perceived to be a cloak-and-dagger affair. Large sums of money can often change hands to secure enough votes to be in the running. And elevation to the post of President is viewed as a similarly contentious affair."

"Then are we to trust Mr. Kildare?"

"It is hard to say. One or two of my well-placed contacts view him as a force for good. He has vowed to improve the governance and status of the Society and has already set about making some key changes. On his appointment six months back, he let all of the existing employees go and recruited a new household staff. While he received the backing of the Paradol Chamber, there was some disquiet about the decision."

"Perhaps that is what lies behind the threatening letter – possibly one of the disgruntled employees?"

It seemed a reasonable assumption, yet Holmes frowned at the thought. "I'm inclined to believe otherwise, Watson. These are dark waters, and I'm convinced that the motivation runs much deeper."

"What of the other chamber members – did you manage to find out anything about them?" I then asked.

Holmes had clearly eaten as much of the shepherd's pie as he was inclined to, a little less than a third of the generous serving that Mrs. Hudson had given him. He placed his knife and fork on the plate and gently slid it away from him. "A mixed bunch. Sir Peter Daines enjoyed a meteoric career, brought to an abrupt halt when he seduced the then-wife of the French Foreign Minister. By all accounts, he is something of a serial philanderer. Claude Ponelle, the journalist, writes for a scurrilous French newspaper and is often challenged in the courts for defaming high profile politicians. Nicholas Lamboray, whom Kildare described somewhat euphemistically as 'an international banker', appears to have made his money through a number of fraudulent investment schemes, most notably providing the funding for Sarah Emily Howe's infamous Ladies' Deposit Company in Boston, which swindled twelve-hundred unmarried women out of their savings seven or eight years ago.

"The American, Austin Cantwell, has a similarly inglorious background. He used strong-arm tactics to force a number of Texas ranch owners off their lands, which he then purchased for his own cattle empire, making himself quite a fortune. And lastly, we have Damian Gastineau, the antiquarian book dealer. In short, he deals only in one specific, and highly lucrative, trade – that of rare pornographic texts. The Berlin apartment building he owns is rumoured to be one of the most expensive private properties in the city."

I was staggered by the revelations. "A veritable bunch of charlatans then. And what of Anthony Kildare? Does he have a dubious past as well?"

Holmes grinned. "Now there is the biggest conundrum. He seems to have led an exemplary life. A dedicated and talented professional who was well regarded in the art world. As well as making himself and his clients rich through the sale of their art treasures, he has been something of a visionary philanthropist, donating vast sums to alleviate street poverty in Paris."

"Then he really does appear to be a force for good. So why would the others have rallied to support his presidential candidacy?"

He drained what remained of his red wine and beamed. "I said that he *seems* to have led an exemplary life. It does not follow that he has been virtuous in all respects. The art world is one of the most criminally corrupt trades in existence. Fakes and forgeries abound. Fortunes are made and lost. Art, like beauty, is indeed in the eye of the beholder. It is my

357

contention that Mr. Kildare has occasionally dabbled in art fraud. The only difference between him and the other members of the Paradol Chamber is that he has never been caught or exposed for his nefarious activities."

The following morning we set off in good time to reach Wellington House for our nine o'clock appointment. A thick fog had descended upon the capital and our cabbie drove both slowly and cautiously given the limited visibility. The temperature was unseasonably cold and the fog deposited a fine layer of mist on our thick overcoats. Holmes seemed not to notice the inclement conditions, but I shivered throughout most of the journey.

Wellington House was a grand three-storey building set within a half-acre plot. Two sizeable columns framed the main entrance, the solid double doors of which led us into an ornate and heavily marbled foyer. As we entered, we were greeted by a uniformed concierge. "Good morning, gentlemen. You must be Mr. Sherlock Holmes and Dr. Watson. Mr. Kildare is expecting you, but has been somewhat delayed by the unfortunate incident in the boardroom. It's a terrible business, to be sure. The doctor is still here."

Holmes addressed the concierge very directly. "What was the nature of this *unfortunate incident*? Has someone been hurt?"

"It's Mrs. Throckmorton, the housekeeper. Her body was found in the boardroom earlier this morning. She must have suffered some sort of fit or heart attack. Mr. Kildare says that she has been there all night, as it was her final job yesterday to clean and polish the silverware in the boardroom. She retained a key to a door at the back of the house, so we all assumed she had finished the polishing and had gone home for the evening."

"I see. Would it be possible for us to see the body? It may have some bearing on our investigations."

The concierge had clearly not been told about the nature of our enquiries and looked bewildered as to why we would want to view the corpse. He looked towards me for some reassurance or explanation. I responded accordingly, "It wouldn't hurt to have a second opinion. I'm sure that the other doctor would not mind."

The concierge pointed us towards the central staircase and invited us to ascend to the third floor. The landing on which we emerged was spacious and exquisitely decorated. A glittering chandelier hung above our heads and all along the walls to the left and right were large oil paintings and the occasional plinth, on which were sat bronze heads and well-executed plaster-cast busts. I could see that Holmes was surveying each in turn.

We were greeted by a fraught-looking Anthony Kildare. "Gentlemen, my sincere apologies. I'm sure that Mr. Hargreaves, the concierge, has alerted you to the sad demise of our housekeeper. The doctor we called is still with the body and I hope that he will attend to all of the formalities required." His manner was considerably more congenial than it had been the previous day. "Would you like to step this way? I will take you along to my office."

Holmes was in no mood to be moved on. "I would be most obliged if you would allow Dr. Watson and me to see the body. I take it that the boardroom is this way, to the left?" He turned and began to walk along the corridor without waiting for an answer.

Kildare looked momentarily confused and then began to trot along behind him. "Of course, Mr. Holmes. But I don't see how this is likely to be relevant to your enquiries. Mrs. Throckmorton was not in the best of health. It was only recently that she managed to overcome a bad case of influenza."

I followed Kildare, and at the end of the corridor we were faced with two heavy oak doors which led into the Society's boardroom. The door to the left was open, revealing a small rectangular room, down the centre of which sat a large oval table and solid refectory chairs. Along both walls were plaques of various kinds, some listing what I imagined to be current or previous members of the Paradol Chamber. At the far end were some ornate glass cabinets containing a large collection of silver trophies and plates.

While the room had no windows, it was lit by a sizeable glass skylight set high above. I could already see the doctor squatting on the floor beside the body of the late Mrs. Throckmorton, his medical bag resting by his right knee. Holmes gently swung the right-hand door open to its fullest extent and stepped cautiously into the room. He then invited me to do the same, but asked Kildare to remain in the corridor.

"Doctor Trent," said the man facing us. "Can I help you, gentlemen?"

"Sherlock Holmes," replied my colleague. "And this is Dr. Watson. We are currently investigating a threat that has been made to prominent members of the Prévost-Paradol Society. I would welcome your opinion as to the nature of the housekeeper's death and, in particular, whether it was the result of natural causes."

Trent smiled uncomfortably. "Are you from Scotland Yard?"

"No, I am a private detective, and my associate is a medical man just like yourself."

The man looked from Holmes towards me and smiled once more. "It is a pleasure to meet you, Dr. Watson. Your arrival is very timely, for I would very much welcome your professional view alongside my own. There are some complications which I had not anticipated."

I stepped over to join Dr. Trent at the head of the body. The cadaver was lying face down, the head twisted slightly to the right, and the housekeeper's arms were stretched out before her in the direction of the door. Holmes seemed content for me to confer with the good doctor, which I began to do in hushed tones, aware that Mr. Kildare was at that time pacing up and down in the corridor behind us. In his inimitable fashion, Holmes then began to survey every inch of the room with his magnifying glass, at one stage lying on the floor and looking up at the skylight. It was a good ten minutes before he re-joined us at the entrance to the boardroom, stepping out briefly to invite Kildare to enter.

Our client looked none too pleased as he took his place beside Holmes. The detective then directed his attention towards him. "Who was it that found the body?"

"My personal assistant, Peregrine Cattermole. He arrived at work at eight o'clock this morning and was unable to locate Mrs. Throckmorton. Ordinarily, our housekeeper spends most of her time on the ground floor, overseeing the work of the maid, chef, and bookkeeper. When Mr. Hargreaves confirmed that he had not seen anything of her, Peregrine came up to the third floor and found the poor woman as you see her now."

"Were the doors to the boardroom locked when Mr. Cattermole arrived?" asked Holmes.

"No, that I can say with certainty, for there are only two sets of keys to the boardroom. I retain one, while Mrs. Throckmorton held the main set. Each door must be unlocked from the outside to gain entry. You can see that both of her keys are still in the outside locks, so she could not have locked the doors from the inside."

A troubled look passed briefly over Holmes's face. "I see. And did no one query Mrs. Throckmorton's absence prior to that? Presumably, she lived somewhere close by and had a family who might have been troubled by her non-appearance yesterday evening?"

"No," replied Kildare once again. "She lived alone, with only a handful of cats for company. It was one of the reasons I employed her. She had no other distractions or responsibilities and was dedicated to the job. She was always prepared to work late or start earlier than normal and was a first-rate housekeeper. Nothing much escaped her attention."

I felt his closing remark was delivered with just a hint of cynicism, but did not challenge him. Holmes then said, "Thank you, Mr. Kildare. I don't have any further questions at this stage. I'm sure that this is a straightforward case of death by natural causes, but will ask my medical colleagues here to brief me on what they have found before the body is removed. Is it possible that Watson and I could join you in your office in a short while?"

Kildare voiced no objection, adding only that, "My office and apartment are to the right of the main staircase. I'll wait for you there. I will also arrange for you to meet Peregrine Cattermole. His office is on the second floor. Should I ask him to join us, or would you prefer to meet him down below?"

Holmes was most direct. "I would much prefer to speak to Mr. Cattermole alone. And a little later it would be useful to speak to the other members of the household staff."

"As you wish," replied our client, turning and heading off along the corridor.

It was as if all three of us knew instinctively to wait until Kildare had departed before resuming our discussions. A moment later Holmes confided in Dr. Trent. "I am sorry for my little charade, Doctor, but at this stage, I am not sure what to make of our Mr. Kildare. Now, I believe you are about to tell me that Mrs. Throckmorton died as a result of a pulmonary edema – the fluid accumulation in her lungs making it difficult for her to breath and resulting in respiratory failure."

Dr. Trent looked astonished. I myself was intrigued to know how he could have made the diagnosis without examining the body, but it was Trent who spoke first. "How did you know that? While Dr. Watson and I were conferring, you did nothing but amble around the room with that eyeglass of yours." His tone then became a little more antagonistic. "But then I wonder if you already knew what to expect?"

I felt I had to step in to protect Holmes's reputation, if not his safety, for Dr. Trent's easy-going countenance had given way to something approaching hostility. "Doctor. Please do not be alarmed by my friend's pronouncement. He has a rare set of talents and an ability to observe things that others so easily overlook. I'm sure that he will happily explain himself."

Holmes took my cue and sought to reassure Trent. "My good man, I apologise for unnerving you. Watson will tell you that I have a terrible habit of announcing conclusions without explaining the facts, reasoning, or logic behind them. On entering the room, I looked first towards the body. The position and outstretched arms were highly suggestive – as if the housekeeper was attempting to make for the doors and had fallen forwards. A trolley containing all of the paraphernalia for cleaning and polishing the boardroom's silverware still sits at the far end of the room, obscured from where we are now by the position of the table. A duster and a tin of silver polish lie discarded on the floor. Clearly, she had been working before something had induced her to try and leave the room.

361

"The frothy pink sputum, visible at the sides of the mouth, shows that she coughed up some blood before dying. The pale skin and bloodshot eyes lend further weight to the idea that respiratory failure was the cause of death. Yet this was not the result of heart failure, for the pulmonary edema was triggered by a chemical agent."

Trent interjected, "Are you saying the woman was *poisoned*? Dr. Watson and I had already identified that that was one of the possibilities, but agreed that a *post mortem* would be needed to prove it."

"Yes. To be precise, she was asphyxiated by phosphine gas. You will know that the ordinarily odourless respiratory poison starves the body of oxygen and causes the lungs to fill with fluid. On the far wall, to the right of the boardroom, is a metal handle which extends upwards and enables a section of the skylight to be opened for ventilation purposes. It is clear that this has been opened and then closed again recently. A small amount of grit and debris – which most likely accumulated on the glass of the skylight during the winter months – has fallen to the floor. It is my contention that the gas was pumped into the room through the skylight and, being heavier than air, descended slowly to the floor, seeping into Mrs. Throckmorton's lungs. Time has allowed the remaining gas to disperse, but close to the floor I detected a faint whiff of rotting fish – clear evidence of the crudely manufactured phosphine gas which contained one or more trace contaminants."

"Truly remarkable!" cried Trent. "Then it's a case of murder."

Holmes nodded. "The killer most likely believed that the crime would not be detected. We know that Mrs. Throckmorton had not been well recently, and you said yourselves that poisoning was only one of the possibilities you had identified. It would be easy to conclude that this was a natural death given the women's age and health."

Dr. Trent still looked stunned by the revelation. "But why would the culprit go to such extraordinary lengths to kill this poor woman? There would have been far easier ways to dispatch her."

Holmes looked thoughtfully towards the body. "I fear it was but a prelude to a much more elaborate scheme. Having tested the efficacy of his method, I believe our killer will attempt to strike again."

I knew he was alluding to the upcoming meeting of the Paradol Chamber, but he seemed reluctant to say any more. I then voiced a practical consideration. "Should we not inform Scotland Yard about the murder?"

"I've reflected on that, but believe it might harm our chances of catching the killer. It is in our interests for him to believe he has carried out an undetected homicide. That way, he will carry on and we will have every chance of acting to prevent further death. I will, of course, be guided by you, Dr. Trent. This is very much in your professional domain."

The appeal to the doctor's professional integrity was a clever move. Trent thought for a few seconds and then announced he was comfortable to comply with such a plan. "I will note all of the findings I had made prior to your arrival and record that the death is, at this stage, *unexplained*. That will give me sufficient leeway to carry out the *post mortem* where evidence of the poisoning should be evident. At that stage, I will alert Scotland Yard."

"Rest assured – if you have any difficulties in dealing with the police, Watson and I will be pleased to step in and assist. We have built a good rapport with many of the senior detectives in the metropolitan force and can use that to our advantage."

"That is kind of you, Mr. Holmes. I will arrange for the body to be taken from here to my surgery in Wilton Street, and will be sure to share the findings of the autopsy with you. Dr. Watson has given me his card."

We left Trent at that point and set off down the corridor towards the landing of the third floor. On three occasions, Holmes stopped and paid particular attention to some of the paintings lining the wall. On the final stop, he extracted his magnifying glass from an inside pocket and examined the oil painting at close quarters. "Extraordinary!" he whispered.

"What is extraordinary?" I asked quietly.

"Three of these paintings are extremely rare and undoubtedly very valuable. And yet they hang here with very little protection."

"Yes, I suppose that is surprising."

He looked at me with some disgruntlement. "No, that is not the extraordinary factor. The surprising fact is that they are genuine." Without elaborating, he moved on, leaving me to pick up the pace as he strode purposefully towards Kildare's office and private quarters.

Our client was at work within a light, spacious, and sumptuously decorated office. The walls were decorated with more oil paintings and a number of his own framed certificates. From the window behind Kildare's large, leather-clad desk he had an incredible view out over the mansions and well-appointed gardens of Belgravia. He beckoned for us to take the two seats which sat in front of the desk and then gestured towards a drinks cabinet on his left. "May I offer you some refreshments?"

Holmes declined, but reached for his pipe and matches. I felt it only courteous to accept the offer and asked for a small sherry. As Kildare poured the drink, my friend lit the pipe and sat back in his chair looking around the room. "Now, that is curious, Mr. Kildare. I had understood you to be a man of the arts, and yet it seems your talents extend into other fields as well."

Kildare followed Holmes's gaze, which was now centred on a framed certificate on the wall to the man's left. "A-ha! I see that your reputation as a detective is well deserved. Few people know that before I started my career in the art world, I had studied at the Ecole Supérieure de Commerce de Paris. That was where I developed my deep affection for the city. While I was born in Cambridge, I see Paris as my adopted home, and retain an apartment there to which I return whenever I can. Now, how is your investigation progressing?"

"Very well," replied Holmes. "I am convinced that the threatening letter is genuine, and believe that some attempt will be made on the lives of those attending the Paradol Chamber meeting next week."

"I see. And do you have any plans to thwart this attempt?"

"Yes. With your permission, Watson and I would like to sit in on the meeting, fully armed. That way, we can respond to any threat which may present itself."

"Excellent!" replied Kildare. His face lit up with undisguised joy. "And do you have any idea who might be behind all of this?"

"I have my suspicions, but need to confirm a few more details. I do believe it to be the work of someone within the Society, but would prefer to say no more at this stage. Could I confirm that you have not told anyone else about the contents of the letter?"

"You can take that as read. I briefed all of the staff about your visit today, but explained only that you were helping me with an investigation into some irregularities regarding the finances of the Society. They have been told to answer any questions you may wish to put to them."

"That is most helpful. I would suggest that Watson interviews all of the staff on the ground floor – whom I believe to be the concierge, chef, bookkeeper, and maid. At the same time, I will speak to Mr. Cattermole on the second floor. Does he keep records relating to the membership of the Society and minutes of your chamber meetings?"

Kildare confirmed that this was indeed the case. Holmes then had one final request. "Would it be possible for us to meet the other five members of the Paradol Chamber in advance of the meeting?"

The request seemed to surprise Kildare. "I have no objection, but in practical terms the only opportunity you will have to do so will be tomorrow evening. On Saturday, we are hosting one of our regular soirees with around a hundred attendees. The drinks reception begins at six-thirty, and after an hour or so the members are free to choose how they spend their time. We have four different rooms which offer our gentlemen various forms of entertainment according to their particular interests. I would be pleased to arrange for you to attend the drinks reception. That would not breach any of the Society's accepted rules."

It was all I could do not to laugh at Kildare's euphemistic description of the event. He was clearly trying to maintain the charade that the Prévost-Paradol Society was a respectable gentlemen's club. Holmes also remained straight-faced and merely thanked our client, saying that we would be pleased to depart at seven-thirty.

At that point, I placed my sherry glass down on Kildare's desk and rose from the chair, believing our meeting with the man to be at an end and reflecting on the sorts of questions I might wish to ask of the staff on the ground floor. To my surprise, Holmes remained seated and proceeded to ask Kildare a rather obscure question. "I noticed along the corridor that you have three exceptional oil paintings. If I'm not mistaken, one is by Paul Cézanne and two by Pierre-Auguste Renoir. I'm curious to know how you came by them, and whether you allow your maid to dust them regularly."

Kildare took a second or two to answer, no doubt curious as to what Holmes was driving at. "The paintings are on loan to us and belong to two of the members of the Paradol Chamber. The Cézanne is owned by Damian Gastineau, while the two paintings by Renoir are the property of Austin Cantwell. They have agreed that the paintings will be displayed until they cease to be members of the chamber. As to dusting, I wouldn't let the maid anywhere near them. They are far too valuable."

Holmes chuckled and rose from his chair. "That is perfectly understandable. Now, to work. Watson, I will speak with Mr. Cattermole, while you head to the ground floor. Thank you again for your time, Mr. Kildare. It has been most useful. I dare say we will need no more than a couple of hours to conclude our business here today."

We shook hands with the man and made our way back down the corridor. At the top of the stairs, Holmes paused and whispered to me. "It would be best not to share our thoughts at this stage, for I'm sure that our conversation will be overheard. Could I suggest that we confer on the way back to Baker Street when we've finished here today?"

I had no objection and left Holmes when we reached the second floor. At ground level, I began my own interviews with a visit to the concierge, taking careful notes of what I considered to be useful and relevant facts. Bill Hargreaves was an affable fellow, with a solid military background. He was concerned to know what the doctor had concluded about the death of Mrs. Throckmorton. I didn't wish to reveal any of the details and stated only that the examination had proved inconclusive and a *post mortem* would be needed.

Asked about his work, Hargreaves said that he adopted a "no nonsense" approach to his dealings with both the household staff and members of the Society. Generally, he found them to be pleasant enough, although he had reservations about the banker, Nicholas Lamboray, whom he described as "a jumped-up, arrogant, and manipulative man, who thinks he's better than everyone else". He believed Anthony Kildare to be a capable figurehead, but admitted that on a day-to-day basis he saw little of him. Similarly, he rarely encountered Peregrine Cattermole, who apparently spent most of his working hours shut in his office and always left at five o'clock each afternoon. The only exception to this routine was on the first of September, the previous year, when he had been required to take the minutes of his first Paradol Chamber meeting.

My final question to Hargreaves had been something of a throwaway remark, but elicited a most curious response. I said I was aware of the colourful nature of some of the Society's social events and wondered if he had ever seen anything which had surprised him. He admitted that as a long-serving sergeant in the British Army he had encountered his fair share of lewd behaviour and bawdy entertainment. That did not concern him. But what he did find odd was the nature of the supplies which Mr. Kildare ordered in on a regular basis and required him to carry up to the third floor. In recent months, this had included paints, oils, turpentine, and sealed containers of chemicals with strange sounding names. On one occasion, he had asked Peregrine Cattermole about the deliveries, and the personal secretary said that he understood Kildare to be preparing for the decoration of his apartment. And yet, to date, no decorators had been employed to carry out the work.

My discussions with Pierre Sabatini, the resident French chef, revealed little of interest. He had a full workload, preparing all of the food required in the household – morning, noon, and night. For the Society's events he employed additional kitchen and serving staff as required. He rarely saw the other members of staff and avoided contact with the members of the Society whom he described, rather cuttingly, as "spoilt rich men".

Tilly Norton, the housemaid, was also able to provide little by way of information. Like the other members of staff, she didn't live in, and her hours of work were strictly "eight 'til four". She had been very close to Mrs. Throckmorton, who had directed all of her work, and seemed tearful at the mere mention of the housekeeper's name. When first employed, she had occasionally helped out as a waitress at some of the Society's dinners, but had asked the housekeeper if she might be relieved of such duties as she found the attentions of some of the members to be "unsavoury". I did not press her further on the matter.

My final interview was with Stanley Dunn, the Society's bookkeeper. He was a skinny, pale-faced man in his mid-thirties, with unkempt sandy hair and a dishevelled appearance. There was something likeable about the

366

fellow and I found him to be open and forthcoming in his response to my questions. He revealed that he had found clear evidence of widespread fraud and irregularities in the Society's accounts stretching back for a number of years. Previous members of the Paradol Chamber had used their position to claim expenses they had not incurred and had authorised illicit payments for a variety of dubious activities. Mr. Kildare had employed Dunn on the understanding that all of this activity was to stop and the financial probity of the Society should be an integral part of its continued operation. The President had been wholly supportive of Dunn's work to strengthen all of the governance arrangements within the organisation.

Like the concierge, Dunn asked about the doctor's conclusions regarding the death of Mrs. Throckmorton. I responded as I had with Bill Hargreaves. He said he respected the housekeeper, who had always worked to the most exacting standards, keeping Wellington House in good shape. He had been about to leave his office the previous evening at the time when Mr. Kildare came down to ask for the silverware in the boardroom to be polished. The door to Mrs. Throckmorton's small office had been ajar and he was able to hear fragments of their conversation. The housekeeper had said something about "painting Mr. Cattermole's office" which seemed to agitate Kildare. He then asked Mrs. Throckmorton if she could ensure that the silverware in the boardroom was polished before the light faded. Dunn heard her readily agree to the task, but she had asked politely whether it could wait until the morning. Kildare had apparently insisted that it must be done there and then. The bookkeeper had been surprised by this as it was a task usually undertaken by the housemaid.

With little more to be gleaned from the staff, I made my way back to the entrance and spent a few minutes chatting to Bill Hargreaves about my own military past. Holmes then descended the stairwell with the broadest of grins and a distinct skip in his step. I could already tell that his afternoon had borne fruit. We thanked Hargreaves and said our goodbyes, explaining that we would be attending the drinks reception the following evening so would see him again then.

On the thoroughfare outside of the drive to Wellington House we were able to hail a cab within five minutes. It was just as well, for the fog had lifted, giving way to a light shower, and the temperature seemed not to have risen at all. The hansom carried us slowly but steadily back to Baker Street, and for whole of the journey Holmes was mired in thought.

It took me some time to warm through, sitting before the fire in 221b with my hands outstretched. Having arrived back, Holmes busied himself responding to a couple of telegrams that he'd received that afternoon from a lawyer in Brussels, a client in a kidnapping case which had been brought

367

to a successful conclusion two weeks earlier. When he finally took to his seat, he was eager to hear what I had discovered from my interviews with the staff. "Do not overlook any facts, my good friend. This case is becoming clearer by the minute, yet a few crucial items still elude me." I was gratified to hear him say this, for I felt no nearer to understanding what lay behind the case than I did the previous day.

I spent the next twenty minutes running through the notes I had made, with Holmes interjecting once or twice on some small points of detail. When I had finished, he congratulated me wholeheartedly. "You've done a splendid job, Watson. Alongside my own efforts this afternoon, I believe we have now laid bare all of the pertinent facts behind this dastardly scheme. And not before time. Had we not done so, there would surely have been a further eight deaths next Tuesday."

I was taken aback. "Eight deaths, you say? But there are only six members of the Paradol Chamber."

"You are forgetting Peregrine Cattermole, the private secretary, who will be taking notes."

"Accepted, although that still only accounts for seven."

"It must be clear to you now that our mystery assailant is Anthony Kildare. He has it in mind to murder Cattermole and all five of his chamber colleagues. In addition, he believes he has hoodwinked you and me in agreeing to attend the meeting so that we also fall prey to his deadly poison."

I was shaken by the disclosure and the thought that our short-sighted client was behind such an elaborate plot. "But why come to us in the first place? Surely it would have suited his purpose better if he'd been able to carry out his plan without the complication of our involvement?"

Holmes tapped the ash from his pipe into the hearth and began to refill the bowl with some rough shag tobacco. "*Hubris*. I said so earlier. Kildare believes himself to be a master manipulator. I believe that my work has, in the past, caused him some material hardship. Some years back, I was commissioned by the Swiss government to intercept a shipment of paintings stolen from a gallery in Zurich. While I managed to successfully locate and return the missing masterpieces, I was never able to identify the orchestrator of the audacious heist. I now believe that person was Kildare, and can imagine that he would take great delight in laying before me a case which would ultimately lead me to my death.

"It was clear from the outset that Kildare knew of my work and reputation. When he came to Baker Street, he knew immediately that I was the detective and not your good self. He claimed his personal secretary had told him about me, yet in my discussions this afternoon it soon became clear that Peregrine Cattermole had no idea who I was. And when I quizzed

Kildare about his certificate from the Ecole Supérieure de Commerce de Paris, he admitted that my *reputation as a detective was well deserved.*"

"I can see all of that," I replied, "but what of the cryptic letter?"

He smirked as he retrieved the letter from the inside pocket of his jacket and passed it across to me. "We will come to that in due course. Let us begin by establishing Kildare's basic motivation in becoming President of the Prévost-Paradol Society. Does it surprise you to learn that he has engineered everything thus far for financial gain?"

On this I felt I had to challenge my friend. "It would. You said yourself that your contacts had described Kildare as a force for good in his stewardship of the Society. He has made changes to improve its governance and the bookkeeper was adamant that the President is committed to maintaining the financial integrity of the organisation."

"Indeed, he may be. But the financial gain was to come not from the Society, but from two members of the Paradol Chamber. While I was with Cattermole, I asked to see the membership records of the Society and other relevant documentation. This revealed that while Sir Peter Daines and Claude Ponelle have been long-standing members, Kildare, Lamboray, Gastineau and Cantwell all joined at the same time – only eight months ago. In fact, when asked, Cattermole confirmed that Lamboray and Kildare have been friends for some years, and he understood Gastineau and Cantwell to be clients of the international banker. Clearly, the four men conspired to elevate themselves to the Paradol Chamber, using their own wealth to buy votes from other members. Having done so, they agreed that Kildare would take on the role of President. Since that time, they have voted as a bloc on all key decisions. While Daines and Ponelle have voiced some dissension, they cannot outvote the others."

He paused to take a further draw on his briar pipe, then continued. "Now we come to the crux of the deception. Kildare managed to persuade his associates that all of the existing staff should be replaced. They agreed to back the decision, although Daines and Ponelle voted against it. He did this firstly – as any new leader might – to allow him to introduce reforms that would improve the reputation and standing of the organisation. With what he had in mind, the last thing he wanted was the unnecessary scrutiny of anyone on the outside. But the changes also enabled him to employ a new member of staff in a post that had not previously existed. Namely, that of Peregrine Cattermore, the personal secretary. The Paradol Chamber may believe him to be a suitably experienced administrator, but I can assure you he is not. The minutes he took at his first, and only, chamber meeting last year are appalling, and it is quite clear that he is no typist."

I interposed, confused as to where this was leading. "Then why would Kildare employ such a fellow? The other staff seem very competent in comparison."

Holmes seemed to relish the challenge. "Cattermole was recruited for one specific purpose. When I entered his office today, my olfactory senses were stimulated by a number of distinct odours: The faint smell of oil paint, a hint of turpentine, and the aroma of linseed oil. While he had tried to wash his hands of all traces, he still had tiny spots of oil paint on both his hands and shirt cuffs. The man is no secretary, but an artist of the highest calibre."

I could see how this tied in with one of my earlier discussions. "That would explain the odd delivery of supplies that Hargreaves, the concierge, referred to."

"It does. So at the heart of this is an attempt to commit art forgery. I believe that Lamboray convinced his banking clients Gastineau and Cantwell to lend the Society three extremely valuable paintings. No doubt they are insured, and through their dealings with Kildare, both men are likely to believe him to be the perfect caretaker for their masterpieces. My examination of all three works showed that they had been removed from the wall and put back frequently – hence my question to Kildare about whether the maid had been allowed to polish the paintings. Piecing together all that we now know, it is clear that Cattermole has been commissioned to create forgeries of the paintings. And once these fakes have been hung on the wall of the third floor, Kildare will be able to sell the genuine canvasses through his network of contacts across Europe."

"Incredible! And yet, you believe he also plans to outwit both Lamboray and Cattermole by poisoning them with the others?"

"Exactly. As neat a scheme as could ever be devised. And the unfortunate Mrs. Throckmorton presented Kildare with the perfect opportunity to test his deadly phosphine. I think the bookkeeper was mistaken when he said he heard the housekeeper refer to 'painting Mr. Cattermole's office'. I believe that what she really told Kildare was that she had seen *a painting in Mr. Cattermole's office.* This set him on edge, for he realised that the scheme could easily unravel with what she had witnessed. Knowing that Cattermole had left work at five o'clock, and no one else was likely to be around on the third floor besides himself, Kildare hastily asked Mrs. Throckmorton to collect her trolley and go up to the boardroom in order to polish the silverware. While she collected her things, he made his way to the room and opened up the skylight. He then re-locked the double doors and waited for her to appear. When she had unlocked both doors using her own set of keys and had gone into the boardroom, he locked her in from the outside. He then made his way onto

370

the roof through a door in his office and surreptitiously pumped the phosphine gas in through the skylight. Later he returned to unlock the doors to the study, but did not open them. He knew that the calculated quantity of gas he had released would be largely dispersed overnight, leaving little trace in the morning."

The genius of this twisted execution had to be acknowledged, but my thoughts turned quickly to the excruciating death the poor woman must have faced. It then occurred to me. "How did you know that Kildare had a door leading to the roof?"

"I didn't at first. But realised there had to be some way of getting on to the roof to clean and maintain the skylight. When we were in Kildare's office, I observed a small doorway in the far corner on which was a printed sign reading '*Maintenance Only*'."

"Very neat," I acknowledged, "but how was he able to procure the gas? I recollect that the chemist Paul Thénard was able to generate phosphine from calcium phosphide in the 1840's, but it is by no means an easy process. To produce a sufficient quantity of gas would require some industry. I also seem to remember that the gas can be spontaneously flammable in air."

"You are quite correct. But a sufficient quantity of gas could be produced by simply heating phosphorus in an aqueous solution of potash – Philippe Gengembre did so as early as 1783. I'm certain that Kildare has the chemical and technical knowledge to overcome the production challenges. The certificate on his wall showed that his studies in Paris were in *Engineering and Natural Sciences*. And while he sought to distract my attention away from it, with the talk of his affection for the city, I already knew from my research that he spent some time working as an industrial chemist before entering the art world. Some of the odd supplies carried up to the third floor by the concierge were almost certainly the strangely-named chemicals he needed to manufacture the gas. If he has already installed some sort of gas pumping system near the skylight, he is certain to have a make-shift laboratory set up on the roof."

It was a terrifying thought, and I realised all too clearly how dangerous our adversary was. But I still did not understand how the cryptic letter fitted into the plan and unfolded it once more to try and make sense of it.

"That was the easiest part of all," admitted Holmes, "and my first clue that Kildare was behind this himself. The missive is clumsy and seeks to implicate Cattermole. The secretary has a typewriter in his office which was the machine used to produce the letter. The way that the type stamps out the letter '*d*' is quite distinct and can be seen on other records and correspondence. Kildare typed the letter himself and is considerably more accurate than his secretary. The stationery is the same as that used by Cattermole."

"But you still haven't explained the coded name," I said with growing anticipation.

"The rhyme was simplicity itself. *I start with the sixth, so easy to discern* gives us '*F*' – the sixth letter of the alphabet. *Find gold in a table, a symbol to learn* is a little more obscure, but you will recollect that Dmitri Mendeleev produced his '*Periodic Table*' in 1871, arranging all of the chemical elements by their atomic mass and assigning each a symbol. In his table, gold is symbolised as '*Au*'. *Derived from the gimel, in temperature and time* requires us to consider the ancient Semitic languages, in which *gimel* is represented by the letter '*C*' or '*G*', for both have the same derivation. Yet as the rhyme refers also to *temperature and time* we can assume that the fourth letter is '*C*', as in '*centigrade*' and '*century*'. *With almost a single, to finish my rhyme* is simple wordplay. A single would be '*One*', *almost one* could be interpreted as '*On*'. So, taken together, our name reads *Faucon*."

"The French for *Falcon*! Thus pointing us in the direction of *Peregrine* Cattermole!"

"Indeed. And with the progress we have made today, I believe a treat would be in order. What say you to supper at the Criterion?"

I arose somewhat later than planned on the Saturday morning to find Holmes already breakfasted and in a jubilant mood. Bright sunlight was already streaming into the sitting room and the weather looked as if it had improved considerably. I sat down at the table with a warming cup of tea and two thick slices of toast.

"Good morning, Watson! Any later, and half the day would have been gone! This evening will be essential in strengthening the case against Kildare. I have but one hour to ensure that the trap is sprung. And I will need you to be at your most gregarious in talking to the members of the Paradol Chamber and thus distracting them from my activities."

"Then your request to meet the chamber members was no more than a ruse?"

"Precisely. Our case hinges on the physical evidence of the forged paintings and confirmation of the existence of the phosphine gas. At present, both are hypothetical. I have conjectured that they exist, but have not seen them first-hand. So while you are at your most genial this evening, I plan to slip out and visit both Cattermole's office and the rooftop laboratory. If I fail in the task, our case will be severely weakened."

The challenge facing us occupied my thoughts throughout the morning. In contrast, Holmes seemed unperturbed and decidedly resolute, brushing down his expensively-tailored dinner jacket and seeking out his best top hat in readiness for the evening reception.

Around two o'clock, Mrs. Hudson knocked on our door and announced the arrival of a telegram. It was from Dr. Trent and summarised the results of his autopsy, saying simply: "*PM completed – Clear evidence of gas poisoning – SY informed*". Holmes was not surprised, but looked momentarily irritated. "I had hoped that Trent might be a little tardy in undertaking the *post mortem*," he declared, reaching for his ulster and hat. "I will have to square this with Inspector Lestrade at the Yard, otherwise we are likely to have half the Metropolitan force running amok on the corridors of Wellington House. The timing could not have been worse."

So saying, he set off down the stairs, promising to be back in good time for our journey to Belgravia. For the rest of the afternoon I did my best to catch up on some neglected paperwork from my medical practice, and was relieved to hear my colleague's familiar footfall on the stairs a little before five-thirty.

"Success, I believe, Watson. Lestrade was not pleased, but has agreed that his men will not take any action at present in investigating the death of Mrs. Throckmorton. I had to reveal to him the full facts of what we have discovered. He seemed highly skeptical about the whole affair, but wished us well in our exploits this evening. However, he has insisted on a heavy police presence next Tuesday when we bring Kildare to justice. I have still to arrange the choreography of that with him."

"Then we are all set," I replied, no less nervous than I had been five minutes earlier.

It seemed fitting that we should book a four-wheeler to transport us to Belgravia. We followed two other carriages along the short drive to Wellington House and finally stepped into the foyer of the building at around six-twenty. Bill Hargreaves gave us an effusive welcome, shaking our hands with some vigour and pointing us towards a long corridor which led to the Society's palatial ballroom.

It was certainly a lavish affair, with canapés, choice cut meats, and the very freshest seafood. I had never seen so many fine Champagnes assembled on one table, and the pretty waitresses who were endlessly circling the oval-shaped hall were dispensing it with little regard for the costs involved.

I heard Anthony Kildare before I chanced to see him in action – his loud, clipped diction cutting through the ceaseless babble of voices in the high-ceiled room. He was wearing a long, crimson dinner jacket with his black bow tie, and his head was adorned with what looked to be a tartan tam-o'-shanter. It set him apart from every other guest, all of whom were bedecked in more traditional evening wear. It was clear that he enjoyed holding court, for a small band of younger men appeared to be hanging on his every word. When he eventually saw Holmes and me, he broke free and approached us with an ebullient welcome.

"Gentlemen, you have arrived in good time. All of my colleagues from the Paradol Chamber are here somewhere. Ah! There is Nicholas Lamboray – perhaps we should start with him."

What followed was an awkward twenty minutes of being dragged from one side of the hall to the other in order to meet the five. We both made polite small talk, and I realised how accomplished Holmes could be in feigning interest in people with whom he had not the slightest interest. It was only when I began to talk for a second time with Sir Peter Daines, that I realised Holmes was no longer by my side and had left the room.

I had known my friend to be stealthy on many of our adventures together, but that night he excelled himself. It couldn't have been more than seven or eight minutes since I had first noticed his absence when I turned to find Holmes by my side once more. While pretending to wave across the room at one of the other guests, he whispered that he had managed to get to the second floor and had picked the lock to Cattermole's office, where he had seen the three forged paintings. Taking a sip of champagne from a glass he had just accepted from a tall, blonde waitress, he then added, "Very well executed they are, too!"

We spent a few moments re-engaging with Kildare in order to avert any suspicions that he might have had about our movements. I asked him his views on the Norwich School of painters that I particularly favoured, and he talked at length about the considerable talents of both John Crome and John Sell Cotman. In doing so, he seemed not to notice Holmes's departure.

My final conversation was a second encounter with Damian Gastineau, a decidedly seedy and furtive old man with a foul mouth to match. The time was fast approaching seven-thirty and Holmes had yet to reappear. Four doors where opened off the main ballroom and many of the members began to file towards these. Gastineau cast a glance at one of the passing waitresses and winked lasciviously. He then turned to me. "Now the fun begins, Doctor. It's such a shame that you'll not be here to sample the delights on offer."

He walked away towards a door which already seemed to be attracting a lot of interest. I glanced towards it and could see two or three scantily-clad young women stood within the entrance having little trouble enticing the men in. I had no doubt that each of the other rooms had its own unique inducements. As my gaze fell upon the back of Anthony Kildare for the final time, I felt a hand touch my elbow and a familiar voice whisper in my ear. "It's done, Watson. Time to go."

374

It need hardly be stated that Holmes's conjecture on the scheme being perpetrated by Anthony Kildare proved to be accurate in every respect. On the flat roof of Wellington House he discovered that a maintenance room used to house the essential workings of the building's heating system had been filled with all of the paraphernalia required to produce his noxious gas. A gas line ran from the building to a small, double-barrelled air pump which sat close to the skylight. From this ran a shorter, more flexible piece of hosing – the means by which the phosphine gas could be hand-pumped down into the boardroom.

The meeting of the Paradol Chamber had been arranged for two-thirty on the Tuesday. We played our part in assembling in the boardroom alongside the others, reintroducing ourselves and again making small talk. In his chairing role, Kildare indicated that he had asked us to attend in order that we might observe the conduct of the meeting. The members did not seem unduly bothered. A moment later he announced that he would suspend the meeting for just a few short minutes as he had forgotten to bring with him his full set of minutes from the previous meeting. He invited everyone present to refresh their coffee cups and then left the room. I chanced a glance at Holmes, who merely smiled. We both knew that the boardroom doors were now locked and Kildare would be making for the roof.

In order to ensure that no one was placed in any immediate danger, Inspector Lestrade worked with the ever-dependable Bill Hargreaves to have his officers secreted on each floor. So it was that when Kildare reached the roof, entered the maintenance room, switched on the gas, and started up the air pump, he was greeted by two burly detectives from Scotland Yard who were only too pleased to place him in handcuffs and shut down his infernal device.

At the same time, the doors to the boardroom were unlocked by Lestrade who entered quickly, flanked by three more of his men. Their arrival caused some consternation and a few choice words from Nicholas Lamboray. Young Peregrine Cattermole looked close to tears, as both he and Lamboray were led away to face questions about their involvement in the art forgery scandal.

When we left the room, Holmes was able to assure the dutiful inspector that the three French oil paintings hanging along the corridor on the third floor were indeed forgeries. A subsequent search of Kildare's office revealed that his bags were already packed, including a map case housing the genuine canvasses. In a small travelling valise, the detectives also found a ticket for a channel crossing that very evening. Having killed everyone and made off with the stolen artwork, Kildare had planned to flee to the Continent that very same day.

There was to be one final twist in the convoluted case of The Paradol Chamber. Having been tried at the Old Bailey, Kildare was sentenced to death for the murder of Mrs. Throckmorton and the attempted murder of eight others. Lamboray and Cattermole were each made to serve a minimum of seven years for their part in the art fraud. But on the day before his hanging, Kildare was found dead. He had used his influence to arrange for a kitchen knife to be smuggled in to him and had slit his wrists, bleeding to death in his holding cell only hours before he was due to face the hangman. He left one final, pencil written note, which read simply:

> *Death awaits us all – You too will go to Hell one day, Mr. Sherlock Holmes.*

Reflecting on the case after we had been notified of his death, Holmes poured us both a large brandy and sat before the fire. "Hubris can be a repellent trait, Watson. You may wish to remind me of that if I ever let my pride overrule my head in the way that Anthony Kildare did. Remember the words of Heraclitus, that '*Character is destiny*' – what you are largely dictates what you become. It is a simple adage that we would all do well to remember."

> *The year '87 furnished us with a long series of cases of greater or less interest, of which I retain the records. Among my headings under this one twelve months I find an account of the adventure of the Paradol Chamber . . . .*

– Dr. John H. Watson
"The Adventure of the Five Orange Pips"

Wolf Island
by Robert Stapleton

To this day, I have no idea why my friend, Mr. Sherlock Holmes, decided to accept that particular call upon his precious time. Indeed, as a man of logic and science, his subjective methods of making such decisions often left me baffled. For whatever reason, the selection my colleague made on that bright spring morning in 1887 would lead us both to a case so singular that it would remain seared upon our memories for many years to come.

From the pile of correspondence stacked upon our table that morning, Holmes picked up one item after the other and, after a cursory glance at the contents, dropped each one into the basket of wastepaper. He finally remained holding this one letter, examining it with intense curiosity.

"What do you think, Watson?" said he, handing the sheet of notepaper out toward me.

I took the letter and read it through. Although, because of the brevity of the correspondence, that did not require much in the way of time or energy. "Somebody is calling on you for help," I replied, seeing no specific reason why this missive shouldn't join its fellows in the basket. "And yet that person appears to give little or no information upon which to make a judgement."

"On the contrary. This item of correspondence tells us a great deal."

I turned the letter over a couple of times, examined the envelope, and looked up at Holmes in bewilderment. "Well, I for one cannot make anything of it."

"Employ my methods."

I looked closer. "The post-mark tells us it was mailed in Beaconsfield."

"You are making progress."

"But that reveals little."

"Until you remember that Beaconsfield lies among the Chiltern Hills."

"Buckinghamshire. A pleasant area of rolling countryside. But what else?"

"The letter is brief: '*Help me, Mr. Holmes. The hermit has gone, and now they are coming for me.*' A *crie de Coeur* if ever I heard one."

"But from whom? The note is simply signed '*M*.'"

"Let us examine the letter itself," said Holmes, sitting back in his chair and inspecting the dust motes floating in the rays of morning sunshine. "You will note that the paper on which it has been written is of good quality. If you hold it up to the light, as I did just now, you can clearly make out a watermark naming the Black Lion as the likely place of origin – no doubt one of the many coaching inns in that town."

"The handwriting is of poor quality. Suggesting perhaps a member of the waiting staff there."

"Perhaps," he said doubtfully. "The handwriting is undoubtedly that of a woman, whose education is limited. But the fact that she has written to me suggests a young person who is reluctant to reveal her name out of fear for her life."

"Certainly dramatic." I looked up. "But who is this mysterious *M*?"

"Time will reveal it to us, Watson."

"And the hermit?"

"Landed gentry often opened their estates to visitors, with attractions such as flowerbeds, rockeries, lakes, woodlands, and occasionally a so-called ornamental hermit, a man dressed perhaps in a cloak, sitting in a cave, giving his opinion and wisdom for the entertainment of credulous visitors."

I chuckled. "I wonder who might be the more eccentric – the landowner or the hermit?"

"Quite."

"Do you know of any estates in the Chilterns that might fit that description?"

Holmes purse his lips thoughtfully. "I know of one. An estate owned by a gentleman by the name of Andrew Grice Paterson."

I reached for our copy of *Who's Who* and searched through the listings. "Ah, here we are. Sir Andrew Grice Paterson is the elder son of the owner of a shipping line, who inherited the business on the death of his father only a couple of years ago."

"I recall reading of the father's death," mused Holmes. "But the entry suggests there might be another brother somewhere. Pray continue, Watson."

"A note that you added in the margin tells us he has an office in London, to which he commutes twice a week, from his home at Stevendale, some ten miles north of Beaconsfield."

"Today being a Tuesday, he is unlikely to be at his London office. Therefore, it should be easy enough for us to pay the man a visit. I can send him a telegram in advance to warn him of our impending arrival. But first we must call upon our mysterious correspondent. Come, Watson – a day out in the countryside should do us both some good."

Taking the train west from Marylebone Station, we arrived at Beaconsfield by mid-morning, and quickly made our way to the Black Lion Inn. As Holmes had surmised, the building was a typical eighteenth-century coaching inn. The smell of wax polish and cooking, common to such establishments by mid-morning, greeted us as we made our way through the grand front entrance.

The hotel manager, a business-like and well-dressed man sporting bushy side-whiskers, looked thoughtful as we explained the purpose of our visit.

"You are looking for a young woman whose first name begins with 'M'," he mused. Opening the visitors' book, he turned it toward us and pointing out one particular entry. "See, gentlemen. Three days ago – that will be last Saturday – a young lady came to stay here. She gave her name as Mary Smith.

"The young lady confined herself to her room," added the manager. "She seemed to be in fear of something or somebody. But our chamber maid gained her confidence and managed to learn that her real name is Muriel Oakwood."

"And for an address?"

"She seemed reluctant to provide one, but finally gave a location in St. Albans."

"Presumably that of her parents."

"We may assume so."

"And how long was this young woman intending to stay here?" asked Holmes.

"She paid in advance for three nights, with the stated intention of leaving on the fourth day – today. But yesterday afternoon, two men came and escorted her away. By the look on her face, I was certain that she was being taken against her will, but the men told me they were taking her to visit her uncle, so I considered it none of my business to interfere."

Holmes nodded. "May we see the room where she was staying?"

"Certainly." The manager handed him the key. "But she appears to have taken the few possessions that she brought with her."

We made our way up to the second floor bedroom.

With the door closed upon the world, Holmes set about examining the room in his habitual manner, scouring the furnishings for the minutest detail which might prove relevant to his investigation.

"The carpet shows the imprint of several sets of men's shoes. The two visitors and the manager, perhaps. There are also two sets of women's shoes. Muriel and the chambermaid. But no sign of any struggle."

He searched the drawers of the bedside table, and then those of the dressing table. On opening the bottom left hand drawer of the latter, Holmes drew out a printed magazine. "Now, what have we here? A copy of *Beeton's Christmas Annual*. I believe that they publish stories of various kinds."

He handed it to me.

"It has Muriel Oakwood's name on the top," I noted. Then I pushed the magazine into my coat pocket. "I shall keep it safe for her until we locate our missing lady."

"Here is something else that belongs to her," said Holmes as he lifted something else out of the drawer.

"How do you know it belongs to Muriel Oakwood?"

"A crudely inscribed letter '*M*' on the handle makes the suggestion more than likely. But the big question is why a young woman would leave behind such a personal item as her hand-mirror, concealed beneath a magazine."

"She forgot it."

"I hardly think she would forget something so intimate."

"Perhaps it carries a message for us."

"How insightful of you, Watson. Yes. The glass appears to carry some writing on the glass, made with the use of a sliver of soap. The message contains two simple words. '*Wolf Island*'."

"'Wolf Island'. Where on earth is that?"

"Perhaps our visit this afternoon will furnish us with an answer."

After a reviving meal at the Black Lion, Holmes and I hired a four-wheeler and made our way out to the Stevendale Estate, the home of Sir Andrew Grice Paterson. We presented our visiting cards to the butler and followed him into one of the front reception rooms, containing brown furniture and potted plants. I noticed that the walls were lined with pictures, paintings, and photographs of ships, both sailing and steam-driven.

Grice Paterson himself arrived, a man of sartorial sophistication, wearing a dark suit, highly polished shoes, and a wing-collared shirt. He invited us to sit down.

"As you can see, gentlemen," he said, after we had introduced ourselves, "my business lies in shipping. It is a line which involves me in a great deal of work and worry, to say nothing of the demands made upon me by the estate which I recently inherited from my father."

"In that case," began Holmes, "it is extremely good of you to spare us your time."

"You hardly gave me much choice, did you?" he returned acerbically.

"Then we must come directly to the point of our visit."

"An excellent idea."

"This morning, we visited Beaconsfield, in response to a letter we received from one of your employees – a lady by the name of Miss Muriel Oakwood."

Grice Paterson stiffened. "That young lady, if I may employ the term, is no longer in my service, Mr. Holmes. She left Stevendale on a sudden impulse three days ago, and none of us has seen her since."

Even I could tell that the man in front of us was being evasive.

"And I'm surprised that a man of your standing, Mr. Holmes, a man with better things to do with his time, should take seriously any correspondence from a semi-literate house maid such as Miss Oakwood."

"And you have no idea what has become of this lady."

"As I said. And now you tell me she has gone missing."

"So it appears."

"Then I am quite unable to assist you."

"But you have also recently lost another member of your staff – a man who played the part of a hermit."

"You are well informed, Mr. Holmes. I presume you mean Gordon Caldy."

"I don't have his name."

"Yes. I believe Caldy and this young woman were close, in which case, it is hardly surprising that they should both have left at the same time."

"Can you tell me the reason for his leaving?"

"Theft. He simply packed his bags one day and left, taking with him a sheet of paper that he had stolen from my study."

"Can you tell us any more about him?"

Andrew Grice Paterson tugged on a bell-pull. "The estate manager will answer any further questions you might have about Caldy."

"One final question then, if you wouldn't mind my asking: Does the name 'Wolf Island' mean anything to you, Sir Andrew?"

Our host glared back at Holmes and said nothing by way of reply.

The door opened and a man dressed in a tweed three-piece suit entered.

"Ah, Talbot," said Grice Paterson. "Would you please show these gentlemen around the estate, reply to any questions they have about Caldy, and then make sure they leave the premises directly you are finished."

The estate was indeed as we had expected. The house itself was large and rambling and the grounds extensive. An orangery and kitchen garden stood on one side of the house, whilst the front looked out over a landscape of pasture and woodlands.

"What exactly do you wish to see?" asked the estate manager.

"Anything that will help us discover the whereabouts of Gordon Caldy."

"You won't find him anywhere near here, Mr. Holmes," said Talbot. "He was a Scottish man, so he has more than likely gone back north again. The master regards him as a thief."

"What did he steal?"

"A sheet of paper that had been consigned to the waste-paper basket in Sir Andrew's study. You see, Mr. Holmes, all papers generated by the Grice Paterson shipping line, which are superfluous to requirement, are taken outside and burned. By myself. But before I could incinerate that sheet, Caldy snatched it up and disappeared. Rapidly."

"Hardly a crime, one would think."

"Perhaps."

"Do you know what was on the paper?"

"No."

"You say he left in a hurry."

"Very much so."

"Presumably Caldy normally resided somewhere in the house. He would hardly have slept outside in all weathers."

"He did have a small bedroom here. But Sir Andrew told me to empty his room immediately after he left, and burn any papers and correspondence that I found there."

"Where did you burn it?"

"We have a brazier on a patch of waste ground on the far side of the house."

"May we see it?"

"Certainly. For all the good it might do you."

The brazier was full of gray ashes, leaving little hope that anything substantial could be salvaged from among Caldy's belongings. Nevertheless Holmes insisted on searching through the incinerated remains. He finally stood up, slipped something between the pages of his pocketbook, and shook his head.

It was my turn to enquire after the former hermit. "Tell us, Talbot, how did Caldy come to be employed in that position?"

"He was engaged as a general handyman on the estate. He had been with us less than a year when the master came up with the idea of establishing a hermit in the grounds. He thought it might encourage more paying visitors to explore the estate, and therefore had a roughly built grotto cut into the cliff-side down in the woodland. Gordon proved to be quite a character and was indeed popular with our visitors."

Upon our return to London, Holmes insisted that we pay an immediate visit to Scotland Yard. There we found Inspector Gregson ready to hear our story.

"I see no reason for alarm, gentlemen," said the tall, fair-haired inspector. "Two people have gone missing, but you have no evidence whatsoever of any foul play."

"One has gone missing of his own volition, whilst the young woman might have been abducted."

"That sounds a little speculative, even for you, Mr. Holmes."

"Except," said Holmes, as he reached for his pocketbook and removed a small fragment of singed paper, "that I managed to retrieve this one piece of burned paper from the brazier."

He placed the fragment onto a sheet of white paper and examined it in the light of the inspector's gas-lamp.

"It might prove to be nothing at all," said Holmes. "Which is why I said nothing to Watson here, but it carries part of an address in Glasgow. And I should like you to look into the matter for me, Gregson."

The inspector looked closely at the paper. "A complete address would be more helpful, Mr. Holmes, but I can tell you at once that this is most likely to be the offices of the local Customs Department in Glasgow."

"Customs?"

"Coast Guard."

"Interesting."

"I could send a message to them, and mention the name of Gordon Caldy. If there is more to this business than meets the eye, then they might want to speak with you."

The telegram arrived so early the following morning that I was packed and on the train before I was awake enough to completely realize what had happened. The noise and smoke of Euston Station filled the air around me, as Holmes hurried me across the crowded platform and into the waiting carriage.

With the door closed against the cacophony of the station, I sat opposite Holmes and looked to him for something in the way of an explanation.

"We have been invited to travel to Glasgow to meet an official from the Coast Guard," he told me. "They have news for us about our missing hermit. It seems, from what Gregson has to tell me, that we've stumbled into a live and ongoing investigation into a smuggling operation."

"What kind of smuggling? I thought the illegal running of spirits was mostly a thing of the past."

"No doubt all will be revealed when we reach Glasgow. For the moment, though, please feel free to renew your interrupted slumber."

It was early afternoon when we arrived at Glasgow's Central Station. We had already eaten, and were both eager to make the acquaintance of our host north of the border."

A man dressed in a uniform resembling that of an officer of the Royal Navy stood waiting for us on the platform as we descended from the train. He was young, fresh of face and with signs of copper-colored hair beneath his peaked cap.

"Mr. Holmes and Dr. Watson, I presume," said the man. "I am Lieutenant Donald McBruar, a Coast Guard officer working with the Customs and Preventive Authorities to counter the smuggling of untaxed goods."

"Good afternoon, Lieutenant," said Holmes as he shook the man's proffered hand. "We're keen to hear what you have to tell us about our missing Gordon Caldy."

"Ah, yes. Caldy. In that case, please come with me, gentlemen. I have a boat waiting to take us 'doon the watter', as they say in these parts."

"Down the water?"

"Aye. The River Clyde. The lifeblood of Glasgow. We are taking a cutter normally used for coastal and river patrols. Once on board, we can talk more freely about the current business."

"Where are we going?" I asked.

"I am going to show you the Island of Uffa," said McBruar. "That is where you will find the answer to your questions."

I found our journey down the river to be a fascinating experience. Ship-building yards lined the banks, vessels were making their way both up and down stream, and the sounds of heavy industry assaulted us from all directions.

"Now, Lieutenant," said Holmes, as he settled into his seat in the rear of the steam cutter. "Please tell us something about the Island of Uffa."

"It lies to the southwest of the much larger island of Arran, and comes within the estate of the Dukes of Hamilton. It covers an area of just over one square mile, and is divided into three or four crofts, together with a larger building occupied by a man by the name of Grice Paterson."

"A-ha. Is this man any relation of Andrew Grice Paterson of Stevendale, the steamship owner?"

"This is his brother, Alexander. He has been in residence on Uffa for only the last year or so, but we have reason to believe that the two brothers are now involved in a smuggling operation centered on that island."

"Are you suggesting that this man is using his brother's ships to smuggle goods into the country?"

"Not only into the country, but out of it as well."

"Please explain."

"Very well. The smuggling of spirits used to be a lucrative business throughout the United Kingdom. Rum and brandy in particular. And untaxed whisky was also smuggled around the country. It could be a particularly violent business at times, but that mostly ended long ago, with the passing of the Excise Act of 1823, which licenced the distilling of whisky, reduced the tax levied on its production, and opened up free market trade. The smuggling of whisky ceased to be lucrative, but a small amount still goes on."

"But the situation has changed."

"Indeed. In recent years, the French vineyards have been ravaged by disease – the phylloxera beetle, to be precise. Consequently, the production of French brandy has been severely hit, almost to extinction. This has opened up a new area of trade between this country and France: Scotch whisky."

"Including the trade in untaxed whisky," concluded Holmes.

"Precisely the problem we now face, Mr. Holmes. And it is mostly centered on the Island of Uffa. We are convinced that small unlicenced distillers have been transporting their produce to the island for storage until it can be collected and exported in bulk to France. Any profits made would be augmented by the fact that no duty was expended at this end of the trade."

"Can you not simply close them down?"

"We need to catch them in the act."

"And where does our friend Gordon Caldy fit into the picture?"

McBruar set his face hard as flint. "First, you must understand that Caldy is *our* man. He has been acting as an informer for us for several months now. We placed him at Stevendale so he could pass on information about the operation from that end of the business, but recently he believed that Andrew Grice Paterson had become suspicious of him. That's when we decided to remove him from Stevendale, but in the meantime, he had formed an emotional attachment with a young lady there."

"Muriel Oakwood."

"He gave her some money and hid her away in a hotel room with the intention of moving her to somewhere safer as soon as every possible. But we now know that Grice Paterson's men found her before that could happen and have spirited her away somewhere else."

"Have you any idea where?"

"None at all. But Caldy is reluctant to help us, for fear that it might place her life in peril."

"Understandable."

"By such intimidation, they are forcing him to remain quiet and not to rock the Grice Paterson boat."

"Why did you choose Caldy for this surveillance job?"

"Because, Mr. Holmes, Caldy is himself from Uffa. He was born there, and knows the island better than anybody."

"He managed to steal something at Stevendale."

"Oh, he certainly did. We learned that the smuggling operation is to take place imminently. He stole a duplicate letter that was addressed to the captain of one of Grice Paterson's ships, the *Rockhopper*. It instructed this man to collect a cargo from Uffa and transport it to a certain port in France."

"And do you have a date for this?"

"No, but the night of the full moon would seem to be an appropriate opportunity."

"And when is the next one?"

"The thirtieth of this month."

"Today is the twenty-sixth, so time is short."

"Even shorter if they bring the date forward."

"And where is Caldy now?"

"He's on the island. In hiding. Watching."

We passed the various industrial towns lining the river until it widened into the Firth of Clyde. From here it was a long trip down the Firth, along the east side of the Isle of Arran. But the weather was fair and the sights were pleasant, especially when Lieutenant McBruar pointed out the main points of interest. For the rest of our journey, Holmes sat smoking, and keeping his thoughts to himself.

Later in the afternoon, we rounded the southern point of Arran, passed the lighthouse on the island of Pladda, and turned due west.

Facing into the afternoon sunshine, I could see very little, but Lieutenant McBruar explained that our destination lay directly ahead of us. "We are heading for Campbeltown, a port on the east coast of the lengthy Kintyre Peninsula."

"And what is that island to the south-west of us?" I asked, indicating a small island silhouetted against the afternoon skyline.

"That, Dr. Watson, is the Island of Uffa itself," said McBruar.

"And the name?" I asked again. "What exactly does Uffa mean?"

"Apparently, Uffa comes from an Old Norse word for 'wolf'."

"Ah," said Holmes, now taking a keen interest in our conversation. "So, *that* is Wolf Island."

386

When we reached Campbeltown, McBruar headed for the Customs House, leaving us time to refresh ourselves at the hotel before enjoying an evening meal.

Later, as darkness crept across both sea and land, we joined McBruar outside and together we climbed up onto a high-point overlooking the ocean. As we looked south across the water with the aid of McBruar's telescope, we could see the now dark and somewhat sinister shape of Uffa.

"Tell us more about that place, McBruar," said Holmes.

"The island of Uffa is small, perhaps no more than a mile-and-a-half in length, and one mile in width. The cliffs are steep and rugged, making access limited. The main landing stage is situated directly below the house that you can just see on the clifftop. From here, in good weather, the journey down to the island is easy enough."

I noticed a light flashing against the darkness of the island. "It seems that at least somebody is at home there."

"That will be Grice Paterson."

"He is using Morse Code to communicate with a confederate over here on the mainland," said Holmes. "From their conversation, it seems to be general knowledge that we have now arrived. I should like to meet him."

"You will have the opportunity in the morning," said McBruar. "He'll be here to collect the mails. We may be a long way from London here, Mr. Holmes, but we are still within the reach of civilization. And the payment of taxes."

"I look forward to that meeting," said Holmes, his eyes still fixed upon the flashing light.

There was no denying the fact that Mr. Alexander Grice Paterson was the brother of the man that we had met at Stevendale a couple of days previously – two beans from the same pod, so to speak – except that this one was dressed in tweeds, and had the bearing of a country squire.

McBruar introduced us as if he and the man from Uffa were on the best of terms, but a coldness in their eyes showed that this was nothing more than an illusion.

"Mr. Holmes and Dr. Watson," said Grice Paterson. "Welcome to the west of Scotland. I can only conclude that you are here at the behest of the Coast Guard. I wish that McBruar would learn to leave honest citizens to their own devices without threatening them with unjust interference."

McBruar snorted his derision, then turned and left us to our conversation.

387

Grice Paterson was engaged in examining the letters that he'd retrieved from the Campbeltown Post Office, having opened and begun to read the one that seemed to him to be most interesting.

"It's from my brother," announced Alexander Grice Paterson, without any apparent change in attitude toward us. As he returned the letter to its envelope, he looked up at us. "Gentlemen, I should be delighted if you would do me the honor of dining with me and my wife this evening."

"On the island?"

"Indeed."

"That would certainly be a great pleasure," said Holmes. "Don't you agree, Watson?"

"Oh, yes, indeed," I replied. "Thank you."

"Excellent. In that case, I shall arrange for my boat to collect you both from this landing-stage at four o'clock."

Holmes and I joined McBruar as he visited one of the licenced distilleries in the vicinity of Campbeltown. We learned about the process of distillation, and the monitoring by the Customs officials. In this way, we passed our time waiting for the hour appointed for our visit to Uffa.

At precisely four o'clock, a steam launch drew up against the Campbeltown jetty. A man, dressed in a smart but practical uniform climbed out of the boat.

"Mr. Grice Paterson has sent us to collect Mr. Holmes and Dr. Watson."

"In that case, you have found them," I said.

"Please, come this way, gentlemen. The master is waiting to welcome you to his domain."

After a journey of several miles, we found Alexander Grice Paterson himself waiting for us as we approached the landing-stage at the foot of an imposing cliff. At the head of this wall of rock loomed a large gray building, which looked more like a castle than a house, with high walls and solid but extensive masonry. It was built of the same sandstone rock that made up the island.

"Welcome, gentlemen, to the Island of Uffa." Our host greeted us with warmth in his voice, and with an outstretch hand of welcome. "Kindly follow me up to the house. We call this place Craigdoon, the 'Castle on the Rock', and you can see why."

Even Holmes was showing signs of wilting by the time we reached the clifftop.

"Is this the only access to the island?" I enquired.

"The island is surrounded by steep cliffs, rising in places to a couple-of-hundred feet," he replied. "Access to the shore is by precipitous descent from any direction. We do however have a winch and pulley system here to raise heavy items, but for the able-bodied, climbing is the only way."

"In that case, you must have very few visitors."

"True. The weather is another limiting factor. Being on such an elevated site, we are somewhat exposed to the elements. But not so much that our residents cannot make a living from the land, poor though the soil might be. We have three crofts, or homesteads, which provide all we need for our immediate needs."

I looked out across the rugged landscape of the island and found it difficult to believe that anybody could survive here, let alone raise a family.

"Come and take a look around, gentlemen," said Grice Paterson. "You will admit there is little here of interest to anybody used to the bustling life of London."

Our host led us across the rough landscape, following the trackways made by sheep and humans that criss-crossed the island. The homesteads were sturdily built, and each lay surrounded by a plot of thin topsoil which sustained a crop of spring vegetables, and grass which fed several chickens, a few sheep, and occasionally a couple of cows.

As the daylight began to fade, Grice Paterson led us back to the big house, and there we were glad to warm ourselves in the glow of a peat-fire in the grand living room.

Alexander Grice Paterson introduced us to his wife, Thelma, who informed us that dinner would be ready within ten minutes. The couple gave the impression of being people of culture, and our host instantly turned to the drinks cabinet and poured us each a glass of dry sherry.

Small-talk began, and continued as we made our way into the dining room and sat down at the large table.

Alexander placed another set of glasses before us, and proceeded to pour out a plentiful quantity of Scotch whisky into each.

Holmes declined, but I was happy to indulge, not wishing to give offence to our generous hosts.

The evening meal consisted of a warming soup, followed by a serving of venison and various vegetables, and a pudding to finish. As he poured me a second glass of whisky, Grice Paterson began to ask searching questions. "May I ask what brings you all this way, Mr. Holmes?"

"I am a private consulting detective, Mr. Grice Paterson, so that my work frequently takes me into the most unusual places," replied Holmes. "My present client has called upon my services because she was fearful that somebody wished to do her harm."

"Of what kind of harm is she afraid?"

389

"That wasn't made clear, and the waters were made even murkier when she disappeared."

"Dear me," exclaimed our host.

"There was also another man who went missing," added Holmes. "Our investigations into both disappearances have brought us to you."

"To me?" Grice Paterson appeared horrified. "I fail to see how I can be of any help whatsoever. What is the name of this lady client of yours?"

"Her name is Miss Muriel Oakwood."

He shook his head. "That name means nothing to me."

"And the name Gordon Caldy?"

"Again, it means nothing, Mr. Holmes. I can only suggest that you are here on a wild-goose chase. You would be better returning to London to continue your investigations."

"And what exactly is your line of work, Mr. Grice Paterson?" Holmes asked. "You hardly make a living out of this island."

"Of course not, Mr. Holmes. My business is in commerce, and involves the import and export of goods. I have an office in Glasgow which, as you have discovered, is no more than a small boat journey from here."

"In fine weather."

"We certainly need our sea legs here."

"And you work in consultation with your brother, presumably."

"Oh, you have met Andrew, have you?"

"You know that we have, Mr. Grice Paterson. That letter you received this morning no doubt told you about us."

For a moment, the atmosphere in the room turned icy cold. Then our host burst out laughing. "You are of course quite right, Mr. Holmes. That letter may have mentioned you in passing, but its main content concerned exports."

"Of untaxed whisky?"

"McBruar and his crew have been leading you astray, Mr. Holmes," said Grice Paterson. "He thinks he is clever. He imagines that we are storing whisky on this island, in preparation for transferring it to some ship owned by my brother. That is of course quite ridiculous. I have shown you around the island, and I hope you appreciate how difficult it is for anyone to arrive or leave. Quite apart from the landing immediately below this house, the two-hundred-foot cliffs make such a thing utterly impossible

The discussion turned to myself as Alexander Grice Paterson leaned over and refilled my glass with whisky. I had lost count of how many I had imbibed, and I could feel myself losing control of what I was saying. But for some reason, I could hardly stop myself. My garrulous nature took over, and I began to tell tales of my time in the Army.

When the meal was over, Holmes and I joined our host in the withdrawing room, where we smoked and I continued to drink.

It was only when Holmes announced that it was time for us to leave that I discovered to my horror that I was quite unable to stand up unaided.

"Oh dear, Dr. Watson," said Grice Paterson, taking me by the elbow. "I fear that you've had a little too much to drink."

"So it seems," I replied, but the thought crossed my befuddled mind that it was more than mere alcohol that was impeding my movements. I was convinced that some kind of sleeping draft had been mixed with my drink during the evening.

"Well, you cannot go back to Campbeltown in that condition," declared Grice Paterson. "But not to worry. We have a bed already made up in anticipation of visitors, and you are welcome to spend the night there."

"That is very kind of you, sir," I told him. "I have no option but to accept your kind invitation."

"In the meantime, I can arrange for Mr. Holmes to return to Campbeltown."

I noticed a look of deep concern cross the face of my friend, but we both realized that we had no option but to submit to our host's suggestion.

"Dr. Watson can remain here for as long as is necessary," said Grice Paterson.

"And exactly how long will that be?" asked Holmes.

"Until the weather and business allow."

"That sounds like a threat."

"Merely a statement of fact, Mr. Holmes. You will see the matter more logically in the morning."

"In that case, I must reluctantly take my leave of you," said Holmes. "Thank you for a most entertaining evening, and for a delightful meal." He turned to me. "Sleep well, Watson. You will need your strength and wits for the morrow."

The next thing I remember was waking to find myself in a strange bed, with the gray light of a new day filtering in through the window. My head hurt, no doubt as a result of the alcohol and sleeping draft I had taken in on the previous evening. I sat up, sipped from the glass of water that I discovered at my bedside, and then slowly climbed out of bed. I was dressed in a borrowed nightshirt, and my clothes were missing.

I drew open the curtains and looked out of the latticed window. I was facing westward, and I could see the rolling countryside of Kintyre, overhung with heavy clouds racing toward me on a strengthening wind. The ocean looked gray and wild, with waves breaking into a multitude of white horses. Rain rattled against the glass, whilst wind howled down the chimney and whistled through gaps in the woodwork.

As I collected my thoughts together, I tried the handle of the door. It was locked. I concluded that I was now a prisoner, or at the very least a hostage – for exactly what reason, I could only speculate. It undoubtedly had something to do with Lieutenant McBruar's presence in Campbeltown, but I had little wish to embark on a small boat journey in this weather, all the way back to the mainland, or anywhere else.

What a fool I had been to drink so much on the previous evening, and to leave myself defenceless against Grice Paterson's scheming. What exactly did Grice Paterson have planned for me? What was Holmes going to do now? And had I made ruin of McBruar's plans to break this trade in untaxed whisky?

I sat back on the bed, and awaited developments.

Within a few minutes, the key turned in the door lock, the handle rattled, and the door opened.

In the doorway stood a man I had met at one of the crofts the previous evening.

"Good morning, Dr. Watson," the man said. "My name is Donald, and the master has sent me to invite you to take your breakfast downstairs in the kitchen."

He stood aside to allow a young girl of no more than thirteen years of age to enter, carrying a jug of hot water which she placed upon the wash-stand on the far side of the room. Then she turned and left.

I noticed that Donald was carrying my clothes, neatly ironed and folded. These he left on the wooden chair standing beside the window.

Before I had time to interrogate him further, Donald had taken his leave, but this time closing the door without locking it.

Downstairs I enjoyed an ample breakfast, and was just finishing off my second cup of coffee when Alexander Grice Paterson himself appeared in the doorway of the kitchen.

"Ah, Dr. Watson. I see you are being well provided for."

"Indeed, thank you" I replied. "But I do wonder what you have in mind for me now."

"My plans are merely for your safety and convenience," he told me. "As the weather is inclement, you will remain on this island. Please feel free to make yourself at home here at Craigdoon. You're free to occupy the living room, the kitchen, the library, and your bedroom. Only you must not venture outside. At least, not on a day as stormy as this."

With little else to do, I made my way into the library, and settled down with a copy of Mr. Stevenson's recently published novel, *Kidnapped*. It seemed most appropriate to my present predicament.

Alexander's wife, Thelma, joined me in the library and sat at the far end of the room, knitting. It was clear that she was keeping an eye on me. I felt isolated. I had no way of contacting Holmes, so I resigned myself to spending the morning, and perhaps most of the day, in reading, and trying to dampen down a developing sense of paranoia.

I joined Alexander and Thelma around their table for the evening meal. The master asked me about my day, which I was able to answer in very few words. He was equally unforthcoming about other events on the island. Thus, with darkness fallen, I finally bade a goodnight to my hosts, and made my way to bed.

By now, the wind had eased, and I felt content to entrust myself into the arms of Morpheus for the night. Perhaps the god of dreams might help me make sense of whatever was going on here.

In the darkest part of the night, I was awoken by the sound of scraping. I sat up, and looked around at the darkness. "Is somebody there?"

I became aware of a movement in the gloom, and of a figure walking across the room toward the door. Light from a dark lantern illuminated that half of the room.

"I see they've locked it again," came a man's voice, carrying the lilt of a lowland Scotsman. "Good. That is hardly surprising, but it will do nothing to confine us to this room."

"Now, come along," I exclaimed. "Who the blazes are you?"

"Me? I thought you might have guessed by now, Dr. Watson. I am Gordon Caldy."

"Ah, Caldy. McBruar told us you were on this island."

"Keeping an eye on the Grice Patersons. I have been living in the ruins of an abandoned croft on the far side of the island. It might be a bit exposed, but nothing to a man whose job has been sitting outside in a hermit's cave."

"How did you get in here?"

"There are passageways in this house that even Grice Paterson himself knows nothing about. As somebody who was born and raised on this island, I know this place better than anybody else alive. One of the panels in this room opens onto a stairway that leads down to ground level."

"And what are you doing here in the middle of the night?"

"I have something to show you, Doctor. Now, get dressed as quickly as you can and follow me."

In the thin light of Caldy's lantern, I followed him into the hidden passageway and down a flight of stone steps, until he pushed open a small doorway and led me outside into the cold night air.

"Now where?"

Caldy held his finger to his lips and put out the lantern. "Hush. Our lives will be in danger if anybody finds us out here."

As quietly as possible, and crouching down to reduce the chance of being observed, we followed the top of the cliff along the western edge of the island. After several yards, Caldy stopped abruptly and, in the light of the nearly full moon, I noticed that the edge of the cliff had been eroded at this point.

Caldy led the way down a slope, until we reached a flight of steps cut into the rock.

"Grice Paterson assured us there was no other way onto the island," I said.

"You didn't believe him, did you?"

I followed, trying to keep alert to any danger.

Caldy proved more alert than I was. He stopped, listened, and then pulled me aside so that we both stood with our backs against the bracken-crowned rock, but with our presence concealed by the night.

Through the blackness, I could make out three men, climbing up the steps toward us. They were talking. Trying to keep my breathing steady, I watched as the men drew closer. I recognized one of them. It was, without doubt, my host, Alexander Grice Paterson. I could hear very little of what they were saying, but one phrase stood out. "High-tide." That sounded significant.

After the three men had passed us and had disappeared beyond the top of the pathway, we waited for another couple of minutes before continuing our descent.

At the bottom, we reached a small cove, with encompassing cliffs making its entrance all but invisible from the open sea. Behind a narrow shingle beach, I noticed a cave, also well concealed, stretched back beneath the cliff-side. The overhang hid this cave from both the weather and from observation by anybody approaching it from the sea. On closer inspection, I noticed that the cave contained casks and barrels stacked together.

"Contraband," breathed Caldy.

To one side of the beach, we reached a concrete landing stage, which gave access to a wooden jetty stretching out some fifty yards toward the sea and hidden by the rocks.

Just visible through the darkness, I could see a small fishing boat slowly making its way out into the Kilbrannan Sound, and heading west.

"They have offloaded their whisky for the night," said Caldy. He relit and uncovered one segment of his lantern, and was rewarded by an answering light from several yards away to the north-west.

394

Another small fishing boat approached the calm waters of the cove and crunched onto the shingle beach. The boat appeared to be full of fishermen. A rougher looking bunch I never wished to meet on such a dark night.

The toughest of them jumped down from the boat, and approached me. "Ah, there you are, Watson," he said.

"Holmes. I never would have recognized you dressed like that."

"I trust you had a restful day as a guest of the Grice Patersons."

"I used it as best I could, but there was one thing of note that occurred during the afternoon. Grice Paterson received a couple of visitors. He took them to his office, so I had difficulty following what they were saying, but I am sure they were speaking French."

"French, eh?"

"But more importantly," Caldy chipped in. "We heard Grice Paterson mention high-tide."

"We can only assume he means the one tomorrow night. Then, high-tide will be at about midnight. That has to be the time of the scheduled transfer."

"So," I said, "you plan to return tomorrow night."

"Not just my plans, but those of McBruar as well. Success now depends upon keeping secret that we know their intentions."

"But they will know when they find me gone."

"Then you will have to return to your room, Watson."

"And remain a prisoner? Surely you cannot be serious."

"Never more so."

"Don't worry, Dr. Watson," said Caldy. "I'll take you back the way we came, and collect you again tomorrow night."

A low whistle sounded from the other end of the beach. We saw one of the fishermen stand up and wave. "Mr. Holmes. Dr. Watson. You must come here, now."

As we approached the wooden jetty, we could both see something floating in the water, bobbing among the waves. I had seen enough human bodies to immediately recognize it as such.

It was Gordon Caldy who waded into the water to retrieve the corpse, and drag it to land.

I turned the man onto his back, and quickly confirmed that he was dead. "His throat has been cut. And not very long ago, judging by the way the blood is still oozing out."

Caldy knelt down and looked the fellow over. "I know this man," he said, with bitterness in his voice. "His name is Alan Randlestone – one of the few people left who were born on the island. He was always a man of honor, and perhaps objected to whatever was going on here."

395

"So they killed him," said Holmes.

"And left his body to drift out to sea," I added.

"Most of the people on the island now are incomers," explained Caldy. "Strangers. People intent on making gain rather than retaining any love for the place."

"The finger of guilt inevitably points to Alexander Grice Paterson," growled Holmes. "Either he committed the murder himself, or else he knows about it. He is a dangerous man."

"We have to take the body with us," said Caldy, reaching down and lifting the corpse into his arms. "Not only was he my friend, but his body is our evidence against Grice Paterson."

"And you still want me to spend another day in that house?" I asked Holmes.

"We have no choice, Watson," he replied. "But take this with you."

He handed me my service revolver. In the dim light of the lantern, I checked that it was loaded, and slipped it into my pocket.

I felt a sense of disappointment as I watched the small boat push off from the beach, taking Holmes with it, and heading back toward Campbeltown. I was alone once more – albeit with Caldy still on the island. But this time, I knew myself to be grave danger.

The following day passed much the same as the previous one, with the exception that I now regarded Grice Paterson through more guarded eyes, as one would a coiled snake or lurking tiger. From time to time, I could hear people entering and leaving the building. Indeed, I gained the impression that the number of people on the island had somewhat increased. I could see men outside, coming and going with singular intent. I had a distinct impression that they are working up to something significant.

At supper that evening, I thanked the Grice Patersons for their hospitality. "But when exactly will I be able to return to the mainland?"

Alexander leaned over and refilled my whisky-glass. I gained the impression that they were trying once more to render me intoxicated. But this time I was more diligent in counting the glasses.

"Tomorrow morning," replied Alexander Grice Paterson. "I promise you, Doctor. By then the weather will have improved sufficiently to make the crossing smooth enough so as not to inconvenience you with the danger of seasickness."

With the encouragement of my hosts, I retired as soon as the clock in the entrance hall chimed ten. With the bedroom door once again locked, I lay on the bed, fully-dressed, and waited. Then, in the light of my candle,

I noticed him. Sitting in the chair by the window, with bright eyes patiently watching me.

"Holmes," I gasped. "What are you doing here?"

"Keeping an eye on you, my old friend," he told me. "I had no intention of leaving you alone for a second night in the same house as that murderer."

"Have you been here all day?"

"Much of it. Caldy knows every corner of this building, including a place where one can rest in peace and remain undisturbed by the rest of the household." He allowed a knowing smile to cross his face. "He showed me another room, almost empty, but with signs of recently having been filled with bags of tobacco and boxes of cigars."

"Contraband?"

"It looks like it."

"So the smuggling is going out as well as coming in."

"We're in dark waters here, Watson. This is becoming a much bigger enterprise than anyone first imagined."

At that moment the hidden door opened, and Gordon Caldy appeared as if by magic, looking pleased with himself. "Are you both ready?"

"Indeed I am," I told him.

Holmes stood up, and nodded. "Remember to take your revolver with you, Watson."

"You will also need to wrap your coat tightly around you," added Caldy. "The weather has turned cold again, and we might have a long wait, though I suspect not."

Once more down in the cove, I noticed that the collection of fishing boats had increased in number. At the far end of the line of vessels, I found the one Holmes had been using the previous night.

"Hurry up, Watson," he told me. "This place will be swarming with Grice Paterson's men before long. We must leave before that happens."

The three of us – Caldy, Holmes, and myself – climbed into the small fishing boat, and one member of the crew pushed off from the shore, whilst others raised the darkly stained mainsail.

A few hundred yards out, the crew turned the boat to face shore, took down the sail, and let out a sea-anchor from the stern.

We all sat down to await events.

Soon, the sound of voices reached us from the shore as a couple of dozen men climbed down the pathway and assembled on the shingle beach. With Grice Paterson giving the orders, the men began to move the casks and barrels from their places in the cave and deposit them at the far end of the jetty.

Holmes tapped me on the shoulder and pointed toward the south. I could see a light somewhere across the water, and it was moving.

"A ship," I whispered.

"*The* ship," he replied.

We watched as the vessel drew closer, turned in a circle, and approached the end of the jetty. With her port beam against the pier, the ship was secured fore and aft.

The ship was a small coastal-trading steamship of less than five-hundred tons and perhaps three-hundred feet in length. A central bridge separated the two small holds, with a forecastle in the bows and a long quarter-deck with a tall smoke-stack rising immediately forward of the ship's boat. On the rusted stern, the ship displayed her name: *Rockhopper*.

"One of Andrew Grice Paterson's vessels, if I'm not very much mistaken," said Holmes. "The very one mentioned in Caldy's stolen paper."

Caldy confirmed it as the ship was secured fore-and-aft to the bollards on the jetty.

Through the darkness, we could hear Alexander Grice Paterson issuing further orders and could see the small army of men hurrying to load the myriad barrels and casks. Working with the vessel's crew and using the ship's derricks, they quickly had the cargo loaded into the holds.

Grice Paterson shouted further orders, and the derricks unloaded casks and bundles, onto the jetty.

"Tobacco and rum," whispered Caldy.

From there, the smuggled goods were spirited away, some onto the waiting fishing boats, and some into the cave behind the beach.

All this we observed from our fishing boat, hidden from their view in the darkness of the night.

When all was done, the men in the boats pushed off from the beach, whilst others climbed back up the pathway, leaving Alexander Grice Paterson talking with the ship's captain, and exchanging papers and money.

As the ship prepared to leave, with a plume of pungent smoke billowing from the funnel, Holmes ordered our boat to draw closer to the ship, on the side away from the island.

"It is my considered conclusion," announced Holmes, "that this ship contains our client, Miss Muriel Oakwood."

"If you're going to board that ship," returned Caldy, his eyes flashing, "then I'm coming with you."

Taking my revolver into my hand, I followed Sherlock Holmes onto the deck of the steamer – just in time, for as the ship pulled away, we crossed the deck to where one member of the crew was stowing the ship's mooring rope.

From behind, Caldy wrapped his arm around the man's throat, whilst Holmes pressed his own revolver against the fellow's head.

I could only imagine the look of surprise on the man's face.

"Where is the girl?" demanded Holmes.

The crewman remained silent.

"The logical conclusion has to be that she is on board this ship, somewhere. Take us to the girl, or you will be taking a dip. Do you understand?"

The man nodded, and Caldy loosened the grip on his throat.

"You lead the way, and remember, we are directly behind you."

The crewman led us along the side of the superstructure and in through a doorway. From there, he led us down a companionway until we halted outside a locked door. The man unfastened the door, and pushed it open.

Inside, in the darkness of the cabin, a young woman cried out in alarm at our abrupt appearance.

"Good evening, Miss Oakwood," said Holmes. "I am Sherlock Holmes, and this is my companion, Dr. John Watson."

In the subdued light, Muriel Oakwood noticed Gordon Caldy and, with a cry of delight, threw herself into his arms.

Holmes turned to the man who had led us here. "What were your orders about the girl?"

"We were to take her with us to France," replied the man. "And leave her there, along with the whisky."

"You had better stay out of sight," said Holmes. "I would hate to be in your shoes when your skipper discovers we're on board – which he will do soon."

He turned to me. "Are you ready, Watson?"

"For what?"

"We are taking over the ship."

"Oh, is that all? Of course I'm with you."

As we made our way farther along the quarter-deck, I heard the sound of the engine change, and felt the ship turn sharply to port.

"What now?" I asked.

"We have company," cried Holmes. "Look. A thousand yards away, off the starboard bow. Another ship."

I strained my eyes. "Now I see her. She's rounding that headland. And I am prepared to bet she's a warship, Holmes. A cruiser."

"She ought to be. Our friend McBruar is supposed be organizing a reception for this ship."

"Well, bravo for McBruar, and the Royal Navy, for turning up right on cue."

I followed Holmes along the deck, and then up a ladder toward the bridge, an open structure, protected from the elements by nothing more than a canvas skirting.

I hung back as Holmes stepped up onto the bridge.

There he found the captain standing beside the ship's coxswain at the helm. Holmes pointed the revolver toward the captain. "You have no hope of escape, Captain. You can never outrun a warship."

The captain turned round, greatly surprised to find Sherlock Holmes behind him, and regaled him with a torrent of choice phrases. "We're not finished yet!" he replied. "And you'll not live long enough to enjoy any victory!"

From where I was, standing unseen in the shadows, I noticed another figure emerge from the far corner of the bridge. A man. I saw him approach Holmes from behind, and reach beneath his jacket. I realized he was about to bring out a gun. I slipped silently onto the bridge, and immediately pressed the muzzle of my revolver against his neck. The man stopped, and allowed me to reach in and extract the gun – a heavy automatic.

"I see that the mate has joined us, Holmes," I cried.

Holmes turned and nodded. "Good work, Watson."

A megaphoned voice reached us from across the water. "I call on you to heave-to, and prepare to receive a boarding-party."

"That sounds like McBruar's voice," I said, pushing the mate to join his companions in the center of on the bridge.

"Do are he says," Holmes growled to the captain.

The captain rang the telegraph, and the ship slowly drew to a halt, bobbing in the swell coming in from the Atlantic Ocean.

A few minutes later, a steam-launch arrived and a party of sailors swarmed onto the ship.

"Welcome aboard, Lieutenant McBruar," called out Holmes. "I'm glad you could make the appointment. I have already taken over the bridge and command of the ship."

"Mr. Holmes," the other man shouted back. "You have done a good night's work, but we are here now to take over from you."

Holmes looked down onto the deck below. "It seems, Watson that this most singular case of ours is now at an end."

I also looked down, and noticed two figures, embracing, oblivious to whatever was going on around them. "Gordon Caldy and Muriel Oakwood," I noted. "The hermit and the house-maid. I hope they have a happy future together."

"After all those two have been through, they certainly deserve it, Watson," replied Holmes. "Which is more than can be said for the Grice Patersons of Uffa. Smuggling is one thing, compounded by abduction, but murder is quite another matter altogether. They are about to face justice. Their singular adventures are finally at an end, and we can safely say that Craigdoon will shortly be looking for a new tenant."

The year '87 furnished us with a long series of cases of greater or less interest, of which I retain the records. Among my headings under this one twelve months, I find an account . . . of the singular adventures of the Grice Patersons in the island of Uffa . . . .

– Dr. John H. Watson
"The Five Orange Pips"

The Etherage Escapade
by Roger Riccard

Chapter I

On a Saturday afternoon one summer, I was enjoying a pipe and reading the latest issue of *The Lancet* in the sitting room of the private consulting detective, Sherlock Holmes. He was occupied at his chemistry table, performing some experiments with small amounts of gunpowder mixed with various other substances. An occasional popping sound would emanate from that corner of the room, as certain mixtures proved more explosive than others.

I had rather tuned out this intermittent cacophony to the point that I did not hear the ascending steps of Mrs. Hudson and a guest until the knock came to our door. I rose from my chair to open it finding our good landlady in the company of Scotland Yard Inspector Morgan Smith.

The stocky fellow with the porcine face burst through the door past Mrs. Hudson and quickly located Holmes as he scanned the room. "Holmes! There you are! I need your help, man!"

At that moment the loudest explosion of the day set up a white cloud of smoke. Smith threw an arm up to cover his face as he ducked. Mrs. Hudson retreated and closed the door behind her. Holmes merely pulled off his goggles and made a note on the tablet next to him.

"Good God, Mr. Holmes!" cried the Scotland Yarder when he straightened up again. "Have you turned to bomb-making now?"

My friend stood to walk over toward our sitting area, "Calm yourself, Inspector. Merely a chemical experiment. Have a seat by Watson there and tell us what brings you to our door in such a state of rude agitation."

Smith sat on the sofa next to me, removed his bowler, and wiped his wide brow with a large handkerchief. Holmes filled his churchwarden with tobacco from the stuffed Persian slipper hanging on the mantel and took the seat opposite us. Smith began speaking, even before Holmes had lit his pipe.

"It's this missing lawyer business," Smith began. "It's fairly plain what's happened, but the widow wants a definitive answer and her father, old Judge Shipley, is putting pressure on the Yard to solve the case."

"You are referring to the disappearance of the solicitor, Etheredge?" I asked, having read the news story earlier that week.

"The very same," replied Smith.

"*The Times* gave few details, Inspector," noted Holmes. "Yet it seemed straightforward enough that I found it to be of little interest. Please give us the precise facts."

I took that as a cue to bring out pencil and paper and began jotting down the story Smith relayed to us. He cleared his throat and began.

"A week ago yesterday morning, Mr. Andrew Etherege left for his office at eight o'clock. He was dressed in a black suit with a grey checked waistcoat, black overcoat, black square-toed shoes with grey spats, and wearing a black-and-burgundy four-in-hand tie. He carried a black leather briefcase which he used to transport papers to the office and various appointments.

"He is fairly young to be so successful, as he is but twenty-eight. However, he began working for his father at the office when he was twenty-one. He inherited the business two years ago, upon his father's death from a stroke. He is five-feet-seven inches tall, weighs about one-hundred-sixty pounds. He has short, wavy brown hair and a neatly trimmed moustache. I have a photograph for you here."

He pulled a sepia portrait of the young man, standing next to a seated woman, from his inner breast pocket, handing it to Holmes. Both wore serious expressions, as was common for formal portraits. He was to the left of the chair with his left hand behind his back and his right on top of the chair back. The young lady, whom Smith noted was Millicent Etherege, his wife of six years, sat up straight with both hands atop the handle of a parasol. A garland of white flowers perched on her hair, which piled up behind the adornment and rolled down the sides of her round face with large curls.

"That was taken shortly after their wedding," continued Smith. "Etherege's office is a small space in a building in Cannon Street. There is a sitting area for customers and two enclosed offices for private consultations. Behind those, a back room containing supplies, files, and a fairly substantial safe. Etherege hasn't hired anyone since his father's death and runs the office by himself. Of course, he spends considerable time at the Stock Exchange, as most of his clients are corporations whom he advises on things like mergers and acquisitions. Mostly contract law, you see. He is generally in the office for at least two hours after the Exchange closes. As a result, he often returns home between seven and eight o'clock for dinner.

"On that Friday, he had yet to return by ten o'clock. Mrs. Etherege had not been overly concerned, as he occasionally goes out with fellow businessmen after work, or to his club. Usually, however, he informs her ahead of time and is always home by ten. She contacted her father and he reached out to the Yard. Of course, in his position, priorities were rearranged and I was assigned the case. Examination of his office showed signs of a struggle, some blood, and an empty safe. The next morning Etherege's coat, with significant amounts of blood on the collar, was found below the north bank support of Blackfriars Bridge. Dragging the Thames has proved fruitless thus far. We've concluded that he was robbed, injured in a struggle, and then kidnapped for ransom. Perhaps his injuries proved fatal, or he attempted an escape which led to his death. In any case, he has not returned home, nor has any unidentified man of his description appeared in any of the city's hospitals. Two days later, his briefcase turned up in a pawn shop in the East End."

"How did you identify the coat and briefcase as his?" asked Holmes.

"The coat was his size and the label was his tailor, Gieves and Hawkes of Saville Row. The briefcase had his initials, *ATE*, inscribed upon it."

"You seem to have the case in hand, Smith. What would you have me do?"

"Judge Shipley is insisting that we enlist your aid, Mr. Holmes. He has heard of your reputation. Even though we reminded him that you are an amateur, he is adamant that we leave no stone unturned."

If the word "amateur" rankled Holmes, he hid it well. Removing the pipe from his lips, he pointed the long stem at the inspector and replied, "Then I suggest we start at the scene of the crime. While we do so, Inspector, would you please get word to Mrs. Etherege that we should like to come around to speak with her this evening at six o'clock? I presume you wish to come along, Doctor?"

I put the pencil and paper into my pocket and replied, "Certainly, if I may be of assistance."

"There's a good fellow. Well, Smith," he said, rising from his chair." Let us be off to Cannon Street."

Chapter II

It didn't take us long to traverse the four miles to Etherege's office. It was in a building full of small business establishments. Smith led us up two flights of stairs and down a hall to the last office in the row. He opened the door and stood aside to let us enter.

Holmes stood in the doorway, taking in the layout of the floorplan. Over his shoulder he asked the inspector, "How many of your people have been in here since the constable discovered the scene?"

Smith looked down at his hands, as if counting the personnel on his fingers. "The constable, his sergeant, a doctor from the coroner's office to test the stains we found, and myself. That's all I'm aware of."

"Yes, your shoeprints are readily apparent," replied Holmes, "as are the prints of the two policemen with their standard footwear. If you'll wait here, gentlemen, I should like to examine the carpet more closely."

My friend entered, walking sideways along the edge of the path that lead through the lobby and bisected the two offices. Carefully he eyed the marks in the carpet, which were all but invisible to the untrained eye. He stopped just short of the two office doors which faced each other perpendicular to the hall created by their presence. He took particular notice of the floor outside the office to the right. Smith called out, rather condescendingly, I thought, "Etherege's office is the one on the left, Mr. Holmes."

Holmes ignored him, opening the door to the right hand office. Still peering down at the carpet, he crouched, swiveling his head to-and-fro. He then rose, his gaze taking in the room's contents like a hen gathering her chicks, nodding his head slightly as some observation became tucked into his brain. He did an about-face and stepped across to the already-open door of Etherege's office. He repeated his observation process from the doorway, and then stepped inside, gesturing for Smith and me to come wait by the door. From where we stood, I could see that Etherege's umbrella and overcoat still hung on the coatrack – a foreboding sign to my mind.

We watched as the detective circled the perimeter of the room, attempting to replay activities indicated by the footprints he could see. "It was foresighted of you, Smith, not to allow the cleaning staff in here. Their carpet sweepers would have destroyed valuable evidence."

The bulky inspector smiled at the compliment, "I never thought I'd have to call you in, Mr. Holmes, but I did wish to leave the scene intact for as long as possible – especially with the judge's son-in-law involved."

"I see that a woman has been here recently," remarked Holmes. "May I presume that Mrs. Etherege was allowed to come in?"

Smith tugged at his collar and cleared his throat, "Ahem! Yes, we allowed her the courtesy to visit the scene. We watched her carefully though. She wasn't allowed to remove any evidence, save for her husband's cheque-book in order to pay her bills. The cheque-book was in the safe, in the room at the end of the hall."

Holmes walked to the window, which looked out on rooftops below and a park in the distance. Even from where we stood, I could see that it was capable of being opened out onto a fire escape. Smith spoke up, "No one came in that way. The frame is swollen and impossible to open without noise. You can see that the latch hasn't been jimmied."

"Yes," replied Holmes in that distracted voice I've heard often. Then he asked, "What was Mrs. Etherege's countenance when she came upon the scene of the crime a mere two days after its occurrence?"

Smith seemed a bit taken aback, "How did you know it was two days later?

Holmes merely turned back toward us and gave him a look, as one does when asked a foolish question.

"Er, yes, of course," replied the inspector. "She remained calm and business-like, though she did give a slight gasp at the sight of the bloodstain on the floor by the safe."

Holmes said, "Yes, I can imagine."

He sat in the chair with the window behind him and examined the layout of items on the desk, as well as the contents of the drawers. One drawer, the second down of the left side, drew his attention. It was completely empty. He pulled it all the way out laying it across the desktop, examining it with his lens. Then, running his fingers over the bottom, he smelled his fingertips, nodded thoughtfully, and returned the drawer to its place.

At length he stood and said, "Let us go examine the safe room, Inspector."

Smith led us to the end of the hall and opened the door. There was no carpet in this small room, just solid oak flooring. There were also file cabinets and storage shelves for supplies. The safe was a large Chubb model with a combination dial. It stood about four-feet-high by three-feet-wide. The door was open. There were several empty sections.

Off to the right, beyond the open safe door, was an irregularly shaped red stain on the floor. Holmes knelt by it, using his magnifying lens to examine it closely. He even used his penknife to scrape up some of the discolored wood slivers. Then he waved me over.

"Take a look, Watson," he murmured. "Note particularly the color, smell, and shape."

"What's that, Mr. Holmes?" called out Smith.

My companion stood and replied, "Just asking Dr. Watson to take some notes for a more precise medical opinion. I presume you realized that the location of the stain would indicate the assailant was likely left-handed."

"How can you know that?" asked Smith, with some skepticism, folding his arms across his wide frame.

"Observe," replied the detective. "Etheredge stands here, opening the safe under threat of harm, no doubt. Once it's opened, his knowledge is no longer needed. He's knocked unconscious and falls to the floor. By falling to the right, he was likely struck on his left side. It is more probable that a

406

left-handed man would swing his arm that way, rather than a right-handed man hitting him with a backhanded blow, though I do not discount that possibility entirely.

"Has anyone gone over the contents of the safe to determine what is missing?"

"'Tis impossible to say, Mr. Holmes," replied the Scotland Yarder. "He had no partner, nor did his wife know anything of his business affairs."

"May I have your permission to examine what is left in the safe?"

"Yes, indeed, sir. We have been given that authority by the Judge."

"Very well," replied Holmes. "I should like to do so this evening, after our visit to Mrs. Etherege, if you will inform your guard."

We began walking back out, but Holmes abruptly turned into the office that he'd first observed. Smith and I followed him in, but stayed back by the door. The inspector huffed, "There's nothing here. This was young Etherege's office before his father died and he moved across the hall. It hasn't been used since, except to store the books on the shelves and files in the cabinets."

Holmes answered back over his shoulder as he opened a double-door cabinet perpendicular to the desk which faced the doorway, "Yes, I can see you came in and did a quick walkabout, Smith. But, there are other footprints here – from our victim, no doubt – which indicate he still put this office to some use recently, as they are not obliterated by the carpet sweepers."

We couldn't see into the cabinet he had opened, as one of the doors blocked our view. However, we immediately went to Holmes's side when he declared, "Well then, what have we here?"

What he had revealed was a counter with a sink bowl and water pitcher atop a lower cabinet. There was a mirror above the sink with candle sconces on either side. What was unusual was that, on the inside surface of the two doors, were mounted two full length mirrors.

"Merely a closet vanity," remarked Smith. "Nothing related to our case."

Holmes opened the top drawer of the lower cabinet and found a shaving kit, toothbrush and powder, moustache wax, towels, and the like. He ran his fingers around the sink and checked the water level in the pitcher. He examined the towels and countertop with his lens, sweeping some small fragments into one of his ever-present envelopes for later examination. Leaving the cabinet doors open, he sat in the chair behind the desk, swiveling to face the mirrors. Examining the desk drawers, he found little of interest. He did spend some moments noting indentations in the carpet to the left of the chair and made a quick measurement of them.

At last, we stepped back out between the two offices and faced the entryway. Holmes asked Smith, "What is your working theory, Inspector?"

The stout official gripped both his lapels in his hands while making his statement:

"Late on that Friday, likely just after the normal closing of business hours when the rest of the building was nearly empty, two unknown persons came in to see Etherege. It may have been by appointment or they may just have burst in unannounced. They confronted the victim in his office, forcing him to go back and open the safe. He was struck him down when the task was complete. They took what cash and redeemable certificates they could, stuffing them into Etherege's own briefcase. Perhaps they realized that they needed his signature on certain papers, or perhaps kidnapping was a part of the original plan.

"They dragged the victim to the door. You can see the drag marks of his heels there on the carpet. They carried the unconscious man down to a waiting conveyance – perhaps prepared to explain to anyone they ran into that Etherege was ill and they were taking him to a hospital. We believe he was initially taken for ransom. At some point he may have attempted to escape and slipped out of his coat when they grabbed for him. He was probably killed in the attempt, or succumbed to his original head wound. They disposed of his body and coat in the Thames, but his coat washed up on shore. Without being able to offer proof of life, they abandoned their ransom scheme. Neither they nor Etherege have been heard of since. The pawnshop owner could only tell us that the person who brought in the briefcase was tall, thin, and wore a moustache."

Holmes nodded, "You seem to have created a plausible theory based upon the facts you have in hand, Inspector. After we make our call upon Mrs. Etherege and examine the papers in the safe this evening, perhaps I can offer some suggestions."

"I would be grateful, Mr. Holmes," replied the harried man. "I have other cases vying for my attention. This seems like a waste of valuable time."

"Until tomorrow then, Smith," answered Holmes.

Chapter III

While returning to Baker Street, Holmes stared out the window of our cab in silent contemplation. I knew better than to interrupt his train of thought. Instead, I merely went over the notes that I'd taken, ensuring I had everything in order. Upon arrival at home, we stepped out onto the pavement. Holmes stared up at our sitting room window.

Shaking his head, he murmured, "It will not do, Watson."

"What's that?" I asked.

"Can you imagine you and me carrying a third person between us down the steps from our room to the foyer? These supposed kidnappers had to carry Etherege twice that far, in a public building, then out to a waiting vehicle."

"It was likely after dark by the time they did so," I suggested. "On a Friday evening, most of the other offices would certainly be closed. I admit that three men abreast, two carrying the other, on that stairwell is unlikely, but what other explanation is there?"

"What indeed?" he said, as he opened the door to 221b and we returned to the comfort of our sitting room. He immediately went to his chemistry table, retrieved the envelopes from his pocket, and began running experiments. I poured myself a brandy, took a seat on the sofa, looked at my notes, and contemplated what I had seen and heard.

Some forty minutes later, Holmes looked up from his microscope. "What was your opinion of the bloodstain, Doctor?"

"Yes, I have a note on that," I replied, flipping through my pages. "Ah, here we are. The color and consistency were unusual. It was far too red for what should have been dried blood. It was rather thick and smooth. I would have expected it to be a crusty texture and reddish brown in color. I can think of no medical condition that would cause blood to congeal in such a fashion. Also, there was only the puddle where he fell. There was no splatter from the initial blow."

"Excellent, Watson!" cried Holmes. "My chemical analysis confirms your findings. We are entering deep waters, my friend. A cunning mind is behind this case. We can take nothing at face value, which is the error Smith has made."

I nodded in agreement, then asked, "Why didn't you request to see the scene where Etherege's coat was found?"

"After a week's worth of tides coming and going, there would be no evidence left to be found. If it indeed washed up on shore, there was no way to know where it entered the water. I have no reason to believe that it is the actual scene of any crime."

"Why would you conclude that?" I asked.

"Let me recall your attention to the unique contents of the coat rack in Etherege's office."

"His umbrella and overcoat were still there."

"Indeed, those were the unique contents," Holmes smiled enigmatically. "I should like to step out for a bit, Watson. I shan't be long, then we can proceed to interview our victim's wife."

409

Holmes returned in plenty of time to retrieve me. Then on we went to the Etherege home in Clerkenwell. We arrived just before six o'clock at a well-appointed house with a colorful flower garden out front of its red brick Georgian façade. We strode up the steps and Holmes rang the bell. A matronly woman opened the door. "Would you be Mr. Sherlock Holmes, sir?"

Upon his affirmation, she invited us in to a modest foyer, took our hats and overcoats, and placed them by the door. "This way, gentlemen," she said. We followed the lady to a parlour where Mrs. Etherege sat by the fire. It was a well-furnished room with several pieces of the French Provincial style. She was reading a book but looked up when we were announced. Placing the bookmark where she left off, she set the volume aside, stood slowly, and then held out her hand. She was about five-foot-four and a bit heavier than she had appeared in the picture we'd been given. Her voice was high-pitched and rather strident, I thought. Holmes and I each bowed over her hand in turn. She waved us to the sofa to sit down.

"Now then, Mr. Holmes, I understand from my father that you are some sort of detective with a fair reputation for solving unusual mysteries. Did you discover anything in my husband's office that may give us hope of finding him alive?"

Frankly, I found her attitude to be a bit cavalier. Were someone I loved missing for a week, I would be frantic. Yet this woman seemed as if she were merely inconvenienced. Holmes replied to her enquiry with one of his own.

"I found several interesting clues, Mrs. Etherege, but I need time to follow them. I should like to ask you, has your husband any enemies or unhappy clients of late?"

"We do not discuss his business at home, Mr. Holmes. So long as his income maintains our lifestyle I care nothing for his work."

I could not resist a question of my own, "How long have you and your husband known each other, Mrs. Etherege?"

"What an odd question, Dr. Watson. We've known each other since childhood. Our families were always very close. It was just naturally expected that Andrew and I would marry."

Holmes asked, "Did Mr. Etherege always wish to follow in his father's footsteps?"

"Of course!" she answered, matter-of-factly. "He studied for it at Cambridge."

"Does he have an office here at home, or a desk where he works? I should like to go over it for any further clues."

"Yes, he has a study upstairs. I'll have Marian show you." She rang a bell on the table next to her. The same lady who had shown us in appeared. "Yes, madam?"

"Marian, please show these gentlemen to Master Andrew's study."

We followed the servant upstairs and into what appeared to be a converted bedroom. This was decidedly more utilitarian with solid oak furnishings. Paintings on the walls by Millais and others depicted scenes from Shakespeare. There was a single bed against one wall, but the rest of the room was taken up by a filing cabinet, a heavy chair with a burgundy upholstered seat and arms, and a roll top desk. Holmes, however, first stepped over to the closet making a mental inventory of the clothes therein. He also took note of hats on the top shelf, as well as shoes, and a full set of luggage on the closet floor.

While he was doing that, I was tasked with examining the filing cabinet. My findings were insignificant, as it contained mostly older files which were likely kept for only historical reference.

Satisfied with the closet, Holmes stepped over to the desk. The top was down and locked, but using his picks, he had it open in mere seconds. He went through each of the cubby holes and drawers, examining various papers and notebooks. One file in particular caught his interest. After he scanned its contents he handed it over to me. I opened it to find programs from various theatres and numerous plays. The file itself was labeled, "*Theatrical*". I did not see why he felt it significant.

"Theatrical companies always need investors, Holmes. It's not as lucrative as the stock market, but certain parties do like to support the arts. He probably kept these as a portfolio of sorts to determine which companies were most successful for his clients' investments."

"Oh, I quite agree, Watson," he replied. "That is why I would like to retain that particular file."

"You think an investor whose money went into an unsuccessful play is responsible for Etherege's disappearance?"

"What I think is that there is more to this little drama than meets the eye."

He took two more files, handing them over to me. Then he closed and locked the desk. Before leaving, he also made a cursory examination of the bed, pulling back the covers, checking the bedding, even sitting on the mattress. Standing again, he threw the covers back over the pillows. Marian immediately entered, straightened them, and tucked them smartly back in.

"I believe that is all we need glean at this juncture, Doctor. Let us bid our hostess farewell."

411

This time the lady remained seated and merely let the book drop to her lap as she asked with a sigh, "Did you learn anything, gentlemen?"

"Possibly some helpful data. I shall be taking these files to compare them with papers I'll be examining at your husband's office tonight. I'll see that you are kept informed as to any progress."

"Very, well. Good night, gentlemen."

She went back to her novel and the maid saw us out. As we stood on the pavement hailing a cab, I remarked, "I cannot understand her attitude. She seems almost disinterested in her husband's case."

"What does that tell you?" my companion asked.

"Well," I hesitated over the thoughts that occurred to me. "Either she has completely accepted her husband's fate, or she is somehow involved in his disappearance."

A hansom pulled up, Holmes held the door for me as he said, "Excellent! I have no doubt that Mrs. Etherege has played a significant role in this act."

Chapter IV

He refused to expound any further. We rode in silence to Etherege's office. The constable on duty snapped to attention at our appearance, though Holmes merely waved him to sit back down at his station in the waiting room.

"First of all, Watson," he stated as he crouched in the doorway, "take a close look at these drag marks made by the heels of our solicitor's boots."

I gently lowered myself to the floor where I could get the best angle on the indentations in the carpet. "What am I looking for?"

"Note how the depth isn't consistent. Every eighteen inches or so, there is a slight hump in the track. This tells me that nobody was dragged to the door. Rather, the marks were made by a man dragging a pair of boots along as he moved backwards on his knees. At the end of each pass, he let up to re-position himself and start again. Note that every so often you can still see the indentations made by his knees."

Holmes helped me to my feet, realizing that my war wound was not conducive to this activity. "Now, let us examine that bloodstain again."

We walked back to the safe room and, this time, he didn't require me to kneel. "You saw for yourself that this fluid resembles fresh blood. However, after a week it should not."

He pulled a vial from his coat pocket and poured a small amount about a foot from the original stain. In appearance and consistency it matched perfectly. I sounded him out, "Something tells me that's not human blood with a strange medical condition. What is it?"

"Indulge me, Watson," he replied. "There's more. Wait here one moment."

He went into Etherege's office. Seconds later he stuck his head back out, "Watson, I wish you to pretend that you are Etherege. Come into this office and do what you think he would do if he were just arriving from being out."

I walked in as if I were a businessman coming to work for the day. I took off my overcoat and hat and hung them on the coatrack, which Holmes had emptied, along with my walking stick. I then moved to the desk, pulled out the chair, and sat down. "Did you wish me to go through the motions of working on papers?"

"That won't be necessary, just open the second drawer down on the left."

I did so, noting that this was the drawer with the stain on the bottom. "Is this stain significant?"

"It adds intrigue to the scene. That stain is from gun oil."

"So there was a pistol here in the drawer?"

"Very likely," said my companion.

I could see he was warming to the task and so enquired, "You have a theory. Out with it."

He rubbed his palms slowly together just below his chin while he sat in one of the guest chairs, an upholstered affair with green velvet on a mahogany frame which matched the desk and other furnishings.

"Consider the layout of the items on the desk and the location of the gun. Etherege was obviously left-handed, which begs the question, why did he not use the gun so close at hand? It also explains why the bloodstain landed where it did. He staged it in his mind and didn't take into account that an assailant would likely be right-handed. Now, note the coat rack. What do you see?"

"My hat, overcoat, and stick."

"And what was left behind after our victim's disappearance?"

"His overcoat and umbrella . . . no hat!" I realized.

"Very good. Now, suppose you were going to carry a man out of here. Would you bother to put on his hat?"

"Not likely," I replied.

He nodded and said, "Now, come next door."

We walked into what used to be the younger Etherege's office and Holmes opened the doors to the vanity again. The mirrors reflected our images multiple times. Holmes opened the drawer, then turned to me.

"While the water had evaporated, I did find some dried shaving soap and several hairs on this towel. There was enough to convince me that our

413

missing man had shaved off his moustache. Note also the wear pattern in the rug on this side of the room."

I looked down, noticing that it was far more worn than the rest of the room. I said, "He obviously always came and went from this side of his desk. That would make sense, since this is the side where the closet vanity is located. Being left-handed, coming around this side of the desk would seem natural."

"An excellent surmise, though not quite complete. Now, step over here."

He led me behind the desk, pointing out the marks on the rug which he had noted on our earlier visit, "What do these suggest to you?"

I leaned over my cane, which I had retrieved from the coat rack, and peered at the circular indentations. There were four marks in a rectangular pattern, roughly eighteen-inches-by-six-inches. Too large for a briefcase. Then it struck me.

"A carpetbag?"

"Precisely."

"So you're saying that Etherege staged this disappearance, right down to the fake blood, the abandoned coat, and the pawned briefcase? To what end, and where is he?"

"The method he chose is interesting. As to motive, and his current location, that will require more investigation. I suggest that tomorrow we pay a visit to Judge Shipley. I also need to send out some telegrams tonight. For now, I intend to go through the files he left behind and compare some information with what we've brought with us."

We returned to Etherege's office and pulled files from the cabinets there. Holmes gave me some indication of what to look for. We spent the better part of two hours in a hunt for pertinent data. I was fortunate to find some relevant papers, as did my companion. Together, we managed to compile quite a little scenario – circumstantial, I admit, but suspicious nonetheless.

It was quite late when we returned to Baker Street. Mrs. Hudson, bless her soul, had left us a note indicating that a cold supper was in the kitchen. I prepared a plate for myself. Holmes, as usual when on a case, chose to forego food, going straight to his indexes and newspapers. He also wrote out telegrams to send in the morning. He was still at it when I decided to retire.

As I lay in my bed, contemplating the day's activities, my mind drifted into various possibilities. Not for the first time, I marveled at how Holmes's mind worked to make sense of such variable facts.

414

Chapter V

The next morning I awoke to find Holmes gone off to who knew where. He did leave me a note, stating that he'd asked for a meeting with Judge Shipley at one o'clock and hoped that I would be available.

I requested breakfast from Mrs. Hudson and enjoyed a splendid meal. I was grateful for the fact, as we would likely miss lunch while traveling to Shipley's home. Being Sunday, I had no patients scheduled, nor rounds at St. Bartholomew's Hospital. Thus I settled at my desk and organized the notes I had taken thus far. I was interrupted twice by telegrams addressed to my fellow boarder. I set them on the table next to his favorite chair by the fireplace.

It was on about eleven o'clock when Holmes finally returned. Once removed from his hat and coat, he greeted me heartily, fell into his chair, and took up the flimsies I had set there. He tore open the first. It confirmed that the judge had accepted our meeting. The second was a bit longer. He read it carefully and at last he sat back and crossed long legs. Staring off into the distance, he tapped the telegram against his chin. I was tempted, but refused to interrupt his thoughts. I waited until at last he folded over the paper and placed it into his waistcoat pocket. When he still did not speak, I broached the subject.

"What have you learned? You seem to have a look of satisfaction."

"Pieces are falling into place," he replied. "A plot is developing, but like any good writer, we must gather our inspiration from facts as they come to light. I believe that the Judge may provide another spotlight or two."

At one o'clock we arrived at a stately home not far from that shared by Etherege and his wife. This one was more masculine in its furnishings and décor. Oak paneling prevailed in the interior. A bearskin rug lay before the hearth. Mounted heads of deer and boar adorned the walls of the judge's den, which also featured the Shipley coat of arms with its black diamond against a white shield. A gun case stood off to one side of the judge's desk, filled with shotguns, rifles, and a pair of pistols.

Judge Shipley sat behind his desk, commanding the scene as if it were his courtroom. He didn't stand upon our entrance. Instead, he bade us to sit down. We settled into black, leather-bound wingback chairs with brass buttons.

"Mr. Holmes, Dr. Watson," he intoned with his stentorian voice. "How are you progressing in finding my son-in law's killer?"

Holmes folded his hands in his lap as he crossed his legs, defying the formality of the situation. "I have been tracing several leads, your

415

Lordship. I need not remind you that no body has been found, so there is still hope that he is alive."

Shipley sniffed, "Come now, Holmes. Even though circumstantial, surely the bloodstain, the coat found by the river, and the pawned briefcase point to Andrew's demise."

My companion tilted his head in acknowledgement and replied, "Strong indicators, certainly, but not proof by any means. I presume no ransom demand has been forthcoming?"

"None at all. What leads have you been following?"

I was curious as to how Holmes would answer Shipley's question. He chose to be vaguely promising, "I'm looking into disgruntled clients and other possible enemies. Not all of his investments or legal advice on behalf of his clients have been successful. I have also gone as far as contacting Cambridge to ensure no old school grudges may be surfacing."

"Cambridge!" cried the Judge, "Hah! You're wasting your time there, Holmes. He was a highly popular student, an excellent half-back. He even performed with the Amateur Dramatic Club. No, you should stick to your disgruntled client theory, or look for a criminal gang."

"Do you know which members of his club that he was close to?"

"The Garrick? I don't recall him being particularly close to anyone. I believe he has mentioned a fellow named Thomas, but I don't know if that was a first or last name."

I made of note of that while Holmes asked his next question.

"What about his finances, your Grace?" asked the detective. "Could he have made a poor investment or borrowed from the wrong people?"

"Impossible! He inherited a fortune as well as a successful business, which he has grown even greater. Marrying my daughter also brought him a very substantial dowry. No, I cannot imagine he has any money trouble. I would have heard something, especially from Millicent. She can be very – shall we say – *boisterous* in letting her feelings be known."

"I take it she has never been in want for anything?" said Holmes.

The Judge acted offended as he replied, "Certainly not! I've never denied her any desire that could be afforded. That's what money and success are for, after all."

"And their marriage is quite happy, I presume?"

"Well, of course. He is a successful young man and keeps her in the lifestyle to which she is accustomed."

"Forgive me for being so bold, Judge. What will become of her, if Andrew is indeed deceased?"

The Judge hesitated slightly at the thought, as if he were truly contemplating the full meaning of it for his daughter for the first time. Then he replied, "She will be a wealthy young widow. I will certainly see

416

to her care, but I'm sure there will be no shortage of suitors after a decent mourning period."

He sat up straighter. If he had his gavel, I'm sure he would have pounded it on the desk as he said, "You need to find his body or his killer before that can happen, Holmes. So, I suggest you get to it!"

We took that as an order of dismissal and left him with assurances that all our efforts would be concentrated on his case.

As we stood on the pavement out front attempting to hail a cab, I asked my companion, "I'm sure you have good reason for not voicing your theory that Etherege is still alive. May I ask why?"

"For the same reason that the police theory is based upon circumstantial evidence," he replied. "My theory has yet to be proved, though I believe it more viable than Smith's. Still, without absolute proof, I prefer not to raise anyone's hopes. The coat by the water may have been a plant by Etherege, but it may also have been the result of a falling out with a co-conspirator. The only thing I am sure of is that Etheredge left that office alive and deliberately."

A four-wheeler came by. Holmes bid the driver to take us to the Garrick Club. We were delivered to Drury Lane, where we disembarked in front of the massive two-storey structure with its facade noted by its long rows of arched windows and a large, oaken front door. Since its founding in 1831, it had remained one of the most distinguished clubs in all London. Membership was limited to actors, lawyers, and journalists. As we entered, Holmes stopped to note its wall-mounted heraldry with the motto stating "*All the World's a Stage*".

I noted his look and commented, "Recalling your days in the theatre?"

He shook his head with a slight smile, replying, "Just ruminating on the truth of that statement, Watson."

A porter came up to us and asked our business. Holmes questioned if Thomas Kent was about. The gentleman asked us to wait while he enquired. It was only a minute or two when he returned with a tall string-bean of a fellow. Holmes introduced me to Mr. Kent, a reporter with *The Daily Telegraph*. The gentleman took us off to a side room where we could talk in private. Once settled in some chairs around a card table in a quiet corner where we would not be overheard, he asked in a high, reedy voice, "Have you a story for me, Holmes, or are you seeking information today?"

"Information for now," replied my friend. "And confidentiality is paramount. I do promise you though, that you will receive an exclusive from me at some future date."

"Ah, how intriguing," replied the journalist as he took out his cigarette case and offered it to each of us. Holmes accepted, so I did as well.

417

Once we had shared a match, Kent continued, with an easy smile, "Well, you've always been as good as your word. What can I tell you, that the great Sherlock Holmes does not already know?"

Holmes smiled and replied, "You are aware of the missing solicitor, Andrew Etherege, of course. My investigation has led me here to seek out a friend of his named 'Thomas'. I believe that man is you, and I have some questions."

Kent paused, taking the cigarette from between his lips. He rubbed the thumb of his other hand across his moustache, then curled his fist, with the knuckle of the index finger under his nose and his thumb rubbing under his chin as his elbow rested on the chair's arm. He stalled for time by taking another puff of his cigarette, then flicked ashes into the receptacle on the table.

Finally he spoke, "I admit, I do know of Etherege, but only as a fellow club member. After all, he is a lawyer and I'm a theatre critic, who only dabbles in news stories when someone like you brings one my way. What could I possibly tell you?"

Holmes leaned across the table and looked him directly in the eye. "I believe quite a bit, sir. Let me start with a piece of information I have discovered: *Cambridge, A.D.C.*"

Kent looked to the ceiling, took a deep breath, then, stubbed out his cigarette. "I'm sorry, Holmes. Just as I would not break a confidence with you, I'll not break one with him."

He started to rise, but the detective waved him back to his seat, "Two minutes, Kent. Let me tell you what I have already deduced. At that point, you can decide whether to let me help your friend, or leave me to expose the truth on my own, which shall surely lead to scandal and possibly incarceration."

Kent sat back down. Holmes poured out a tale which I now understood. I berated myself for not having assembled all the clues my companion had pointed out along the way.

When finished, he extinguished his cigarette and held an open palm out to the journalist, "Well, what shall it be?"

Chapter VI

This time Kent did stand and looked down upon us. "I will not break his confidence, Holmes. I will convey to him what you know, as well as what you propose, then leave it up to him. I want your word as a gentleman not to follow me, or report this conversation to the police. I will meet you at Baker Street tomorrow morning at nine o'clock with his answer."

418

Holmes stood and shook the journalist's hand in agreement. Kent showed us to the door. We obtained a cab for home.

The next morning, as we sat expectantly before the morning fire at precisely nine o'clock, Mrs. Hudson announced that we had visitors. While I wondered at the plural, Holmes gave that quick smile of his, that one can miss if one blinks, and nodded for her to show them up.

We stood by the entry as our landlady led the gentlemen to our door. She asked if we would care for coffee or tea. Holmes looked to Kent's companion who bowed to her, responding, "Tea would be lovely, madam. Thank you."

I looked upon the gentleman. He was the right size and weight for Andrew Etherege, but the resemblance stopped there. He was clean shaven with long, straight black hair with sideburns. He wore tinted, silver-framed eyeglasses and a grey suit, which, most certainly, did not come from Saville Row. He also carried a large manila envelope.

Holmes extended his hand to each man. Without hesitation, he called Etherege by name. I also shook their hands in welcome. My friend waved toward the sofa by the fire as we took up the chairs opposite them.

Etherege got right down to business. "Thomas tells me you know everything, Mr. Holmes. Before I share my story, I should like to know how you discovered my secret."

Holmes folded his hands together, elbows on the armchair, index fingers steepled just below his chin as he gazed upon the solicitor. "Very well, sir," He finally answered letting his hands fall into his lap and crossed a leg over his knee.

"To start with, there weren't enough footprints upon the carpet to indicate anyone other than the police, the doctor, you, and your wife had been in your office since its last cleaning. Then there was the blood. You used stage blood to make sure you had enough to indicate a serious injury. Since I was called in a week after your disappearance, it should not have retained the bright red color and smooth texture. Your gun was missing from its accustomed place in your desk drawer, yet there were no indications that you used it to defend yourself. You faked the drag marks of your boot heels on the carpet by having to stop periodically, thus not having them be of consistent depth. I also found evidence that you had shaved your moustache. Finally, you left your overcoat and umbrella but took your hat. An unlikely action of a kidnapper."

Etherege spoke up, "My hat was supposed to be found with my coat."

"It was not," replied the detective. "Most likely it was blown away by river breezes."

419

Mrs. Hudson arrived with her tea tray at that moment. I poured for all of us. With cups in hand, Holmes continued his summary.

"Now convinced that your abduction was a prevarication, I began to look for motive. Examination of papers left in your office and home led me to believe that you had created a bank account under a false identity, then transferred a significant amount of funds and bonds to that new institution. I also noted that the vast majority of your cases were in a state of completion or close enough that they could easily be taken up by another solicitor. I commend you on your loyalty to your clients."

Etherege saluted with his cup, "My clients did not deserve to suffer for my situation. I made it as easy as possible for them to carry on without me."

Holmes nodded. "In your old office, there was a wear pattern to the carpet along the side of the room where the closet vanity was located and in front of the vanity itself. The larger mirrors told me another story. You are not a vain man, but you felt a need to observe your appearance. The most likely reason is that you were contemplating a change in career to one that required you to project a specific presence. If you were going to become a barrister, where you would be required to appear in court, that might explain it. However, the pacing up and down on that side of the room and the change in your appearance told me a different story. When I went to your home and discovered the file on theatrical productions and the Shakespearean paintings on the wall of your study, I felt I was on the right track. I wired to Cambridge. Thus, I discovered your participation in the Amateur Drama Club. This confirmed to me that your pacing was the result of your process of memorizing lines."

"If you've been to my home, I assume you met Millicent?" he asked.

"Yes, I also noted the condition of the bed in your study. It is far too worn to be merely a daybed or a sickbed."

"Couples often sleep in different rooms, Mr. Holmes," replied Etherege. "Especially if one of them is a prodigious snorer."

I noted that he didn't indicate which one. Recalling Mrs. Etherege's strident voice, I could easily conclude to whom he was referring.

"I also noted that after six years of marriage, you have no children."

Etherege stiffened, "I prefer not to discuss intimate matters with you, Mr. Holmes. Infer what you will, I'll not speak of such things except to her alone."

"As you wish, sir," said Holmes, retreating diplomatically. "Regardless, I determined you wished to leave your present situation behind to embark on a career in theatre. Judge Shipley recalled that you had a friend at the Garrick named 'Thomas'. I have known Mr. Kent for several years. If he was not the Thomas I sought, he would likely know who was. I questioned him accordingly, and here we are."

Etherege finished his tea with a gulp, setting it down on the table. "Thank you, Mr. Holmes. At least I know I did enough to fool the police. I hadn't counted on the Judge calling you in.

"My intention was to let Millicent twist in the wind for years until she could legally have me declared dead. It was fitting for what she has put me through. It would also have saved any other poor fool from falling into her clutches until, perhaps, she mellowed with age. You have made that impossible. Thus, I am forced to take another tack."

He pulled some papers from the manila envelope and flipped to the last page. "This is my declaration of divorce, gentlemen. I intend to sign it, having you two sign as witnesses. Then you may deliver it to her to make it legally binding. She is entitled to none of my savings or income and is wealthy in her own right, thanks to her father spoiling her all these years.

"I am sailing for New York today to pursue my new career. I would appreciate your delaying delivery until it is too late for her to ask the Judge to stop me."

Holmes leaned on his elbow to one side and placed an index finger to his lips as he considered Etherege's proposal. I, on the other hand, asked a question. "What of your marriage vows, sir?"

The gentleman, having placed the papers on the table before him in preparation for signing, leaned forward with his elbows on his knees as he replied, "In all your experience, Dr. Watson, have you not run across a situation where a woman was forced into an arranged marriage with a man who was totally wrong for her? Did you not feel sorry for her, being required to endure this lifetime of unhappiness?"

"Well, yes, but . . . ."

"It's the same thing here, Doctor. Only in this case, *I* am the one who is stuck in a loveless marriage and forced to carry on in my father's footsteps. The advantage I have is that, as a man, I have a legal right to put an end to it. I am doing so at last. She will be free to pursue someone who can make her happy, if such a person exists. I will be free to pursue my own dreams. Perhaps even find a true love. In any case, it puts an end to a bad situation. Is that not reasonable and best for all, sir?"

I looked at him and could see the sincerity in his eyes. I glanced at Holmes, who merely nodded, then I stood and retrieved pen and ink from the desk across the room.

After the departure of Etherege and Kent, I asked Holmes, "How long should we wait?"

421

"It matters not, Watson," he replied. "First, we must report this to Inspector Smith so he can be relieved of his search. Then, there will be plenty of time to inform Mrs. Etherege.

The trip to the Yard and finding Inspector Smith took the better part of an hour, as he was in a meeting on another matter. He was relieved to discover that Holmes had found Etherege alive. An unsolved murder would not reflect well on his record. He was sorely disappointed that we didn't have the name of the ship Etherege would be sailing upon. He felt duty-bound to curtail a matter of family abandonment. Holmes merely pointed out there would not likely be many ships sailing for New York that day. If he hurried, perhaps he could still catch the rascal.

As we left the Yard and headed for Mrs. Etherege's home, I said to my friend, "I noted that you neglected to mention Etherege's change in name and appearance. I presume that was a purposeful omission?"

"It matters not, Watson," he replied. "Even with a description, Smith's first effort will be to send a telegram to check the passenger manifest and stop Etherege from boarding. He will not find Etherege's name. Assuming Etherege is sailing at all, it will be under his new identity, which only we know, due to the bank account we discovered. There is only one ship sailing for New York today. Smith will be too late to stop it. Kent knew that when he set the time for our meeting. He will barely reach it in time."

"You said *assuming he is sailing?*"

My companion smiled, "Etherege has been very clever throughout, although some of his execution has been less than perfect. It wouldn't surprise me if his statement was meant merely to throw us off, in case we should not keep our promise. With his new look, name, and profession, he could go anywhere in England. He could even remain here in London, with no one the wiser, save his friend Kent. If he chooses a stage name on top of his new identity, the only trace we would have to him would be through his bank account. It would not surprise me if he changes his name and bank again, just to keep us at bay."

We arrived at the Etherege home at half-past-eleven. We were told by Marian, the housekeeper, that Mrs. Etherege had gone out to a luncheon and would not be returning until two o'clock.

As we stood there, I asked Holmes if we should deliver the papers to the Judge.

He replied that these were a private communique, and only Mrs. Etherege could decide who should see it. "Besides, Watson, Judge Shipley is likely to be on his bench all day. You know how busy the courts are on Mondays."

Thus we left the papers with Marian and returned to Baker Street. The next day, very early, we were set upon in our sitting room at breakfast by Inspector Smith and Judge Shipley. The elderly jurist was furious, demanding Smith arrest us for aiding and abetting Etherege's escape.

Holmes, still in his dressing gown, asked me to ring for Mrs. Hudson. She soon joined us. He then went into his defense. "First of all, your Lordship, we were engaged merely to find proof of what happened to your son-in-law. At this we were successful. I have every right to bill you for my services, though I have decided to forego my charges in this instance. I am not the official police, and therefore had no power to arrest Mr. Etherege. I remind you that he still had his pistol as well as a rather large bodyguard was with him. Isn't that right, Mrs. Hudson?"

As he said this, he raised his palm several inches above his head, indicating to her that he meant Kent's height, not his bulk. She took the hint and readily assured our accuser, "Oh it's true, sir. He barely fit through the door. I'd certainly not want to confront such a man myself."

"Thank you, Mrs. Hudson," said Holmes. "You may go."

He now turned back to our visitors, "As you can see sir, we signed as witnesses under a threat that hung in the air like a choking cloud. I also remind you, as soon as they left us, we immediately made our way to Scotland Yard to inform Inspector Smith. Afterward, we set out and delivered the papers to your daughter. We have acted in good faith throughout. Should you persist in this false arrest, I will see to it that every newspaper in town be informed of your daughter's situation. I have no wish to expose her scandal, but neither do I desire to sit in jail, even temporarily, for doing what I was tasked to do."

Fuming, the Judge sputtered as he tried to form a reply. Finally he merely said to his companion, "Come along, Smith. We'll arrange to have the bastard arrested when he lands in New York. Then we'll see, Mr. Sherlock Holmes, just how true your testimony is."

He stomped out with the inspector on his heels. Holmes walked over to the landing watching them descend the stairs and storm out the front door. Then, he called to Mrs. Hudson for a fresh pot of coffee.

As he returned to the breakfast table, I commented, "Very clever use of words, Holmes. All true enough, but not accurately portraying the situation. I was wondering about your use of the word 'threat', however."

"Ah, Watson, recall that I did not say Etherege threatened us. It was the threat of our exposing him to which I referred. Dear, Mrs. Hudson!" he cried as she brought forth a steaming pot of coffee. "You were quite the heroine this morning. Thank you."

"You're welcome, I'm sure, Mr. Holmes," she replied with a wink and left us to finish our breakfast.

423

Two months later, Holmes and I had heard nothing more from Smith nor Shipley. We were taking in a performance of *Hamlet* when Holmes nudged me with his elbow, leaned over and whispered, "Observe Polonius, Doctor."

I took up my opera glasses and trained them upon the evil counselor. Even with his stage makeup on, I recognized the fellow and looked back at my friend who merely replied quietly, "All the world's a stage, Watson. Our friend has found his part in it."

"I came to you, sir, because I heard of you from Mrs. Etherege, whose husband you found so easy when the police and everyone had given him up for dead."

– Mary Sutherland
"A Case of Identity"

The Dundas Separation Case
by Kevin P. Thornton

Through the early part of the Twentieth Century, I didn't see my friend Sherlock Holmes as often as I would have liked. Since he had gone off to be a Bee Squire on the Sussex Downs, our lives perforce intersected much less than before when we had shared rooms in Baker Street. I had my own life and responsibilities in London, and Holmes had taken to cultivating honey, altogether less exciting than what had once been our shared existence. Consequently, I was delighted to receive a letter from him inviting me to visit.

"*I have need to go to Arundel on any Wednesday in the next two months for the midweek market,*" he wrote. "*If you can find the time to visit, it would be good to see you again, my dear friend.*"

That was all the invitation I needed. I rearranged my affairs to create some time to be away, answered Holmes in the affirmative, and departed the following Tuesday.

I took the LB&SCR train (London, Brighton, and South Coast Railway) to Horsham, changed to the Littlehampton all-stopper, and soon found myself in Arundel. Unlike trips north, which frequently trundled through industrial pallor and smoke-laden cities, it was a pleasant trip down to the south coast. We travelled through the gentle Surrey farmlands before crossing the county border into the wonderfulness of the Sussex Downs, much of which was unchanged since time immemorial. All told the journey was scarcely more than two hours, and a delightful manner to while away the time.

Holmes, now firmly settled into his life in the wilds, met me at the station dressed in a robust tweed suit, both well-made and well worn. He looked hale and hearty, and if he caught me giving his outward health a professional glance, he said nothing of it. "We will be staying at The Swan, down by the harbour and near the site of tomorrow's market. I have not stayed there before. Normally when I come to town for business, I like to get back to my bees on the same day. However, it seems right to indulge ourselves a little. The *Kimpton's Guide* reports it has good accommodations for travellers, wines and spirits of superior quality, and a kitchen that serves excellent food. I've also heard the landlord has an 'in' at the inn with some murky people. As a result, there is nearly always a tickled trout or a well-hung pheasant available. If you can stand the immorality of it, we shall dine well tonight, and in the morning, we shall peruse the market before we go on to my home. There is a man putting up some excellent honey from a valley on the other side of Tortington, and I must have a jar or two to analyse his work."

"And who watches over your bees while you are away?"

"They fend for themselves, mostly," said Holmes, "but there is a young girl, a neighbour, who will mind them when I am away. Come my friend, let us repair to the hotel and dine and talk. How is London? I miss it terribly and yet I also never want to return to it. Such is the dichotomy of life."

As Holmes had promised, we ate well. We talked easily, as old friends do. I was glad to see him so well and so outgoing, which was unusual for the man I remembered as the great detective. He told tales of bees and the quiet life, making it all seem so glamourous all the while complaining of the tedium. "Had I not discovered bees to keep my mind occupied," he said at one point, "I would have withered away. As it is, I am finding some fascinating uses for honey that may well revolutionize medicine."

I admit in all candour to drifting away somewhat during this part of our discourse, returning only when the landlord joined us for an after-dinner drink, and Holmes proceeded to regale us with an exposé of how poachers tickle for trout.

"It is an art," he told us. "I had thought it to be an old wife's tale until I chanced upon a poacher down on his luck who offered to teach me how it's done. As you can imagine, I was delighted to speculate on his skills, and it was well worth the coin. He took me to a stream where he'd had notable success and, as we stood back from the water, he described what he was about to do."

"'Now then, Mister Holmes,' he said, 'you need to find a spot where the fish'll rest on their way upstream, generally under a rock that diverts the flow so they can take a breather. Then you come up behind them as quiet as you can, lie down on the water's edge, roll your sleeve up and gently put your hand, palm upwards, under the tail of the fish. Then you gently stroke the underside, all the while moving slowly forward until your hand reaches the gills. Then you hoicks it up onto the river bank and club it over the 'ead.'"

"That's very fanciful," I said and the landlord smiled.

"It works," he replied, "Otherwise you'd have had roast mutton this evening. You can thank Squire Holmes here for the delights of your meal." He stepped away to the kitchen and I looked at Holmes in horror.

"If you have need of supplementing your income in this way, you could have asked me for help."

426

"Stuff and nonsense, Watson. I did tickle for the trout, and though the Duke of Norfolk seems to own all of this part of Sussex, I had no need to poach from him. There is part of his trout stream that meanders off his land for a hundred yards or so and it is there I practiced my skills."

"But why?" I asked.

"For the joy of life. It is an idea you should try sometime."

We retired to the lounge. Holmes's words had stung a little, but they had also played into my hand. Although I was always delighted to see my friend, I had come on this trip with an ulterior motive.

"I do have a hobby that brings me the same *joie de vivre* as your beekeeping and nocturnal activities," I said "There was a time when I would quite happily sit and write of your adventures, telling your stories in my own manner, and delighting that they were published and enjoyed. I have – for obvious reasons – not done much of this since your retirement, but I was re-reading one of your cases recently when I realized that there was mention of an inquiry you handled without my involvement. I carried on looking through the tales and found that there were many such instances. I was hoping that if I could trouble your memory for a few of these. If I could hear, in your own words, anything you could tell me about these adventures, I would go home to London fuelled with inspiration to write more."

"Watson, my dear old friend and companion. Many is the time you stood by when I needed your strong arm and steady aim. Even though I would normally detest such regurgitations of my investigations, I shall nevertheless do what I can to make you happy. I assume you have a couple in mind."

"As it happens, I do. When I wrote the story that was published as 'A Case of Identity', I mentioned in it the headlines in the paper of that day." I reached into my pocket.

"No matter," said Holmes and he began to quote verbatim from the beginning of the fourth paragraph.

I smiled and shook my head. "I can quite understand your thinking so." I said. "Of course, in your position of unofficial adviser and helper to everybody who is absolutely puzzled, throughout three continents, you are brought in contact with all that is strange and bizarre. But here – " I picked up the morning paper from the ground. " – let us put it to a practical test. Here is the first heading upon which I come. 'A Husband's Cruelty to His Wife.' There is half-a-column of print, but I know without reading it that it is all perfectly familiar to me. There is, of course, the other woman, the drink, the push, the blow, the bruise, the sympathetic sister or landlady. The crudest of writers could invent nothing more crude."

"Indeed, your example is an unfortunate one for your argument," said Holmes, taking the paper and glancing his eye down it. "This is the Dundas separation case, and, as it happens, I was engaged in clearing up some small points in connection with it. The husband was a teetotaler, there was no other woman, and the conduct complained of was that he had drifted into the habit of winding up every meal by taking out his false teeth and hurling them at his wife, which, you will allow, is not an action likely to occur to the imagination of the average story-teller."

"Holmes, that is extraordinary. I don't know what to say. I knew you had read my stories – how else could you disparage them so – but that you can quote one so readily, and the exact one that I wished to discuss. Pray tell how this came about. This is the utmost in wizardry."

"Sadly not," said Holmes, "although I wish it were so, as I see how it would delight you. It is nothing more than the application of logic. I had noticed you were writing and publishing less than before, and I deduced, correctly as you have just confirmed, the reason why. Had you not mentioned the topic, I may very well have brought it up anyway, to encourage you to write again. As to the Dundas separation case, I looked through your tales and made a decision based on how much you had mentioned of an unspoken case. Many references were just a castaway line, but there were three that seemed to be likely candidates. This was one of them, and I found myself thinking as you would Watson – wondering what to write that would be the most fascinating. As it turns out, I chose correctly. As to memorizing the relevant passage – well that was no more than an intellectual exercise. I find as I get older that I devise these little tests to make sure my mind remains sharp. Remembering the relevant passages from the three incidents I identified was a way of warming up the little grey cells."

"What were the other two?" I asked.

"I may enlighten you later. Let us see how the time passes in the telling of this tale."

Holmes began thus . . .

"There are various parts of the empire named after Lord Dundas. The first Viscount Melville, as he was also known, was in his time a very important and powerful man. Even though he barely travelled to any of the places that honoured him, he was recognized quite by the people in power as a means of currying favour with him. In Upper Canada, for that is the relevant part of the world for this story, there were several sycophants who wished to be in his good books. As a result, two counties and a parish, a military road, a street in Toronto, an island in British Columbia, and another in the frozen north were all named after him. There was also a town, strategically placed at a control point of the trading route from west to east, named Dundas. Though there is no record of the Viscount or his descendants ever using these geographic locations as access points to the darker recesses of the empire, others were less scrupulous."

"Is there not a Clan Dundas?" I asked him

"Indeed," said Holmes. "And even though it is not the most common name in Scotland, it is frequent enough that another, unrelated Dundas, Arthur John of East Kilbride in Lanarkshire, was delighted to find such familiar names when he went to the land shortly after the Confederation of their nation in 1867. He and his family settled in the Canadian hamlet of Kilbride at first, before realizing that it would do his business opportunities no harm if he were to make his home in the community whose name he shared."

"So Dundas went to Dundas," I said.

"The Dundas family moved to the gateway of the Great Lakes: Dundas, Ontario. Arthur John, his wife Helen, and their four sons – Brian, Francis, John and Paul. They are important to the story, as you will soon see."

"You have become a better storyteller, Holmes, but do hurry along."

"At first Dundas was successful," he continued, "buying low and selling higher. Canada was a country rich in the resources needed to build an empire, and the local traders' assumptions of his probity due to his surname did his business no harm. In fairness, Arthur John did what he could to honour such assumptions. He traded fairly and honestly, but he was nearly undone twice by unscrupulous merchants at the London Docks. Only the loyalty of his suppliers in Canada allowed him to survive, but Arthur Dundas knew that another failure would end his business. He needed a man he could trust in London. Naturally enough, he thought of his only other family member, his younger brother Andrew."

"This would be the Dundas of the false teeth," I said. "That is the part that most puzzles me. Indeed, it was on the hope you would explain why a man repeatedly used such an item to attack his wife that made me think of writing this tale."

"Patience, Watson, all will be revealed. There was significant age gap between the two brothers, but Arthur knew Andrew was the man for him, and in truth Andrew needed the help. He had been in Brazil trying to make a living trading in rubber and coffee, and while he had managed to acquire a wife there, he had also been hit with a disease that waylaid him and had periodontal implications."

"A-ha!" I said. "You are setting the scene quite nicely Holmes."

"Patently," he said. "And the exposition continues. Did you know that dentures are made from many different substances, most but not all of which are brittle. Wood, resins, porcelain, for example, as well as the one exception, vulcanite, which you may well know as a form of hardened rubber."

"Excellent," I said.

"Anyway, the years passed, the Dundas families did well, and every now and then Arthur would send a son over to stay with Andrew while completing his education. Poor Andrew and his wife were never able to have children, so they gladly opened their home to their nephews, and Andrew and Maria endeavoured to set a fine table, especially of an evening where he encouraged his nephews in the Catholic pieties of his youth. The boys had all been brought up in the church, but they were not as faithful as their uncle and aunt. They tolerated his wishes though, because they were fond of their uncle, and he never pressed too hard if they missed a visit to church on Sunday, or were late for the family rosary night.

"The two younger sons, John and Paul seemed set to join the family business. Both travelled to England and indentured in their trades, eventually qualifying, John in accounting and the Paul as a lawyer. The third son, Francis was a slight disappointment to Arthur, as he became a priest, and while his uncle was delighted, his father would rather have put his brains into the family business, as he was by far the smartest of them all."

"You mentioned only three of the sons. What happened to the oldest?"

"Yes," said Holmes. "At the time he was considered the wastrel, and although no less hard-working than the others, his field of expertise was *magic*."

"Magic?" I said. "There is no such thing."

"And yet the music halls and theatres of London were, and no doubt still are, full of its practitioners. Come, Watson, must you take everything so seriously? Brian, the oldest son, came to London to apprentice with a third-rate prestidigitator. Then he moved up to a second-rate card trickster, a fairly well-known illusionist, and finally a top ranked showman. If I were to tell you the name Brian Dundas plies his trade as now, you would be astounded. Although considered the failure of the family back then, he now only needs to perform a dozen times a year to live a lifestyle of grace

430

and ease. He frequently plays Monte Carlo, Berlin, and New York, and is the favourite of Kings, Queens, Presidents, and Prime Ministers. Now tell me, Watson – have you worked out the mystery yet?"

I confessed I had not.

"Very well," he said, "but do stop me when you have it all. The lives of the Dundas families would have proceeded happily, no doubt, had Arthur Dundas not enjoyed his drink, His wife, perhaps recognising his weakness, always managed to keep him reined in. Arthur Dundas loved his wife, so he behaved himself and was seen as a man of rectitude and sobriety within the business world of the Upper Canada gentry. And none of this might have happened had she not taken ill one winter and died."

"That is a terrible time for any man," I said.

"Indeed," said Holmes. "Within a year Arthur Dundas had nearly run the business into the ground. His consumption of alcohol, exacerbated by his inability to cope with the death of his wife, was driving the business into ruin. With his four sons all in various stages of their tertiary education in the mother country, the managers of the Canadian side of the Dundas business laid out the dire straits that the company faced in a missive to the sons and heirs. Dundas Trading (Canada) needed an influx off money to stave off the wolves at the door, and it needed the sons to step up and take over."

"What of the kindly traders?" I asked. "All those who had banded together and helped the company through its early days."

"The camaraderie that is shown to a struggling neophyte businessman," said Holmes, "rarely resurfaces when his struggles from the top of the trading world are made manifest. Those clucking mother hens who nurtured him in his beginnings turned into hovering buzzards as his star fell. The four brothers came together – priest, lawyer, magician, and accountant – and resolved there was only one course of action. They approached their uncle, who treated them as a joke."

"Indeed," I said.

"Even though they explained the situation and the importance of timely intervention, and begged him for financial aid to prop up the Canadian end of the business until such time as they could gain control of the situation, he turned them down. We can only surmise that either his piety or his business nous prevented him from helping out his drunken brother, even though to do nothing would ruin their combined business. I heard during my investigation that it could also have been that the plan the brothers presented seemed flighty and unrealistic. Let us not forget that none of them were yet proven in their respective fields. Andrew Dundas may simply not have wanted to throw good money after bad. Whatever the case, and for whatever the reason, he refused them."

431

"Did you ever find out the reason?" I said.

"No," said Holmes, "because it was only the result of that meeting, not the content, that had any relevance to my investigation. All that happened afterwards was because he refused to help his family, and that was all I needed to know in order that I might unravel the mystery."

Holmes took a moment to light his pipe. "It was an unusual case," he continued. "When my client came to me, it was clear who the perpetrators were likely to be. The real question was how they caused it to happen. Andrew Dundas appeared to be going mad, and I needed to determine how it was happening, and prevent it."

"How did you come to be involved?"

"I was asked to study the behaviour of Andrew Dundas and the effects they were having on his marriage."

"Who was your client?" I said.

"His wife Maria. She came to me and laid out the entire story as she knew it. It was an intriguing tale. She was strong-willed woman of Portuguese descent. Her family had made a go of ranching in Brazil, so there was some considerable resilience to her. I can remember our conversation as if it were yesterday . . . ."

"Mister Holmes," she said, "my husband is a good and honourable man. He is a regular churchgoer and communicant and a diligent and hardworking soul – at least up until this last month."

"And what has changed?"

"Since his nephews came to him for help with their father's situation and he turned them down, the atmosphere has been difficult. We have treated these four young men as if they were our own sons, welcoming them to London and our homes. We were so proud when Francis was ordained a priest, equally when John received his accounting papers, and Paul was accepted to the Bar. We even supported Brian in his career and lifestyle on the stage and have seen his talents bloom. Not only is he a prestidigitator of note, but he has a side show in mesmerism, and while I do not fully approve of such malarkey, Brian is happy. They all seemed to be doing so well – up until this last month."

"Please explain how things have changed."

"When they told us of the problems facing their business in Canada and their father's waywardness following his wife' death, I thought my husband would help them and was surprised when he refused.

"Initially life was tense in the household. My husband encouraged his nephews to go back to Canada and help their father seek professional help. The consensus of opinion among the four of them was that without the necessary funding there was nothing left to go back to. I know they went

432

to the City, separately and together, to try and raise the money. They had no luck. The first question from all parties referred to their successful uncle. Because he was reluctant to reinvest in the Canadian arm of Dundas trading, this reluctance shut the doors to all conventional forms of investment. Thereafter the atmosphere in the house was charged, as if there was an internal war going on. On the one hand, my husband blithely carried on as if there was naught the matter. The stares and barely disguised anger of his nephews were as water sliding off a swan's feathers. My nephews did little to disguise their enmity – so much so that after some days of this I addressed them all sharply at the dinner table and told them that while they would always be welcome in our house, they would need to be polite and civil. This last seemed to help, and after a day or two of neutrality, I was pleased to see them trying to behave as if nothing was wrong. Indeed, Brian ventured up to visit his uncle in his office, and they spent several hours together.

"Do you know the nature of their conversations?" Holmes asked.

"No," Maria Dundas replied. "I was just glad life was returning to normal. Or so I thought."

"What happened next?"

"It has always been our habit to have a breakfast buffet as the schedules of the men vary, and while I would like for us all to sit together and eat, it was nigh impossible in the mornings. Similarly, most of them are not even in the house for the midday meal. Consequently, I insisted that we all sit together for the evening meal insofar as possible and I tried to make it formal. We dressed for dinner, and as a Catholic household we said our traditional prayers of grace both before and after the meal.

"About a week after the enforced rapprochement, I asked Father Francis to intone the prayer at the end of dinner, which is usually the signal that all may rise and depart. He had barely finished when I felt a sharp pain on my chest. I looked down and right there in front of me were my husband's false teeth.

"My first thought was that they had sprung from his mouth by accident. It had never happened before, but the mind tries to rationalize, does it not? Later I asked one of the maids what had happened, and she told me that my husband had taken them out of his mouth and flung them at me so that they bounced off my chest and landed on the table. I can tell you, Mister Holmes, that I was surprised and hurt. My husband has never been violent to me, not once in all the years of our marriage. For him to assault me so, and in front of family and the servants . . . well it was scandalous. Not to mention all the fine china and the Waterford crystal he very nearly damaged.

"It's a fine throw," said Holmes. "Across the length of a table. Your husband played cricket, I assume. Did he explain himself later?"

"Not to my satisfaction. When I asked him, he seemed mystified, as if he couldn't remember it."

"What happened then?"

"Nothing until the next night. After dinner, he threw his teeth at me again. This time they bounced off my forehead. I was trembling with anger and I picked up his teeth, marched to the other end of the table, held them in front of his face, and shouted at him."

"What did he do?" said Holmes.

"He took his teeth off me and put them back into his mouth, as if nothing had happened."

"How long has he had these dentures? Are they uncomfortable?"

"I suspect not," said Maria, "as they are his first pair, and the ones he always seems to return to. After he was sick, these dentures were the only ones easily available in Brazil. They are made of rubber, and thank God for that. If he had been throwing around his expensive teeth, they would likely have shattered by now."

"How long did this go on?"

"It is still happening every night. The only difference is I have learned to duck. Now I have my nephew Father Francis looking into an institution where we can place my husband. He says that such behaviour is often the first sign of madness. Oh, Mister Holmes, please can you help me? Every day, my husband sits at table as if nothing is wrong, but I feel that I am losing him."

Holmes opened his eyes and looked at me. I was willing to bet that his remembrance was near verbatim, even after all these years.

"Do you see it yet, Watson? I have given you all the pieces."

"I believe I see some of the picture. It was the nephews who were responsible for the events. I assume they wanted to have their uncle declared incompetent. Then they could use Dundas Trading in London to rescue Dundas Trading in Canada."

"Correct my friend. Your perspicacity is finally developing into a useful tool."

I smiled at this. Every time I thought my friend mellowed, he reminded me of his talent for backhanded compliments.

"Tell me the rest."

With Mrs. Dundas's connivance, we organized that one of the staff would be away for a couple of days, and it was arranged that I would drape myself in servile disguise and take his place. That way I could see how they triggered this behaviour, and find a means to prevent it. It was

434

apparent already that they were not totally evil young men. They had hatched a complicated and sophisticated plot to gain control of their uncle's business without killing him, when doing so would have been quicker and achieved the same result. Oh, don't look so horrified, Watson. We came across plenty of cutthroat murderers in our time. That the Dundas brothers were trying to avoid such finality counted in their favour."

"It seems to me that the four brothers, working in concert, would have most of the skills needed to effect such actions as they deemed necessary to take over the business."

"Precisely," said Holmes. "The accountant, John Dundas, was readily able to ascertain the healthy state of the London side of the business, and knew it could be plundered to rescue their Father. The priest, as was mentioned, was trying to get his uncle declared unfit to run his company, which meant, according to the lawyer brother, that his male next of kin would take over. The grand part of the plan was making him seem mad – and this, I must tell you was a stroke of genius."

"Holmes, tell me now. I must know."

"It was the fourth brother, the magic student. He hypnotized his uncle."

"Is that even possible?"

"What was that phrase that you ascribed to me? 'If you have eradicated the inconceivable, whatever is left, no matter how unlikely, must be real'."

"No, Holmes. It was 'When you have eliminated the –'" Then I looked up to see the rarest sight in our friendship. Holmes was laughing.

"Ho, Watson, it is still a delight to lead you up the garden path via an assiduous leg-pull."

"My dear Holmes, if I had known how the countryside would have improved your health so, I would have prescribed it sooner."

"Quite. It seemed an unlikely way to deal with the situation. Brian Dundas had the opportunity and the ability to hypnotize his uncle, but it was an audacious plan. They needed only convince one person, their Aunt Maria, of their uncle's mental weakness. Brian Dundas needed to get him to do something insane, yet mostly harmless. He doubtless knew of his uncle's prior illness and the false teeth he was forced to wear. What could be more disgusting, more convincing to Maria Dundas that her husband's sanity was failing in his mentality?

"I can see where you think it to be brilliant," I said.

"Indeed," replied Holmes "No doubt they told her it was a temporary stopgap. They would have him committed until he was well again. Meanwhile they would run the company, rescue their father's company, and get him the help he needed back in Ontario."

"The way you explain it," I said, "it almost seems logical."

"And it would have worked had Maria not come to me."

"What a noble woman," I said. "Seeking you out to rescue her husband."

"That is not exactly true," said Holmes. "Maria Dundas wanted the truth, but she also wanted the company. If her husband was mad, she was prepared to have him committed. She hired me to find out what her nephews were up to and to stop them."

"What was the trigger?" I asked. "How did they get him to do this thing only once a day, and not in the boardrooms of the city, or in his club?"

"It was in the incantations after the meal," said Holmes. "The Catholic prayer known as Grace after meals contains a phrase nor heard anywhere else. I was there for three days, watching carefully before I spotted it. The prayer is as follows:

"We give thee thanks, Almighty God,
For these and all thy benefits,
Which we have received
Through Christ our Lord.

"It's the second line, Watson: *For these and all thy benefits*. It is an obscure phrase, almost nonsensical. It fits nowhere else in any prayer in English, not is it a phrase used anywhere except this one place. As such it was the perfect trigger phrase, and every time Andrew Dundas heard it, he took his false teeth out and threw them at his wife. So there you have it, my friend."

"And how did it all end? Happily?"

"Somewhat," said Holmes. "I took Brian Dundas into his uncle's office, positioned him in front of his uncle, repeated the magic phrase and ducked. Brian Dundas was not as quick and ended up with a nasty rubber bite mark on his ear. When faced with the evidence, and when I told him who I really was, he confessed to all. I sat in the room and watched him de-hypnotize his uncle. Then we told him everything."

"I was an assiduous reader of the newspapers of the time, and do not recall any notice of arrests or prosecutions.

"I advised Andrew Dundas not to call the police," said Holmes. "Faced with the evidence of the ingenuity of his nephews, he struck a deal with them. The younger brothers would run the Canadian business after Andrew Dundas gave it the necessary financial uplift it required. Father Francis was allowed to stay in the priesthood and now runs a parish in Putney. Brian promised to behave himself and not use his powers of hypnotism for bad ends again – which he did, as far as I know. There were casualties however."

"Arthur Dundas?"

"Indeed. He remained under the grips of alcohol for the rest of his short life. The family tried to do right by him, but he wandered out onto a frozen lake with a large quantity of rum inside him, and the lake was not as solid as he thought."

"That is sad," I said, "but his sons were lucky they had a kind uncle and aunt, or else they could have seen the inside of a gaol cell."

"Hmm," said Holmes. "There was one last casualty: The marriage of Andrew and Maria Dundas. Maria was surprised at how easily her nephew had managed to manipulate her husband, so she read everything she could about mesmerism and hypnotism, and she learned a lot. Chief among these was the advice for entertainer hypnotists: Make sure you pick the right victim."

"What do you mean?" I asked.

"Most people who go to a magic show are prepared to suspend their logic for the evening in the chase of a good time. If they are invited to be hypnotized and are in turn made to cluck like a chicken, it becomes a great story to tell their friends. These are the kinds of people hypnotists choose, victims who are ready to do something strange. But you cannot go against ingrained behaviour. You could never get a nun, by way of example, to undress herself. It would be so foreign to her natural law that no amount of hypnotism could change that. Maria Dundas read variations of that fact in every bit of research she did."

"But when it came to hypnotize her husband," I said, "the will not to harm her was not as engrained as Maria Dundas might have wished."

"Exactly. Her husband, who had been a perfect gentleman all her life and never laid a hand in her, had a dark side brought out by her mesmerizing nephew. Brian was able to get Andrew Dundas to attack his wife, and that possibility was enough for her. She eventually leaked the tale to the newspaper, and they saw fit to write it as '*A Husband's Cruelty to His Wife*', the headline that started this entire conversation all those years ago.'

"Did she divorce him?" I asked.

"There is no justice in the divorce courts. Quite apart from being painted as a woman outside of polite society, her chances of being paid full recompense for her years of service were non-existent. Maria Dundas was much smarter than that. She persuaded her husband that she needed to go home to Brazil to see her dying mother at the same time that Andrew Dundas needed a large sum of bearer bonds delivered to a trader in Venezuela. Maria took the bonds with her, and was never seen again."

"Holmes, that was illegal. How could you condone that?"

"You ate dinner tonight convinced the trout was poached. That was illegal, so in your heart you condoned breaking the law. Most lawbreakers have a sliding scale in their head as to what laws can be broken and what ones cannot. Is it all right to steal a loaf of bread if your child is starving? Most would say yes. Is it all right to kill five women and disembowel them in Whitechapel? Most would say no. Ever other crime is in between.

"This is the Dundas separation case, and, as it happens, I was engaged in clearing up some small points in connection with it. The husband was a teetotaler, there was no other woman, and the conduct complained of was that he had drifted into the habit of winding up every meal by taking out his false teeth and hurling them at his wife, which, you will allow, is not an action likely to occur to the imagination of the average story-teller."

– Sherlock Holmes
"A Case of Identity"

The Broken Glass
by Denis O. Smith

Between the years 1881 and 1891, I had the privilege of studying the methods of Sherlock Holmes, the foremost criminal investigator of the period, and of making a record of his more interesting cases. In truth, there were very few of his cases which were *not* interesting. If a case made no appeal to his taste, if it appeared to possess none of those *outré* features which so delighted his artistic temperament, he would not infrequently decline to take it up at all. My note-books therefore contain some of the oddest, most surprising, and most puzzling problems which ever beset the mind of man.

As I turn the pages over, I find there the strange case of the Honourable Reginald Langdale, a young man who fell asleep in an armchair at his club, in London's West End, and awoke to find himself in a small hotel in Wick, in the far north of Scotland. There, also, I find an account of the true identity and puzzling disappearance of the Countess of Lytton, and the full facts in the singular case of Henry Cartwright of Kensington. Cartwright, a physician, often purchased a flower for his button-hole from an elderly flower-seller outside South Kensington station, but found to his very great surprise one morning that slipped into his hand along with his change was a cryptic and disturbing note, which the flower-seller denied knowing anything about.

Any one of these cases, or countless others, would make a suitable addition to this series of tales in which I have sought to depict the remarkable and varied career of my friend, Sherlock Holmes. In this instance, however, I am inclined to select for my text the memorable and surprising Blackwell Lane Mystery, in which, perhaps more than in any other case, absurdity rubbed shoulders with tragedy, and apparent disorder and chaos concealed a cold and ruthless calculation.

It was a dull and chilly day towards the end of October '87. All day long, from dawn to dusk, the clouds had been low and heavy, and as I looked from our sitting room window, just before seven o'clock, I saw that a fine drizzle had now begun to fall, and the cold glimmer of the street-lamps was reflected back from puddles of rain in the street.

"You will no doubt be glad you haven't been called out upon such a dismal evening," I remarked to my companion as I turned away from the window with a shiver.

Holmes looked up from where he was sitting at his chemical bench, examining the contents of a flask into which he had just tipped a few drops of some violet-coloured liquid. "On the contrary," said he in a brisk tone, as he gave the flask a shake, "I should be very glad if I *were* to be called out, Watson. It has been a dull and boring day – not the first I have had to endure recently – and needs something a little more stimulating than this mundane chemical experiment to redeem it. After all, if something seizes our interest, then the weather becomes as nothing, a trifle we are scarcely even aware of – as I'm sure you would agree."

My features must have betrayed a less than whole-hearted endorsement of this proposition, for my friend abruptly burst out laughing in that strange, silent way which was so characteristic of him.

"Well, well," said he at length, when he had recovered himself, "we shall see. Or perhaps we shan't," he added with a wry smile, as he glanced at the clock. "I doubt that we shall have any callers now."

In this speculation, however, my friend was mistaken. Our supper had been cleared away and we had settled to a quiet evening of, in my case, reading and, in Holmes's case, further chemical experiments, when there came the sound of a cab pulling up outside, followed almost at once by the jangling of the doorbell. Holmes had paused in what he was doing and now remained perfectly still, his head cocked slightly on one side, like an old hound listening for a rustle in the undergrowth.

"They are coming upstairs, Watson," said he in a sharp whisper. "But the cab has not been dismissed. Evidently it is retained for a further journey. I think we shall be required after all!" He put down the test-tube he had been holding and sprang to his feet. As a knock came at the door, he pulled it open instantly. "Yes?" said he in an eager tone.

To my surprise, a smart young police constable stood behind the maid, towering over her. "I have been instructed to ask if you will accompany me back to Clerkenwell, sir," said the policeman.

"Instructed?" queried Holmes. "Instructed by whom?"

"By Inspector Jones, sir. He told me to tell you that it is something in your line."

"Oh? What is it, then?"

The policeman hesitated and glanced at the maid, who was still standing beside him. "It is not yet clear, sir. It may be murder."

"Very well," said Holmes, rubbing his hands together enthusiastically. "I shall come. That will be all, Mary," he said, addressing the maid. "Kindly tell Mrs. Hudson that I'm going out. Ask her not to put the bolt on the door, and I shall let myself in when I return. Will you come with us, Watson?" he continued, turning to me.

I did not answer at once. I felt tired. Our sitting room was warm and cosy, and it would undoubtedly be cold and wet outside. On the other hand, I could see from his expression that Holmes wished me to accompany him, and I knew that if I did not go, and the case turned out to be an interesting one, I should regret it. "Yes, of course," I replied.

"Good man!" said Holmes. "Your hat and coat, then, and let us be off!"

In the cab, Holmes asked the constable what it was that had occurred.

"I'm not certain, sir," the other replied. "Someone has died. There's a doctor there who thinks he might have been poisoned, although whether deliberately or accidentally, no one seems sure."

"Whereabouts is it, precisely?"

"Blackwell Lane, sir."

"Ah! A narrow street of large warehouses, as I recall."

"Yes, sir, that's correct. But there seems to be a club there, which is where the incident occurred."

"A club? Blackwell Lane seems an odd location for a club."

"Yes, sir. It's in the basement of a furniture warehouse."

"What sort of club is it? A gambling club, perhaps?"

"No, sir. Leastways, I don't think so. The gentlemen are all very shabby-looking, like a collection of tramps and beggars, but they're very well-spoken – like vicars, sir, or solicitors."

"How very curious!" said Holmes with a frown.

"Yes, sir, it *is* a bit odd, I must say. I've never seen anything like it!"

As our cab turned into Blackwell Lane, the rain was falling steadily, and the pavements glistened wet under the street-lamps. The street itself was as Holmes had described it, an unbroken row of towering warehouses hemming it in on either side, like the walls of some deep, dark canyon. Half-way along on the right, an open doorway threw a bar of bright light across the pavement, and beside the doorway stood a uniformed policeman.

Through this doorway we were conducted by our guide, and down a wide stone staircase to a lower level. There, in the dusty stair-well, three or four plain wooden doors faced us. So far, what we had seen of the building was as one might have expected: A bare, somewhat dirty, plain, and unadorned commercial building. As our guide then pushed open one of the doors, however, we were met by a most surprising sight, for beyond the door was a large room decorated in the most amazingly opulent fashion. Above our heads hung a huge, dazzlingly-bright chandelier, and all around us, reflecting this light, were walls of beautiful polished wood, hung with all manner of exotic and colourful tapestries and curtains. About the room were a large number of small oblong tables, on the top of which

441

numerous glasses of all shapes and sizes were scattered, as if a meeting had taken place there which had been hurriedly abandoned. At one end of the room, on a larger table, were wine bottles, whisky bottles, and the like, and in the centre of the room stood our old friend Inspector Athelney Jones, in conversation with a small, bald-headed man in a dirty-looking jacket and ragged trousers. They turned as we entered.

"Ah! Mr. Holmes!" said Jones. "And Dr. Watson! I'm very glad you were able to come, gentlemen. It's a bad business, I'm afraid!"

"I'm sure we are very glad to be here," returned Holmes. "What is this place, Jones?"

The policeman snorted. "They call themselves 'The Amateur Mendicant Society'," he replied. "Mr. Quantick here is chairman of the society. I'll get him to explain it all to you in a moment."

"Must I?" asked the small man in a querulous tone.

"Is there some reason you don't wish to?" demanded Jones, his voice suffused with suspicion and menace.

"No, not at all, Inspector," said the other quickly. "It's just that I've explained everything at least twice already."

"Well you should be getting better at it, then," said the unsympathetic policeman. "But first, please guide us to the room where the deceased is lying. It's like a rabbit-warren down here," he added for our benefit, and then, as Quantick pulled open a door at the other side of the room, "Brace yourselves, gentlemen!"

I had been conscious of a distant, muffled hum of conversation from somewhere as we had been speaking to Jones and Quantick, but now, as the door was opened, this hum became a roar. The room before us – similar in size to the one we had just passed through – was full of men, a few sitting, but most standing, and all dressed in the same sort of ragged garments as Mr. Quantick. The room was evidently used as a dining room, for there were several neat rows of tables, each covered with a white cloth and laid for a meal.

Abruptly, as we entered, the room fell completely silent, and all eyes turned in our direction. Quantick nodded silently to the crowd, and then someone called out "Can we leave now?"

"No, you can't," returned Inspector Jones quickly. "I'll let you know when you can go. We are investigating a very serious business here. We'll take statements from you all in a moment."

With that, we made our way through the crowd, which parted like the Red Sea to let us through. Mr. Quantick then led us through a door on the other side of the room, which gave onto a plain and unadorned corridor. "This is the way to the kitchens, and various store-rooms," said he.

Twenty yards along the corridor our guide pushed open a door on the left and we found ourselves in a small, plain room. On the floor a blanket had been spread out, and on the blanket lay the body of a man, clad in ragged clothing. A professional-looking gentleman was kneeling beside the body, making notes in a pocket-book. He looked up as we entered.

"This is the police surgeon, Dr. Archer," said Jones. "When the incident occurred, Mr. Quantick here sent for the nearest doctor, a man called Plummer, who came in about five minutes. He pronounced this poor devil dead, but thought the circumstances were suspicious, so he sent for us, and waited until we arrived. He's gone now."

"What struck him as suspicious?" asked Holmes.

Dr. Archer rose to his feet. "When Dr. Plummer first got here," he said, "he was told that one of the members had had a heart seizure, or something of the sort. But when he examined the body, he thought that the symptoms did not really match that diagnosis, but suggested, rather, some type of poisoning."

"Cyanide?" said Holmes.

"Yes. How did you know?" asked the doctor in surprise.

"There are several indications," said Holmes, "the most obvious perhaps being the red flush on the cheeks. May I?" He bent down and put his nose close to the dead man's mouth. "Yes," he said as he stood up once more. "There is the unmistakable bitter-almond smell of Prussic Acid – in other words, hydrogen cyanide."

"Are you an expert?" queried the doctor with a raise of his eyebrow.

"On poisons I am. You may have come across a small pamphlet of mine listing the most obvious and significant symptoms of forty-three different poisons, in the form of a practical field-guide for non-experts. Have the members of the society been informed of these suspicions?" he continued, turning to Inspector Jones.

The policeman shook his head. "Mr. Quantick here knows all about it, but we have kept it from the others so far."

Holmes nodded. "Now, Mr. Quantick, if you could tell me precisely what occurred here earlier, I should be obliged."

"Well, sir," said Quantick, who appeared impressed by Holmes's authoritative manner, "I must tell you first very briefly about our association, the Amateur Mendicant Society. Our members are all from the most respectable levels of society. We meet here at least once a month – sometimes more often – when we dine together, and one of our number presents a paper for discussion.

"Four times a year, however, we have a special meeting. Today is the day of our Michaelmas meeting, which is one of the four. On these days, each of our members must abandon for the day his usual respectable

443

clothing, and dress in the rags of the most disreputable-looking beggar. He must then spend the day begging in the streets, before attending the quarterly meeting here. At the meeting, each member must show what he has managed to accrue during the day. The man who has gained the most is then acclaimed as the society's honorary president for the next quarter-year."

"Forgive me for mentioning it," interrupted Jones in a sarcastic tone, "but surely it would be simple for anyone to fill his pockets with coppers before leaving home in the morning, and later claim he had gained them all in the course of the day?"

"In theory, that might, I suppose, be possible," said Quantick in a tone of distaste, "and the statutes of the society recognize the possibility, however remote it may be, by providing the most severe penalties for anyone engaging in such deceitful behaviour. In short, anyone whose conduct has fallen to such a level renders himself liable to immediate expulsion from the society with no possibility of appeal. But we have never had to invoke that clause in the constitution. Our members are all men of the very greatest integrity and honour, to whom such a course of action would probably never even occur. Indeed, I would go so far as to say – "

"What happened this evening?" asked Holmes, interrupting the other's flow, "and who is the dead man?"

"His name," replied Quantick, "is George Wyndham. To begin with, his identity was established from some papers which were in his pocket. Although I know him well, as I do most of the members, I had not recognized him in his begging disguise. Some of our members are exceedingly creative with paint and other materials for changing their appearance, I must say.

"Anyway, the members began arriving here about half-past-six. They were all having a glass of something, and talking, very loudly and boisterously, in the reception room you saw back there, when there came a sudden sharp cry, as of pain or distress, which cut through the hubbub, and the rest of the room fell silent. I hurried forward and found one of our members lying on his back on the floor."

"Was he still alive then?" asked Holmes.

"Yes, but he was breathing very rapidly, in a hoarse, shallow sort of way. I thought he must have had a seizure. I loosened his collar and sent Thompson – the head waiter, who was in charge of the drinks table – to fetch a doctor straight away. The doctor was only a few minutes in coming, but by the time he arrived Wyndham was already dead."

Holmes nodded. "We had best speak now to those who were near him when he had his attack."

444

We returned to the main dining room and, again, the crowd fell completely silent as we entered. Quantick introduced Sherlock Holmes, who then addressed the assembly.

"The deceased gentleman was George Wyndham," said Holmes. "Will those who were speaking to him, or were standing close by him when he had his seizure, please step forward?" At which four or five men pushed their way to the front of the crowd. "Was the deceased speaking or listening just before he cried out?" Holmes asked them.

"A bit of both," replied one man, who identified himself as Hodgetts. "We were all exchanging anecdotes of our day in the streets. It was a lively and humorous conversation. The deceased gentleman had, as far as I recall, spent most of his day down Cheapside way."

"That's right," agreed one of the other men, who identified himself as Howe. "He seemed in good spirits. There didn't seem anything wrong with him."

"Did any of you know at the time who he was?" asked Holmes, at which most of them shook their heads.

"We were all pretty much anonymous," said one man. "Even now I couldn't tell you who many of these – my fellow-members – are, despite the fact that I know a number of them personally." This remark was met with a murmur of agreement from the assembled throng.

"I knew who he was," said Howe. "I recognized his voice when he spoke, and then saw who it was, but I couldn't have recognized him from a distance. He was telling me that this might be his last mendicants' meeting. He said he was sorry, because he would miss it, but he might not be able to attend in future."

"Did he say why?"

"Something about moving out of London. I gathered that he owned a rural property in Surrey – near Woking, I believe – and was considering moving out there."

"I see," said Holmes. "Can any of you recall if Mr. Wyndham had a glass in his hand at the time of his seizure?"

"Yes, he did," responded Hodgetts. "He had one in his right hand. It was a small tumbler – he was drinking whisky. I remember at some point he smacked his lips and said 'Ah! Good old plain whisky! I don't know why anyone ever adds anything to it!'"

"Had he finished the whisky?" asked Holmes.

"No," said Hodgetts. "He'd only had a couple of sips. But he'd only had it in his hand a moment or two, so that's not surprising."

"Had he only just arrived, then?" asked Holmes.

"No, he'd been here a while. But that wasn't his first drink."

"How are you so sure?" asked Holmes.

"Because I happened to notice while we were talking, without really thinking about it, that he had a practically empty glass in his hand at some point, and then later had a glass in his hand which wasn't so empty. Whether he went up and got a refill for himself, or someone got one for him, I really couldn't say, as I was talking to other people, too, and moving around a bit."

"Very well," said Holmes. "Pray proceed with your account."

"As Mr. Wyndham cried out," Hodgetts continued, "he stuck his right arm out towards me in a stiff sort of manner, so I took the glass from his hand."

"What did you do with it?"

"I put it on a table that was just behind where I was standing. I put my own glass down there, too, and tried to help Mr. Wyndham. He was shaking, and appeared to be unsteady, as if he might collapse to the floor at any moment – which, in fact, he did, before anyone could prevent it."

Holmes turned to Quantick, who was standing next to him. "Do you know how many members are present this evening?" he asked.

"Not exactly. I'm not sure yet who is here and who isn't."

"Would anyone know the precise number?"

"Thompson should. He was standing by the door when members started arriving."

Thompson, the head waiter, stepped forward. He was the only man in the room not dressed in rags and tatters.

"Did you mark off the members in a register as they arrived?" Holmes asked him.

"Not exactly, sir."

"What, then?"

"Each of the members has a specially engraved metal disc, bearing the initials of the society and a membership number, which they are to show at the door to gain admittance to the meeting."

"Did everyone who entered show you such a disc?"

"Most of them, sir."

"I have told Thompson not to be too strict in his execution of the regulations, if some of the members have not brought their membership discs with them," Quantick interjected. "Sometimes discs get lost, or simply forgotten. We would not wish to deny a member entrance just because of such a minor infraction of the rules."

"So some people did not show such a disc?" Holmes asked Thompson.

"That is correct, sir. One or two members had forgotten theirs, and then, at about ten minutes to seven, the rain started falling heavily. There was quite a crowd in the street at the time, trying to get in. I didn't think I could leave them all out in the street in such wretched weather, so I opened the door wide, and the whole crowd pushed their way in. Whether they all had their membership discs with them or not, I really couldn't say."

"Quite right, too," said Quantick with emphasis.

"What is all this?" demanded a tall man at the front of the crowd. "What does it matter who had a disc and who didn't? Poor old Wyndham – if that's who it is – has had a heart seizure. Why are the police here at all, asking all these questions?"

"The police always attend sudden, unexplained deaths," said Inspector Jones in a portentous tone. "Do you have some particular reason for not wishing the police involved?"

"No, no, of course not," said the tall man, clearly somewhat abashed by the policeman's manner. "I just don't see the point of all these questions."

"Nor me," said one of the other men. "I don't imagine anyone would wish to go ahead with the supper after what has happened, so we might as well get off home now."

"Patience, gentlemen," said Holmes in a mollifying tone. "The questions are nearly over – for the moment at least. But first, we wish to know how many members are here, and as no one made a record of it when you arrived, we shall have to count you all now."

There was much grumbling at this proposal, but at length, after several false starts, as the members milled around like a flock of reluctant and disobliging sheep, it was established that, including Mr. Quantick, twenty-six members were present.

"Including Wyndham, then," said Holmes, "that makes twenty-seven. "Is that the number you were expecting this evening, Mr. Quantick?"

"Yes," said the chairman. "That is the full complement of our membership at the moment."

"Now," said Holmes, addressing the crowd once more, "did you all have a glass of something when you arrived here?"

This question was met with a general affirmative murmur, but as the men were all speaking at once, it was difficult to be certain what anyone had said. Holmes frowned. "Let me put it another way: did any of you *not* have a glass of something?"

At this, the room was perfectly silent. "Very well," said Holmes. "So you all had a drink. And all the glasses were left in the other room – or did anyone carry his glass through to this room?" This question, too, was met with silence. "Very good," said Holmes. He asked Mr. Hodgetts, the man who had taken the glass from Wyndham's hand, to accompany him, then, signalling to me that I should do likewise, he led the way through to the reception room. As we left the dining room, I heard Jones telling the crowd

447

that he would have to take the name and address of everyone there, a suggestion which elicited groans, protests, and complaints. "Because," I heard him say, in a loud, irritable voice, "you are all witnesses, and all witnesses must be recorded."

As we passed into the reception room, Holmes closed the door behind us to shut out the noise of the crowd. "Now, Mr. Hodgetts," said he, "if you would indicate where you and Mr. Wyndham were standing when you took the glass from his hand and he fell to the floor, I should be most obliged."

"It was just here," replied Hodgetts, positioning himself by an oblong table which stood against the wall to the right of the doors to the dining room. "I had my back to the table, and Wyndham was facing me, along with two or three other men. When I took his glass, I turned and put it down here, and put my own glass next to it. See, they are still here, the two of them together."

"You are certain those are the two glasses in question?"

"Yes, I'm sure they are."

"Very well. You may return to your colleagues now, Mr. Hodgetts. I am grateful for your assistance. And now," continued Holmes, as the door closed, "let us see if either of these glasses bears the scent of bitter almonds. That one doesn't! And nor does that one! Would you mind examining them, Watson, to see what you think?"

I did as he requested, holding each glass in turn close to my nose, but neither of them bore that deadly scent.

"Hmm!" said Holmes, rubbing his chin in a thoughtful way. "Perhaps someone has swapped the glasses round. We shall have to examine them all, then. But first, let us count them!"

This we did, independently, then compared our totals. "I make it twenty-eight," I remarked.

"So do I," said Holmes. "That is interesting! Let us examine them all, then! Try to be methodical, so that you don't miss any." I started from one end of the room, Holmes from the other, and for several minutes we moved round the room in silence, examining each glass in turn. At length, we had examined every glass we could see. I had found none bearing any scent other than one might expect – wine, whisky, sherry and so on – and I could tell from his features, without needing to ask him, that Holmes, too, had drawn a blank.

"Twenty-seven members and twenty-eight glasses," he said, "and none bearing the deadly scent of Prussic Acid! Let us at least see if we can account for the extra glass!" He opened the door to the dining room, called loudly for silence, and then asked the assembled throng if any of them had used two glasses. This query was met at first with silence, then one man put his hand up to attract attention and called out.

"I had two separate drinks," he said, "but took them both in the same glass."

"So did I," called another man, followed by several others.

Holmes turned to the head waiter, Thompson, and asked him if he himself had taken a glass of anything.

"Certainly not, sir," came the prompt reply, a note of indignation in his voice.

"Can you recall, then," asked Holmes, "if any of the gentlemen brought a used glass back to you and asked for a fresh one?"

"I can, sir, and none of them did."

"Very well," said Holmes. "Carry on giving your names and addresses to Inspector Jones and his men."

With that he closed the door again and looked round the reception room once more. "We appear to have met with a check," said he. "But wait a moment!" he cried all at once, as much to himself as to me. He strode purposefully across the room to the large table from which, as was evident from the large number of bottles atop it, Thompson had been dispensing the drinks to the club members. Then, bending down, he pulled out a couple of large cardboard boxes from underneath the table. "Here are some spare glasses," he remarked, "and here are some unopened bottles of various types of liquor. The glasses all appear to be clean and unused."

Then he pulled out from under a smaller table, to the side of the large table, another cardboard box. "More glasses," said he. "All clean. Anyone who wished to could have helped himself to a fresh glass from here." Then he pulled out a sort of large wicker waste-paper basket. "What have we here?" he murmured, as he began to remove the contents of the basket one by one. One or two wine bottles came first, then some smaller bottles, and then he paused. "Come and look at this, Watson!" he cried.

I joined him where he was crouching down by the waste-paper basket. "See!" he cried, as he dipped his hand to the bottom of the basket, and slowly and carefully lifted it up again. In his grasp was a large, jagged chunk of a broken glass. Carefully he held this dangerous-looking lump of glass to his nose. From the expression on his face, I could tell that he had at last found what he was looking for. Then he placed the piece of glass on the floor and invited me to examine it.

I raised it to my nose. There could be no doubt: The scent of Prussic Acid was unmistakable.

"I think, Watson," said my friend, "that we are permitted at this juncture to say 'Eureka!'"

"Indeed," I returned. "This glass was undoubtedly the one that conveyed the poison to Wyndham's lips."

Holmes nodded. "There is the scent, also, of something else – bitters, I think. There is an opened bottle of bitters on the drinks table – which was probably added in an attempt to disguise the presence of the cyanide. But it seems likely that Wyndham still didn't care for it overmuch, which I think explains his remark to Hodgetts about the 'good old plain whisky' of his second drink."

"Yes, I'm sure you must be right," I agreed. "But now we have twenty-seven members and twenty-*nine* glasses! The matter becomes more confusing all the time!"

"It is certainly not entirely clear yet," said Holmes, "but we have made definite progress. Now we must ensure that we make further progress. Come!"

We returned to the dining room. Inspector Jones and the two constables were just finishing taking the names and addresses of everyone there.

A stout man with a dirt-smeared face, whose hair was sticking up in odd clumps, approached the inspector. "I must go now," said he in an imperious tone.

"In a moment," returned Jones, without looking up from his notebook.

"Do you know who I am?" the man demanded. "I am head of one of the oldest private banks in the City."

"I congratulate you," said Jones. "But it doesn't make any difference who you are – the formalities must still be observed. I'm sure if it was you lying dead in that room along the corridor you'd be hoping that people would show you a little respect!"

"But why keep us here?" said another man. "We haven't done anything wrong."

"Oh no?" said Jones in a sarcastic tone. "Are there any lawyers among you?" he added, looking over the crowd. One or two men answered back that they were solicitors. "Well, then," said Jones, "you should know that under the Vagrancy Act of 1824, it is an offence to beg on the streets. If I wished to, I could have you all clapped in the cells for the night in the next five minutes!"

This announcement quietened the crowd a little, but after a moment, a small man at the front protested. "But we don't keep any of the money we collect for ourselves," he said. "We donate it all to various charitable causes."

"Oh, *do* you?" said Jones. "That makes no difference to the fact that you got it by begging. And am I to understand that you don't need the money yourselves?"

"No, of course not."

"In that case I could have you all clapped in the cells on a charge of fraud and imposture. Now, just be quiet for a moment. Mr. Quantick wishes to say something to you."

"But first," interrupted Holmes, "I wish to ask you a question."

"What?" came the general clamour. "More questions?"

"Did any of you break a glass?" asked Holmes, ignoring the uproar. The response was complete silence. "So, no one broke a glass? No? Very well. Did any of you see or hear anyone else break a glass?" Again, the response was silence, then one man put his hand up and spoke:

"I thought I heard the sound of breaking glass earlier on," he said. "It was just behind me. But when I turned, I couldn't see anything, and as someone was speaking to me at the time, I didn't give it another thought."

"Where were you standing?" asked Holmes.

"Near Thompson's drinks table, with my back to it."

"Did you recognize any of those standing behind you?"

"No, not at all."

"You did not hear a glass break?" Holmes asked Thompson, at which the head waiter shook his head.

"And now," said Quantick, "if you would come forward one by one, identify yourselves, and tell me how much you collected during the day, I can tick you off my list, and you can leave your takings in a general pile on this table here. Then," he continued, turning slightly towards Inspector Jones as he spoke, "I can arrange to have it taken to the charitable institute we chose for this month."

Athelney Jones left the amateur mendicants to their business and drew Holmes to one side. "What is all this about a broken glass, Mr. Holmes, and how does it relate to what has happened here this evening?"

"We have found what you might term the murder weapon," replied Holmes. "Come and see!"

The policeman followed us into the reception room, where Holmes recounted our examination of all the glasses, and the discovery of the broken glass.

"I should keep these tainted fragments of glass safe," said Holmes. "Apart from the condition of the dead man himself, they constitute the only evidence we have that Wyndham's death was not a purely natural one."

451

"Yes, certainly. I had, of course, intended to examine the glasses when I had finished with that crowd in the other room. What do you think we should do now?"

"There is little more we can do here," replied Holmes after a moment's thought. "I suppose you're thinking of notifying Wyndham's household of his death?"

"Yes, precisely. It's something I've got to do, of course, but it's the part of my job that I like the least, as you can imagine – being the bearer of bad news. Anyway, I've got his address from Quantick. It's not far from here, as it happens – in Bertram Street, just off the Gray's Inn Road. I was thinking of walking round there now, when we have finished with those people in there."

"Then we shall come with you, if we may, and see if we can learn anything."

"Certainly. I am a little reluctant to leave Quantick at large, but I have his address if I need to lay hands on him again."

"You harbour some suspicions of Quantick, then?"

"He is my number one suspect, if that's what you mean."

"On what grounds?"

"On the grounds that he has been the chairman of the society for years, and must know all of them pretty well. I don't believe for one moment that he couldn't recognize them this evening. On the grounds, also, that his manner all evening has seemed to me suspicious. I don't yet have sufficient evidence to arrest him, but as soon as I do, I'll have the darbies on him and have him in the cells before he knows what's hit him!"

Outside, the rain was now falling steadily, and the streets were deserted. Jones had left two of the uniformed policemen behind, to finish dealing with the members of the club and supervise the removal of the body, and he brought one of them, Constable Burton, with us.

"I must say," I remarked to Jones, as I turned my coat-collar up against the icy rain, "that Quantick doesn't look very guilty of anything to me. What about the head waiter, Thompson? It seems to me that no one would have been in a better position than he was to have added something unpleasant to one of the glasses of liquor he was doling out. And no one would have been in a better position than Thompson to put the tainted glass in the waste-paper basket and deliberately break it."

"That's true, Dr. Watson," the policeman replied. "All in all, I shouldn't be surprised if we find, when we get to the bottom of the matter, that Quantick and Thompson were acting in concert, together. What do you think, Mr. Holmes?"

Holmes shook his head. "It seems to me too early to reach any firm conclusions," he replied after a moment.

452

"Come, come, Mr. Holmes," said Jones. "You must at least have a theory. You are usually such a great one for theories! You have seen the evidence. Does it suggest nothing to you?"

"There are indeed some suggestive points," returned Holmes, "but most of them are open to more than one interpretation. I would rather restrain my urge to theorize for a little while longer. Incidentally, Jones, with regard to your theory, what do you suppose Quantick's motive might be?"

"That we don't yet know," Jones conceded, "but considering that it now seems more than likely that he and Thompson are in league in the matter, it must be something to do with their precious society. Perhaps Quantick has been pocketing for himself the society's takings from their begging activities, rather than passing it on to the charities he referred to, and Wyndham had threatened to expose him. Whatever it is, we'll get to the bottom of it eventually, you mark my words!"

A brisk walk of a little under ten minutes brought us to Bertram Street. On either side of the street were unbroken terraces of neat, attractive old houses, set back a few feet, behind low walls and railings. Beside the front-door of some of them, bushy shrubs had been planted, including outside Number 54, which was the house we sought. Holmes paused for a moment before this bush, which was a good eight feet tall, and seemed very taken with it.

"This is a very fine specimen," said he in a tone of admiration. "It is, I believe, a cherry laurel."

"It is always pleasant to see a little greenery in these otherwise plain brick streets," I remarked, somewhat surprised at my companion's enthusiasm.

Jones had to knock twice before there came any sound from within the house, but, at length, the door was opened to us by a pleasant-faced young man, clad in a smoking jacket.

"Pray excuse the delay," he began with a smile. "The servants have been given the evening off, and I'm the only one in. It's been so quiet that I'm afraid I fell asleep in my chair. What can I do for you, gentlemen? If you were hoping to see Mr. Wyndham, he's out at his club, although he should be back later."

"Might I inquire to whom I am speaking?" asked Jones in a sombre voice.

"My name is Ventnor," returned the young man, a frown of puzzlement on his features. "I'm a second cousin of old Wyndham's, and I'm staying with him for a few days. I can take a message for him if you wish."

Jones produced his card. "I'm a police officer," said he, "and I'm afraid I have some bad news for you."

"Oh?" said the young man, his mouth falling open in surprise. "You'd better come in then."

He opened the door wider, and Jones, Holmes, and I filed through into the hall, Constable Burton being instructed to wait outside. Ventnor pushed open a door, and we followed him into a warm and well-lit sitting room, where a fire blazed in the grate. Upon the walls, in addition to a number of paintings, were several glass display-cases of butterflies and moths.

"Now," said Ventnor, "what exactly has happened? Wait a moment," he added quickly. "Where is your colleague?"

I looked round. I had thought that Holmes was standing behind me, but he was nowhere to be seen. Ventnor returned to the hall, and Jones and I peered out of the sitting room doorway, to see what was happening. Holmes was crouching down with his hands on the floor and his face just a few inches above it, as if looking for something on the carpet.

"What are you doing?" asked Ventnor in a puzzled tone.

"I do beg your pardon," said Holmes, looking up and blinking. "My eyes must be playing tricks upon me. They're not very good today! I thought I saw one of my companions drop something onto the floor, but I must have been mistaken." He rose to his feet, shaking his head, and we all returned to the sitting room.

"Now," said Ventnor, addressing Jones, "please tell me. What is the bad news you have brought for us?"

"Your cousin, Mr. Wyndham, has met with an accident."

"An accident?" repeated Ventnor. "Good grief!" he cried, seating himself on the arm of a chair. "Is he all right?"

"I'm afraid not," said Jones. "I'm afraid he is dead."

"What!" cried Ventnor, rising sharply to his feet again. "Surely not! What on earth has happened to him?"

"He appears to have had a seizure of some kind," replied Jones, "possibly a heart seizure. Do you know if he had a weak heart?"

"No," replied Ventnor, shaking his head. "Not at all. But I understand that those sorts of conditions do not always manifest themselves very clearly. Where did it happen?"

"At his club, the Amateur Mendicant Society."

"Oh, how terrible!" said Ventnor. "He always enjoyed going to their meetings so much! It was, I think, his biggest pleasure in life."

"Was he also a lepidopterist?" inquired Holmes abruptly, bending forward and peering very closely at a case of butterflies on the wall, as if his eyesight were very poor.

454

"Yes he was," said Ventnor with a frown of surprise, "as you can see."

"I mean," persisted Holmes, his eyes just an inch or two from the glass case, "did he catch all these specimens himself, or did he purchase them somewhere?"

"He caught them all himself. He used to go off on expeditions to heaths and places like that." Ventnor turned to Inspector Jones with a pleading expression on his features. "Who is this man?" he inquired, indicating Holmes. "He doesn't seem much like a police officer to me. Why is he asking me all these ridiculous and irrelevant questions about butterflies when my cousin has just died?"

Jones cast a brief, nonplussed glance in my direction. "This is Mr. Holmes," he said after a moment. "No, he isn't a regular police officer, but he is an expert in cases such as this one, and is assisting me in the present investigation."

"Why do you refer to it as a 'case'?" asked Ventnor, "and an 'investigation'? I understood you to say that Mr. Wyndham had died of heart failure – surely a medical man would be of more use than another policeman?"

"My other assistant, Dr. Watson, *is* a medical man," responded Jones, indicating me.

"We understand," interjected Holmes, "from what we heard from one of the other club members, that Mr. Wyndham was considering moving out of London. Can you shed any light on that?"

"I don't think so. No, wait! That might be a reference to an old cottage he'd inherited from someone, somewhere near Woking, I think. But I can't believe he was seriously considering moving out there. From the only reference I heard him make to it, I got the distinct impression that he intended to sell it and pocket the proceeds – which wouldn't amount to very much, so he said." Ventnor turned to Jones. "Do you wish me to come with you and formally identify the body?" he asked.

"First of all," said Holmes, before the policeman could respond, "we should like to inspect Mr. Wyndham's wardrobe."

"His wardrobe?" repeated Ventnor. "What on earth for?"

"I speak metaphorically, of course," said Holmes. "My colleague, Dr. Watson, wishes to assess Mr. Wyndham's clothing from a medical perspective."

"I don't understand," protested Ventnor. "You have already told me that Wyndham almost certainly died of a heart seizure."

"That is true," said Holmes, "but heart seizures are, almost always, brought on ultimately by something else – such as, to take a simple example, tight clothing. A tight collar, for instance, constricts the blood

455

vessels in the neck, putting stress and strain upon them, which in turn puts stress and strain upon the heart. Dr. Watson must put all that sort of thing in his report."

I had listened to this outpouring of nonsense with increasing stupefaction. I had not the faintest idea what Holmes's purpose might be in making such absurd statements, but I guessed that, whatever it was, he would wish me to go along with it. I therefore did my best to adopt a serious and earnest expression. Athelney Jones glanced my way and caught my eye, and I could see from his features that he was as much in the dark as I was.

"Oh, very well," said Ventnor in an impatient tone. "Come this way."

We followed him from the sitting room and up a narrow flight of stairs to a landing, where three or four doors faced us. Before Ventnor could indicate which of these was the door of Wyndham's bedroom or dressing room, Holmes lumbered forward in a clumsy, uncharacteristic manner, his back bent as before and his head thrust forward as if his eyesight were poor, and seized hold of one of the door-handles and pushed the door open.

"That's not the right door," said Ventnor in a sharp tone. "That's my room." He interposed himself between Holmes and the doorway, and pulled the door firmly shut again. "This is the way," he continued, opening one of the other doors and inviting us to enter, "although it seems a complete waste of time to me, I must say."

We followed him into the room. "Now," said he, addressing me, "what is it you wish to look at?"

"I'll start with the shirts and collars," I replied, in as natural a manner as I could muster.

Ventnor pulled open one or two of the drawers in a large tallboy. "There you are," said he. "Help yourself." He turned to me as he spoke, and I saw his expression abruptly change, from one of boredom to one of alarm. "Where has that other idiot gone?" he cried, as he pushed past me.

I turned quickly to find that Holmes had disappeared again. Barely a second later, I heard a cry of anger and a great crash, as if a piece of furniture had been knocked over. Jones and I hurried from the room. There was no one on the landing, but the door of Ventnor's room was ajar.

As we reached the doorway, we heard Ventnor cry out.

"You impudent scoundrel! How dare you force your way into my room!"

"How dare you murder your cousin!" came Holmes's swift reply.

"You lying hound!" cried Ventnor, as he flung himself at Holmes and seized him by the throat.

456

Jones and I dashed forward and pulled Ventnor away. "What in the name of Heaven is going on here?" demanded Jones, who kept a tight hold on the young man.

"This idiot you have brought with you has accused me of murdering Mr. Wyndham!" said Ventnor in a loud voice.

"So I have," said Holmes, "because it is true." He bent down and picked up a bundle of clothes from behind a chest of drawers and flung it onto the bed. I saw at once that it was a ragged, grubby-looking outfit. "This was the costume of a beggar you wore this evening at the Amateur Mendicants' Club," continued Holmes, "when, as you had carefully planned, you murdered George Wyndham in cold blood!"

"It's a lie!" cried Ventnor, "a complete and unmitigated lie! Yes, I wore that outfit earlier in the day for a lark, when I was out with Wyndham on his begging round. But I am not a member of his club – and didn't have a booking, anyway – so when he went on to the meeting, I came home. I never set foot in his precious club! I was back here between half-past-four and five, and never left the house again."

"You're lying," said Holmes. "These clothes are soaking wet. But it didn't start raining until well after six o'clock. You couldn't possibly have got so wet if you had returned when you claim you did!"

"Perhaps I got the time wrong," said Ventnor. "I don't know precisely what the time was. I wasn't wearing a watch."

"You lie every time you open your mouth," said Holmes. "Let us see! Ah!" He had picked up the ragged jacket, and, turning it upside down, had tipped out the contents of the pockets onto the bed. Among a few small objects – coins, a box of matches and so on – was a small glass phial. This, Holmes picked up, and, removing the rubber stopper, he held it up to his nose. The smell was evidently a strong one, for I saw Holmes recoil slightly as he sniffed it. "Here, Watson, have a smell of this – but be careful – it's had a very concentrated distillation in it!"

I took the phial and sniffed it. The smell of hydrogen cyanide was penetrating and unmistakable. I then held it up to Jones's nose, and he recoiled from it, as Holmes had done. "That settles the matter," said the policeman. "If you would be so good as to get Constable Burton up here, Dr. Watson, I'll get the darbies on this villain!"

The evening was far advanced when there came the jangling of the doorbell. I hurried downstairs to open the door, for I knew that the landlady and the servants would have been long abed. It was, as I had expected, Inspector Athelney Jones, who had said he would call round to discuss the case with us when he had completed all the necessary formalities connected with Ventnor's arrest.

457

"Yes, I will have a glass of something, Dr. Watson," said he, as he seated himself beside our blazing fire. "It is a chilly night now, although somewhat less chilly than it might have been had we not solved the Wyndham case! You certainly had a stroke of luck in finding Ventnor's begging disguise, Mr. Holmes!"

"Luck doesn't come into it," retorted Holmes, clearly nettled by the policeman's remark. "I found it because I was looking for it!"

"Oh, yes, of course, I realise that!" said Jones quickly. "I'm certainly glad that you and Dr. Watson came along to Wyndham's house with me – don't think I'm not! The case had seemed nothing but chaos when we were at the mendicants' club, but then seemed to clarify itself when we got to Wyndham's house. But what was the point of all that talk about the butterflies and moths? Were you just filling in time until you could think of a way to search for his begging outfit? Or were you trying to trick Ventnor into giving himself away in some way?"

"Not at all. I'll tell you how I saw the case from the beginning, and then you can follow my train of thought."

"Certainly, certainly," said Jones. "I should like nothing better!"

"First of all," began Holmes after a moment, "when we reached the premises of the Amateur Mendicant Society, we heard that one of the members had had some kind of fatal seizure. We were then told, in confidence, that the medical men were not entirely satisfied that the death was a natural one, and that the deceased might have ingested some poisonous substance. This we were quickly able to confirm for ourselves, and positively identify the poisonous substance as Prussic Acid, that is, hydrogen cyanide.

"Now, hydrogen cyanide is, as you're no doubt aware, relatively quick in its effects, and as no one at the club had yet had anything to eat, but all, it seemed, had had one or two glasses of liquor of one sort or another, it seemed practically certain that the poison had been in Wyndham's drink. No one else had been affected, however, so the poison could not have been in one of the bottles, but must have been added to Wyndham's glass. Finding that glass took a little time, until we looked in the waste-paper basket, where it had presumably been dropped in and deliberately broken by having a wine bottle dropped on top of it. Whether this was to prevent anyone else accidentally using the tainted glass or to try to remove it from any future investigation, we cannot say. From the murderer's point of view, it no doubt seemed to serve both purposes.

"Having found the glass that Wyndham must have drunk from, we were at once faced with another puzzle, for although *twenty-seven* members of the society were present, including the deceased, *twenty-nine* glasses had been used, including the broken one. As it was clear that the

458

glass in the waste-paper basket was the one from which Wyndham had imbibed the poison, then the glass in his hand when he had his seizure was one of the two extra glasses. But whence came the other one? It was possible, of course, that someone was lying, or had simply forgotten that he had used two glasses, but that seemed so unlikely as to be scarcely worth considering. What seemed more likely was that someone had been present earlier but had already left. This person I took to be the murderer. Clearly, he had left after Wyndham had drunk from the poisoned glass – because he had been present long enough to put that glass in the waste-paper basket – but probably before Wyndham had had his seizure – because he would not wish to draw suspicion to himself by being seen to slip away just as Wyndham was crying out, nor immediately afterwards. But a little earlier, with all the members milling about the room, and the conversation no doubt very loud, it would have been relatively easy for someone to slip out of the room and up the stair to the street – there was no one on the door at that time, if you recall, Thompson being occupied at the drinks table.

"If, then, as I believed, the extra glass had belonged to the murderer, who was no longer there, that raised a further question as to his identity. According to Quantick's list, every member had turned up for the meeting, and all of them were still present. Who, then was the murderer, the man who had left early? Clearly, he was not a member, yet he must have been dressed in the same sort of ragged garments as everyone else, or his appearance there would have caused comment. But if he was not a member, who, then, was he?

"As I considered what must have happened with Wyndham's drinks, the matter became clearer to me. The only way, it seemed to me, that the poison could have been added to Wyndham's first glass was if someone else had fetched it from the bar for him. Obviously, Wyndham would not have added it himself, and as all the men would have been standing up, talking and laughing, no doubt each holding his glass in his hand, I doubted that anyone else could have then done so. Furthermore, despite your speculations, Watson, I could not imagine that Thompson, who was no doubt thronged by thirsty members at his bar, would have been able to do it unobserved, either. But someone who was fetching a drink both for himself and for Wyndham could have turned away from the bar carrying the two glasses, paused momentarily at that small side-table, and, with his back turned to everyone else – who would probably have all been concentrating upon getting to the front of the queue – added the cyanide to Wyndham's drink, into which he had already added a large dash of bitters while at the bar.

"Similarly, the only way that Wyndham's first glass could have been hidden and deliberately smashed was if someone else had taken that glass away and brought Wyndham his second drink in a fresh glass. But no one but the murderer would have had any reason to do that, so clearly this was the same person in both cases – that is to say, the murderer. As this person was not a member of the society, but had twice fetched a drink for Wyndham, the overwhelming likelihood was that he was some crony of Wyndham's who had accompanied him in his begging activities during the day, and gone with him to the club."

"That seems reasonable enough," I remarked, and Jones grunted his agreement.

"When we set off for Wyndham's house, then," Holmes continued, "my principal aim was simply to try to learn something there which might shed light on the matter, perhaps including the name of some acquaintance of Wyndham's who might have accompanied him today. I was not really expecting to encounter such a person at Wyndham's house, or find that he was currently staying there. When we reached Bertram Street, however, I was at once struck by the shrub which had been planted by the front door."

"The laurel?" Jones repeated in a dismissive tone. "What on earth is striking about a laurel? Why, it must be one of the most common plants in London!"

"Common plant it may be," returned Holmes, "but it is also one of the best and easiest sources of cyanide. Collectors of butterflies and other insects have often used crushed laurel leaves in their glass 'killing jars', as the fumes released when the leaves decay kill the specimen quickly without damaging it. For keener or more frequently active lepidopterists, it is not too difficult to prepare a concentrated solution of cyanide from the crushed leaves, a few drops of which on a pad of cotton wool in the bottom of a glass jar will serve the same purpose more conveniently. In the laurel bush, therefore, I saw simply a ready source of cyanide. It was no more than that, but, still, it struck me as an odd coincidence, and raised the possibility that Wyndham's death might have been caused by poison from his own house.

"When we entered the house, I succeeded by a simple ruse in feeling the carpets, both on the stair and in the hall, and was able to confirm to my own satisfaction that both were damp, and that someone had therefore entered the house that evening, after the rain had begun to fall, and had gone upstairs. This gave the lie to Ventnor's account of his 'quiet evening', in which he implied that nobody had been in or out of the house since the servants had left in the afternoon. When we entered the drawing room, the first thing I saw were the cases of butterflies and moths on the wall. A simple question to Ventnor established that Wyndham had caught his own specimens, which probably meant that there was indeed cyanide in the house. I had therefore established in my own mind, first, that Ventnor was almost certainly lying about not having been out that evening and, second, that he almost certainly had access to some sort of distillation of cyanide. I was therefore convinced that Ventnor was the mysterious extra person who had been at the amateur mendicants' club, where he had poisoned Wyndham's drink, taken the first glass away and smashed it, and brought the second glass before quickly leaving. All that remained, to make the case conclusive, was to find the clothes which Ventnor must have been wearing earlier in the evening, which, as you saw, I managed to do while he was distracted by Watson's trawl through Wyndham's shirts and collars."

"You make it all sound so straightforward and obvious," I said with a chuckle, "which is not how it seemed to me at the time."

"Nor to me," admitted Athelney Jones with a rueful expression. "I am certainly very glad you agreed to join me this evening, Mr. Holmes. We might not have got to the bottom of the business so quickly without your help! I wonder," he added after a moment, "why Ventnor plotted to murder his cousin in such a public way. You might have expected him to choose a dark, deserted alley-way somewhere, rather than a brightly-lit club, packed with people!"

Holmes shook his head. "Dark alley-ways bring their own problems for the murderer," he said. "First of all, deaths in such circumstances will always be regarded as suspicious, and then there is the problem of how to lure your victim there in the first place, the likelihood of encountering a constable on his beat, and the fact that in the absence of any other suspects, attention will inevitably be turned in your direction. To murder someone in what you describe as a 'brightly-lit club', however, avoids all these problems. Ventnor probably hoped that, if he was lucky, no one would even realise that a murder had occurred, and would believe that Wyndham's seizure was the result of his having been out walking the cold streets all day and having then consumed several glasses of whisky in rapid succession. He would know, also, that if the true cause of death *were* discovered, then the circumstances would instantly provide nearly thirty ready suspects to occupy the attention of the authorities, and confuse their analysis of the matter. He must have been confident that he himself would escape suspicion, for, after all, Ventnor's presence at the club was known to no one except Wyndham himself. All in all, hideous and diabolical as it was, I think Ventnor's scheme was also highly ingenious and cunning – as clever as any murder plot I have ever encountered."

"Perhaps you are right," Jones conceded. "But what do you imagine Ventnor's motive to have been?"

461

"We can't yet say," replied Holmes, as he reached for his pipe and tobacco, "but I shouldn't be at all surprised if it has something to do with that property which Wyndham had recently inherited in Surrey."

Holmes's speculation on this last point proved accurate. Official investigations, which Inspector Jones later relayed to us, revealed that what Ventnor had described to us as simply "an old cottage" proved to be a substantial house and estate, worth a considerable sum of money. Subsequent investigations further revealed, first, that although only Wyndham's second cousin, Ventnor was nevertheless his closest relative and thus stood to inherit whatever Wyndham might leave, and, second, that Ventnor himself had recently been living far beyond his means, and had contracted very large debts. The true character behind the smiling face which he presented to the world was perhaps best revealed by the fact that instead of trying to find an honest way out of his financial difficulties, his answer to it all had been the cold, calculated, and cruel plot to murder his cousin and thus inherit all his possessions – including, of course, the property in Surrey. His plan was certainly a devilishly clever one, and I think it no exaggeration to say that it might very well have succeeded, had it not been for the perceptive intervention of my good friend, the inestimable Sherlock Holmes.

The year '87 furnished us with a long series of cases of greater or less interest, of which I retain the records. Among my headings under this one twelve months, I find an account of . . . of the Amateur Mendicant Society, who held a luxurious club in the lower vault of a furniture warehouse . . . .

– Dr. John H. Watson
"The Five Orange Pips"

Appendix:
The Untold Cases

The following has been assembled from several sources, including lists compiled by Phil Jones and Randall Stock, as well as some internet resources and my own research. I cannot promise that it's complete – some Untold Cases may be missing – after all, there's a great deal of Sherlockian Scholarship that involves interpretation and rationalizing – and there are some listed here that certain readers may believe shouldn't be listed at all.

As a fanatical supporter and collector of pastiches since I was a ten-year-old boy in 1975, reading Nicholas Meyer's *The Seven-Per-Cent Solution* and *The West End Horror* before I'd even read all of The Canon, I can attest that serious and legitimate versions of all of these Untold Cases exist out there – some of them occurring with much greater frequency than others – and I hope to collect, read, and chronologicize them all.

There's so much more to The Adventures of Sherlock Holmes than the pitifully few sixty stories that were fixed up by the First Literary Agent. I highly recommend that you find and read all of the rest of them as well, including those relating these Untold Cases. You won't regret it.

David Marcum

A Study in Scarlet

- Mr. Lestrade . . . got himself in a fog recently over a forgery case
- A young girl called, fashionably dressed
- A gray-headed, seedy visitor, looking like a Jew pedlar who appeared to be very much excited
- A slipshod elderly woman
- An old, white-haired gentleman had an interview
- A railway porter in his velveteen uniform

The Sign of Four

- The consultation last week by Francois le Villard
- The most winning woman Holmes ever knew was hanged for poisoning three little children for their insurance money

- The most repellent man of Holmes's acquaintance was a philanthropist who has spent nearly a quarter of a million upon the London poor
- Holmes once enabled Mrs. Cecil Forrester to unravel a little domestic complication. She was much impressed by his kindness and skill
- Holmes lectured the police on causes and inferences and effects in the Bishopgate jewel case

The Adventures of Sherlock Holmes

"A Scandal in Bohemia"
- The summons to Odessa in the case of the Trepoff murder
- The singular tragedy of the Atkinson brothers at Trincomalee
- The mission which Holmes had accomplished so delicately and successfully for the reigning family of Holland. (He also received a remarkably brilliant ring)
- The Darlington substitution scandal, and . . .
- The Arnsworth castle business. (When a woman thinks that her house is on fire, her instinct is at once to rush to the thing which she values most. It is a perfectly overpowering impulse, and Holmes has more than once taken advantage of it

"The Red-Headed League"
- The previous skirmishes with John Clay

"A Case of Identity"
- The Dundas separation case, where Holmes was engaged in clearing up some small points in connection with it. The husband was a teetotaler, there was no other woman, and the conduct complained of was that he had drifted into the habit of winding up every meal by taking out his false teeth and hurling them at his wife, which is not an action likely to occur to the imagination of the average story-teller.
- The rather intricate matter from Marseilles
- Mrs. Etherege, whose husband Holmes found so easy when the police and everyone had given him up for dead

"The Boscombe Valley Mystery"
NONE LISTED

"The Five Orange Pips"
- The adventure of the Paradol Chamber
- The Amateur Mendicant Society, who held a luxurious club in the lower vault of a furniture warehouse
- The facts connected with the disappearance of the British barque *Sophy Anderson*
- The singular adventures of the Grice-Patersons in the island of Uffa
- The Camberwell poisoning case, in which, as may be remembered, Holmes was able, by winding up the dead man's watch, to prove that it had been wound up two hours before, and that therefore the deceased had gone to bed within that time – a deduction which was of the greatest importance in clearing up the case
- Holmes saved Major Prendergast in the Tankerville Club scandal. He was wrongfully accused of cheating at cards
- Holmes has been beaten four times – three times by men and once by a woman

"The Man with the Twisted Lip"
- The rascally Lascar who runs The Bar of Gold in Upper Swandam Lane has sworn to have vengeance upon Holmes

"The Adventure of the Blue Carbuncle"
NONE LISTED

"The Adventure of the Speckled Band"
- Mrs. Farintosh and an opal tiara. (It was before Watson's time)

"The Adventure of the Engineer's Thumb"
- Colonel Warburton's madness

"The Adventure of the Noble Bachelor"
- The letter from a fishmonger
- The letter a tide-waiter
- The service for Lord Backwater
- The little problem of the Grosvenor Square furniture van
- The service for the King of Scandinavia

"The Adventure of the Beryl Coronet"

467

NONE LISTED

"The Adventure of the Copper Beeches"
NONE LISTED

The Memoirs of Sherlock Holmes

"Silver Blaze"
NONE LISTED

"The Cardboard Box"
- Aldridge, who helped in the bogus laundry affair

"The Yellow Face"
- The (First) Adventure of the Second Stain was a failure which present[s] the strongest features of interest

'The Stockbroker's Clerk"
NONE LISTED

"The "Gloria Scott"
NONE LISTED

"The Musgrave Ritual"
- The Tarleton murders
- The case of Vamberry, the wine merchant
- The adventure of the old Russian woman
- The singular affair of the aluminum crutch
- A full account of Ricoletti of the club foot and his abominable wife
- The two cases before the Musgrave Ritual from Holmes's fellow students

"The Reigate Squires"
- The whole question of the Netherland-Sumatra Company and of the colossal schemes of Baron Maupertuis

The Crooked Man"
NONE LISTED

The Resident Patient"

- [Catalepsy] is a very easy complaint to imitate. Holmes has done it himself.

- . . . and paid a short but interesting visit to the Khalifa at Khartoum
- Returning to France, Holmes spent some months in a research into the coal-tar derivatives, which he conducted in a laboratory at Montpelier [*sic*], in the South of France
- Mathews, who knocked out Holmes's left canine in the waiting room at Charing Cross
- The death of Mrs. Stewart, of Lauder, in 1887
- Morgan the poisoner
- Merridew of abominable memory
- The Molesey Mystery (Inspector Lestrade's Case. He handled it fairly well.)

"The Adventure of the Norwood Builder"
- The case of the papers of ex-President Murillo
- The shocking affair of the Dutch steamship, *Friesland*, which so nearly cost both Holmes and Watson their lives
- That terrible murderer, Bert Stevens, who wanted Holmes and Watson to get him off in '87

"The Adventure of the Dancing Men"
  NONE LISTED

"The Adventure of the Solitary Cyclist"
- The peculiar persecution of John Vincent Harden, the well-known tobacco millionaire
- It was near Farnham that Holmes and Watson took Archie Stamford, the forger

"The Adventure of the Priory School"
- Holmes was retained in the case of the Ferrers Documents
- The Abergavenny murder, which is coming up for trial

"The Adventure of Black Peter"
- The sudden death of Cardinal Tosca – an inquiry which was carried out by him at the express desire of His Holiness the Pope
- The arrest of Wilson, the notorious canary-trainer, which removed a plague-spot from the East-End of London.

"The Adventure of Charles Augustus Milverton"

470

"The Adventure of the Six Napoleons"
- The dreadful business of the Abernetty family, which was first brought to Holmes's attention by the depth which the parsley had sunk into the butter upon a hot day
- The Conk-Singleton forgery case
- Holmes was consulted upon the case of the disappearance of the black pearl of the Borgias, but was unable to throw any light upon it

"The Adventure of the Three Students"
- Some laborious researches in Early English charters

"The Adventure of the Golden Pince-Nez"
- The repulsive story of the red leech
- . . . and the terrible death of Crosby, the banker
- The Addleton tragedy
- . . . and the singular contents of the ancient British barrow
- The famous Smith-Mortimer succession case
- The tracking and arrest of Huret, the boulevard assassin

"The Adventure of the Missing Three-Quarter"
- Henry Staunton, whom Holmes helped to hang
- Arthur H. Staunton, the rising young forger

"The Adventure of the Abbey Grange"
- Hopkins called Holmes in seven times, and on each occasion his summons was entirely justified

"The Adventure of the Second Stain"
- The woman at Margate. No powder on her nose – that proved to be the correct solution. How can one build on such a quicksand? A woman's most trivial action may mean volumes, or their most extraordinary conduct may depend upon a hairpin or a curling-tong

The Hound of the Baskervilles

- That little affair of the Vatican cameos, in which Holmes obliged the Pope

- The little case in which Holmes had the good fortune to help Messenger Manager Wilson
- One of the most revered names in England is being besmirched by a blackmailer, and only Holmes can stop a disastrous scandal
- The atrocious conduct of Colonel Upwood in connection with the famous card scandal at the Nonpareil Club
- Holmes defended the unfortunate Mme. Montpensier from the charge of murder that hung over her in connection with the death of her stepdaughter Mlle. Carere, the young lady who, as it will be remembered, was found six months later alive and married in New York

The Valley of Fear

- Twice already Holmes had helped Inspector Macdonald

His Last Bow

"The Adventure of Wisteria Lodge"
- The locking-up Colonel Carruthers

"The Adventure of the Red Circle"
- The affair last year for Mr. Fairdale Hobbs
- The Long Island cave mystery

"The Adventure of the Bruce-Partington Plans"
- Brooks . . .
- . . . or Woodhouse, or any of the fifty men who have good reason for taking Holmes's life

"The Adventure of the Dying Detective"
NONE LISTED

"The Disappearance of Lady Frances Carfax"
- Holmes cannot possibly leave London while old Abrahams is in such mortal terror of his life

"The Adventure of the Devil's Foot"

- Holmes's dramatic introduction to Dr. Moore Agar, of Harley Street

<u>"His Last Bow"</u>
- Holmes started his pilgrimage at Chicago . . .
- . . . graduated in an Irish secret society at Buffalo
- . . . gave serious trouble to the constabulary at Skibbareen
- Holmes saves Count Von und Zu Grafenstein from murder by the Nihilist Klopman

The Case-Book of Sherlock Holmes

<u>"The Adventure of the Illustrious Client"</u>
- Negotiations with Sir George Lewis over the Hammerford Will case

<u>"The Adventure of the Blanched Soldier"</u>
- The Abbey School in which the Duke of Greyminster was so deeply involved
- The commission from the Sultan of Turkey which required immediate action
- The professional service for Sir James Saunders

<u>"The Adventure of the Mazarin Stone"</u>
- Old Baron Dowson said the night before he was hanged that in Holmes's case what the law had gained the stage had lost
- The death of old Mrs. Harold, who left Count Sylvius the Blymer estate
- The compete life history of Miss Minnie Warrender
- The robbery in the train de-luxe to the Riviera on February 13, 1892

<u>"The Adventure of the Three Gables"</u>
- The killing of young Perkins outside the Holborn Bar
- Mortimer Maberly, was one of Holmes's early clients

<u>"The Adventure of the Sussex Vampire"</u>
- *Matilda Briggs*, a ship which is associated with the giant rat of Sumatra, a story for which the world is not yet prepared
- Victor Lynch, the forger
- Venomous lizard, or Gila. Remarkable case, that!

473

- Vittoria the circus belle
- Vanderbilt and the Yeggman
- Vigor, the Hammersmith wonder

"The Adventure of the Three Garridebs"
- Holmes refused a knighthood for services which may, someday, be described

"The Problem of Thor Bridge"
- Mr. James Phillimore who, stepping back into his own house to get his umbrella, was never more seen in this world
- The cutter *Alicia*, which sailed one spring morning into a patch of mist from where she never again emerged, nor was anything further ever heard of herself and her crew.
- Isadora Persano, the well-known journalist and duelist who was found stark staring mad with a match box in front of him which contained a remarkable worm said to be unknown to science

"The Adventure of the Creeping Man"
NONE LISTED

"The Adventure of the Lion's Mane"
NONE LISTED

"The Adventure of the Veiled Lodger"
- The whole story concerning the politician, the lighthouse, and the trained cormorant

"The Adventure of Shoscombe Old Place"
- Holmes ran down that coiner by the zinc and copper filings in the seam of his cuff
- The St. Pancras case, where a cap was found beside the dead policeman. Merivale of the Yard, asked Holmes to look into it

"The Adventure of the Retired Colourman"
- The case of the two Coptic Patriarchs

About the Contributors

The following contributors appear in this volume:
The MX Book of New Sherlock Holmes Stories
Part XXII – Some More Untold Cases (1877-1887)

Ian Ableson is an ecologist by training and a writer by choice. When not reading or writing, he can reliably be found scowling at a clipboard while ankle-deep in a marsh somewhere in Michigan. His love for the stories of Arthur Conan Doyle started when his grandfather gave him a copy of *The Original Illustrated Sherlock Holmes* when he was in high school, and he's proud to have been able to contribute to the continuation of the tales of Sherlock Holmes and Dr. Watson.

S.F. Bennett has, at various times, been an actor, a lecturer, a journalist, a historian, an author, and a potter. Whilst some of those things still apply, she has always been an avid collector, concentrating mainly on ephemera and other related items concerning Sherlock Holmes and British science-fiction of the 1970's. To date, she has written articles on aspects of The Canon for *The Baker Street Journal*, *The Sherlock Holmes Journal*, and *The Torr*, the journal of *The Sherlock Holmes Society of the West Country*. When not collecting, she can be found writing science-fiction and mystery stories, and has contributed to several anthologies of new Sherlock Holmes pastiches. Her first novel was *The Secret Diary of Mycroft Holmes: The Thoughts and Reminiscences of Sherlock Holmes's Elder Brother, 1880-1888* (2017). She is also the author of *A Study in Postcards: Sherlock Holmes in the Golden Age of the Picture Postcard* (*Sherlock Holmes Society of London*, 2019).

Brian Belanger is a publisher and editor, but is best known for his freelance illustration and cover design work. His distinctive style can be seen on several MX Publishing covers, including *Silent Meridian* by Elizabeth Crowen, *Sherlock Holmes and the Menacing Melbournian* by Allan Mitchell, *Sherlock Holmes and A Quantity of Debt* by David Marcum, *Welcome to Undershaw* by Luke Benjamen Kuhns, and many more. Brian is the co-founder of Belanger Books LLC, where he illustrates the popular *MacDougall Twins with Sherlock Holmes* young reader series (#1 bestsellers on Amazon.com UK). A prolific creator, he also designs t-shirts, mugs, stickers, and other merchandise on his personal art site: *www.redbubble.com/people/zhahadun.*

Derrick Belanger is an educator and also the author of the #1 bestselling book in its category, *Sherlock Holmes: The Adventure of the Peculiar Provenance*, which was in the top 200 bestselling books on Amazon. He also is the author of *The MacDougall Twins with Sherlock Holmes* books, and he edited the Sir Arthur Conan Doyle horror anthology *A Study in Terror: Sir Arthur Conan Doyle's Revolutionary Stories of Fear and the Supernatural*. Mr. Belanger co-owns the publishing company Belanger Books, which has released numerous Sherlock Holmes anthologies including *Beyond Watson*, *Holmes Away From Home: Adventures from the Great Hiatus*, *Sherlock Holmes: Before Baker Street*, *Sherlock Holmes: Adventures in the Realms of H.G. Wells*, *Sherlock Holmes and the Occult Detectives*, *Sherlock Holmes and the Great Detectives*, and *Beyond the Adventures of Sherlock Holmes*. Derrick resides in Colorado and continues compiling unpublished works by Dr. John H. Watson.

Bob Bishop is the author of over twenty stage plays, musicals, and pantomimes, several written in collaboration with Norfolk composer Bob McNeil Watson. Many of these theatrical works were first performed by the fringe theatre company of which he was principal director, The Fossick Valley Fumblers, at the Edinburgh Festival Fringe between 1982 and 2000. Amongst these works were four Sherlock Holmes plays, inspired by the playwright's lifelong affection for the works of Sir Arthur Conan Doyle. Bob's other works include the comic novel, *A Tickle Amongst the Cornstalks*, an anthology of short stories, *Shadows on the Blind*, and a number of Sherlock Holmes pastiche novellas. He currently lives with his wife and three poodles in North Norfolk.

Chris Chan is a writer, educator, and historian. He works as a researcher and "International Goodwill Ambassador" for Agatha Christie Ltd. His true crime articles, reviews, and short fiction have appeared (or will soon appear) in *The Strand*, *The Wisconsin Magazine of History*, *Mystery Weekly*, *Gilbert!*, *Nerd HQ*, Akashic Books' *Mondays are Murder* web series, *The Baker Street Journal*, and *Sherlock Holmes Mystery Magazine*. His latest book is *Sherlock and Irene: The Secret Truth Behind "A Scandal in Bohemia"*

Leslie Charteris was born in Singapore on May 12th, 1907. With his mother and brother, he moved to England in 1919 and attended Rossall School in Lancashire before moving on to Cambridge University to study law. His studies there came to a halt when a publisher accepted his first novel. His third one, entitled *Meet the Tiger*, was written when he was twenty years old and published in September 1928. It introduced the world to Simon Templar, *aka* The Saint. He continued to write about The Saint until 1983 when the last book, *Salvage for The Saint*, was published. The books, which have been translated into over thirty languages, number nearly a hundred and have sold over forty-million copies around the world. They've inspired, to date, fifteen feature films, three television series, ten radio series, and a comic strip that was written by Charteris and syndicated around the world for over a decade. He enjoyed travelling, but settled for long periods in Hollywood, Florida, and finally in Surrey, England. He was awarded the Cartier Diamond Dagger by the *Crime Writers' Association* in 1992, in recognition of a lifetime of achievement. He died the following year.

Ian Dickerson was just nine years old when he discovered The Saint. Shortly after that, he discovered Sherlock Holmes. The Saint won, for a while anyway. He struck up a friendship with The Saint's creator, Leslie Charteris, and his family. With their permission, he spent six weeks studying the Leslie Charteris collection at Boston University and went on to write, direct, and produce documentaries on the making of *The Saint* and *Return of The Saint*, which have been released on DVD. He oversaw the recent reprints of almost fifty of the original Saint books in both the US and UK, and was a co-producer on the 2017 TV movie of *The Saint*. When he discovered that Charteris had written Sherlock Holmes stories as well – well, there was the excuse he needed to revisit The Canon. He's consequently written and edited three books on Holmes' radio adventures. For the sake of what little sanity he has, Ian has also written about a wide range of subjects, none of which come with a halo, including talking mashed potatoes, Lord Grade, and satellite links. Ian lives in Hampshire with his wife and two children. And an awful lot of books by Leslie Charteris. Not quite so many by Conan Doyle, though.

Sir Arthur Conan Doyle (1859-1930) *Holmes Chronicler Emeritus*. If not for him, this anthology would not exist. Author, physician, patriot, sportsman, spiritualist, husband and father, and advocate for the oppressed. He is remembered and honored for the purposes of this collection by being the man who introduced Sherlock Holmes to the world. Through fifty-six Holmes short stories, four novels, and additional Apocryphal entries, Doyle revolutionized mystery stories and also greatly influenced and improved police forensic methods and techniques for the betterment of all. *Steel True Blade Straight.*

Steve Emecz's main field is technology, in which he has been working for about twenty years. Steve is a regular trade show speaker on the subject of eCommerce, and his tech career has taken him to more than fifty countries – so he's no stranger to planes and airports. He wrote two novels (one a bestseller) in the 1990's, and a screenplay in 2001. Shortly after, he set up MX Publishing, specialising in NLP books. In 2008, MX published its first Sherlock Holmes book, and MX has gone on to become the largest specialist Holmes publisher in the world. MX is a social enterprise and supports three main causes. The first is Happy Life, a children's rescue project in Nairobi, Kenya, where he and his wife, Sharon, spend every Christmas at the rescue centre in Kasarani. In 2014, they wrote a short book about the project, *The Happy Life Story*. The second is the Stepping Stones School, of which Steve is a patron. Stepping Stones is located at Undershaw, Sir Arthur Conan Doyle's former home. Steve has been a mentor for the World Food Programme for the last several years, supporting their innovation bootcamps and giving 1-2-1 mentoring to several projects.

Mark A. Gagen BSI is co-founder of Wessex Press, sponsor of the popular *From Gillette to Brett* conferences, and publisher of *The Sherlock Holmes Reference Library* and many other fine Sherlockian titles. A life-long Holmes enthusiast, he is a member of *The Baker Street Irregulars* and *The Illustrious Clients of Indianapolis*. A graphic artist by profession, his work is often seen on the covers of *The Baker Street Journal* and various BSI books.

Denis Green was born in London, England in April 1905. He grew up mostly in London's Savoy Theatre where his father, Richard Green, was a principal in many Gilbert and Sullivan productions, A Flying Officer with RAF until 1924, he then spent four years managing a tea estate in North India before making his stage debut in *Hamlet* with Leslie Howard in 1928. He made his first visit to America in 1931 and established a respectable stage career before appearing in films – including minor roles in the first two Rathbone and Bruce Holmes films – and developing a career in front of and behind the microphone during the golden age of radio. Green and Leslie Charteris met in 1938 and struck up a lifelong friendship. Always busy, be it on stage, radio, film or television, Green passed away at the age of fifty in New York.

John Atkinson Grimshaw (1836-1893) was born in Leeds, England. His amazing paintings, usually featuring twilight or night scenes illuminated by gas-lamps or moonlight, are easily recognizable, and are often used on the covers of books about The Great Detective to set the mood, as shadowy figures move in the distance through misty mysterious settings and over rain-slicked streets.

Christopher James was born in 1975 in Paisley, Scotland. Educated at Newcastle and UEA, he was a winner of the UK's National Poetry Competition in 2008. He has written three full length Sherlock Holmes novels, *The Adventure of the Ruby Elephant*, *The Jeweller of Florence*, and *The Adventure of the Beer Barons*, all published by MX.

Roger Johnson BSI, ASH is a retired librarian, now working as a volunteer assistant at the Essex Police Museum. In his spare time, he is commissioning editor of *The Sherlock Holmes Journal*, an occasional lecturer, and a frequent contributor to *The Writings about the Writings*. His sole work of Holmesian pastiche was published in 1997 in Mike Ashley's anthology *The Mammoth Book of New Sherlock Holmes Adventures*, and he has the greatest respect for the many authors who have contributed new tales to the present mighty trilogy. Like his wife, Jean Upton, he is a member of both *The Baker Street Irregulars* and *The Adventuresses of Sherlock Holmes*.

Susan Knight's newest novel from MX publishing, *Mrs. Hudson Goes to Ireland*, is a follow-up to her well-received collection of stories, *Mrs. Hudson Investigates* of 2019. She is the author of two other non-Sherlockian story collections, as well as three novels, a book of non-fiction, and several plays, and has won several prizes for her writing. She lives in Dublin where she teaches Creative Writing. Her next Mrs. Hudson novel is already a gleam in her eye.

David Marcum plays *The Game* with deadly seriousness. He first discovered Sherlock Holmes in 1975 at the age of ten, and since that time, he has collected, read, and chronologicized literally thousands of traditional Holmes pastiches in the form of novels, short stories, radio and television episodes, movies and scripts, comics, fan-fiction, and unpublished manuscripts. He is the author of over sixty Sherlockian pastiches, some published in anthologies and magazines such as *The Strand*, and others collected in his own books, *The Papers of Sherlock Holmes*, *Sherlock Holmes and A Quantity of Debt*, and *Sherlock Holmes – Tangled Skeins*. He has edited fifty books, including several dozen traditional Sherlockian anthologies, such as the ongoing series *The MX Book of New Sherlock Holmes Stories*, which he created in 2015. This collection is now up to 24 volumes, with more in preparation. He was responsible for bringing back August Derleth's Solar Pons for a new generation, first with his collection of authorized Pons stories, *The Papers of Solar Pons*, and then by editing the reissued authorized versions of the original Pons books, and then volumes of new Pons adventures. He is now doing the same for the adventures of Dr. Thorndyke. He has contributed numerous essays to various publications, and is a member of a number of Sherlockian groups and Scions. He is a licensed Civil Engineer, living in Tennessee with his wife and son. His irregular Sherlockian blog, *A Seventeen Step Program*, addresses various topics related to his favorite book friends (as his son used to call them when he was small), and can be found at *http://17stepprogram.blogspot.com/* Since the age of nineteen, he has worn a deerstalker as his regular-and-only hat. In 2013, he and his deerstalker were finally able make his first trip-of-a-lifetime Holmes Pilgrimage to England, with return Pilgrimages in 2015 and 2016, where you may have spotted him. If you ever run into him and his deerstalker out and about, feel free to say hello!

Stephen Mason has been the Third Mate (President) of *The Crew of the Barque* Lone Star scion society in Dallas/Fort Worth for over seven years. He is also the Chair of the Communications Committee for *The Beacon Society*, a national educational scion society. With Joe Fay and Rusty Mason, he produces the *Baker Street Elementary* comic strip each week, the first adventures of Sherlock Holmes and John Watson.

Mark Mower is a member of the *Crime Writers' Association, The Sherlock Holmes Society of London*, and *The Solar Pons Society of London*. He writes true crime stories and fictional mysteries. His volumes of Holmes pastiches include *A Farewell to Baker Street*, *Sherlock Holmes: The Baker Street Case-Files*, and *Baker Street Legacy* (all published by MX Publishing) and he has contributed multiple stories to the ongoing *The MX Book of New Sherlock Holmes Stories*. He has also had stories in two anthologies by Belanger Books: *Holmes Away From Home: Adventures from the Great Hiatus – Volume II – 1893-1894* (2016) and *Sherlock Holmes: Before Baker Street* (2017). More are bound to follow.

478

Mark's non-fiction works include *Bloody British History: Norwich* (The History Press, 2014), *Suffolk Murders* (The History Press, 2011) and *Zeppelin Over Suffolk* (Pen & Sword Books, 2008).

Sidney Paget (1860-1908), a few of whose illustrations are used within this anthology, was born in London, and like his two older brothers, became a famed illustrator and painter. He completed over three-hundred-and-fifty drawings for the Sherlock Holmes stories that were first published in *The Strand* magazine, defining Holmes's image forever after in the public mind.

This work represents **Richard Paolinelli**'s fifth published Sherlock Holmes pastiche. He began his writing journey as a freelance writer in 1984 and gained his first fiction credit serving as the lead writer for the first two issues of the Elite Comics sci-fi/fantasy series, *Seadragon*. Following a twenty-year newspaper writing career, he returned to his fiction writing roots and has since published several novels, two non-fiction sports books, and has appeared in several anthologies. His novel, *Escaping Infinity*, was a 2017 Dragon Award Finalist for Best Sci-Fi novel. He also writes weekly short fiction on his website, *www.richardpaolinelli.com*

Otto Penzler, proprietor of The Mysterious Bookshop in New York City, founded The Mysterious Press in 1975, and publishes e-books through *MysteriousPress.com*. Penzler has won two Edgar Awards, *The Mystery Writers of America*'s Ellery Queen Award, and The Raven. He has been given Lifetime Achievement awards by Noircon and *The Strand Magazine*. He founded two new publishing companies in 2018, Penzler Publishers, reissuing American Mystery Classics in hardcover and trade paperback, and Scarlet, which publishes original psychological suspense novels. He has edited more than sixty anthologies.

Tracy J. Revels, a Sherlockian from the age of eleven, is a professor of history at Wofford College in Spartanburg, South Carolina. She is a member of *The Survivors of the Gloria Scott* and *The Studious Scarlets Society*, and is a past recipient of the Beacon Society Award. Almost every semester, she teaches a class that covers The Canon, either to college students or to senior citizens. She is also the author of three supernatural Sherlockian pastiches with MX (*Shadowfall, Shadowblood,* and *Shadowwraith*), and a regular contributor to her scion's newsletter. She also has some notoriety as an author of very silly skits: For proof, see "The Adventure of the Adversarial Adventuress" and "Occupy Baker Street" on YouTube. When not studying Sherlock, she can be found researching the history of her native state, and has written books on Florida in the Civil War and on the development of Florida's tourism industry.

Roger Riccard of Los Angeles, California, U.S.A., is a descendant of the Roses of Kilravock in Highland Scotland. He is the author of two previous Sherlock Holmes novels, *The Case of the Poisoned Lilly* and *The Case of the Twain Papers*, a series of short stories in two volumes, *Sherlock Holmes: Adventures for the Twelve Days of Christmas* and *Further Adventures for the Twelve Days of Christmas*, and the new series *A Sherlock Holmes Alphabet of Cases*, all of which are published by Baker Street Studios. He has another novel and a non-fiction Holmes reference work in various stages of completion. He became a Sherlock Holmes enthusiast as a teenager (many, many years ago), and, like all fans of The Great Detective, yearned for more stories after reading The Canon over and over. It was the Granada Television performances of Jeremy Brett and Edward Hardwicke, and the encouragement of his wife, Rosilyn, that at last inspired him to write his own

479

Holmes adventures, using the Granada actor portrayals as his guide. He has been called "The best pastiche writer since Val Andrews" by the *Sherlockian E-Times*.

Geri Schear is a novelist and short story writer. Her work has been published in literary journals in the U.S. and Ireland. Her first novel, *A Biased Judgement: The Diaries of Sherlock Holmes 1897* was released to critical acclaim in 2014. The sequel, *Sherlock Holmes and the Other Woman* was published in 2015, and *Return to Reichenbach* in 2016. She lives in Kells, Ireland.

Award-winning author **Dr. Liese Sherwood-Fabre** doesn't remember a time she didn't know of Sherlock Holmes – be it the old Basel Rathbone movies, Tom and Jerry in deerstalker hats, or the original Conan Doyle tales. During her thirty-plus years as a federal employee, Dr. Sherwood-Fabre worked and lived in various countries, including Mexico and Russia, finding inspiration for stories based on events taking place around her. She garnered a prestigious Pushcart nomination for a short story inspired by her experiences in Mexico, and having lived through the tumultuous years of Russia's budding democracy, her first published novel, *Saving Hope*, centered around an unemployed Russian microbiologist who must choose between saving her daughter's life or working with a former KGB agent to stop the sale of bioweapons to Iran. After returning to the United States, Dr. Sherwood-Fabre revived her early interest in Sherlock Holmes and the Victorian period. For the past six years, she has shared her knowledge with other Sherlockians by contributing regularly to several society newsletters, as well as the prestigious *Baker Street Journal* and *Canadian Holmes* publications. Besides her own recently launch series *The Early Case Files of Sherlock Holmes*, she has contributed to Sherlockian anthologies through *Mocha Memoirs* and *The Crew of the Barque Lone Star* scion – and now MX Publishing. Visit her Website *www.liesesherwoodfabre.com* for more about her publications and to sign up for her newsletter.

Jacqueline Silver is the newly-appointed Headteacher of Stepping Stones School. She has developed her career from her early days as an accomplished Drama teacher and has a strong background in school leadership. She has always had a passion for creating nurturing and positive school environments for mixed ability children. Her recent career history has seen her spearhead pastoral care provision at a number of schools where she has also been resolute in her vision for safeguarding, particularly of the most vulnerable children in our society. Since her recent appointment as Headteacher of Stepping Stones School, she can realise her prime personal focus for improving the employability of young people with learning needs. Quality of life, independence, and positive engagement with society are linchpins of Jacqueline's vision for the future. Stepping Stones will flourish under her leadership.

Denis O. Smith's first published story of Sherlock Holmes and Doctor Watson, "The Adventure of The Purple Hand", appeared in 1982. Since then, numerous other such accounts have been published in magazines and anthologies both in the U.K. and the U.S. In the 1990's, four volumes of his stories were published under the general title of *The Chronicles of Sherlock Holmes*, and, more recently his stories have been collected as *The Lost Chronicles of Sherlock Holmes* (2014), *The Lost Chronicles of Sherlock Holmes Volume II* (2016), *The Further Chronicles of Sherlock Holmes* (201). He also wrote a Holmes novel, *The Riddle of Foxwood Grange* (2017). Born in Yorkshire, in the north of England, Denis Smith has lived and worked in various parts of the country, including London, and has now been resident in Norfolk for many years. His interests range widely, but apart from his dedication to the career of Sherlock Holmes, he has a passion for historical mysteries of all kinds, the railways of Britain and the history of London.

Robert V. Stapleton was born and brought up in Leeds, Yorkshire, England, and studied at Durham University. After working in various parts of the country as an Anglican parish priest, he is now retired and lives with his wife in North Yorkshire. As a member of his local writing group, he now has time to develop his other life as a writer of adventure stories. He has recently had a number of short stories published, and he is hoping to have a couple of completed novels published at some time in the future.

Tim Symonds was born in London. He grew up in Somerset, Dorset, and Guernsey. After several years in East and Central Africa, he settled in California and graduated Phi Beta Kappa in Political Science from UCLA. He is a Fellow of the *Royal Geographical Society*. He writes his novels in the woods and hidden valleys surrounding his home in the High Weald of East Sussex. Dr. Watson knew the untamed region well. In "The Adventure of Black Peter", Watson wrote, "*the Weald was once part of that great forest which for so long held the Saxon invaders at bay.*" Tim's novels are published by MX Publishing. His novels include *Sherlock Holmes and the Nine Dragon Sigil. Sherlock Holmes and The Sword of Osman, Sherlock Holmes and the Mystery of Einstein's Daughter, Sherlock Holmes and the Dead Boer at Scotney Castle*, and *Sherlock Holmes and the Case of The Bulgarian Codex*. His collection of Holmes short stories is called *A Most Diabolical Plot.*

Kevin P. Thornton is a seven-time Arthur Ellis Award Nominee. He is a former director of the local Heritage Society and Library, and he has been a soldier in Africa, a contractor for the Canadian Military in Afghanistan, a newspaper and magazine columnist, a Director of both the *Crime Writers of Canada* and the *Writers' Guild of Alberta*, a founding member of *Northword Literary Magazine*, and is either a current or former member of *The Mystery Writers of America, The Crime Writers Association, The Calgary Crime Writers, The International Thriller Writers, The International Association of Crime Writers, The Keys* – a Catholic Writers group founded by Monsignor Knox and G.K. Chesterton – as well as, somewhat inexplicably, *The Mesdames of Mayhem* and *Sisters in Crime*. If you ask, he will join. Born in Kenya, Kevin has lived or worked in South Africa, Dubai, England, Afghanistan, New Zealand, Ontario, and now Northern Alberta. He lives on his wits and his wit, and is doing better than expected. He is not one to willingly split infinitives, and while never pedantic, is on occasion known to be ever so slightly punctilious.

William Todd has been a Holmes fan his entire life, and credits *The Hound of the Baskervilles* as the impetus for his love of both reading and writing. He began to delve into fan fiction a few years ago when he decided to take a break from writing his usual Victorian/Gothic horror stories. He was surprised how well-received they were, and has tried to put out a couple of Holmes stories a year since then. When not writing, Mr. Todd is a pathology supervisor at a local hospital in Northwestern Pennsylvania. He is the husband of a terrific lady and father to two great kids, one with special needs, so the benefactor of these anthologies is close to his heart.

The MX Book of New Sherlock Holmes Stories

Part XXIII – Some More Untold Cases (1888-1894)
and
Part XXIV – Some More Untold Cases (1895-1903)

Hugh Ashton was born in the U.K., and moved to Japan in 1988, where he remained until 2016, living with his wife Yoshiko in the historic city of Kamakura, a little to the south of Yokohama. He and Yoshiko have now moved to Lichfield, a small cathedral city in the Midlands of the U.K., the birthplace of Samuel Johnson, and one-time home of Erasmus Darwin. In the past, he has worked in the technology and financial services industries, which have provided him with material for some of his books set in the 21st century. He currently works as a writer: Novelist, freelance editor, and copywriter, (his work for large Japanese corporations has appeared in international business journals), and journalist, as well as producing industry reports on various aspects of the financial services industry. However, his lifelong interest in Sherlock Holmes has developed into an acclaimed series of adventures featuring the world's most famous detective, written in the style of the originals. In addition to these, he has also published historical and alternate historical novels, short stories, and thrillers. Together with artist Andy Boerger, he has produced the *Sherlock Ferret* series of stories for children, featuring the world's cutest detective.

Thomas A. Burns, Jr. is the author of the *Natalie McMasters Mysteries*. He was born and grew up in New Jersey, attended Xavier High School in Manhattan, earned B.S degrees in Zoology and Microbiology at Michigan State University, and a M.S. in Microbiology at North Carolina State University. He currently resides in Wendell, North Carolina. As a kid, Tom started reading mysteries with The Hardy Boys, Ken Holt, and Rick Brant, and graduated to the classic stories by authors such as A. Conan Doyle, Dorothy Sayers, John Dickson Carr, Erle Stanley Gardner, and Rex Stout, to name a few. Tom has written fiction as a hobby all of his life, starting with The Man from U.N.C.L.E. stories in marble-backed copybooks in grade school. He built a career as technical, science, and medical writer and editor for nearly thirty years in industry and government. Now that he's truly on his own as a novelist, he's excited to publish his own mystery series, as well as to contribute stories about his second-most-favorite detective, Sherlock Holmes, to *The MX Book of New Sherlock Holmes Stories*.

Leverett Butts teaches composition and literature at the University of North Georgia. His poetry and fiction have appeared in *Eclectic* and *The Georgia State University Review*. He is the recipient of several fiction prizes offered by the University of West Georgia and TAG Publishing. His first collection of short fiction, *Emily's Stitches: The Confessions of Thomas Calloway and Other Stories*, was nominated for the 2013 Georgia Author of the Year Award in Short Fiction. The collection of the first two volumes of his *Guns of the Waste Land* was nominated in 2016, and the third volume of the series won honorable mention in the 2018 Georgia Independent Author of the Year Award in historical fiction. He recently completed the fourth and final volume, *Desinence*. He lives in Carrollton, Georgia, with his wife, son, their Jack Russell terrier, and an antisocial cat.

Mike Chinn lives in Birmingham UK with his wife Caroline and their guinea pigs. He has published over sixty short stories, some of which have found their way into two collections: *Give Me These Moments Back* (The Alchemy Press, 2015) and *Radix Omnium Malum*

(Parallel Universe Publications, 2017). He has edited three volumes of *The Alchemy Press Book of Pulp Heroes* (2012, 2013 and 2014) and *Swords Against the Millenium* (2000) for The Alchemy Press. The first publication of his Damian Paladin collection, *The Paladin Mandates* (The Alchemy Press, 1998), was short-listed for the British Fantasy Award in 1999, and a second Paladin collection, *Walkers in Shadow*, was published by Pro Se Publications in 2017 (who are due to republish an expanded and revised edition of *The Paladin Mandates* in 2020). He sent Sherlock Holmes to the Moon in *Vallis Timoris* (Fringeworks, 2015), and in 2018 Pro Se published his first Western: *Revenge is a Cold Pistol*.

Barry Clay is a graduate of Shippensburg University with a BA in English. He's dug ditches, stocked grocery shelves, tutored for room and board, cleaned restrooms, mopped floors, taught cartooning, worked in a bank, asked if you'd like fries with that (and cooked the fries to boot), ordered carpet for cars, and worked commission sales at Sears. Currently, he is a thirty-two year veteran of the Federal employee workforce. He has been writing all his life in different genres, and he has written thirteen books ranging from Christian theology, anthologies, speculative fiction, horror, science fiction, and humor. His Sherlockian volumes include *The Darkened Village* and *The Leveson-Gower Theft*. He volunteers as conductor of a local student orchestra and has been commissioned to write music. His first two musicals were locally produced. He is the husband of one wife, father of four children, and "Opa" to one granddaughter. He is honored to have been asked to contribute to this collection.

Craig Stephen Copland confesses that he discovered Sherlock Holmes when, sometime in the muddled early 1960's, he pinched his older brother's copy of the immortal stories and was forever afterward thoroughly hooked. He is very grateful to his high school English teachers in Toronto who inculcated in him a love of literature and writing, and even inspired him to be an English major at the University of Toronto. There he was blessed to sit at the feet of both Northrup Frye and Marshall McLuhan, and other great literary professors, who led him to believe that he was called to be a high school English teacher. It was his good fortune to come to his pecuniary senses, abandon that goal, and pursue a varied professional career that took him to over one-hundred countries and endless adventures. He considers himself to have been and to continue to be one of the luckiest men on God's good earth. A few years back he took a step in the direction of Sherlockian studies and joined the *Sherlock Holmes Society of Canada* – also known as *The Toronto Bootmakers*. In May of 2014, this esteemed group of scholars announced a contest for the writing of a new Sherlock Holmes mystery. Although he had never tried his hand at fiction before, Craig entered and was pleasantly surprised to be selected as one of the winners. Having enjoyed the experience, he decided to write more of the same, and is now on a mission to write a new Sherlock Holmes mystery that is related to and inspired by each of the sixty stories in the original Canon. He currently lives and writes in Toronto and Dubai, and looks forward to finally settling down when he turns ninety.

John William Davis is a retired US Army counterintelligence officer, civil servant, and linguist. He was commissioned from Washington University in St. Louis as an artillery officer in the 101st Air Assault Division. Thereafter, he went into counterintelligence and served some thirty-seven years. A linguist, Mr. Davis learned foreign languages in each country he served. After the Cold War and its bitter aftermath, he wrote *Rainy Street Stories, Reflections on Secret Wars, Terrorism, and Espionage*. He wanted to write about not only true events themselves, but also the moral and ethical aspects of the secret world. With the publication of *Around the Corner*, Davis expanded his reflections on conflicted human nature to our present day traumas of fear, and causes for hope. A dedicated Sherlockian, he's contributed to telling the story of the Great Detective in retirement.

Harry DeMaio is a *nom de plume* of Harry B. DeMaio, successful author of several books on Information Security and Business Networks, as well as the thirteen-volume *Casebooks of Octavius Bear.* He is also a published author for Belanger Books, the Dear Holmes series, and the MX Sherlock Holmes anthologies edited by David Marcum. A retired business executive, former consultant, information security specialist, pilot, disk jockey, and graduate school adjunct professor, he whiles away his time traveling and writing preposterous books, articles, and stories. He has appeared on many radio and TV shows and is an accomplished, frequent public speaker. Former New York City natives, he and his extremely patient and helpful wife, Virginia, and their late, lamented Bichon Frisé, Woof, live in Cincinnati (and several other parallel universes.) They have two sons living in Scottsdale, Arizona and Cortlandt Manor, New York, both of whom are quite successful and quite normal, thus putting the lie to the theory that insanity is hereditary. His e-mail is *hdemaio@zoomtown.com* and you can also find him on Facebook. His books are available on Amazon, Barnes and Noble, directly from MX Publishing and at other fine bookstores. His website is *www.octaviusbearslair.com*

Matthew J. Elliott is the author of *Big Trouble in Mother Russia* (2016), the official sequel to the cult movie *Big Trouble in Little China, Lost in Time and Space: An Unofficial Guide to the Uncharted Journeys of Doctor Who* (2014), *Sherlock Holmes on the Air* (2012), *Sherlock Holmes in Pursuit* (2013), *The Immortals: An Unauthorized Guide to* Sherlock *and* Elementary (2013), and *The Throne Eternal* (2014). His articles, fiction, and reviews have appeared in the magazines *Scarlet Street, Total DVD, SHERLOCK,* and *Sherlock Holmes Mystery Magazine*, and the collections *The Game's Afoot, Curious Incidents 2, Gaslight Grimoire, The Mammoth Book of Best British Crime 8*, and *The MX Book of New Sherlock Holmes Stories – Part III: 1896-1929.* He has scripted over 260 radio plays, including episodes of *Doctor Who, The Further Adventures of Sherlock Holmes, The Twilight Zone, The New Adventures of Mickey Spillane's Mike Hammer, Fangoria's Dreadtime Stories*, and award-winning adaptations of *The Hound of the Baskervilles* and *The War of the Worlds*. He is the only radio dramatist to adapt all sixty original stories from The Canon for the series *The Classic Adventures of Sherlock Holmes*. Matthew is a writer and performer on *RiffTrax.com*, the online comedy experience from the creators of cult sci-fi TV series *Mystery Science Theater 3000* (*MST3K* to the initiated). He's also written a few comic books.

Tim Gambrell lives in Exeter, Devon, with his wife, two young sons, three cats, and now only four chickens. He has previously contributed stories to *The MX Book of New Sherlock Holmes Stories*, and also to *Sherlock Holmes and Dr Watson: The Early Adventures* and *Sherlock Holmes and The Occult Detectives*, also from Belanger Books. Outside of the world of Holmes, Tim has written extensively for Doctor Who spin-off ranges. His books include two linked novels from Candy Jar Books: *Lethbridge-Stewart: The Laughing Gnome – Lucy Wilson & The Bledoe Cadets*, and *The Lucy Wilson Mysteries: The Brigadier and The Bledoe Cadets* (both 2019), and *Lethbridge-Stewart: Bloodlines – An Ordinary Man* (Candy Jar, 2020, written with Andy Frankham-Allen). He's also written a novella, *The Way of The Bry'hunee* (2019) for the Erimem range from Thebes Publishing. Tim's short fiction includes stories in *Lethbridge-Stewart: The HAVOC Files 3* (Candy Jar, 2017, revised edition 2020), *Bernice Summerfield: True Stories* (Big Finish, 2017) and *Relics . . . An Anthology* (Red Ted Books, 2018), plus a number of charity anthologies.

Jayantika Ganguly BSI is the General Secretary and Editor of the *Sherlock Holmes Society of India*, a member of the *Sherlock Holmes Society of London*, and the *Czech Sherlock Holmes Society*. She is the author of *The Holmes Sutra* (MX 2014). She is a corporate lawyer working with one of the Big Six law firms.

Paul D. Gilbert was born in 1954 and has lived in and around London all of his life. His wife Jackie is a Holmes expert who keeps him on the straight and narrow! He has two sons, one of whom now lives in Spain. His interests include literature, ancient history, all religions, most sports, and movies. He is currently employed full-time as a funeral director. His books so far include *The Lost Files of Sherlock Holmes* (2007), *The Chronicles of Sherlock Holmes* (2008), *Sherlock Holmes and the Giant Rat of Sumatra* (2010), *The Annals of Sherlock Holmes* (2012), *Sherlock Holmes and the Unholy Trinity* (2015), *Sherlock Holmes: The Four Handed Game* (2017), and *The Illumination of Sherlock Holmes* (2019).

Dick Gillman is an English writer and acrylic artist living in Brittany, France with his wife Alex, Truffle, their Black Labrador, and Jean-Claude, their Breton cat. During his retirement from teaching, he has written over twenty Sherlock Holmes short stories which are published as both e-books and paperbacks. His initial contribution to the superb MX Sherlock Holmes collection, published in October 2015, was entitled "The Man on Westminster Bridge" and had the privilege of being chosen as the anchor story in *The MX Book of New Sherlock Holmes Stories – Part II (1890-1895)*.

John Linwood Grant is a writer and editor who lives in Yorkshire with a pack of lurchers and a beard. He may also have a family. He focuses particularly on dark Victorian and Edwardian fiction, such as his recent novella *A Study in Grey*, which also features Holmes. Current projects include his *Tales of the Last Edwardian* series, about psychic and psychiatric mysteries, and curating a collection of new stories based on the darker side of the British Empire. He has been published in a number of anthologies and magazines, with stories range from madness in early Virginia to questions about the monsters we ourselves might be. He is also co-editor of *Occult Detective Quarterly*. His website *greydogtales.com* explores weird fiction, especially period ones, weird art, and even weirder lurchers.

Arthur Hall was born in Aston, Birmingham, UK, in 1944. He discovered his interest in writing during his schooldays, along with a love of fictional adventure and suspense. His first novel, *Sole Contact*, was an espionage story about an ultra-secret government department known as "Sector Three", and was followed, to date, by three sequels. Other works include five Sherlock Holmes novels, *The Demon of the Dusk*, *The One Hundred Percent Society*, *The Secret Assassin*, *The Phantom Killer*, and *In Pursuit of the Dead*, as well as a collection of short stories, and a modern detective novel. He lives in the West Midlands, United Kingdom.

Paula Hammond has written over sixty fiction and non-fiction books, as well as short stories, comics, poetry, and scripts for educational DVD's. When not glued to the keyboard, she can usually be found prowling round second-hand books shops or hunkered down in a hide, soaking up the joys of the natural world.

Stephen Herczeg is an IT Geek, writer, actor, and film-maker based in Canberra Australia. He has been writing for over twenty years and has completed a couple of dodgy novels, sixteen feature-length screenplays, and numerous short stories and scripts. Stephen was very successful in 2017's International Horror Hotel screenplay competition, with his scripts *TITAN* winning the Sci-Fi category and *Dark are the Woods* placing second in the horror category. His work has featured in *Sproutlings – A Compendium of Little Fictions* from Hunter Anthologies, the *Hells Bells* Christmas horror anthology published by the Australasian Horror Writers Association, and the *Below the Stairs, Trickster's Treats, Shades of Santa, Behind the Mask,* and *Beyond the Infinite* anthologies from Oz*Horror.Con, The Body Horror Book, Anemone Enemy,* and *Petrified Punks* from Oscillate Wildly Press, and *Sherlock Holmes In the Realms of H.G. Wells* and *Sherlock Holmes: Adventures Beyond the Canon* from Belanger Books.

Paul Hiscock is an author of crime, fantasy, and science fiction tales. His short stories have appeared in several anthologies and include a seventeenth century whodunnit, a science fiction western, and a steampunk Sherlock Holmes story. Paul lives with his family in Kent, England, and spends his days chasing a toddler with more energy than the Duracell Bunny. He mainly does his writing in coffee shops with members of the local NaNoWriMo group, or in the middle of the night when his family has gone to sleep. Consequently, his stories tend to be fuelled by large amounts of black coffee. You can find out more about his writing at *www.detectivesanddragons.uk.*

In the year 1998 **Craig Janacek** took his degree of Doctor of Medicine at Vanderbilt University, and proceeded to Stanford to go through the training prescribed for pediatricians in practice. Having completed his studies there, he was duly attached to the University of California, San Francisco as Associate Professor. The author of over seventy medical monographs upon a variety of obscure lesions, his travel-worn and battered tin dispatch-box is crammed with papers, nearly all of which are records of his fictional works. To date, these have been published solely in electronic format, including two non-Holmes novels (*The Oxford Deception* and *The Anger of Achilles Peterson*), the trio of holiday adventures collected as *The Midwinter Mysteries of Sherlock Holmes,* the Holmes story collections *The First of Criminals, The Assassination of Sherlock Holmes, The Treasury of Sherlock Holmes, Light in the Darkness, The Gathering Gloom, The Travels of Sherlock Holmes,* and the Watsonian novels *The Isle of Devils* and *The Gate of Gold.* Craig Janacek is a *nom de plume.*

Steven Philip Jones has written over sixty graphic novels and comic books including the horror series *Lovecraftian, Curious Cases of Sherlock Holmes,* the original series *Nightlinger, Street Heroes 2005,* adaptations of *Dracula,* several H. P. Lovecraft stories, and the 1985 film *Re-animator.* Steven is also the author of several novels and nonfiction books including *The Clive Cussler Adventures: A Critical Review, Comics Writing: Communicating With Comic Book , King of Harlem, Bushwackers, The House With the Witch's Hat, Talisman: The Knightmare Knife,* and *Henrietta Hex: Shadows From the Past.* Steven's other writing credits include a number of scripts for radio dramas that have been broadcast internationally. A graduate of the University of Iowa, Steven has a Bachelor of Arts in Journalism and Religion, and was accepted into Iowa's Writer's Workshop – M.F.A. program.

Susan Knight *also has a story in Part XXIV*

John Lawrence served for thirty-eight years as a staff member in the U.S. House of Representatives, the last eight as Chief of Staff to Speaker Nancy Pelosi (2005-2013). He has been a Visiting Professor at the University of California's Washington Center since 2013. He is the author of *The Class of '74: Congress After Watergate and the Roots of*

Partisanship (2018), and has a Ph.D. in history from the University of California (Berkeley).

David Marcum *also has stories in Parts XXIII and XXIV*

Will Murray has been writing about popular culture since 1973, principally on the subjects of comic books, pulp magazine heroes, and film. As a fiction writer, he's the author of over 70 novels featuring characters as diverse as Nick Fury and Remo Williams. With the late Steve Ditko, he created the Unbeatable Squirrel Girl for Marvel Comics. Murray has written numerous short stories, many on Lovecraftian themes. Currently, he writes The Wild Adventures of Doc Savage for Altus Press. His acclaimed Doc Savage novel, *Skull Island*, pits the pioneer superhero against the legendary King Kong. This was followed by *King Kong vs. Tarzan* and two Doc Savage novels guest-starring The Shadow. *Tarzan, Conqueror of Mars*, a crossover with John Carter of Mars, was just published. *www.adventuresinbronze.com* is his website.

Gayle Lange Puhl has been a Sherlockian since Christmas of 1965. She has had articles published in *The Devon County Chronicle*, *The Baker Street Journal*, and *The Serpentine Muse*, plus her local newspaper. She has created Sherlockian jewelry, a 2006 calendar entitled "If Watson Wrote For TV", and has painted a limited series of Holmes-related nesting dolls. She co-founded the scion *Friends of the Great Grimpen Mire* and the Janesville, Wisconsin-based *The Original Tree Worshipers*. In January 2016, she was awarded the "Outstanding Creative Writer" award by the Janesville Art Alliance for her first book *Sherlock Holmes and the Folk Tale Mysteries*. She is semi-retired and lives in Evansville, Wisconsin. Ms. Puhl has one daughter, Gayla, and four grandchildren.

Tracy J. Revels *also has stories in Parts XXIII and XXIV*

Jane Rubino is the author of *A Jersey Shore* mystery series, featuring a Jane Austen-loving amateur sleuth and a Sherlock Holmes-quoting detective, *Knight Errant*, *Lady Vernon and Her Daughter*, (a novel-length adaptation of Jane Austen's novella *Lady Susan*, co-authored with her daughter Caitlen Rubino-Bradway, *What Would Austen Do?*, also co-authored with her daughter, a short story in the anthology *Jane Austen Made Me Do It*, *The Rucastles' Pawn*, *The Copper Beeches from Violet Turner's POV*, and, of course, there's the Sherlockian novel in the drawer – who doesn't have one? Jane lives on a barrier island at the New Jersey shore.

Brenda Seabrooke's stories have been published in a number of reviews, journals, and anthologies. She has received grants from the National Endowment for the Arts and Emerson College's Robbie Macauley Award. She is the author of twenty-three books for young readers including *Scones and Bones on Baker Street: Sherlock's (maybe!) Dog and the Dirt Dilemma*, and *The Rascal in the Castle: Sherlock's (possible!) Dog and the Queen's Revenge*. Brenda states: *"It was fun to write from Dr. Watson's point of view and not have to worry about fleas, smelly pits, ralphing, or scratching at inopportune times."*

Shane Simmons is the author of the occult detective novels *Necropolis* and *Epitaph*, and the crime collection *Raw and Other Stories*. An award-winning screenwriter and graphic novelist, his work has appeared in international film festivals, museums, and lectures about design and structure. He was born in Lachine, a suburb of Montreal best known for being massacred in 1689 and having a joke name. Visit Shane's homepage at *eyestrainproductions.com* for more.

Dacre Stoker is the great-grand-nephew of Bram Stoker, and the international best-selling co-author of *Dracula the Un-Dead* (Dutton, 2009), and *Dracul* (Putnam 2018). Dacre is also the co-editor (with Elizabeth Miller) of *The Lost Journal of Bram Stoker: The Dublin Years* (Robson Press, 2012). A native of Montreal, Canada, Dacre taught Physical Education and Sciences for twenty-two years, in both Canada and the U.S. He has participated in the sport of Modern Pentathlon as an athlete and a coach at the international and Olympic levels for Canada for twelve years. He currently lives in Aiken, SC, and together with his wife Jenne, they manage The Bram Stoker Estate.

Joseph W. Svec III is retired from Oceanography, Satellite Test Engineering, and college teaching. He has lived on a forty-foot cruising sailboat, on a ranch in the Sierra Nevada Foothills, in a country rose-garden cottage, and currently lives in the shadow of a castle with his childhood sweetheart and several long coated German shepherds. He enjoys writing, gardening, creating dioramas, world travel, and enjoying time with his sweetheart.

Kevin P. Thornton *also has a story in Part XXIV*

D.J. Tyrer is the person behind Atlantean Publishing, was placed second in the Writing Magazine "Local Reporter" competition, and has been widely published in anthologies and magazines around the world, such as *Disturbance* (Laurel Highlands), *Mysteries of Suspense* (Zimbell House), *History and Mystery, Oh My!* (Mystery & Horror LLC), and *Love 'Em, Shoot 'Em* (Wolfsinger), and issues of *Awesome Tales*, and in addition, has a novella available in paperback and on the Kindle, *The Yellow House* (Dunhams Manor) and a comic horror e-novelette, *A Trip to the Middle of the World*, available from Alban Lake through Infinite Realms Bookstore.
His website is: *https://djtyrer.blogspot.co.uk/*
The Atlantean Publishing website is at *https://atlanteanpublishing.wordpress.com/*

Jan van Koningsveld was born in Emden, Germany, having both the German and the Dutch citizenship. He has been a fan of Sherlock Holmes and Dr. Watson since 1982, when a TV series starring Geoffrey Whitehead and Donald Pickering was aired in Germany. The first Holmes story that he read was *A Study in Scarlet*. In his study, he has a library containing more than 1,000 books regarding Sherlock Holmes, and he is a collector of different versions of *The Hound of the Baskervilles* in different languages. He is married and father of three children, works as an account and instructor, and is the author of the books *The Mental Calculator's Handbook* (with Dr. Robert Fountain) and *Become a Human Calendar in just 7 Days*. He is the organizer of multiple events regarding Mental Calculation (such as the World Championships for students), and also a tutor for workshops, all non-profit. HE is the creator and maintainer of the Pi World Ranking List (since 2001) *www-pi-world-ranking-list.com* and the holder of more than twenty world records in Mental Calculation, a 4-time World Cup winner, and a 2-time Memoriad winner. He is a consultant for German TV shows regarding math, and has made several appearances on German and Dutch TV shows. His German website is: *www.janvankoningsveld.com*

Margaret Walsh was born Auckland, New Zealand and now lives in Melbourne, Australia. She is the author of *Sherlock Holmes and the Molly-Boy Murders*, *Sherlock Holmes and the Case of the Perplexed Politician*, and *Sherlock Holmes and the Case of the London Dock Deaths*, all published by MX Publishing. Margaret has been a devotee of Sherlock Holmes since childhood and has had several Holmesian related essays printed in anthologies, and is a member of the online society *Doyle's Rotary Coffin*. She has an ongoing love affair with the city of London. When she's not working or planning trips to London. Margaret can be found frequenting the many and varied bookshops of Melbourne.

I.A. Watson is a novelist and jobbing writer from Yorkshire who cut his teeth on writing Sherlock Holmes stories and has even won an award for one. His works include *Holmes and Houdini, Labours of Hercules, St. George and the Dragon* Volumes 1 and 2, *Women of Myth*, and the non-fiction essay book *Where Stories Dwell*. He pens short detective stories as a means of avoiding writing things that pay better. A full list of his many works published works appears at:
http://www.chillwater.org.uk/writing/iawatsonhome.htm

Marcia Wilson is a freelance researcher and illustrator who likes to work in a style compatible for the color blind and visually impaired. She is Canon-centric, and her first MX offering, *You Buy Bones*, uses the point-of-view of Scotland Yard to show the unique talents of Dr. Watson. This continued with the publication of *Test of the Professionals: The Adventure of the Flying Blue Pidgeon* and *The Peaceful Night Poisonings*. She can be contacted at: *gravelgirty.deviantart.com*

489

The MX Book of New Sherlock Holmes Stories
Edited by David Marcum
(MX Publishing, 2015-   )

"This is the finest volume of Sherlockian fiction I have ever read, and I have read, literally, thousands." – Philip K. Jones

"Beyond Impressive . . . This is a splendid venture for a great cause!
– Roger Johnson, Editor, *The Sherlock Holmes Journal,*
The Sherlock Holmes Society of London

Part I: 1881-1889
Part II: 1890-1895
Part III: 1896-1929
Part IV: 2016 Annual
Part V: Christmas Adventures
Part VI: 2017 Annual
Part VII: Eliminate the Impossible (1880-1891)
Part VIII – Eliminate the Impossible (1892-1905)
Part IX – 2018 Annual (1879-1895)
Part X – 2018 Annual (1896-1916)
Part XI – Some Untold Cases (1880-1891)
Part XII – Some Untold Cases (1894-1902)
Part XIII – 2019 Annual (1881-1890)
Part XIV – 2019 Annual (1891-1897)
Part XV – 2019 Annual (1898-1917)
Part XVI – Whatever Remains . . . Must be the Truth (1881-1890)
Part XVII – Whatever Remains . . . Must be the Truth (1891-1898)
Part XVIII – Whatever Remains . . . Must be the Truth (1898-1925)
Part XIX – 2020 Annual (1882-1890)
Part XX – 2020 Annual (1891-1897)
Part XXI – 2020 Annual (1898-1923)
Part XXII – Some More Untold Cases (1877-1887)
Part XXIII – Some More Untold Cases (1888-1894)
Part XXIV – Some More Untold Cases (1895-1903)

In Preparation
Part XXV – 2021 Annual

. . . and more to come!

The MX Book of New Sherlock Holmes Stories
Edited by David Marcum
(MX Publishing, 2015-)

Publishers Weekly says:

Part VI: *The traditional pastiche is alive and well. . . .*

Part VII: *Sherlockians eager for faithful-to-the-canon plots and characters will be delighted.*

Part VIII: *The imagination of the contributors in coming up with variations on the volume's theme is matched by their ingenious resolutions.*

Part IX: *The 18 stories . . . will satisfy fans of Conan Doyle's originals. Sherlockians will rejoice that more volumes are on the way.*

Part X: *. . . new Sherlock Holmes adventures of consistently high quality.*

Part XI: *. . . an essential volume for Sherlock Holmes fans.*

Part XII: *. . . continues to amaze with the number of high-quality pastiches . . .*

Part XIII: *. . . Amazingly, Marcum has found 22 superb pastiches . . . This is more catnip for fans of stories faithful to Conan Doyle's original*

Part XIV: *. . . this standout anthology of 21 short stories written in the spirit of Conan Doyle's originals.*

Part XV: *Stories pitting Sherlock Holmes against seemingly supernatural phenomena highlight Marcum's 15th anthology of superior short pastiches.*

Part XVI: *Marcum has once again done fans of Conan Doyle's originals a service.*

Part XVII: *This is yet another impressive array of new but traditional Holmes stories.*

Part XVIII: *Sherlockians will again be grateful to Marcum and MX for high-quality new Holmes tales.*

Part XIX: *Inventive plots and intriguing explorations of aspects of Dr. Watson's life and beliefs lift the 24 pastiches in Marcum's impressive 19th Sherlock Holmes anthology*

Part XX: *Marcum's reserve of high-quality new Holmes exploits seems endless.*

Part XXI: *This is another must-have for Sherlockians.*

The MX Book of New Sherlock Holmes Stories
Edited by David Marcum
(MX Publishing, 2015-)

MX Publishing

MX Publishing is the world's largest specialist Sherlock Holmes publisher, with several hundred titles and over a hundred authors creating the latest in Sherlock Holmes fiction and non-fiction.

From traditional short stories and novels to travel guides and quiz books, MX Publishing caters to all Holmes fans.

The collection includes leading titles such as *Benedict Cumberbatch In Transition* and *The Norwood Author*, which won the 2011 *Tony Howlett Award* (Sherlock Holmes Book of the Year).

MX Publishing also has one of the largest communities of Holmes fans on *Facebook*, with regular contributions from dozens of authors.

www.mxpublishing.co.uk (UK) and *www.mxpublishing.com* (USA)

Lightning Source UK Ltd.
Milton Keynes UK
UKHW040727270521
R2744800001B/R27448PG383924UKX00001B/1